Palisade Trilogy – Omnibus Books 1-3

AN EPIC FANTASY ADVENTURE

Amber L. Werner

Published by Werner Ink
Norristown, PA

Chapter Header Art by Lauren Kratz
Front Cover Illustration by Robert Ardy
Typography and Paperback by Getcovers
Map designed by Inkarnate
Edited by Claire Ashgrove
Paperback ISBN: 978-1-960073-08-2
Library of Congress Control Number: 2025905342

AMBER L. WERNER

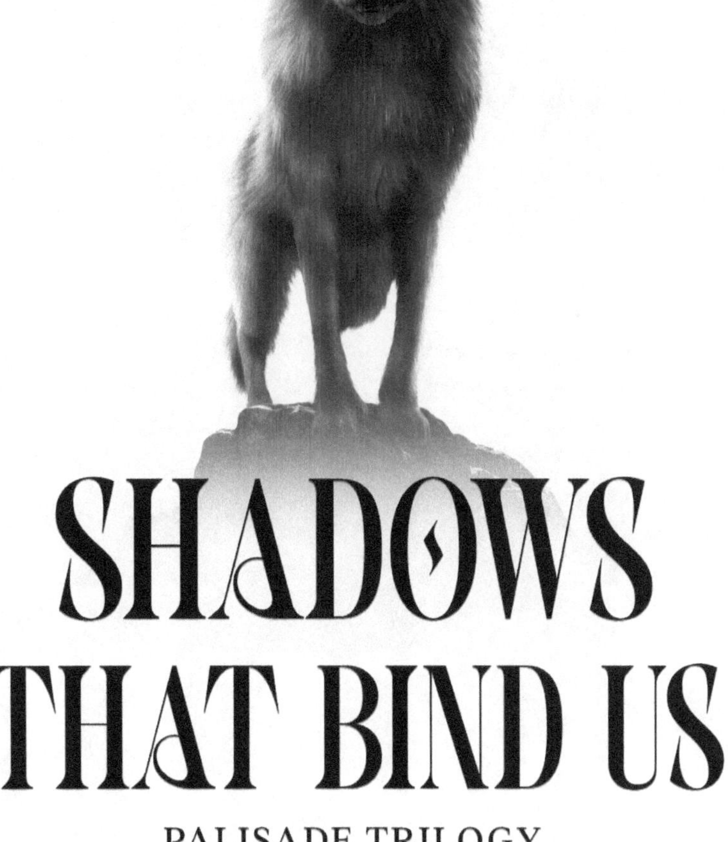

SHADOWS THAT BIND US

PALISADE TRILOGY

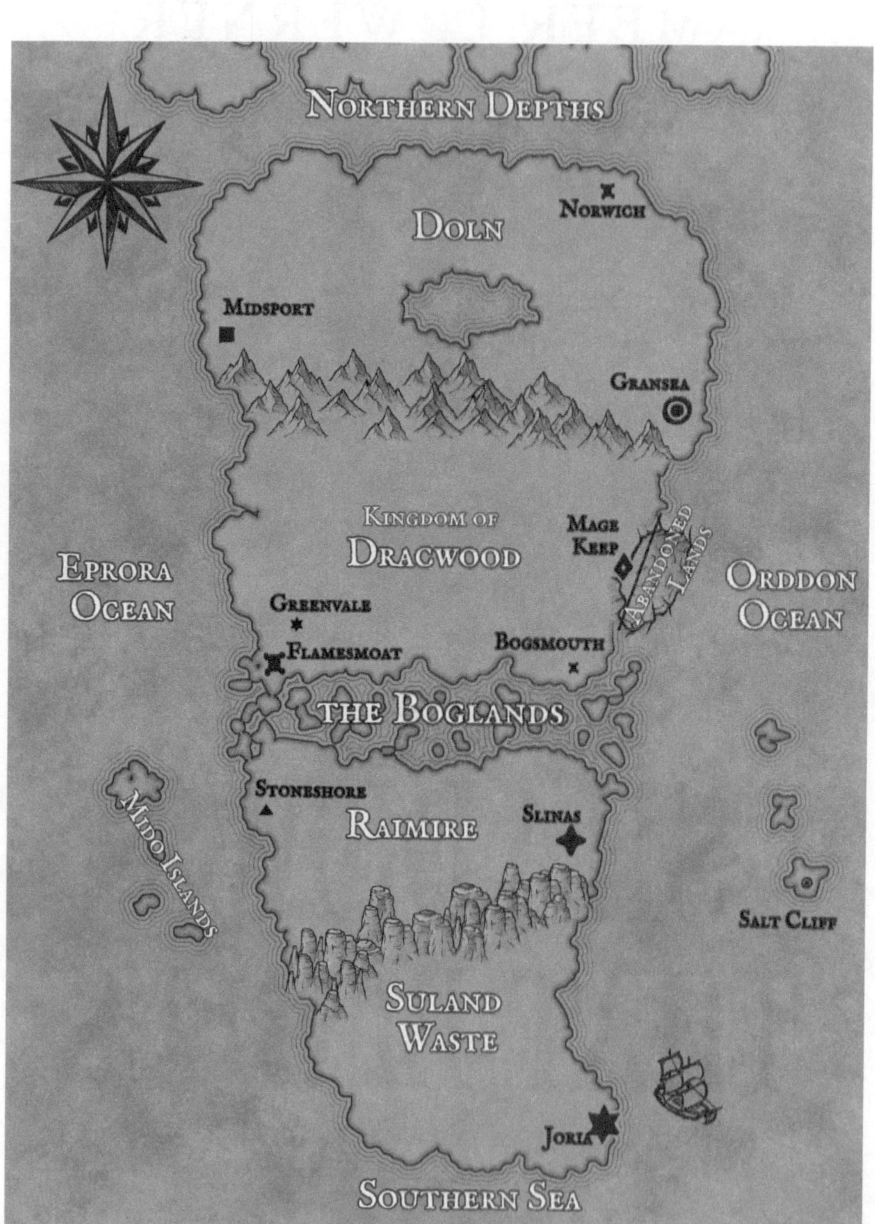

NORTHERN DEPTHS
NORWICH
DOLN
MIDSPORT
GRANSEA
KINGDOM OF
DRACWOOD
MAGE KEEP
EPRORA OCEAN
ABANDONED LANDS
ORDDON OCEAN
GREENVALE
FLAMESMOAT
BOGSMOUTH
THE BOGLANDS
STONESHORE
MIDO ISLANDS
RAIMIRE
SLINAS
SALT CLIFF
SULAND WASTE
JORIA
SOUTHERN SEA

Prologue

Appearances can be deceiving. Delyth knew that better than most. She stood atop a ridge, surveying an expanse of fertile land. Lush fields sprawled on rolling hills, laced with trickling streams and wildflowers. In the far distance, dancing waves kissed the sandy shore, the ocean sparkling in the midday sun. Most would agree it was a scene fit to adorn a finely crafted tapestry.

Delyth knew the truth. Hiding just below the surface, evil lay in wait.

"They're here, Sade Prim," said a voice behind her.

Delyth turned, tossing her long, gray braid over her shoulder. A dozen young men and women gathered nearby, clothed in pristine white robes that matched her own. They were so young. Such a pity what they were being asked to do. What she was asking them to do.

She drew a deep breath, focusing on each of them before speaking. "By now, you've all learned about our noble mission. Destiny has gifted you great power. We can teach you to harness that power to become a Palisade Mage. But before you can learn to control the elements, you must be willing to sacrifice some of that power for the protection of us all. For only those who are noble of heart may join our ranks."

She studied the young initiates again. Not one was fully still. They twitched and gazed around curiously, but they seemed at peace with their decision to be there. All except for one.

At the end of the line of initiates stood one girl, who looked on the verge of tears. While the others returned Delyth's gaze—some even smiling or blushing at the attention—this girl stared at the ground. She twisted her hands together, taking breath after shaky breath.

Delyth approached the girl and lifted her chin gently. "There's no shame in admitting you aren't ready to pay the price, child." She peered into blue eyes wet with tears.

She recognized her. Amora, the daughter of Remon, a skilled water mage. Delyth had met little Amora many times over the years, but this was the first time she'd spoken to her so closely. She was beautiful, even with her face reddened and puffy from tears, and no more than sixteen years old.

Perhaps she should take her aside for a private word? No. All of these initiates deserved to hear what she said next.

Delyth released Amora's chin and raised her voice, gazing at the entire line of initiates. "You've all been told what to expect, but don't forget—this choice is binding. The Palisade will be here next year, and the year after. I was a woman fully grown with a child of my own when I stood where you stand now. There's no harm in enjoying your youth before joining our ranks." She turned back to Amora.

This time the girl met her gaze, hands still at her sides. "Thank you for your kind words, Sade Prim." She rolled her shoulders back. "I'm ready." Her shaky voice grew steadier with each word. "I've been ready for this for a long time. I want to be a mage. I want my power to be awakened." She stood tall, her tears banished.

Delyth inspected the initiates once more. Her chest swelled with pride to see so many willing to join their ranks. They were brave. And ready. Ready as any of them ever were for what came next.

"Let's begin." Delyth stepped to the edge of the ridge. Taking a deep breath, she pulled at the surrounding air, drawing it closer, shaping it to her will. Air filled her lungs, comfortable and familiar, like slipping into her favorite robe at the end of a long day. The sky crackled with electricity. The hairs on her skin stood straight on end. She visualized what she wanted and exhaled. A massive wall appeared, stretching out from north to south as far as the eye could see.

A collective gasp rose from the initiates. The Palisade towered over them all, taller than the highest tree, blocking the view of the valley below. At first glance, it appeared to be made of metal that shined in the sun. Upon closer inspection, it became clear the structure was not wrought by a blacksmith, for it glittered strangely and pulsed, as if alive.

"Place your hands against the Palisade," Delyth instructed.

As one, the initiates complied.

Delyth gritted her teeth. No matter how many times she watched this ritual, it never got easier or less unsettling.

Each instant the initiates touched the wall, they aged. Delyth watched the man closest to her as the years sped by on his skin. Wrinkles and age spots that should take decades to form appeared in mere moments. His hairline receded, and a bald spot emerged; his black locks thinned and turned gray before her eyes.

This was the price they paid to keep the Palisade standing. And sooner or later, it wouldn't be enough.

"Sade Prim," her assistant for the ritual whispered at her side, a tense expression on his weathered face. "Shouldn't it be over by now?" His gaze darted over the initiates' faces.

Delyth patted his forearm, opening her mouth to speak just as the class let go of the Palisade and fell to their knees. She smiled at him instead and turned to address the initiates.

"Welcome back, my friends." Her smile widened, arms lifting skyward. "Let me be the first to congratulate you on taking the first step to becoming a Palisade Mage. Please, everyone return to Keep Hall. There's a celebration waiting for you."

The new mages murmured among themselves as they staggered to their feet. Delyth drew air into her lungs again to return the Palisade to its typical invisible state. It took a moment of concentration to complete the task, after which she gazed at the beautiful landscape laid out beyond the unseen wall.

No one had seen a trace of the creatures trapped beyond the Palisade for hundreds of years. No one even knew for sure what they looked like. The stories of the time were the stuff of myth and legend.

Some doubted they ever existed. They thought the mages fools to waste their time and power—their very lives—to keep watch over what appeared to be nothing more than an idyllic, untouched piece of land.

They were all wrong. They didn't know what she knew. But even before reading the journals of her predecessors, and her journey to the Northern Depths, she'd sensed the truth. She could feel it in her bones every time she looked at the Abandoned Lands. Something was out there still, waiting. Something evil.

Turning to return to the hall, she spotted one of the new mages still with her on the ridge. Amora rested on her knees, slowly tracing the new lines on her face, eyes closed in reflection. Her eyes shot open as Delyth drew closer, and her hands dropped in her lap.

"Don't worry, my dear." Delyth closed the distance between them. "You'll get used to it quickly." She patted Amora's back sympathetically. "The first time I looked in the mirror after my own ritual, I had a good long cry." She tugged the gray braid resting against her shoulder. "My hair used to be so glossy and thick. Now look at it." She sighed. "But no matter. Come tomorrow, you'll be so busy learning to use your magic you won't have a spare moment to stare at your reflection."

"I'm sure you're right," Amora said wistfully, a wry smile curving her lips. She grasped a vial necklace dangling on her chest, one common among mages. Eyes lighting up, she twisted the stopper free, spilling the contents into her cupped hand. Then she closed her eyes and pursed her lips, fingers straightening until her palm displayed a tiny pool of liquid. Slowly, an orb of water materialized in Amora's outstretched hand. It started out the size of a marble, slowly growing until it was the size of a large apple.

Delyth watched, her head tilting slightly. Her skin prickled with goosebumps as moisture whispered through the air.

Amora's eyes opened, widening with wonder. Then the water orb splattered to nothing, soaking her hand and sprinkling her robe with droplets. She laughed, shaking the remaining moisture free from her fingertips.

"I knew it would be water." Amora's eyes sparkled, her smile wide and infectious.

Delyth couldn't help grinning with her. "There will be time for practice tomorrow. Let's join the others." She pulled Amora to her feet. Together, they trekked down the ridge toward the hall where their brethren gathered.

They didn't have far to travel. Mage Keep, which served as both home and school for the Palisade Mages, rested beneath the ridge opposite the Abandoned Lands, south of the Palisade River's banks. The sprawling compound contained a jumble of different-sized buildings, none of which had ever been praised for their beauty or architecture.

Nevertheless, the sight of the keep warmed Delyth's heart. Though she'd traveled far in her youth and seen many areas much more beautiful, Mage Keep was the only place she'd ever consider home.

The keep appeared deserted as they approached, but that was no surprise. Everyone would be inside Keep Hall for the celebration.

Not quite everyone. A solitary figure strode in their direction. Delyth turned to Amora, sending her a small smile. "Head in without me. I have to speak to my daughter."

Amora nodded and picked up her pace, trading a glance with Ereni as they passed. Ereni hid her shock at Amora's transformation, but Delyth knew her daughter well.

"I didn't know Amora was joining the ritual today," Ereni said, once they were close enough to speak without being overheard. She raked a hand through her long brown hair, her blue eyes staring at Amora's retreating back.

Delyth pulled Ereni into a hug. At nineteen, she'd long outgrown the need for constant affection from her mother, but Delyth didn't let that stop her. Sometimes she needed to remember there were more things in life than ancient evil, magic, and responsibilities.

Delyth gave a final squeeze and released her daughter from the warm embrace. She grasped her shoulders, holding her at arm's length. Ereni was dressed plainly in a brown tunic and trousers. Still, it was like staring at a reflection of her former self. They shared such a close resemblance they could've been mistaken for sisters had they been the same age. As it was, she looked more like a grandmother to her daughter.

"I'm glad you're here, Ereni." Delyth dropped her hands but remained close, ignoring the confusion on her daughter's face. She spoke quietly. "I have something very important I need you to do. It's time. Pack your traveling bag and head to Flamesmoat. I have a letter that must be delivered, and you're the only one I trust to do it. Wait for a reply and return with it, personally." Delyth leaned in closer, voice whisper soft, though she remained smiling, as if relaying a pleasant anecdote. "If anyone should discover either letter, kill them."

Ereni's eyes widened slightly, but she showed no other sign of surprise at the request. "Of course, Sade Prim," she said with a smile.

Prior Boaz crept through the graveyard south of the church in the dead of night, leading a goat. The tiny lamp High Prior Sander carried brightened the shadows just enough to see a few paces ahead. Still, he stumbled more than once, his feet catching on rocks and roots littered in the crumbling cemetery.

They must be a strange sight—two old men in black hooded robes, clambering around in the dark. He clutched tightly to the rope, his heart swelling with pride to be chosen for such an important mission.

"We're almost there, son," High Prior Sander said. "You must memorize this route. When I'm gone, the responsibility will fall to you."

Boaz nodded, tugging the rope. The goat snorted, following closely. Boaz' brown eyes flicked over the battered gravestones. The names and dates carved on them had been worn smooth, lost to time.

Sander saw him looking. "Every so often some builder will come to you, offering to tear this place down. 'No one buries their dead anymore,' they'll say. 'Think of all the wasted space.'" His brow furrowed, and he stared at him intensely. "You must shut them down without question. This is a holy place. The holiest. Never forget."

Boaz gulped, shaking his head vehemently. "Of course, High Prior. I'll do exactly that."

"I'm not getting any younger, Boaz. After this year's Harvest Festival, I'm going to step down as High Prior. I want you to replace me."

His chest swelled even more. "I would be honored, sir."

"I'm glad to hear it, son." Sander stared ahead. "Now, let me introduce you to your most important responsibility." He shuffled forward and pulled a key from his waist pocket. He inserted it in a rusty lock on a small mausoleum. It opened with a *click*. "Since the first days of the church, every high prior has brought a goat to this spot on the same night each year."

Sander swung open the door, revealing—nothing. The tiny room was bare except for a large hole in the bottom. The slanted floor sank down into the earth.

Boaz tilted his head. "I didn't think we condoned sacrifice?"

"It's not a sacrifice exactly. More like a duty. The most essential of duties. Bring the animal," High Prior Sander commanded.

Boaz tugged the rope again, ushering the goat into the stone structure. The opening was barely wide enough, but Sander gave the beast a shove. Soon the small room engulfed the animal, and it clambered down the sloping path in the darkness.

"Where is he going?" Boaz asked.

"To his fate," Sander replied solemnly. He slammed the door, replaced the rusty lock, and spun to face him. "Every year, on this day. Don't forget."

He nodded, his stare glued on the tiny room. The goat's bleating reverberated behind the stone door, muffled but distinct. Suddenly the sound cut off mid-bleat, replaced by a sickening crunch.

He jerked back, inhaling sharply. A moment later, light flickered behind cracks in the stone door, and he fell to his knees, his heart hammering madly in his chest.

Sander squeezed his shoulder gently. "You see. Never let anyone shake your faith. We are doing god's work."

Boaz nodded again, his eyes full of tears.

"C'mon, son. We can still catch a bit of rest before the morning sermon."

He lurched up, following High Prior Sander back through the crumbling graveyard with tears rolling down his cheeks and a smile on his face.

Chapter 1

A hawk soared, gliding through an updraft before swooping down behind the tower looming on the edge of the Royal Grounds. Princess Kayda sighed, watching from her perch in her favorite oak tree. The summer breeze rustled the leaves, dry and hot but bearable in the shade. A well-worn book lay open in her lap, neglected today while her mind wandered.

The crunch of footsteps below broke her reverie. Her grandfather, King Quinton, and her half-brother, Prince Tarquin, strode nearby. They were dressed for hunting in russet-brown trousers and tunics, both carrying a bow and a quiver of arrows.

The family resemblance was staggering this morning, in their matching attire. Both were strikingly handsome. Tall and muscular with cornflower-blue eyes and dark-blond hair, although the king's hair was streaked through with gray. Behind them, a handful of house servants and courtiers trailed at a distance, where they could watch without overhearing the men's conversation.

She should climb down. Say hello. But then she'd have to talk to Tarquin. He might be blood, but she loathed the man.

Kayda suppressed a shudder, staying put among the thick foliage. Luckily, she'd chosen a fern-green dress today. Chances were good they would stroll past without noticing her. She did her best to stay motionless as the men drew closer, and their conversation rose to her ears.

"Ah, there's nothing better than the breeze in your hair and a good gallop about," King Quinton said, a genuine smile lighting his face. He was certainly in good spirits today.

Kayda grinned. She almost reconsidered staying hidden, so she could bask in his good mood. It was a rare sight to see him so happy and carefree.

"It would be much nicer if we need not be afoot. Let me buy a nice stallion for you, sire. It would be my pleasure." Tarquin's voice dripped with sincerity, but she knew it to be false.

Quinton's smile faded. "I'm afraid that won't be possible." His steps slowed, and his gaze shifted to that strange, far-off stare he wore so often.

Her blood boiled. Leave it to Tarquin to ruin someone's day. He knew better than to make that offer, yet he did it anyway.

"Oh, Grandfather, I can't believe I forgot. Of course, you can't." Tarquin's face was the picture of remorse as he wrapped an arm around the king's shoulders. "Please forgive me. It's just I have so much on my mind."

Kayda rolled her eyes. It was typical behavior for her brother. He had a way of saying the most cutting remark in one breath and begging for forgiveness with the next. What's worse was no one could see through the act, her grandfather included.

"It's all right, my boy," the king said, sounding distracted. "No harm done." He patted Tarquin's hand, staring off into the distance.

Tarquin withdrew his arm from the king's shoulders and moved to stand in front of him, halting a few paces away from her oak.

Kayda stifled a groan. Her nose picked the perfect time to need scratching. She wiggled her nose back and forth, keeping her hands glued to her lap, silently praying the men would continue walking.

"I wonder if you could help. You see, I've been approached by a group of merchants from Joria," Tarquin said.

Kayda's ears perked up. Her mother had been born in Joria.

"They've expressed interest in entering into a new trade deal with our great kingdom." Tarquin leaned in close. "An exclusive agreement," he added with a sly grin.

"An exclusive deal with the Jorians? Why, that's excellent news." The king's eyes regained their focus. His face lit with interest.

"I was hoping you would agree, sire. The deal would be mutually beneficial and would allow us to stop relying on those heathen Dolnmen to act as middlemen, of course." Tarquin's teeth gleamed in his self-satisfied smile.

"Ha, you're right on that account," Quinton said. "I would kill to see the look on Chief Aundrea's face when he hears the news." He laughed then, loud and long.

Kayda smiled in response until the motion set that traitorous itch traveling to her cheek. She closed her eyes briefly, praying the men would start moving again.

Her prayers were soon answered. The king patted her brother's shoulder and started walking. "Well, don't keep me in suspense. What are the details?"

Tarquin puffed out his chest, smiling widely.

Kayda's fingers curled in her lap. Her brother loved nothing more than being asked to talk.

"It was an impressive bit of bargaining I did," Tarquin matched steps with King Quinton. "You will be pleased to know I managed to convince the largest merchant group in Joria to agree to abandon Gransea port and to trade exclusively with us." He combed a hand through his hair, his eyes shining. "We'll save a fortune on goods that would normally have to run through Doln before reaching our ports."

"That's excellent news," Quinton said, "but what do they expect from us in return?"

"Just for us to build a new port on our eastern shores."

"Are you mad?" Quinton stopped in his tracks, his face flushing. "Absolutely not. We will not be building anything on our eastern shores."

The smug smile dropped from Tarquin's face.

Kayda stifled a smirk.

Tarquin quickly masked his disappointment, turning wide eyes toward the king. "Don't tell me you believe there's anything out there, sire. It's been hundreds of years since anything has been seen."

"Of course, I believe it." The king pressed his fingers to his brow, drawing in a deep breath. "Tarquin, our entire kingdom exists solely to protect the world from that cursed place. Has that drunkard father of yours taught you nothing?"

Tarquin flinched at the king's tone, pinching his lips together. "It's just a shame we can't use that land. Perhaps we could send an exploratory team beyond the Palisade and see what's out there? I'm sure the mages could be convinced to—"

"We will not be stepping foot inside the Abandoned Lands," Quinton said through gritted teeth. His voice was hard, brooking no argument. "That's my decision, and it's final."

"Of course, Grandfather." Tarquin adopted a nonchalant air, though she could tell by the set of his shoulders he was not as relaxed as he appeared.

The itch, forgotten while she listened to the argument below, returned to plague her. But they looked far enough away she could chance a scratch...

She slowly lifted her shoulder while moving her cheek to meet it, using the rough cloth of her sleeve to finally bring some relief. Eyes half closing, she spotted Tarquin's gaze lift in her direction.

Oh, no. Kayda gulped reflexively, remaining stock still. If only he would look away without noticing her. The moment seemed to stretch out infinitely until he finally looked away, taking a few steps forward toward the king.

In a single, fluid motion, Tarquin spun to face her, lifting his bow and nocking an arrow. Eyes bulging, Kayda had less than a heartbeat to scramble backward before the arrow hurtled through the sky. Weightlessness and the slap of leaves on her skin assaulted her as she lost her seat on the branch. Eyes closing in fear, she shrieked, clutching blindly for a grip to stop her fall and finding nothing but air.

But the hard wallop she expected never came. She cracked open an eye and found herself dangling from the tree upside down. The arrow pierced the hem of her dress before lodging in the tree branch, arresting her fall, leaving her hanging just above the ground.

"Why, Kayda, is that you, dear sister?" called Tarquin's voice from behind her, full of false surprise. "Whatever were you doing in that tree?"

With her heart racing and blood pooling in her ears, she couldn't think of a reply before her skirt ripped. She fell, thudding her head into the ground and landing in a heap on the grass. She groaned, rushing to fix her skirts and sit properly.

Her grandfather crouched beside her. "Little red, good gracious. Are you hurt?" The king's weary gaze traced her body as he clutched her shoulder to steady her.

She winced slightly and rubbed the back of her head. The panic and fear of the last few moments receded as she gazed at her grandfather. "I'm all right, I think."

"I can't believe I almost shot you." Tarquin chuckled, moving in front of her. "I saw that red hair of yours and thought I'd spotted a squirrel." He laughed again and crossed his arms, leaning against the tree, looking far too amused for someone who'd just barely escaped killing a sibling. "Don't you have better things to do with your time than hide in trees?" he added, raising an eyebrow.

Spotting her book to her left, Kayda snatched it off the ground. "I was only looking for a quiet place to read." Her voice was shaky, laced with a petulant tone she couldn't contain that made her grimace.

"Oh, please don't be mad," Tarquin pleaded, splaying a hand on his chest and crouching down beside the king. "You know I would never hurt you on purpose. I'm so sorry."

"Sure you are." Kayda pushed to her feet. Quinton and Tarquin followed suit. She glanced behind her and spotted the servants approaching.

Great. The story would be all anyone would talk about for days. She cursed inwardly. She considered saying more but settled for an icy glare. It wouldn't be seemly to argue. Besides, Tarquin would just make her look like the one at fault and he the victim.

Turning to her grandfather, she warmed instantly. He leaned toward her, his brow furrowed and lips pursed as he scrutinized her.

"I'm fine, sire, I swear. I'll head back. Enjoy the rest of your hunt." She forced a small smile and turned, crossing the field toward Kings Keep.

Kayda kept her head down as she passed the servants, not wanting to see them snickering. It wasn't everyday they witnessed a member of the royal family with half of their skirts dangling in their faces. Her cheeks burned, and though she tried to give the men's followers a wide berth, she could still hear their excited murmuring as she passed.

The nerve of Tarquin, shooting at her! She had no doubt he'd seen her sitting there and shot at her to teach her a lesson. There's no chance he'd mistaken her for a squirrel. He was an expert marksman. If he'd been aiming at her hair, he wouldn't have missed. No, he just wanted her to look like a fool.

Her shoulders drooped as she slinked away, picking up speed. He certainly never missed a chance to mock her appearance either. Her Jorian heritage meant she didn't have the dark blond hair and light skin the rest of the royals shared. Tarquin never forgot to remind her she was different. As if her having a Jorian mother made her lesser than him somehow.

She'd long ago realized Tarquin would take any opportunity to make her look bad. She lost count of all the chances she'd given him over the years. He always let her down. One might think a man nearly ten years her senior would've grown tired of teasing his little sister, but that was unfortunately not the case.

Like the day a few years back, when she begged him to remove a spider from her chambers. She shuddered at the memory. She'd trusted him that day when she confided her fear of the creepy insects. He'd acted so sweet and understanding, coming to her rescue. The next evening, she strolled into her chambers and found the entire room crawling with spiders. And of course, his laughing face was there to greet her as she raced screaming through the keep.

She'd called him out on it, but he had a way of spinning every situation like it was her fault. He would never do anything to hurt her. It was all for her own good, or just a joke. What a load of crap.

Kayda had lived in Kings Keep her whole life and knew the way by heart. Speeding through the immaculate gardens and manicured lawn, her mind reeled with outrage. She made her way inside through the back servants' entrance and headed swiftly toward her quarters.

She couldn't stop picturing the arrow coming straight for her. And the moment she lost her seat on the branch and plummeted through the air. She'd feared she was done for—that she'd break her neck, crack her skull, and force her grandfather to watch her bleed to death before his eyes.

All her life she'd dealt with Tarquin's bullying, but this was on a whole new level. He could've killed her.

As she opened the door to her room, his smug laughter replayed in her mind. She would give anything to wipe that stupid look off his face.

Her bedroom was her sanctuary. The one place in the crowded keep she could be guaranteed a little peace and quiet. Surrounded by light-blue walls and plush pastel bedding, she could relax and unwind. But not today. She still couldn't shake off the anger and humiliation burning inside her.

Feeling a chill sweep over her, she leaned down to check if any embers remained in her fireplace. A faint orange glow of flame appeared as the sound of her brother's awful gloating laughter rose again in her memory.

The flames leapt to life with a blast. She flew backward, landing hard on her behind. Her heart seized as the flames swallowed the fireplace, licking the edges and threatening to envelop the entire wall.

Gulping, she scooted backward away from the heat and bumped into something hard. Craning her neck up, she discovered her nurse, Izora, staring at the flames.

"What are you doing just sitting there, child?" Izora said, as calm as if gazing out an open window instead of at a raging inferno. "Fetch some water." She deftly grabbed the largest vase perched on the bedside table, tossed the flowers aside, and dumped the remaining contents on the flames.

Kayda sprang into action, thankful for her nurse's habit of bringing her a bouquet of flowers every morning. Within moments, the two women emptied half a dozen vases full of water on the flames, effectively extinguishing them. Surveying the wreckage of flowers, ash, and water, Kayda sucked in several gasping breaths and calmed her raging heart before turning a rueful smile toward her savior.

"Thanks, Izora. I don't know how that happened. The flames just appeared out of nowhere."

Izora shook her head, her short white curls bouncing with the motion. "I know what happened." She set a vase down on the side table and whirled to face her with a knowing grin, her eyes gleaming. "You did this. You conjured the flames. You have a talent for fire magic, Princess."

Kayda's breath caught. A fire mage... her? "No, that's not possible. The royal family has always possessed bonding magic, not elemental."

Was it even possible for someone to possess both types of talent? Shaking her head, she backed away from the steaming fireplace and sank down on the edge of her bed.

It couldn't have been her who'd done that, could it?

The bed shifted as Izora sat beside her. She smoothed the skirt of her flint-gray servant dress. "Believe it, child. The royal family may have always had bonding magic, and you may still have it, too. But you're forgetting one thing, my dear." She paused until Kayda turned from the fireplace. Izora stared straight at her, brown eyes warm, smiling tenderly. "Magic can be inherited from both parents."

Kayda gasped. "My mother was a mage?"

Izora had been her mother Solenne's companion before becoming her nurse when Solenne died from complications of childbirth. There was no one in the keep who'd known her better. But had she really been a mage? How could that be possible when Kayda had never heard a whisper of a rumor?

Izora's wrinkled hand landed atop Kayda's hand on the bedspread, her dark brown skin a few shades darker than her own. "I know you never got to know her. Your mother was an amazing woman. And yes, a powerful mage. She would've been very proud of you. I see so much of her in you."

Kayda teared up and wiped the moisture away with the back of her hand. Proud of her? What a joke. She had a father who ignored her and a brother who went to desperate lengths to embarrass her. Her grandfather always treated her with kindness, but with how busy he was ruling the kingdom and dealing with his own demons, she barely saw him.

A day would soon come when he would be gone, and she would be at the mercy of the new king and prince, who only cared if she married, mage or not. It was the blood that mattered most, after all. Since her brother and father showed no signs of bonding talent, it would be her duty to continue the royal bloodline. She was nothing more than a broodmare in her family's eyes. How could her mother be proud of that?

Izora must have sensed her internal distress. She squeezed her knee with surprising strength for her age. Kayda's gaze shot to her nurse's face, and she flinched from her intense glare.

"She would be proud. You'll be the first in your family—perhaps even the first in the entire world—to be a mage and have a bondmate. You are going to do amazing things, Kayda. Amazing, incredible things."

A ghost of a smile crossed Kayda's face. She could always count on Izora to cheer her up. She returned the squeeze with a much gentler one of her own. "What now? We'll have to tell my family what happened first, I expect. Then send word to Mage Keep—"

Izora's laughter cut off Kayda's words. "Don't be ridiculous, dear. We won't be telling anyone."

"You can't mean that. Why can't we tell anyone?"

"You don't belong at Mage Keep. Your place is here. And besides, the longer you keep your talent hidden, the better. If you ever end up in trouble, you'll have a secret weapon at your disposal."

"But I'll need training. And there's no way we can keep this a secret."

Izora walked to the far wall, reaching out toward the lit candlesticks adorning the walls. "You'd be surprised what secrets people keep." She closed her eyes.

A chill ran up Kayda's spine. Then, to her astonishment, a ball of flame slowly formed on her nurse's outstretched hand.

Eyes opening, Izora smiled. "I'll clean up this mess. You need your rest tonight. Your training starts tomorrow."

Chapter 2

Crouching to inspect the empty trap in the underbrush, Conall caught a glimpse of ominous storm clouds peeking through the dense canopy above. His shoulders slumped. A storm was exactly what he needed to add to his day. He still had two more snares to check, and with his unwanted company in tow, there was no doubt in his mind he would end up drenched.

"Storms brewing." Brows furrowing, he stood, pointing to the break in the tree cover. "Maybe you ought to head home early. I can handle the rest on my own."

"Head home? From a little rain? I'm a man, not a mouse, boy," muttered his companion, Gael.

Gael was a large man, as broad as he was tall. His bulk suited him fine for the many chores they shared running their family farm, but was ill suited to tracking game.

Conall hadn't seen a single creature that day with Gael noisily trudging along, alerting all the wild game to their presence. It was strange he'd insisted on tagging along today, when he'd shown no interest in joining him in the past.

Then again, Gael had been acting strangely ever since Rhea, Conall's mother and Gael's wife, died a few weeks ago. Conall might not be overly fond of the man, but there was no denying Gael loved his mother deeply. He couldn't fault him for wanting some companionship during his grief. Even if he was scaring away all the game.

Steeling himself for more of the plodding pace and stilted conversation, he gestured to the left. "All right, the last set of traps are this way. Follow me."

Conall led the way through the forest, carefully avoiding the brambles and nettles that caused Gael to curse in frustration as they caught on his brown wool trousers.

He inhaled the salty tang of impending rain mixed with the familiar scent of wood and fresh vegetation. These woods were like a second home to Conall. He'd been hunting and trapping in them most of his life.

In the first few years, before the farm began to produce enough food to feed his family, his hunting and trapping had been essential to their survival. He had been only a child then, but hunger and desperation kept him coming back, practicing the few meager skills his father taught him.

He struggled at first, but with daily practice, it wasn't long before he became proficient enough with the bow to hunt small game. And through trial and error, he managed to find the best spots for his traps on their land.

Conall smiled, recalling the look on his mother's face the first time he'd brought home a kill. She'd been heavily pregnant with his sister Lark and heard the news his father died only days before. She'd moped around for days, barely getting out of bed, surviving on stale bread and watered-down broth that had nearly run out. When Conall placed that scrawny hare in her lap, her face lit up like it was a candy apple at the Harvest Festival.

Pain flashed inside his chest. His mother had been an amazing woman. Generous, loving, and so strong.

Those early years at the farm, after his father died, she managed to get it up and running with no help and two small children underfoot. She was always there with a smile and a helping hand for those who needed it, earning a reputation in nearby Greenvale as a great neighbor and friend.

Conall did his best to help, but he was only six when they moved. He hunted and did his fair share of work tending the vegetable garden, but the farm didn't make a profit until his mother married Gael.

Glancing back where Gael struggled uphill, Conall sighed. He had to admit, Gael saved their asses.

The money his mother received for their father's death at sea had run out before long, and she'd been more interested in following her late mother's footsteps as a healer than running a farm. She constantly made house calls, curing all the village folk of their aches and pains. She'd never been one to demand payment, always happy to help out of the kindness of her heart.

Gael had shown up around the time Conall turned fourteen. Within a year, he was married to his mother, doing the majority of work around the farm.

Conall hadn't liked him at first. Truthfully, it was hard to see how his mother found him attractive. He was a balding, coarse, hulk of a man.

His father had been so different. His mother claimed Conall had grown into the spitting image of his father. As the years passed, he struggled to picture his face clearly, but he remembered his father being tall and strong, with shaggy brown hair and hazel eyes that were always full of laughter, much like the image he saw when he looked into the mirror.

It was strange she could love two men who were so very different from each other. But Gael wormed his way into his mother's heart somehow. And despite his bristly attitude when working on the farm, he treated his mother like a queen and Lark like a princess, so Conall had grudgingly learned to live with the man.

As the trail became steeper, Gael's pace slowed even more. "You didn't tell me we had to climb a mountain today." He gripped tree branches and roots to steady himself with his right hand while keeping a tight grip on his bow with his left.

"There's a stream at the top of this hill, just ahead. It's a good spot for trapping." Conall kept the small smirk on his face hidden as he crested the ridge ahead of his stepfather. The old man should've stayed at home if he couldn't keep up.

The top of the ridge hadn't changed from his last visit. He stood on a flat area of grass with a small stream cutting through the middle. The stream began somewhere inside a rocky cliff that rose beyond their path and tumbled into a waterfall to the west, where a sheer drop gave way to the forest floor below.

Water splattered his nose. As he brushed the droplet away, he glimpsed gray fur in the forest to the east, along their much more gently sloped route home.

Finally, some luck. Fur that color likely belonged to a hare. The animal was mostly hidden behind a set of bushes, twitching, as if foraging in the underbrush. Inexplicably, a strange urge to leave the animal to its business came over him, but he shook off the feeling with a shrug.

Reaching into the quiver on his back, Conall's fingertips brushed the fletching of an arrow as Gael crested the ridge with a loud *thump*, and the mystery creature retreated with speed.

Nostrils flaring, Conall dropped his hand from his quiver and spun toward his first snare, which rested close to where the stream burst through the mountainside. He could see from where he stood it was empty.

"Conall, could you slow down for a moment?" Gael inquired, panting. "We need to talk."

Conall stopped, eyebrows raising. Gael was not the type for heart-to-heart conversations. At least now, his insistence on coming along today was starting to make sense.

"It's Lark." Gael frowned. "She's still got that fool idea in her head to go join the bloody mages."

Turning to inspect his trap again, Conall rolled his eyes. "Lark has been set on becoming a Palisade Mage for years. And she has the talent for it. Why stop her?"

"She's too young, for one."

"She'll be sixteen at harvest. They take initiates as young as thirteen, I hear." He knelt down to replace the bait in his trap. Gael and his mother had advised Lark against joining the mages in the past, but this was the first time either of them included him in the discussion.

Gael glowered at him.

"You know Lark. She's always been set on finding adventure. She could probably use it in her life now..." Conall trailed off as he finished setting the trap carefully back in place.

Lark had taken their mother's death hard. They'd been so close, spending practically every moment of the day together. It was as if part of her died with their mother. Grief cast a shadow on her heart, tormenting her. If becoming a mage could be the thing to bring joy back into her life, he wasn't going to stand in her way.

Raindrops fell in earnest, and the sky darkened to a sinister gray. He rose and picked his way toward the second trap, which sat closer to the waterfall and the cliff's edge. His brown tunic and trousers dampened and stuck to his skin.

Gael grabbed his shoulder, spinning him. "Those witches are not who you think they are, boy. They're liars and thieves."

He shrugged Gael's hand off. "What are you talking about, Gael? That's ridiculous. The mages are the most respected people in the kingdom."

Gael rubbed the back of his neck, staring off into the distance. "There's a reason your mother and I got on so well. Both of us had been in love before, you see. She had your father, and I had Seren. Seren was the love of my life." A wistful smile crossed his face, then he grew serious, meeting Conall's eyes. "No offense to your mother."

Conall nodded, and Gael took a deep breath before continuing.

"She had talent, too, you see. Decided she was going to become a mage. Protect the realm and all that nonsense." Gael shook his head vehemently. "What a load of crap that was."

"I don't understand..."

"They stole her youth."

"Her what?"

"I followed her to Mage Keep. I hid on the hillside while they performed her initiation ceremony. I saw that wall suck the life out of her before my eyes." Gael clenched his bow tightly with both hands.

Conall gulped, his mind brimming with questions. "When you say it sucked the life out of her, what do you mean?"

"Seren was eighteen when she walked up that hillside. After she touched the Palisade, she could've easily passed for fifty."

Conall's jaw dropped. He racked his brain for anytime in the past he'd seen a young mage. He'd spotted them countless times while at market or a Harvest Festival. His stomach clenched. He couldn't remember a single mage who wasn't gray-haired or wrinkled. "Surely, there must be a reason..."

"I found Seren after the ceremony. She told me they all give up a bit of power to keep the Palisade working. They do it to protect the realm from some ancient evil beyond the wall." Gael's stare turned flinty. "I saw beyond the wall. Stood there staring at it for half the day. There's nothing out there. Whatever they trapped, it's long dead. Those witches are forcing anyone with talent to waste their lives guarding a bunch of empty fields."

Conall let his words sink in. "Seren told you they forced her to do it?"

"Well, no." Gael's eyes lost focus. "She said it was her choice. Told me to go home. She had chosen her path, and it didn't include me."

Conall patted Gael's shoulder. No wonder he was so insistent Lark not join the mages. But Conall knew Lark. Forbidding her from going would only make her want to go more. She'd always been impulsive and hated being told what she couldn't do.

"Gael, you need to tell Lark what you just told me. She should be the one to decide," Conall said firmly.

"And what if she still wants to go? You would let your sister go, knowing the next time you see her she'll be as old as your mother?" Gael asked, voice cracking on the final word.

It would be strange, for sure, to see Lark aged prematurely. But what was the alternative? Keeping her a prisoner in her own home? And she would gain so much in return. The Palisade Mages were revered by everyone, welcome in every town. Plus, she would get what she always wanted—a life full of adventure and magic.

Conall met Gael's eyes and patted his shoulder once more. "I would. She deserves to know. And she deserves to choose for herself."

Gael stared back at him, his face blank.

Conall smiled, speaking gently. "Let me check this last snare, and we'll go back. We'll talk to her together."

He carefully made his way to the edge of the ridge, where the waterfall disappeared over the steep ledge. His trap nestled in a patch of mossy grass that often attracted birds. Conall sighed as he crouched down to add fresh bait. Another one empty.

"Jump." Conall startled.

How strange. He heard a voice in his head, clear as day. He ought to get some rest if his mind was playing tricks on him.

"Listen, little brother. He's aiming a killstick at you. Jump!" For a moment Conall knelt motionless, beyond confused.

Little brother? Killstick?

Then the full import of the message struck him, and he stood. He whirled around just as an arrow sailed through the sky, impaling his shoulder. Searing pain exploded, and his boots slid across the slippery moss. He staggered, trying desperately to ignore the pain and find his balance.

Dizziness struck him as gravity took over, but not before he caught a last glimpse of his stepfather glowering, bow drawn. His final thought before he slipped over the edge echoed in his ears, all the way down.

Gael, why?

Chapter 3

Stopping short, Lark peered nervously across the wide wooden bridge. Her stomach churned in time with the Riddle River below them. "You didn't tell me we'd have to go to Southmoat, Aunt Brenna."

Brenna was a plump, jolly woman, who wore her brownish-gray hair pulled back in a bun with strands escaping every which way. Both boots already planted on the wooden planks, she turned to address Lark, causing the hem of her simple brown dress to swing round her knees. She smiled.

"Don't tell me you're getting cold feet." Brenna motioned her forward. "The mages are at the docks, of course. I know the way; come on."

Lark frowned, standing on the cobblestone path in Northmoat. "Isn't it dangerous over there?"

Dozens of cramped buildings lined the street across the bridge. They were dingy and gray compared to the brightly colored shops and houses they'd passed in their walk through the Northmoat section of Flamesmoat.

Brenna positioned herself directly in front of Lark, blocking her view. "I've lived in Southmoat all my life. I won't let anything happen to you. Besides, it's only dangerous there at night, and we'll arrive where we're going long before nightfall." Brenna moved to her side, linking their arms together. "If we get a move on, that is."

Lark allowed her aunt to move her along, keeping pace with her along the creaking bridge. A cool river breeze swirled her brown skirt around her legs. She shifted the pack across her tan tunic that held a few snacks and a change of clothes.

Slowly, her apprehension subsided, replaced with excitement. This was it. The start of her first real adventure. She was going to become a mage.

A grin crept across her face. "I wonder why the mages don't keep their headquarters in Northmoat?"

"I imagine they want to be close to the port to welcome all the recruits coming from other parts of the world," Brenna said.

Lark's heart sped up. She hadn't considered that. She would meet people from all over the world. How thrilling!

They made it across the bridge and swung west toward the port section of town. Now that she stood on the streets of Southmoat, her stomach settled. Refuse lingered in the street gutters, and the wooden and brick structures were covered in faded, chipped paint. But although the buildings were more run down than the well-kept villas of Northmoat, they didn't seem so scary up close.

The streets bustled with activity. Children played while mothers strung wet washing on clothes lines between buildings. Men and women, young and old, stood talking animatedly with each other or moved through the streets toward some unknown destination.

Shaking her head, Lark giggled, attracting the attention of a young couple passing by, who smiled in her direction. "I don't know why I was so afraid to come here. It's just like back home in Greenvale. Although a bit more crowded."

She slowed and glanced inside the shop to her left. The smell of freshly baked bread drifted toward her, and her stomach growled.

"If I know my brother, I'm sure he's filled your head with stories of pickpockets, slavers, and thieves." Brenna chuckled, her pudgy face jiggling. "Truth told, Southmoat is not all bad. Why, your mother and father were from here, too, if I'm not mistaken."

Pain throbbed in Lark's chest. It should've been her mother taking her to meet the mages. If only she'd been able to save her...

Pushing the thought aside, she forced a smile. "You're right. They lived here before I was born. Then Father inherited the farm from some distant cousin, and they moved to Greenvale." Her smile brightened. "Do you think we have time to stop by Mother's old job? She's told me so many stories about the place."

"What place?" Brenna asked. "If it's on the way, we can stop for a moment."

"It was an inn called the Boggy Beaut. That's where my parents met. Mother was a barmaid, but on the night she met Father, she was filling in as the entertainment." She leaned in, voice hushed. "According to my mother, it was love at first sight. He was enthralled with her singing, and she with his charm."

Lark's smile faded as she noticed the pinched look on her aunt's face.

"I'm afraid that's nowhere near where we're headed." Brenna frowned sympathetically. "Another day, perhaps?"

Lark nodded, her heart sinking. "Of course. It was just a thought."

She sighed. It was probably better not to reminisce about her mother today. Today was about starting her future, not wallowing in the past.

As Brenna led the way through the crowded streets with the ease of a native, Lark was overwhelmed with gratitude. "Thank you again for taking me today, Aunt Brenna. I would've been lost without you. These streets are like a maze."

"Think nothing of it. You know I would do anything to help my brother." Brenna patted her arm gently. "And you, too, of course."

A pang of discomfort rose in her breast. Brenna was being so nice to her without realizing her help was something Gael would definitely not appreciate.

She lost count of all the times Gael advised her against joining the mages. She should've told Gael the truth in person, but she couldn't stand the thought of him trying to talk her out of leaving again.

With her mother gone, he was the closest thing she had left to a parent, and she couldn't bear disappointing him. When he returned from hunting with Conall that afternoon and found her goodbye letter on his pillow, he would not be happy.

She needed to tell Brenna the truth, at least. Brenna had been so kind these last few weeks, coming to help at the farm after her mother's death. She shouldn't have led Brenna to believe she'd be doing Gael a favor by guiding her through Flamesmoat. But when she'd woken up and found Gael and Conall headed out to hunt, and Brenna announced her plans to return to the city, she jumped at the chance to tag along.

The scent of saltwater grew stronger, and the first of many warehouses populating the dock section of Southmoat emerged in the distance. She needed to say something soon, or she would lose the chance.

"Aunt Bren." Lark's voice trembled. "I need to tell you something." She shuffled along, her eyes downcast. "Gael and Conall weren't exactly expecting me to leave today. I left them each a letter to explain, but you might not find they're happy I followed you the next time you head over for a visit." She snuck a peak at Brenna's face, and her eyes widened.

A grin stretched across her aunt's face. "Oh, I already knew that," she said with a chuckle.

"You did? And you helped me anyway?"

"Of course." Brenna smiled. "I do what I can to help my brother. Sometimes that means doing something he doesn't agree with. Any fool with half a brain could see you don't belong on that farm. He'll see it, too, eventually." She lifted her gaze to the darkening sky and frowned. "Let's pick up the pace. Looks like a storm is coming. It's not much farther."

It seemed the townsfolk had the same idea. The twisting streets became less crowded as everyone sought shelter from the storm.

Lark kept pace with Brenna easily. The older woman huffed with exertion but doggedly pressed on until she reached a large warehouse at the docks' edge.

Planted in the middle of a long line of buildings built of red brick common to the area, the warehouse appeared deserted from the outside. Lark didn't notice a number or any distinguishing feature to set it apart from the surrounding buildings, but Brenna marched purposefully to the back door and knocked without hesitation.

A few moments passed without reply. Just as Brenna lifted her fist to knock again, the door opened, revealing a middle-aged man with bloodshot eyes and a frown plastered to his face. He stuck his head out and looked left to right before focusing on Brenna and addressing her directly.

"Come in." He opened the door fully and disappeared inside.

Lark's heart sped up, fluttering as fast as a hummingbird's wings. Should she really be doing this? Leaving her family and everything she'd ever known?

A small part of her screamed to turn back. Head home. Forget this foolishness and return to the family she'd abandoned.

No. This was it. Her future was about to change. All she had to do was cross the threshold. Taking a deep breath, she strode forward and followed her aunt inside.

The warehouse was dimly lit. It took Lark a few moments to adjust to the darkness before she could make out most of her surroundings.

The building was enormous and almost completely filled with crates and boxes. Some were stacked neatly, others more haphazardly, lining the walls and forming row upon row of makeshift walls in the center.

As she continued to scan the building, the smile she'd been wearing faded away to nothing. This was not what she'd been expecting. Where were the mages? She shifted from foot to foot, waiting for someone to round one of the stacks and greet them.

Turning to take another peek at the man who'd invited them inside, she found him standing beside the closed door. He was of average height and build with brown hair and eyes, and he had one of those faces that was only remarkable in that nothing about it was particularly remarkable. He wore plain brown clothing, not the spotless white robes the Palisade Mages favored.

The hair stood on the back of her neck. He silently watched her, inspecting her body, the same way Gael looked at livestock. Why wasn't anyone talking? Brenna stood beside the man, watching him eye her up. Was this some test prospective mages needed to pass? Was he scanning her for talent?

"Are you a mage?" Lark blurted out, breaking the silence.

The man's eyes shot to her own, and he raised a brow. "Mage, me?" He exchanged a look with Brenna before returning his gaze to Lark and smiling, revealing a set of straight, yellow teeth. "No, I'm not a mage. I just work for them." He turned and gestured toward a door on the far right of the warehouse. "Come on; they'll want to meet you."

They followed closely behind the man, keeping their distance from the stacked boxes as best they could. A sour smell wafted around them, one that seemed vaguely familiar. What were they storing in here that smelled so unpleasant?

They stopped in front of the door. The man knocked twice and opened the door without waiting for a response, ushering Lark forward into the brightly lit doorway. "After you."

She smoothed her hands along her dark brown curls, wishing she had a mirror to check her appearance. Brenna grabbed her hand and gave it a gentle squeeze. "Go ahead, Lark. You look lovely."

Lark started through the doorway, breathing deeply through her nose. The smell assailed her again as she passed the man. This time, she recognized it. The stale scent of alcohol. It must have been coming from the man all along, not the boxes. She wrinkled her nose in distaste, squinting in the bright light after so long in the dimly lit warehouse.

Blazes, she must be making the most ridiculous face with her eyes scrunched up and her nose wrinkled. She fought to return her face to a neutral expression before the mages wondered what was wrong with her.

As her eyes adjusted, she found herself alone in a small room. It was empty except for a set of high, narrow windows lining the top of the far wall and a single cot that'd seen better days. She spun around as the door slammed shut behind her. The lock clicked shut.

"Let me out," she screamed, banging on the door. Her heart thundered, her stomach dropping as dread filled her.

This must be some mistake. Perhaps her aunt had teamed up with her stepfather to teach her a lesson about the dangers of Southmoat? Yes, that must be it. She would open the door, and they'd all have a good laugh. "C'mon, Aunt Bren, it's not funny. Let me out. Please!"

Her aunt didn't answer. The door stayed firmly closed no matter how much she pounded. The gravity of her situation sunk in. Tears welled in her eyes, and she clutched her neck, unable to scream or even make a sound.

She was so stupid. Something had felt off, but she'd ignored her feelings, trusting Brenna to lead her here safely. Never again.

She pressed her ear to the door. She could hear her aunt and the man talking on the other side.

"What did I tell you? Those hazel eyes, those bouncy, brown curls. I told you she'd be lovely. You'll score a fortune for her in Doln."

Doln? She stiffened. The man didn't work for the mages. He was a slaver, and he was going to sell her to a Dolnman!

"You didn't tell me she would be talented, Bren. I've half a mind to set her free here and now and forget the whole thing, lovely or not. Damn mages are more trouble than they're worth."

"Don't be so dramatic, Rasmus. You know talent doesn't matter a wit without training. You're not planning to stop by Mage Keep on the way to Doln, are you?" Brenna snorted.

How long had her aunt been planning this? She'd obviously met this Rasmus before. Lark had to at least try to gain some answers. And if she could hear them through the door, they could hear her.

"You can't leave me in here," she yelled, pounding on the door again. "Gael will come for me. You know he will." She stopped pounding, her chest aching as she remembered the letter she'd left on his pillow. "If not him, then Conall will come." A tiny smile lit her lips. "I promised to write him. I promised! When the letters don't show, he'll come looking for me."

Conall *would* come. Her brother would walk to Mage Keep himself if he didn't hear from her. Lark held her breath, waiting for some response from the other side of the doorway.

"Don't give me that look, Ras," Brenna said, her voice dripping with contempt. "She won't have anyone coming to her rescue. She doesn't know my brother at all."

"What are you talking about?" Rasmus asked, his words harsh and clipped.

"Oh, just that Gael would rather stay put where he is, on his precious farm. And with his wife and stepson dead, and his stepdaughter off to join the mages, he'll have exactly what he wants. It'll be so sad to lose his son to a tragic hunting accident this afternoon, won't it?"

Lark clasped a hand over her mouth, falling to her knees against the door. Her stomach filled with knots, her head reeled. She couldn't believe it. Gael wouldn't do that to Conall. It couldn't be true. They were family.

"Bren, you're colder than I thought. You really talked him into offing the boy for the inheritance?" Rasmus sounded impressed.

She was going to be sick.

"He worked his hands to the bone to turn a profit at that farm, only to be cut off by some boy when his bitch wife died. It ain't right." Her jolly aunt was like a different person, her voice laced with disdain. "Besides, you know I'd do anything for my little brother."

The world spun. How could she have been so blind? To think she had been worried about Gael being mad at Brenna for taking her to meet the mages. Her aunt must have been laughing at her the whole time while she confessed, knowing she was about to betray her.

She clutched her stomach, lurched away from the door, and collapsed on the worn cot. As the sound of talking quieted to a soft murmur, Lark laid silently and cried.

Chapter 4

Conall came to slowly, consciousness returning, bringing with it confusion and pain. He hurt everywhere and wanted nothing more than to sink back into blackness and escape.

No sooner had his mind awakened than he heard the voice return. The voice he now knew with certainty was not his own.

"Don't move, don't speak, don't move, don't speak," it said, repeating like a litany.

As if he could, he thought ruefully. *"Why?"* he asked the voice in his mind. *"Who are you? What's happening? Have I gone insane?"*

It was all too much. The voice. The pain. He wanted to cry out but heeded the voice, staying motionless and silent.

"We are the same, you and I. We shall meet soon enough. For now, be still. He watches."

He watches. Gael. He was still there?

He was so consumed with the voice and his aching body he'd forgotten what that snake had done. The pain in his shoulder was from him. It felt like the arrow was still lodged in his skin, the throbbing intensifying as he concentrated on the spot.

And the fall must have caused the rest of it. He wouldn't learn more with his eyes closed and lying still, but he could already tell he'd been struck in multiple places as he'd fallen down the ridge to the forest floor.

"You live, little brother. Your body will heal in time. So long as he thinks you dead, he will leave, and you will have time to heal. Just... don't... move."

"Yes, I won't."

Conall itched to open his eyes. To confront his stepfather. To show him his treachery had been wasted and he lived. But he knew that would be foolish. He'd likely only earn another arrow for his trouble.

He fought to ignore the pain. Warm rain fell on his face. The cold ground was hard against his back and legs. He listened to the soothing rain and the nearby trickling of the small waterfall. Had his body not been in agony, it would've been enough to lull him to sleep.

The water was loud in his ears, but not loud enough to drown out all the sounds around him. One particular sound he heard faintly, but nonetheless clear and unmistakable. A man crying.

Gael was crying for him? The realization almost made him laugh. He had no business feeling sorrow after what he'd done. They shared a home and family for years. Years. Worked alongside one another, celebrating birthdays and festival days together. And he'd shot him over a simple disagreement? It was crazy.

"My boy, my boy, what have I done?" Gael cried out between sobs, his voice filled with anguish. "Brenna... bloody blazes, I should've never listened to you."

Conall's confusion deepened. Brenna had something to do with this? Gael's sister had come to stay with them at the farm a few weeks ago, during the days leading up to his mother's funeral.

He racked his brain, trying to recall anything suspicious about her, but he'd been so filled with grief for his mother, so lost in his own memories of her, he'd not given the woman much thought.

Brenna had been a great help, taking over the everyday household chores of cleaning and cooking that his mother and sister always shared. Lark was happy to allow it, especially at first. She'd still been recovering from the sickness that infected both women and killed their mother. The familiar ache of grief rose in his chest, thinking of her.

Eventually, Lark recovered enough to return to her daily routine. Brenna seemed eager to return home to her life in Southmoat. But maybe not. Maybe her kindness was all an act. An excuse to creep close, to whisper plans of murder in her brother's ear. But why? What could she possibly want?

The farm. They wanted the farm.

Bile stung his throat. In retrospect, it was painfully obvious. Conall had been to Flamesmoat. He spent the first years of his life in the slums of Southmoat. No one in their right mind would be eager to return.

He should have known. He should have suspected. Now, his sister would be alone with those murderers. Trapped in that house with the only family she had left, not knowing they were responsible for her brother's death.

Not for long. Conall vowed to return to her. He'd pull his broken body along the forest floor if he had to, but he'd find a way to get back to Lark. He would save his sister.

The sounds of water and crying went on for ages. Conall's thoughts drifted back to the voice. It was silent now, but he had no doubt if he called out to it in his mind, he would receive a response. He didn't know who it was, or what exactly was happening, but he sensed instinctively he could trust it.

Twice it saved him. It said they would meet soon, and he found himself looking forward to it, if only for the opportunity to meet his savior and thank them properly.

He had a suspicion it would be more than a simple meeting. That it would change the course of his life. It was a curious thought, but one that brought him a measure of comfort. Despite the pain, or perhaps because of it, he fell asleep.

He awakened with a start. After listening carefully for a time and hearing no crying, he chanced opening his eyes to a tiny slit. The rain had stopped, and night was not far off. Unless Gael planned to spend the night fumbling through the darkened forest, he'd taken off hours ago.

Fully opening his eyes, he shifted on the cold ground, regretting the decision instantly as the pain that had become dull while he rested came into sharp focus. The agony stole his breath. Gritting his teeth, he lifted his head enough to look down at his body in the evening light.

He saw the damage the fall caused for the first time and shuddered. The arrow stuck out from his shoulder like a snapped twig; the fletching was broken and parts missing. He noticed his clothing was soaked, torn, and stained with blood in more places than he could count before the pounding in his head demanded he close his eyes.

He lay still, cursing his luck, gathering the strength to open his eyes. To find some way to move his battered body. He had to find shelter, build a fire, pull the arrow out. He'd not forgotten his vow. In fact, if it hadn't been for his burning desire to see his sister safe, he would've likely lay there and succumbed to the pain.

A twig snapped to the left. His eyes shot open. A large gray wolf sat on its haunches near his feet, studying him.

Conall should've been afraid. He should've been quaking with fear to find a predator so close, with him in no condition to defend himself. But gazing into the wolf's golden eyes, gratitude and tranquility washed over him. Something inside of him knew. The voice, his savior, was here.

"Little brother, you live." The wolf stood, pacing closer. A quick check told him he was male.

"Brother? You keep calling me that," Conall replied.

"What else would you have me call you?" The wolf tilted his head.

"My name's Conall. What's yours?"

"My name? I don't have a name." He yawned, lying down. *"Call me whatever you like."*

"All right, I'll think of something." Conall felt oddly comfortable talking with the wolf in his mind. It was so strange, like they'd known each other all their lives, although they'd only just met.

Magic. It was bonding magic. He was ready to admit what he'd only guessed at. What he'd only dreamed of. He was bonded to this wolf.

It made an odd sense to him. He always had a thing for dogs, for as long as he could remember. He loved them, and they loved him back.

As a child, he fantasized about owning a dog, but his family didn't have the means to take care of a pet. He befriended every stray in Southmoat, no matter how mean-tempered, sneaking little bits of scraps to them whenever he could. But it would be many years before he had a dog to call his own.

It was actually Gael who'd given him his first pup, Sunny. Shortly after proposing to his mother, he'd gifted Conall the sweetest, yellow mutt. From day one, he and Sunny shared a connection unlike any other in his experience. He raised her like a child and treated her more like a treasured friend than an animal. She was the best gift he'd ever received.

Looking back, that was the moment he'd started to accept Gael as part of the family. The realization stung, especially considering Sunny would treat Gael as her new master when he never returned from their hunt. One more reason he had to make it back. He had to survive.

"Do you think you can help me, brother?" The title would have to do until he thought of a name.

The wolf must've approved. His ears perked up, and his tail wagged. *"Always."*

"I have to get this arrow out. I'm going to break the bottom off, as best I can. Can you grab the sharp end with your teeth and pull it out from behind?"

"Arrow?" He rose and walked closer, examining Conall inquisitively.

Conall remembered the warning. *"Killstick. You called it a killstick."*

"Yes, I can try."

Conall sat up. Blackness clouded his vision. A fresh wave of pain slammed into him, and he struggled to concentrate on the task at hand. He better finish this quickly, while he still had the strength.

"Listen, I'm probably going to black out when you pull the arrow out. Do you see that tree?" He pointed to a massive star oak nearby. *"The ones that drop these?"* He used his knuckles to nudge an acorn resting next to his hand across the grass. *"If you can get some of the bark for me... like the skin, you know, of the tree... I can make a medicine when I wake up to stop infection."*

He'd listened to his mother and Lark enough to learn a few things. The fast-growing star oak trees, named for their star-shaped leaves, grew like weeds in Dracwood. Its scrawny branches made for poor climbing, but its bark might be the difference between life and death for him today.

"I can bring you the tree skin, little brother." His tail wagged again. *"Conall,"* he added.

Conall smiled. Maybe it was his imagination, but he felt like having the wolf here to help gave him a boost of fortitude. With him here it didn't seem so crazy to think this mad plan would work. That he might actually survive. He drew in a deep breath and got to work.

He'd lost his bow and quiver during the fall, but luckily, the pouches he wore strapped to his belt remained attached. Ignoring his body's protests, he reached into the pouch on his right-hand side and closed his eyes in relief when his fingers brushed against a smooth leather object inside.

It was a small blade he used to cut the twine for his snares and traps. He pulled it out, sliding his finger and thumb to remove the leather sheath covering the sharp edge. This ought to help.

Just that small movement had him panting. Sweat poured off his brow, plastering his brown locks to his forehead and stinging his eyes, despite the forest's coolness at dusk.

Should he start a fire? No. There was no time. He had to remove the arrow now. Before the wound started to fester and while he still had enough daylight to see what he was doing.

Now that he sat, the arrow dangled at an angle, swinging lightly with each heaving breath he took and sending little shockwaves of agony through his skin.

He just had to decide where to cut. The largest bend in the shaft close to his shoulder looked like it could work. He gritted his teeth, lifted the blade with his right hand, and began sawing.

On the first stroke, he screamed. The sound was so loud and jarring it sent the wolf scurrying back, tail between his legs. The second stroke brought forth a curse, uttered gutturally while his body shuddered. On the third stroke, the arrow broke, falling on his lap with a *plop*.

"Now, brother," he whimpered in his mind. Blackness already crowded the edges of his sight.

The wolf disappeared behind him. He heard him sniffing before the shooting pain in his shoulder told him the wolf had clasped onto the arrow with his powerful jaws.

"Pull!" he screamed.

His brother pulled. The last image he remembered after falling backward was the wolf standing over him with the broken, blood-soaked arrow clenched between his teeth.

Chapter 5

The storm had come and gone, the raindrops echoing strangely as they pelted the huge warehouse roof. Lark allowed herself to cry while the storm raged, but when the rain stopped, she let out one last heaving sob and dried her eyes on her sleeve. She forced the despair and humiliation deep down inside and sat up on the cot.

The warehouse was silent. The room she was trapped in dimmed as the sun worked its way closer to the western horizon. It truly was bare.

She pressed a hand to her temples. There was nothing in the room she could use to escape. She still had her pack, but the few pieces of clothing and half a loaf of bread would be less than useless as weapons.

In those last moments while the rain fell, she'd made up her mind. She *would* escape. She'd fixed that thought in her mind and was intent on seeing it through. There was no way she would end up as some Dolnman's slave.

No, she was going to find a way out of this mess. And after she was free, she would return to the farm and make them pay.

Her insides contorted with pain... Conall.

Brenna and Gael did not get to kill her brother, sell her to slavers, and steal their farm. No. They would *not* win. She was going to escape. She had to.

Determination fueling her, Lark stood and took another look around. After dropping her pack on the dirt floor, she climbed atop the cot. Despite her petite stature, by balancing on her toes, she could just peer through the bottom of the high, narrow windows.

Hope blossomed in her chest. Some kind stranger might be out there. She would call out to them, and they would come to her rescue—but of course, the street was deserted. Worse, it wasn't a street at all, but a tiny alley filled with even more crates and boxes, most looking decrepit and abandoned. Her heart sank. She wasn't likely to find help there.

After hopping down from the cot, she peered under it. Her eyes widened when she spotted something shoved to the back. Kneeling down, she reached under and slid out a large enamel pot. She opened the lid, then retched at the smell and closed the lid with a clatter.

That at least answered one question she had in the back of her mind, but it wouldn't be much help to escape. Although, it was rather heavy.

She sat back on her heels, an idea forming. Maybe she could land a lucky strike to Rasmus' head and slip out in the mayhem. She would need to distract him first with some ruse that would make him enter and turn his back. If she could just think of something...

A door slammed in the warehouse, and she almost jumped out of her skin. She shoved the chamber pot back under the cot but placed it within easy reach, just in case. After hopping up off the floor, she tip-toed to the door and pressed her ear against the wood.

"Well, well, well." She heard Rasmus' muffled voice. "What do we have here?"

"Pretty, ain't she?" said a second man, his voice deep and gravelly.

"Very, very, nice. Where did you find this gem?"

"The Joria Rose brothel. Seems her previous benefactor had enough of her." The new man laughed cruelly. "Don't want any other rich pigs around town sniffing at her, either. One of those 'don't play with my toys' types, I gather."

"Brothel, did you say?" Footsteps pounded across the room before Rasmus spoke again. "Pax, you know you aren't supposed to damage the merchandise."

"She was like that when I got her, I swear." Pax laughed again.

"Fine, fine. Stick her in the back room with the other one. Then come help me pack the wagon. We're leaving."

"Whatever you say, boss."

Footsteps headed in her direction. Lark scrambled back from the door and hopped onto the cot. She wrapped her arms around her knees and tucked her chin against her chest as the lock clicked and the door swung open.

One of the ugliest men she'd ever seen stepped into the room. He was completely bald, hulking in size and had a scar across his left eyelid that puckered the skin, leaving the eye looking like it was perpetually squinting. He gripped the forearm of a girl who looked not much older than she was.

Unlike the man, she was undeniably gorgeous, all soft lines and curves, her face so striking she would earn stares from any man with a pulse. She had dark brown skin and golden-brown eyes that were wide open in fear.

Pax let go of the girl's arm and dragged his hand through her short brown curls, gripping them tightly and forcing her head back. He stared into her eyes with a smirk and said, "I'll see you later, beautiful," before releasing his grip on her hair. Then, he shoved her inside and slammed the door shut. It locked with a *click*.

The girl smacked into the floor, catching herself on her hands and knees. Lark leapt up, intending to help her to her feet, but she backed away when the girl flinched at her touch and scrambled away, banging into the wall.

"I'm sorry. I didn't mean to frighten you." Lark perched on the cot and offered the girl a half smile. "I was only trying to help you off the ground."

The girl peered at her, silent and unsmiling. She was clothed in a tight-fitting, flimsy brown dress. The fabric blended into her skin so well she almost appeared nude. There was a bruise on her chin and a set of fresh scratches on her neck that looked red and angry.

"I got here right before the storm started. I had a look around, and there doesn't seem to be any way out of this room... Well, there is a chamber pot under the bed." Lark shook her head sheepishly, rubbing a hand on her neck, realizing she hadn't bothered to supply a name. "I'm Lark, by the way." She stared at the ground, wishing the girl would speak. "What's your name?"

"I'm Tiora," she said, after a moment of silence. Her voice was beautiful, too; a sweet alto.

Lark's gaze shot back to Tiora's face, and she found her staring out the window at the last rays of sunshine filtering through the glass. She looked forlorn, but her eyes held no tears.

"I would say 'pleasure to meet you,' but that doesn't seem right in these circumstances." Lark scooted sideways on the cot, patting the lumpy mattress' empty half. "You don't have to stay seated on the hard floor. It's not much better up here, but you're welcome to share the cot with me."

Tiora glanced at the bed before returning her gaze to the dimming view. "I'm fine here, thanks."

Lark's brow furrowed, but she didn't push the matter. She sighed. The chamber pot was out now. With two villains here, there was no way she could surprise them both. But she might get Tiora on her side. They had little chance of overpowering the men, but maybe the two of them working together could come up with a plan to outsmart them.

Before she could think of something to say to enlist the older girl's help, the sound of footsteps pounded in her ears. She sat stock still, gaping at the door.

Pax threw it open and sauntered into the room with an evil grin plastered to his ugly face. He was so large his muscles strained at the cloth of his brown tunic and trousers.

Lark couldn't stop the shudder that overtook her body when his eyes locked with her own.

"Blazes, how did I miss you earlier?" Pax licked his lips and prowled closer. "This is gonna be a fun trip. I'm gonna enjoy getting to know you two." He wagged his eyebrows suggestively, grinning even wider.

Lark's stomach clenched at the implication behind his words.

"Hands off that one, Pax. She needs to arrive unspoiled if we want the best price." Rasmus stepped inside and pulled the door closed behind him.

Lark's shoulders relaxed, until she glimpsed the items he carried, and her back knotted up again, worse than before.

Rasmus held rope and long strips of rough, black cloth. Handing half to Pax, he stumbled forward, and a whiff of liquor wafted off of him.

Lark angled her nose away in disgust. It only awarded her a brief moment of relief, for he came closer still; the smell grew much stronger.

"I'll take care of her." Rasmus glanced back over his shoulder. "Tie up the whore."

Lark's body rooted to the spot. She stared up at Rasmus as he unwrapped the rope between his hands. "You're not going to give me any trouble, are you, little bird?"

Lark's mind raced, her gaze flicking to the door. Could she make a run for it? Snatch the chamber pot and clobber Rasmus, race past Pax…

She considered it briefly, but the glint of silver at her captor's waist drove the thought from her mind. A man willing to trade in slaves would likely have no problem hurting or even killing a troublesome girl. Especially a slaver who'd been drinking.

She shook her head slowly, looking into the man's cloudy eyes. "Never mess with a man deep in his cups," her mother used to say. She would play the part of the obedient prisoner for now and bide her time until she could see a way out of this.

"Give me your hands." Rasmus' face displayed no sign of glee like Pax's but was just as frightening for all his stoic indifference.

She stuck her hands in front of her, and Rasmus went to work. The rope scratched her wrists, the loops dug into her skin. He wrapped the rope expertly, finishing it all with a knot and pulling it tight. She gulped, her stomach churning as he held up the strip of cloth he'd strung over his shoulder while he was busy with her hands.

"You're not going to blindfold me, are you?" she asked, her voice shaky.

He wobbled a bit as he slid the strip between his hands, then stretched it out. "Open your mouth."

Lark obeyed, shuddering as the rough cloth made contact with her tongue. Rasmus knotted the cloth tightly behind her head, then grabbed the rope around her wrists and tugged, pulling her to her feet.

She managed to catch a glimpse of Tiora tied in identical fashion, still staring impassively out the windows, before she was forced to follow Rasmus' lead.

He led her through the warehouse, weaving between the stacked boxes, and then through the back door. The street was much the same, except for a black horse and wagon that stood at the ready beyond the door. The wagon looked sturdy and the horse spritely and young. It pulled gently at its reins and nickered as they approached.

Rasmus tugged on her bound hands, leading her to the back of the cart. "Get in." He lifted the black tarp covering the back of the wagon enough so she could squeeze in.

She sat down on the edge and scooted backward but apparently not far enough.

"Further." Rasmus nudged her shins with his fist.

Lark scooted back as far as she could until her back pressed against something hard and unyielding. Tiora was made to squeeze in as well. The wagon was so crowded they were forced to sit crammed together like children vying for the best seat at the Harvest Festival parade.

Once Rasmus was satisfied they were arranged to his liking, he lifted the wooden, slatted tailboard and dropped the tarp. He sealed them in, shrouding them in darkness.

The cart swayed as the men boarded and Rasmus called out to the horse, "Ya." Then the cart surged forward, slamming her back against the hard object behind her.

Lark's chest rose and fell as she struggled for air. This was really happening. Her life was over. Everything she'd known and loved was lost to her. Even her pack lay back in that warehouse room, abandoned and forgotten.

She tugged at the gag, franticly trying to dislodge it now that the men weren't watching, but it was tied so tightly it wouldn't budge. She tried desperately to calm her rushing heart, scanning the darkness for something to calm her panic. There was nothing. Only the taste of wet cloth clogging her mouth and the rough rope digging into her skin.

Suddenly, movement brushed her side. Tiora pressed her thigh against Lark's more firmly, and a moment later, a pair of bound hands landed on her knee. That small reminder that she wasn't alone helped immensely. Slowly, her breathing evened out, thanks to the kindness of the stranger beside her.

Time passed. Lark's eyes adjusted to the darkness. There were a few spots ahead of her where light leaked through the wagon slats. Leaning forward, she pressed her eye against the nearest spot and watched Southmoat as they drove through dusk. It was nearly evening, but there was still enough light for her to see.

Her stomach lurched. So that was the reason for her aunt's winding route earlier in the day. The wagon headed directly west, and the sights she saw were a far cry from the poor, but still respectable, neighborhood Brenna was so careful to showcase.

Beggars sprawled in the streets, a few covered in weeping sores or missing limbs. Dilapidated buildings crowded the dirty streets. Many appeared abandoned or like they might fall over in a stiff breeze. Children still ran in the streets, but they did not play. Instead, they fought one another or slinked in doorways, looking half-starved and desperate.

The wagon rolled on, the darkness outside deepening until all she could see was shadow broken by occasional glimpses of light shining from the seedy buildings. Finally, she leaned back, her shoulders and neck protesting after so long spent leaning forward.

What she wouldn't give for a hot bath. And a warm meal. Her chin trembled, and she closed her eyes. Would such simple pleasures ever be hers again?

The *clip-clop* of hooves on the hard-packed dirt slowed, and then halted, as the wagon rolled to a stop. Lark tensed, holding her breath.

"I'll just be a moment," Rasmus said. The wagon swayed with his shifting weight. "Have to stock up on libations. Stay with the wagon."

Lark peered through the slats but couldn't see much in the darkness. Just a rectangle of light and the sound of raucous merriment spilling out of a building as Rasmus slipped in. The moment dragged out with no sign of his return.

The wagon vibrated with the *tap-tap-tapping* of a booted foot. After an eternity of tapping, Pax cursed. The wagon jolted as he jumped down, followed by sounds of merriment once again breaking the night's silence.

Her heart skipped a beat. This might be their chance.

With all her strength, Lark shoved her fists into the tarp, looking for any weaknesses. A heartbeat later, Tiora joined in, and their fists pounded together in concert, like a crazed drummer in a frenzy. But it was no use. The tarp was tied on expertly, and their pounding had no effect.

Changing tactics, she kicked the wooden tailboard. Tiora joined in again, but being so cramped, it was soon obvious they wouldn't have the leverage needed to force open the lock. Shaking from exertion, Lark stopped kicking. Tears welled in her eyes.

Shuffling footsteps sounded from the opposite direction of the pub. Lark's breath caught. Had their attempt at escape attracted someone who might help?

A sound crinkled above her head, and a tiny corner of tarp peeled back, revealing the face of a stranger.

An old woman, wrinkled and gray-haired, peeked in at them, her brown eyes as big and round as the wheels of their wagon. "Oh dear, you poor things."

Lark tried to speak, to cry out help, but the gag only allowed her to mumble unintelligibly.

"There, there, little ones. Oh, I wish I could free you, but I haven't a knife for the rope—and the back—I haven't the key."

Staring at the woman with pleading eyes, Lark's heart filled with dread as she began to drop the tarp and leave.

The woman stared through the hole, remorse painting her face before disappearing. An instant later, she shoved her hand through and dropped something into the wagon. "I'll pray for you," she whispered, then she shuffled away.

Lark groped around in the darkness with her bound hands, searching for whatever the woman gifted them. After a moment, she found it, and a tear dripped from her lashes. The unmistakable softness of a fresh-cut flower flattened under her fingertips. She screamed her frustration into the gag, tears rolling down her face.

The pub door opened, and Lark pressed her eye to the slat. Pax exited, half dragging, half carrying out Rasmus, who had a bottle slung under his arm and another clenched in his fist.

Shoving the flower into her skirt pocket, she rubbed her face against her sleeves, brushing away the tears as the wagon rocked.

"Get up there, you lush," Pax said. He lifted the tarp's corner and eyed them both before hopping onto the cart and setting it in motion.

They traveled for ages. She'd long ago given up looking through the slats, for night had fully fallen. After they left the confines of Flamesmoat and entered the forested countryside, there was nothing to see, anyway. Just an endless expanse of woods and trees.

Her body was sore all over, muscles aching from being crammed in the back of the wagon for so long. When they stopped, relief washed over her, if only for the chance to climb out and stretch.

The wagon shifted, and a single *thud* landed on the ground before someone came round and unlocked the tailboard. Pax's face was revealed in the moonlit night. "Out," he said.

Lark moved to comply.

He looked at her stone-faced and shoved her back with his palm. "Not you." He pointed at Tiora. "You, out."

Tiora shrank back, but Pax grabbed her by her wrists and tugged, spilling her out onto the ground. He slammed the board back into place, locked it, and returned Lark to the darkness.

For a moment, she rejoiced. With Tiora gone, she had room to spread out, which she did at once, groaning as her muscles stretched.

Then came the sounds. Moaning. Skin slapping. Grunting and cursing.

Her blood boiled. Rasmus, no doubt blackout drunk, was not stopping it. She could do nothing to stop it.

Her stomach kinked up in knots with every disgusting groan. The momentary relief was long gone, replaced with disgust and guilt. She would gladly spend an eternity cramped together with Tiora to spare her this.

As she lay there listening, the cold night air chilling her skin, she made another promise to herself. One she was just as determined to keep. Before she escaped, she would see both of these men dead.

Chapter 6

Izora rapped on the door to Kayda's bedchamber early on the morning after Kayda summoned for the first time. The sun had barely crested the eastern horizon, but Kayda was already dressed in a cream and ivory-striped dress, ready for training.

Despite her nurse's instructions, she hadn't slept much. That night, her mind had brimmed with questions. And the morning had been no better. She was so full of excitement and apprehension about the day to come.

Izora breezed in without waiting for a reply. "Good morning, Princess." She placed a vase of flowers on her bedside table. "Up early, I see."

"Yes, I'm ready." Kayda jumped up from her bed, smoothed the bedspread, and nodded with satisfaction. "Are we training in here? Or shall we go to your quarters?" She was hoping for the latter. The musty scent of yesterday's events still lingered in the air.

"Neither." Turning on her heel, Izora led the way to the door, calling over her shoulder, "Follow me."

At this hour, the castle was quiet. Likely, there were servants awake in the kitchens and stables, but in the southeast wing, where the royal family slept in their private chambers, they were the only ones stirring.

Her rooms were the smallest in the wing, comprising a modest bedchamber, a closet-sized dressing room, and a cramped sitting room. They sat close to the corridor leading to the central hall, which Izora headed toward.

They called it the royal corridor. The entire path was hung, floor-to-ceiling, with portraits. Kings and queens of the past stared stoically out of the frames.

One day, her own portrait might be up there. Kayda suppressed a smirk. At least she would add a little variety to all the pale blondes and brunettes with her light brown freckled skin and auburn hair.

As they neared the corridor's end, they approached the largest painting. It was her favorite. Something about it always made her gaze linger on it as she passed.

It was a portrait of the first King of Dracwood, King Algernon the Great. According to legend, he'd been instrumental in blocking the Abandoned Lands, helping the mages along with his bonded animal, a dragon named Dru. Unlike most of the others, he was smiling, his tawny-brown eyes sparkling on the canvas. The painter must have been a genius of the time. The image seemed so alive.

Her favorite part of the piece was in the background. A casual viewer might even miss it, but Kayda's gaze always locked on the little detail. In the top left corner, camouflaged among trees, was the tip of a black-scaled tail.

She couldn't stare long today, so she settled for a passing smile and followed Izora out of the royal wing.

The central hall was the largest building in the castle and was rectangular, with four wings attached on each corner by a corridor. The royal corridor let out into the drawing room, a cheery canary-yellow room dominated by oversized settees and chaises, which connected to the main foyer and great hall.

Izora passed through the drawing room without pause and led Kayda through the great hall, which was brightly lit with daylight and deserted. Their footsteps reverberated through the cavernous hall. They scurried like mice, taking no time to admire the many colorful tapestries adorning the whitewashed brick walls.

Izora turned right at the back of the great hall and headed through the music room. Instruments of all shapes and sizes—the wood and metals polished to a gleaming shine—adorned the walls or sat waiting atop shelves and display racks. Today, the room was silent and still.

They passed through quickly, into the corridor leading to the northwest wing of the castle. This wing contained one of Kayda's favorite places in the whole keep, the library.

"You can't mean to teach me to summon fire in the library," Kayda whispered as they hurried down the corridor. "That would be disastrous."

She shuddered, picturing the wing going up in flames. Destroying all the tomes the library held would be a crime she could never forgive herself for.

"Don't fret for your books, child. We won't be training here." Izora smiled as she opened the door to the library.

They slipped in, and Kayda smiled, too, breathing deeply the familiar woody scent of the written word. Much like the royal corridor, the walls were loaded from floor to ceiling, only with shelves instead of pictures. Books sat neatly upon them in all sizes, shapes, and colors, covering a wide variety of topics. So many she could never read them all in her lifetime. She loved it here.

Kayda arched her brow. "Well, what are we doing here if we won't be training?" She crossed her arms. "Am I to study some books on magic before I'm allowed to practice?"

"No, don't be silly." Izora strode across the library toward a closet tucked away in a corner. On the way, she grabbed a large, three-armed candelabra off one of the shelves and lit it in the fireplace before motioning Kayda forward. "In through here."

Kayda followed, cramming herself inside behind her nurse, and then closing the door. The scent of lye soap permeated the room. She drew her elbows close, avoiding the stacked cleaning supplies while the dusty air tickled her nose.

"I don't see how you expect me to get much practice done in here. I can hardly move."

"Patience, my dear," Izora said. "Just a moment."

Kayda couldn't see what she was doing, but it was clear her nurse was doing something besides standing motionless in the closet. Before she could question her, the answer became obvious when the closet's back wall swung inward, revealing a stone stairwell leading into darkness.

Kayda squealed with delight. She'd thought she knew everything about the castle, but this was new.

She was about to follow her nurse into a hidden room... Forget reading about adventures; she was about to experience one for herself. Taking a deep breath, she lifted her skirts and followed Izora into the passage.

The steps were narrow, so they traveled single file. Kayda focused on the candles' bobbing light and held the rough brick wall to keep her balance. Her heart pounded with excitement.

It wasn't long before they made it to the bottom of the steps. In the candelabra's dim light, she could see the beginnings of an underground chamber of some sort. "What is this place?" Kayda squinted into the darkness.

The light dimmed even more. Kayda looked back at her nurse as a chill filled the air.

Izora cupped a hand near one of the candles, eyes closed. When she opened her eyes, the candle's flame split into four distinct balls. The flames separated, then floated to the corners of the room, pausing just below the ceiling and hanging suspended as if from invisible dangling sconces.

"Wow," Kayda exclaimed, impressed with the display of Izora's talent as much as the underground chamber's size. It was massive, comparable in size to the great hall. The walls were made of brick and stone, but the floor appeared to be hard-packed dirt.

There were several doorways hewn into the stone walls. Most of them were open to reveal passages leading off into more darkness, but one on the far wall had a wooden door that blocked her view of what lay beyond.

Kayda itched to explore it all. Especially that door. What would she find if she walked through that doorway? Forgotten treasures? Ancient relics of the people who once inhabited this keep? A voice inside of her hummed with wonder and curiosity and called out to open that door and discover what hid behind it.

"I never knew this was down here. How did you find this place?" She turned and found Izora watching her.

"Oh, I have my ways. These rooms were once used as storage. At some point, they stopped using them. From the looks of it, they're prone to flooding." She nodded toward the discoloration shading the bottom of the brick walls. "This room should serve us fine for our training."

"All right, but what about the rest of this place?" Kayda stood on tip-toe, peering into the darkness beyond the closest opening. "Have you been down all the halls and passages?"

"I've been through some. It's all the same—just more empty rooms like this one and locked doors."

"Oh." Her shoulders slumped. It wasn't the mystery she'd been hoping for, but she wouldn't let a few empty rooms dampen her enthusiasm. She was about to learn how to summon fire. "So, how do we start?"

"Before we begin practicing, there are a few rules you need to learn." Izora planted herself in front of her, meeting her eyes, her face serious. "Never try to summon without your source element nearby. Luckily, the fires in this old castle are always lit, but that won't always be the case everywhere you go."

Izora removed something from her skirt pocket and placed it into Kayda's hand. It was an oblong metal box about the size of a deck of cards. Kayda smoothed her fingers across the top, admiring the intricate etching of a flame engraved upon it.

"It's a tinderbox. It has flint and steel inside," Izora explained. "I'll teach you how to use it."

"Thank you." Kayda lifted the lid and peeked inside. "But I don't understand. Why can't you just summon flames from nothing?"

"You can, dear. But that doesn't mean you should. Using a source that's already there—you'll find it's as easy as breathing. Summoning a flame from nothing—that's much harder to do, and it has a cost."

"A cost?" She snapped the tinderbox lid shut and placed it in her skirt pocket.

"Yes. Sometimes it might take your energy. Mages have been known to black out when they lose their source and still try to summon."

"That doesn't sound so bad. I mean, you would recover quickly, at least."

"Well, that's just for simple things. Like the little trick I did earlier to light the room." Izora nodded toward the closest fire orb, still suspended from the ceiling. "But if you try to accomplish something bigger without a source—well, the price is a bit steeper."

"What would happen then?"

"You pay with your life."

"It... kills you?"

"In extreme cases, it can. More likely, it will age you. Years of your life, gone in the blink of an eye." Izora sighed. "It's a steep price indeed."

Kayda gulped, eyes widening. Years of her life... The thought of having to pay that price was frightening, but it wasn't enough to stop her from wanting to learn all she could. "All right, so always use a source. What else?"

"You have to remain close to your source if you want the magic to last." Izora held up the candelabra at eye level, the flames dancing merrily. "If I snuff out this candle right now, the flames I summoned will disappear, too. I could use my talent to keep them lit for a short while, but without the source, the magic will only have my own energy to use for fuel."

"And then the costs... Yes, I see." Her brow furrowed. "Hmm, it's too bad I don't have air talent. I bet they don't have to worry about any of this."

Izora chuckled. "Some of us do have it a bit easier than others, I'm afraid. But that's life. You have to work with whatever talents you're given." She backed up a few paces and placed the candelabra on the dirt floor. "Remember those two rules, and you'll be fine. Are you ready for your first lesson?"

Kayda nodded eagerly. "Yes. What should I do?"

Izora sidestepped a few paces, watching Kayda intently. "Approach the candle. That flame will be your source. You don't have to touch it, but you should be close enough to feel the flame's heat."

Kayda complied. The candle warmed her skin. It didn't feel any different today after learning about her talent then it had all the multitude of other times in her life she warmed her hands around a flame. There had to be more.

"This is the part that will take practice. You have to visualize what you want the flames to do. Concentrate. See the flame take shape in your mind."

Kayda bit her lip, flinching away from the flame. It couldn't be that simple, could it?

Izora must have seen the confusion on her face. "It's not as easy as it sounds. At least, not at first. You'll have to learn to empty your mind of all else in order to concentrate and visualize properly. But once you've mastered the basics, you'll find you can shape the flames into whatever you desire."

Kayda's jaw dropped. "Anything I desire... Wait, then why didn't you make the flames disappear from my fireplace yesterday?"

Izora chuckled. "I could have, but I didn't want to scare you before we had a chance to talk. But there's a reason I brought a vase full of water to your room every day. I've been waiting for this day for a long time." She rested a hand on her shoulder, giving her a squeeze. "I know you can do this, Kayda."

She still hadn't wrapped her head around this incredible gift she'd been given. Her whole life, she'd been expecting a completely different talent. Now she could control flames, too.

It was a lot to get used to, but she was up for the challenge. Setting her shoulders back, she reached forward, and the flame's heat kissed her skin once more.

"Try to clear your mind. Start with something small, a ball of flame floating in your hands. Visualize it clearly, the heat... the shape..." Izora instructed, backing away a few paces.

Kayda closed her eyes and tried to empty her mind. She started to picture a ball of flame resting in her palms, but a question interrupted her concentration.

"Wait, if you have to clear your mind, then how did I summon the flames in my room?" She turned to her nurse, raising a brow. "My mind wasn't clear at all."

"Sometimes, when a mage first discovers their talent, it's an instinctual response to extreme emotions. More often than not, it's a response to danger, a life-or-death situation." Izora raised an eyebrow of her own. "If the rumor floating around the keep is to be believed, then you had quite the scare yesterday."

Kayda shivered. The arrow streaking toward her flashed through her memory. She recalled the terror of that moment, and the anger she felt later as she stirred the coals in her fireplace. That must have been the trigger.

A smile crossed her lips. Just this once, she could be thankful for her brother's bullying. If he hadn't shot at her yesterday, she wouldn't be down here learning to summon.

Izora cleared her throat, interrupting Kayda's musing. "Try again, please."

Kayda nodded. She focused on the flame topping the middle candle. She pictured the color of it. The heat. The way it danced in the air. Closing her eyes and lifting her right hand, she tried to picture the flame moving, forming a small sphere floating above her palm. She emptied her mind and thought of nothing else but the flame. The warmth, the power.

A chill swept through her, like an icy breeze stroked every inch of her skin. Lifting her lashes, she squealed with glee when she saw a fireball the size of an apple resting exactly where she pictured it above her outstretched palm. She turned to share her excitement with Izora, only to witness the fireball vanish when her concentration broke.

"Blazes." Kayda frowned. "I had it for a moment, at least."

Izora squeezed her arm. "No, no. That was excellent, Kayda." She tilted her head, a smile stretching across her face. "You're a natural, just like your mother."

Kayda's chest swelled with pride. She was going to be a mage, like her mother. She beamed.

Izora dropped her hand from Kayda's arm and took several steps back. "Again."

Chapter 7

Conall awoke dazed, with a luxurious warmth pressing against his face. A musky scent wafted off his pillow. His nose twitched. The pillow twitched back. He startled, rolling away in surprise, jostling his battered body and awakening fully.

"Blazes." He groaned and clamped his eyes shut, breathing deeply through the pain. His skin was scratched and bruised all over, like he'd been through a thresher. His shoulder burned where the arrow had been, and his body screamed in a dozen places.

The sound of water was missing.

Opening his eyes, he took stock of his surroundings. Shadows blanketed the walls of a shallow cave. It was small, just wide enough to fit a man and wolf inside, with a little room to spare. The cave roof loomed high above, ensuring he could stand without smacking his head on the ceiling, but he would have to crawl to get out. The only light came from the mouth of the cave, by which he could tell a new day had dawned outside.

"How did we get here, brother?" Conall eyed his silent companion, who yawned lazily before replying.

"I pulled you in when you would not awaken. It's not far from where you fell."

"Thank you." He smiled. That was a good call. Sleeping on the wet ground next to a waterfall would've been a bad idea in his condition. The wolf had saved him again. Time and again, he proved himself a true friend.

Hmm, maybe he could call him Buddy? No... that wasn't quite right.

"Did you get the bark?"

"Yes." He rose from his stomach and stretched out his hind legs before walking back a few paces to the cave wall, picking up the bark with his jaw, then depositing it in Conall's outstretched hand.

Conall inspected the bark and sighed. He grabbed his waterskin from his belt loop and swigged a few long swallows before casting his gaze about for a large rock he could use to grind the bark into a paste.

There. *"Please, can you bring me that rock?"* He pointed to it and grimaced as he raised himself into a seated position.

The wolf rolled it with his snout until it landed next to his thigh. Conall got to work, using the stone floor and the rock to grind the bark, adding water one splash at a time until he made an ugly concoction that would hopefully be enough to stave off infection. He'd watched his mother and Lark enough times to know what to do, although he doubted they'd ever worked with such primitive tools.

He smiled crookedly at the soggy mess. They both would've laughed at his attempt and made him start again had he been home with them. For today, it would have to do.

Grimacing again, he unbuttoned the top few buttons of his tunic and peeled back the bloodstained cloth covering his shoulder. The wound looked as bad as it felt—red and black and swollen, weeping fresh blood from where his shirt had been glued.

He suppressed the urge to heave and scooped big globs of the oak paste onto the wound. Though he couldn't see the exit wound, he heaped paste onto his back, gritting his teeth with agony.

He pulled a bit of folded rag out of one of his belt pouches. He always kept some with him when trapping, for cleaning his hands and knife after handling a fresh kill. His empty traps had been a stroke of luck, after all. The fabric was old and worn but blessedly clean.

Holding one end with his teeth, he tossed half the fabric over his shoulder, then smoothed the rest over the front of the wound. That would have to do for now. He rolled his sleeve back in place, ignoring the searing pain as he jostled his wound, and lay down on the cave floor, totally spent.

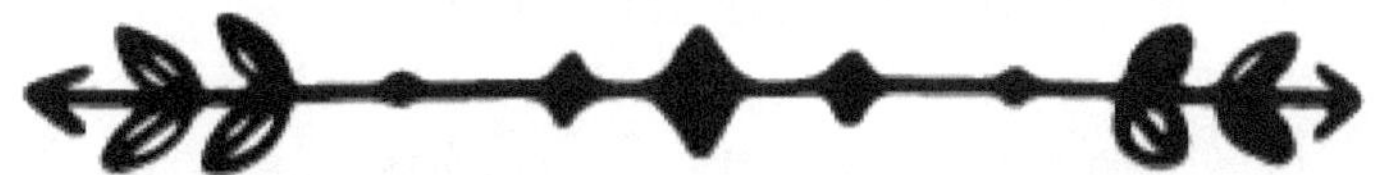

He must've slept. When he opened his eyes, the cave shadows had lengthened. Was it afternoon outside, or dusk? Feeling a pressing need to know and to relieve his aching bladder, Conall decided to venture out and explore.

The wolf was no longer in the cave. Perhaps he had similar thoughts.

Rolling up to sitting, he groaned. That hadn't yet gotten any easier. His body protesting, he leaned forward on his knees, and being careful not to put much weight on his left arm, he crawled through the mouth of the cave into the forest.

From the sun's position, it appeared to be late in the afternoon as he knelt, squinting. The cave let out into a small clearing surrounded by trees. The waterfall peeked out behind trees to the left, a few dozen paces away. He smacked his dry lips together. He ought to head there, to fill his waterskin before dark.

He tried to stand. That was a mistake. His right ankle screamed in pain as he placed his weight on it. Falling back to his knees, tears pooling at the corners of his eyes, he crawled between the trees, searching—there.

He grabbed a large stick just the right size for a crutch. Once again, he stood. With the stick under his right armpit, he hobbled toward the waterfall, pausing behind a tree to take care of his other pressing business.

It appeared so close when viewed from the clearing, but his injuries and hobbling pace made it feel like twice the distance. When he made it to the trickling stream, he collapsed next to it in relief, bathed in sweat, wishing he'd remained resting in the cave. He quickly emptied his waterskin with a few gulps and refilled and emptied it twice more before his thirst was quenched.

Scanning the cliff wall, he spotted the path his body had taken on its way down. Below the top of the ledge lay freshly turned earth, dislodged roots, and torn plants that told the story. A story of betrayal.

Even now, so many hours later, darkened stains marred the spot where he'd lain bleeding, shot, and pretending to be dead. A shiver swept down his spine. He should be dead, but he wasn't. He was alive, and he would set things right. He must.

His stomach rumbled, reminding him he hadn't eaten since yesterday's breakfast. He reached for his belt pouches, planning to nibble on the dried meat he'd brought with him, but at that moment, the wolf appeared. His tail wagged, a freshly killed hare dangling from his jaws.

"Little bro—Conall, you're awake. Good, good. I brought meat." He dropped the hare at Conall's feet, tongue hanging, looking particularly pleased with himself.

Hunter? No... still not right. The name had to be perfect.

"You can still call me little brother, if you like. I don't mind it," Conall said.

"Good." His tail wagged again, a bit faster. *"It is a habit of all wolves to call each other brother, sister, and the like. Sometimes, I forget you are not a wolf. I went searching for a*

pack of my own, and I found you, so to me, we are brothers." He nudged the hare with his snout. *"Eat up, little brother. You need to regain your strength."*

"All right, all right, but not before I cook it." He picked up the hare and grabbed his blade.

"Cook?"

"Gather some dry sticks, and I'll show you."

Conall skinned the hare quickly. He grimaced with pain every time his shoulder jostled, but luckily, years of practice left him so deft at the task he could do it in his sleep.

The wolf spent the time waiting gathering sticks as requested. Then he watched Conall spear the hare's carcass with a stick, licking his chops as Conall stabbed the end of the long branch into the ground.

Conall rinsed his hands in the stream and stacked the wood for a fire. He pulled out a worn metal tin, dented and scratched in a dozen places. He popped it open, grabbed what he needed, and within moments, the scent of smoke filled the air as the fire caught.

"Brother. Fire. Fire!" The wolf backed away from the smoke, pacing, tail between his legs, reminding Conall of his dog Sunny during a thunderstorm.

"It's safe. It's how we cook. The fire won't spread, I promise."

His words seemed to comfort the wolf, but he was still wary. He stayed far back from the fire, until he caught the scent of roasting meat, then he began licking his chops again and creeping closer.

"C'mon, brother. It's almost done." Conall beckoned the wolf forward.

The wolf appeared at his side as he was ready to pull the meat from the spit. Conall used his knife to split the hare in half and placed the wolf's portion in front of him.

He sniffed the steaming meat before licking it cautiously. *"It's warm,"* he said before taking a bite, then proceeding to devour it with relish. *"I like it,"* he proclaimed between bites.

Conall laughed. He ate his own portion more slowly but with just as much pleasure. There was nothing else quite like a simple meal over a campfire with good company. He inhaled, lifting his nose, the scent of wood fire and foliage calming some part deep inside him.

Could that be the answer? Woody... Forest? No, still not it.

He rubbed the back of his neck, polishing off the last of his meat. It would come to him. Perhaps after a night's sleep. Drowsily, he made his way with his brother back to the cave, eager for rest and a chance to heal.

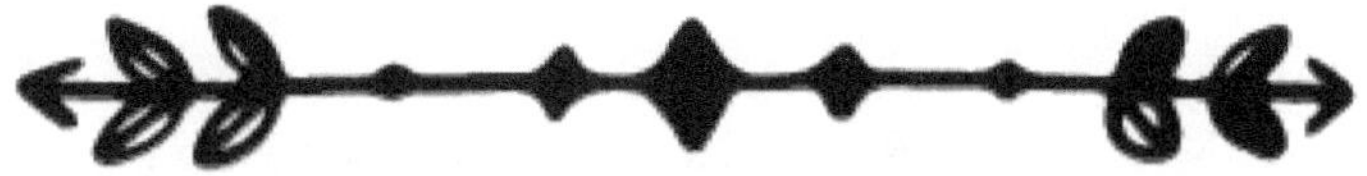

He awoke in the night, bathed in sweat, awash with pain and screaming at some half-forgotten nightmare.

The wolf was at his side in an instant, curling up next to his good arm, staring at him with golden eyes in the dark. *"It's all right, Conall, I'm here."*

He clutched a fistful of fur, comforted instantly, but still scared witless, knowing the infection he'd hoped to avoid was the cause of his state. He hoped with all his might he would overcome this. That his battered body still had enough fight left in it to see him through this fever and alive on the other side.

He spent the night drifting in and out of consciousness, plagued by unrelenting visions. Lark was trapped in the farmhouse while it burned. He stood outside watching but could not move to save her, no matter how he tried. His heart raged as he listened to the torturous cries, the pleas for help. It drove him half mad with agony.

Suddenly, he was in front of a wall that gleamed and pulsated with a life of its own. Lark was there, too, and he watched the life being sucked out of her. He screamed, glued to the spot, unable to move. His throat ached like he'd swallowed broken glass before she heard him, only to turn her ancient face his way, looking drugged.

A smile split her face, ear to ear. She held on tight to the wall, forcing him to watch while the ravages of time wore on her. Her skin decayed, ending with only bone. Her skull still stared back at him, smiling... always smiling.

He saw his own face, glowering at him with shame. Or... it was his father. His own face so similar, those hazel eyes gazing into his own with regret. He'd sacrificed his life on that ship to ensure his family's survival, and what did he get in return? A weakling, a victim. Couldn't protect his own.

No—those were not his father's thoughts. They were his own fevered imaginings.

There were monsters. Great behemoths in the waste, trying to drag him under. Sand filling his throat, hot and choking.

Reptiles slithered in the water, waiting for the moment he let down his guard to plunge him into the salty depths.

Phantoms stalked him through an unending expanse of snow. The cold and fear froze deep in his bones.

His whole body, covered in vermin. The squirming, squealing bodies full of sharp teeth. They would eat him alive.

Darkness blanketed the sky. A black creature, so huge and fearsome, soared through the clouds. Swooping down, it rained fire on the ground, surrounding him with flame. Panic turned his blood to ice.

Run. He had to run.

He awoke with a start, heart still pounding. But his nightmares receded, the way such things do, until they were only a feeling. A niggling discomfort he couldn't fully banish.

Dragging the back of his hand across his forehead, he huffed out a sigh. The fever had passed. His body was weak and his throat drier than it had ever been. He grabbed his waterskin and emptied it, not minding the way it sloshed out from the edges and dribbled down his sweat-soaked neck.

Something twitched to his right. The wolf—his brother—lounged beside him, head resting on his front paws, watching him. Gratitude washed over Conall. He gently stroked the wolf's fur, and soon, fell into a dreamless sleep.

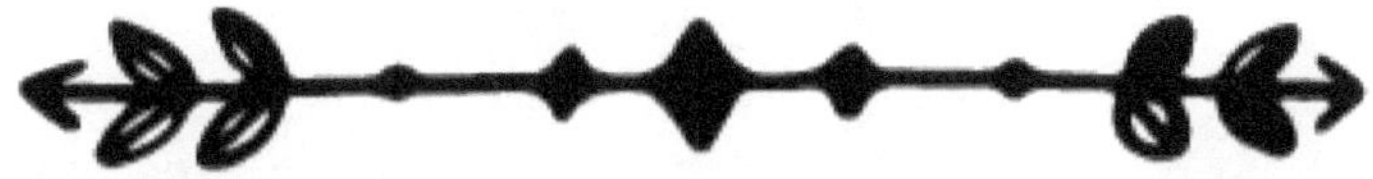

Days passed. The wolf hunted by night while Conall slept, and they feasted each morning. Before long, Conall's body began to knit itself back together. The pain receded slowly. He feared his shoulder would never be the same, yet that, too, began healing.

Throughout it all, the wolf stayed with him. Following him out wherever he went, glued to his side. Then one day, it came to him.

"Shadow. I think I shall call you Shadow, brother." Turning to gaze into his companion's golden eyes, he waited for a response.

"Shadow... Yes, I like it. I'm Shadow." Raising his head to the sky, he let out a single, heartfelt howl.

Conall placed his hand on Shadow's back. Looking at the mouth of the cave, he smiled, feeling bittersweet. *"I hope you're ready for a journey. Tomorrow, we're leaving. I have to save my sister."*

"We will, little brother. Together."

Chapter 8

The days passed by in a flurry of activity for Kayda. Every morning she rose with the sun and crept through the sleeping keep with Izora to practice her magic in the forgotten depths of the castle.

Steadily, her skills improved until she could call the flames at ease. Izora tested her concentration at every turn, distracting her in a million ways. At long last, she became adept at keeping the flame burning, no matter what her nurse did to divert her attention. A bud of pride bloomed in her chest, but she knew she'd only just begun. She was eager to continue her training, relishing learning to control her talent with a fervor she'd not yet known in her life.

Early one morning, Izora did not come to meet her at their usual hour. Refusing to sit and wait, Kayda pulled on a simple turquoise dress and set out to discover the reason for her absence. Stealthily, she made her way through the castle, searching all the common areas on her way, but finding them empty and silent.

Had Izora gone on ahead without her?

She made her way to the tunnels through the library. After the first day, her nurse had shown her the secret that revealed the entrance to their training room. A simple lever hid in a decorative pattern inlaid in the closet wall, which served as clever camouflage.

But when she opened the hidden door, she found the room still swathed in darkness and closed the door hastily after calling down, "Izora...?" and hearing no reply.

Perhaps she'd overslept?

She headed to Izora's quarters in the keep's northwest wing. She made her way quickly through the library and music room. Then she skirted the back of the great hall, avoiding a servant with his head and shoulders in the main fireplace, likely stirring the coals, preparing to rouse the fire to life for the day.

She opened the door into the staff corridor that bordered the greenhouse and slid inside the candlelit hallway. The cramped, windowless passage enabled the staff to reach the northwest corridor from the keep's back entrance without being seen by the royal family or any visitors who came to enjoy the lush vegetation and exotic flowers in the greenhouse.

She paused. A sound from the greenhouse caught her attention.

Who could that be at this hour?

Her curiosity piqued, Kayda tiptoed to the adjoining wall, placing her ear on the cold plaster. It was obvious this wall had not quite been made up to the keep's high standards. But the thin walls afforded her the ability to hear a bit of what was said.

Tarquin. Kayda recognized her brother's arrogant, self-absorbed tone, though she couldn't make out all the words. She listened carefully but only picked out perhaps two words out of every ten Tarquin uttered.

"Old man... mages... port... regret..." It made no sense to her but raised her hackles nonetheless. What was he doing up this early?

A voice answered him, so quietly, or from such a distance, she couldn't make out a single word, only an incomprehensible whisper. The tone differed from Tarquin's, but in such a register, she couldn't be certain whether the speaker was a man or woman.

Who could he be meeting at this hour? She had half a mind to sneak outside and peek at the pair through the greenhouse windows, but the conversation ended. Silence returned to the keep, broken by the sound of a door opening and closing in the distance a moment later.

Sighing deeply, she removed her ear from the wall and tried to push the mystery aside. She could not forget her purpose. She had to find Izora.

As she approached the door to the northwest wing, she tried to remain calm. It was not like Izora to forget to tend to her. She was always there, the most constant presence in her life. Izora had even been known to drag herself out of bed while suffering from colds and injuries to check on her young charge. Kayda couldn't help but worry something was very wrong with her nurse.

The door slammed behind her, and Kayda grimaced. Well, if Izora overslept today, she was probably awake after that. But at least she'd made it to the staff rooms. Within a few steps, she was at Izora's door and knocking gently upon it.

"Come in," came Izora's voice from within.

Breathing a sigh of relief, Kayda set a stern look on her face, opened the door, and stepped inside. Upon seeing her nurse sitting on her single bed in her small, neat room, the stern look dropped from her face as if it had never been there.

Izora sat there in her flint-gray dress, clutching a letter, looking lost and miserable. "Oh, Kayda. I thought you were someone else. What are you doing here?" Izora straightened her shoulders, pasting a smile on her face.

"When you didn't come for our lessons, I worried something had happened... Has something happened? Are you all right?" Kayda eyed the letter warily, her brow furrowing.

"Yes, dear, I'm well. Just a bit of bad news from an old friend. Nothing you need concern yourself with."

Izora rose from the bed and strode toward Kayda. She rubbed her shoulder and glanced at her with a sad half smile. "Thank you for worrying about me, Princess, but as you can see, I'm quite all right. I'm afraid we'll have to skip our lessons today." She maneuvered them both so Kayda was poised to leave the small room. "Why don't you take the day off, do something fun? Read a book. Take a walk. We'll get back to it bright and early tomorrow."

Kayda withdrew, feeling even more confused than before. What was in that letter? Who was it from? If she knew anything about her nurse, she would let her know when she saw fit and not a moment sooner. Her shoulders sank as she made her way back through the staff corridor and through the door to the great hall.

"Got ya!" a familiar voice accosted her.

Kayda nearly jumped out of her skin.

"What a surprise to find you here, sister," Tarquin said, seeming not to care that his words echoed off the vast room's walls in the early morning stillness. He was dressed in a flashy blue silk tunic and spotless tan trousers today, topped with his haughtiest glare. "It's not enough for you to spy on my hunt with Grandfather, you have to spy on my trysts, too?"

"I wasn't spying on you." Kayda's cheeks burned, and she shot him a sour glare.

"That's a load of horseshit." His jaw jutted out at an angle as he leaned in, pointing at the door she'd just exited. "I heard you slamming doors in the servant's corridor while I was engaged with my paramour in the greenhouse." He smirked. "I mean, it really isn't seemly to lust after your own brother. Perhaps we should find you a husband quickly, before you do something rash."

Kayda saw red. Of all the disgusting, egotistical things he could have said, that was the foulest.

"I was checking on Izora. If you must know, she's not feeling well. The world doesn't revolve around you." She stepped around him, heading for her quarters. "And I couldn't care less what you do, or who you do it with."

The fact that he stuck around to confront her—would've likely confronted anyone who came out of that corridor next—made Kayda even more suspicious. He shouted so loudly about his supposed paramour she suspected the whispering party with him in that room was anything but. What was he hiding? She *knew* he was up to something.

He caught her arm before she could get far and spun her to face him. "Don't leave like that, sister. You know I didn't mean to offend. We'll go our separate ways as friends, no—as loving family—ought to." He smiled, flashing that fake vacuous grin he wore so often.

Raising an eyebrow, she pulled her arm free from his grasp. "Sure, let's." She turned and exited the great hall.

What was that? Tarquin being Tarquin, or an attempt to displace her suspicion?

She returned to her quarters and sank down onto the oversized chaise that took up most of her cramped sitting room.

Try as she might, she couldn't set the incident out of her mind. Those few scattered words replayed in her ears. She couldn't help wondering if this secret meeting had some connection to the trade deal Tarquin had discussed with her grandfather. The four words she overheard certainly seemed to suggest a connection.

Tarquin had no love for the mages. It likely stemmed from the seers' announcement the family talent had skipped him. But he was always eager to be useful despite his lack of bonding talent. He trained with the castle guard habitually and jumped at every opportunity to be seen at public events with the king.

Could he still be planning to move forward with his plans to build a port on the land the mages protected? Behind her grandfather's back, no less?

Oh, it was no use. She could sit around guessing his motives all day, but without knowing more of what was said in that room, she couldn't be sure. All she had was a feeling. An aching wrongness she felt to her core.

It was time to pay her grandfather a visit. She would share what she learned with the king. Perhaps he knew something that could help set her mind at ease. At the very least, she would gain some company and a fresh perspective.

It was not far from her suite of rooms to the king's. She knocked, bouncing on her toes as she waited for an answer.

Quinton's personal servant, Evander, slid open the door, but only halfway. His bushy white eyebrows knitted together as he stared down at her. She was tall for a girl of fifteen, but Evander always made her feel like a child.

He swiveled his neck in both directions, checking that she was alone, no doubt. "I'm afraid the king is feeling poorly today. Can you come back later?"

"Who is it, Evander?" the king's voice called from within.

Evander frowned, turning to speak over his shoulder. "It's your granddaughter, Your Majesty. She can come this afternoon, when you're feeling more yourself."

"Nonsense, man. Send her in. If anyone should see me like this, it ought to be her."

Evander frowned again, the lines on his forehead so deep they could swallow a coin. He obeyed, opening the door wide and stepping aside.

Kayda entered, swallowing reflexively and stopping just inside the doorway.

Evander pulled the door closed without a sound and disappeared into the king's dressing chamber.

These rooms were the best in the keep. No expense had been spared to make King Quinton comfortable. The large sitting room was upholstered in the finest Jorian silk. Knick knacks and curiosities from all over the world were displayed on shelves decorating the walls.

Normally, she loved to spend time here and came whenever offered an invitation. But something was off this morning that had Kayda's palms sweating.

The room was a wreck. Clothes were strewn everywhere. All the carefully collected artwork and collectibles lay scattered or broken. Some had obviously been thrown into the walls and even the fireplace, if the multicolored ash and broken shards of pottery inside were any indication.

In the middle of all this disarray, wearing only a crimson robe and his underclothes, was her grandfather, sprawled unceremoniously on a large settee, holding his head in his hands.

He glanced up as she drew closer, a lopsided smile spread across his face. "Sorry for the mess. It just gets a little too... crowded in here sometimes." He shoved some clothes and the battered remains of a map off the sage-green settee cushions and then gestured for her to join him.

She approached warily and perched on the cushion's edge. She'd heard the rumors—the same rumors everyone had. Until today, she hadn't truly believed them. In spite of all his quirks, her grandfather had always been good to her. Good to everyone, all throughout the entire kingdom.

It couldn't be true... that his use of bonding magic had driven him mad. She gulped, taking another long look at the mess scattered around her. It was the same magic she was expected to inherit.

"Have I told you about the time I flew?" Quinton blurted out, a wild grin flashing across his face. "Oh, it was amazing. Right over the Riddle River. Ha!"

Kayda quirked a brow, clenching her dress in her hands.

The King didn't seem to notice her discomfort. He rambled on, a faraway look in his eye. "It was all good fun until the damn harbormaster caught me. Blazing big-mouth, had to go tattle to my father."

"The harbormaster caught you flying..." Kayda said, the word trailing off into silence.

"Quiet!" King Quinton exclaimed out of nowhere. He closed his eyes and applied pressure to his temple with his fist.

"Maybe I should come back later," she said after a moment, moving to stand.

"No." His arm shot out sideways, blocking her from standing. His abrupt tone set her heart jolting.

"I've kept you sheltered from my condition your whole life, but you should see." Quinton opened his eyes. They were strangely murky and stared at some point above her shoulder. "You should look and see what your future might hold." His voice cracked on the final word, and his eyes met hers.

His arm fell, coming to rest between them. Some of the cloudiness in his eyes retreated. "I'm sorry. What was I saying?"

Kayda shook her head and forced a smile. "Nothing important, Grandfather." She patted his hand gently, deciding not to burden him with her suspicions. "I just came to invite you to breakfast, that's all."

He stared at the wall again, his voice distracted. "No, not today, dear. I've some... things that require my attention, I'm afraid."

"I understand. I'll leave you to it then." She squeezed his hand, then stood.

"Little red, fetch Evander for me before you leave, please."

She nodded once, then picked her way across the mess to the dressing room. Same as the sitting room, it appeared as if it'd been caught in the midst of a storm. She found Evander standing tall in his servant's uniform, setting things to rights.

He continued his work, smoothing the wrinkles from one of the king's tunics. "He gets this way, sometimes. Ever since his second bondmate passed." He stared at her directly, compassion filling his eyes. "You'll do well to learn from this, Princess. The king is not wrong in that." He placed a wrinkled hand on her arm. "Don't bond more than once, if you can help it."

Evander's brows knitted together, his words earnest. "Their voices will never leave you. Can you imagine having your dearest friends living only inside your own mind? Being the only one who can hear them? The constant reminder of them—you never get the chance to heal your grief. It must be maddening." His hand dropped from her arm, falling to his side.

A shiver raced down her spine. Her only thought was to escape. "I... have to go now," she replied lamely. "He's asked for you." She turned on her heel, left the king's rooms, and leaned against the door, shaking in the hall.

Was that what her future would be like? Locked away in her rooms, tortured by voices in her mind?

A portrait of King Quinton hung across the hall. He smiled at her, young and carefree. His arms draped around his beautiful queen and his beloved brother, both now deceased. All three of them looked so merry. The man in that wreck of a room was a shadow of his former self. So afraid of what might happen were he to bond with another that he hadn't set foot in a stable in over a decade.

She'd spent most of her life eagerly waiting to discover her bonding talent. It was what made her family special. The royal trait might skip a generation but always bestowed someone in the royal family the gift to speak to an animal companion.

For her grandfather, it was horses. He told her stories about his love for the beasts. Even as a boy, he'd been drawn to them.

Before, when he would tell those stories, she ached inside, like something was missing. Despite being introduced to all manner of creatures during the course of her life, she'd never experienced the instant connection he described.

She had longed for it so badly. For the first time in her life, she felt grateful instead.

Before long, she calmed enough to head back to her rooms. Her thoughts returned to Tarquin and his suspicious meeting. She began second guessing her decision to not tell her grandfather, but seeing him like that... it would've been selfish to add more worry to his day.

She paused outside her father's rooms. Maybe he could help? She wouldn't know if she didn't try. She planted her feet in front of the door and knocked.

"Bloody blazes," a slurred voice shouted from within. The next instant a crash sounded as something thudded into the door, vibrating the wood. "Leave me alone."

She let out a heavy sigh and escaped down the hall. She couldn't say she was surprised. It was a sad fact that all he cared about was having enough to drink.

Perhaps Izora? No. She was clearly dealing with some disaster of her own, if that letter was any indication.

Kayda would have to shoulder this burden alone, but that didn't mean she was giving up. She would learn the meaning of those scattered words, one way or another.

Chapter 9

The days melded together for Lark. They traveled by day, with Lark and Tiora crushed together, sweltering under the tarp in the heat. Every night they stopped to rest and parked the wagon somewhere off the road in the forest. Rasmus would sneak off to the nearest tavern or drown himself with the bottles of liquor he stashed in the front of the wagon. And every night, without fail, Pax took Tiora. Lark sat there shivering and seething, locked in the back of the wagon, night after night, wishing she were anywhere but there.

After the first night, Rasmus removed their bonds and gags, but not without threatening to replace them should either of them try to escape. Though Lark spent many hours scheming about how to do just that, an opportunity had yet to present itself where she could put the idea into action.

At least without the gag, she could talk to Tiora. It took Lark a few tense days to convince the older girl to open up, but eventually, they started sharing stories with one another. They whiled away the dull days of travel with conversation that began with unemotional descriptions of their respective homelands, but quickly became more personal, until Lark felt a closeness to Tiora she'd previously only shared with her mother and brother.

One afternoon, Lark fanned herself in the back of the wagon while the sun beat down unmercifully on the tarp above them. "Tell me again about Joria."

Sunshine slipped through cracks in the wooden slats, brightening the wagon just enough for Lark to note Tiora's wistful smile. "We lived south of Joria on the eastern banks of the Peat River. It was hot, just like this, all year round."

Lark groaned. "I don't think I could stand it."

Tiora giggled. "Well, it wasn't all bad. We spent the hottest part of the day resting in the shade. Or better yet, swimming in the river."

"Swimming would be amazing right now." She pictured the cool river water rushing over her skin, sighing. "It sounds so nice. Why did you leave?"

"My mother—she got sick. She was a dyer, contracted with traders in the city. When she couldn't meet her quota... someone had to do something."

"I don't understand. What about your father?"

Tiora scowled. "He was long gone. Only stuck around long enough to give my mother me and my sisters. Then he disappeared to parts unknown."

"So, it was up to you to take care of your family."

"Exactly. I would do anything for my mother and sisters. There was only one way I could get the money we needed. I made sure it was more than enough to pay for a healer for my mother." Tiora's fingers tangled in the hem of her brown dress. "I walked to the city and sold myself to a Jorian slaver." She grimaced, her eyes downcast. "You must think I'm so stupid."

"No, no." She grabbed Tiora's hand, her heart breaking for her. "I understand. My mother got sick, too." Lark's voice was thick with pain. "I would've done anything to save her. It's one of the biggest regrets of my life that I couldn't." Tears welled in her eyes.

Tiora squeezed her hand. "I'm so sorry, Lark."

"I miss her like crazy." She sniffled. "I couldn't save her."

"You can't blame yourself. People get sick every day. Even if you were trained as a healer, it's not your fault."

Lark scrubbed her cheeks, fighting for composure. Tiora was sweet to say that, but deep down, she knew it was her fault. Nothing was going to change that.

"It must have been exciting to be a healer. Did you ever birth babies?" Tiora asked.

Lark smiled. Those, at least, were happy memories. "Yes. Many times."

"Wow, what was that like?"

"Incredible. There's nothing like seeing a mother hold her child for the first time." Her smile fell, brows knitting together. "It could be awful sometimes, too. When the babies or mother didn't make it."

"That must be hard to watch."

"You can't even imagine." She let go of Tiora's hand and hugged her knees to her chest. "Once there was a baby. A boy. My mother handed him to me after his mother birthed him while she tended to the mother. It'd been a long, hard delivery, and the baby, he wasn't crying."

"Oh, no." Tiora frowned, listening raptly.

"I tried everything. Slapped his bum, rubbed his back, cleared his mouth and nose. Nothing worked."

Tiora's hand rose to cover her lips, eyes wide. "Was he dead?"

"My mother thought so. But I wasn't ready to let him go. I grabbed some of my mother's salve and started rubbing it on his chest." She shook her head slightly. "I'm not even sure why I thought it would work. It's supposed to treat skin irritation. But I rubbed and rubbed and rubbed some more."

"And it worked?"

She laughed. "No... But then I placed my hand on that little babe's chest." Lark closed her eyes, recalling the moment so clearly it was almost as if she was back there with the babe nestled in her arms. "I closed my eyes and wished. I wished with everything I had in me he would just breathe." She opened her eyes, smiling slowly.

"And did he?"

"I felt something then. A tingling vibration, like the ground was quaking beneath me and shaking my whole body. Some power moved through my hand into the boy's chest. Then he let out the biggest, most beautiful cry."

"It was a miracle." Tiora smiled, eyes bright.

"No—it was magic."

Tiora's smiled dropped.

"My mother told me that day, my grandmother, she'd been talented, too. That salve had a few ingredients, all of them from the earth."

Tiora's mouth fell open. "You're an earth mage? Why didn't you tell me before?" She punctuated the question with a punch to Lark's knee.

"Hey, no need to get violent." Lark rubbed her knee. "And I'm not a mage. At least, not yet."

Tiora's eyes darted back and forth. Lark could practically see the wheels spinning in her mind.

"But you summoned. If you summoned once, you could do it again." Tiora grabbed her hand, squeezing tightly, those golden-brown eyes staring into her own with such intensity. "You can do it, Lark. You can free us."

Lark looked down, breaking eye contact. "I can't... I've only been able to summon that once. I don't know how it happened in the first place, or how to do it again."

The wagon stopped. Tiora dropped Lark's hand and shuddered.

Lark tensed, waiting for the rocking of the wagon and the thudding of the men's footsteps. She'd been so caught up in their conversation that she hadn't noticed the light in the wagon slowly diminishing.

The tarp lifted a few moments later. Fresh air rushed in to greet her. She sighed as a breeze swept through, cooling off her sweat-soaked skin. She caught sight of Pax watching her, that scarred eye winking at her lasciviously, and she snapped her mouth shut, wrapping her arms around her chest.

The villain laughed, reached behind his back, and tossed something at Tiora. She flinched but caught the waterskin, then opened it and hastily drained a portion before passing it to Lark. She drank, too, the lukewarm water a blessing after the afternoon spent sweltering under the tarp.

Rasmus appeared, retrieving the key he wore dangling from a length of cord wrapped around his neck. He opened the backboard and motioned for Lark to hop down. "I'll take this one first. Get a fire started," he said to Pax.

Lark jumped down, her muscles protesting from so many hours spent cramped in the back of the wagon. She took a moment to stretch and heard Pax call out to Tiora behind her, "Make yourself useful and gather some sticks, whore."

Fire spread through her veins, but she said nothing and followed Rasmus across the clearing.

She searched for a sign of anything to tell their location, but it was no use. They were in a clearing, much the same as any other she'd ever been in. Trees loomed on all sides, and there was no sign of a road, stream, or anything else she recognized. The sweet melody of a sparrow broke the forest's stillness. From a distance, she could hear running water, though she couldn't see its source.

Rasmus stopped behind a star oak tree, trampling a patch of dandelions. "Be quick about it." He shuffled a few steps to the left but kept his stare trained on her, his face impassive.

Though he watched with little interest, Lark's cheeks burned all the same as she crouched behind the tree and relieved her aching bladder.

They returned to the clearing. Lark was made to collect sticks while Tiora took her turn with Rasmus. The hair on her spine raised as Pax watched Lark's every move. His eyes on her felt much different from Rasmus', and she was thankful to see the pair return, so she no longer had to be alone with the hulking man.

Soon, the fire roared, and the scent of meat roasting made her stomach rumble. Rasmus made them sit back in the wagon but left the tarp pulled back and the backboard down, which was a luxury after so long spent crouched beneath it. He handed each of them a stick with a piece of meat dangling off it; the aroma made her salivate. She'd just begun to tuck in when a voice called out beyond the clearing.

"Hello, my friends."

Lark jolted, almost dropping her dinner, as she searched the forest for the voice's source.

A man stepped out of the trees to their left, beaming and waving both hands. He was middle-aged, with dark brown skin and long, dark brown hair plaited in a multitude of small, neat braids that were decorated with beads in every color of the rainbow. His tunic was multicolored, too; the bright silk covered his lanky frame and glittered in the firelight.

"I saw your fire from the road and smelled the delicious aroma of roasting meat. Would you care for some company tonight at your campsite? My group of travelers and I are stopping for the night. We'd love to trade some entertainment for a full belly and the pleasure of meeting some new friends." He spoke with his hands and projected his voice in a strong, pleasant tone that marked him as a natural showman.

Excitement stirred in her breast as the man bowed with a flourish.

"I am Dausius of the Wandering Bards. It's a pleasure to make the acquaintance of such fine folk as yourselves."

Rasmus and Pax watched the man curiously, both with a hand on their sword hilts. They exchanged a look, then Rasmus spoke. "I think a bit of entertainment would be a welcome diversion. I'm Rasmus, and this is Pax." He nodded in his direction. "You can go fetch the rest of your group and share our fire tonight."

Dausius' smile never wavered as his gaze slid over Lark and Tiora, seeming to note the fact they'd not been introduced but not pressing the matter. He bowed again and disappeared back into the forest, presumably to go fetch the rest of his group.

A traveling show! Lark's pulse quickened. Maybe she could use this turn of events to her advantage. Visions of her and Tiora escaping while the slavers were distracted played in her mind. She did her best to hide her excitement, chewing her meat silently while she waited for the return of Dausius and his group.

They didn't have to wait long. Dausius returned moments later, leading a white and brown spotted horse and wagon.

The wagon was similar in size to the one they sat in, but his brought a smile to her face. Bright paint and intricate patterns decorated the sides in all the colors of the rainbow. The bed was uncovered, and perched in the center, among a number of trunks and boxes, sat a large hawk upon a wooden tree branch.

Lark's breath caught as she stared at the majestic creature. She'd never seen a bird of prey from such a close distance before. Its strength and power, even at rest, was a magnificent thing to behold.

Three people trailed the wagon. Each of them dressed identically to Dausius—minus the beaded hair. The rainbow silk threads of their multicolored tunics gleamed in the evening light.

The first two, a short-haired boy and girl with a single, long braid, appeared so similar she was sure they were related. The pair appeared to be in their late teens, with olive skin, brown hair, and brown eyes.

A young man, wearing a large, brimmed hat that obscured much of his face, lagged a few paces behind. He was much paler than the rest but taller and more muscular, too.

He wore a thick leather glove on his right hand and had a finely made lute strapped to his back.

Dausius stopped and parked the horse and wagon in the clearing. Then he raised his voice and swiveled toward the men seated at the fire. "Please, allow me to introduce my companions and fellow performers." He spread his arms wide, smiling broadly, adopting a theatrical voice. "Hailing from the exotic jungles of Raimire, I present to you, Mazen and Meital."

The brown-haired pair stepped forward, both offering a shallow bow and a mischievous grin.

Dausius continued, "They learned their deadly knife skills fighting for their lives against jungle cats and venomous snakes, but the only danger these twins face now are each other."

They reached behind their backs in unison, each of them revealing a set of four small daggers that glittered dangerously in the setting sun's light. Without a word, they casually juggled them, tossing them in ever-widening circles and flawlessly swapping them.

Lark gasped with delight. Glancing sideways, she saw Tiora's gaze dancing as she traced the blades' flight through the clearing.

The pair ended the display by throwing each knife into the grass, all eight lined up neatly in a row.

Lark and Tiora clapped, earning a wink from Mazen. Tiora giggled until Pax glared in their direction, cutting her laughter short.

Dausius broke the tension, stepping forward with an exaggerated bow. "Thank you, thank you., You are too kind. Please, save some applause for the last members of our group."

The tall man stepped forward, lifting his gloved arm and whistling. The hawk flew to him and landed on his outstretched arm.

"Behold, the beautiful and fierce hawk Whisper and his handler, Aren," Dausius said.

Aren reached into a pouch on his belt with his free hand. Whisper's eyes locked onto the movement, and he looked like a coiled spring, ready to fly at any moment. Aren tossed some small morsel into the air. Whisper flew at lightning speed, snatching it mid-flight in his beak, and then landing back on his wagon perch.

Lark and Tiora clapped once more, as Dausius spoke again. "Thank you, Aren and Whisper. Please take a bow."

The hawk tilted its head forward repeatedly, and Tiora laughed again, but Lark's attention was caught entirely by Aren.

Before bowing, he removed his hat, revealing a face that rivaled Tiora's for its beauty. He had light blond hair cut short and ice-blue eyes that sent a shiver down her spine when they locked on her own. Her hands stilled their clapping as she returned his stare, and she found herself leaning forward without consciously deciding to.

He looked away first, straightening from his bow and replacing his hat.

Lark blinked, shaking off her strange reaction.

"Bravo." Rasmus clutched one of his bottles in his fist and took a long swallow. "Come, join us 'round the fire and have a bite to eat."

"You're most kind, good sir." Dausius swaggered in the fire's direction, the beads in his hair clacking as he signaled his performers to follow. Meital and Aren headed over directly, but Mazen detoured in their direction, a playful smile on his face.

Lark's brow wrinkled when she realized his intentions.

Tiora was still admiring Whisper and didn't notice the boy's gaze zero in on her as he approached.

"Will you lovely ladies be joining us?" Mazen asked, glancing at her and returning his gaze to Tiora.

Tiora jolted at his voice, her mouth dropping open as she met his stare.

Dausius spun to view the scene and shot daggers with his eyes at Mazen.

"No, they will not," Pax announced, his voice hard and cold. He stood with his fists pressed on his hips, a feral grin flashing across his face.

Tiora's shoulders slumped, and an echoing disappointment spread inside Lark's chest.

"Toss me the key, Ras." Pax thrust out a hand.

Rasmus shrugged and pitched the keys at him.

Pax caught them and strode to the wagon, shooting a glare at Mazen, who retreated with his hands in the air, a pleasant expression plastered to his face.

"It's bedtime for the lovely ladies." Pax stalked closer, grinning maliciously.

Tiora's eyes shone with unshed tears. She made herself small on the wagon floor, preparing for the tarp and backboard to lock them in. Lark let out a heavy sigh, took a final look at the traveling show, and did the same.

It wasn't long before Pax shrouded the wagon in darkness. The setting sun and shadowy tree cover permitted little light to shine through the cracks of the wooden slats.

Lark fumed, clenching her fists together so hard her nails dug into her palms. Her hopes to sneak away during the performances were dashed, and as she noted the sounds outside, she realized Pax was preparing to hitch the horse back up to the wagon. The bastard wasn't even going to allow them the simple pleasure of listening to the performers.

The wagon jerked forward. Quiet sniffling broke the silence inside the wagon bed.

Tiora never cried. Not even after that monster returned her to the wagon each morning. It looked like missing out on the show was the final straw for her. Lark wrapped an arm around her, pulling her close. Tiora's tears wet the linen of her tunic as she shuddered.

The wagon stopped, and Pax jumped down, slapping a hand on the side. "Pleasant dreams, ladies." His laughter faded as he strolled back to the fire.

Lark held Tiora while she cried and silently prayed for that to be the final time they saw Pax that evening. She fell asleep with the sound of a lute whispering in her ears.

She startled awake at the sound of the backboard opening. It was Pax, coming for Tiora. Lark's arms were still wrapped around her friend, and seeing that vile man's profile lit in the moonlight, she clutched her closer, even as her friend moved to go with him.

"No," she whispered.

Then Tiora's hands closed on her own, prying her fingers free of her arms. "It's all right, Lark. I can do this."

Lark shook her head, tears filling her eyes, but she released Tiora and let her climb down from the wagon. She covered her ears when the sounds began but couldn't block them out entirely. The familiar grunts and groans seemed more forceful tonight and were joined by a new, more frightening sound. Cries of pain.

Anger burned in her chest, and shame. How could she sit here night after night listening? It was killing her to do nothing, but she had to be smart and bide her time. She rubbed her wrists, remembering the rope biting into her skin. All hope would be lost if she got herself wrapped in bondage again.

Pax returned Tiora to the wagon as the first rays of dawn brightened the sky. Lark scooted back, her stomach clenching.

Tiora's cheek was swollen, and from the way she winced as she sat on the hard wooden slats, she suspected that wasn't the only injury she'd sustained that night. Despite the pleading look Tiora sent her, Lark couldn't help glaring at Pax as he slammed the backboard shut with a laugh, obviously not caring about the damage he inflicted on her friend.

"Tiora, what did he do to you?" Lark whispered. The sound of Pax's footsteps trailed off into the distance. "I'll kill him, that bastard!"

Tiora reached out her hand, managing a sly smile despite her swelling face. "I hope so." She deposited a fistful of fresh soil on her palm.

The cool dirt slid across Lark's fingers, its earthy scent filling her nostrils. She nodded. "I'll try." She owed it to Tiora, to herself, to do something. She stuffed the dirt in her pocket to wait for her chance.

Tiora winced again, and a pang of sympathy struck Lark. "Can I do anything? Do you want me to check your injuries?" she asked, wishing she had her mother's book and the right herbs so she could tend to her properly.

"No, I'll be all right." She sighed deeply. "I just wish we could've watched the show last night. It's been so long since I've heard any music."

Lark's face lit up. "Well, we'll fix that." She closed her eyes briefly, and when she opened them, she began to sing. It was a cheerful song, one her mother had sung to her as a child.

Tiora listened with her eyes closed and a small smile on her face. When the song was over, she lifted her sleepy lids and whispered, "That was beautiful. Your mother named you well." She closed her eyes again before she noted the blush warming Lark's face.

It wasn't long before the sounds of the camp rising and the performers making ready to leave echoed throughout the clearing. By the time Rasmus came around to give them each a chance to empty their bladders, the other wagon was gone.

Lark's stomach quivered as their own wagon rolled along the bumpy forest trail. Pax had stayed too far away for her to try anything with the dirt that morning. They had another long, sweaty day of travel to finish before she would have another opportunity.

Tiora spent the day resting, and Lark refused to wake her after the night she'd been forced to endure. She rested, too, or tried at least, but often her mind wouldn't allow it, replaying all she'd overheard that night, keeping her anger smoldering.

Finally, the wagon stopped for the night.

"Pax, I'm going to ride into that town we passed a few miles back. You can handle feeding the girls tonight on your own." Rasmus jumped down from the front wagon seat.

"Whatever you say, boss," Pax replied.

The horse whinnied, and soon the sound of galloping echoed in her ears. It quickly faded away.

Lark wet her lips, rubbing her sweaty hands against her skirt. She'd expected to feel fear in this moment; instead, giddy anticipation tingled up her spine as the backboard swung open and Pax sneered in at them.

"Please, take me, I have to go now," Lark blurted out before he said anything, making a show of pressing her thighs closed and bouncing her knees up and down.

She expected him to say something cruel, even make her wait just because he could, but he surprised her.

"Fine." He moved aside so she could hop down. "Then back in with you, and me and the whore will have some fun," he added, leering at Tiora as he shut the backboard again, leaving them alone in a clearing practically identical to the last.

Lark dug in her pocket while his back was turned, scooping the pile of loose soil into her palm. This was it. She was going to kill him.

As soon as he whirled around, she pretended to trip, catching herself with her palms on his chest. She started to wish, like she had with the babe, but before she had the chance to set the thought in her mind, Pax shoved her away. The handful of soil sprinkled down his shirt and landed on the grass at his feet, and Lark's heart dropped to her stomach.

"Watch it, you clumsy bitch," he spat, not noticing the dirt dusting his clothing.

Lark cursed inwardly, her mind spinning as she tried to think of some excuse to place her hand on his chest. She grimaced, realizing what she would have to do and prayed there was more dirt in her pocket.

As he led the way behind a nearby tree, she searched her skirt pocket as circumspectly as she could. At first her fingers only brushed cloth, and her heart thundered madly. Then she dug further and found something flat and crinkly, crushed in the far corner. The flower! She said a silent thank you to the old woman who'd gifted it to her on their trip out of Southmoat so many days ago. Tucking the dried flower into the center of her palm, she put her plan into action.

"I was lying, just now." She slowed, eyes half lidded and a sly smile on her lips. "The truth is, I've been feeling a little left out."

Pax stared at her, raising a brow, that scarred eyelid looking even more grotesque with the action.

Lark swallowed her disgust and closed the distance between them. "It's not fair I have to stay locked away in that wagon while the whore gets to have all the fun." She followed the statement with a pout and pressed her chest forward, drawing his gaze downward.

This had to work. She held her breath, hoping it had been enough to bait him.

Time stretched out, neither of them moving. His eyes searched hers, then zeroed in on her upturned lips. Had he seen through her seduction? Sweat beaded on her forehead. She was sure he was a heartbeat away from laughing in her face and pushing her to the ground. But then he struck.

Shooting out a hand, he gripped the brown curls at the nape of her neck and jerked her head back. His mouth landed on hers, hot and oppressive, and she shuddered as his tongue invaded her mouth. Her body screamed at her to spit out the vile thing, to pull away. Instead, she pressed closer and wedged the flower between them, flattening it directly over his heart.

She remembered the sounds. The awful, disgusting sounds clogging her ears every night. The bruises that evil monster left on her friend. She closed her eyes and wished. She wished with every fiber of her body for his heart to stop beating.

She felt it then. Her whole body thrummed with energy, the same as before. The vibration coalesced in her palm, her skin tingling. Then it jolted through her hand and entered his chest.

For one excruciating moment, panic filled her. It hadn't been enough. He was still at it, tongue still moving, choking the air from her mouth. His fist still clenched around her curls.

Then he pulled back and clutched his chest, eyes bulging. His vile tongue still dangled from his mouth, a string of spit hanging.

Lark backed up slowly, a smile spreading on her lips.

He saw her smile, and his eyes filled with fear and panic. He reached for the hilt of his sword, but it was too late. With a sickening *thump*, he collapsed, slumping face-first in the grass.

Lark stared at his back, covering her lips as she fought to overcome the intense disbelief raging inside her. Then she drew her sleeve across her lips, wiping off his foul taste. She crouched down, fished the cord and key out of his tunic, and hurried to free Tiora from the wagon.

Tiora gaped at her as she let down the backboard. She hopped down, heading straight for where Pax's booted feet sprawled on the ground still twitching, the front half of him hidden behind a large oak tree. Lark let her go and watched silently as Tiora screamed with rage, and the *thud* of her boots kicking that monster sounded over and over again.

Finally, Tiora stopped and rounded the tree, her brown dress covered with flecks of red. "You did it." Her face lit with joy. "Lark, you did it!" She ran to her, pulling her into an embrace and bursting into tears.

Lark's muscles relaxed, and she sagged against Tiora. They stood there, clutching each other and crying. Lark was so overwhelmed with relief, she didn't register the sound of a horse's footfalls approaching.

"Ho, Pax, just forgot my coinpur—" Rasmus' voice trailed off as he took stock of the scene.

The girls sprang apart, backing away slowly from the horse. Lark's heart hammered with the rat-a-tat-tat rhythm of a woodpecker.

No. No, no, no! He shouldn't be back. They were free.

There was no way she could repeat the same trick with Rasmus. He would tie them both up again, keep them trapped in the wagon, bound and gagged, until they reached Doln.

His brow furrowed as he spotted Pax's body lying still and half hidden behind the tree. He dropped the reins, gripping his sword hilt. His mouth opened, and Lark gulped, preparing herself for the order that would come next.

Instead, his body shook as a wet *thunk* interrupted the clearing's stillness. His eyes bulged, his mouth widened, and blood poured out. A scarlet flood coated his chest in an instant. He slumped forward, a blade lodged in the back of his neck.

Lark's mouth dropped open at the crunch of footsteps.

Meital stalked forward from the forest, shoved Rasmus' body from the horse, and retrieved her dagger. Then she whistled sharply, and Lark flinched, her wide eyes searching the forest as more footsteps sounded.

Dausius strode into the clearing, Mazen and Aren following closely. "I'm sorry, we've not been properly introduced, my ladies." He smiled. "Which one of you is the singer we heard early this morning?"

Lark stared, tongue tied, still trying to process the events of the last few moments.

Tiora spoke up. "I'm Tiora, and this is Lark. She's the one you heard singing."

Dausius' smile widened. Leaning toward them, he offered his hand. "Tiora, Lark, it's a pleasure to meet you. Have you ever considered joining a traveling show?"

Chapter 10

"What do you think?" It was early morning on the day they'd chosen to return to the farm. Conall stood staring at the sheer wall of rock and dirt he'd tumbled down so many days ago. *"If I can make it up there, it will cut out a full day of walking, maybe two."*

"What about your shoulder?" Shadow sat beside him, his golden eyes shining like wheat caught in a sunbeam. *"You'll need two arms for that climb."*

Conall shrugged his shoulders and winced at the answering twinge where the arrow had been wedged. He grimaced, taking a last look up at the wall, and spun to face south. Had he been in better shape, he could've made that climb, but Shadow was right. He couldn't chance it. Another fall could set him back weeks in recovery time if it didn't kill him outright.

"All right then, we'll take the scenic route."

"Wise choice, little brother." Shadow's tail wagged.

The day was bright and cool. The forest sang with activity from insects, birds, and all manner of creatures.

Conall inhaled deeply, gazing at the waterfall and cave that had been his home during his recovery. It was an adventure he wouldn't soon forget—living off the land with a wolf as his only companion—but he was ready to head back to civilization. It was time to say farewell to the forest and set things right at home.

They set out heading south. This part of the forest was new to Conall. He'd always stopped at the top of the ridge, never choosing to venture down the cliffside.

Shadow, at least, was at home in these woods. He trotted happily by Conall's side, leading the way whenever the trail split.

"How is it you know these woods so well, brother? Did you learn the paths by heart while you hunted for us?" Conall asked, watching as he expertly wove between trees and branches on the trail.

"No, I've been here many times." Shadow's tail stilled its wagging, and he slowed his pace. *"This land is part of my pack's territory."*

"Your pack... I thought you said you left your pack?" Perhaps now he might learn more about his bondmate. Shadow had been vague so far about his past.

"I did. And I found you, little brother." His tail wagged again, and his ears perked up as he stared off into the brush to their right.

Conall lifted a brow. *"I didn't realize you were so close to me all along."* It was strange to think they might have crossed paths before this.

"The pack's territory is very large. We weren't always so close. This is near the edge." Shadow stilled, his eyes and ears the only thing moving as he tracked something.

Conall stilled as well but saw nothing. *"Huh, I guess that's why we haven't seen any of your brothers and sisters so far."*

"They're not my brothers... not any longer." Shadow darted into the nearest bush, spooking a hare, and then tearing off into the distance, fast on its trail.

Conall sighed. Every time he brought up Shadow's pack, he found an excuse to dodge the subject. He had to find a way to let his friend know he could talk to him about anything. It was obvious there was something in his past he was reluctant to think about too closely.

Conall headed after Shadow, his steps lingering as he waited for his bondmate's return. He still had problems with his own family to consider. He clenched his fists, kicking the dirt trail.

There was the question of what to do about Gael. The part of him that still burned with anger wanted to creep into the barn at night, grab his second-best bow and quiver, sneak into the farmhouse, and shoot an arrow right through that murderer's heart while he slept. It would be a fitting end for a man who would shoot his own stepson and leave him for dead.

Conall sighed again. As much as he wanted revenge, he could never go through with that plan. The smarter play would be to head for town, tell the townsfolk and magistrate his tale—with the broken arrow and still healing wound for proof—and bring the town's wrath down on that villain.

Conall smiled. He wouldn't have the pleasure of pulling the trigger himself, but he would watch Gael hang. He would get the farm back the right way. It was his by rights, inherited from his father, and he had every right to march inside and tell him to leave...

But there was no way he was going to just let Gael leave. He wanted justice, and he would get it.

The one decision he was wrestling with was what to do about Lark. She was still there on the farm with Gael. Every moment she spent in his presence was another moment he might harm her.

He thought back to their argument in the forest. Gael acted so concerned for her, so eager to keep her from becoming a mage, but after what he'd done to him, Conall couldn't be sure he wouldn't do something just as thoughtless to Lark. What if she put her foot down and insisted on leaving? Would he shoot her, too?

His stomach churned. Could he head straight to town to tell his tale when he couldn't be sure what Gael was doing to Lark on the farm? He could go to her first, but then he might show his hand to Gael. If Gael realized he was still alive, he would have the chance to flee, escaping justice for attempted murder.

A movement in the brush ahead, and a flash of gray fur signaled Shadow's return. He trotted up beside him, the hare clutched in his jaws.

Conall grinned. *"I suppose now is as good a time as any to stop for breakfast."*

Shadow dropped the hare, sitting on his haunches and licking his chops.

As much as he wanted to race back to the farm, he couldn't push his body too hard. Though his ankle had healed, his shoulder still pained him. And though he didn't want to admit it, he still had a way to go before his energy was back where it'd been before the fall.

After breakfast, they walked again. Conall took breaks every so often, careful not to overtax his body, but they made good time through the forest despite the stops. Shadow was an expert guide, never taking them down a path that required much exertion. By the time they stopped for the night, they'd covered a fair distance and drew close to where they would turn toward the farm.

Conall constructed a simple shelter out of sticks and leaves and started a fire before night fell. He gazed at his bondmate, feeling immensely grateful for his presence. Without Shadow, the loneliness that washed over him while he sat in these woods, away from his family and friends, would be overwhelming.

Still, it was a beautiful night for camping, and despite the circumstances, he found himself smiling as the last rays of daylight faded in the sky. It felt good to be doing something. His journey home had begun, and he would soon set things right on the farm.

His shoulder and feet ached, but his heart was at peace as he fell asleep that night, curled up next to his brother under the stars.

They woke the next morning to find a fog had rolled in while they slept. When they set out for the day, it had not yet dissipated entirely, forcing Conall to step carefully in the haze.

Shadow seemed on edge, ears and eyes constantly roaming, searching the forest. *"Brother, could you do me a favor? This fog has me all turned around. Do you think your shoulder can handle a climb today?"*

Conall lifted his shoulders a few times. His left was still sore, but if he kept most of his weight off it, he suspected he could manage a climb. *"What did you have in mind?"*

"That tree there." Shadow approached a large pine. *"It looks plenty tall. Can you get to the top and tell me if you see a stream off to the right? I don't want us headed in the wrong direction."*

Scrutinizing the tree, Conall nodded in agreement. *"Good eye. That looks like an easy climb."* The tree branches were spaced evenly and close to each other. *"Shouldn't take long at all."*

He made it about a quarter of the way up without having to put much weight on his left shoulder, then he paused for a breath and smiled. He glanced down, spotting Shadow pacing back and forth. *"Don't worry, my shoulder is holding up."*

He climbed up halfway and glimpsed water off in the distance to the right, where Shadow expected it to be. He shifted, preparing to climb down and tell his bondmate the good news, but he stopped in his tracks as the haze parted and revealed three large wolves stalking toward Shadow.

"Brother, watch out," he cried.

"I see them, little brother. Stay where you are." Shadow headed toward them, hackles raised, growling, and looking ready to fight.

What was he doing, going after them all on his own? There was no way Shadow could win this fight—three against one.

All three wolves were large, with gray hair and strong, lithe forms. As they caught sight of Shadow's aggression, they snarled and growled in kind, circling in on him as a team.

He had to get down there. He had to help his brother. But what could he do? His bow was lost, and his arrows lay broken and discarded beside the waterfall. The only weapon he had was the tiny crafting blade he used for his snares. That would be practically useless in a fight with wolves.

Conall's breath caught in his throat as he realized Shadow sent him up that tree to get him out of the way.

Down below, the biggest wolf stalked forward, his left ear missing a sizable chunk of skin and fur at the tip. He was ferocious. His jaws snapped, lips curled back, his stare locked onto Shadow's neck.

Shadow stood strong, looking fierce and fearless despite the odds stacked against him.

Conall's stomach dropped to his feet. The other two had disappeared, probably using the trees and fog to hide their movements, preparing to jump at Shadow from behind.

He had to do something. Tearing his gaze from the tense standoff below, Conall searched the forest in vain, desperate to find a weapon or some way of causing a distraction. The snarling intensified as he spotted a dead branch of a star oak, caught up in the pine above him.

That could work! He just had to reach it.

He climbed, then gritted his teeth as he stretched his left arm to its limits to grab it. He pulled. At first, the stubborn branch refused to move. Then he pulled harder, ignoring the shooting pain in his shoulder until it finally dislodged.

Yes! He stashed the branch in the crook of his arm, balancing carefully as he dug in his belt pouch and retrieved his tinder box.

He chanced a glance below and grimaced. The lead wolf dashed toward Shadow, his jaws snapping. Shadow deftly avoided him, spinning on his hind legs and closing his jaws on the attacker's haunches, drawing blood.

There was movement in the bushes behind Shadow. *"Look out behind you,"* he called, just as the second and third wolf sprang out of the fog-shrouded forest. Shadow let the leader go, barely managing to leap away before the other wolves pounced.

Conall gulped. His fingers felt fat and sluggish as he raced to light the dried leaves on fire.

This had to work, and fast. Shadow couldn't last down there much longer.

The three wolves backed up, snarling and snapping. They were poised to attack in tandem.

A chill swept over him as he fumbled with the flint, striking against the steel, praying a spark would catch. It had to.

An ember caught, bursting into flame faster than he thought possible. He gasped, holding the makeshift torch tightly and raced down the tree as fast as he could. He dropped to the ground, landing directly behind Shadow.

"Get out. Get away, you bastards," he screamed, his own voice gruff and foreign in his ears after so many days of silent communication.

The wolves jerked back and stared at the fire.

Conall strode in front of Shadow swiping the stick in an arc. "Get out of here, you filthy mutts!"

Conall's heart pounded wildly. He was certain the wolves would attack at any instant, but his fears were negated a moment later when two of the wolves took off, tearing through the woods in the direction they'd come. The wolf with the torn ear sent a final snarl in Shadow's direction before he joined his companions, fleeing the flames.

Conall stumbled back a step, his legs wobbly. He turned to Shadow, lowering the flaming branch but keeping hold of it, in case the wolves still watched from the trees. *"Are you okay?"* He searched his bondmate, not picking out any obvious injuries.

Shadow stood at attention, staring off into the forest where the wolves disappeared. *"I'm fine, thanks to you, little brother."* His shoulders relaxed, and he circled the area, peering closely into the forest. *"I do not think they will return, but let's be on our way just to be safe."*

"Who were those wolves?" Conall dropped his torch and stomped out the remaining flames before they began picking their way through the forest. *"I thought you said this was your pack's territory?"*

"That was my pack." Shadow's head dropped. *"Or what's left of it. I told you when we first met, we're the same."* His head lifted, those golden eyes staring at him. *"My father died. The new alpha didn't want me around anymore. Leave or die. Those were his orders."*

Conall's heart twisted. No wonder they were bonded. Both of them had been betrayed. *"The one with the torn ear... was that him?"*

"Yes." The fur on his back quivered as he snorted. *"You're not the only one who has someone out to kill him. I'm glad you were there with me, Conall."*

He smiled, tussling the fur on Shadow's head. *"Always, brother."*

"Can I ask you something?" Shadow tilted sideways, leaning into Conall's hand as he scratched him behind the ear. *"What did you say when you were swinging around that branch?"*

"What do you mean?" Conall stopped scratching, glancing at his friend curiously. *"You didn't understand me?"*

"No. Did you understand what I said to the alpha?"

"That was talking? I just heard you two growling and snapping at each other." Conall rubbed his shoulder, massaging the ache that reignited during his climb. For some reason, he'd assumed they would understand each other when they spoke, but it was good to know their communication's limits. *"I called them filthy mutts."*

Shadow snorted again and wagged his tail. Conall grinned, sensing his friend's amusement.

Then Shadow stopped, body tense and nose raised, scenting the air. Conall tensed as well, stopping next to him. They'd turned toward the farm, and the woods had finally begun to look familiar. He noticed nothing out of sorts.

"What is it? Why have you stopped?"

"Smoke... I smell smoke. A lot of it. Something ahead is burning." Shadow's gaze darted all over as he sniffed. *"Something big."*

The farm—Lark. Even though he couldn't see the flames, something inside of him knew. It was his home burning. He gazed at his brother, eyes speaking volumes, and without either of them saying or thinking a single word, they took off running.

Chapter 11

"Are you sure about this?" Dausius asked. His hands were still for once, resting on his hips as his brown eyes searched her face.

Lark pressed her lips together and nodded. "I'm sure. This is the perfect time. With everyone in Greenvale watching the show, I'll have no trouble getting in and out without being noticed."

Her nerves thrummed with anticipation. They stood in the forest outside the town's limits. She'd waited days for the show to reach her hometown. And as luck would have it, they arrived at the perfect time.

Everyone had already gathered in town to head for Flamesmoat in the morning for the annual Harvest Festival. Gael never missed it, so she could be sure to have the privacy she needed to retrieve her belongings. She was ready to go back to the farm. She had to know for sure if what Brenna had said in that awful dock warehouse was true.

Dausius pursed his lips and crossed his arms. "I just wish you weren't going alone."

Footsteps crunched behind her. "She won't be." Tiora strode out from behind a tree, wearing a multicolored tunic and trousers borrowed from Meital, a knapsack strung on her back. "I'm going with her."

Lark smiled and linked her hand with Tiora's. "Don't worry, Daus. We'll be in and out, I promise. Then we'll meet back here after."

Dausius shrugged his shoulders dramatically, letting out a loud sigh. Then his long arms pulled both of them into a tight hug. Tiora stiffened beside Lark, but after a moment she relaxed and wrapped her arm around Dausius, returning the hug.

Lark laughed, reveling in the embrace. They'd only been with this strange crew for a few days, but they'd already begun to feel like a family.

"Stay safe, girls," Dausius said at last. He ended the embrace and waved as he joined the others on the trail to Greenvale.

Lark turned to Tiora as Dausius disappeared into the trees. "You don't have to do this, you know. Gael will be in town watching the show and preparing to trek to Flamesmoat in the morning, just like everyone else. I won't be in any danger."

"Danger or not, you shouldn't have to do this alone, Lark. You were there for me while that vile man—" Tiora's voice caught, and her chin quivered, but she drew a deep breath and continued, "You were there for me, and I'm here for you."

Lark nodded, blinking quickly to stop the moisture filling her eyes. "All right then, let's do this."

Leading the way with a confidence born of familiarity, she started down the well-worn trail that led to the outskirts of Greenvale and her family's farm. The trail was devoid of people, but the solitude didn't help calm her nerves. Her senses were strained, searching for signs of any stragglers on their way to the show, ready to vanish into the trees should anyone appear. The last thing she needed was for someone to recognize her and tell Gael she was headed to the farm.

It was late afternoon when they started down the trail, but when they made it to the turnoff to the farm, the sun was setting. The sight of her home, surrounded by the pink, purple, and orange clouds of sunset, stole her breath.

Not so long ago, she'd thought she'd never have the chance to return. Now, instead of racing inside and reuniting with her loved ones, she crept through the woods like a thief in the night. She set her jaw, straightened her shoulders, and headed for the barn.

Tiora had been silent as they hiked through the forest, but as they began their trek across the wide, green grazing field surrounding the barn, she spoke. "Lark, there's another reason I wanted to come with you today." Her eyes were downcast, her voice barely above a whisper. "I know you trained as a healer." She gulped, her stride slowing. "I... there was this awful-tasting tea they made us drink at the brothel." She cleared her throat. "Do you think—"

Lark squeezed Tiora's arm. "I know it well. When we get inside, I'll brew a pot. My mother ought to have stored all the herbs we need." Her heart ached as relief flashed across Tiora's face, and she wished she could kill that bastard Pax all over again.

They crossed the field and stood poised to open the barn door. Lark closed her eyes, whispered a silent prayer, then pushed.

Growling resonated from the building's shadowy depths. "Sunny?" she called, stepping into the large barn. The musty scent of animals assaulted her nose.

Her brother's mutt darted forward, her tail wagging like a flag caught in a storm wind.

"Sunny, I missed you, girl." She laughed and crouched down, stroking her soft golden fur.

Tiora giggled as Sunny sniffed her hand and licked her fingers.

"I have to check something in here before we head inside the house." Lark led the way inside the barn, passing the goats and cattle, all tucked into their pens for the night and indifferent to their presence. "My brother always comes in here when he gets home. It's where he stores all his bows and trapping gear." Lark reached a ladder and grabbed a worn, wooden rung, staring at the top of the loft where a high window lit the space with the last of the day's sunlight. "I have to see if the letter I left for him is still there."

She climbed in a few quick steps and held her breath as she took her first look around. Her heart filled with glee. The letter—it wasn't where she'd placed it, atop the trunk where her brother stored his trapping supplies. Did that mean... was Conall alive?

But as she stepped off the ladder, she spotted the white parchment lying beside the trunk, and her heart fell. She lifted it with shaking fingers. It was still sealed. Even worse, two of the hooks her brother used to display his bow and arrows on the wall lay empty. She sank to the loft floor and clutched the letter to her chest, letting out a gasping sob.

She'd hung onto hope for so long that Brenna had been lying. That her brother was still alive. She'd prayed Gael would not have the heart to go through with the evil plan his sister whispered in his ear. Now she had to face the facts. Conall was gone. There was no way he would've missed her letter. Even if it had fallen to the loft floor immediately, it was still right there in plain sight. Her brother was dead.

Tiora climbed up after her and hugged her as she cried. "It's all right, Lark. I'm here."

Lark clutched her friend, grateful not to be alone. She let herself feel the grief of her brother's death for the first time and wept with abandon.

Her brother and her mother were both gone. She couldn't do anything to bring them back, but she could do something to make things right. She remembered her vow. There was no way she was going to let Gael and Brenna win.

Lark wiped her tears and pulled free from Tiora's arms. "C'mon, we better go in the house."

The light in the barn had dimmed even more as she cried. She ruffled Sunny's fur as she stepped back onto the barn's packed dirt floor. "I'll be back for you, girl. I promise. But for now, you'll have to stay in the barn." She offered the old mutt one more gentle pat on her head, then shut the barn door and turned toward the farmhouse.

Passing her mother's herb garden, Lark shook her head. Weeds strangled the once neat little rows. As they approached the house, she shivered. The darkened interior no longer buzzed with life and laughter but stood empty. She opened the back door and wrinkled her nose. It even smelled off. No longer full of the scents of food baking or fresh herbs hanging to dry, it reeked of sour ale and rotting vegetables.

She froze in the doorway, her gaze the only thing moving. Dirty dishes and empty bottles crowded the kitchen counter and packed the washbasin. A single place was set at the table, the used cutlery and dish still waiting to be cleared away. Pain stabbed her chest. This was not her home any longer.

Lark opened the door and ushered Tiora inside. "This is it. Sorry about the mess." She winced as the stench of stale alcohol sparked a flashback of Rasmus. "...and the smell." She picked her way past empty bottles, treading carefully across the soiled floor that likely hadn't been swept since the day she'd left. "I'll put the kettle on. Have a seat." She stirred the hearth in the center of the room, bringing the fire back to life.

Tiora's chair skidded across the floor. "It's a lovely home if you ignore the mess. It must've been nice growing up here."

A wistful smile tugged at Lark's cheeks. "It was. It was wonderful." Her smile dropped, and she left the hearth. She stood on her tiptoes and opened a nearby cabinet bordering the ceiling. "That's over now. After today, I'll be glad when I never have to set foot in this house again."

She pulled out an old book and rubbed her hand across the smooth leather cover. Her mother's book. She leafed through it, sighing as she noted her mother's familiar handwriting filling the pages. She stopped on one of the first pages and bustled about the kitchen, visiting several shelves and cabinets until she'd assembled a variety of different-sized jars and containers on the table.

The kettle whistled, and she returned to the hearth to grab the steaming pot. "I'll have that tea ready for you in no time. Let it steep while it cools, then you can drink it while I collect the rest of my things." She set to work, adding a pinch of this and a dash of that to her favorite ceramic mug. She set it in front of Tiora and squeezed her shoulder gently.

"Thank you." Tiora gazed into the cup with obvious trepidation. "I wish I didn't need this, but I can't..." Her eyes teared up, and she sniffled. "I just can't."

Lark bent down, staring into Tiora's watery brown eyes. "You don't have to. And you don't need to explain why to me or anyone else." She saw the pain written all over her friend's face, and her blood boiled with rage. "I'll be back in a moment. I just have to grab a few things from my room."

It wasn't fair her friend had to deal with these consequences. Both of them had been forced to change their lives so drastically, through no fault of their own.

All her life she'd followed the rules and listened to her elders. She'd helped her mother heal countless people, often without asking for a single thing in return. Look where that had gotten her. She was sick of other people thinking they could walk all over her and take advantage of her kindness. And she'd learned the hard way not all of her elders deserved respect.

Lark charged into her room and collected the pouch of herbs she'd come for. Grabbing a knapsack from her closet, she packed the fragrant bundle inside, along with a change of clothes. She grabbed a few more things that looked like they might fit Tiora and clutched them in her arms.

Her eyes welled with tears as she surveyed the room. Memories of her childhood flashed in her mind. Her mother brushing her hair and reading her bedtime stories. Conall playing dolls with her on the floor, humoring her, despite being six years older and likely bored to tears. But that was all in the past now. She took a steadying breath and a final look around, then shut the door.

She found herself drawn to Conall's door. She slipped inside, the metal hinge squeaking as it swung open to reveal the room—cold and desolate.

Lark exhaled a shaky breath. A part of her had been hoping he would be there, curled up in his bed, ready to jump up and yell at her for leaving without a proper goodbye. Now that would never happen. Gael and Brenna had seen to it that he would never greet her again. She gritted her teeth, shut the door, and spun on her heel.

Tiora set down the empty mug as Lark reentered the kitchen. "Did you find everything you needed?"

"Just about." Lark dropped the bag on the table and handed the clothes to Tiora. "I thought you might like these." Then she grabbed the spell book, stashed it inside the bag, and pulled the cord closed. She slung the bag around her shoulders. "That's everything. Let's get out of here."

Tiora rose from the table, stuffing the clothes in her knapsack. Brow furrowing, she inclined her head toward the table, still littered with jars and containers. "Do you need help putting these back where they belong?"

"No. Leave them." Lark lifted the lid off the closest container, giving the contents a sniff before casually dumping the aromatic herbs in a heap on the wooden floor near the door. She grabbed the next pot, sliding it aside without opening it and picking up a large jar behind it. She walked a circuit of the room, scattering handfuls of brown herbs all along the floor, atop cabinets and walls.

"I thought you wanted to be in and out with no one the wiser?" Tiora asked from the open doorway, frowning. "What's the mess for?"

"My mother taught me a lot about herbs." Lark glanced up from her task, setting the empty jar on the table and selecting another. "Gael wanted this farm so badly he killed my brother for it." She lifted the pot's lid and tossed the contents down the hall leading to the bedrooms and family room. "I'd rather watch it burn than let that monster stay here."

Carrying the empty vessel to the hearth, she used a set of metal tongs to place a smoldering coal inside. She strolled over to join her friend in the doorway. Tiora backed away slowly, staring at the jar glowing ominously in the moonlight outside.

Lark spun to face the kitchen, letting the jar warm her hands as she took a last look at the house that had once been her home. She expected to feel reluctant, even sorrowful, but all she felt was a burning conviction that this was the right decision. That murderer did not deserve this place. This home that was once so full of love and warmth did not belong to him.

Lark stared down into the glowing jar and upended it. She dumped the coal into the pile of herbs near the door and backed away as the dry leaves burst into flames.

Shoving the door closed with her boot, she turned her back on the house, grabbed Tiora's elbow, and hurried toward the barn. "C'mon, we better let the animals out to graze. The flames probably won't spread to the barn, but you never know when the wind might change direction."

They set the cattle and goats free. Sunny helped, weaving around the stragglers and nipping at their heels to encourage their exit.

As they abandoned the empty barn, she gazed at the house. The kitchen was already engulfed in flames, and the fire spread quickly into the center of the house. A loud *thud* caught her attention, coming from the back bedroom.

Her breath stilled. That was her mother's room. Gael's room.

Tiora stumbled back, her hands shaking. "Lark, did you hear that?"

Lark's heart thudded madly as she remembered the empty bottles littering the kitchen floor. Could he have been asleep in the bedroom the whole time they were inside?

"Bloody blazes," a voice from within exclaimed.

Rage burned in her veins. She knew that voice.

Gael coughed loudly between curses. Another *thud* sounded, closer to the front door. It was him, staggering drunkenly through the burning house, making his way toward fresh air and the freedom of the night. The freedom her brother would never again enjoy.

Lark sank to the ground, digging her fingers into the soil. Her gaze never left the house as she concentrated on the spot where she'd heard the sound. She wasn't going to let him leave.

With everything inside her, she wished for that bastard to be buried inside the house he wanted so badly. Closing her eyes, she pictured the ground opening up and swallowing the house. A tremor struck her, pulsating through her bones and rattling her teeth. The power flew into the earth through her fingers. Then a great bellowing *crunch* made her eyes fly open.

Blazes. The unburnt side of the house now rested halfway into the ground.

She gasped, pulling her hands from the ground and covering her mouth. As she knelt in the dirt with Tiora and Sunny standing motionless beside her, what was left above ground of the front door—just the very top—jolted wildly as Gael attempted to shove it open. Smoke, and the sound of his hacking coughing, were the only things that escaped.

Finally, the door stilled. Lark stood and turned her back on the farm. Tiora stared at her hands, still covered with the wet, brown soil.

Brushing her fingers along her tunic, Lark rubbed the dirt from her skin. "Let's go. We're done here." Without looking back, she set off for the forest trail.

Chapter 12

Kayda hurried along the cobblestone path. Red silk swirled around her legs, the crimson color dulling in the thick fog that had arrived in Flamesmoat overnight. "I can't believe we're late. Grandfather will not be pleased," she said to Izora as they approached the centuries-old brick cathedral. The bell tower rang, signaling the start of the Harvest Service.

"Oh, I'm sure he'll just be happy you came at all this time," Izora replied with a chuckle.

Kayda clasped her hands together and rubbed her knuckles.

If she'd only gone to the renewal ceremony this spring, she wouldn't be so late today. She thought she'd allotted enough time for dressing after her morning training session, but she hadn't counted on the growth spurt she'd been through this year requiring alterations to be made to her ceremonial frock. They had to summon a trio of seamstresses to the castle, who added several inches of silk to the bottom edge and the bust of the gorgeous, cumbersome gown.

Now she would have to scurry past everyone already assembled to take her place at the front of the pews. She shuddered, picturing all those eyes upon her, whispering under their breath.

The path split. Izora grabbed her hands, unclasping them and giving them both a gentle squeeze before placing her hands at her sides. "You look lovely, Princess. I'll see you later, at the feast." She sent a gentle smile her way and set off down the path to the front entrance.

Kayda swallowed her apprehension, approaching the side door to the church. Thankfully, that entrance was reserved solely for the royals. She wouldn't have a dozen sets of eyes on her as she navigated the stairs with the thick layers of fog-dampened silk bunching about her legs and threatening to trip her.

Her eyes widened. A pair of men stood closely atop the steps, speaking in hushed voices. With the bell tower still chiming, she had no chance of overhearing what they said. How strange to find them cloistered here outside of the service, when everyone was meant to be inside.

She didn't recognize the man facing her, but she noted his features—dark eyes and hair, light skin and a full beard—before he spotted her staring. He said a final word to his companion and hustled down the steps, onto the path she'd just exited. She paused, watching the black-cloaked stranger's back retreating in the fog before she turned to address the second man as he spun to greet her.

"Hello, Tarquin."

Her brother was dressed in a suit of matching red silk. He looked down at her from atop the stairs, his brows scrunching together before he plastered a wide smile across his face. "I see I'm not the only one making a dramatic entrance." He moved sideways, making room on the top step. Then he offered his elbow, quirking a brow mischievously. "Shall we?"

She stared up at him, eyeing his proffered arm like a snake in the grass until the smirk dropped from his face.

"I can tell you're nervous." His expression warmed. "You don't have to walk in alone. C'mon, I promise, no tricks."

She swallowed, considering. Just when she thought he could not be any more awful, her brother did something sweet. She should hold her head up high and march in on her own. But the part of her that remembered the handful of good times they'd shared as children insisted she give him the benefit of the doubt.

Well... they were both late. Kayda linked her arm with Tarquin's. He opened the door, and they entered as the church bells concluded their chiming. As all eyes flicked to them, she let out a shaky breath, grateful she had her brother to share the spotlight. With him there to lead her, his grin spread from ear to ear, she could set her gaze to the ground and ignore the dozens of eyes inspecting her.

They strode down the polished, tiled aisle, their footsteps echoing in her ears despite the muffled chatter of the assembly. They reached the front pew as High Prior Sander emerged from the curtained alcove at the front of the building.

Everyone stood to honor the prior's entrance. The king, wearing a crimson silk suit identical to her brother's, smiled at her and Tarquin as they slipped in next to him in the front pew. He showed no sign of displeasure at their tardiness. Her father, Prince Gideon, was absent, as usual.

As Kayda's stomach settled, her attention was drawn to the High Prior.

High Prior Sander was a somber man who rarely sported a smile on his wrinkled face, and today was no exception. He adjusted his black robe that was lined with red silk stripes down the side—the color a perfect match for the bright crimson the royals wore, but the fabric was not nearly so fine. He marched out front and center and mounted the podium steps that raised him high enough so all those in the back of the spacious building could view his speech.

"Please be seated." High Prior Sander's deep voice boomed through the room.

Kayda smoothed her gown and admired the decor as she waited for the room to quiet and the sermon to begin. The Church of the Dragon was palatial and imposing. Brightly colored tapestries adorned the walls, along with majestic stained-glass windows with intricate etchings—muted today in the foggy morning—that rivaled those in the great hall of Kings Keep.

The centerpiece hung suspended from the ceiling above the prior's head; the massive skull of a long dead dragon, so huge it made High Prior Sander—one of the tallest and stoutest men she had ever met—seem puny in comparison. She shivered as she marveled at its size and imagined the ferocity of the extinct creatures who had such large, sharp teeth.

"Thank you all for coming to join us in prayer this morning. Today, we ask the Lord Dragon to bless our harvest..." High Prior Sander's voice was strong and soothing. It wasn't long before Kayda's mind wandered, tuning out the message she knew by heart after attending these services her entire life.

Her gaze slid sideways. She smiled at her grandfather. He was clear-eyed today, staring intently at the prior as he delivered his sermon. He'd always been so devout, his bonding talent proof enough for him to take every word as truth. It was the church who upheld their right to rule, stating in their holy text that those of the bloodline of the first King of Dracwood would inherit the gift of bonding and prove essential in the future when the Lord Dragon tested the world again.

Tarquin sat on the other side of the king, fingers tapping repeatedly on his knee. His stare was fixed not on the priest, but out the stained-glass window behind him. Kayda returned her gaze to the prior, keeping her face impassive. For her grandfather, and the assembled public, she would at least give the impression of listening, even though the droning sermon was not inspiring her rapt attention.

Her half-brother ignoring the sermon was no surprise. Though Tarquin pretended to be as devout as their grandfather when they were in public, she suspected his belief in church teachings was not the driving force behind his actions. He certainly behaved like he didn't believe there was any higher power out there, ready to reward or condemn him for his actions in the afterlife. No, Tarquin lived every day doing exactly as he pleased, with no thought to any rules of behavior the church espoused.

As for herself, she wanted to believe. She tried her hardest to live by the church's teachings. She sought to embrace their highest values of honesty, kindness, and charity in her daily life. For the rest—if she were honest with herself—she had her doubts.

Her gaze was drawn again to the skull, suspended above them like a menacing chandelier. She didn't doubt dragons had once existed, but she found it harder to believe they would return to save them all from some future danger. Add to that the idea that her children, or even herself, would have some role to play in that conflict, and her skin moistened with sweat under all those layers of silk.

"Please, join me in asking the Lord Dragon to bless the royal house of the Kingdom of Dracwood." High Prior Sander's voice interrupted her musing.

She took a deep breath and stood with her family, turning to gaze upon the parishioners. Her heart raced as all those adoring eyes fell upon her standing in her crimson dress, the color a visual reminder of the blood the royals carried.

The common people held so much love for her family. They expected so much from them. Kayda couldn't help but feel uneasy with their eyes upon her and unworthy of their devotion. She bowed her head and lowered her lashes as the prior prayed, grateful to escape the public's scrutiny.

"Holy Father Dragon, spread your protective wings over our king and his heirs, so they may serve your children and all who believe. Bring to them, on this day of harvest, all the great fruits of our world, so they may reap the benefits of your everlasting love in this time of plenty. Finally, please bless them with your wisdom and bestow them with your strength to weather the storm to come."

A moment of silence stretched out. Then the prior raised his voice again. "King Quinton, please do us the honor of lighting the holy oil. As our Father Dragon's flame burned bright, so too, shall the fire that burns in our hearts."

Her grandfather strode forward. Kayda lifted her head and spun forward again, watching the king clasp hands with the prior and smile fondly at his old friend. "Thank you so much for your prayers, High Prior Sander."

He plucked a taper from a candelabra on the wall and used it to light the wick of the laumarle oil lamp that the prior settled on the podium for all to see. The rare oil sent a bright white light flickering into the air. Despite costing a fortune, the oil would be left to burn all day long, warming the hearts of all who visited the church.

The king turned to address the parishioners, "Thank you all for your great faith in the Lord Dragon and our kingdom. Everyone is welcome to join us at the feast to celebrate the coming harvest."

Cheers erupted throughout the room, and voices rang out calling, "Bless you," and "Long live King Quinton."

Kayda smiled. The love the people felt for her grandfather washed over her like a warm wave. He sauntered forward, grinning and waving at the common people. He gracefully made his way to her side, offering his elbow to escort her to the feast. She accepted and made her way down the church aisle, Tarquin following closely behind them.

They exited the church from the front, where another group of people waited outside to watch the royal family's procession through the outskirts of Flamesmoat and the great field surrounding the city. The fog had lifted, chased away by the bright morning sun.

They were met by a large group of the castle guard, around thirty or forty armed men. Their silver, ceremonial armor glittered as they circled them, providing a buffer between the royals and the common people as they strode down the streets of Northmoat.

Kayda kept her eyes trained forward and a tight grip on her grandfather's arm as they strolled through the city. The shops and houses on the route were decorated with bright flowers and shimmering ribbons. Townspeople ringed the streets, and children perched on their parents' shoulders, grinning as they passed.

The king seemed to enjoy himself, waving at all the people lining the streets.

Kayda's stomach wobbled. She loved seeing her grandfather in such good spirits but couldn't help feeling uncomfortable being on display.

They drew closer to the edge of the city, their steps sinking as they traversed through the shallow gully ringing the city. Centuries ago, it was erected to protect the people within, filled with flame, giving the city its name. But it had been out of use for so long it was overgrown with grass and barely discernible from the surrounding fields, allowing them to pass through easily.

Throngs of people amassed outside, waiting for their arrival at the feast site. Tumblers and jugglers wove through the crowds, delighting children with their antics. A bouquet of delicious smells wafted in their direction, making her mouth water. People sat upon blankets of all shapes and sizes, drinking, eating, and laughing with family and friends.

Kayda sighed as she spied the nearby tables. Most were already full of people, many she recognized from the castle, but the grandest table of them all sat empty, except for the great heaping plates of food piled high upon it. Her grandfather spotted it and ambled in that direction.

A scuffle of some sort broke out to the right. Several guards peeled off from their procession, headed toward it.

Kayda tore her gaze from the waiting feast, craning her neck. The guards and townspeople closed in on the source of the disturbance so quickly she couldn't see anything.

"Don't worry, my dear." King Quinton patted her hand, which rested in the crook of his elbow. "The guards will take care of it."

She turned to her grandfather, abandoning her attempt to view the commotion that had only increased in size and volume since the guards rushed into the fray. As she met the king's eyes, she spotted movement behind him. Then some unreadable emotion flashed on his face, his body shuddering violently.

She gasped, clutching him as he collapsed, a knife lodged firmly in his back. She fell with him, unable to hold up the king's dead weight. Her eyes glistened with tears. Her mind swirled with horror and disbelief. She held his gaze, unable to look away as the light disappeared from her grandfather's eyes.

As if from somewhere far away, chaos erupted as the crowd took note of the king's fate.

Tarquin yelled, "The king, the king's been murdered. Catch the villain, you fools!"

The guards attempted to close in around them while simultaneously trying to find the man who'd stabbed the king.

An old man burst through the crowd, his pristine white robe and imposing bearing marking him as a Palisade Mage. "I'm a healer. Let me through," he said calmly, slipping between the guard and crouching down beside her.

She shook her head, blinking furiously, her mouth opening and closing soundlessly. The mage's wrinkled hand pried her fingers from the king's shoulders, then he rolled him onto his stomach.

Kayda pulled herself into a seated position, watching the mage as he set his hands on her grandfather and examined the wound.

After reaching into a pouch on his belt, he pulled out something small enough to hide in his fist. Then he spread his hand on the king's wound and pulled the knife from his back. He closed his eyes, his palm covering the wound tightly.

Kayda held her breath, watching. A tremor tingled over her skin. It was there and gone in the space of a heartbeat.

The mage opened his green eyes, staring into her own and smiled weakly. "I've done what I can. The rest is up to him."

"Thank you," she whispered. She reached for her grandfather and gasped at the wound. The skin was perfect and unmarred, as if the knife had never been there. Hope erupted in her chest. She stared into the mage's face. "You've healed him. Bless you!"

The mage shook his head slightly. "I've healed the body only. We have to wait and see if his soul returns." He turned his attention to the guardsmen surrounding them. "What are you men waiting for? Get the king and princess back to the keep."

A wagon appeared, surrendered willingly from some folk in the crowd. The guards made quick work of lifting the king and carrying him to the back of the cart. By the time they held him aloft, dozens of people had offered their blankets to cushion the wooden boards. Their tear-stained faces crowded around the guards, and the sound of wailing reverberated as the masses wept for the fallen king.

Kayda allowed herself to be moved, still in a state of disbelief. An armored man ushered her into the back of the cart to sit beside the king. She searched her grandfather's ashen face. His eyes were closed, his features slack. His scarlet suit was covered in dirt and grass, soaked with a dark stain that could only be from his blood. As the cart began to move, pulled by a brown mare and driven by a set of armored men, she grabbed her grandfather's hand and squeezed it tightly.

"We'll be back home soon, Grandfather. You're going to be fine." She stroked the back of his hand with her thumb. The panicked thudding of her heart slowed as they made their way closer to the keep.

It had all happened so fast. There'd been no time to think, but now that she had a moment to reflect on the attack, one image returned to her, and her mouth dropped open.

She'd seen the face of the man who'd stabbed her grandfather. The stranger—it was him! The same man that had been engaged in a whispered conversation with Tarquin this morning just tried to assassinate the king.

She dropped the king's hand, wringing her own together as the implications of that fact dawned on her. Tarquin had been involved. Her stomach turned. She didn't have any proof, but she *knew*. All those secret meetings she'd happened upon, all his suspicious behavior, it had all led to this.

If only she'd told her grandfather like she'd planned that day in his chambers. Her heart pounded again, and she snapped her eyes closed, dizziness washing over her. Tarquin was behind this, and she was the only one who knew... What was she going to do?

The wagon jostled violently, and her eyes shot open as she bounced off the side of the wagon. "Hey, take it easy." She steadied herself before she fell on top of her grandfather.

The two guards up front didn't respond, and Kayda's eyes bulged when she spotted where they were headed. "Why aren't you heading for the Keep?"

Her gaze locked on the tower. It grew closer with every passing instant as they sped straight for it.

"Take us to Kings Keep." She crawled on her hands and knees to the front of the wagon. She grabbed the man's shoulder who steered the reins, her hand closing on the cold metal of his armor, and she jostled him—hard. "Listen to me. We need to go to the Keep!"

The driver sat unmoved, her attempt to grab his attention as effective as a child screaming at a storm cloud. But the second man swiveled to face her, his features shielded by his helm, so all she could see was a set of piercing brown eyes glowering at her. "The tower is more secure. You'll be safe there, my lady." His gauntleted hand rose, aiming for her fingers that still clutched his companion's shoulder, but Kayda snatched her hand back before he touched her.

"No." She slammed her fist against the wooden slats, then pointed to the Keep. "Take us to Kings Keep. That's an order."

"We are following orders. Prince Tarquin's orders." He spun forward again, and Kayda sat back, covering her mouth with her palm.

No... it couldn't be true. The guards were under orders from that sneaky bastard, and she was about to be locked up in the tower. She reached instinctively for her skirt pocket. The one where she kept the tinderbox Izora had gifted her. But her hands only slid over the smooth silk of her ceremonial dress.

Damn. She had no pockets, no tinderbox, and no way to call forth the flames. Even if she had, she couldn't summon. What would she do? Kill the guards and steal the king? There was no way she could leave him, not now.

Even if she succeeded, she'd have nowhere to go. The sad fact was Kings Keep was all she knew. Except for the occasional jaunt in the countryside or sightseeing trip, she'd spent her entire life here. And there was no one she trusted enough to take them in. She grimaced, realizing she had little choice but to go with the guards and hope her inaction in this moment didn't destroy what chance she had of stopping her brother.

The tower loomed above them. She crawled back to the king and grabbed his hand. "Don't worry, Grandfather... I'll think of something," she whispered. "I'm going to figure out what he's up to and stop him." She cupped a hand on his face, eyes filling with tears, her jaw set firmly with determination. "I'll find a way to make him pay for what he's done... I swear it."

Chapter 13

Smoke and ash filled the air. Conall slowed to a stop, panting in the forest just outside the farm. He gripped the side of his chest. His lungs burned, and the taste of metal lingered in the back of his throat as he swallowed breath after gasping breath.

They'd made it to the farm in record time, running at full speed through the forest. It was a miracle neither of them had stumbled in the fog-shrouded underbrush. Now, they were here—and it was too late.

He fell to his knees as he caught sight of the wreckage for the first time. Fire had torn through the entire house, leaving smoldering debris in its wake. His heart, still racing from the run, wrenched. It was gone. His home was gone.

Shadow sidled up beside him. Conall draped an arm around him, accepting the comfort he offered. He sucked in another gasping breath, resting his cheek on the soft gray fur on Shadow's back as he tried to wrap his mind around the loss of his home. All those hours in the cave recovering, all the miles he'd trekked, all the pain he'd endured... it had not been enough to save his home.

He closed his eyes, shutting out the devastation in front of him, and said a silent prayer for his sister. She was probably sitting at a neighbor's house right now or out tending to a sick child in town. There was no reason to assume she'd been in there when the fire blazed through. She would show up any moment, just as surprised as he was to see the farm in ashes. He opened his eyes, refusing to believe otherwise. She had to be all right.

"I have to go check things out. I need you to stay here, Shadow."

"Are you sure?" The wolf's muscles stiffened below his cheek as Shadow tensed. *"What if Gael is there?"*

"I'm sure. The barn is still standing. If the animals are in there, you'll only spook them. Besides, this is a farm town. With all the livestock here, the people don't have a great fondness for wolves. If anyone happens by, they're likely to shoot first and ask questions later." He took to his feet, exhaling through his mouth and adjusting the pouches on his belt. *"I'll be all right. Wait here. I'll be back as soon as I get some answers."*

"All right, brother, I'll be right here waiting. Call for me if you need me."

Conall nodded and set off across the grazing field on a straight course for the barn. The building still stood, but it was empty. The doors were thrown wide open, and the noise of animals was gone.

He walked into the shadowy interior. The familiar musty scent was absent, overpowered by the smoky bonfire that had been his home. It was a good sign. Lark had probably set the animals free, then set off with Sunny to bring them round to a neighbor's house.

He sighed as he spotted the worn wooden loft ladder, still standing. He climbed, careful not to put any weight on his aching shoulder. Gazing upon his things, a small weight lifted off his chest. He dug through his trunk for a change of clothes and grabbed his second-best bow and quiver off the wall, where it hung waiting.

It took only a moment to replace his filthy clothes with a brown tunic and wool trousers. Then he stood there—the familiar heft of smooth wood in his hands, his clothes free of bloodstains and shredded holes—feeling refreshed and better prepared but still at a loss for what to do next.

He spotted a crumpled piece of parchment lying on the loft floor near the ladder. As he bent to pick it up, Shadow's voice rose in his mind. *"Conall, someone is coming."* Stuffing the paper into his pocket, he crouched down on the loft floor. He nocked an arrow and aimed his bow at the barn door.

"I saw you heading in there, boy," a weathered voice called out. "We don't take kindly to thieves in these parts. You better drop whatever you're stealing and show yourself before I send for the magistrate and you end up losing a hand."

Conall let his bow arm relax. He knew that voice. "Barrow, it's me, Conall."

The bewildered face of his closest neighbor peeked through the barn door. He looked the same as he always had, his white hair unbrushed and wind-tossed, dirt-dusted overalls covering his lanky frame. Conall climbed down the ladder, holding his bow in his left arm.

When he turned around, Barrow gaped in surprise. "Conall? Blazes. It is you!" He pulled him in for a hug. "We all thought you were dead. I'm so glad to see you."

"What's happening? Do you need my help?"

"No, stay where you are. It's just my neighbor," he told his bondmate as he returned Barrow's embrace. The old man squeezed his shoulder a bit too tightly, and he grimaced. *"Maybe he'll have some answers."*

"You thought I was dead?" Conall stepped back a few paces.

Barrow threaded a hand through his messy locks. "Gael came into town a few weeks back. Told everyone how you'd fallen to your death while out trapping in the forest." He set his tanned hands on his hips, brown eyes searching him intently. "A few of us didn't believe him. We demanded he take us out there to see where it happened."

"And he did?" Conall's brow furrowed. That would've been risky. If anyone spotted him there pierced with an arrow, Gael's story would be revealed as a lie.

"He didn't want to at first, but the magistrate convinced him. A few of us trekked out there the next day. All that was left when we got there was a trail of bloodstains and the tracks of a wolf nearby on the streambed. We all figured you'd been dragged off into the woods." Barrow's wrinkles deepened as he frowned. "I'm sorry we didn't look harder for you."

Conall stared at the ground, shaking his head. They'd been out there searching for him? He must have been in the cave, fighting off the fever that had nearly killed him. A bitter smile crossed his face, there and gone in an instant, before he returned his attention to Barrow.

"It's all right. You couldn't have known I was out there." Conall aimed for the open doorway and took a few steps in that direction before Barrow stopped him.

"What happened out there in the forest, Conall? Was what Gael said the truth?" Barrow's bushy brows knitted together. "Did you slip and fall?"

"Yeah, I fell." Conall pulled the neck of his tunic to the side, revealing the red puckered flesh of the still healing wound on his left shoulder. "But not before that lying bastard shot me."

"Blazes." Barrow leaned closer, examining the wound. His mouth dropped open, and his eyes bulged. Then his jaw snapped shut, and his brows furrowed as he met Conall's eyes again. "Well, he got what was coming to him, at least."

"What do you mean?" Conall headed outside.

Barrow kept step with him, nodding at the wreckage as they stepped out into the daylight. "The fire caught in the night. Everyone was in town, watching some traveling show and camping on the village green before heading to Flamesmoat for the Harvest Festival. I decided to stay home for a little peace and quiet. I happened to speak to Gael earlier in the afternoon. He told me he was skipping the feast this year, too. And, well, I was out in my field stargazing when the fire started. I watched it all from a distance."

Barrow glanced down at the ground before looking back at the smoldering remnants of the building. "It started in the kitchen. Then the rest of the house—it was the strangest thing—it sank right into the ground like the floorboards collapsed and it all tumbled into the cellar." He clasped Conall's shoulder. "By the time I made it here, the place was completely engulfed... No one made it out."

The words pummeled Conall like a punch to the gut. He closed his eyes, scrubbing at the lids with his fingertips. There's no way Gael would have let Lark go camp on the village green alone. And no one made it out...

Gael and Lark were gone. He clasped his head in his hands, pressing his fingers into his temples. No... not Lark... please, not her.

"I'm so sorry to be the one to tell you, Conall." Barrow rubbed his back gently.

Conall dropped his hands at his sides and stared ahead blankly. It couldn't be true. If only he'd just climbed that damn ridge like he'd planned, maybe he would've made it back in time. Now he'd never see his sister again.

Barrow continued, "I came to make sure I hadn't missed any animals. They were out to graze when the fire rolled through. I brought them all to my farm. Was planning to sell them and send the money round Mage Keep to your sister, but I suppose now you'll be wanting them back."

Blinking rapidly, Conall whirled to face his neighbor. Did he hear that right? "Lark is at Mage Keep?"

Barrow nodded. "She left the same day you had your fall. Went with that chubby sister of Gael's into Flamesmoat before traveling to Mage Keep." He chuckled. "Gael was plenty steamed about that when he found out... He kept shoving her letter in everyone's face, jabbering on about the mages stealing her youth or some such nonsense. Was why he didn't want to take us into the forest to look for you. He was dead set on setting off for Flamesmoat after her, instead."

Conall clutched his chest, his lungs full enough to burst. Lark was alive! And she'd left Gael a letter. He smiled and pulled the crumpled parchment out of his pocket, smoothing the paper, revealing the word written on the sealed envelope.

He sighed. There was his name written in his sister's unmistakable handwriting. "You have the animals at your farm. Is my dog Sunny with them?" Conall folded the letter carefully and placed it in his pocket, his smile fading as Barrow clasped his hands together, frowning.

"I'm sorry, son. I haven't seen your dog."

Conall swallowed, his heart crushed. She must've been inside with the only master she had left, Gael. Poor Sunny. She should've been with him, not that murderer.

Tendrils of smoke escaped from the charred remains of his home. His stomach clenched. He would never again tousle Sunny's golden fur or feel the warm weight of her against his side as he slept. He gritted his teeth, his hands curling into fists at his side.

"What now?" Barrow asked. "Should I bring the animals back? Will you rebuild?"

He blinked repeatedly, trying to focus. The house might be gone, but the land was still his. He'd better decide what to do with it. One thing was certain. He wouldn't be around to take care of the animals anytime soon.

"You were willing to sell the animals for Lark... would you mind doing the same for me?" Conall raised a brow.

"Sure, I could handle it. It's the least I can do after how Lark and your mother saved Leda and my new grandbaby last winter." Barrow pulled a worn leather coin purse out of his pocket and dumped the contents into his hand. "This ought to cover about half of it. Come on down the road to my house, and I can fetch you the rest."

Conall shook his head, holding out a hand for the coins. "Thanks, Barrow, but I want to head into town, tell the magistrate what happened here, and let him see I'm not dead before I leave for Mage Keep."

He was going to see his sister. He hadn't forgotten Gael's warning. She deserved to know the truth. And he had to tell her the facts of what had happened with him and her beloved step-father.

The coins landed in his palm, clinking together before he dropped them into his belt pouch. "I wouldn't want to travel with too much coin on me. Mind if I pick up the rest when I get back?"

"No, won't be any trouble. Tell the magistrate I witnessed the fire, and he can come find me if he has any questions. I'll keep an eye on the farm for you while you're gone." The old man took another long look at the smoldering rubble. "So, you are planning to come back and rebuild?"

"Yes, I'll be back. You can count on it." Conall joined his neighbor in staring at the destruction as a snippet of conversation from earlier came back to him. "Hey, you said earlier the house sank, didn't you?"

Barrow nodded.

Conall stepped closer to the wreckage, pulling the neck of his tunic over his face to shield his nose from the smoke wafting in the air. The fiery debris' heat rose to greet him.

"Yep, this side of the house." Barrow walked beside him, peering at the part of the house sunken much lower in the ground than the other half. He coughed, then shielded his face with his sleeve. "One moment it was there, and the next, it was halfway buried in the ground. One of the most bizarre things I ever saw... But if the floorboards were on fire, and the whole section dropped into the cellar—well, that would do it, I suppose."

Conall tilted his head, pursing his lips. "Yeah, that's the strange thing, Barrow. We didn't have a cellar."

The door to the Greenvale Inn slammed shut behind him. Conall trudged away from the inn, headed for the forest trail that would lead him to his sister. He'd just finished telling the magistrate his tale. He sighed deeply, shading his eyes from the midday sun.

All the gory details would be known throughout town in a matter of days. Although he'd tried to relay his tale quietly, the acoustics in the inn made the feat impossible. And with practically everyone in town away at Flamesmoat for the annual Harvest Feastival, the few stragglers who stayed behind had gone quiet as he spoke, leaning in close to discover how he'd returned from the dead.

His eyes adjusting to the light, he lengthened his stride. At least it was over and done with now. He could rest easy knowing that although the farmhouse lay in ruins, the land would be there waiting for him when he came back from Mage Keep.

The inn door creaked open and shut. Hurried footsteps followed. "Hello. I couldn't help but hear you were headed for Mage Keep. Care for some company?" inquired a female voice behind him.

Conall slowed and turned to examine the young woman walking toward him.

She smiled, her sun-kissed, white cheeks a pretty pink. At first glance, she appeared to be close to his age and was attractive despite her plain traveling clothes, with long brown hair pulled into a simple ponytail and bright blue eyes. He didn't recognize her, which was strange, as their small farming town wasn't a place that typically had many visitors.

"You're going to Mage Keep?" he asked, stopping to await her answer.

"Yes, I'm on my way back. Just passing through this little town after completing an errand for my mother." She stuck out her right hand, still looking at him directly. "I'm Ereni."

His gaze jumped to her hand, then back to her face before he grasped her hand and shook. "Conall."

Her grip was firm and her hands soft as she shook back. "So, what about it? Shall we travel together?" She dropped his hand and strode forward, toward the trail he planned to use. She wore sturdy leather boots and had a knapsack strung around her shoulders as if prepared to leave that instant. "I was planning to leave today, and it looks like you are as well. It would be nice to have a little company." She cocked her head sideways, peering at him.

Conall walked, too, keeping pace with the girl as he considered her proposition. It would be nice to have some company to help stave off the loneliness he felt without his family and friends. And she'd said she was headed back, so it sounded like she'd been there already. It couldn't hurt to learn some inside information about the keep before they arrived. But what about Shadow?

"Brother, there's a girl here that wants to travel with us to Mage Keep... Do you have any objections to her joining us?"

"I won't eat her, if that's what you're asking."

Conall couldn't stop the chuckle that escaped him. Ereni looked his way, eyebrows raising.

He cleared his throat. "My hound is waiting for me in the woods." It was his turn to raise his brows. "You're not afraid of big dogs, are you?"

Her face lit up, her arms swinging as she entered the trail. "I love dogs."

Conall led the way to his bondmate. He was curled up below a star oak, resting in the shade. When they neared the tree, Shadow rose to his feet, leisurely stretching and staring at Ereni.

He had to give her credit. She didn't balk at his size or the wild intelligence of his stare. The only sign of her surprise was the slight hitch in her voice when she spoke next.

"You weren't kidding. You keep big dogs in Greenvale, I see."

Conall shrugged. "Not Greenvale. Just me. This is Shadow."

She knelt down, offering her fist. "Hi, Shadow. I'm Ereni."

"Go on." Conall slid his gaze from Shadow to Ereni's fist. *"I told her you're my hound."*

"Your hound?" Shadow snorted and backed up a pace, shooting him a glare. Then he padded forward, gave her fist a single sniff, and sat on his haunches.

Her gaze lingered on the gray fur above Shadow's head. For a moment, he was certain she would pet him, but she retracted her hand and stood. "You two ready? Mage Keep is this way."

They walked, the late summer breeze humming through the leaves. The wind and the shaded trail made for a comfortable hike, despite the lingering heat.

She edged closer until they strolled side by side, tilting her head toward him. "I couldn't help but overhear your story in the inn."

He winced, staring down at the dirt path. "Yeah. Kind of crazy, I know."

She nodded, her brows sinking as she concentrated on him. "Sounds like you've been through a lot. And now you're going to Mage Keep to tell your sister?"

"That's the plan."

The mention of Lark had him tapping his pants pocket, sighing as the fabric crinkled beneath his fingers. He'd been so busy planning what he'd say to the magistrate on the way into town he hadn't opened her letter.

They spent the afternoon walking and chatting. When the sun sank down behind the trees and they stopped to make camp for the night, he pulled the crumpled parchment out of his pocket and unfolded it.

"What's that? A goodbye letter from your sweetheart?" Ereni perched on a fallen log, digging through her pack.

He shook his head. "It's from my sister."

He scanned Lark's elegant handwriting from where he sat on his bedroll, next to a small campfire. Shadow was off hunting, leaving them alone in a clearing surrounded by trees, a short distance away from the trail they'd hiked all day.

"What's it say?" she asked.

He scrunched his nose and glanced over, spotting parchment sticking out of her bag. "You've got a letter in your pack. Are you gonna read it to me?"

She chuckled and pulled a shiny red apple out of her pack, then cinched it closed. "If I did that, I'd have to kill you."

Conall rolled his eyes before dropping his gaze back to the letter. "It doesn't say much. Just that she's going to Mage Keep, and she'll write to me as soon as she gets there." He folded the letter again and stuffed it into his pocket.

Ereni pulled a knife from her belt, sliced the apple in half, and handed him a portion.

He accepted the fruit and nodded to her bag. "What about yours?"

She shifted on the log and crossed her legs. "I don't know. It's for my mother." She sheathed her knife, then spun the apple half over and over in her hands.

"Was that the errand you mentioned? Your mother sent you to deliver a letter?"

"Mm-hmm. She's not just my mother. She's my boss, too."

He cocked a brow.

She bit her lip, looking down at the dirt. "My mother is Sade Prim. Leader of the Palisade Mages."

Her mother was the mages' leader? He took a bite of the apple, taking his time chewing to let his shock subside. A smile tugged at the corner of his mouth. "So, you're like a princess mage, then?"

She shook her head once. "No. More like a lapdog." She smiled sheepishly. "Not that I mind, actually. I've always loved to travel."

"You'll get along with my sister. Lark's always wanted to travel, too."

Her smile widened. "If she's anything like you, I imagine I'll like her just fine." She bit into her apple and leaned back, stretching out her legs.

The tips of his ears warmed. Was she flirting?

He stole another glance at her. She made a pretty picture, reclining on the log, smiling slightly as she chewed, relaxed and open. It wouldn't be the worst thing in the world if it were true.

He cleared his throat. "Funny that your mother wouldn't send someone else to be her letter carrier. You don't see a lot of young girls traveling alone through the forest."

She snorted, her eyes twinkling with mischief. "That blade's not just for cutting fruit. Don't get any ideas."

Conall gulped. Not flirting, then. He watched her, lounging in the clearing, slowly chewing on her apple. How far could he trust her?

"Can I ask you something?"

She swallowed. "Sure."

"My stepfather... He told me the Palisade steals youth from mages."

She narrowed her eyes and sat up straight, crossing her legs again. "And?"

"Is it true?"

"In a way. I wouldn't call it stealing. The initiates know what they're giving up. It's not exactly a secret, but it's not something the minstrels sing about either."

So, it was true. He scratched his jaw, the bite of apple weighing down his stomach like a stone. "I don't get it. Why would anyone make that sacrifice?"

She shrugged and stared at her feet. "It's the way it's always been. If you want to be a mage, you have to pay the price." She glanced his way. Her gaze softened, and she reached over to squeeze his knee. "Don't worry about your sister. She won't be forced. Maybe she won't even go through with it. Not everyone does." She pulled back her hand, offering a small smile. "It'll take us weeks to travel to Mage Keep. I'll tell you all about it while we travel. You'll see it's just a place like any other, magic or not."

He exhaled, a small weight lifting off his shoulders. It sounded like no matter what, Lark would have a choice. He turned toward Ereni, gazing at her inquisitively. "What about you? Will you go through with it?"

She rubbed her arm, gazing into the fire. "My family can trace our talent all the way back to the first mages that helped conjure the Palisade." She sighed. "It's always been my fate to be a mage."

Shadow reappeared then, a freshly killed hare dangling between his teeth. Conall let the conversation drop, but he didn't miss the fact that she hadn't answered his question. It must be hard having to live up to her mother's expectations.

In a way, he could relate. All these years, his father's last words to him hadn't ceased echoing in his ears. "Watch over your mother and the new baby," he'd said that fateful day before he'd left for the ocean journey he'd never returned from. Conall spent his whole life seeking to fulfill that request.

His gaze lifted to the sky before returning to his new companion. He sent her a smile. Maybe together they could satisfy their loved one's expectations. At the least, he'd have another friendly face to talk to.

Ereni smiled back, licking her lips. "You gonna skin that hare, or should I?"

Chapter 14

A late summer breeze blew through the clearing, raising goosebumps on Lark's tanned arms and whirling the brown wool of her skirt around her legs as she strolled toward the colorful wagon.

Whisper sat tethered to his perch, sunning himself with the last rays of daylight. Sunny watched Lark's passage across the clearing from the back of the plain wagon Lark and Tiora had taken ownership of, while happily chewing on a stick.

Nearby, the rhythmic *thunk* of knives hitting wood echoed. Tiora did her best to stand perfectly still and smile without flinching as the twins took turns throwing knives with expert precision dangerously close to her limbs. All three of them glittered in their multicolored garb.

Every night when they stopped to rest, Dausius monopolized all of Lark's time, teaching her the lyrics and melodies to dozens of beautiful songs from his homeland. Tonight, he'd let her off easy, only asking her to practice on her own before disappearing into the woods on some mysterious errand. But instead of repeating the same tunes over and over, she headed for Whisper.

She could finally examine the gorgeous hawk up close. Maybe it was to be expected, since she shared her name with a songbird, but she'd always loved birds. Her mother claimed a meadow lark landed on the window sill the moment she gave birth and serenaded them. The bird's feathers were a perfect match for the brown curls she'd been born with, so her mother thought it only fitting to name her after the bold songbird.

It led her to become a little obsessed with the delicate creatures. She'd learned the names and songs of dozens as a child. But though she'd dreamed of owning a bird one day, she'd had to content herself with viewing them from afar, until now.

She smiled as she walked to within a pace of the wagon and stopped to admire Whisper. He gazed back at her, then tucked his pointed beak into his chest, scratching his glossy brown and white feathers.

"He likes you." Aren appeared between two trees and sauntered up beside her.

Lark flinched but stopped herself from gasping out loud. "Do you think so?" She stole a glance at Aren. He'd taken off the oversized hat since they stopped in the clearing and donned the long leather glove on his right arm. "How can you tell?" She tore her gaze away from his handsome face, focusing on Whisper.

"He's preening. Hawks don't let down their guard to take care of their feathers if someone has them on edge."

Whisper lifted his head from his chest, looked at her again, then with great agility proceeded to turn his neck, scratching the long, brown feathers on his back with his beak.

Lark giggled. "I wish I could scratch my back like that."

"Do you want to see something?" Aren strode to the front of the wagon and rustled around in the open bed.

Lark lost herself for a moment, admiring the cut of his shoulders. The muscles of his back bunched and released through his silk shirt as he bent over. She gulped and forced her gaze away as it wandered lower, stealing a glance at his trousers. Lowering her face, she prayed the tan she'd acquired these last few days on her otherwise light skin, along with the shaded, late afternoon sun, would be enough to disguise the blush warming her cheeks as Aren turned around.

He held his right arm out stiffly. On his leather glove was a hooded bird, much smaller than Whisper.

All thought of her burning cheeks faded. She lifted her chin, leaning close, and traced the bird's features with her gaze. Feathers of gold, brown, and white covered its body and wings, with a few small, fluffy white feathers peeking out from beneath the bottom of the hood. Its clawed feet clutched the leather glove, its head pivoting in all directions. Sensing the bird's nervous energy, Lark reached out to stroke its chest.

Aren pulled his arm out of reach before her fingers connected with the silky-looking feathers. He sent her a small smile. "Most birds don't like being touched. You wouldn't want to lose a finger." The bird seemed even more restless now, digging those sharp talons into the leather gauntlet.

"I'm sorry. She's just so beautiful. I don't know why, but I thought if I touched her, I could calm her down."

Strangely, while she'd been speaking, the bird stood perfectly still, as if intently listening to her voice. The moment she quieted, the bird was back at it again, twisting and twitching under the hood.

"I found her this morning. She's only a few months old, still learning how to fly. You can see she still has some baby down on her neck. Are you familiar with falcons?" Aren asked, holding his arm steady despite the bird's movement. "Or did you guess she's female?"

Lark shrugged. "Just lucky, I guess." She peered at the falcon again, still itching to touch her, though she kept her hands plastered to her sides. "Can I see her face?"

Aren shook his head. "It's not a good idea to take off her hood while she's so agitated. Though I wonder..." He shifted his weight, leaning closer. "Could you sing?"

Lark's gaze darted to Aren's face, her stomach fluttering. He'd heard her sing before. Dausius would often call him over to accompany her on his lute as she practiced around the campfire each night. For some reason, the request felt much more intimate with just the two of them there and him staring at her so closely.

"Are falcons fond of singing?" She dropped her gaze back to the beautiful bird, sucking in a nervous breath.

"Can I tell you something?"

Aren's softly spoken question drew her gaze again. She nodded.

"That first night we met, Meital and I... well, we're both light sleepers."

Lark's stomach twisted. First from the image of Aren and Meital sleeping together. Then, as the meaning of his words sunk in, it twisted even harder from the memory of what had happened that night.

Aren glanced at the ground, leaning away slightly. "We both woke up when Pax... did what he did to Tiora." He grimaced, then met her eyes again. "After we realized what was happening, we woke up Daus, but by that time, it was over. We tried to convince him to come up with a plan to free you both. But he hadn't heard what we had... He said it was too dangerous."

He frowned, his Adam's apple bobbing as he swallowed. "I thought Meital and I would have to handle it alone—until you started to sing. I took one look at Daus' face, and I knew he heard it, too. You have something special, Lark. I don't know if you've ever noticed, but when you sing, the whole forest listens. All the owls, the crows, the songbirds, they go quiet. It's... kind of amazing."

Lark's cheeks burned again. She'd always known she could sing. It was a talent she shared with her mother. But this was the first time anyone had ever called her voice amazing.

She studied the falcon still wriggling on Aren's arm and drew in a deep breath. "I guess it can't hurt to try." She cleared her throat and sang.

The effect was immediate. As Lark sang the first words to one of the songs Dausius had taught her, the falcon stilled. Her head swiveled toward the sound, and her whole body, from the tip of her tail to her wings and talons, relaxed.

Lark felt lighter than air. She kept singing with a smile peeking through between words.

Aren was smiling, too. He pulled the black hood free, revealing the falcon's face for the first time.

The bird's stare fixed on Lark, and a rush of something—some incredible, indescribable feeling—filled her as she locked eyes with the bird for the first time.

She kept singing, studying her, those black eyes staring back at her hypnotically. Her voice burst forth from her effortlessly; the words rolled off the tip of her tongue. The song she'd practiced only a scant handful of times sprang forth like it had been written for her.

It was as if, for the first time, she wasn't just singing with her voice. Something inside her soul sang, too.

From the corner of her eye, she caught movement. She broke eye contact with the bird but continued the song as Dausius returned from the woods. He wore his multicolored tunic, his arms loaded with fruit. Apples and berries overflowed from a small basket he carried in his dark brown arms. His expression made Lark blush yet again. His eyes were wide and a grin split his face from ear to ear as he hustled toward them, his beaded hair clinking musically.

"Brilliant, gorgeous, transcendent even," he exclaimed as Lark sang the final word to the ballad. "You are going to make us famous, my dear." He ambled to the back of the wagon and placed the basket of fruit on the wooden boards. "I saw these beauties growing wild and couldn't resist gathering a few." He plucked a shiny red apple from the top of the pile and bit into it with a loud crunch. He closed his eyes briefly, letting out a tiny moan, his lips puckering.

Dausius opened his eyes and finally took note of the falcon. "Well, who do we have here?" He strolled toward the bird. "Another new addition to the show?" He quirked a brow in Aren's direction.

"I'm not sure yet." Aren pulled the hood over the falcon. She squirmed around, agitated again. "My father always said female birds weren't worth the challenge. Too smart for their own good. This one seems anxious, too. I might set her free, once I'm sure she can fly on her own."

Lark's heart skipped a beat. "No, you can't." She grabbed his arm and looked up at him imploringly. She stared, unblinking, as he returned her gaze, then dropped her hand from his arm and backed up a step, dropping her gaze to the ground. "Just give her a chance. Please?"

She glanced back at Aren's face, and his expression softened. "All right. I will." He smiled. "Maybe you'd like to help with her training?" he added, cocking a brow toward Dausius. "If you don't mind your new star spending some time with us animals?"

Dausius looked back and forth between the two of them, crunching away on his apple. His face was full of amusement, like a child munching on popcorn while watching a play.

Lark bit her lip, staring at Dausius while he chewed.

He finally swallowed, swinging the half-eaten apple around as he performed an exaggerated bow. "By all means. You heard the girl sing... I don't have much else I can teach her."

Lark's face lit up, and she bounced on her toes, nodding emphatically. "I would love that."

Aren's smile deepened. "Would you like to give her a name?"

It came to her instantly, sliding off her lips breathlessly. "Muse."

Dausius paused with the apple—only a core now—in front of his lips. A peel of laughter burst out of his mouth, spraying tiny chunks of yellow fruit in the air. He laughed so loud it echoed around the clearing. Mazen and Meital halted their practice, sending curious glances in their direction.

"I think you better get used to working with females, son." He thumped Aren on the back and wiped a tear from the corner of his eye. "Our star needs her Muse." He turned to Lark, winked, and tossed the core into the woods.

Chapter 15

Movement outside the window caught Kayda's eye. A hawk landed on the sill, folding broad, brown and white checkered wings into its sides. It swiveled its head to stare inside the glass.

She imagined what the bird must be seeing. A plain, freckled girl, sitting on the cold stone floor in a crumpled red dress. Her long red hair spilling wild down her back, darkness encircling her tired, brown eyes.

An old man, his pale skin yellow and sickly. The strength he'd always exuded slowly ebbing as he lay unmoving on a cot, wrapped in the multi-colored blankets of his subjects.

The hawk looked in for a moment, then turned its head and flew away.

Kayda sighed. If only it were that easy for her to leave.

A full day and night had passed since she'd been brought to the tower and locked inside one of the top floor's bare stone rooms. She spun away from the window and clenched her hands together in her lap. She was going to go mad in this place if she didn't escape soon.

The tower was home to the castle guard. They lived and worked in the bottom levels of the converted prison. Those floors had been full of noise and life as they led her inside. Several men paused their activities to peek at her as she traversed the building, trailing along behind the soldiers who carried the unconscious king.

From what she'd glimpsed during their hurried passage through the halls, they'd renovated the space into something much warmer and more welcoming than the old prison had been. Weapons and armor of all kinds festooned the walls, with detailed scenes of battles painted in the common areas.

But the tower's top floors had been unoccupied for countless years. Despite the thorough cleaning she'd insisted on when they arrived, their room still felt barren and cold, no matter how hot the hearth in the corner blazed.

The room they were in belonged to the former warden. While technically not a prison cell, it was serving the same purpose for her and the king. The door remained locked, and no matter how much she begged and cajoled the men who brought food and drink every few hours, she could convince no one to listen to her pleas for release. They were all steadfast in their commitment to keeping them safe and following Tarquin's orders.

Tarquin...

She shuddered, remembering his treachery. There was no doubt in her mind he'd been involved. Every moment that passed without him appearing to check on her grandfather's condition made her even more positive about his betrayal. She should be out there, finding the proof she needed to implicate him in the king's assassination, not forced into hiding.

Kayda's shoulders drooped. Proving her brother's involvement seemed impossible when she couldn't even convince the guards to let her leave a single room. Why would they listen to her, a mere girl, rather than the prince who'd trained with them daily, year after year?

She scratched her thigh. At the least, they could send her a change of clothes. Her ceremonial dress had not been designed for comfort.

Her attention was drawn to the hearth fire. She itched to summon. She could burn down the door, set fire to anyone who got in her way, and be outside in the fresh air before they knew what hit them.

Kayda tore her gaze off the flames. No. She wouldn't have all those deaths on her conscience. The guards were only doing their jobs. Following the prince's orders was protocol for them, with the king incapacitated. The only person who could override him was her father, but he was probably too busy staring at the bottom of a bottle to even notice she was missing.

She walked away from the window to the cot where her grandfather rested. The guards had sent the castle healer up to examine the king. He'd echoed the mage's assessment, insisting all they could do was wait and hope the king would recover. He ordered her to keep a close eye on him and to call for him if he showed any improvement, but so far, there had been no change.

She let out a shaky breath, looking down at her grandfather's prone form. If only he would wake up...

Her stomach buckled. She couldn't do this alone. She couldn't shake the feeling that she wouldn't be enough to stop Tarquin.

The steady clunk of footsteps sounded in the hall outside. They were muted at first but steadily became louder until they reverberated throughout the silent room and stopped outside the door. The sound of a muffled conversation followed, brief enough that she barely had time to wonder who was speaking before the lock clicked and the door swung open, revealing the familiar face of Izora framed in the doorway.

Kayda raced forward as Izora stepped into the room. They both threw their arms open wide and collided together, clasping each other tightly. After a moment, Kayda pulled free, the soft press of cloth brushing along her back as Izora's arms slid off her.

"I brought you some fresh clothes, Princess." Izora placed a large bag into her arms. "I'm sorry I didn't come earlier. Those fools downstairs wouldn't let me up."

"It's all right." She smiled for what was likely the first time since she'd seen her grandfather's stabbing. "I'm just glad you're here now. I'm going crazy locked up in here, not knowing what's happening."

Kayda carried the bag to the far side of the room, where a second cot had been set up with a curtain dangling down from the ceiling. She pulled the curtain closed, dropped the bag on the bed, and dug through it.

"Tell me what I've missed while I dress." Kayda breathed a sigh of relief as she spied one of her favorite dresses in the bag, along with more clothes and the little tin tinderbox.

"I don't know where to begin. It's been madness." Izora's boots tapped in rhythm as she paced the wooden floor. "Utter and complete madness. There's been rioting in the streets. The guards are spread thin, keeping a constant force around this tower and trying to help the local forces to keep the peace. If the Guard Captain hadn't gone out this morning to help in Southmoat, I don't even know if they would've let me in to see you today."

Kayda frowned as she listened, while shucking off the crimson silk gown and sliding on new undergarments. "I don't understand. Why wouldn't they let you see me from the start? You've been my nurse since the day I was born." She slipped into the simple turquoise frock and fastened the buttons lining the center between her breasts.

"Tarquin's orders, apparently. You and the king are not to be disturbed under any circumstances." Izora punctuated the statement with a derisive snort. "From what I gather, the Guard Captain had to be persuaded to even let the castle healer in. That's how serious he is about following that idiot's orders to the letter."

"Why is the Guard Captain in charge?" She circled the curtain, feeling much lighter in her clean clothes. "Where's Tarquin?"

Izora leaned close and pitched her voice low. "No one's seen him since the feast. He took off in pursuit of the villain who stabbed the king. Left with an entire contingent of the guard and headed east into the forest. None have been back, except for a lone rider bearing a letter for the Guard Captain that detailed the prince's orders."

"Am I to be stuck in here until Tarquin returns?" Kayda turned to her grandfather, praying for the hundredth time he would open his eyes. "I don't know if I can do it, Izora." Her voice broke. "I can't watch him die."

Izora was there in an instant, wrapping her arms around her. Kayda inhaled her familiar floral scent, comfort enveloping her as tears rolled down her face and wetted her nurse's tunic. It had all gone so wrong, so quickly. Her entire life unraveled in an instant as the knife pierced her grandfather's flesh.

In the warm embrace of the only woman she'd ever loved, Kayda let herself feel the pain and loss she'd shoved deep down inside. She grieved for her grandfather. For herself. For the suffering the entire kingdom experienced and she could do nothing to fix. She let the agony surface from deep within her soul where it burned, and she wept.

Izora held her, rubbing her hands tenderly along her back, and said nothing until she ran out of tears. Then Izora broke their embrace but remained close enough to touch. She pulled a finely crafted silk handkerchief out of her skirt pocket and wiped the tears off Kayda's face. "You can handle much more than you give yourself credit for, Kayda. Just like your mother. She had the heart of a warrior, like you. Born of the sand."

Kayda shook her head gently. What was Izora going on about? Her mother was the daughter of traders.

Izora finished wiping away the moisture but kept one dark hand on Kayda's face, tipping her chin up and staring into Kayda's watery eyes. "Don't give up hope for the king. He's strong, too. Just like his granddaughter."

Izora pitched her voice low, speaking in a hushed whisper. "I'm working on getting you out of here. I have a plan, but I don't have all the pieces in place yet." She glanced away, her gaze darting to the window. "I don't know if they'll let me visit you again, so on the day I have all the pieces ready, I'll send you a signal at dusk. You'll see it from your window."

Kayda's heart jumped. She searched Izora's face, backing up a step. Her old nurse was going to sneak her out past a whole building full of guards? It sounded too good to be true. "But how?" she asked, her voice just as quiet.

Izora smiled and tucked the handkerchief back into her pocket. "You didn't think I've spent over fifteen years of my life here without making a few friends and earning a few favors, did you?" Her smile dropped, and her face turned serious. "There's too much for me to tell you right now. Just know I have a few friends within the guard. On the night I send the signal, the door to this chamber will be left unlocked, and you can walk out with no resistance. I'll be waiting for you once you get outside."

She opened her mouth to ask Izora a few more questions, but before she got out a single word, the lock clicked on the door. Kayda snapped her mouth shut as the door swung open and a gruff voice called in, "Time to go."

Izora pulled her in for a last hug goodbye. "I'll see you soon," she said as they parted, then strode out the door.

The door closed behind her with a *click*, and Kayda marched across the room to the window. She caught sight of a hawk, perhaps the same one as before, circling the woods nearby. The lone hunter zeroed in on its prey before plunging down for the kill.

As the bird disappeared into the tree cover, she smiled. A few more days, and she would be out there, too, hunting for Tarquin. She flexed her fingers and stared through the glass as the hawk swooped into sight again with a small bird clutched in its talons.

When the signal came, she would be ready to fly.

Chapter 16

Applause echoed all around Lark, bouncing off the walls inside the modest country inn. She stood next to Aren, their shoulders pressed together, crammed into the corner behind the scores of townspeople who'd gathered to watch the show. He finished plucking the strings of his lute as clapping thundered around them.

Dausius hopped up from his seat. "Thank you. Thank you all. You're too kind." He grinned and squeezed through the crowd to stand beside them. "We'll be back with more entertainment after a quick break."

The applause died down at his announcement, and the crowd thinned. Lark picked her way through the throng to the table the rest of their group shared. She sank down on the hard wooden bench beside Tiora. "I don't think I'll ever get tired of this."

"That's easy for you to say. You don't have to stare down the sharp end of a knife at every performance." She giggled and elbowed Meital, who sat beside her and offered a wobbly grin. "I can't say it's the worst job I've ever held, though."

Lark slung an arm around her shoulder and squeezed gently. The silk of their matching multicolored tunics slid against her wrist. They were full members of the show now, matching outfits and all.

Lark's gaze trailed along the faces in the crowd. Seeing the pure enjoyment on their faces as she sang—there was nothing quite like it. She'd always sought to help others. She'd spent her entire childhood helping her mother as a healer. This was still helping others, in a way, but it was so much more *fun*. And didn't she deserve a little fun in her life after everything she'd been through?

Aren leaned across the table. "Busy in here. I'm gonna grab a drink from the bar. Can I get something for you?"

Lark nodded. "Water would be lovely."

Mazen rose from the bench. "I'll go with you. We can grab a pitcher and some glasses. Maybe some ale to go with it." He grinned.

They left together, leaving her with Tiora and Meital. Dausius was a few tables away, chatting merrily with some townspeople.

"Rot and decay," Meital muttered.

Lark turned to her, raising a brow. Meital stared at a pair of young men headed their way. It seemed a table of three young women alone was easily interpreted as an open invitation. Aren and Mazen hadn't even worked their way through the crowd to the bar before the strangers descended on them.

The larger of the two, a beefy fellow with straw-colored hair, spoke first. His gaze zeroed in on Tiora, and he licked his lips like a glutton staring down a delicious morsel. "It's been a long while since our little town has had any ladies so fetching as you three."

Tiora dropped her gaze to her lap, her shoulders tensing. Lark's eyes widened, and she tried to think of something clever to say. Something pleasant and innocuous that would send them on their way.

"You're too kind, sir," Meital said smoothly. "But I'm afraid we're all spoken for."

Lark nodded in agreement, but one look in the man's glassy brown eyes had her stomach sinking.

"Is that so?" He wobbled a bit before leaning closer, a flagon of ale clutched in his left hand. "I don't see any rings."

Meital smiled and flicked her long brown braid over her shoulder as she reached behind her back. Her hand slid back into sight with a blade resting across her knuckles. "Look again."

The man's companion's freckled arm shot out, gripping his shoulder, his brown eyes wide. "Shouldn't we be getting ba—"

The big man shrugged off his friend's hold and leaned closer, trying to catch Tiora's eye. "What about you? Where's your ring, beautiful?" The ale on his breath wafted across the table and sent a prickle of revulsion up Lark's throat.

Tiora twisted her hands in her lap, her gaze flicking up and back down.

Meital didn't wait for her answer. She stabbed her blade into the wooden table directly in front of the man. Her voice was a dagger drenched in honey, sickly sweet and deadly sharp. "Here it is. Would you like to see the rest?" Another blade appeared in her hand, flashing silver. "I'd love to show them to you up close."

Dausius rushed up to the big man's side with a wide grin. "Fellas, have a drink on me, hmm? Let's go grab a round at the bar." He twirled the pair and launched into a story, his voice pitched low as he ushered them away from their table.

"You certainly have a way with words, Meital." Lark grinned.

Meital shrugged, making her blades vanish as quickly as they'd appeared. "I guess you could say so." She nudged Tiora with her elbow. "You all right, Ti?"

Tiora nodded, offering a smile that didn't quite reach her eyes. "Yeah, thanks."

Lark gave Tiora's hand a gentle squeeze. Would things ever be normal again for the two of them? Times like these, normal seemed so close and yet so far all at the same time.

Soon Aren and Mazen returned with drinks. They spent a pleasant quarter hour chatting and laughing. The room buzzed with merriment, and some of the villagers stopped by with a kind word or the occasional tip.

Then Dausius joined them with an indulgent smile and a wink for the twins. "I was ready to regale the crowd with a tale, but I'm afraid I need a rest after handling that mess. You're up next."

Mazen splayed a palm on his chest with a laugh, brown eyes twinkling. "Don't look at me, Daus. I wasn't even here."

Meital stood, her lips curling into a smirk. "I was getting bored, anyway. C'mon, Ti."

Lark settled back to watch as the twin's knives sailed through the air. The crowd curled back, giving them room at the front of the building, none eager to stand too close to the sharp blades.

As the room quieted and all eyes fell upon the trio, Lark couldn't help but overhear a pair of voices talking quietly behind her between the *oohs* and *aahs*.

"Haven't you heard? The king's been stabbed," declared a woman, her voice raspy and tinged with sadness.

Lark's heart skipped a beat. Not King Quinton?

"No. Surely that's only a rumor?" replied a man.

"I heard it straight from my cousin in Flamesmoat," the woman continued. "He was there at the Harvest Festival when it happened. He saw it all with his own eyes."

"Did they catch who did it?" the man asked.

"No. It's such a shame." She *tsked* softly.

Lark leaned forward in her seat and rubbed her temple. Aren reached across the table, grabbing her glass and refilling it from the water pitcher. He quirked a brow. "Something wrong?"

The twins chose that moment to pull off their final trick, and the crowd roared with applause. Lark sent Aren a small smile and shook her head. Now was not the time. She'd share what she'd overheard with the group later.

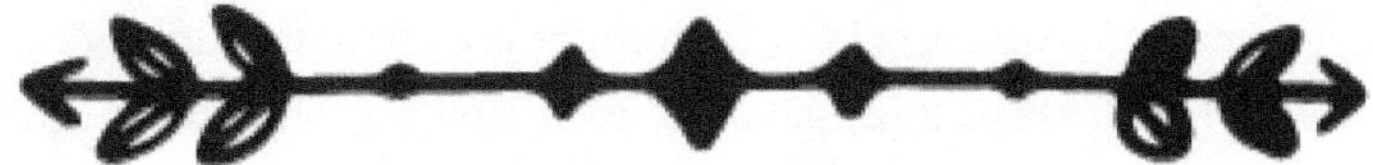

Lark plopped down beside Sunny atop a pile of hay in the barn behind the inn. Dawn was not far off. They'd just wrapped up their last performances for the night, leaving a crowd still buzzing with excitement and a portly innkeeper grinning with undisguised glee.

She groaned. "I feel like I could sleep for a week."

Tiora sank down beside her and yawned. "Me, too."

Dausius stuck his head in the horse stall. "Have a good long rest, girls, you earned it." His beaded hair tinkled gently as he swung around and raised his voice. "That goes for all of you. I've arranged it so we can stay and play one more night at this inn before moving on."

Lark hopped up and caught Dausius at the door before he disappeared into another stall to rest. "Wait. I overheard some news in there. They're saying the King of Dracwood's been stabbed."

Aren whirled around, his eyes widening. He abandoned his efforts to tend to the birds and strode closer. "The king's been stabbed? Are you sure?"

Dausius frowned. "I heard much the same, I'm afraid. From what I gather, he's been locked away since it happened, with no word on his fate."

Mazen's hand stilled as he brushed down one of the horses. "What does that mean for us?"

"I imagine once the news spreads, there'll be even more folks in need of entertaining." Dausius' gaze flicked over them all. "We've an important job to do, my friends. It's not all fun and games. People need folk like us more than ever in such trying times." He smiled. "Get some sleep. We're back at it again tomorrow night." Then he disappeared into a stall, closing the door behind him.

Lark slid the door to their stall closed, joining Tiora and Sunny atop the fragrant hay pile. She closed her eyes, her fingers tangling in the soft golden fur on Sunny's back.

Dausius was right. They were doing important work. Not as important as healing, but useful just the same.

Lark sighed. Was it so bad for her to take a few months of her life to enjoy traveling the world with these amazing people, learning new skills and bringing smiles to people's faces? There would still be time for her to become a mage. She hadn't forgotten about her calling. She would receive the training she needed one day. But did it have to be now?

She kept telling herself it would be all right. That she'd earned the right to a little pleasure in her life after all the hardship she'd been forced to endure. She'd lost everything. The father she'd never met. Her mother and brother. Her home.

She snuggled closer to Sunny, holding tight to the last physical remnant of her former life. No matter what else happened, she could never go back. She'd never again feel her mother's warm embrace or hear Conall's laughter. The memory of all she'd lost still haunted her, especially in quiet moments like this.

Was it wrong to grab the one thing in her life that brought her joy? The Wandering Bards might not be changing the world, but they weren't hurting it either. And she couldn't discount the role they'd played in saving her and Tiora. Didn't she owe it to them to at least help with the performances until they reached Mage Keep?

It couldn't hurt to spend some time getting to know this incredible group of people. Deep down, she knew a few months spent on the road living the life of a traveling entertainer was no crime. But a small part of her kept nagging her to give up this foolish dream and become a mage like she'd always envisioned.

Lark forced the questions aside as sleep dulled her thoughts. She fell asleep with the memory of applause echoing in her ears and a smile on her face.

Chapter 17

The sun sank behind the tallest trees to the west. Conall dragged his feet, his pace slowing. "I think we ought to find a place to camp soon."

"Sure. Maybe we can find a stream or a river. I've been sweating like crazy." Ereni tugged the neck of her brown tunic.

The day had been particularly hot. One of those early fall days that hung onto the remnants of summer. He would kill to submerge himself in a river or to splash some cool water over his face and neck.

"Any sign of a river nearby?" he asked, careful not to show any sign of his silent communication on his face.

Conall still hadn't told Ereni about his bond. He couldn't think of the words to explain without sounding crazy. And every day that passed without him bringing it up, the more it built up in his mind, like a snowball let loose to roll down a hill, gaining mass with every rotation. Would she believe him when he told her? Or would she be angry he hadn't mentioned it from the start?

"No, but there's something else," Shadow replied. He was a few paces ahead of them on the trail, just out of sight. *"A town."*

Ereni gasped. She'd spotted a signpost sticking out of the trail with an arrow leading down a well-worn footpath to the north. "It's even better than a river." She smiled, standing on tiptoe and peering between the trees. "We can stay the night at an inn."

Conall rubbed the back of his neck. "I don't know. What if they don't allow pets?"

Ereni shrugged. "Then we'll sneak him in." She tugged his elbow, towing him toward the footpath. "C'mon, it's been nearly a week since we left Greenvale. I'm dying for a bath and a proper bed, aren't you?"

Well, it would be a shame to pass up a good night's rest and a chance to clean up. He grinned, keeping pace with Ereni down the trail. "C'mon, Shadow," he called over his shoulder.

"We're going to spend the night indoors for a change," he added through the bond.

"Do you think that's wise?"

"Just stick close to me. We'll say you're my hound."

Shadow snorted, catching up to them on the path.

"It worked with Ereni," Conall added. *"And she'll be there to back me up."*

Shadow made no other complaint, so he let the matter drop. They'd be all right. What's the worst that could happen? They'd be asked to leave and have to spend another night camped outdoors?

The little town nestled in a large clearing in the middle of the woods. A handful of wooden houses rested alongside an empty building that vaguely resembled the Church of the Dragon in Flamesmoat—only on a much smaller scale—and a large wood and brick inn and stable.

They turned straight for the inn, ignoring the stares of the few people who ambled about on the neatly swept dirt streets. As they approached, they were met with a lovely sound spilling out from behind the inn's walls. One he vaguely recognized.

"Is that a lute?"

"Sounds like it." Ereni grinned. "What luck! I hope you're not too tired for a dance or two." She winked, sweeping past him and shoving open the door.

He held back the frown that threatened to spread at her request. He'd never been much of a dancer. Then the image of her smiling in his arms, cheeks flushed as they took a turn on the floor, rose in his mind, and he shrugged. He could probably stand a dance or two.

Conall followed her inside. The room was so packed he couldn't even see the musician through the crush of people dancing. Live music must be as much of a draw for the people of this village as it was back in Greenvale.

Fresh stew bubbled on the hearth, filling the air with a delicious aroma. Conall breathed deep and followed close on Ereni's heels as she slipped through the throng, headed for the bar. Shadow walked by his side, eliciting a few gasps and wide-eyed glances from those he passed.

Ereni slapped a handful of coins on the bar. That was enough to grab the innkeeper's attention. "We'd like rooms for the night, please. And some of that stew you have boiling."

The innkeeper leaned over, his bald head glistening with sweat. "We've plenty stew for ya, but I'm afraid I've only one room to let tonight."

Conall's stomach sank. Only one room?

Ereni glanced at him briefly. "We'll take it."

The innkeeper nodded, pocketing the coins. "Will ya be wanting the stew brought up to the room, or will ya be eating down here?"

"Oh, I think we'll stay and enjoy the music while we eat," she said.

Just then, the lutist began to sing. Conall grimaced. Ereni shot him a look, then grabbed the innkeeper's sleeve before he bustled off. "On second thought, we'll eat in the room."

The innkeeper laughed. A hearty belly rumble that sent his jowls jiggling. "I understand. Too bad ya weren't here a few days past. We had a full show in here. Let me tell you what, that lass could sing circles around this fellow." He chuckled once more, rounding the bar. "Follow me, then. I'll show ya to your room."

The innkeeper caught sight of Shadow and gasped. "Blazes. I didn't see your—dog standing there." He backed away warily. "Don't think I can house him in the stable. The horses wouldn't like it."

Conall stepped forward, pulling a coin from his belt pouch. "He can stay with us in the room. He's house trained."

The innkeeper frowned but accepted the coin, then turned aside with a nod. "All right, but damages will be extra."

He led them up a wooden staircase to the third floor. The door swung open to reveal an attic room with two large windows hanging open on opposite walls to let in a cross breeze. A large bed sat in the center, the only piece of furniture except for a single chair and a tiny table tucked into the far corner.

They crowded inside. Shadow curled up beside an open window. *Awful cozy in here. Sure you don't want me to meet you outside of town in the morning?*

And be alone with Ereni and that single bed... What would she say, if he sent Shadow away? *No, stay.* Conall ducked his head to avoid bashing it on the low roof.

"I'll send up a girl with the stew. Enjoy." The innkeeper spun on his heel to leave.

"Wait." Ereni stopped him with a hand on his sleeve.

Conall drew in a breath. Was she about to call off the whole thing? They couldn't spend the night together in this tiny room, could they?

But she smiled, another coin winking in her fist. "Where can a lady get a bath in this town?"

The innkeeper frowned. "You'll be needing much more coin for that here, my dear. We've only got the one well. How about a bowl of hot water and a washcloth? I'll have the maid set up a screen for privacy."

Ereni sighed. "I suppose that will do. Thank you, sir." She tossed him the coin, and then he was gone, closing the door behind him.

Conall shucked off his bag and sank down on the bed. "Are you sure you're all right sharing a room? Shadow and I can camp outside."

She waved a hand and pulled off her bag, settling down beside him. "It's not a problem. We've been camping together for days. All that's different is we're indoors." She shrugged. "We're not even really alone. Shadow's here with us."

Conall nodded. Seems he'd been right to ask Shadow to stay with them. He couldn't argue with her logic. Still, he had to admit to being flustered, knowing she wasn't the least bit uncomfortable sharing a bed with him. There were times the last few days when he could've sworn she was flirting. There'd been countless little quips and side-eyed glances. And now this. Was she happy to allow it because she knew nothing would happen, or was she hoping something *would* happen?

There was a knock at the door. A trio of maids piled in. The first two carried trays. One held two bowls of fragrant stew, and the second, two bowls of steaming water. The last carted a slatted wooden screen and an armful of towels. They settled the bowls on the table and the towels on the chair, unfolded the screen, and left.

No sooner had the door closed than Ereni hopped up off the bed with her pack. She grabbed a bowl of stew and handed it to him. "Here, eat. I'm going to clean up first."

She disappeared behind the screen, leaving him alone on the bed, trying his best not to picture what she was doing back there.

The screen did its job. He couldn't see a thing behind it except for the top of her head peeking out above it. But he could hear everything. The *thud* of her boots hitting the floor. The gentle *pop* of buttons being unfastened.

Food. He scooped up a bite of stew and stuffed it into his mouth. The sound of his chewing dampened some of the noise distracting him.

"Mighty hungry tonight, I see." Shadow's voice sounded amused. *"Careful you don't choke."*

Conall glared at him, not bothering to respond.

He kept shoveling in bite after bite, chewing methodically. But though he was hungrier than he'd been in ages after a full day of walking, the stew sat like a stone in his stomach. As the splash of water sounded behind the screen, he strode across the room to the window.

He placed the bowl on the floor beside Shadow. *"Here, you can have the rest."*

"What are you doing?" Ereni called out from behind the screen. Her voice sounded a bit off. Breathless.

"Nothing." He returned to his spot on the edge of the bed. "I was just passing Shadow the last of my stew."

"Oh." Water splashed again. She was dipping the washcloth back in the bowl. Then came the gentle dribble as she rang it out. Next, she'd be sliding it across her skin. "You like it?"

Conall's heart skittered. "Huh?"

"The stew. How's it taste?"

"It was fine." He tugged the neck of his tunic. "Hot."

He caught movement in the corner of his eye. Her bare arm snaked out from behind the screen to grab a towel off the chair.

He exhaled slowly. At least that was over. The light in the room was dim, the sun well on its way to being fully set. Soon they would be sleeping, then back on the road again in the morning. Back to normal.

A moment later, she reappeared and lifted her bowl of stew off the table. She wore a fresh change of clothes. Brown trousers and tan tunic, the long sleeves rolled up to her elbow, her feet bare.

The bed sank as she settled beside him cross-legged and scooped up a bite of stew. She paused with the bite halfway to her lips. "Go on." She nodded to the screen. "Your turn."

Conall gulped. He'd forgotten he'd be expected to wash up as well. He stood, keeping his neck bent to avoid smacking his head on the ceiling, and rounded the screen.

He grabbed the second bowl of water. The wood vessel warmed his hands as he settled it on the floor beside him. Then he cast his gaze about for a washcloth.

"Where did you find the washcloth?" he asked.

"It was atop the pile of towels. I think they only brought the one. I hung it on the screen for you."

Conall gulped again and lifted the damp square of fabric. He tried not to picture where it had just been. Sliding across her skin. Everywhere on her skin. He closed his eyes and exhaled.

He had to get this over with. Fast. He tore off his clothes and got to work, scrubbing his skin with the cloth. Surely, he'd never washed as quickly in his entire life. Within a few moments, he reached out to grab the towel off the chair. Then his stomach sank.

Shit. His bag. He'd left it sitting on the floor beside the bed. He eyed the sweaty pile of clothes he'd just shucked off.

He sighed and wrapped the towel around his waist. "Ereni, could you do me a favor?"

"Depends what you're asking," she replied. Was it his imagination, or did her voice sound different again? Deeper, almost husky.

"I left my bag on the floor. Could you hand it to me?" He stuck his arm out the side of the screen, his hand open. He listened to the soft tap of her bare feet on the wood. Then came the slide of cloth on his hand as she settled the strap against his palm. "Thanks," he said, his voice a hoarse whisper.

He waited for the sound of her footsteps to retreat before he dropped the towel and dug out a change of clothes. It was nearly fully dark now in the little room. He slid out from behind the screen and took careful steps on the wooden boards until his toes tapped the bottom of the mattress.

He sank down on the edge, sitting upright on the side. "Maybe I should sleep on the floor. I've got my bedroll."

Silence greeted his statement. Then movement on the mattress. "Don't be silly," Ereni said, finally. "There's plenty of room. I scooted over for you."

"All right." He laid down stiffly, keeping close to the edge. If she was fine, then so was he. They were both adults. Fully clothed. No reason this had to be awkward. They were only going to sleep.

He smiled as his head sank into the plush pillow. It was much nicer than the hard ground beneath his bedroll. He closed his eyes, his muscles relaxing as his breathing slowed.

"Conall?"

His eyes shot open in the dark. "Yeah?"

"Sorry, were you sleeping?" The bed shifted as Ereni turned. Her breath wafted against his face.

"No." What could she want from him now? Together in bed. In the dark.

"I thought you might like to hear another story about Mage Keep."

"Oh." Of course, that was all. But he couldn't stand the thought of her whispering voice sliding across his ear. He shook his head. "Can you tell me in the morning?"

"Sure." She shifted again, turning away.

He sighed and closed his eyes again.

"Can I ask you something?"

His eyes popped back open. "Hmm? Sure."

"What will you do after you find your sister?"

He slid an arm behind his neck. "Go back to Greenvale, I suppose. Rebuild the farm. Marry eventually and have a few kids. I know it's not as exciting as traveling the world and all that, but it's what I've always planned."

"No, it sounds lovely." She sighed. For a moment he was sure she'd ask him more, but then she said, "Goodnight, Conall."

"Goodnight."

He took a deep breath, trying to find the peace he needed to slip off into sleep. But though the bed was soft against his back, and Ereni remained on her side of the mattress, he couldn't stop his thoughts from turning over in his mind.

Why was she so curious about his future? Did she want something more from him? He couldn't help but wonder if she felt even a tiny sliver of the attraction he felt for her. If he reached across the bed and touched her, would she recoil? Or would she welcome his embrace?

As he listened to the soft sound of her breathing, he realized it was not a question he would answer tonight. Finally, his thoughts slowed, and sleep found him.

He awoke sprawled out on his side on the edge of the bed with a warm weight pressed against his back. He looked down and spotted an arm wrapped around his waist, the fingers slack. Ereni. He sucked in a breath, and her fingertips grazed his shirt, pressing gently against his skin.

What was she doing? Had she rolled against him as she slept? He should slip out of bed. Get ready for the day. But as the soft rise and fall of her chest pressed against his back, he closed his eyes and lay still. His skin tingled as the warm wash of her breath glided across the back of his neck.

Another moment, and he'd get up. Just one more moment.

Ereni stiffened behind him. Her hand slid off his waist, and she rolled away. Then the bed rose, and her feet tapped on the floor.

He lay still, his eyes closed, trying not to let the fact that she'd immediately gotten up bother him. He'd let her think he was still sleeping. That he hadn't awoken and caught her holding onto him and then just remained there like a fool.

After a moment, he stretched and made a show of yawning, long and deep. "Good morning."

"Good morning." She sat on the single chair, lacing up her boots. "Let's see if they have some breakfast downstairs before we hit the trail." She smiled.

He sat up. Nodded. He grabbed his boots and shook off the last vestiges of the attraction that lingered in his mind. He could tell by her actions this morning nothing was going to happen between them. When she'd awakened to find her arm draped over him, she couldn't bolt up fast enough.

In the cold light of day, he had to face the facts. Ereni was just a girl he'd met on the road. After they made it to Mage Keep, he'd probably never see her again. He had to stop imagining feelings from her that didn't exist.

"All right," he said. "Let's go."

Chapter 18

The light of dawn spilled in through the high tower window. Kayda rubbed the sleep from her eyes. Her gaze was immediately drawn to the bed where her grandfather rested.

She crept across the cool stone floor. Her chest ached as she stared down at his prone form. It was five days now since he'd been stabbed. Five whole days of him lying unmoving on the lonely cot. How much longer could he last without food and water? She knew the answer to that question—she wished she didn't.

Her chin quivered, and she turned aside to cross the room to the cold hearth. She crouched down and poked at the coals, then threw more wood on the pile and coaxed the flames back to life.

She settled down beside the fire. She might as well spend some time practicing. It would be a shame to lose all the progress she'd made training with Izora. And at least it would give her something else to concentrate on, besides her poor grandfather.

Reaching out her hand, she took a deep breath. She emptied her mind. Pictured the flames taking shape before her eyes. A wave of cold spread across her skin as her talent responded, and the fire materialized in the air, floating at eye level. She made the flame grow. She made it dance. Sent it to the ceiling and flying across the room.

Then Kayda glimpsed movement out of the corner of her eye. The flame disappeared, and she gasped.

It was the king, sitting upright in bed. She raced over.

"Grandfather?" She crouched down in front of him and stared into his cloudy eyes. "Grandfather, you're awake." She sat next to him on the bed and took him into her arms, squeezing him tightly.

Yes! He was awake. He was finally awake. Her heart soared, so full of relief she almost squealed aloud. All those days and nights waiting—he'd finally pulled through.

But something was wrong. He didn't return her embrace. She loosened her arms, peeking up into his face. He stared at the ceiling, his eyes glassy and unfocused.

"Grandfather?" She gripped his shoulder and shook gently. "Grandfather!" She shook a little harder. "Grandfather, please, say something." He didn't respond. Tears pooled in the corners of her eyes.

The healer. She would call for the castle healer. He'd know what to do.

She rose from the bed and strode to the door. She slid her fingers against the knob. It didn't move. Damn. For a moment, she'd forgotten she was a prisoner in this blazing room.

She banged on the door instead. "Help us. We need the healer. The king is awake."

Footsteps sounded in the hall outside. The door opened, revealing the face of one of the guards who'd been bringing food and drink every few hours. He stuck his head inside, his eyes wide as he caught sight of the king sitting upright on the cot.

"What are you doing, man? Call for the healer," Kayda demanded.

The guard nodded and slammed the door shut without a word. The lock *clicked*. Kayda rubbed a hand down her face. It was too much to hope he'd be lax and leave it unlocked.

How long would they be? She prayed the healer would come soon and break her grandfather out of this stupor. She wrung her hands, returning to his side.

He must be starving. And thirsty. She rushed across the room and grabbed the pitcher of water she'd been left last night. Water trickled into the wooden cup as she poured. She lifted it with a shaky hand and returned to her grandfather's side.

Could he even drink in this state? There was only one way to find out.

She raised the cup to his lips. "Here, Grandfather. I brought you some water," she whispered, tilting the cup toward him. For a moment, she was certain nothing would happen. That the water would come spilling out the side of the cup, wetting his face and neck. But when the cup brushed against his lips, he opened his mouth and drank.

Kayda smiled gently. If he was drinking, then there was hope. He would live. They could nourish his body and give his mind the time it needed to heal completely.

Soon, he'd drained the cup. She returned to the table and lifted a half loaf of bread left over from last night's dinner. The crust crunched beneath her fingers. It might be a little stale, but it would do until she could call for something fresh.

She walked back to the cot, broke a tiny chunk off the loaf, and lifted it to her grandfather's lips. He opened his mouth dutifully, like a baby bird ready to be fed. She watched his throat work as he chewed and swallowed.

"It's all right, Grandfather. The healer will be here soon, and we'll get you all fixed up." She patted his hand where it rested, slack in his lap, and kept feeding him.

The castle healer arrived as she was feeding the last bite to her grandfather. His dark cloak billowed around him as he slipped into the room and shut the door behind him, a wide smile on his weathered face.

"Sire, it's good to see you awake." He strode across the room before he noted Quinton's blank stare. When he did, the smile fell from his face. "Has His Grace spoken yet?"

Kayda shook her head. "He's been like this since he woke. He'll eat and drink if you feed him, but he hasn't said a word. He just keeps staring. Do you know what's wrong with him?"

"Hmm. I'm not sure. We'll figure it out. Don't fret." He set his bag down and leaned over, examining the king with his shrewd gaze.

The door opened again, revealing the Guard Captain. The hulking man barreled in, his dark brow dampened with sweat. He slammed the door behind him, shoving his lanky brown hair out of his eyes. "I heard the news. The king lives?"

Kayda rose to her feet and met the Guard Captain in the center of the room. "He's awake, yes. Eating and drinking. Perhaps now we can return to Kings Keep? I'm sure the king would recover much faster in his own bed."

The captain's brow furrowed, and his gaze fell to the ground. "I'm afraid I can't allow it, Princess. Not without orders." He met her eyes. "But now that the king has awakened, we will of course follow his wishes to the letter."

"I'm afraid that won't be happening today," the healer stated, not looking up from his examination. "The king is not yet speaking."

The Guard Captain grimaced. "Well, then I'm bound by duty to keep you here under my protection." He turned to leave.

"Wait." Kayda grabbed his sleeve. "My father. Did you call for him like I asked?"

The captain spun to face her, his eyes hard. "Prince Gideon has not answered. He's been holed up in his rooms since the king's attack." His face softened. "I'm sorry, Princess."

Kayda sighed. Was it too much to ask for her father to take even a tiny smidge of responsibility? Even in the face of the king being attacked? Her heart sank as she realized she would remain a prisoner in the tower, even now, after the king had awakened.

Her gaze slipped to the window as the Guard Captain left the room. At least she still had Izora to count on. And now that her grandfather had awakened, she could be sure she'd not be leaving him here to die all alone when she escaped.

She turned back to the cot. The healer gathered his bag and stood.

"You can't be leaving already?" Her voice rose on the final word. She clutched her chest. "Can't you fix him?"

"My lady, I will try. I must go retrieve some more things from my chambers. Take heart, my dear. This is a good sign. The king lives." He sent her a small smile and retreated from the chamber, leaving her alone again with the silent king.

Kayda sank back on the cot beside her grandfather. She lifted his hand from his lap and gave it a gentle squeeze. "Grandfather, can you hear me?" she asked gently. "Please, I need you to come back. I need your help. I can't do this all on my own."

Her words had no effect. Her grandfather stared, unfocused, at the wall.

She laid her head on his shoulder and smiled. It would be all right. He was alive. At least he was alive.

Chapter 19

F ire crackled, shooting sparks into the night sky. Conall basked in the campfire's warmth, his belly full and feet aching slightly from the day's exertion.

A *crunch* sounded beside him. Shadow was busy with the bones of their latest kill, cracking them open to suck the marrow from inside.

Conall's eyelids drooped. He yawned as he relaxed on his bedroll and watched the stars winking in the sky through a hole in the forest canopy, which shone with fall colors splashed among the green leaves.

A feminine moan made his eyes shoot open. Ereni was seated opposite him with the fire between them. Her fingertips kneaded the bottom of her bare left foot. One sturdy boot sat next to her, standing straight up and empty with a long, tan sock folded neatly atop it.

Conall heard something strange in his mind. *"Did you just snicker at me?"* he asked Shadow.

"Told you." Shadow glanced at him, then his gaze changed direction, his long snout pointing across the fire. *"This proves it."*

"Don't be ridiculous." He shot his bondmate a sideways glare.

Shadow kept trying to convince him Ereni was interested in him. But he couldn't be right. If anything was going to happen between them, surely it would've happened back in that little inn.

He glanced across the fire again. She still held one slender foot in her hand, her half-lidded eyes staring off into the darkened trees surrounding the small clearing they'd stopped in for the night.

"She's not even looking at me."

The thought had barely escaped his mind before she moaned again. Her eyelids lifted lazily, blue eyes connecting with his own. Her slack mouth curved upward in a smile of pleasure.

Conall gulped.

Shadow snickered again. *"You still have a lot to learn."* He rose from his spot, arching his back and stretching his muscles before standing fully. *"I'm off to hunt."* He disappeared into the darkened trees.

Ereni's fingers stilled. She dropped her naked foot to the ground and stretched out her booted right leg to roll up her trousers. "So, are you going to sleep while Shadow hunts? Or would you like to hear another story about Mage Keep?"

Ereni had been true to her word. She'd told him much about the keep in the time they'd traveled together. Her stories of growing up with the mages did a great deal to ease his misgivings about his sister joining their ranks.

She clearly looked back on her childhood fondly, regaling him with tales of pranks she and the other children pulled on the mages that had him laughing and blushing despite himself. And according to her, the mages took it all in stride. She described them like one big family, all taking great pride in molding the next generation of mages.

The *clunk* of a boot hitting the ground broke his train of thought. He gazed back across the fire and watched her pull the sock from her leg slowly. Well... he definitely wasn't tired now. "What story do you have for me tonight?"

"I think I've told you all the good ones from when I was a child. Would you like to hear about how I became a seer for Mage Keep?"

"Sure."

The sock was off now. She folded it methodically and placed it neatly atop her boot then stood both boots next to each other before she spoke. "I'm sure you know magic talent is inherited. In most families, it skips a generation. Sometimes even two. But some families, like mine, are blessed with magic that doesn't skip."

Ereni folded her leg, readying her fingers to perform the same action on the bottom of her right foot. Then she seemed to change her mind. She stretched out both of her feet instead and wiggled her toes near the fire.

"It was always assumed I would grow into my powers one day. What I didn't realize was I had been born with a special talent. One so rare that even at Mage Keep no one recognized it until a chance encounter when I was eight years old."

Conall's interest was piqued. He tore his gaze from her delicate little toes and looked at her face.

Ereni stared at the fire, her features relaxed.

What talent could be so rare?

"I'd spent my whole life knowing I was different. Destined for greatness, if you will. I thought what I saw, all mages could see. I mean, why wouldn't I?" She scoffed, shaking her head gently. "Really, it was like spending your whole life viewing a world full of color, only to one day discover the rest of the world could only see in black and white."

"I'm not sure I follow..."

She glanced at him, a lopsided smile crossing her face before she stared back into the flames. "Sorry, it's a little hard to explain. For me, when I look at someone with talent, I can see something—a glow."

Conall's stomach clenched. She could see talent?

"My whole life at Mage Keep, I always knew who'd inherited talent and who'd been skipped. But I didn't realize it was anything special." She stared at the fire, leaning back on her bedroll. "Until one day, we had a special visitor come to the keep. King Quinton. My mother introduced me, and I asked her why he glowed red, and not blue."

Her stare bored into his, and she lifted a brow. "We've been traveling together for weeks. Were you ever planning to tell me?"

Conall sat up and rubbed the back of his neck, grinning sheepishly. "I haven't told anyone yet... I'm still trying to wrap my head around it myself, actually."

Her brows lowered, but she didn't smile, only stared back at him with a flat expression.

"So, you've known this whole time? When I walked into the inn that day back in Greenvale—you saw me glowing red?"

She gazed at the fire again. "Yes, and no... Shadow glows red." Her blue eyes connected with his once more. "You glow purple."

He quickly connected the dots. "Red and blue... you're telling me I can summon?" His gaze dropped to the forest floor, his brow furrowing. It made sense, in a way. His grandmother had been talented. His sister was talented. But the revelation still crashed around him like a shock wave. "I can summon," he repeated. His mouth went dry, and he shook his head slowly.

Ereni stood and walked toward him, her bare feet leaving prints behind in the loose soil. She lowered herself and sat in front of him on his bedroll, folding her feet to the side, resting an elbow on her thigh. She lifted her ponytail off her chest and tossed her long brown tresses over her shoulder, drawing his gaze to her tunic.

His heart picked up speed. The top three buttons were undone, revealing the creamy skin beneath.

"There's something else you need to know about being a mage."

Conall sucked in a breath, lifting his gaze from that enticing bit of flesh to look into her eyes. She was so close. His fingers itched to touch her. Was Shadow right? Did she want him to touch her?

"What should I know?" he asked, his lips parting.

She dropped her gaze to the bedroll. "Since talent is inherited, we're all strongly encouraged to have children before we become full-fledged mages." She took a deep breath, her breasts lifting.

He fought to pull his attention away from her chest as the meaning of her words struck him. Her eyes drifted back to his, her gaze earnest. He gulped.

"I've always thought I would be one of the few who took my vows without a child. But now..."

Conall's mind raced. Shadow was right! But she didn't just want a quick diversion in the woods. She wanted a child. With him. He'd always pictured his future with children, but this was so sudden. Blazes. They'd never even kissed. He gulped again.

"Tell me, what are you thinking?" Her eyes darted back and forth across his face.

There she was, vulnerable, open, willing to share her life story with him. In the weeks they'd spent together, he'd grown to care for her. She'd done a great deal to banish the loneliness that plagued him when he thought of his family. She was sweet and funny. Beautiful. He'd never considered himself an impulsive man, but as gazed into her eyes, he made the decision instantly.

"Brother, can you find somewhere else to sleep tonight?"

The snickering was back, louder than before. *"Already done, little brother."*

Conall reached across his bedroll and pulled Ereni into his arms.

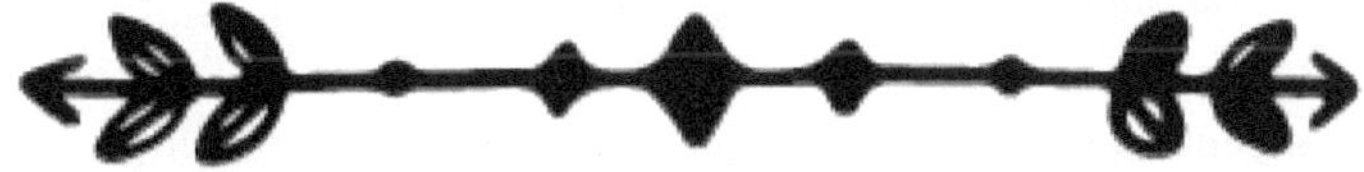

A yawn stretched Conall's face, but he didn't let it slow his pace through the dense forest. Despite averaging less sleep the last few nights—which he didn't regret in the least—they'd kept on schedule during their days of traveling and almost made it to Mage Keep. Shadow was somewhere up ahead, scouting. He expected to hear him announce through their bond at any moment that he'd sighted their destination.

Conall pushed a breath out through his teeth. He should be ecstatic right now. He was on the cusp of finding Lark and finally setting his mind at ease. She would be safe and happy, thrilled to see him. And now that he knew about his own talent, he might even do more than stop for a visit. He might have cause to stay.

Perhaps that was what had his stomach quivering nervously as they approached. It was a lot to consider. Unlike Lark, he hadn't spent years of his life dreaming of becoming a mage. He always had simpler dreams for himself. Settling down on the farm. Maybe a wife and children, one day.

He'd certainly complicated matters in that regard. His gaze drifted to Ereni as she strode beside him, her pale cheeks pink from exertion. He sighed, then found himself smiling. He could get used to complicated.

She caught him staring and sent a grin in his direction. With her eyes lifted from the forest floor, she didn't see the root sticking up that tried to send her tumbling to the ground. Conall caught her elbow and steadied her.

"Thanks." She straightened her brown tunic after planting both her feet firmly on the ground. "Do you mind if we took a break, just for a moment?"

"All right." He spied a large rock to the left of where they stood. He seated himself upon it, patting the smooth stone beside him in invitation.

Ereni settled beside him. "You know, I always thought I kept a pretty fast pace, but you and Shadow are a challenge to keep up with."

"Sorry." He frowned. "You should've said something earlier. We could've slowed down."

The smile never left her face as she reached for her waterskin. "Oh, I'm not complaining. It just reminded me of something..." She lifted the skin to her mouth and took a long drink.

"What's that?" He admired the graceful curve of her neck as she swallowed.

She finished her drink and reattached the skin to her belt. "I read a book, once, about bonding magic. Did you know bonds don't just let you hear each other's thoughts? You share certain physical attributes as well."

"Really?" His mouth dropped open. "That's incredible."

"I'll have to see if I can find it again in the keep library. There was a chart in it that listed all the different enhancements bonding pairs had reported." Her gaze lifted skyward, her head tilting sideways. "I can't remember them all, but I remember each animal brought unique skills to the bond."

"Do you remember what skills wolves enhance?"

"I'm pretty sure sense of smell was one of them. And increased stamina."

Enhanced sense of smell? He couldn't recall noticing anything different with his nose lately. As for the second thing she'd listed. "Well, that explains a few things." He smiled at her mischievously.

She laughed and poked his side with her elbow. "That's what made me remember. You certainly have the stamina part." She grinned shamelessly. "You know what else is great, too?"

"What?"

"The skill humans bring to a bond is always the same. The bonding animal's lifespan is lengthened significantly. Doubled in most cases."

"Really? That's great news."

It had crossed his mind that wolves had much shorter lifespans than humans. Doubling Shadow's years still wouldn't give them as much time together as if he were human, but he would take whatever he could get.

It was strange to think they'd only been together for a few short months. Shadow was already such an integral part of his life. The thought of one day going on without him... He shook his head. He didn't even like to think about it.

"You all right?" Ereni asked, gazing at him closely.

He forced the thought away and sent her a smile. "Yeah. You rested enough?"

"Yes, I'm ready." She rose from the rock and held out a hand to help him to his feet. He took it, his fingers tingling as they slid across the soft silk of her wrist. He stood but didn't release her hand and pulled her close.

Her blue eyes fluttered closed as she tilted her head upward. Conall drew in a breath through his nose, concentrating on the gentle aroma he could sense surrounding her.

They drew closer. Her breath warmed his skin. Was that lavender in her hair? His lips curved into a tiny smile as they brushed her petal-soft lips. Maybe that whole enhanced sense of smell was working. Her tongue collided with his own then, and all thoughts of magic fled his mind.

Shadow interrupted the haze of desire swirling inside him a moment later. *"I found it. Mage Keep is not far ahead."*

Conall broke the kiss and stepped back, putting distance between them. "Shadow says the Keep is just ahead." He tugged his sleeves, composing himself.

"Conall, something seems off about this place... Hurry."

His eyes widened as he received Shadow's warning.

Ereni didn't miss his change of expression. "What is it?" she asked, already in motion, heading for the Keep.

"I'm not sure. He said to hurry." They exchanged a look, then both took off running.

Chapter 20

The morning air was cool and crisp. The woods were awash with yellow, orange, and red, which joined the vibrant green of the forest canopy. The wind tousled Lark's brown curls, and leaves crunched beneath her feet as she strolled by the river's edge.

She tensed her fingers within her new leather gauntlet. Her gaze was drawn upward as Whisper and Muse took to the sky, searching for prey. She'd grown to love these early morning outings. Watching Muse learn to hunt brought her a thrill unlike anything she'd experienced.

Every day traveling with the Wandering Bards was a pleasure. It was like the world had seen fit to reward her for her past suffering with the experience of a lifetime.

She spent her nights singing in small towns all over the countryside, reveling in the applause and pure pleasure on the faces in the crowd. Her days, she spent traveling with a group of people she'd grown to love who treated her like family. And best of all were mornings like these, where she watched Muse fly, full of grace, strength, and cunning.

She stole a glance beside her at Aren. He kept step with her on the riverside, occasionally prodding a bush or tree with a long stick, hoping to flush out prey for the birds. His oversized hat shaded his pale face from the morning sun.

He'd been so patient and kind, helping her learn the basics of falconry, but there was still so much she didn't know about him. Of all the performers in the group, he was the most mysterious. While the rest of the group were happy to share stories of their lives prior to joining the show, he'd yet to share anything but the barest details of his past.

"So, I've been wondering something…" She blurted when her curiosity became too strong to bear. "When Daus introduces Tiora and the twins, he always tells the story of where they're from. He's been making a big deal about me being from Dracwood, too… but with you, he says nothing."

"And you're wondering why that is?"

"Yeah. Are you on the run or something?'

He laughed. "No… I'm from Doln."

She blinked. "Oh."

"That reaction is why he doesn't mention it. Raimire and Joria are exotic and exciting to the people here. But your people and mine aren't exactly on the best of terms."

"Might have something to do with the whole slavery thing…"

He tipped back his hat so he could look her in the eye. "I haven't traveled as much as some, but I've seen enough to know that there are good and bad parts of every country. I know you had an awful experience with slavers, Lark. But really, Doln is a lot different than the people here imagine it to be."

She raised a brow, noting the serious look on his face.

Her trip through Southmoat had proven there were bad parts everywhere. But while slavery surely existed in some form in Dracwood, it was hidden, relegated to the seedy parts of large cities. It must be so strange to live in a land where it was accepted by rulers and common folk alike.

She decided to at least hear him out. "How so?"

He readjusted his hat, covering his face again. "Well, most slaves are treated well."

Lark scoffed. "Really?"

"It's a tradition from the days when both sides of the country were ruled by competing clans. There's Minsport on the Magus River's western side and Gransea to the east. The chiefs on both sides would kidnap high-ranking members from rival clans and try to convert them to their side. It was worth the ultimate bragging rights if they could convince one of the kidnapped clan members to pledge their loyalty to the new clan chief. Once that happened, they'd become a full member of the new clan, no longer considered a slave. But if they held onto their loyalty, chances were good their home clan would save them in a future raid."

"That's not how it works anymore, is it?" She looked away as the memory surfaced of being squeezed in the back of the wagon with Tiora that first night. She shuddered, remembering the terror that had overcome her when she discovered she was headed for Doln's borders. "Now they want slaves from other lands instead."

"You're right. The clan chiefs squashed their rivalry centuries ago, and stealing rival clan members fell out of favor. Slavery was around there for so long it became a big part of the culture. These days, having a foreign house slave is fashionable, like a status symbol. Some clan chiefs even favor slaves as wives. But you'd be hard pressed to find one who's treated poorly. It's a manner of honor in Doln to treat all those who work in your household with respect and honor."

"I still don't like it. Keeping someone against their will is wrong, even if you treat them nicely." She frowned. "Not that I don't find that part a bit hard to believe."

"Well, you'll believe it when you see it. We're planning to take the show to Doln next spring. I'll introduce you to a few slaves in Clan Chief Aundrea's household, and you can ask them all about it, if you're still interested."

Lark swallowed, not sure what to feel about the prospect of visiting the county she'd escaped being sold to. "You know slaves?"

"Sure. I grew up as a member of Clan Chief Aundrea's house. My father was Clan Huntsmaster. And my mother was music teacher for the clan's children."

"Well, that explains how you ended up talented at falconry and the lute." She raised a brow, tilting her head. "But if it's so great there, then why did you leave?"

"Wanderlust, I suppose." He grinned, adjusting his hat for more shade as they circled a bend on the riverbank, the splash of some aquatic creatures echoing in the distance. "All of you have such interesting tales about your lives before joining the show. I'm afraid my life was boring in comparison. I wasn't orphaned and made to live by my wits on the streets like the twins, nor am I a healer, like you. I never had to make a horrible choice to save my family, like Tiora. I'm just a guy who lived a normal life with loving parents until I woke up one morning with an itch to see the world."

Could that be why he never spoke up when everyone was talking about their pasts? He was worried about being boring? She stole another glance at him, then returned her gaze to the sky. He wasn't boring at all.

"Help, someone, please help!"

Lark stopped in her tracks, scanning for the source of the desperate voice shattering the calm morning.

Aren caught sight of him first, staggering up from the riverside. He raced ahead as soon as he spotted the panicked child. "What's wrong?" Aren approached the boy, steadying him as he tripped in his haste to reach them.

Lark arrived on his heels, scanning the boy for injuries. He had to be less than ten and wore plain homespun clothes. His trousers were soaked from the waist down. His face and hair were splattered with mud.

"Please, mister, you gotta help him." His voice cracked, and he gestured wildly behind him. "My little brother, he fell in the river."

Aren didn't hesitate. He shucked off his hat and leather gauntlet. In a few short steps, he reached the river's edge and dove into the water.

The boy spoke again, and the sorrow in his voice broke her heart. "Please, Lord Dragon, let him be okay."

"It's all right. Aren will find him. Just you watch." She crouched down, and brown, terror-struck eyes stared back at her. "I'm Lark. What's your name?"

His lip quivered. "Kaleb," he whispered. "I knew I shouldn't let Nico come with me." Tears spilled down his face, leaving tracks on his mud encrusted cheeks. "He begged and begged, promised to stay out of the water. I should've never let him come. It's all my fault."

Lark held him as he cried. She stared at the river, searching for any sign of Aren or the boy. It was taking too long. Her stomach wrenched as she watched the deep, placid water.

Aren surfaced downriver. Lark jumped to her feet, spotting the boy clutched in his arms. "C'mon, he found him."

They raced forward, meeting Aren as he struggled out of the water and placed the unconscious child gently on the muddy riverbank.

Kaleb fell to his knees beside his brother and grabbed his shoulder, shaking his lifeless form. "Nico—No!"

Tossing her own gauntlet on the ground, Lark knelt and pushed him aside hastily. "I'm a healer. Let me look at him."

Kaleb backed away on his hands and knees, his face screwed up with pure anguish. "Please, you have to save him!"

Nico was much smaller than his brother, perhaps only five or six. His pale face had already taken on a bluish tinge.

Lark placed a hand on his breast and felt nothing. The steady thump of his heart was absent and his chest still. She prayed it was not too late to save him. She grabbed a handful of mud from the riverbank.

Closing her eyes briefly, she placed her mud-filled hand on his chest. Her heart pounded out of control; her entire body filled with anxiety and doubt. Lark took a deep breath. She'd done this before; she could do it again. She let out the breath and wished.

For a moment, she thought nothing would happen. Then she felt it. The tingling tremor of energy flowed through her body. A pulse rose from his chest to vibrate her palm. Then another. His heart had started.

But one look at his face, still that unnatural blue, banished the smile that threatened to escape. He still wasn't breathing.

"Help me turn him on his side," she said to Aren, who crouched on the other side of the boy.

Together, they rolled him sideways. Lark climbed on her knees, holding him steady with one hand and beating on his back with her fist.

"What are you doing to him?" Kaleb's voice was wobbly, full of distress.

"He breathed in water. We have to get it out." She thumped over and over. His body quaked with the force of her fist; his blue face darkened into purple. She held her breath, her heart pounding with each blow she landed on his back.

Finally, he coughed, spewing a huge mouthful of water into the air. She smiled as she tilted his face downward so he could finish expelling the water on the muddy ground.

She'd done it! He was breathing. For one blissful instant, she rejoiced. Then, she glanced up at Aren, and the relief vanished. He looked green, his stare locked on the back of the boy's head.

She followed his gaze, and her stomach plummeted. How had she missed that? Nico's head was caved in from behind, covered with a huge, jagged laceration. Blood gushed from the wound, and bits of white bone peeked through his dark hair.

Her mind spun and bile rose in her throat. She couldn't fix that.

Kaleb cradled his head in his hands, crying silently. Her chest ached. She had to try. She had to at least try.

She grabbed another fist full of mud and slathered it on the head wound.

"Is that going to work?" Aren whispered, staring at her incredulously.

"I don't know," she admitted.

Her mind raced with thoughts and memories. The baby, Pax... her mother. She closed her eyes, praying and wishing with everything inside her for this to work the way it had worked before. But doubt kept forcing its way to the surface. Her mother's face returned to haunt her, looking exactly the same as it had the day she'd held her as she took her last breath. She waited for the vibration to fill her. But deep inside, she knew. She didn't have it in her to fix this child, the same way she couldn't save her mother.

She opened eyes flooded with tears. Nico's wound was unchanged. Cold mud and warm blood mingled in her palm and gushed between her fingers. Her chin quivered, and she gently lowered his head to the ground, the rise and fall of his chest already slowing. It hadn't been enough to save him.

Kaleb lifted his head. The grief and pain on his face stabbed her like a knife through her breast. "Is he... is he going to be all right?"

Lark wet her lips, tears burning a hot trail down her face. "I'm sorry, Kaleb. I'm so sorry."

"Kaleb, Nico?" A man's voice reached them just before he emerged from the woods. The man was tall and muscular, dressed in simple homespun clothes like the boys.

"Father..." Kaleb leapt to his feet and raced into the man's arms, crying hysterically, anguish pouring off him like a flood.

It took the man a moment to notice Nico lying dead in the mud, but when he did, he gasped, his face contorting with pain. "Oh no, not my boy." His gaze jumped around the scene. Lark's heart tore apart as she watched the realization dawn on him that what he was seeing was real. "Who are you people?" he demanded. "What's happened to my son?"

She opened her mouth to speak but found herself unable to form a single word in the face of his anger. Tears flowed freely down her face. Her lungs burned.

Aren stood. "We heard your son call for help. I managed to pull Nico from the river, but his wounds were too much. I'm so sorry, sir."

She shook herself out of her stupor, reaching again for the boy. "I'll try aga—"

"No." The man's harsh demand made her retract her hands. "You've done enough."

The man stared at them again. Aren soaked to the bone. Lark covered in mud, blood, and tears.

He let out one gasping sob, clutching Kaleb tight. Then he set his mouth in a grim line and gently set Kaleb aside. "It's going to be all right." He stared down at the boy's tortured face. Then, he plodded forward and picked up Nico's small, battered body from the muddy ground. "Thank you for trying," he said as he approached where Aren stood. "Let's bring Nico home," he said to Kaleb, then disappeared back into the trees.

Kaleb's eyes met her own one last time. She knew with absolute certainty his face would be burned into her memory forever. He dropped his gaze, then trudged off after his father into the woods.

As the boy's back retreated into the woods, his shoulders slumped, his body shuddering with the force of his grief, something inside of her snapped.

She had allowed herself to forget her purpose. She'd ignored her calling. No longer. She couldn't keep letting the thrill of singing and the camaraderie she felt with the performers stop her from becoming a mage.

She rose to her feet and retrieved her leather gauntlet from the ground. Her hands closed on the rough fabric. It would be so easy to slip it on. Slip back into this life she loved. A life that let her forget all about the people she'd killed and the ones she'd not been strong enough to save. Her gaze lifted to the sky where she could still see the pair of birds circling the woods in the distance, and she clenched the leather, painting it red and brown with the muck on her fingers.

Her heart breaking once more, she walked forward and thrust out the gauntlet, placing it into Aren's hands. He stared down at the glove, then met her eyes. "Lark... I—"

She shook her head, the words tumbling out before he said anything to change her mind. "I have to speak to Daus."

Chapter 21

Dusk was upon them. Kayda sat beside the window, her legs curled beneath the skirt of her favorite turquoise dress, watching the clouds light up with color from the setting sun.

The first few days after Izora's visit, she'd watched the sunset with bated breath, her stomach churning and nerves on edge as she waited eagerly for the promised signal. Then days stretched into weeks. She was beginning to think the signal would never come.

She glanced sideways to where the king sat staring blankly out the window. Was he admiring the colorful sky? Could he even see at all? She sent a small smile in his direction and wiped a tiny bit of spittle from his chin with a handkerchief.

The king hadn't awakened from his stupor. He spent every day like a statue. Staring blankly. Never talking. Content to sit or stand in the same position for hour upon hour, unmoving.

The healer tried countless things to snap him out of it. Bleeding, potions, and tonics by the dozen. But nothing had worked.

Now, she spent every day taking care of him. Feeding him like a child. Leading him to the privy and from bed to chair and back again.

She kept telling herself as long as he was up moving and eating, there was hope. But every time she looked into his dull blue eyes her heart ached. His body was alive, but his mind was gone. She didn't know if she'd ever see him smile or hear him call her "little red" again.

Her gaze returned to the window. Where was the signal? Had she missed it somehow?

Every night, she cursed herself again for not taking the time to question Izora more carefully about what to expect. If she'd missed her chance... Her chest squeezed at the thought.

No, she just had to be patient. Izora would come through. She had to.

The sun dipped down below the horizon at last. The last rays of daylight lingered as she stared out at the castle, resigning herself to another day as nursemaid and prisoner. She leaned back and was on the verge of turning away from the window when she saw it.

There was a light high up on the keep. It flashed erratically, as if someone held a torch out an open window and flailed it about in all directions. She gasped as it dropped. The flame careened down the side of the stone keep, twisting end over end before sputtering out on the ground.

Her heart sped up. Finally!

She rose to her feet, her wooden chair skidding against the stone floor in the silent room.

This was it, the moment she'd been waiting for. She would leave this tower and put an end to whatever fiendish plot her brother had become embroiled in.

She told her feet to move, but they remained fixed in place. Her gaze slid to her grandfather's face. She bit her lip, her hand raised to her throat that'd suddenly gone dry.

Was she insane to leave him here? He was already lost inside his own mind. Was she really going to leave him alone in truth?

She strode forward, crouching down and looking at her grandfather face to face. His foggy eyes stared blankly ahead, not focusing on her, even when she was close enough to smell his stale breath.

"I'm sorry, Grandfather. I... have to go. I'll do my best to set things right, I promise." She started to say more but backed away, wiping the corner of her eye with her sleeve.

What was the use? He wasn't listening.

She stood once more, her gaze glued to the door. A few steps later, she stopped before it, her hand shaking as she reached out to turn the knob.

Wait—her bag.

She raced to her bed and shoved aside the dangling curtain, fishing out the sack Izora had brought her from beneath the cot. It took only a moment to strap the bag to her back, then she was back at the door.

She grabbed the knob and the smooth, cold metal turned beneath her fingers. She smiled. But before she could shove the door open, she heard a terrible sound—the steady *clunk* of footsteps in the hall headed toward her.

Her heart sank. If only she'd left at the first sign of the signal, she would be outside already. Blazes, she was so stupid!

She let the knob go slowly, praying whoever stood in the hallway didn't notice it twisting from the other side and backed away from the door. She just had time to shuck off the bag and shove it beneath her grandfather's cot, out of sight, before the door swung open.

Kayda's jaw dropped. "Father?"

After weeks of begging the guards to speak to him and dozens of letters, he had to show up now? Right when she was poised to leave?

Prince Gideon lingered in the doorway. Like the rest of the men in the family, he was tall, blond-haired, and blue-eyed, but unlike Tarquin and Quinton, the years had not been kind to him. His pale skin was yellow and sallow. His body was no longer muscular and trim but bulged with fat, making the black tunic and trousers he wore appear a few sizes too small.

He stepped forward, his stare fixed on the king's back where he sat by the window. Then he swung to face her, his face flat and unreadable as he strode inside, closing the door behind him.

He walked straight to her, grabbed her upper arms, and stared down into her upturned face. "I'm so sorry, Kayda. I've been worse than useless for years. But I'm here now. You don't have to be alone any longer." He pulled her close, embracing her tightly.

Kayda held herself stiffly in his arms. She steeled herself for the sour stench that would surround her—but it never came. She pushed free from his embrace and searched his face. His eyes, so often bloodshot, were clear tonight. His cheeks were missing their familiar rosy hue, and his voice had not slurred in the slightest.

"Did you stop drinking?" Her brow furrowed.

Gideon's stare locked onto her own. He nodded. "Yes. It was the hardest thing I've ever done, but when I heard about the attack on Father…" He glanced at the king's back again, then refocused on her face. "I locked myself in my room and ordered my man to keep me there, no matter what, until I was off the stuff. I should have done it long ago, Kayda. I'm so, so sorry. All those years wasted—I want to do better. I will do better."

His face burned with intensity, but Kayda shook her head in disbelief.

Her entire life, she could count on one hand the number of times her father had said so many words to her at once. And he'd never apologized. Who was this man standing before her?

Her eyes filled with tears. "Why didn't you? We could've been so much more if you'd only cared enough to try."

He frowned at the floor. "I don't know. My life… just didn't turn out the way I expected. I should've faced my problems, dealt with them. But I drowned them instead."

"What problems? You're a prince." She narrowed her eyes and backed away another pace.

"I know it sounds crazy. I should've been able to be happy... but I just... couldn't." He sighed and met her eyes. "I wasn't always this way. Growing up, knowing the royal talent had skipped me, I could handle that. When it skipped your brother—that's when everything went to shit."

His face screwed up, and he shook his head. "I couldn't get it out of my mind. He should've had it. Bonding magic skips a generation in our family, but it always comes back... always. I couldn't stop thinking that his mother had been untrue. She denied it, of course, but I just knew. It was the only explanation that made sense. When she got sick later that year and died, I was glad." He laughed, a single joyless sound that echoed through the room. "I was glad to be rid of her lies. Glad to remarry and try again. She'd robbed me of my birthright. Bringing the next royal with talent into the world. But then the rumors started..."

Kayda's mind roiled with uncertainty. She'd heard the rumors. Everyone had. When Tarquin was born without talent and his mother died of a mysterious sickness a few short months later, it didn't take long before people began whispering that her death hadn't been natural. That Gideon had poisoned her.

When she first heard the story as a child, she'd brushed it off, not inclined to think so poorly of her father at the time. But she'd remembered, her view of the man forever colored differently thereafter. It was always there in the back of her mind, unanswered. Was her father a killer?

"It's not true. I swear it." His gaze sought out hers, full of fervor. "It might as well have been, though, for all the trouble it caused me. No one would allow their daughter to marry me after that. Father and I searched for years in Dracwood before we accepted that we'd have to look elsewhere for a bride. By that time, I wanted nothing more to do with it. I would've rather let the bloodline die than force some unwilling foreign wife to bed me. But my father convinced me..." He scowled. "For duty."

Kayda's stomach turned. She was more similar to her father than she realized. She knew all about the pressures that came with keeping the royal bloodline alive.

"Your mother—she was a sweet girl, but she didn't marry me by choice. If it hadn't been for the trade deal that Father negotiated with her family, then she wouldn't have had anything to do with me. But we did our duty. And then there you were."

He sent a rueful smile her way. "You don't know the relief I felt that day when the seers announced your talent. But your mother died during childbirth." His upper lip curled back. "The rumors flew again. I started drinking. I couldn't stand to see the veiled accusation on everyone's faces, and the drink, it let me forget. After that, it became a way of life for me. I'd done my duty. Who cared if I drank myself to death?"

Tears stung her eyes. "Who would care? I did. Your daughter."

He flinched, but she refused to lower her voice or temper her emotion.

"I needed you, and you ignored me. My entire life, you acted like I wasn't even there. How do you think it made me feel, knowing you'd rather drink yourself into oblivion than spend time with me?"

He raked a shaky hand through his hair, staring at the floor again. "I know. I'm so sorry, Kayda. If I could go back and do it all over, I would. I would be the father you deserve. Please... just tell me what I can do to make it right?"

Her gaze shot to the fireplace. It would be so easy to call forth the flames. Part of her wanted it. To watch him burn.

No. She balled her hands into fists and looked away. "Let me leave. I don't want to be a prisoner in this blazing room any longer."

His gaze raised from the floor, and he nodded. "Done."

"And don't let him die." Her arm shot out, pointing directly at the king. "Don't you dare." She stepped closer and stared straight into his eyes, her voice laced with venom. "If Grandfather isn't still breathing when I return, you won't get the chance to drown yourself again when all the rumors start."

His eyes bulged, and he backed away a pace, staring at her strangely. She expected him to say something, to chide her not to speak to her elders in such a way, but he only nodded again.

Kayda spun on her heel, knelt down to retrieve her bag, and fled the room before he could change his mind. She stormed through the tower in a daze, disappointment and anger boiling in her veins. Maybe one day she could forgive her father for his faults. Not today.

Chilly autumn air hit her face as she emerged outside, cooling her rage. She inhaled deeply, the fresh air a welcome relief after the stuffy tower room. Spinning around slowly, she gaped at the scenery. She spent so long in that single room, staring out the lone window toward Kings Keep. She finally escaped, only to be greeted with the night's darkness.

As she turned east, she was met with a strange sight that sent a shiver up her spine. The full moon perched there in the sky, blood-red. From where she stood, it appeared to hover over the path to Mage Keep.

"Kayda!" Izora stepped out in the moonlight from a shadowed alcove in the brick tower, her black-hooded cloak blending into the darkness. "What took you so long? Did someone stop you on your way out?" She grabbed her elbow, towing her toward Northmoat. "Never mind, it doesn't matter. There's no time. We have to hurry."

"Why are we rushing?" she asked as they sped up. "Please, you have to explain what's happening."

"Do you remember the mage who healed the king?"

Kayda nodded. She would never forget that kind man's face.

"His name is Vespen." Her voice became increasingly labored, but she didn't slow. "He's waiting for you outside the Royal Grounds to take you to Mage Keep."

"Mage Keep?" She stopped and shook her head vehemently. "No, I have to find Tarquin. I didn't have time to tell you when you came to see me. He was involved in the attack on the king."

Izora tugged her arm again, starting her moving. "I don't doubt it. That boy is always up to no good. No one's heard from Mage Keep for days now. Something's happening there, and I won't be surprised to find out that fool is behind it." She jolted to a stop, panting. "I can't go with you, child. I'd only slow you down. Go find out what's happening at Mage Keep. I'll stay behind and keep an eye on the king."

"My father is with him now. He promised to keep him alive."

Izora's face blanched, all the color draining from it in an instant. "What did you say? Your father..." She gasped, a hand on her breast.

"Izora, what's wrong? Are you okay?"

She pulled in another breath, struggling for air. "That man is not your father."

The words struck her like a slap to the face. "What are you talking about?"

Izora shook her head, her white curls bouncing beneath her hood. "There's no time. I have to get back, and you have to go. The Sade Prim, Delyth, she can tell you everything when you reach Mage Keep." She clutched her tightly. "I love you, my princess," she whispered before she let go. Then she hurried off, disappearing into the darkness.

Kayda stood silently, trying to wrap her head around Izora's shocking revelation. Gideon was not her father? How could that be true? She almost raced after her to demand an explanation. How could she reveal something like that and just leave?

Then, a commotion started somewhere nearby. The unmistakable clash of violence resounded in the night, and she jogged off toward Northmoat. She'd been given this chance to set things right. She wouldn't waste it.

Her bag bounced on her back as she sprinted toward the light of the blood-red moon. The sounds of fighting faded as she approached the edge of the Royal Grounds, and her stomach sank. That meant Kings Keep was under attack. She stopped, turning around to stare in the keep's direction as a cold sweat broke out on her skin.

"Princess," said a voice behind her. "I'm glad you made it."

The mage from the feast, Vespen, rode up to greet her. He was seated atop a black stallion and held the reins of a chestnut mare in his hands. He'd exchanged the white robes for dark brown traveling clothes, and he perched upon his steed with that steady expression Kayda remembered so clearly.

"It's too late. If you head for the mages, we're all doomed."

Kayda gasped, immediately realizing what the voice meant. She raced forward and placed her hands on the second horse. *"Are you my bondmate?"* She rubbed the horse's silky mane as Vespen stared at her. *"I'm bonded to horses just like Grandfather?"*

"*A horse?*" Laughter filled her mind. "*No, I'm definitely not a horse. But I am your bondmate. I need you to find me.*"

"My lady, we have to go," Vespen said.

She ignored him and dropped her hands from the horse, backing away. "*Where are you?*"

"*Hard to say. Underground somewhere, in the darkness.*"

A locked door flashed in her memory. Instinctively, she knew. Her mind raced. She had to get back in the keep.

"I have to go back." She looked up at Vespen as she backed away slowly.

He frowned. "I promise you, whatever you left behind, we can replace. We have to leave now."

Kayda shook her head. "No, you don't understand. My bondmate is back there."

His eyes widened, and he dismounted. "No, *you* don't understand, Princess. We needed a distraction to secret you out of the city. If you go back there, you'll be walking into a battle."

She gulped but refused to let the news dissuade her. "It doesn't matter. I have to go back. I have to do this."

Vespen stared into her eyes for what felt like ages. Then he drew a breath in through his nose and crouched down to grab fists full of soil, stuffing them into his pockets. He rose, setting his shoulders back and staring straight forward. "All right. Let's go find your bondmate."

Kayda smiled, her heart overflowing with gratitude. Then she squared her shoulders and shoved aside the anxious fluttering in her stomach. "*I'm coming to find you.*"

Chapter 22

Mage Keep was a ghost town. It was no surprise something spooked Shadow when he first set eyes on the sprawling compound.

"Is it ever deserted like this, in the middle of the day?" Conall asked, glancing at Ereni.

She shook her head and frowned. "No, never. Even if there was a mandatory meeting called, there should be someone outside keeping watch."

"I don't like this. I have a bad feeling..." Shadow stood stiffly, staring at the empty keep.

Conall gulped. *"Me, too, brother. But my sister's in there."*

He studied the landscape. Mage Keep nestled at the bottom of a ridge, leaving the back half inaccessible from their position. It was surrounded by great swaths of farmland on all other sides, with a slow-moving river to the north. They were hidden in the woods on the outer edge, but to reach the keep, they would have to traverse a huge, empty field.

He sighed. If they'd arrived a few weeks ago, they might've had some options, but with harvest completed, there was no chance of using the crops for cover. He could see no other way to stealthily approach.

Even waiting for nightfall would be a gamble unlikely to pay out. They were due for a full moon tonight, and the sky was clear and cloudless.

He unslung his bow from his shoulder, the familiar weight a comfort in his hand. "I'll head in first. You two can wait—"

"If you think I'm going to wait in the woods like some helpless maiden, you're sorely mistaken," Ereni said with a huff. "That's my home. We go together."

He considered debating, but one look at her face assured him she would not be swayed. "All right, then we leave Shadow here as backup."

"There's no livestock here." Ereni waved a hand. "Bring him. If there's trouble waiting for us inside, we'll need all the help we can get."

He gazed again at the deserted compound. She was probably right. It's not like Shadow could sneak in any easier to rescue them if something happened. "Together then."

He exchanged a glance with Shadow and nodded toward the keep. *We go together, stay sharp.*

"Always." Shadow edged forward.

Conall followed, gritting his teeth as he exited the tree line. There was no movement from the keep. No arrows shot at them. No blasts of fire or eruptions of magic disrupted the eerie stillness. Just the gentle plodding of their footsteps in fresh-turned earth.

Still, he couldn't shake the sensation of being watched. His gaze slid from building to building, expecting an ambush at any moment. It wasn't until they'd crept past several mismatched buildings, each one as silent and empty as the last, that he was certain they were not alone. A gentle breeze carried a scent to his nose. The foul scent of unwashed flesh.

"Someone's here." He grabbed Ereni and shoved her behind him. At the same time, he reached into his quiver, pulling out and nocking an arrow.

"Drop it," said the gruff voice of an unseen man. "You're surrounded."

Shadow growled, the fur on his back standing on end.

Conall's head jolted all around as he searched for cover. There was a building they'd just passed that might work. Heart pumping, he shuffled sideways, his bow held at the ready, preparing to jump back.

Then the whistle of a dozen arrows flew through the sky and thudded into the ground by their feet.

Shadow's growling intensified. He hopped back, an arrow landing just shy of his snapping teeth.

"I said drop the bow," the same voice yelled, "and calm that hound, or the next round of arrows won't miss."

"They have us surrounded. Calm down, Shadow." Conall scowled. His gaze darted all around as he tossed his bow on the packed dirt road between buildings. Shadow sat down by his side, tucking his tail beneath him.

"All your weapons. You, too, girl."

Conall shucked off his quiver and pulled his hunting knife from its place on his belt. He tossed both down. Ereni stepped forward. Her knife clattered against his own before it landed in the dirt.

Only then did the gruff voiced man reveal himself. He was large, middle-aged, and balding. He charged forward, muscles rippling, and whistled.

The sound had barely cleared his pursed lips before a dozen men revealed themselves, pouring out between buildings, a few vaulting down from the rooftops.

"Restrain them. Put them in with the others," said the leader.

Several men sauntered forward with swords, spears, and bows aimed at them. They wore plain clothes but handled their weapons with the familiarity of constant use.

Were they mercenaries? What could they possibly want at Mage Keep? And why had the mages allowed themselves to be captured? It was all so strange.

A short man with a pocked face approached Shadow, and a growl rose in his throat. The man retreated a step. "That ain't no hound." His eyes bulged, and he trained his bow directly at Shadow's face. "Blazes. That's a wolf."

Conall's heart jumped into his throat. He inched between the man and Shadow, swallowing as the arrow targeted his chest. "He's trained. He's no threat to you."

"Relax, Lonan." The leader said to his man as he marched toward them, a long rope coiled in his hands. Then he turned to Conall. "Here, you tie him up. Round his neck and muzzle." He shoved the rough rope into his hands.

Conall knelt, catching a glimpse of Ereni glowering at a stocky man as he tied her outstretched hands. How were they going to escape now? He uncoiled the rope and gazed down at Shadow's face. *I'm sorry, they want me to tie you.*

Do what you must. We'll think of something, little brother.

He wrapped the rope around Shadow, leaving a long length free to hold like a leash. Then he stood, handed the rope to a waiting man, and stuck out his own hands to be tied.

Lonan slung his bow on his shoulder and got to work with a rope. "C'mon then," he said as he finished.

The rope bit into Conall's flesh so tightly he had no chance to slip free. A group of six men formed up, their weapons held at the ready, and led them away from the leader, further into the keep.

Ereni gasped as they rounded a corner to reveal a large building in similar bondage. Its ground-level windows were boarded with freshly cut wood tacked on from the outside. The door was barred with an iron bar and locked. Lonan detached a key from his belt as they approached, and Conall's stomach turned.

Lonan ushered them in. Ereni went first, her steps quickening as she caught sight of the huddled folk within.

Conall paused, gazing in awe at the massive building. The interior was far grander than he'd expected. Huge wooden tables that could comfortably seat hundreds were lodged in neat lines along the walls. High ceilings shone with massive glass windows, illuminating walls painted a dazzling white. Each of the four walls displayed a brilliantly wrought tapestry depicting mages using one of the four elements.

A shove on his back set him in motion again. He stumbled forward. Shadow followed by his side after the man holding his makeshift leash tossed the lead to the ground and pulled the heavy door closed, sealing them inside.

Ereni had already reached the center of the room. She embraced an old woman wearing the long, white robes the mages favored. Conall approached the pair and scanned the rest of the room, desperately seeking one familiar face in the crowd.

There had to be more than a hundred people staring at them. At least three quarters of them were old and wearing the white robes. The rest were young adults and teens, who wore plain clothes. His heart sank. Lark was not among them.

"What's going on here, Amora?" Ereni pulled free of the old woman's embrace and frowned. "Who are these men? Where are my mother and the children?"

Amora wrung her hands together, her brow furrowing. "Ereni, I'm so glad you're here. We've been stuck here for days. It's been absolutely wretched not knowing what's going on. What did you see on your way in?" Her wrinkled hands tugged at the bindings on Ereni's wrists.

"All we saw was empty buildings before those men ambushed us. Who are they? What do they want?"

Amora's stare fixed on Ereni's hands as she released the final loop of rope. "They're castle guards, from Kings Keep."

Ereni raised a newly freed hand to her lips. "No." Her eyes widened like a hare caught in a trap before she whirled to face him and began loosening his bonds.

"They came last week, with Prince Tarquin." Amora glanced at Shadow but made no move to free him. "You know it's not unheard of for the royals to visit. We welcomed them, invited them in for a feast. It all seemed perfectly normal... until it wasn't. A few of the guards offered to put on a demonstration for the children. Sword fighting. Turns out it was merely a ruse to separate us. Once they had the children, they used them as leverage to herd us all in here like cattle. They threatened us, said if any of us summon or try to escape, they'll kill them."

Ereni finished untying his hands. Her face flushed and her jaw clenched as she listened to the tale. He couldn't imagine what she must be feeling. He wanted drag her into his arms, but he suspected she wouldn't appreciate it with all the mages eyes on them, so he settled for sending her a sympathetic smile before he knelt down to free Shadow.

Ereni spun back to Amora and crossed her arms. "And my mother?"

Amora shook her head. "No one has seen her since that first day. The prince took her with him. What he wants with her, or with any of us, he didn't say. We keep waiting for something to happen. So far, nothing." She turned and stared at him. "What about you, Ereni? Who are your companions?"

Ereni offered a small smile and raised her voice, projecting her answer to the whole assemblage. "I'm so sorry everyone has been through this. I'll see it all gets sorted out, I promise. This is Conall of Greenvale and his wolfhound, Shadow. He is seeking his sister, Lark."

Conall finished removing Shadow's bindings. He stood and thrust out a hand. "Pleased to meet you."

Amora shook his hand, her grip firm and warm.

"I don't see my sister here, now. She left me a letter a few weeks back, said she was heading here for training. We have the same curly brown hair and hazel eyes, but she's a few years younger than me and about this tall." He lifted a hand to the height of his shoulder. "Have you seen her?"

"There's been no one here by that name, I'm afraid." Amora gazed at him intently. "I can recall no visitors in the last few weeks who share a resemblance with you, either. You are welcome to inquire among the rest of the mages, but I don't think you'll find her here."

Conall swallowed, his chest aching. The fear that had subsided when he learned of Lark's intentions to travel to the mages assaulted him once more.

Where could she be? He had no other clues, nothing to go on except for the letter she'd left him. Would he ever find her?

Even worse, now they were caught in the middle of some strange standoff. His mind raced as he examined the sad and fearful faces of the assembled mages. Some sat in small groups, their gazes downcast, eyes ringed with dark circles. Others paced mindlessly or stared dejectedly out the tall glass windows.

They'd been separated from their families just like he had. He had to do something to help them.

"What's going on? Where is your sister?" Shadow sat by his side, looking at the gathered mages, seemingly unbothered by the attention despite rarely being around so many people before.

Conall closed his eyes and pressed his fingertips against his eyelids. *"Sounds like she was never here."* His hand drooped back to his side. *"But those men, they're holding the young of this keep hostage. We have to help them."*

Footsteps pounded outside. The door opened a moment later, and two men carrying food and drink barged in. Several others shadowed them with weapons drawn.

Conall scowled as he saw what was on offer. Was this what he had to look forward to now? Stale bread and ale spread between too many mouths to be satisfying.

His head pounded. How long would they be stuck in here, waiting on the royals to play their political games?

From the corner of his eye, he spied movement. Ereni glided forward, showing no fear even when the guards pointed their weapons straight at her. "Take me to my mother," she demanded.

He clenched his fists, staring a hole in her back. What was she doing?

"I don't have orders to move you, lady," said the same stocky man who'd tied Ereni's hands earlier.

"My mother is the Sade Prim, and I have an urgent message for her. You would be wise to allow me to see her."

The man frowned, then heaved out a sigh. "I'll take you to the prince. He'll decide what to do with you."

Conall started forward, ready to protest, but Ereni sent a hard glare his way and shook her head from across the room. He stopped moving, his nails digging into the palms of his hands as he watched her wrists being bound. Then she was led through the door and out of sight.

Amora squeezed his arm as the iron bar clanged back into place, echoing through the silent Hall. "It's all right. She'll get things sorted. She promised."

He looked down at the old woman and forced his hands to relax. "I hope you're right."

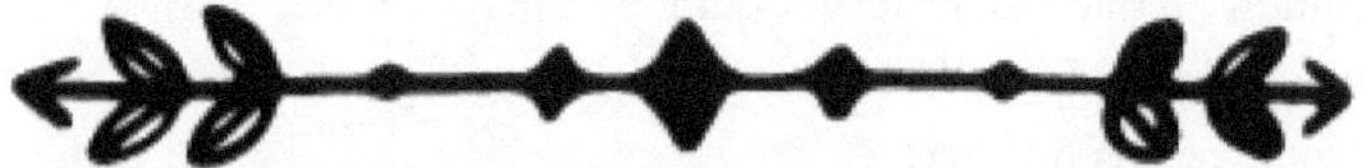

Conall's thighs burned, the muscles in his legs and calves straining as he climbed up the steep rise to the top of the ridge overlooking Mage Keep. He stepped carefully, aware he might not catch himself with his bound hands if he were to fall on the uneven ground.

Beside him marched Shadow and four mages, all bound in similar fashion, and the six guardsmen who'd collected them from the hall. They'd stormed in with a list of names, ordering them to follow but not saying why or where they were heading.

It shocked him when the guards read off their names. Ereni had done it. In the short time she'd spent with the prince, she'd convinced him to let them go. This had to be part of her plan. There was no other way those guards would even know who he was. He hadn't given them his name, or Shadow's.

Eventually, the ground leveled off. Conall was the first to round the summit. He found himself on the top of a flat rise that overlooked both Mage Keep behind them, and a large swath of coastal plains ahead of them. He glanced around, admiring the unspoiled land's majestic beauty, until his gaze was captivated by an unexpected sight.

It was just before dusk, but tonight, the moon chose to grace the land with an early appearance. The entire surface shone a bright, bold red. He couldn't stop the uneasy shiver that slid down his spine. It was like he was face-to-face with an ill omen hovering in the sky before him.

He didn't have long to stare. Amora crested the rise a moment later and gasped aloud. Conall turned as she raced forward and stopped next to a woman seated on the rise's far side. She wore a white robe, her hands were bound, and she had a pair of guards watching over her as she sat stoically gazing into the distance.

He stopped mid-stride as he caught sight of the woman's face. He didn't need anyone to tell him he was looking at the Sade Prim, Delyth. Although her hair was gray instead of brown, the familial resemblance was uncanny. This woman was undoubtedly Ereni's kin.

"Sade Prim, I'm so glad you're all right." Amora knelt, her face lit with joy. "What's going on? Do you know why they've brought us here to the Palisade?"

The other three mages hastened over and crowded around the pair. Their leader didn't speak. Her stare was fixed on the horizon.

Conall walked forward more slowly as he took a second look at the shoreline. He'd missed something with his first glance. He squinted in the fading daylight and spotted a ship moored offshore, along with what appeared to be a camp full of people on the beach. From this distance, the details were unclear, but the unmistakable sight of smoke rose above their campsite. Someone was out there.

A gasp stole his attention. Amora had noticed the scene. She stared at the shoreline, her mouth agape. "They're in the Abandoned Lands? We have to stop them!"

"You'll do nothing of the sort," proclaimed a new voice behind him.

He spun around in time to see a tall blond man cresting the ridge with more guards surrounding him. From his fine silk attire and pompous air, he suspected he was looking at Prince Tarquin. "Say hello to my good friends from Joria. They're going to help me build a port here as soon as you mages take down that blasted wall."

"You have no idea what you're asking, Prince Tarquin," said a woman's voice behind him.

An icy chill spread through his chest. The prince wanted to build a port? Here? Conall backed up, turning sideways so he could watch both parties speak from where he and Shadow stood in between them.

"You've already doomed those men to death," continued Delyth, "don't doom us all." She rose to her feet and tore her gaze from the shoreline, surveying everyone with her steely blue eyes.

"You mages and your silly superstitions." The prince strode forward, smirking. "Those men have been camped on that beach for a week. They've trekked all over the land and found nothing. No creatures jumping out to spook them. No monsters descending on them in the night. There's nothing out there to be afraid of."

Delyth stepped forward, staring at the prince. Until she veered alongside him and Shadow. Her head flicked to the side, studying them both. Conall swallowed, meeting her gaze and seeing something in it he couldn't quite name, but it made his stomach sink all the same.

Delyth's head snapped back, her gaze refocusing on Tarquin. "Where is my daughter?"

Tarquin's smile widened. "She said you were smarter than most. I didn't believe anyone so easily taken in with ghost stories and legends could be, but I see I'm mistaken."

Conall's stomach climbed into his throat. Why was he being evasive? Where was Ereni?

Then he spotted movement coming up the ridge behind him. He smiled. It was Ereni, hiking up to join them, with several young people from the hall following closely behind her. They walked freely with no bonds and no guards trailing them.

She'd done it. He knew she would find a way to free her people.

Something was wrong. The smile fell from his face. His gut ached, a terrible wrongness eating a hole inside him.

She crested the ridge and walked, not toward her mother, or even him. She strode up to Tarquin and stopped beside him, entwining her arm with his. "Hello, Mother."

Conall's head spun. What was she doing with the prince? She hadn't greeted him. She hadn't even looked at him. After everything they'd been through. All those days traveling together. All those nights...

He sucked in a breath through his nose. His jaw clenched tightly as his gaze flicked away from her traitorous face and down at her stomach. He was going to be sick.

Shadow sidled up beside him, brushing against his leg and standing at attention. A growl rose from his throat, no less menacing despite the rope wrapped around his muzzle.

Conall lifted his gaze back to Ereni's face and found her staring back at him. Those blue eyes he'd spent long hours staring into were full of indifference. Those lips he'd kissed, slack and emotionless. His heart wrenched, pain stabbing behind his ribs. He wanted to scream. But all he could do was stare back dumbly in shock.

"Why?" Delyth approached her daughter, her eyes flashing. "You've read the journals. You know what's out there. How could you be a party to this?"

"You're right, I've read them. That's exactly why." Ereni dropped Tarquin's arm. "The Palisade was never meant to last this long. It's weakened us for centuries. Enough is enough." She walked past her mother, striding closer to the edge of the ridge overlooking the coast. "If there is something out there, we must stand and fight while we still have strength." She closed her eyes, her lips parting and her chest slowly rising as it filled with air. She exhaled, opening her eyes.

Conall backed away, the hair on his skin standing on end. A massive wall materialized, blocking the shoreline and gleaming strangely. The Palisade. His breath caught as he stared up at the colossal structure.

Ereni turned, spreading her arms wide. "Take a good look, my friends. You will be the last people to set eyes on this sight. Tonight, the Palisade falls."

Cheers erupted behind him, but he didn't turn. His gaze was glued on her. He watched the smile slowly spread across her face and cursed himself for a fool.

Chapter 23

Lark hopped down from the back of the wagon and wrapped a brown woolen blanket around her shoulders against the chilly night air. She paused, her hand snaking out from beneath the blanket to pat Sunny's head.

"Don't get up, girl," she whispered. "I'll be back in a little while."

The yellow mutt wagged her tail lazily and rolled over, closing her eyes.

Lark sank down on a log next to the remnants of the evening fire. She sighed, half-heartedly poking a stick at the dying embers of a log that had once been nearly as big as the one she sat on.

Everyone had gone to sleep hours ago. She'd tossed and turned for ages, but finally gave up trying. Her mind was on edge tonight and sleep elusive.

Her eyes lifted and instantly widened, mirroring the shape of the full moon. The silver orb had darkened tonight to a brilliant crimson-red.

How strange. A prickle of unease crept across her shoulders.

"Couldn't sleep?"

Lark gasped, clutching her chest beneath the blanket. "Aren? I didn't know anyone was still awake."

He strode forward and crouched by the fire, the corner of his mouth lifting in a smile. "I couldn't sleep either." He grabbed a few twigs and tossed them onto the log, coaxing the fire back to life. "Care for some company?"

"Sure." She scooted over and tightened the blanket across her shoulders. Her fingers tangled in the rough cloth as Aren seated himself beside her.

His eyes lifted to the sky, his ice-blue irises reflecting the red moonlight. "Wow. That's not something you see every day."

Lark tilted her head, her brown curls spilling over her shoulders. "Do you think it means something?"

"Where I'm from, they have a saying. Blood-red moon, tides changing soon."

"Well, that's certainly ominous." Her knees trembled.

"Think that's what's keeping you awake?"

"Maybe. No." She rolled her shoulders. "Daus says we'll reach the turnoff for Mage Keep tomorrow morning."

Aren shifted. His thigh pressed against her leg, sending a frisson of electricity across her skin. "You know, we'll be back this way in a few short months. Maybe you could—"

She shook her head, closing her eyes. "No. I've waited long enough."

Kaleb's grief-stricken face flashed in her memory. Once she reached Mage Keep, she wouldn't fail anyone like she'd failed him. Never again.

It was like she'd been blessed with a deep well of water, but no tools to bore down to reach it. She couldn't keep clawing through the dirt with her hands, praying to stumble across a geyser.

Aren's hand landed on her knee. "Lark, you can't blame yourself for what happened to Nico."

She opened her eyes. Her fingers released the rough cloth and slipped out to give his hand a gentle squeeze. "Please, I don't want to think about that right now. Can we talk about something else?"

Her thumb lingered on the smooth skin of his wrist. She drew in a deep breath, tempted to link their hands together, but she slid her fingers back inside the blanket instead. "What about you? Will you travel with the show much longer?"

Aren lifted his hand from her knee. She shivered, regretting the loss of his warmth.

"Yes, I will." He brushed his fingers through his hair, tousling his light blond locks. "I'm afraid my wanderlust has only grown stronger since I left home."

She smiled up at him. "Is that so?" They were alike in that. The more time she spent traveling, the more she craved it.

He leaned closer, speaking in a hushed whisper. "Can I tell you a secret?"

She nodded.

"In Doln, there's a legend about a hidden land, somewhere beyond the Orrdon Ocean. A paradise full of white sand beaches. The sea so clear, you can look straight down into the water and watch the fish swimming between your toes."

She giggled at the imagery, and Aren grinned.

"My friends back home never believed the stories. They said it was just a myth. A foolish tale to keep the kids entertained while the blizzards raged in the winter." He wrinkled his nose, smiling down at her. "One day, I'm going to set sail and find out the truth of it."

"That sounds amazing." She could picture him on the bow of a ship, that oversized hat of his hiding his face from the sun. "I wish I could join you."

"Well, then you shall. I'll swing round Mage Keep and collect you before I set sail." His grin widened, and he slung an arm around her shoulder, giving her a squeeze. "I'll be getting into plenty of scrapes that could benefit from a healer's touch on that voyage. You'd be a welcome addition to my crew."

Lark smiled back, but she couldn't match Aren's enthusiasm.

When his gaze flicked down to her face, his smile dropped, and he pulled her closer. "Hey, tomorrow, when you go to Mage Keep, it's not goodbye. At least, not forever. We'll meet again. We'll have more adventures together. I promise."

Lark snuggled closer to Aren's chest, watching the flames flickering in the moonlight.

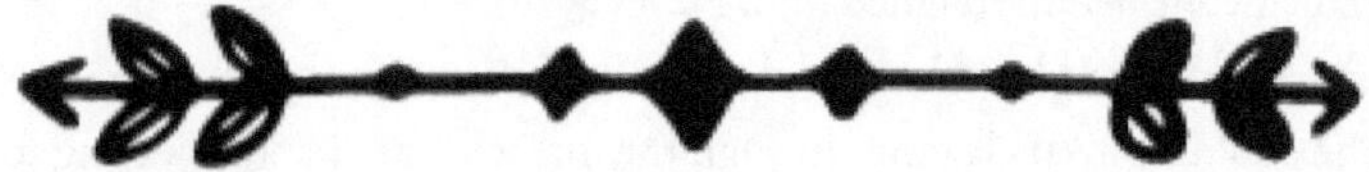

"I wish you would reconsider." Dausius huffed out a dramatic sigh. "The show won't be the same without you."

Lark stood at a crossroads early the next morning. The road before her led to the show's next performance. And the one behind her led to Mage Keep.

"I've made up my mind, Daus. Thank you for putting up with me for so long. And for saving me."

His lower lip quivered. He pressed a palm against his chest and made a show of breathing in and out deeply.

She cocked her head to the side and smiled. Always so dramatic. She was going to miss that. Her heart swelled. She was going to miss them all.

Suddenly, his face lit up. "I almost forgot." He squeezed her arm gently. "I have something for you. Don't move, I'll be right back." He spun around, his beaded hair tinkling musically as he made a beeline for his wagon and scrounged around in the back. "Where is it? Where is it?"

Lark raised a brow, shoving her hands into her dark blue dresses pockets as she waited. Daus was notorious for misplacing things. She might be waiting for a while.

Mazen and Meital stood on the far side of the wagon, chatting among themselves. They'd already exchanged their goodbyes with her. Both expressed regret that she wouldn't be staying for longer.

And Aren. He'd been so sweet last night, not pushing her to stay. Telling her their adventures weren't over. But she couldn't help but worry he'd regret wasting so much time teaching her to handle birds of prey only for her to leave.

She exhaled, shifting her weight from one foot to the other. She would miss those mornings with him and Muse a great deal. But she'd made her decision.

Aren caught her staring and sent her a crooked grin from across the road. Then he whistled, holding out a gauntleted arm to catch Whisper, and strode into the forest.

"I think he's going to be heartbroken for a while." Tiora walked over and joined her, staring at the woods where Aren had disappeared. She wore a golden-brown dress today, the color a perfect match for her eyes.

"Aren? Surely not." She scoffed, her gaze dropping to the dirt road.

"All that time you two spent together, alone in the woods every morning. Don't tell me you didn't realize how much he's in love with you?"

Her gaze shot to Tiora's, and a frown spread across her face. "Don't be silly, Ti. Anyway, he told me about Meital. He's got her to comfort him."

"He told you what about Meital?" Tiora crossed her arms.

"How on the night we all met, they were sleeping together. And that they both woke up and heard me singing."

Tiora laughed. "He told you he and Meital? Lark, that's not true."

"What? Why are you laughing?"

Tiora squeezed her shoulder. "Meital... I've grown to know her very well since becoming part of her act." She smiled fondly, meeting her gaze. "She's not sleeping with Aren."

Lark rolled her eyes, shaking off Tiora's hand. "You know women aren't always willing to admit when they're with someone, for modesty's sake."

Toira shook her head, her smile never wavering. "No, no. She's not being modest. People don't even care about modesty where she's from the way they do here." Her gaze flicked to the sky, as if she were gathering her thoughts, before her brown eyes connected with hers again. "Meital..." She dropped her voice, speaking in a whisper. "She doesn't sleep with men. Any man."

"Oh." Lark's eyes widened. She thought back to that conversation with Aren. Had he said he and Meital were sleeping together? Or had he said something vague, and she'd just assumed? She grimaced. "I suppose it's possible I misheard," she admitted, a pit forming in her stomach.

Tiora sighed. "Well, we'll see you again. You know Daus won't pass by Mage Keep in the spring without checking in on you. Maybe things will be different with you and Aren next time."

Lark lowered her head, her shoulders sinking. She was right, there was the future to look forward to, but it didn't stop her from feeling any less of a fool in that moment.

"Ah ha, I found it!" Dausius jumped down from the colorful wagon, waving something in his hand. With a few steps, he stopped in front of her. He bowed, his body finally stilling enough for Lark to get a clear look at the gift. It was a book with a brown leather cover. "This is for you, my dear." He extended it with a flourish.

She took the book with a grin, her hands sliding over the smooth leather. The pages glided open with a whisper, revealing page after page of handwritten words. No, not words. Songs. The lyrics to every song he'd taught her filled the pages.

"Forgive me if my handwriting is a bit wobbly. It's not easy writing in the back of a moving wagon."

Her eyes welled up as she smoothed the yellowed parchment. "You made this... for me?"

"Songs for my songbird." He chuckled. "Oh, don't cry," he added, as he met her gaze. "It's all in self-interest, I swear. One day, when you decide you've had enough of spells and magic, you'll open this book. All the songs will come flooding back, and you'll return to us." He pulled her in for a quick hug, smashing the book between them. When they pulled apart, his eyes were full of tears.

"Thank you, Daus."

He stared down at her, his expression earnest. "Don't forget. We're going to stay in Bogsmouth for an entire week before leaving for Raimire. You have until then to change your mind and come find us." He sniffled and pulled out a huge, multicolored handkerchief and wiped his eyes. "Oh, I can't bear it any longer." He spun on his heel and waved the handkerchief in the air. "Farewell." Then he disappeared back into the wagon.

"Never a dull moment with Daus around," Tiora said with a giggle.

Lark turned to her friend, and saw her eyes were red rimmed, too, despite her laughter. Her chin wobbled. "I'm going to miss you, Ti. I wish you could come with me, but I know you're excited to see your family again when the show goes to Joria."

"I'm going to miss you, too. One day, when you're a mage, you'll have to come visit Joria with me. I'll take you swimming in the Peat River, just like we talked about." Tiora pulled her in for a hug, clutching her tightly. "Daus is right. The show won't be the same without you."

"Anyone can sing. You'll find someone to replace me soon enough."

Tiora pulled away, frowning. "We might find another singer, but they'll never replace you, Lark." She bit her lip and turned away. "Go on then. Go become who you're meant to be." She met her eyes one more time before drifting back to the wagon.

Lark swallowed. She took one last long look at the wagons before pulling her pack from her back. Carefully tucking Dausius' gift next to her mother's spell book, she cinched the bag closed. She whistled, watching both Sunny's and Muse's bodies perk up at the sound from where they sat on the back of the colorful wagon.

Her stomach sank. If only she could bring them both. She'd decided to leave Muse with Aren. She didn't know what life would be like at Mage Keep, but she doubted she'd have time in her days for flying Muse like she deserved.

But Sunny was getting old and was happy to lie around all day. Dausius told her he'd seen a few hounds around the keep on his last visit, so she was taking the chance of bringing her. Really, she just couldn't stand the thought of parting with the dog. She was the only reminder she had left of her brother.

"Sunny, c'mon, girl."

Sunny rose, stretching and yawning, before hopping down from the wagon. Lark ruffled the yellow fur between her ears as she stopped beside her, tail wagging.

She had one more goodbye she needed to offer. She took a few steps closer to Muse's perch. The falcon's eyes trailed her movements, her body still as she rested in the wagon bed. Tears gathered in the corners of her eyes. For some reason, this goodbye was the hardest of them all.

"I'm sorry I can't take you with me, Muse. I can't give you the care you deserve at Mage Keep. Aren—he's promised to take great care of you." Her voice trembled, and her final words were a choked whisper. "We'll meet again, my friend. Goodbye."

She whirled around, using her sleeve to catch the tear that trickled down her cheek. Then she walked with Sunny down the path to Mage Keep. When she peeked back, the path had curved, and all sight of the wagons and her friends was gone.

Lark inhaled the fresh autumn air, but it didn't help calm her nerves. The pit in her stomach had only grown larger. She had to admit she was afraid of what the future held.

All her life she'd longed to become a mage. She'd watched her mother, Rhea, struggle to live up to the legacy her grandmother left as a healer.

Lark had been too young to meet her grandmother, Simone, but she had her to thank for the talent she possessed. According to her mother, Simone had just enough talent to make her healing spells work, but little enough that the mages turned her away from training.

Her mother had possessed no talent and couldn't match any of the miracles Simone performed while making a name for herself as a healer in Southmoat, but she didn't let that stop her. She spent her whole life learning herbal lore, finding ways to heal with the earth, just as surely as Simone healed with magic.

Lark had vowed to continue her family's mission. The power she'd been born with was much stronger than her grandmother's. Once she was trained, she could live up to the legacy of the women in her family. When she came across another poor child on the brink of death, she would be ready. She would make her mother proud.

She looked forward, steadily plodding down the forest path. Half a day's walk to the keep, Daus had said. She was almost there.

She needed this. On her own, all she'd used her powers for was death. Her head sank, her gaze drifting to the leaf strewn dirt footpath. Would the mages even allow her to train after learning she'd used her talent to murder?

Despite the question, she didn't regret her actions. Pax had been a beast. She would kill him a hundred times over for the pain he'd forced on Tiora.

And her stepfather Gael. A part of her wanted to cry when she thought of what she'd done to him. But then she remembered all he'd been party to. Stealing their home. Selling her into slavery. Killing Conall. Anger and hurt spread through her just thinking about it, paining her like a wound left to fester.

He deserved the death she gave him.

Did that make her irredeemable?

Lark was so lost in thought that at first, she didn't notice the forest coming to life all around her. It was the screeching bird cries that finally made her notice the strangeness surrounding her.

All the creatures in the forest were on the move. Squirrels and hares sped past, squeaking and squealing as they hopped through the underbrush. Birds took to the sky, a cacophony of sounds filling the air as they squawked noisily.

She gulped, realizing where they were all headed. Away from Mage Keep.

From somewhere ahead, a howl tore through the air, sending shivers down her spine. Sunny stopped in her tracks, her ears perking up and her fur bristling.

"Turn around."

Lark shook her head. That was only fear talking. She buried the fear deep down and stepped forward. She'd made her decision. She wasn't going to let anything stop her from becoming a mage. "C'mon, Sunny. Something's happening at the keep. Maybe we can help."

Sunny whined, her tail tucked between her legs, but she followed.

"Run. You have to run!"

She took another step, ignoring the voice. She was done being afraid.

A blur dropped down from the sky and streaked past her eyes. She jerked back, her legs wobbling as she staggered on the uneven ground.

"Muse?" Her brows shot up as the bird slowed and landed on a low branch in the forest beside her.

"Don't you ever listen? I said run!" She hopped along the branch, her wings flapping nervously.

Lark gawked at Muse, rubbing a hand on her temple. *"What the blazes? I'm going mad."*

"You're not crazy. I don't know how or why, but I can talk to you now. There's something happening where you're headed. I can see it from the sky. Something evil has been unleashed, and it's spreading. If you don't turn back, you'll be killed."

Her head spun. Could it be... was this bonding magic? Was she really talking to Muse?

A second howl split through the sky. Sunny cowered and backed away down the forest trail.

"See. She feels it, too. We have to go!" Muse bounced on the branch and spread her wings, her stare glued to where she and Sunny stood on the trail. *"Turn around, you stubborn girl!"*

"No, I can't turn around. I'm almost there." She cursed under her breath. *"What if we can help them?"* She lifted her foot, taking another step forward.

"Stop. You can't help them. Not from this."

Footsteps thundered up the trail. She whirled around, her chest thudding in time with the footfalls as she waited for the person making them to appear.

"Aren?" Her heart skipped a beat. She didn't think she'd see him again for months.

He skidded to a stop. His short blond hair was wind-tousled, and his pale skin was red with exertion. "Lark. I was searching for Muse." He paused, panting. "She took off like she spotted a blizzard brewing. I'm not surprised she found you."

"You can make eyes at each other later. We have to move."

Lark swallowed. "I... Something strange is happening. Muse, came to warn me."

Aren's brow furrowed. "She came to warn you?"

"Yes, I can hear her in my mind."

His gaze flicked between them, then he nodded. "Bonding magic."

"You don't think I'm crazy?"

"No, it makes sense. The way you are with her. The way birds quiet when you sing. I believe you."

Lark smiled, warmth blooming in her chest.

"C'mon. We have to go. Now. If you won't run to save yourself, then do it for them. Save your friends back at the wagons. Save Aren. They're in danger, too." Muse rose into the sky, hovering for a brief instant before lifting into the air. *"Run."*

"What's she saying?" Aren gazed at Muse in flight, his head tilted and lips parted slightly.

"Run. We need to run." She sucked in a breath, her feet glued to the spot. She couldn't abandon her mission. Not again.

Aren strode forward, grabbing her hands. "Lark, I know you mean to be a mage, but you can't go to Mage Keep now. There are more people in this world with talent that can teach you. Come with us to Raimire. I'll help you find someone to teach you. I promise." He dropped her hands but didn't take his eyes off her.

She stared back, her mind racing. He could be right. She knew little about the world beyond her own country. She had a choice. She could race headlong into danger, hoping to find a mage still alive after facing whatever mysterious evil that had Muse and the rest of the forest animals fleeing, or she could run to warn her friends and try to find someone, somewhere, who could guide her in the future.

Lark searched herself, taking stock of her own feelings. She had to admit she could sense it, too. Something was wrong. It was there just beyond her grasp, wriggling across her shoulders, like a pair of eyes watching her from the woods.

She drew in a deep breath. There would not be a repeat of that day so long ago in Flamesmoat. She'd had a goal that day, the same as she had now. She'd ignored the voice that whispered something was wrong. Not today. Today would be different. She remembered the promise she'd made to herself in that tiny, barren warehouse back room. It was time for her to trust her own instincts.

She took off running. Sunny and Aren followed, all three of them with an eye on the sky, watching as Muse led them away from the keep and whatever evil had been awakened.

Chapter 24

"You arranged this as a distraction? What were you thinking?" Disgust tinged Kayda's voice as she stared at the battle spread out before her in the blood-red moonlit night. Hundreds of people swarmed Kings Keep, like scurrying mice fleeing floodwater.

The castle guards were spread thin, struggling to keep up with the sheer number of invaders. As she watched, a pair of guards were overwhelmed, crushed under the mass of bodies that poured in relentlessly. Yet others held their own, using their skill and superior weapons to spray blood through the air, hacking limbs, felling the enemy, one after one, mercilessly.

Bile stung the back of her throat as it dawned on her. There were no skilled warriors among these attackers. The common people of the city were attacking, and they were being slaughtered.

Vespen turned to her, his white hair lit vibrantly by the full moon. "You misunderstand, Princess. We arranged nothing. We merely used an inevitable event to our advantage."

Kayda shook her head. "What do you mean, inevitable?"

"Flamesmoat has been simmering with anger for weeks. Their beloved king was attacked and imprisoned. The castle guard beating down any who speak or act against them, filling the prison in Southmoat full to bursting. It was only a matter of time before their rage boiled over."

Her heart sank. She needed to get in the keep. But how could she countenance slaughtering her own people to clear a path?

She could see no way around it. There was an immense crowd surrounding the back entrance, kept at bay by a half dozen guards on the ground blocking the way. They would have to pass through a hail of arrows raining down from archers posted high on the keep walls to even make it that far. Then somehow, they would need to convince those guards to pause their bloodlust long enough to let them inside.

She gulped. "Please tell me you have a plan?"

"I'll get you to the doors, my lady." Vespen reached into his pockets, pulling out fistfuls of soil. "Stay close to me. Keep up with my pace, no matter what." The soil flew from his hands and scattered through the air in all directions.

A tingling sensation slid over her skin. At first, Kayda stared in confusion, wondering how the flying debris could help them, but then the dirt took shape and formed a sphere around them. She grinned, admiring the ingenuity of the earthen shield.

"Let's go." Vespen started forward. The sphere moved in sync with him, large enough to protect both of them, so long as they stayed within a few paces of each other.

Before long, they were in the middle of the fray. "Make way," Vespen shouted at the top of his lungs. All around them, people leapt aside, fear and shock painting their faces as they spotted the magical shield barreling toward them.

Most people had a healthy respect for mages, and they backed away reverently. Most, but not all. Kayda winced as a tanned man approached them, his face full of rage, a wooden cudgel held menacingly above his head, aimed at them.

Vespen saw him, too. The man swung the cudgel, his battle cry ringing hoarsely through the air. A clump of soil broke free from the shield and flew through the sky to strike him between the eyes. He staggered backward, his cry and assault interrupted, dropping the cudgel to scrub his face.

A rain of arrows flew through the sky. Her heart lurched as silver death winked in the air, coming closer. The shield kept them protected. The arrows hit the top and ricocheted off harmlessly.

But the rest of the crowd was not so lucky. Bodies fell all around her. Cries of agony filled the night.

A man beside them was struck in the eye. Droplets of his blood passed through the shield. His warm, wet blood sprayed Kayda's face before his lifeless form crumpled to the ground.

"Move!" Vespen took advantage of the confusion to shove his way further through the crowd.

Kayda buried the urge to vomit and tore her gaze from the dead man's body, panic driving her feet to move. She had to keep up with Vespen. Keep up or die.

All around her, people fell. She forced herself to ignore the screams and the gore. Death did not touch them beneath their shield. They were safe amid the madness.

Yet with every arrow turned aside, every projectile Vespen sent to displace another maddened attacker, their shield shrank. By the time they neared the door to the keep, the few paces of space they'd started with was gone. They stood shoulder to shoulder, the sphere reduced to a dome hovering close to their faces, the debris no longer protecting their legs.

Luckily, they didn't have far to travel, and the rain of arrows was no longer a threat this close to the handful of guards that held the door. She spotted one ahead. His metal armor was painted red with blood, his body never resting. His swung an axe and wielded a shield he used with just as much vigor, deflecting blow after blow and shoving folk back violently.

The guard spun sideways. His axe slammed into the chest of the man ahead of them with a wet *thud*. He lifted a metal-clad foot and kicked the man in the stomach, dislodging his axe. The kick sent the man tumbling into them, his dead weight rebounding off the remnants of the earthen shield. The rest of the debris fell to the ground, leaving them exposed.

The guard finally paused. Though she couldn't see his face below his helm, surprise was evident in his body language and clear in his voice. "Princess Kayda?" He sprang back in motion immediately. He snatched her away from Vespen and shoved her behind him. "Get her in the keep, now."

Kayda refused to retreat. "Vespen!" Her arm shot out as she desperately searched for the mage in the crowd. Her heart dropped to her feet. He was gone, already lost in the seething mass of people.

A second guard appeared a heartbeat later. His arms wrapped around her waist like a vise and he towed her away from the crowd and opened the keep door. He tossed her inside.

Tears stung her eyes as she landed hard on her behind on the cold stone floor. The door slammed shut, leaving her alone in the dimly lit corridor.

Her breath came flooding in gasps, chest heaving. She scrambled backward, her back smacking the corridor wall. The solid mass at her back helped calm her. She couldn't fall apart now. She clutched her chest, forcing her breath to slow. This wasn't over. She had to get moving.

She rose to her feet. Her heart was heavy as Vespen's face flashed in her mind. She took a step toward the door, the muffled sound of the melee outside reverberating in her ears.

Kayda turned from the door. No matter what guilt she harbored for Vespen's fate, she could do nothing to save him. She rushed through the keep in a daze, her familiarity with the building steering her feet while her thoughts jostled all around.

Somehow, she ended up in the library, the dusty tomes overpowering the scent of blood lingering on her skin. She snatched a candelabra from the wall and placed it on the floor, her shaking hands coaxing the hearth embers back to life.

Glass shattered with a crash. Screams and clashing steel roared in her ears. She couldn't move. She was transported back into the battle, watching from below the shield as death rained down from the sky and bodies fell all around her. Her breath quickened, her heart pounded as the wounded were trampled by their fellows. The dirt ran red and squished beneath her boots.

"*No.*" She clutched her chest. "*Make it stop.*"

She saw the man beside her, the one destined to catch an arrow in the eye, still alive and moving toward the keep. Only this time it was not some random man—it was Vespen. Her soul screamed as the arrow lodged in his skull. Vespen's hot blood splattered across her face. His body crumpled to the ground. "*Please, make it stop!*"

"*You're not in battle any longer, my friend. It's over.*"

The calm voice snapped her out of her daze.

"*It's over and you have to find me.*"

She shook her head, listening. Though the clamor from outside had not calmed completely, it had lost some of its intensity. It wasn't over, but her part in it had ended. She had work to do.

"*Yes. Yes, you're right. I'm coming.*" She lit the candelabra and rose to her feet.

Soon, she found herself standing before the locked door in the forgotten basement chamber. The one that called to her. It called to her still.

This is where she would find her bondmate. She could feel it in her bones.

She turned the knob. The metal was no longer smooth but rough and rusted. Nevertheless, it held fast. She had no skill as a lock pick, but she did have one advantage. The door was wood.

She smiled, cupping her hand around one of the candelabra's three flames. She drew in a deep breath, a chill sinking into her skin. Then the door burst into flames.

She backed away. The water-damaged bottom ignited quickly. The top took a moment to catch before finally succumbing to the flames. While the fire ate away at the wood, a problem arose she'd not anticipated. The chamber was slowly filling with acrid smoke.

Kayda coughed, holding the sleeve of her tunic to her nose. It became harder and harder to breathe. Her throat felt raw, and her eyes stung, but she waited, watching smoke curl through the air as the door burned.

She could take it no longer. Letting out a hacking cough, she concentrated on the wooden door. She pulled at the flames, forcing them to move. Fire floated toward her, leaving the door a pile of crumbling ash at the bottom and smoldering char above.

With a thought, she extinguished the floating flames and strode forward. Using her boot, she tamped down the smoking ash on the ground. Then she bent, and lifting the skirt of her turquoise dress with one hand and the candelabra with the other, she carefully shimmied through.

She stood and smoothed her skirt, a lightness in her chest as she took her first breath from the other side of the door. Then she shivered, holding out the candelabra. Smoke curled through the air in the darkened tunnel. The walls, floor, and ceiling were made of packed dirt and stone. She could see no end of it. It appeared to go on forever.

Her heart sped up. Was she really going to do this? March into a darkened corridor that could lead anywhere? What if the walls collapsed, burying her beneath the castle? No one would ever find her.

She sucked in a breath, setting off another round of coughing. She staggered away, heading forward. At least she would leave behind that blazing smoke. She had to believe the walls would hold. Finding her bondmate was all that mattered.

The tunnel curved and wound through the earth. She walked for what felt like forever. Eventually, she rounded a bend and gasped as she spotted a problem. There, before her, sprawled a pile of stone and dirt that almost completely blocked the tunnel.

A small opening sat at the top of the piled rubble. She clambered up the rough stone and lifted the candelabra, squinting into the darkness. It appeared to lead somewhere. If she lay down on her stomach, she could squeeze through.

There was one problem. The candelabra was too tall to fit. She extinguished two candle flames, trembling as the darkness crept closer. Plucking the single lit candle from the center of the holder, she shoved the candelabra into the bag she'd slung over her shoulder.

There was only one way this would work. She would have to push the bag ahead of her while holding the candle, and then shimmy down the narrow passage on her stomach like a worm wriggling through the dirt. She gritted her teeth and put her plan into action.

Her bag was nearly too big for the small opening; it blocked much of the tunnel ahead of her. Her stomach roiled with discomfort. Only being able to see the scant bit of space between her and her bag was maddening.

Dust rose to choke her with each movement. She squirmed along, trying her best to ignore the sharp rocks stabbing at her belly and legs.

Before long, her entire body was inside the hole. She slid further. Would her next move cause another rockfall? The jungle people of Raimire buried their dead. She shuddered. Thankfully, she'd been born where cremation was the norm.

Time seemed to slow, the way it always did when she was doing something detestable. She tried to stay calm, to remind herself that every tiny lurch forward was one step closer to freedom. One step closer to finding her bondmate.

Then she felt it. The tickling of an insect crawling across her back. Panic overcame her. Immediate and visceral panic.

"Ahhhh!" Kayda shoved forward, heedless of the rocks stabbing her. She slammed her back along the top of the tunnel wall. Dust and debris rained down in a cloud. She had to knock it off. She had to escape.

Her heart hammering, she tossed her bag forward—and it slipped out of her grasp as it fell. Finally! Her breath flew out in a rush. The passage opened ahead. She scrambled forward. She clutched the edge of the opening and pulled herself free.

She tumbled straight down and landed with a jarring *thunk*, her head slamming into something hard. Pain screamed at her. She lost the candle, and the light snuffed out, leaving her shrouded in a darkness so complete it stole her breath.

Blazes.

She grappled in the dark, searching for the candle or her pack but finding only rock and dirt. Then she remembered the crawling sensation on her skin and snatched back her hands. Kayda curled into a ball, terror seizing her. She swept her hands all over herself, frantically trying to rid herself of the crawling bugs.

Get them off. She had to get them off!

She couldn't do this. She needed to see. She needed fire.

All of Izora's warnings came flooding back. Never summon without a source. Remember the cost. The terrible cost.

She didn't care. She would go mad if she had to spend one more instant in this unending black. She gulped a steadying breath and summoned.

Ice filled her veins as a fist-sized ball of fire appeared floating in the air in front of her. Relief washed through her, along with a wave of exhaustion. If she'd been standing, she would have fallen, but luckily, she was still curled on the floor. She wobbled instead, her eyes heavy and her body as weary and spent as a newborn babe.

She struggled to push through the exhaustion. Her teeth chattering, she forced her eyes open. She skimmed her gaze over her body and almost wept with relief. No bugs. Then she shifted her focus beyond the flame and shuddered.

She perched atop a pile of rubble on the tunnel's right side. To the left lay a huge, deep hole in the floor. She gasped, staring down into the cavernous pit.

Her bag was nowhere to be seen. It must've fallen, lost in the earth. Her clothes and food were gone. Worse still, her treasured tinderbox. She exhaled shakily. It could've been worse. She could be the one who'd vanished into that gaping maw.

White wax winked in the corner of her eye. Carefully, she crawled toward it, away from the hole. As her fingers wrapped around the skinny taper, she said a silent prayer of thanks. Pulling the floating flame toward her, she lit the candle with it and extinguished the flame.

The worst of the exhaustion lifted immediately. Her skin warmed. But a bone deep weariness lingered as she stood.

She shook her head. Couldn't be helped. She'd needed fire in that moment as surely as she needed air to breathe. Without it, she could've joined her bag in the pit. A little fatigue was a fair price to pay.

Kayda continued her trek through the tunnel, the light of her single candle barely enough to stave off the shadows. Her weary body dragged her down with each step. She needed rest. Sleep. But she pressed on, sheer determination keeping her feet shuffling forward when all she wanted to do was sink down and close her eyes.

At long last, she stopped before a doorway. Another door loomed there, identical to the one she'd burned at the start of her search. The thought of having to breathe in that choking smoke again started a phantom tickle in the back of her throat. She reached out, twisting the knob.

It turned. She bowed her head and sighed. Then she pushed.

Inside was an enormous chamber. She couldn't see the entirety of it with the scant light of her single taper, but she could sense the size of it nonetheless.

The trickling of water whispered in the distance. A musky scent assaulted her, the odor pungent after so long spent with only moist earth surrounding her.

And from deep within, she sensed something else. Movement. There was someone inside.

She crept forward cautiously. "Hello?" she called out.

"Ah, you made it." The voice in her mind sounded pleased. *"Come in, quickly. I need your help."*

Though she squinted in the dim light, she couldn't see her bondmate yet. She walked a few steps farther into the chamber, her pulse racing.

This was really happening. She was about to meet her bondmate.

Her foot connected with something on the dirt floor. Her gaze slid to the ground as it skidded away.

She gulped. A bone.

Another step. Another. Then her jaw dropped, her eyes blinking furiously.

She must be dreaming. Surely, she'd laid down in the tunnel and let the exhaustion lull her into a dream-filled slumber. This couldn't be real.

She stared into the room, her heart hammering madly. And from the shadows, a creature of myth stared back, eyes red as the flame of her candle.

Her bondmate was a dragon.

Chapter 25

Night had fallen as they waited on the ridge. The red moon rose high in the sky over the Abandoned Lands. Conall and Shadow sat with the five old mages off to the side, under guard.

The pulsating wall glimmered in the moonlight as the young mages and the castle guard roamed up and down from Mage Keep. They carried up boxes of all shapes and sizes. And weapons. So many weapons. For someone convinced there was nothing to fear beyond the Palisade, the prince certainly wasn't taking any chances.

Conall grimaced and rubbed his hands to warm them, ignoring the twinge of pain that shot out from his tightly bound wrists.

He wished they would get on with it. He still wasn't sure what part he had to play in this whole debacle, but he was cold and angry and sick of waiting. If Ereni was so set on the wall crumbling, then let it. He just wanted to get off the ridge and as far away from Mage Keep as possible.

He tore his gaze away from the hypnotic Palisade and found his stare drawn back to her. She talked with Prince Tarquin on the other side of the ridge in hushed tones. He swallowed hard as Tarquin placed a hand on her back and smiled down into her face.

Blazes, he'd been so stupid! How could he have trusted a girl he'd only known a few weeks with so much of himself? His stomach churned with disgust. He deserved this. Every awful feeling roiling within him. He would never make that mistake again.

"Brother, look. I think they're ready."

Shadow was right. The path from the keep was empty, the ridge crowded with everyone milling about among the stacked boxes and weaponry. Anticipation was heavy in the air.

Ereni strode forward, staring at the men standing guard over their group. "Stand them up and bring them forward toward the wall." She spoke in a commanding tone, her voice clear and unwavering. "The wolf and my mother stay."

His heartbeat surged as the man behind him grabbed his elbow and shoved him up onto his feet. Why was he being led to the Palisade? He was no mage.

"You don't have to do this, daughter," Delyth said from the ground. "It's not too late to change your mind."

Ereni ignored her, turning her back and strolling up to where he stood with the four mages, a handbreadth away from the pulsating wall of magic. "To break the Palisade we need four mages. One strong in each of the four elements." She strode between them, her gaze flicking between them as she spoke. "When all four mages join together with one strong in bonding magic"—her stare slid to him, and his stomach burned—"then, and only then, will the magic be broken."

That was why she needed him here. It all made a sick kind of sense now. She had never cared for him at all, only for his magic.

He shook his head. Suddenly, he wanted nothing to do with her plans. "I won't do it."

Ereni quirked a brow, her lips curling into a twisted smile. "Won't you?"

Shadow growled. The guard beside him held the rope leash in one hand and a sword at his neck with the other.

Ereni continued, "You might want to reconsider that, or you'll be searching for a new bondmate when this is all over."

She knew him too well. There was no way he could stand by and watch Shadow be killed while he had a chance to do something about it.

"Leave him alone. I'll do what you want."

She nodded to the guard, who dropped his sword from Shadow's neck. Then she turned her attention back to the mages. "Do I have to remind you what you have to lose? All the children, all of your families. They go free as soon as this is done."

The mages peered around, their fearful gazes connecting with each other's and one by one landing on Delyth.

"It's all right," Delyth said, her voice firm. "You don't have any other choice. No one will fault you for your actions here tonight."

Ereni pulled her hunting knife from her belt sheaf. She walked past each mage and sliced through their bindings.

She saved Conall for last. He stared at her, his face cold. As she reached forward to slice his bindings, her fingers brushed his skin, and he recoiled.

She opened her mouth as if to speak, and her eyes filled with a glimpse of something he couldn't name. As quickly as the look came over her face, it vanished, replaced with a solemn stare. Her mouth slammed shut. Then she grasped his hands and tore away the rope from his wrists.

She stepped away, gone from his side before the rope hit the ground. He rubbed his wrists, his gaze returning to the behemoth of a wall before him.

"On my mark, place your hands flat on the Palisade," Ereni's voice boomed behind him.

He gulped, his heart beating madly.

He was really going to do this. All of Gael's warnings came rushing back. Would he still be the same man when this was over? It didn't matter. Shadow had saved his life. He would be a coward and a snake if he wasn't willing to return the favor.

He looked to the side. All the mages held out their hands, just short of touching the metallic gleam. He mimicked their stance, thrusting his hands forward. What would it feel like? He didn't have long to speculate.

"Now."

His skin made contact, and his face lit up with awe, goosebumps sliding over his skin. He'd expected the surface to feel cool, but it was warm. As warm as a rock that sat soaking up the sun. Even more strangely was how it pulsed, echoing the beat of his heart. Like something alive.

Suddenly, the wonder vanished. Pain rose to fill the void. Pain so intense it stole his breath. He hadn't thought he'd ever feel worse than on the day he'd fallen, his body bruised all over and pierced through with an arrow. But this—this was so much worse.

His every nerve ending was alive with fire. His bones rattled beneath his skin. He wanted to scream but couldn't. His jaw clamped shut. He closed his eyes and moaned instead, praying for the wall to fall before it killed him where he stood.

He opened his eyes to a changed world. He was floating. All around him, in every direction, the Palisade's metallic gleam filled his vision. The pain was gone. So was the ridge, Mage Keep, and all the people who stood watch over him.

"Shadow?"

Panic flooded his chest when his bondmate did not reply. Wherever he was, he was alone.

No. Not alone.

From afar, he spotted something. Someone adrift in the magic like him. He squinted, unsure of who he was seeing, as they floated on the Palisade's undulating surface. If only he could get closer—

He gasped. The idea had barely formed in his mind before he found himself beside the far-off form.

His heart thumped wildly. How was that possible? He pushed the thought aside and took a closer look at the figure beside him.

It was Amora. She floated freely, eyes closed, her face calm and slack, as if asleep. He grabbed her shoulder and shook. "Amora. Wake up."

Her lashes fluttered open. She eyed her surroundings before turning to him. "Conall? Where are the others?"

He shook his head. "I don't know." Then he looked around. Off in the distance, he could just make out another figure floating.

This was it. This was his purpose in this strange void. He had to bring them together.

"Hold on." He grasped Amora's hand. Then he wished they were both beside the floating figure.

It worked! He grabbed the man and jumped again. This time, he found a woman. They jumped once more, with all the mage's hands linked. They roused the final man, and finally, they were all together.

"What do we do now?" asked the man he'd collected on the second jump. He looked older than Amora, his wrinkled skin deeply lined, his bushy white eyebrows raised in question.

Amora thrust out her hand. "We summon."

The words had barely escaped her lips before a ball of water formed on her outstretched palm. The other mages followed suit. The old man held out a ball of fire. The second woman materialized a ball of dirt, and the final man a ball of swirling vapor.

A flurry of sensations filled Conall as he floated beside the mages. His skin tingled from within and prickled on the surface, moisture and cold surrounding him. But despite the strangeness filling the void, nothing changed.

Then he felt it. The surface he floated on began to weaken. His gaze roved around as the shiny substance blurred.

As the void responded to the magic, its shimmering gleam dimming, the pulsating gyrations growing erratic and wild, a new feeling crawled across his skin he couldn't explain. The unmistakable sensation of being watched.

He jolted around erratically, searching for the source of his discomfort. There was nothing but the endless metallic sea. No matter how much he looked, he couldn't shake the squirming itch.

Was something there with them, watching?

A flash of the real world intruded into their shared vision. He saw himself and the mages from behind, all still holding tight to the Palisade. The onlookers gathered around, watching, their eyes stretched wide with horror.

Then the scene disappeared, gone before he could delve any further.

His stomach contorted. Why did their faces look like that? What was so terrifying?

"Conall. Come back." Shadow's voice reached him within the crumbling void, his usual calm tone now frantic. *"You have to come back now."*

His bondmate's terror set his nerves on edge. He could feel it, too. Something was wrong. He had to do something.

The Palisade needed to fall, now.

He stared at the mages. The balls had tripled in size. The void drew on their power, sucking at the elements held in their outstretched palms. They kept summoning, their faces the picture of deep concentration.

He stretched out his own hands, turning them over, staring at his palms curiously. Ereni had said he could summon. Maybe he could tip the scales. But how?

He recalled the way he'd jumped through the void. It had been so simple, action following thought. Could this be just as simple?

There was only one way to find out. He stared at the mages, watching the balls growing slowly. So slowly. He pictured each of those elements rising from his own hands. Then his mouth fell open as power took shape before his eyes.

On his right palm, an orb of fire warmed his flesh. The gently swirling wind tickled his fingertips. His left palm held a cool orb of water, and the earth's heavy weight floated above his left fingertips.

The sensations that started as the mages summoned intensified. His body thrummed with power.

All around him, the void responded. The gleaming fabric of the Palisade grew fuzzier. Weaker. He remembered Shadow's plea. He needed to do more.

He glanced at his hands, and a thought crossed his mind. He had to bring the mages together. Maybe he needed to bring the elements together, too?

He moved his arms close to each other until his palms were cupped together side by side. The power responded, the elements swirling quicker.

He gasped, as the balls conjured by the others responded in kind, creeping closer to each other as they expanded. His body shuddered, his teeth chattering. Yes, this was right. But it still wasn't enough.

He hesitated. The itch was still there, slithering across his skin. The phantom watched with great interest. Though he still couldn't see it, as the Palisade weakened, he could sense a presence there with them. Its sickening glee. It wanted this. For the Palisade to fall.

Indecision battled the certainty from just moments before. The magic on his hands swirled slower, the balls shrinking.

He took a deep breath and slammed his hands together. The elements collided. He was buffeted by a power so intense he lost all sense of time and place. Something inside of him screamed. It was a mistake! He was being destroyed.

Then he blinked. He was back on the ridge. He had just enough time to note the gorgeous scenery, visible again, before he collapsed.

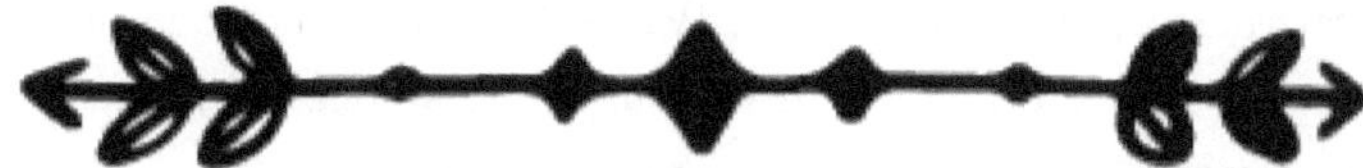

He came to sometime later. It couldn't have been long; the ridge was still swathed in moonlight. People shuffled around uneasily, wearing shocked expressions and staring in his direction.

His mind was fuzzy, and the pain had returned with a vengeance, weighing down his limbs and making it hard to breathe. He sprawled out on the ridge, and someone pressed on his chest. He groaned, staring up into the handsome, dark face of a young man he vaguely recognized.

"He's waking." The man removed his dirt-covered hand from his chest. "I think he'll be all right, eventually." He stood and walked away, joining Ereni's side.

That's right. He was one of the young mages that helped carry the boxes and weapons earlier. Most of them still crowded around Ereni, but a few had broken off to tend to him and the mages he'd joined in the void.

He turned his head sideways, hoping to see the mages awakening as well. The sight he was met with was much grimmer than he'd hoped for. His stomach lurched.

Closest to him lay the oldest man. He was clearly dead, his body emaciated and shrunken. His expression was far from the calm concentration Conall remembered seeing last. Instead, his features were locked in agony.

The man's death stare brought tears to his eyes. He couldn't even remember his name.

Helpful, kind Amora lay with the others he'd barely known but who had helped him break free from that strange, undulating dream world. None of them had made it.

Tears welled in his eyes, the hope he'd held in his heart disappearing just as surely as the magic wall had. If only he'd realized what needed to be done sooner, had he not hesitated, maybe he could have saved them.

A commotion broke out somewhere behind him. The next instant, a warm weight settled by his side. Shadow.

"I heard you calling for me." His head tilted sideways, the fuzzy feeling wrapping around him again. *"Thank you, brother."*

"I'm here for you always, little brother." Shadow looked down at him, his muzzle still wrapped in rope, golden eyes filled with relief. *"You've been through a lot. Rest."*

His eyelids were already drooping. Sleep rose up to claim him.

When he woke next, daylight filled the sky. Two burly men in white robes lifted him atop a long wooden stretcher. Shadow sat beside him, his bonds removed, watching the men as they worked together to place him on the rough boards.

"Shadow, what's happening? Where are they taking me?"

"Good. You're awake." Shadow's tail wagged. *"I think they mean to bring you down this hillside. You're in no condition to do it on your own right now. Just relax and let them do the work for you."*

Conall tried to lift his arm and swallowed hard when it barely rose off the stretcher. He had the strength of a newborn lamb. He resigned himself to being carried.

A face appeared, hovering over his own as soon as the men had him situated on the stretcher. Delyth, the Sade Prim, peered down at him, her piercing blue eyes soft as they connected with his. "Thank you for what you did back there. I know it must have been an incredible trial."

The men stood, one at the foot and one at the head of his stretcher. He rose in the air with a groan. They began walking, jostling his body painfully with each step. They took ten steps before they both froze, their gazes locked on something far off on the horizon.

He lifted his head as much as he could bear. It caused pain to shoot down his spine but afforded him a view of what the men were watching.

His blood pounded through his veins. Down on the beach, where the campfire still burned, men the size of ants ran around screaming. Something was attacking them.

"Hurry," Delyth ordered. "We don't have long now."

"What?" he croaked out, his own voice sounding strange in his ears.

"They'll be everywhere within a few hours. Our only choice is to flee." Delyth kept pace with the men as they tramped down the ridge, back to the keep. "Most of the others have left already, heading for the mountain passes. I'm taking you with me. I'll need your help in Doln."

"Doln? I can't go to Doln." He shook his head, the motion sending a wave of dizziness through his body. "I have to find my sister. That's all that matters to me now."

"Do you know where she is? Do you have even an inkling?"

His stomach wobbled at the reminder. "No."

"What if I told you I knew a woman who could help you find her? The Winter Witch of the North."

He scoffed. "I'd tell you I don't believe in legends and myths."

"She's real. As real as you or I. She'll help you find your sister."

He shook his head again, groaning with pain as he tried to pull himself to standing and rise on his own two feet. "I don't believe you. I'm done with you mages. Shadow and I will find Lark on our own." The stretcher wobbled. The men struggled to keep it steady while he attempted to climb free.

"Lie back, Conall of Greenvale. You're as stubborn as a mule. Just like your father."

The words sent shock flooding through his chest. He fell back, lying still on the stretcher. "You knew my father?"

"Knew him? I know him still."

No, that couldn't be right.

He frowned. "That's impossible. He's been dead for more than a decade."

"I'm afraid you're mistaken." She stared down at him, and he spied the truth written on her face. "Come with us, help me reach the Winter Witch, and I'll tell you where to find him."

Could it be true? Was his father alive? The thought sent a surge of feeling through him. Anger and elation warred within him as he imagined seeing him again. He had to know. He owed it to himself and Lark to find out the truth. And if he could learn his sister's fate at the same time? It seemed he had no choice but to follow Delyth to Doln to seek the Winter Witch.

"She wants us to go with her, through the mountains to the north. What do you think? Should we trust her?"

"Trust her... No. But she is right about one thing. We need to leave. Do you feel that?" Shadow stopped suddenly, letting out an ear-splitting howl.

"What was that for? What are you talking about, brother? I feel nothing but pain." Even as the thought faded, a shiver slithered up his spine. There it was again. That odd tickle in the back of his skull that told him he was being watched. Shadow could feel it, too?

"I have to warn them. All my brothers and sisters out there. Whatever that was on the beach—it's coming." Shadow lifted his muzzle and howled with all his might.

Chapter 26

They caught up to the wagons outside of Bogsmouth. Muse sat atop her perch on the wagon, awaiting their arrival. *"Hurry, we're still not safe here."*

Surprise and delight painted the faces of the show members as they spotted Aren, Lark, and Sunny tearing into the clearing.

"Lark, you're back." Tiora beamed. But the smile fell from her face as she noted her friends' panicked expressions.

"There's trouble," Lark said between gasping breaths, "headed our way." She clutched her stomach, doubling over. "We have to leave, now."

"Leave?" Mazen's brow arched. "We just got here. And this town is always generous with tips."

Dausius hopped down from the colorful wagon and approached them quickly. "What's the trouble?" He reached out a hand to rub her back and stuffed a waterskin in her hands with the other. "Calm down, have a drink, and tell us everything."

She straightened and set the waterskin to her lips, gulped a few quick swallows, then tossed the skin to Aren. He caught it and began drinking while she recounted their tale.

"When I got close to Mage Keep, all the forest animals started going crazy. Running away from something."

"Yes, we saw it, too," Dausius replied.

"That's when Muse found me." She paused, her stomach in knots. "And she spoke to me."

"Lark, have you been drinking?" Mazen asked with a laugh. Meital shoved an elbow in his side, looking annoyed at the interruption.

"Bonding magic." Aren chimed in, handing the skin back to Dausius.

Lark stared at Dausius. His body was still for once, but she could see the wheels turning in his mind. He had to believe her.

Mazen was the first to speak, his voice incredulous. "You have bonding magic *and* elemental? I didn't think that was possible..."

"If Lark says she heard Muse speaking, then I believe her," Tiora said to Mazen, hands on her hips.

"I do, too." Dausius' hands shot out. He grabbed her arms and stared down into her face. "What did she tell you?"

A weight lifted off her shoulders. He believed her!

Her words came out in a rush. "She said some evil had been unleashed and that it was spreading. If I kept heading to Mage Keep, I would be killed. She told me to run." She glanced at Muse, remembering her final warning. "She says we're still not safe here."

Dausius turned to stare at Muse; she shifted from foot to foot on her perch. Whisper was behaving the same way. Both of the birds seemed ill at ease, their heads and eyes jerking all over on high alert.

He whirled back to her, his brown eyes searching her own. "All right. We run." Dausius spun her where she stood, turning her toward the wagons. "Hop in." Then he scooped up Sunny and deposited her inside the plain wagon before hopping into the front of his own. "Follow me closely, girls," he called back as he mounted the driver's bench and grabbed the reins. "We'll head straight for the docks."

Aren jumped into the back of Daus' wagon as it started moving, nodded to Mazen and Meital, and headed over to calm the birds.

Tiora held the reins for their wagon, but she reached over and squeezed Lark's hand as Lark settled next to her on the bench. "I'm glad you're back."

Dausius set a punishing pace. The wagons rattled over the cobblestone streets of Bogsmouth. This town was one of the largest they'd been in, but not nearly as big as Flamesmoat. People dove out of the way of their speeding wagons, cursing and shaking their fists.

Bogsmouth was full of fishermen, perched on the edge of the Boglands that bordered the Kingdom of Dracwood to the south. The Boglands were rumored to be dangerous, filled with carnivorous beasts, but that didn't stop the people of this town from reaping the riches of their waters. The smell of fresh fish filled the air, and Lark spotted a marketplace to the right of their path that appeared to be thriving.

Laughter bubbled in the air. As they rushed around a corner, she spotted the source. A schoolhouse sat to their left. Dozens of children played a game of tag in the yard. Lark's stomach clenched, and she shared a look with Tiora. "Shouldn't we warn them?"

Tiora shook her head, placing a hand on Lark's. "Do you think they would believe you without any proof?" she asked gently.

Lark frowned, her heart shattering. She knew she was right, but it didn't stop the sick feeling stabbing her stomach. She exhaled, tearing her gaze from the schoolhouse.

Soon they approached the dock section of town. Unlike the crowded streets near the marketplace, this area was practically deserted. Dausius pulled his wagon to a stop beside a rickety wooden dock on the far edge. He didn't even wait for it to come to a full stop before he hopped down, heading straight for a fellow sitting in a worn wicker chair.

"Dal, how good to see you, my friend." He sauntered forward with his arms spread open in welcome, a wide grin plastered on his face.

The man rose from his chair, holding up a tanned arm to shade his eyes from the sun. He was fit and trim, dressed in mud splattered overalls, his feet bare, and he appeared to be about the same age as Daus. "Dausius?" His brown eyes squinted. "That you?"

"Yes, it's me. I have a proposition for you. How would you feel about ferrying my friends and I through the Boglands?" He pulled out a coin purse, jingling it noisily. "I'll pay double if we can leave immediately."

Dal quirked a brow. "Make it triple, and you've got a deal."

"Done," Dausius agreed readily. "We'll need at least two boats. Do you have another sailor who can join us?" He tossed the coin purse through the air.

Dal caught it, hefting the bag a few times before stuffing it into his pocket with a smile. "Sure do. Let me grab my boy, Fillan. You and your folks can load what you want to bring in the two biggest canoes down at the end of the dock." His gaze skimmed over the wagons as he walked away from the dock to fetch his boy. "Two ought to handle it, if you pack light. Unless you want to bring the horses?"

"No, they'll have to stay with the wagons, I'm afraid," Dausius announced.

Mazen's face fell. He'd always taken the lead in caring for their horses each night.

Dausius noticed. "Horses don't last long in the jungle, son," he said quietly. "I'm sorry."

Mazen looked sick, but he nodded, then grabbed a crate from the wagon and carried it down the dock.

"All right." Dausius turned to address them. "Let's get those boats loaded. Only bring what we need. Food, a few changes of clothes, props for the show."

"And the animals." Aren grabbed a box and set off down the docks.

"Yes, of course." Dausius climbed into the back of the colorful wagon, dumped out a large bag, and started throwing things around, stuffing clothes and various props inside while discarding others.

Lark counted herself lucky she'd already packed. She grabbed her bag and whistled for Sunny to follow then settled both in one of the boats at the end of the dock. She returned to help with the food, carefully treading on the dock's shifting boards.

With everyone working together, they filled the boats quickly. Lark was just settling down next to Tiora in the largest canoe when Dal came back with a young man who looked like a younger version of himself. He even wore matching overalls and bare feet, though his skin was not so darkly tanned.

The man strolled up to the canoe she was in. He hopped in with a smile. "I'm Fillan. Nice to meet you all." He glanced around the boat, an expectant look on his face.

Tiora jumped in, making introductions. "Hello. I'm Tiora, and this is Lark and Aren."

They all exchanged nods, then Fillan's face lit up as he spotted the birds and Sunny sitting behind them. "You're bringing your pets, too?" His smile widened. "This ought to be fun."

Lark stared beyond Fillan. Mazen stood alone next to the wagons, unhitching the horses.

Fillan glanced over curiously. "Aren't you folks going to sell those horses and wagons before you leave? My dad could get you a good price for them."

"No," Aren said. "We have to leave now."

"Mazen." Dausius rose to his feet on the second boat. "Get on board. We're leaving."

Mazen gave each horse a gentle pat, then sprinted down the dock and hopped into the smaller boat with Dausius, Meital, and Dal. Meital threw her arm around his shoulders as he sat, squeezing tightly. Then Dal and Fillan stood in unison, untying the ropes that kept the canoes tied to the dock.

Lark sighed as they pulled free from the dock. They'd made it.

Then the screaming started.

They'd just pulled free of the docks when the sound blew in on a cool breeze. "What in the world?" Fillan peered back toward Bogsmouth. "Wonder what's going on back there?"

Though they steadily moved through the water away from town, the screams only grew louder. All of them stared in horror at the shore, their eyes peeled for the cry's source. Lark's heart thumped madly, the smiling faces of the children they'd passed on their way to the docks fresh in her mind. What was happening back there?

Movement on the dock's far side captured her attention. Her breath caught as a young woman staggered into sight. Her face was crazed, and she screamed at the top of her lungs. Her arms flailed about wildly, clutching her body.

Something was on her. A blur of motion climbing across her chest.

"What is that?" Tiora's eyes widened with terror.

Lark shook her head. She'd never seen anything like it. The small creature was barely bigger than a squirrel, with brown and silver-striped fur, sharp fangs, and claws. The creature tore a path across the woman's chest, slashing and biting her hands as she desperately sought to dislodge it. As the poor woman opened her mouth to scream again, the creature struck, launching on her face and viciously tearing out her tongue.

Lark's stomach lurched as the woman's screams stopped and she dropped to the ground. The creature held fast, tearing at her face relentlessly.

"Bloody blazes, what is that thing?" Fillan stared at the shore, his brown eyes round. Then he gulped as more creatures came bounding into sight. "How many are there?"

Lark blinked twice, not trusting her eyes. There were so many. Dozens bolted toward the fallen woman, covering her body in a blanket of writhing fur. Others spotted the horses where they stood on the edge of the docks and raced toward them.

The creatures were on them in an instant. Though the horses bucked and brayed with all their might, it was no use. They were overwhelmed by the sheer number of creatures piled atop them, tearing and biting at their flesh.

"I don't believe it," Dal said from the boat beside them. "The scourge. I thought it was just a legend."

"Is that what this is, then?" Dausius asked. "I suppose it must be."

"You know what those creatures are?" Lark grabbed Tiora's hand, clutching it tightly.

Dausius nodded. "There's a legend in these parts about creatures who lived long ago. The people here call them the scourge, but they have many names... *ichneumon*... dragonkillers."

Meital gasped, her arm wrapped tightly around Mazen, who watched the horses being slaughtered with teary eyes. "Those things could kill dragons?"

Dausius pitched his voice loudly, moving his hands animatedly, like when he told stories at the show. "They were said to be fast as lightning, fearless, and full of an insatiable hunger. They'll eat anything that moves, but they delight in finding and devouring eggs. Especially dragon eggs. They could even take down a fully grown dragon, sliding down their throat, tearing them apart from the inside."

Suddenly, the boat she was in lurched backward. Lark tore her gaze from Dausius and spun in her seat to find Fillan shoving a long wooden pole into the bottom of the bog. Tears streamed down his face.

"What are you doing?" Lark asked, her voice shrill.

"We have to go back." Fillan pushed again on the pole. "We have to help them. My friends..."

Tiora stood and placed a hand on his arm. "Listen. It's already too late."

Lark listened, too. She was right. The screams had died down. The scourge had already torn through, decimating the large town in mere moments. Her stomach heaved. All those people. The children.

Fillan broke down, sobbing. Aren stood slowly, the boat wobbling as he removed the pole from Fillan's shaking fingers. "I'm so sorry," Aren said as the boy sank down into a seat, holding his head in his hands.

"Aren." Tiora's eyes bulged, her hands twitching. "I hope you know how to use that pole."

Lark leaned sideways, sweat dripping down her spine. Their canoe still drifted toward the docks. The dragonkillers had spotted them. At least a dozen raced along the rickety structure, their beady eyes watching as the boat glided ever closer in the calm water.

"I'm on it." Aren shoved the pole into the bog, grunting. They stuttered to a stop, then slowly reversed direction.

Lark shivered as the creatures raced to the end of the docks. The one in the lead ran at breakneck speed. Its gaze connected with her own, and she yelped. It was going to jump!

It splashed into the bog barely an arm's length away from where she sat, spraying her face with droplets and disappearing below the murky water. She scrambled back from the side of the canoe as it resurfaced.

Her gaze locked on it, and she trembled, fighting off the nauseous ache that invaded her body from its stare. She stared into its eyes and saw the moment panic set in. It began to struggle. Then she exhaled a shaky breath as it bobbed up and down. The ravenous beasts had at least one flaw. They couldn't swim.

The dragonkillers backed away, making no attempt to save their drowning brethren or to reach the canoe as it steadily picked up speed.

Lark sat still in the canoe as her heartbeat slowed, her mind roiling with conflicting emotions. She was relieved, and so intensely happy to have escaped the savagery that had befallen that town. She looked to Muse, her heart filled with gratitude. There was no question she'd saved her life. All of their lives.

Some part of her had been in disbelief as she watched the scene unfold, but now the gravity of the mayhem she'd witnessed sank in. Those things were a menace. They would tear through the Kingdom of Dracwood, laying waste to everything in their path.

A lump formed in the pit of her stomach. If they'd made it this far, did that mean the mages had already been destroyed? If the strongest among them had fallen, what chance did the rest of them have?

Her heart broke for her friends back in Greenvale. All the gentle souls she'd sang for on their trip across the country as the Wandering Bards. The thousands of people in Flamesmoat. They had no idea what was coming for them.

Chapter 27

Kayda stared wide-eyed in disbelief. She had to be dreaming. She was standing in front of a dragon—and he needed her help?

"Come on, don't be shy. We've shared our thoughts already. Meeting in the flesh should be a simple matter."

She gulped. The single candle flame flickered in her shaky hands as she took a step closer. Her bondmate was covered in black scales that blended into the darkness so well she couldn't accurately gauge the size of him. Based on his head alone, she imagined he must be incredibly massive, at least the size of a small house.

She had every right to be afraid standing before this beast, but she took another step, the fear she expected completely absent. Something within pulled her closer until she stood beside his enormous head.

"I'm Kayda." Her hand reached out as if it had a mind of its own and stroked a hard, smooth scale on his jaw. *"What's your name?"*

"Kayda. It's a little short for my liking, but I suppose it shall do. I am Druturion the Black. Pleased to meet you, Kayda." He leaned into her touch, the motion so forceful it nearly sent her tumbling backward.

The name struck a chord within her. *"Druturion the Black,"* she repeated.

"It is a bit of a mouthful for you humans, I'm told. If you prefer, you may call me Dru for short."

That was it. *"My ancestor Algernon rode a dragon he called Dru..."*

Druturion snorted, and his breath sent her skirts swirling round her legs. *"Yes, yes, we're one and the same. He's pleased to meet you as well."*

Kayda stepped back. Her heart skipped a beat. One and the same? *"You can't mean... but that would make you five centuries old, at the least."*

"Hard to believe, I know, but entirely possible with magic on your side. I'll explain it all when we have the time. But now, we have to get out of here."

She nodded, feeling his urgency through the bond. *"What do you need me to do?"*

"I'm a fire dragon. We don't just spit fire, we need to ingest flames in order to keep up our strength. Could you bring that flame of yours closer?"

Kayda strode forward and lifted the candle up next to one giant, crimson eye.

"No, that won't do. It needs to be larger. Do you have anything else we can use as kindling?"

She shook her head, regretting the loss of her pack. *"No, but I can make it bigger with magic."*

"Good, do it."

Kayda took a deep breath and concentrated on the flickering candle. Instantly, it grew larger, the flame quickly becoming the size of her head. She wobbled on her feet, cold seeping into her skin, and the exhaustion returning with a vengeance. She ignored it, holding the candle aloft. *"How is that?"*

"Good, that should work nicely. Drop it in." His massive jaws opened, revealing a set of huge, sharp teeth that glimmered like deadly icicles in his dark maw.

She gulped but followed his instructions, dropping the candle in his mouth and stepping back. A heartbeat later, his jaw snapped shut, bathing the room in darkness.

Her heart jolted in the black room. She cursed herself for not thinking to leave herself some light. The thought had hardly crossed her mind before Dru swallowed and dizziness washed over her.

The next thing she knew, she sprawled on the ground in the dark, her mind swimming and eyes fluttering open to a world of black.

"You didn't tell me you conjured the flame on that candle. Stupid girl. You could have killed yourself, summoning without a source."

She sat up, cradling her head in her hands. *"Blazes, you don't have to yell. My head is already killing me."*

"Well, at least you won't have to worry about finding a source very often now." He opened his jaw, and she glimpsed a light—a flame—radiating inside his throat. The room was lit enough for her to see again, though much of the enormous chamber remained swathed in shadow.

She rose to her feet, her body feeling strangely heavy. Dropping her hands from her head, she patted her chest, her eyes widening as she palmed the rounded flesh that had somehow grown larger. She took a step, and her legs wobbled. Was she taller, too?

"You're not going crazy. You look a few years older, I'm afraid. The price you pay for summoning without a source."

She gasped, her hands roving around her body. Bloody blazes, of all the times to be stuck without a mirror.

"It's not too bad." Dru's voice was heavy with amusement. *"You were very young to begin with. I'd say it's actually a bit of an improvement."*

"I'm glad you find this funny," she said, trying her best not to scream. Although he had a good point. How many times in the past had she lamented that no one would take her seriously because of her age? Still, she couldn't help feeling like a stranger in her own skin.

Dru stood, and she stepped back, craning her neck, gaping as his head brushed the ceiling.

"Ah, yes. I haven't felt this strong in ages. Quick now, climb beneath me. I'm going to put a hole in the ceiling. This place is much too crowded."

She lifted a foot to follow his instructions, but set it down in the same spot as a thought flickered in her mind. Too crowded. Crossing her arms, she stared up at him. *"Wait a moment. How many bonds have you had?"*

Dru stiffened. His head tilted as a single eye fixed on her. *"Including you? Five."*

"Five?" Kayda's stomach sank. Her grandfather had struggled with two voices in his head. Now she was bonded to a dragon who had four other voices distracting him. What could go wrong?

"It's no challenge for a dragon, I assure you. Now get beneath me before you're crushed by the ceiling."

Kayda rushed forward, ducking beneath his neck and sliding between two clawed feet until she was hunkered down below Dru's chest. Then he rammed his head into the chamber ceiling, and dirt and debris rained down around them. The ceiling trembled with the force of his strikes. She covered her face with her sleeves, holding her breath to avoid choking on the dust swirling in the air.

He struck a half dozen times before a hole appeared in the roof and sunlight flooded into the chamber. She blinked and shielded her eyes from the light. A few more strikes of Dru's massive head, and the hole looked wide enough for him to stick most of his body through.

"That ought to do it," he declared. *"Well, what are you waiting for? Hop on my back. Let's get out of here."*

Her heartbeat picked up speed. She was about to ride a dragon.

Kayda climbed out from beneath Dru, using the piles of dirt to boost herself high enough to grab his long black neck. For a girl who spent much of her childhood climbing trees, it was no challenge. In fact, it sent a strange thrill racing through her as she perched atop his back. Her turquoise dress bunched up around her thighs as she wrapped her arms and legs tightly around his neck.

In the sunlight, she could finally get a good look at her bondmate. What she saw made her eyes widen with wonder. His black scales were not fully black at all but shimmered with flecks of purple, green, and blue. He was indeed as large as a house, but his body wasn't bulky. His long limbs, enormous wings, and svelte torso seemed almost feline in strength and agility.

"Are you ready?" Dru's body tensed beneath her.

Kayda's heart thumped against her ribs. Her skin tingled with anticipation. Part of her still couldn't believe this was real. But the greater part was alive with joy. She was going to ride a dragon!

"Yes, I'm ready."

Dru hopped up from the hole in the ground. A single leap was all it took to send them bounding free of the earth. They landed in the old decaying cemetery bordering the Church of the Dragon.

Kayda smiled. She'd always doubted the church's teachings, but no longer. The certainty she always longed for had found her last night. There was no denying she would have a part to play in the future of her country.

The church door flew open with a bang, and a group of priors clambered out, their faces filled with wonder. Some were crying, others smiling and laughing. A few dropped to their knees, while others clumped together, clutching each other, jumping and hugging.

She ached to stay, if only for a moment, to bask in the joy on their faces, but Dru was already tensing again, preparing to take to the sky. Unfurling his black wings, he pumped furiously. He took two running steps forward, and on the third, they sprang free from the ground.

Tears flooded her eyes. How many times had she wished for this? Countless times spent watching birds in flight, her heart longing for just a small taste of that freedom. The wind flew through her hair, and the world grew smaller as they climbed. And her heart soared with them.

"Who were those men back there in the robes?" Dru pulled to the left, circling the city from above. *"I would've thought the first humans to see a dragon would be quaking with fear, not filled with delight?"*

Kayda stared down at the ground, wondering what Dru was searching for. *"Those were priors from the Church of the Dragon."*

He stopped dead in the air and hovered in place. Kayda jerked sideways, the sudden stop almost sending her rolling off his neck. A sound filled her mind as Dru rumbled beneath her.

Was he laughing? The thought of his many bonds returned to plague her. Was this the first sign of madness?

"Church of the Dragon," he repeated between bursts of laughter. *"You humans will pray to anything, won't you?"*

She bristled, frowning. *"They were right, you know. They said dragons would return one day, and here you are."*

The laughter quieted as he continued circling. *"All right, all right,"* he mumbled angrily.

Kayda held on tightly, her stomach churning.

"I'm sorry," Dru blurted out. *"Algernon tells me it's not polite to mock your religions. I'll be more tactful in the future."*

His apology calmed her racing nerves, if only a little. *"It's all right. Tell me, what are you searching for?"*

They still circled. The city was so small from above. The destruction of the battle in Kings Keep last night stood out in stark relief, but from the looks of things, the castle guard had fought off the worst of the onslaught. Her heart felt heavy, thinking of all the people who'd lost their lives last night.

"I don't see any sign of the scourge. Good, they haven't made it this far."

"The scourge?" Kayda could feel the tension in Dru as the name filled her thoughts. Her body tensed in response. What could scare a dragon?

"You'll see, soon enough. If I've awakened, then so have they. The Palisade has fallen." He pivoted, heading east. Soon, they left the city behind and raced above the forested hills of the Kingdom of Dracwood, toward Mage Keep.

"Tell me, Druturion. I have to know what we're facing."

"Vicious little beasts. A horde of them. I can feel them. Their murderous glee. Their hunger." Panic laced his voice, and his body trembled beneath her. *"They're responsible for the destruction of my brethren. We have to burn them all."*

Her fingers clenched around his neck. What could be so awful, so terrifying, it sent panic through a creature so strong? And how could humanity possibly survive when these mythical beasts had fallen?

They blasted through the air. Her thoughts swirled, dampening the elation that had flooded her as they first took to the sky. She didn't know what to expect, but some part of her, deep inside, quaked with fear. Would she be ready to face the scourge?

Her breath caught as Dru suddenly picked up speed, descending like an angry bolt of lightning tearing through the sky. *"They're here."*

She craned her neck sideways, spotting a town perched on the Bogland's edge. She knew this place—Bogsmouth. Her grandfather had brought her to visit once before. She'd marveled at the open air fish market and admired the small town charm and friendly people.

As they flew closer, she saw all was not well in the small fishing community. Every street swarmed with chaos. Tiny, brutal creatures were everywhere, attacking everything that moved. The scourge.

Dru swooped down on the dock's edge above a large crowd of the silver and brown-furred beasts. His jaw snapped open, and fire blasted through the sky.

Her heart leapt as the first of the creatures burst into flame.

Dru hovered, bathing the beasts with flame.

The scent of singed fur and roasting flesh rose through the air. The piercing screams of pain flooded her ears.

Kayda spotted mangled corpses on the ground; the back of her throat clogged with saliva as she fought the urge to be sick. The people of this town had all been massacred. They were too late. Her soul filled with an anger so intense it burned from within.

From the corner of her eye, she spotted movement heading her way on the rooftops. Cold rage surged within her. Burning with righteous vengeance, her hand shot out. She pulled on the flames that made their home within Druturion's chest, and they answered. Fire flowed from her palms, scorching the creatures that loped toward them. Their beady little eyes filled with fear as the fire licked their skin.

Yes, they would burn them all.

They raced through the city, laying waste to every beast they found. Finally, the crowds of creatures began to thin, but Dru did not relent, painting the town red with fire. Suddenly, he stopped and landed in a large square.

Kayda recognized the space as the same open air market she'd marveled at so long ago. The smiling townspeople she remembered crumpled dead on the ground, their corpses barely recognizable as people, the flesh torn clean from their bones and covered in ash.

Dru strode forward on the ground, approaching a group of burning scourge. Their dying shrieks filled the air.

What was he doing?

He dipped his head, heedless of the fire still burning the creatures, and scooped them up inside his massive jaw.

Kayda held on for the ride, bobbing up and down on his neck as he went back for more, the crunch of bones loud in her ears.

"Shouldn't we be moving on?" She coughed, eyeing the burning buildings warily.

Dru stiffened and shook his head. *"You try sleeping for hundreds of years and not being a little hungry after,"* he said, sounding a bit irritated. But he left the rest of the creatures to burn and lifted back into the sky.

Within moments, they flew above Mage Keep. She'd been here before, too. The mismatched buildings looked deserted from above. She could see no movement in the streets from either people or the scourge.

Though she could see nothing, it didn't stop a strange sensation from scrambling up her spine. The further they traveled, the more the feeling spread, worming through her veins. It was almost as if something watched her approach. Some specter peering over her shoulder, waiting.

They climbed higher in the air, and finally, she spotted movement. There, beyond the cliffside that had once held the Palisade wall, a group of mages and soldiers in full metal armor had built a large circle of magic and fought from behind it.

The sight brought a tear to her eye. Someone had stayed to fight. But it was obvious from above the mages were losing. The scourge had them surrounded, their protective bubble slowly diminishing. They struggled beneath the onslaught of thousands of the beasts that threw themselves at the group relentlessly.

Dru saw it, too. He swooped down and flew in a tight circle around the group. Fire flowed from his mouth, burning the scourge from above. A cheer erupted from the people below, and her heart filled with pride. She added her own flames to the sky, sending the creatures skidding back from the group. They'd earned the mages a momentary reprieve.

"Can you land beside them?" she asked. *"We have to help them."*

He slammed down a moment later. The mages faces were filled with astonishment as she dismounted, her boots crunching on ash and stomping out cinders. A man jolted forward and pulled the metal helm from his face. A man she recognized.

"Kayda?" Tarquin's jaw hung low as his gaze flicked over her body. "Is that you? On a dragon?"

"Tarquin. What did you do?"

The bastard had the audacity to smirk. "Oh, you don't like what I've done with the place? It'll make a great port town after a little pest control. Come to help, have you?"

Kayda breathed in deeply through her nose, itching to slap the smile off his face. "You fool. You bloody, blazing fool. How could you be so stupid? You've condemned the whole world to deal with this evil, so you could build a seaport?"

"Don't be so dramatic, sister. We'll have this all under control by day's end. Just watch."

"Under control?" She shook her head. "You've already lost, and you don't even know it."

A brown-haired mage pushed forward, rolling her shoulders back and blinking rapidly. "What do you mean, Princess?"

"We just came from Bogsmouth. The scourge destroyed the entire town. They've already spread."

The mage's face blanched, the blue of her irises shrinking as her pupils dilated. She turned to face Tarquin. "It's over. We have to retreat to Flamesmoat."

"Retreat to Flamesmoat? Don't be ridiculous, Ereni. We have these creatures on the run."

"Kayda, get back now," Dru said, his mouth opening and spewing forth flame as the scourge circled back with a vengeance.

"Listen to her, Tarquin." Kayda raced back to bound atop Dru's back. "Retreat while you still have a chance."

Dru took to the sky.

"C'mon, let's clear a path for them," she said.

He swooped down again, and they both got to work shooting flames at the ground. More and more scourge popped free from the ground, swarming toward the group. All the while, that strange tingle slid over her skin, like eyes on her back she couldn't shake. They circled once, twice, three times, until they had a clear path away from the field and toward the forest bordering the keep.

The mages departed, leaving Tarquin and the guardsmen behind on the field. She cursed inwardly. The idiot was going to get himself killed.

She should be grateful to be rid of him. He'd plotted to kill her grandfather. And he'd never treated her like anything more than a nuisance and amusement, but she found herself absurdly upset at the thought of him dying at the hands of these vicious creatures. No one deserved that kind of death. Not even him.

"Take us closer," she ordered, holding tight to Dru's neck. He complied and hovered in the air near the guardsmen.

"Tarquin, please. Listen to reason," she yelled down from atop her perch on the hovering dragon. "I can't protect you from all of these creatures, and the mages are retreating. You have to join them."

His laughter set her stomach on edge. "You don't have to protect me. We men can handle ourselves."

The guardsmen's answering whoops reverberated in the air.

She couldn't help it any longer. She screamed. The stupid idiot of a man! He would lead them all to their deaths.

The guardsmen backed away in the face of her rage but did not move to retreat.

Fine. If he was set on dying on this bloody field and she couldn't stop him, then she at least wasn't going to let him go out without a fight.

"Let's burn them all down, Druturion."

He flew forward, flames spewing from his mouth. *"With pleasure."*

They blazed across the sky in ever widening circles. Their magic rained down on the scourge, sending all who touched it to a fiery death. The crowds began to thin. They were forcing them back, making them think twice about rising from the ground to quench their unfathomable hunger. For a moment, she thought it might be enough to save her brother.

Fear grabbed her, seizing her mind. The ghostly presence she'd nearly forgotten surged around her like a crushing wave. Her heartbeat thrashed in her ears. Then her heart shattered as dozens of the vile creatures broke free from the earth beside Tarquin's group. *"Dru!"* she cried out, *"Please, we have to help them."*

He spun in a flash, but Kayda could see it was already too late. Their circling path had driven them too far, and the dozens swiftly turned to hundreds. Their massive numbers overwhelmed the small group of guardsmen. In the blink of an eye, they collapsed under a wave of gnashing teeth and writhing bodies.

The last man fell, and something inside of her—something primal—screamed its rage into the sky.

Magic pooled within her, like ice in her blood. The fire burned, raging on the tips of her fingers. As they raced to the mound of fallen men and squirming, raving beasts, she thrust out her hands and screamed. Fire rained down, pouring out of her hands like a wave of death. She gripped Dru with her legs, her teeth bared and nostrils flaring.

Together, they set the scourge on fire.

Chapter 28

They floated just beyond the docks, neither Dal nor Fillan making any effort to quicken their speed as grief for all the people they'd known and loved in Bogsmouth filled their faces.

Aren crouched beside her in the canoe. "Are you all right?" Lark gazed at him, and he must have seen something in her eyes. "I know what you're thinking, but we can't go back there. Not now."

A shadow blocked the sun for a brief instant, casting their boat in darkness. Lark looked up, her heart hammering. That was no cloud.

A dragon!

He raced across the sky, then swooped down close to the shore. Fire rained down on the scourge from above. They writhed beneath the flames, shrieking in agony.

Her breath caught. Some of the creatures had made their way to the rooftops. They were going to spring on the dragon from above.

Wait. A chill crept up her spine.

A second set of flames blazed to life, stopping the beasts in their tracks. The dragon tilted, and Lark's heart filled with hope. Atop the dragon rode a young woman in a blue dress, her red hair streaming behind her like a flame flickering in the breeze. Fire flowed from her fingers, her face fierce and fearless.

Lark stared at that girl and made herself a promise. As surely as that brave girl fought, she would do the same. She might be running scared right now, but she vowed to return. She would scour the jungle for someone to teach her to control her powers. And one day, she would return to help free her country from this blight.

Her face brightened as the heat from the shore drifted across the water to warm her skin. She would see her homeland again.

"How did you know?" Dal's anguished voice reached her from the second boat. He scrubbed his face and rubbed the tears from his cheeks. "How Dausius?" He stared at him, and the pain she glimpsed in his eyes tore her apart.

"I once knew a girl. Just a slip of a thing. But she had a voice..." Dausius smiled sadly, gazing off into the distance. "I've never in my whole life heard her equal. We traveled together in a different show. I was only a lowly puppeteer, but she, she was the star. People from all over were filled with laughter and tears when they heard her. Her voice was so moving, so sweet."

Dausius swallowed, a frown spreading on his face. "Then one day, she grew ill. The leader of the show wanted to leave her, find a replacement. But she and I, we'd become very close. I refused to leave her to die alone." He sighed, flicking his hand dismissively. "So, they left us both. I stayed with her, held her hand. And I was there in her final moments as she took her last breath."

"That's a sad tale, but what does it have to do with anything?" Dal's brow furrowed. "I asked you how you knew those things were coming."

"I'm getting to that. You see, what I forgot to mention was this girl, she didn't just sing. She had many talents. And when a person with certain talents is close to death, they often see glimpses of things that have yet to pass."

Lark leaned forward, open-mouthed. She'd told him about the future?

"I told her, as she lay there dying, traveling the world with her was my greatest accomplishment. That nothing I did would ever meet the same measure." He closed his eyes, the sad smile painting his lips once more. "She was so weak by that point, barely holding on. But all of a sudden, she sat straight up in bed and gripped my hands with the strength of two men. She stared into my eyes. And the words she said to me, I'll never forget."

Everyone was leaning in now. Even poor Fillan had dried his tears and stared at Dausius expectantly.

Dausius' brown eyes rolled over their boat and landed directly on Lark. "'You have much more left to do,' she said. 'One day, you will meet a songbird. Three times, you will set her free. Listen to her, trust her, help her fly. Together, you will save the world.'"

Lark sat back, her hand flying to her chest. Everyone turned to stare at her. She shook her head in disbelief.

Dausius cleared his throat. All eyes flicked back to him as he continued. "So, when I finally heard another voice that moved me the same way hers did, I listened." He grinned, looking at the twins and Aren. "We set her free. And when that girl"—his voice choked up, tears in his eyes—"our songbird, told me to run, you're damn sure I listened."

Tears welled in her eyes. Could any of that be true? Was she destined to save the world?

She glanced back at the shore. The whole town was bathed in flames. The dragon and rider were nowhere to be seen. Flames and smoke filled the sky as tears streamed down her face. It all seemed so unlikely. Would she ever have power like this? The power to render a whole town to ash?

Aren reached over and held her hand. She smiled at him, at all of them. She didn't know if she would ever be ready to save the world. But at least she had a few friends she could rely on. Whatever the future flung at them, they would face it together.

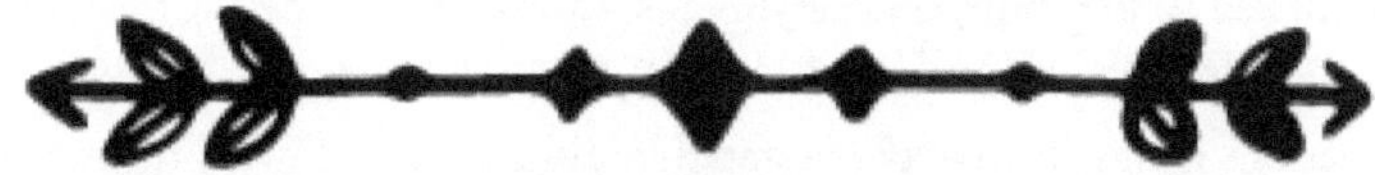

Conall awakened with a start, his breath clouding up before his eyes. He shivered, his nose filled with the scent of smoke. He raised his arm, sighing as it lifted easily and without pain.

"Brother, you've slept half the day away. How are you feeling?" Shadow sat next to him, watching over him.

"Much better." He sat up and rubbed his eyes as he gazed at his surroundings. He was on the stretcher on a mountainside in a large clearing. A few dozen people milled around, mostly children. Some of the youngest played nearby, oblivious to the anxiety filling the older children and handful of adults. *"Where are we? Where are the mages?"*

"We headed north, then they set you down with these people and turned back. I'm not sure why."

Conall stretched, his body stiff but free from pain. He lifted his tongue and winced as he tried to swallow. He grabbed his waterskin, hefting it and finding it empty.

"There's a small lake nearby. I can show you," Shadow offered.

He nodded and followed Shadow through the trees. A few people stared at them but made no move to stop them.

The trees at this elevation were sparse, affording a clear view of the land below.

Conall gasped. It was all on fire. Smoke filled the air, and flames undulated unchecked like a wave of red as the forest burned. Living in a forested country, he was no stranger to the odd forest fire, but this—this was like nothing he'd ever witnessed.

The mages were always called on to contain fires when they erupted. With their mastery over the elements, they could contain even the largest of blazes easily. Dousing it with water or soil. Stilling the wind so the flames would not spread. Even pulling the flame straight from tree trunks and extinguishing them with a thought.

This had to be deliberate. Was this why the mages had disappeared? To build a wall of flame to slow the enemy? A pit formed in his stomach. How frightened they must be if they were willing to set their home ablaze.

What of the mages and guardsmen who'd chosen to stay behind? His chest still burned when he remembered Ereni's betrayal, but deep down, he still felt a connection to her. Would she survive the inferno and whatever evil had awakened?

His thoughts drifted to his sister, and the pit in his stomach grew larger. What if she was out there somewhere, on her way to Mage Keep? Would she get caught in the crossfire?

He closed his eyes briefly and said a silent prayer for Lark. She had to be safe. He opened his eyes, clenching his jaw tightly. He would find her.

The lake lay ahead. Shadow raced forward and dipped down to lap at the water.

Conall hurried to join him, submerging his waterskin into the clear, cold water and draining it quickly. As he knelt down for a refill, he froze.

His reflection. It was all wrong. He stared in disbelief and slowly lifted a hand to his face.

Bloody blazes!

"It happened while you touched that wall," Shadow said. *"You changed as quickly as snow melting in the sun. I'm sorry, little brother."*

The youthful face he'd worn yesterday was gone. The skin on his forehead and around his eyes was wrinkled. His brown hair was full of scattered gray strands. He raked his fingers through his hair and captured a single strand between his fingers. He lifted it up to the sun, inhaling sharply. It shone silver in the daylight.

He shuddered, remembering the emaciated bodies of the mages who'd helped him destroy the Palisade. In a way, he'd gotten off easy. If they'd taken longer in that strange, glimmering void, he could've shared the same fate.

Still, he couldn't help feeling cheated. His stomach ached. Would Lark even recognize him when he found her?

He dropped the hair and watched it float away on the breeze. He sighed.

A twig snapped. Conall turned as Delyth stepped out from behind a tree.

"Well, you're looking much improved. I hope you both are ready to begin our journey," she said.

Conall rose to his feet, frowning. "You mages are unbelievable. Are you really going to leave the people of Dracwood when they need you the most?" He shook his head. "Didn't you take an oath to protect the world from evil? Why are you running scared?"

"Come, I'd like to show you something." She beckoned him to follow.

She led the way down the mountain to a group of old mages, their once pristine white robes covered with dirt, grime, and ash. On the ground beside them, an oval shape sat, shrouded with a dark blanket. The blanket swayed, and a strange snarl reached his ears.

There was something alive inside. Shadow's fur bristled, and he growled.

"It likely won't survive the mountain's extreme cold this late in the year, but the men and women of Doln will listen more closely if they see the carcass with their own eyes." Delyth lifted the blanket, revealing a metal cage with a large rodent inside.

Conall leaned closer and watched the thing cower in the cage, blinking its beady eyes at the light. Something stirred in his chest, a whisper of the same sensation he'd felt while the Palisade fell, but not nearly so strong. "Is that it? That's what has you so scared?"

The creature chose that moment to throw itself at the bars in front of his face. He flinched, backing away. Its vicious teeth snapped, and sharp claws tore at the metal.

Shadow growled at the thing, flashing his teeth. The creature showed no fear, despite facing a wolf ten times its size. Conall had no doubt it would have no qualms attacking them, if the cage were not there to stop it.

"They're called *ichneumon*—the scourge. There are already thousands of them out there, terrorizing the countryside. They've been living underground beyond the Palisade for centuries, mostly sleeping. Eating whatever snakes and mice they can find. Eating their own when they have to." Deylth glared at the creature with obvious disdain. "They breed faster than rabbits. The fire will slow them, but only for a time. Within weeks, they'll have spread throughout Dracwood. When the Boglands ice over this winter, they'll move south. And when the mountain passes thaw in the spring, they'll invade Doln."

She dropped the blanket back on the snarling beast. "The whole world is going to be swarming with *ichneumon* soon. We need time to find a way to stop them. I've sent riders in all directions with orders to send all the folk from the countryside to Flamesmoat. The ancient moat that rings the city will be lit, protecting all within."

Conall's heart thumped. "How do you know the answers you seek will be in Doln?"

Delyth marched forward and stopped before him, staring up into his face. "When I was a young woman, I traveled to Doln. I met the Winter Witch. She helped me see my future, the same way she'll help you find your sister. It's because of that vision I know I must return." She drew in a deep breath, her eyebrows raising. "Do you want to know what I saw all those years ago?"

"What?"

"I saw a girl who made the earth quake. Another girl reborn in flames. And a boy who held all the elements in his hands."

Conall's eyes widened. He hadn't told her what he witnessed while the Palisade fell. He hadn't said a word about what he'd done. How could she know?

"I saw myself as an old woman returning to Doln. Returning to the witch with two companions. A middle-aged man and a wolf."

He swallowed, his reflection in the lake flashing in his mind.

"We're meant to go there." Delyth laid a wrinkled hand on his sleeve. "I have to believe we'll find something there to help us win this fight."

Conall looked behind her at the mountain looming large on the horizon. He was so tired of worrying about the future. Would he ever find his sister? Would he, one day, be reunited with the father he'd thought dead all these years? If Doln held answers, then he was ready to find them.

"All right." Conall smiled. "Let's go meet that witch."

"What have we done?" Kayda and Dru stood atop the ridge overlooking the Abandoned Lands to the east and Mage Keep and the forested hills of the Kingdom of Dracwood to the west.

Mage Keep and the forest surrounding it had already been decimated, reduced to ash and smoldering debris. Fire and charred earth surrounded them in all directions, spreading through the forest to the west, heading inland toward Flamesmoat. Smoke clogged the air, making it hard to breathe. It was like she was living inside a nightmare come to life.

She swallowed and winced, her throat painfully dry. It had taken them most of the day, but finally, the scourge stopped coming. As the sun dipped low in the sky, the last handfuls of the vicious things had retreated, returning to the earth.

"We did what we had to do." Dru raised his neck, his nostrils flaring. *"This is not the last we'll see of the scourge. I can feel them still. They'll regroup. They'll breed. Within a few weeks, a few months at most, they'll be back terrorizing the land."*

She frowned, and her chest tightened at the certainty behind his words. It was the second time he'd said that phrase—he could feel them. His words brought back a shadow of the presence she'd felt during the battle. Had bonding with Druturion let her sense those things, too?

"Dru, how do you know so much about these things?"

His body stiffened. *"I did what had to be done back then, the same as we did just now."*

She backed up and eyed him warily. She rubbed a hand across her face, suspecting she knew what he was about to say.

"It was the only way," he continued. *"Bonding certain species lets you share abilities. It had to be done, so we could survive that long underground."*

"You bonded one of those things?" Her eyes widened as a certain word stood out in her mind. *"Wait a moment. What do you mean, we?"*

"It is very rare to find a human who can bond any species they choose. For dragons, it's much more common. I know there were others who made the decision to bond one of the scourge. We knew one day the Palisade would fall, and they would return to ravage the

world." His shoulders slumped, his red eyes staring off into the distance. *"They slaughtered my kind. Devoured every egg. Destroyed our hope for the future. We will not let that stand. I don't know where the others are, but I intend to find them."*

She sucked in a breath. Suddenly, everything made sense. His weird connection to the scourge. The crazed hunger he'd displayed in Bogsmouth. A new appreciation for her bondmate washed over her. He was so brave to do whatever it took to ensure he would live to win this fight.

And also, definitely a little bit crazy. She could barely even fathom it. How strange it must be to bond one of the creatures responsible for the destruction of his own species...

Still, she couldn't help being thankful for his sacrifice. If he hadn't been there, sleeping beneath the ground, waiting for this day to come, then the events of today would've played out much differently. If there were more dragons out there, waiting to be awakened, then they would find them. She owed it to her bondmate to help him, just as he'd helped her.

Her gaze landed back on a certain spot in the Abandoned Lands. Tarquin. All that time she'd spent hating him, wishing to stop his plotting, had all been for naught. Her mind raced, questioning everything. Every single decision she'd made that led to this moment. All the "what ifs" plagued her. She flexed her fingers, tears pooling in the corners of her eyes. If only she'd been able to figure out what he was up to sooner, they wouldn't be in this mess. Maybe she could've saved him.

Her heart twisted. He'd always been an arrogant jerk. But he was still *her* jerk. She'd wanted to stop him. She'd wanted him brought to justice for the role he'd played in her grandfather's attack. But she didn't want this. She didn't want to watch him die.

She leaned on Dru for support. Her whole body ached. Exhaustion weighed her down. But she couldn't rest. Not yet.

"What now?" she asked. *"Can the Palisade be restored?"*

"No. It took the life energy of hundreds of dragons and mages to conjure the Palisade. And it was never meant to last forever. Honestly, I'm surprised it lasted this long."

She bit her lip. There had to be some way to pen these things in now that they'd retreated beneath the earth. *"What of a normal wall? One made of stone and earth?"*

"The scourge would only dig under it, given enough time. The Palisade went down as deep as it stood tall."

She could see no other options. They had to find some way to stand and fight. *"Can you fly us back to Flamesmoat?"*

Dru tilted his head and stared at the towering inferno that was only just this morning a sea of unending green foliage. *"No, not now. The battle has me spent. I need to rest. In the morning, I could fly through the fire, but you'd never make it without air talent to clear the smoke. We can wait it out or go around."*

She shook her head, and her gaze landed on something else. A large boat anchored offshore. A Jorian shipping vessel.

It reminded her of something. She was supposed to uncover a second mystery today. Izora's hasty declaration that Prince Gideon was not her father.

But the Sade Prim wasn't here to explain. She couldn't be sure if she'd survived the fire and scourge. Even if she had, she could be anywhere by now. There was no point in searching her out if she hadn't a clue where to look. She could question Izora back in Flamesmoat, but it might take them weeks to fly around the smoke and ash.

There was one other place she might find answers. And maybe she could find some others to help win this fight while she was at it.

"Dru, I have another idea. I think it's about time I met the other side of my family. How about a little detour to Joria before we head back home? I have a feeling if the Princess of Dracwood and her new bondmate sail back with the Jorians' lost ship, they'll be willing to talk."

Dru stretched out his wings and crouched down close to the ground. *"I could use a sand bath right about now. Hop on."*

Kayda took a last look at the devastation surrounding her as she vaulted on top of Dru's back and wrapped her arms and legs tightly around his neck. She had to admit she was frightened. Who knew what she would discover when she went digging into her past? Who was her real father? Why make her a princess when she wasn't? And why did Prince Gideon, even now, believe he was the man who'd fathered her?

Despite the fear, she was ready. Ready to find the answers, no matter what they might be. And even if she discovered she wasn't a royal, maybe it wouldn't be so bad. For once in her life, she was free from all the responsibilities of royal life. She had to admit, despite all the death and destruction, she was enjoying the freedom.

She tossed back her head, her long auburn hair blowing in the breeze, and smiled. *"Let's fly."*

Epilogue

The forest burned all around her. Animals that hadn't the sense to flee were incinerated. Dense clouds of smoke clogged the air. Massive, ancient trees toppled over like saplings in a windstorm.

Ereni sucked in a breath of cool, moist air, her skin tingling as magic surrounded her. She and the young mages had a front row seat to the destruction from within their protective bubble of magic. Dozens of them worked together to do the impossible. To survive where all should be destroyed.

Wind mages cleaned the smoke. Earth mages flung dirt to deflect any fiery debris that came too close. The fire and water mages worked in concert to extinguish the flames before them so they could take step after careful step through the burning forest.

She grinned. It was a thing of beauty, to be sure. Just days ago, some of these mages hadn't even known how to summon. For so long, the Palisade Mages had made them wait to learn how to twist the elements to their will. For so long, they had to wait and pay. Pay with their very lives to maintain a dying wall of magic.

Those days were over. Now they could return to the old ways. Where young mages learned of their abilities when they needed them the most. She'd experienced this for herself years ago. How a mage could gain access to their abilities in a time of great stress and great need.

All the young mages around her had learned this, too. As soon as the scourge attacked, all of those who'd not yet manifested abilities quickly received them. And because they'd not been made to sacrifice their power to the Palisade, they were, by far, the strongest mages the world had known in many generations. Together, they would be enough to defeat the scourge. She had faith in them all.

At long last, they broke free of the wall of flame. Ereni turned back to survey the inferno they'd strolled through. The fire stretched from north to south, splitting the entire country in two. It was miraculous they'd survived. Her heart soared with pride. Just think of all they could accomplish.

She gazed at the group of mages beside her. They would never wear the white robes of the Palisade Mages, but they were all living proof that clothes and tradition were not what makes a mage. Every one of them, in their plain traveling clothes, glowed blue so strongly. All of them looked at her expectantly.

She smiled. "Baris, Oriana, head northwest. Edrik, Karina, you two go southwest. Stop in every town you pass. Tell all the people you find who haven't left already to head for Flamesmoat. The rest of us will travel straight west. We'll meet in Flamesmoat, light the moat, and make our stand."

The mages all nodded and separated quickly, leaving on their respective missions. Ereni led the way west, calmly walking at the head of the group until just before sunset.

They found themselves in a small town. It didn't surprise her to find it already deserted. They were still close to the forest fire. Most people in Dracwood knew to flee when they spotted a fire so large, even if only to wait in a neighboring town for the mages to come and extinguish the flames. Little did they know this time would not be like all the rest. This time, they had to let the forest burn.

"We'll rest here for the night," Ereni said. "Roan, you have first watch. Everyone else, spread out and check there's no one hunkered down waiting out the fire."

The mages scattered, all of them listening without complaint or question. Ereni rubbed a hand across her chest and paced down the main street until she found what she was looking for. Then she turned and entered a large building on the outskirts of town.

Perfect. She made her way into a huge, empty bathhouse. It appeared the town they were in had the good fortune of being built atop a natural hot spring. She seated herself on a stone bench in front of a shallow pool of steaming water and began freeing the laces on her sturdy brown boot.

The action brought back the memory of another night not long ago. Taking off the same boot with a set of eyes watching her every move. A bittersweet smile crossed her face.

For her whole life, she'd always tried to live without regret. To be true to herself. To follow her own heart, her own conscience. Until yesterday, she would've thought she'd done a good job of doing just that. Not any longer.

Ereni finished removing her boots. She folded her socks methodically and placed the little folded bundles atop her boots, which she set neatly beside each other.

She sighed. She couldn't stop picturing Conall's face. The way he'd stared at her with hate in his eyes when she'd threatened Shadow. How he flinched from her touch when she'd freed his hands. Her stomach churned as she lifted her tunic over her head and pulled down her trousers. She might wash the smoke and dirt free from her skin, but that look, that feeling, would not wash away so easily.

Blazes. If only she hadn't listened. If only there'd been another way.

She knew in her heart there wasn't. If he had known, there was no way he would have left with her mother while Ereni remained fighting. Not Conall. He would've stayed with her, no matter the cost to himself.

Ereni had chosen to trust her mother, the Sade Prim. When she'd said it was time, Ereni had listened. She'd done her part to set the plan into motion. And when she'd returned and her mother said Conall had to travel with her to Doln, she'd trusted her then, too. She'd done what she had to do to ensure that would happen. She only wished it didn't hurt so much.

If they'd only had more time to think, then maybe they could've thought of another plan without so much lying and subterfuge. She wouldn't have been forced to stand by the prince's side and act like she couldn't care less about Conall, while secretly her heart crumbled into a million pieces.

She sighed again, leaving her pile of neatly folded clothes behind and sinking into the hot spring's warm waters. She would regret the decision to lie to Conall for the rest of her life. But she'd needed to be the villain to save him. To save the world.

Her gaze trailed down her naked belly. At least there was one decision left she didn't regret. Her rare seer eyes had just picked up something new. Something wonderful. Radiating from her lower belly was the most beautiful purple glow.

She traced her fingers over her stomach and smiled.

AMBER L. WERNER

MUSES THAT ALIGN US

PALISADE TRILOGY

Prologue

Ereni stared at a writhing carpet of fur and gnashing teeth from behind a wall of flame. The scourge had come to Flamesmoat.

It took a few weeks for the creatures to arrive. First in numbers so small their forces dispatched them wherever they terrorized the pockets of the countryside that had escaped the unchecked wildfires. After only a few days, they were forced to retreat.

Hundreds of the vile rodents came. Then thousands. And they kept coming. Every hour that passed brought more approaching on the horizon until they swarmed the land like carnivorous locusts feasting on everything that moved.

So far, the wall of flames erected around the capital, and the Riddle River cutting through the middle, had thwarted their advance. Fire and water were all that stopped the scourge from destroying a city of tens of thousands. The mages manning the fire moat held the lives of so many in their hands, working in shifts to ensure the flames stayed lit. But one instant of broken concentration might be enough to send all their defenses crumbling.

It wouldn't hold the scourge back forever. The constant scratching reverberating beneath the roar of flames guaranteed it. The scourge were digging.

They'd posted earth mages in the ancient tunnels ringing the city, desperately seeking to shore up the underground passages, but it was only a matter of time before the relentless beasts found some hole in their defenses. Some small spot to tunnel in and catch them unawares.

"Ereni. You called for us?"

Two young mages approached. Her seer sight picked up a vivid blue halo surrounding them both.

She turned to address them, the heat from the moat warming her back while the bite of an autumn breeze nipped her face. She smiled warmly and beckoned them closer. "Edrik, Oriana, I have an important mission for the two of you, if you're up for it."

Oriana nodded, her bright green eyes eager. "Of course. What do you need?" She curled a lock of brown hair behind her ear and thrust her tanned hands near the flames, warming them.

Edrik joined her, reaching out his hands, the chill air reddening his pale skin. "I'm in, too." His blue eyes reflected red from the flames dancing before them.

"I was hoping you'd say that. There's a ship on the docks in Southmoat waiting for you. We tracked down a captain willing to sail down the southern coast. I need the two of you to journey to Raimire to seek aid."

Edrik snatched his hands back and stuffed them in the pockets of his heavy brown cloak. "I thought that route was impassable. They say it's littered with jagged reefs, and even if you can dodge them, you have to do it all while fighting the strong northern current."

"That's why I'm asking you two to go. You're the strongest water and wind mages we have. I have faith that you can guide the ship there safely."

It was partially true. She had Oriana beat for wind talent, but only just. But there was no way she could leave the front lines. Not with the scourge beating down their doors.

It seemed the tiny lie had the expected effect. Oriana tipped up her chin and flashed a satisfied smile. "When do we leave?" She pulled her dark cloak closed tightly as the wind picked up, sending her long locks blowing in her face.

Ereni flicked the tail of her brown ponytail back, her blue eyes watering in the wind. "In the morning, with the tide. That gives you the rest of the afternoon and evening to pack and say your goodbyes."

Oriana nodded once and strode away, disappearing into Northmoat. That left Edrik. She placed an arm on his shoulder, peering into his face. His brow wrinkled, his mouth drawn into a moue.

"I can find another, if you would rather stay. It's no trouble," Ereni said.

He schooled his features. The pout disappeared, exchanged for a sheepish grin. "No, I meant what I said. I'm in... it's just... I've never been sailing before. You would think a water mage would be the last person to be afraid, but the thought of being stranded out in the water has always given me the creeps. Silly, isn't it?"

"Not at all, Edrik. Fear is a strange thing. It gets the better of us all, sometimes. But I know you can do this." She squeezed his shoulder before dropping her hand and smiling encouragingly.

"Thanks, Ereni. You're right. I've got this." He set his shoulders back and turned to leave. "We'll secure the Raimish aid. You can count on it," he called as he strode off into the city.

She sighed. She could use a touch of that bold confidence right now.

Ereni frowned, taking a last look at the blanket of vermin spread out before her, then left the flaming moat. She roamed through the streets of Northmoat, dodging the tents and ramshackle lean-tos crowding the cobblestone streets. The city was stuffed to the rafters. Folk from all over the country had fled their homes, seeking the protection of Flamesmoat.

Though they'd begun to send boatloads of refugees up north to Minsport, progress was slow. Many city folk refused to leave, due in part to age-old prejudice against the Doln and also from the misguided belief that some solution would soon be found to save the city from their plight. Ereni was not so quick to assume the city would not fall. Not any longer.

She walked without choosing a destination, picking through and examining the tangled mess of plans in her mind while her boots ate up the road. As the sun sank down on the eastern horizon, she found herself standing in the first spot she'd insisted on seeing when they arrived in Flamesmoat weeks ago. The crumbling old cemetery bordering the Church of the Dragon.

The church grounds were just as littered with refugees as the city streets, but one spot of the ancient cemetery was given a wide berth by all. It was here she paused and gazed down into the gaping hole that had recently housed a dragon.

It brought back the same wave of hope that had washed over her when she first stared into the dark recesses that sheltered the majestic creature. Surely, if dragons had returned, they had a chance. They could save the world from the scourge.

Her hands clenched into fists at her sides. Humanity would survive. She would make sure of it.

The crunch of footsteps on grass rose behind her. Ereni turned, relaxing her hands and slipping them into the pockets of her brown cloak. "Hello, sire."

Prince Gideon shuffled forward, wearing a burgundy cloak and fur hat. "I see I'm not the only one who's drawn here. I still can't believe it. My girl... dragon bonded." Pride was clear in his tone, then he sighed, his shoulders slumping. "Any news of Kayda, or Tarquin?"

Ereni shook her head. "I'm afraid not, sire."

The prince hadn't given up hope for his children, no matter how many times he was reminded of the certain doom they'd faced in the Abandoned Lands. Neither of them had been seen since that day. They were all left to wonder whether they'd perished in the flames or at the scourges' hands. Every day that passed without the return of black wings in the sky made death seem more likely.

"How is the king?" she asked.

"The same," Gideon replied with a resigned shrug.

They lingered in a tense silence. Ereni could think of nothing to say, that hadn't been said a dozen times already, to comfort the man. He'd been forced to step up in a time of unprecedented danger and strife. She could sense the weight of rule chafed him.

A dark-skinned woman approached, a gray castle servant uniform peeking out beneath her unbuttoned black cloak. She hustled between tents, surprisingly spry for her old age. A dim blue glow surrounded her.

Izora's sharp brown eyes rested on Ereni briefly, but she pointedly ignored her, stopping before the prince. "Your Highness, there's been news. It's the princess. She's alive."

Gideon spun to face her, his jaw dropping. "She is? She is! I knew it." He clutched Izora's shoulders and stared down into her face. "Out with it, woman. Tell me everything."

"Seems there's a trader in Southmoat that has a fondness for doves. He's trained them to fly back and forth between here and Joria, to a cousin's house. They've been exchanging news regularly for years. The cousin sent word of a shipping vessel hugging the southern coast, on a straight track for Joria Port. A boat carrying a black dragon."

The prince listened closely, a smile slowly spreading across his face. "That's excellent. Excellent." He grabbed her arm and towed her away from the pit. "Come on, let's return to the keep. We must send for this trader. I want the news straight from the source."

Ereni smiled, watching their backs retreating in the setting sun's light. She'd come here seeking hope, and she'd found it.

She sucked in a deep breath and turned, resting her hands on her stomach from inside her cloak pockets as she headed back to the moat. It was time to do her part to hold back the invaders. Help would come. *He* would come. She had faith.

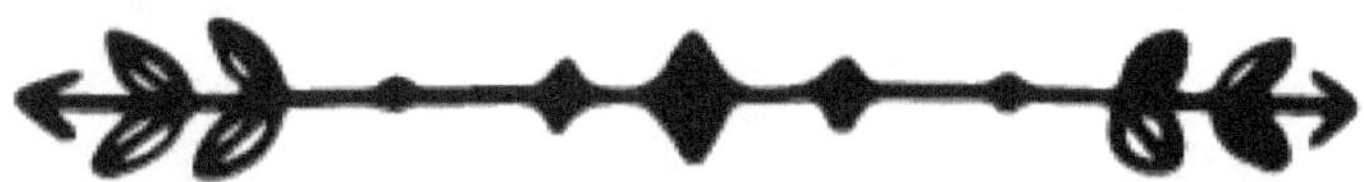

The day was bright and hot. The jungle lit with dazzling flashes of color from the flowers and creatures sprinkled amid the dewy green foliage. A symphony of bird song joined the gentle buzz of insects.

Mika stepped lightly on the overgrown footpath, his curiosity piqued by his companion's hasty demand this morning.

"How much farther?" he asked the young girl who led the way.

Ravenna had barged into his hut just after sunrise and begged him to follow, promising a mysterious creature waited.

She glanced back, not slowing in the least, her long brown braid swinging against her slim shoulders and swishing gently against her luct tunic. "It's just ahead on the coast. It's huge."

"And you really don't know what it is?" He peered at her closely.

She spared him another look, her brown eyes drifting over him appreciatively. "That's why I brought you. You can teach me." Her mouth twisted into a playful smirk.

Mika smirked back but reached out and ruffled the top of her head. "Keep your eyes on the path, and I'll teach you plenty."

She scowled at the dismissive gesture, swatting his hand away and smoothing her hair.

Mika pressed a fist against his lips, hiding his smile. He might be in the prime of his life, with a reputation as a generous lover, but he drew the line at bedding girls that still played with dolls in their spare time.

As they approached the coast, a rotten stench filled the air. He wrinkled his nose, lifting his luct sleeve to block his nostrils briefly before abandoning the action. The sheer green fabric was a blessing for keeping cool in the humid jungle and repelling the biting insects that thrived there, but it did nothing to stave off the foul odor. "What's that smell?"

Ravenna raised a brow. "Didn't I tell you? It's dead."

Mika stopped and rubbed his temple. "You dragged me out of my hut to see a dead animal?" He turned, taking a step back toward home. "I don't have time for this."

Ravenna darted around him, stopping him with her palms flat on his chest. "Please, Mika. We're almost there. You're gonna want to see this—trust me."

He should abandon this foolish errand. A dead animal. Ravenna ought to know he had live people back in the village waiting for his skilled touch.

His lips parted to tell her he was leaving, but the certainty in her eyes made him bite his tongue. He grasped her wrists and gently removed her hands from his chest. "All right, since we're almost there. Quickly."

Ravenna smiled, dashing around to lead the way. Soon, the crash of waves drowned out the chirping birds. That awful stench thickened so much he resorted to breathing through his mouth.

The trail ended at the top of a cliff. Below, the rocky shore met the pounding surf. That was where the carcass rested, brought in on the tide, no doubt.

Mika's eyes widened as he stared down at the massive beast. The bloated body was covered with gulls and crustaceans that picked apart its rotting flesh.

What was it? A whale? It was impossible to tell from up here. He had to get closer.

"I told ya, didn't I?" Ravenna said. "Just look at the size of that thing. It's bigger than my whole hut!"

"Is there a way down to the beach?" Mika tilted his head and scanned the cliffside.

"Sure, if you don't mind a climb." Ravenna walked as she spoke, her steps sure even as she skirted the cliffside's edge. "Some boys carved foot holes last summer that haven't washed away yet. Right... here." She sank down on the edge and swung her legs out below her.

Mika watched her descend until her boots thudded on the pebbly beach. Then he followed.

His heart picked up speed as he navigated the cliffside, reawakening the thrill he'd forgotten since the last time he'd made this climb as a youth. The wind whipped at his dark brown hair. He tasted salt on his tongue as he clung to the footholds, steadily making his way down. It only took a few moments until he landed on the beach, sending tiny rocks skittering across the wet shore.

They approached the carcass. He still couldn't say for sure what it was with all the scavengers feasting on it. Leaning down, he scooped up a handful of pebbles and shell fragments, the smooth stones moistening his skin. Then he flung the stones toward the dead beast and sent the gulls scattering, cawing in anger.

The creature's back was revealed. His breath caught in his throat. That was no whale.

"Ugh, it sure stinks. It must've been dead for a long time, huh?" Ravenna circled the creature and wrinkled her nose.

"Actually, it can't have been dead for long. Otherwise, the scavengers would've picked the bones clean."

"Do you know what it is?"

"I'm not sure. It's unlike any sea creature I've ever seen." He edged around the carcass, staring at it curiously, even as the boldest birds returned to their meal. "It's hard to tell with all the bloat and the missing pieces." The body was covered in green scales in the few spots where the top layer was still intact.

He circled around the top of the beast. The head was missing. No doubt lying on the ocean floor somewhere. As he rounded the creature, he spied another group of gulls tearing at the meat on the front of the body. He knelt down and grabbed another fistful of pebbles, then sent the birds scattering.

He squinted, moving closer to the beast's massive, strangely shaped flipper. Then he reached down and plucked free a bone that lay on the rocks.

How queer... It was hollow. Only birds had hollow bones. Birds and—

Rot and decay. He rocked back on his heels, staring at the beast with wide eyes. Could that flipper be a wing? Was he looking at the freshly killed carcass of a dragon?

"Mika, look." Ravenna stared at the waves, one hand shielding her brow and the other pointing into the distance.

He followed her gaze, gulping. Three more carcasses floated in on the surf. The trail of bodies led to the uninhabited Mido Islands, the largest of which was faintly visible on the horizon.

Were there dragons on that island out in the ocean? Had they survived there all this time, while the world thought them dead? What was killing them? His stomach filled with dread. He wasn't going to stick around to find out.

"C'mon, Ravenna. Let's head back."

"Wait. What is it? Aren't you gonna tell me?"

"It's just a whale. Diseased from the looks of things. You better keep off this beach for the next couple of weeks. Don't want you getting sick. Do me a favor, spread the word around to the rest of the kids, too."

She bristled and puffed out her chest. "I'm not a kid anymore, Mika."

He forced a smile. "Sorry. Just tell them, will ya?"

"Fine. I will." She headed back to the cliffside.

Mika followed, stuffing the bone in his satchel. He had a bad feeling those bodies would be the first of many.

Chapter 1

Bitter.

The word epitomized his life. The bitter cold of the Turney Mountains was his constant companion. From sunup to sundown, it never ceased chilling him to the bone. Bitterness burned deep in his chest when he remembered all the years stolen from him. It stared back at him in every puddle and sheet of ice. And worst of all, when he thought of Ereni, her betrayal, the bitterness grabbed hold and wouldn't let go.

An elbow jabbed Conall in the side, hard enough to be felt beneath layers of fur. He glared down into the eager face of a boy at that awkward age where he was no longer a child but not yet a teen. His pale, freckled cheeks and nose flushed red in the chilly air.

"Shouldn't you be out there?" His bright green eyes sparkled, head tilted sideways.

Conall looked away, turning his glare on the mages training in a circle on the mountain plateau in the dusky light. "I'm no mage."

"That's not what I heard."

He ground his jaw, hazel eyes narrowing. "Don't believe everything you hear, boy."

"I'm Quent." He stuck out a gloved hand and tilted forward, aiming a smile up at him. "You're Conall, right? I heard all about how you brought down the Palisade. They say you can summon all the elements."

Conall glanced down at Quent's hand but made no move to shake it. "They talk too much. Like you."

Quent dropped his hand and backed up, staying at his side.

Conall sighed. Kid wouldn't take a hint. Not that he could blame him. The company in these mountains was decidedly lacking.

How had this become his life? Weeks of traveling at a snail's pace, plagued with grumpy old mages used to a warm keep. And children. So many boisterous youths and stinky babes.

He frowned. Even his bonded wolf, Shadow, had made himself scarce. He spent his time hunting for the group. Stalking the wild mountain goats that managed to thrive on this barren mountainside. Not that Conall could fault Shadow for that. He wasn't exactly the liveliest companion these days.

"Excellent," Delyth, the gray-haired mages' leader exclaimed, as she studied an old man forming a sword of ice. "Though, I'd wager you'd use less energy and fell more enemies if you made a dozen daggers instead." Her eyes connected with Conall's from across the plateau, and she nodded her head inward, toward the circle.

Conall held her gaze and remained perfectly still against the cliff wall. The Sade Prim was relentless in her attempts to sway him to train. But his answer was always the same. He was no mage.

One of the few young adults in the camp burst out of a large tent. She hadn't taken time to throw on any furs or gloves. Her hands shook, her voice loud and shrill. "Dena!" she screamed. "Eddena, this is no time to play hide and find."

Delyth approached the young woman, tugging the hood of her gray fur cloak as the wind sought to force it off her head. "What's wrong? Can we help?"

"Sade Prim, it's Eddena." The woman's breath clouded the air with each panicked breath she drew. "She was sleeping in the children's tent. I just closed my eyes for an instant, and now she's gone."

"It's all right, we'll find her." Delyth patted her shoulder.

The mages had already begun searching. "Over here," called a voice behind the large tent shared by the children whose parents weren't at Mage Keep when the Palisade fell. "I see tracks her size leading this way."

Within moments, a search party formed and headed in that direction while the remaining mages barged inside every tent, leaving Conall alone on the plateau. Well, almost alone.

"Dena's always wandering off." Quent shook his head and stuffed his gloved hands into his pockets. "I'm actually surprised this is the first time she's disappeared on this trip."

Conall scowled. "Dangerous place to be a child all alone." He paced forward to the plateau's edge and gazed down the steep slopes that sprawled below. Jagged gray rocks dotted a sea of white. One wrong step around here could be a death sentence.

"Brother," he reached out with his thoughts. *"There's a child missing from our camp. You don't see her by any chance?"*

"No, little brother," Shadow replied. *"Just goats over here. Do you need me to head back?"*

"No, keep hunting. I'm sure they'll find her soon, and everyone will still need to eat."

He stole one last look at the lower slopes, then turned back. Seems Quent finally decided to look for more entertaining company. The boy was gone from sight. Conall was about to head back to his own tent, to make sure the mages had wrecked none of his things in their search, when he spotted movement in the corner of his eye.

Blazes. There was the girl, Eddena. She couldn't have been more than five, and she was blissfully wandering off in the opposite direction of everyone searching, above and to the right of where he stood. He pivoted, trudging through the snow toward her.

He got about halfway to her when a second figure emerged from behind a snowbank, arms spread out to grab her. Quent.

Conall stopped in his tracks. Good, someone else could be the hero for a change.

The boy caught up to her and crept up from behind. Eddena seemed oblivious to his presence until he crouched down and scooped her up in his arms.

She noticed then. She shrieked, the screech deafening and sharp. She struggled within Quent's arms, causing him to stagger atop the snow. Conall grimaced, resisting the urge to cover his ears as the ear-piercing noise echoed all around.

Whoomph. A new noise sounded, a heartbeat before Quent and Dena started sliding.

Conall's stomach plummeted to his feet. Avalanche.

He flew into motion. He cleared one leaping step as Quent's eyes widened with fear.

The second step saw the girl give up her struggle, clutching tight to Quent as they torpedoed down the slope.

A third step. They were almost upon him, picking up speed so quickly.

He took a final leap and dove headfirst toward them as the boy fell, unable to keep his balance on the shifting snow.

A wall of cold slammed into him, forcing his breath out in a rush. He clamped his jaw shut before he got a mouthful of snow for his trouble. Groping forward, blinded by white, he clasped onto something. He prayed the object he clutched was one of the children and not some random tree branch. He held fast for an eternity while the snow tumbled him away.

Finally, it stopped.

He opened his eyes and shuddered. He was well and truly buried, surrounded on all sides, squashed so tightly it was hard to breathe. Squirming, he tried to move, only to realize his entire body was locked in place by the blasted snow.

Wait. Not his whole body. The hand still clutching—something—could move.

Was some part of him lucky enough to end up above the snow? There was only one way to find out.

He dropped hold of whatever it was and shoved his fist side to side, expanding the hole. An instant later, he jolted when something rubbed his wrist. He craned his neck up as the hole widened and spotted a pair of gloved hands joining in, digging from the other side. Conall breathed out a sigh. Those were the same gloves he'd refused to shake earlier.

He kept working, expecting at any moment to burst into the fresh air on top of the snowbank. When he finally pulled himself free, he collapsed into a heap, not atop the snow, but in a small spherical cave.

He stared so long and hard he forgot to blink, his jaw slack. The cave was perfectly circular—except for the spot where he'd burst through—and made entirely of snow. It was darkened inside but somehow light enough to see. Perhaps the sun still shined on them from above. "How in the world…"

"I don't know," Quent replied. "We just ended up in here somehow."

There was only one explanation that made sense. "What type of magic runs in your family, Quent?"

The boy's mouth fell open, his voice rising in pitch. "Air."

Eddena had been quiet until now, but she chose that moment to speak. "I want my daddy."

Her wobbly voice tore at Conall's heart. She curled up on the cave floor and clutched her knees to her chest, shivering so violently her brown hair vibrated, flicking little motes of snow into the air. The poor thing was dressed only in a sweater, trousers, and black boots.

"There, there, little one." He had to warm her. The cold was already seeping into his skin below all his layers of fur. She wouldn't last long in that garb.

He scooted closer to her, leaning down and forcing what he hoped was a reassuring smile onto his face. "Come snuggle inside my fur, Dena. I'll keep you safe. I promise." He unbuttoned his fur as he spoke, then opened it wide in invitation.

There was that bitter cold again, rushing in to greet him. Eddena stared up at him with tear-filled eyes. At first, he feared she would refuse, but then she crawled forward and climbed onto his lap, wrapping her little arms around his back. He shuddered as her bare fingers tangled in his shirt, tiny icicles spearing his skin through his tunic. Then he re-buttoned his fur, shrouding the girl in warmth.

"What now?" Quent smacked his gloved hands together, knocking the snow off them. "Do we dig?"

Conall shook his head. "It's too risky. We could dig the wrong way up into a huge snowbank, or cause the cave to collapse."

Quent gulped, his gaze darting around the small sphere.

"Don't worry." Conall squeezed the boy's shoulder. "Shadow will find us. Just give me a moment. I'll call for him."

Brother, I need your help. There was an avalanche. I'm buried in the snow, somewhere on the slopes below camp, to the east. He dropped his hand from Quent's shoulder.

Shadow answered almost instantly. *Are you all right, little brother?*

"Yes, for now. I'm in a pocket of air, with two children. You need to find us."

I'm on my way.

Conall sent a small smile to Quent. "He's coming. When we hear him digging, we'll know which direction to dig."

Quent stared down at his gloves. "Are you sure he'll be able to find us?"

"Of course, he will. Wolves have the keenest sense of smell. Besides, Shadow's never let me down. He'll find us."

Time passed slowly. The darkness in their buried cave grew more complete as they sat in silence, waiting. A vibration pulsed along the cave wall. Was that their rescue? No... just Quent shivering so strongly the snow wall shook with the force of it. Conall shuffled beside him and wrapped an arm around him, pulling him close.

He cursed inwardly. If only he hadn't been so stubborn, maybe he would be skilled enough by now to melt the snow around them and free them from this bitter prison. As it was, he'd been less than useless. If not for the boy's bubble of air, they'd all be dead by now.

If he made it out of this frozen tomb—no, *when* he made it out—he wouldn't make the same mistake twice. He would swallow his pride and learn how to summon. Somehow, he would bury the bitterness in his heart and find a way to live with what had happened to him.

He was through letting the bitter rule his life. It was time to learn what he must to protect himself and the people around him.

I've made it back to camp. I can see the path where the snow carried you. Hang on, little brother. Shadow's voice warmed his heart, even as the cold seeped deeper into his bones.

"We're still here, brother. Hurry."

"He's c-coming," Conall whispered through chattering teeth.

Beneath his fur, Eddena remained still. Was that a good sign, or bad? He closed his eyes and prayed she'd warmed enough from his body heat that she'd fallen asleep. *Please, let her only be sleeping...*

For some time, the cave had been getting dimmer, but as he sat there waiting, blackness overwhelmed the cave, leaving only the barest shadow of light. Did that mean night had fallen outside? As cold as it was, without the sun, it would only become colder.

On top of the temperature, the air became increasingly stale. His head throbbed dully, his breath coming faster than it should, like he was running and not sitting motionless. How long could they survive without fresh air? Would Shadow find them in time?

"If I don't make it out of here, will you do something for me?" Quent's voice was calm, steady. His body no longer shivering.

That couldn't be good. Conall's body shuddered so violently he could hardly force out any words. "You're g-gonna make it out of here, Q-Quent. Shadow will f-find us."

"Please, just listen. I need you to find my mother, wherever she is. Tell her I'm sorry." Quent's chin wobbled on his shoulder. "Tell her I love her." He pulled free from Conall's arm, his breathing speeding up. "Is it hot in here, all of a sudden?"

Conall sat dumbfounded, struggling to see what the boy was doing. Then something landed in his lap. He lifted it close to his face. Was that a glove? The *swoosh* of fabric on the ice told him the boy had shucked off its twin. Then came the pop of a button as he worked at removing his fur.

"N-no—are you m-mad? Leave it on." Conall lurched forward and grabbed the boy's fur, wrenching it closed.

Then he heard the *scritch-scratch* of an animal furiously digging in the snow. He laughed, grabbing the still struggling Quent and clutching him tight. "Listen. He's h-here. Shadow's f-found us!"

He sat still, or as still as he could while shivering uncontrollably, trying to determine the direction the sound was coming from. Before he could figure out where to dig, the snow around them simply dissolved.

He blinked, shielding his face from the sudden appearance of torches. Ahead of him stood Shadow, next to the same old man who he'd watched craft a sword of ice that evening. He held his arms out wide, eyes closed in concentration. Then he opened his eyes, and smiled.

Delyth strolled forward and clasped the mage's shoulder, holding a torch up in the moonlight. Her shrewd gaze flicked between him and Quent. When she spoke, her voice was shaky. "Eddena—is she with you?"

Conall nodded, even as Shadow raced forward and ducked beneath his arm, lending him strength and warmth. "She's h-here, b-beneath my furs. She's n-not moving."

Delyth exhaled, immediately composing herself and barking out orders. "Quick, now. Bring them to the closest tent. We'll need healers, blankets, warm clothes. Let's move."

How he arrived there was all a blur, but before he realized it, he was somewhere warm, and a mage was rubbing something on his bare chest.

He gasped and jolted up. For the first time in so long, the cold—that awful, bitter cold—was finally gone. Tears filled his eyes. He spun to the left and found Delyth watching him. "Quent, Eddena... are they all right?"

She nodded and pointed to a table to his right. Quent sat wrapped in a blanket, looking dazed but whole and unharmed.

He craned his neck around, searching for Eddena. Suddenly, a warm weight plopped onto his lap. Staring down into the little girl's smiling face—who he'd promised to keep safe—he grinned crookedly and hugged her close. And here he'd thought it was someone else's turn to be the hero.

He turned back to Delyth and met her eyes. He had a feeling from the way she stared back at him she already knew what he was about to say, but he said it anyway. "I'm ready."

Chapter 2

The sun beat down on Kayda's back as she lowered the spyglass on the bow of the *Sea Silk*. Even the cool ocean breeze so late in the fall wasn't enough to bring relief from the sweltering heat this far south.

Her boots thudded on the wooden deck, her scorched blue dress long ago exchanged for a pair of cotton trousers and a bright yellow button-down tunic pilfered from the former captain's room. She made her way to the bridge, a bead of sweat rolling down her spine beneath the loose-fitting silk.

"Is that what I think it is ahead of us?" she asked the tall, shirtless man at the helm.

"Aye, Princess." Jayan was clothed only in a pair of tan shorts, his dark brown skin glistening. "We'll be ready to dock before day's end."

She nodded and shifted to survey the *Sea Silk*. The wooden vessel was huge, equal in length to half a city block in Flamesmoat. Overhead, massive sails billowed in the wind.

Her bondmate, Druturion, lounged on the midship deck, seeming unbothered by the heat. In fact, he reminded her of the tiny lizards she used to spot basking in the sun in the Royal Grounds during the summer.

A handful of people milled on deck. Some bustled about, handling the many tasks that came with sailing a ship so large. Yet others stood staring at the rolling waves with uneasy expressions or fanning themselves in whatever shade they could find.

It had been a stroke of luck to find so many souls aboard this vessel. When she and Druturion commandeered it after the battle in the Abandoned Lands, she hadn't realized the work needed to bring the huge trading craft safely back to port.

When they'd first landed, she'd spent a few confused moments trying to make sense of the many ropes, sails, and dozens of other unfamiliar things. She quickly understood she had no chance of sailing the ship back to Joria on her own. If it hadn't been for the sounds she'd heard below deck, and her subsequent discovery of the slaves in the hold, the *Sea Silk* would still be anchored offshore the Kingdom of Dracwood.

Her hand curled into a fist. It was no wonder they all wanted to be above deck. She'd found them chained to the walls, half-starved, and begging to be freed. A fact made even more cruel when the ship had a galley packed full of salted meat, beans, and enough flour to feed an army. And now she was dragging them all back, within grasp of their captors.

"Dru, we're almost there. Time to make yourself scarce."

His eyelids lifted lazily, those crimson eyes connecting with her own. *"Are you sure about this? It's not too late to change the plan."*

A flutter tickled her stomach, but she drew a deep breath and nodded. *"I'm sure."*

"All right, I'll see you soon." He rose and unfurled his shimmering black wings. Then he backed up to the far railing, causing a few panicked people to scramble out of the way. He took two running steps and leapt into the air.

Kayda's breath caught as she watched him soar away. Her bondmate was truly magnificent. His svelte form soared through the clouds, full of power and beauty. Black scales glittered with flecks of purple, blue, and green.

Sometimes it still felt like a dream. Was she truly bonded to a dragon?

"Where's he going?" asked a lanky man, his voice thick with the desperation of someone certain he was watching his last chance of salvation being torn from his grasp. He stared at Kayda with wild eyes. "You can't mean to take us back there alone!"

Jayan spoke up before she could formulate a response. "Eh, that's *princess* to you, dust eater."

Kayda shot Jayan a glare and strode forward to the nervous man. She placed a hand on his shoulder and pitched her voice loud enough that all could hear above the wind and surf. "Don't worry. Druturion will return. We have a plan to assure everyone's freedom when we pull into port. I've not forgotten the promise I made to you all. You will not feel the bite of chains on your skin again. Not if I have anything to say about it."

A few people clapped or cheered. But most stared at her warily or avoided looking at her all together as they shuffled their feet and shook their heads.

At least the lanky man seemed to relax. Some of the tension in his shoulder lifted as Kayda gave him a squeeze and released him.

"Bless you, Princess." He backed away reverently.

Kayda smiled and turned back to Jayan, smoothing her long auburn hair. "You don't have to speak up for me. I can handle myself."

He raked a hand through his short, curly black hair, dark brown eyes twinkling. "Sorry, Princess. You just remind me so much of my sister, Nova. If I saw someone disrespecting her, I'd do much the same."

"You're forgiven." She grinned, then she narrowed her eyes. "Just don't pull the same trick when we arrive at port. I want the port master to know I don't need anyone fighting my battles for me."

"Aye, Princess," he said with a wink.

Kayda rolled her eyes and turned away. Jayan was a strange man, but he'd been instrumental in their voyage. Unlike the others, she'd found him chained up in the captain's room. From the way he knew every nook and cranny on this ship, she suspected he was much more than the captain's personal slave. He was the true captain of this vessel.

She strolled to the starboard rail and leaned against it, watching the city of Joria grow large as they approached. The city was immense. Far larger than Flamesmoat, with buildings sprawled up and down the coast, spreading out from the city center.

Huge factories rested on the Peat River's banks, home to the silk mills and dye-houses the region was famous for. In the distance, a handful of beautiful palatial mansions dotted the shore on the Peat's far side. The gorgeous buildings were a stark contrast to the crowded city center, which was overrun with tiny shacks and storefronts.

Soon, they altered course, heading for the massive wharfs lining the Port of Joria. Kayda's stomach churned as they sailed closer. The crowded docks were alive with activity. Dozens of boats were moored already. Sailors and slaves packed the walkways, carrying goods, making ready to depart or unload.

It was into this organized chaos they landed. Jayan expertly glided their large ship into port with the ease of a natural sailor.

A short, pudgy fellow, dressed in a suit of fine blue silk, barreled down the wharf, his tanned face reddening with each step. Kayda made her way down the gangplank, on a course to intercept him.

"The *Sea Silk*, back in port? No, no, no. You're not supposed to be here." The man pulled up short and scanned her up and down with a frown. "Who, pray tell, are you? Where is Captain Kent?"

"Dead, I'm afraid," she answered, hopping off the gangplank and onto the wharf. "Are you the port master? I claim finder's rights to this vessel."

"Finder's rights," he exclaimed, shaking his head vehemently, his jowls wobbling with the motion. "Are you mad? Don't you know who this ship belongs to?"

"Yes." She grinned. "This ship belongs to me. I found it unmanned off the Abandoned Lands' coast, all the crew dead. I sailed it back. And now I claim the ship and all the cargo, as is my right." She paused, doing her best to hold back laughter as the man's face turned redder still, until he looked ready to explode. Then she leaned in close, ignoring the crowd of curious onlookers gathered around to watch. "Now, point me in the port master's direction, please."

"I am the port master," he said through gritted teeth.

"Well, why didn't you say so?" She strolled forward, her hands clasped behind her back. "We'll be changing the name. Mark it down in your ledger. This boat is now *Nova's Champion.*" She spun sideways and sent Jayan a wink of her own, where he stood watching from the side rail.

Then a handsome dark-skinned man, clothed in an even finer suit than the port master's, his a deep burgundy, came upon the scene. Though he carried himself with the bearing of a man twice his age, it was clear he was barely older than she, perhaps in his early twenties.

He strode forward, and as the folk crowded around spotted him, they parted hastily. He marched past them all with his nose in the air, as if they were beneath his notice. Within moments, he stopped before her, eyeing her just as vigorously as the port master had.

"I see the *Sea Silk* has returned ahead of schedule. And who do we have to thank for her safe return?" He raised a brow.

Who should we thank, he'd asked? So, this pompous man must be the owner. Time to play her cards.

"I'm afraid you're mistaken. As I just finished informing the port master, this vessel is now *Nova's Champion*, and she's mine, along with all her cargo, by finder's rights." She turned aside dismissively and raised a hand to her face, pretending great interest in her nails.

"I see you don't quite understand how finder's rights work, girl. You have to make every effort to find the found property's owner before claiming it as your own." He smirked and spread his arms. "It appears you're in luck. You found me." He strode forward, headed for the gangplank.

"So, you admit to treason, then?"

He stopped in his tracks and swiveled slowly to face her. "Excuse me? I said nothing of treason."

"But you admit to owning this vessel. The same vessel that sent a landing party into the Abandoned Lands, breaking the Palisade Treaty." She leaned back on her heels as a chorus of gasps spilled from the onlookers. "That sounds an awful lot like treason to me."

"That's where you're wrong, girl." He stepped closer, leaning close to her face, a lock of his perfectly coiffed curly brown hair falling forward on his forehead. "That treaty has expired."

"I'm afraid you're the one who's wrong. I've read that treaty. It's void only after 500 years have passed since the death of each member present at the signing."

The man scoffed, his chin lifting. "That happened over a decade ago. Believe me, we checked."

She let a smile spread slowly across her face. *"Dru, that's your cue."*

She took a step closer, standing toe-to-toe with the man, looking directly into his dark brown eyes. "Are you sure about that?"

At that moment, the crowd spotted Druturion flying through the sky. Chaos erupted as dozens of people screamed and scuttled away, bumping into each other in their haste. Some of the terrified onlookers jumped into the ocean rather than face the fearsome dragon, their splashes echoing and water erupting in the air. Dru hovered briefly, then thudded down on the wharf, causing the entire structure to shift with his weight.

As the wharf came to rest, the man and the port master stared at Dru, their mouths hanging open.

Kayda strolled forward, reaching out to stroke his massive head. "This is Druturion the Black, in the flesh. If you check the treaty again, you'll find his name listed among the signatories."

The man turned his wide eyes to her again, his brows furrowing. "Who are you?"

"I'm Kayda."

She watched recognition strike the man. Both his brows shot up and he took a step back. "Would that be *Princess* Kayda of Dracwood?"

She grinned. "It would."

Then the man surprised her. He slapped the port master's back, nearly sending the poor fellow tumbling off the dock into the ocean. He grinned even wider than she had, showcasing a set of perfect, white teeth. *"Nova's Champion* is a fine name. I'll have the papers drawn up. The ship and all the cargo are yours."

A cheer erupted from the ship's deck as the former slaves heard the news.

Kayda was not so quick to celebrate. "That's it? It's all mine?" She lifted a brow and cocked her head sideways.

"Of course, of course. We are family, after all." The man laughed and strode forward, pulling her into an embrace. "It's nice to finally meet you, cousin."

Kayda gulped, holding herself stiffly in his arms. This arrogant stranger was her kin? A man who traded in slaves and had no problem flouting the customs of her kingdom by striking a deal with the prince behind the king's back?

He released her and gazed down at her with that wide grin. "I'm Wyll. Come, let me introduce you to the wonders of Joria. And after, we'll head home, and you can meet the rest of the family."

She backed up, considering his offer. *"Dru, what should I do?"* She didn't need to explain. She'd learned aboard the ship that Druturion had spent enough time with humans he could understand humans' speech, but he could only speak to those he bonded with.

"Go, meet your family. I'll stay here on the ship. No sense in scaring half the city into the ocean. If you need me, just say the word, and I'll find you."

Her heart racing, she stepped forward. This was what she'd come here for, after all. She looked to Wyll—her cousin—and smiled. "After you."

Chapter 3

They sailed through a maze. Twisted mangroves loomed on all sides of the canoe, their gnarled roots plunging into the salty waters. The stench of decay lingered in the air. Croaking, chittering reptiles and the splash of hidden creatures echoed in her ears.

Just one more day. One more day until they reached Raimire, and this place would become a memory. Lark shuddered and stroked Sunny's yellow fur. It couldn't come fast enough. This place gave her the creeps.

"Cheer up, blue bird. We're almost there," said a voice in her mind.

Lark rolled her eyes and swatted a bug off the back of her hand. *"Please, no. Not this again."* The weeks spent traversing the Boglands' tangled waters had been a chore in more ways than one. *"Can you quit it with the nicknames already? Each one is worse than the last."*

Her bondmate, Muse, sat preening on her perch in the center of the canoe. The strangeness of speaking with a falcon in her thoughts had morphed into familiarity during their travels. But sometimes Lark wished she wasn't quite so familiar.

"Don't be so morose. Your face, your thoughts, they're so dark." Muse paused scratching her feathers and lifted her beak from her chest. *"Ha, dark Lark. That's a good one."*

Lark groaned. *"No, it's not."*

"Everything all right?" Aren tipped back his wide-brimmed hat, his blue eyes peering at her curiously.

Her stomach fluttered. She sent her handsome companion a crooked smile. He sat behind her in the crowded canoe, wearing plain brown traveling clothes and a leather gauntlet on his right arm.

"It's nothing. Just Muse thinking she's funny when she's clearly not." She punctuated the statement with a glare at her bondmate, but Muse only went back to preening, fluffing the gold and white checkered feathers on her chest.

Aren smiled. "It must be amazing, your bond. I have to admit I'm envious. I would give anything to know what Whisper is thinking." He lifted his gloved arm and whistled. Whisper, Aren's trained hawk, cocked his head at the sound, then dutifully flew from his perch at the front of the canoe and landed gracefully on his outstretched arm.

"What's he saying?" Muse turned, watching Aren toss a small morsel to Whisper.

"He wishes he could understand Whisper the way I understand you."

A strange sound filled her mind. Was that a scoff?

"Ha, he's lucky he can't. He would be bored to tears by that one, trust me." Muse shifted on her perch, her talons digging into the wood.

"She's probably restless. It's about time for their afternoon hunt." Aren whistled twice. The sharp blares sent Whisper soaring. Muse reacted just as quickly. Both birds blasted into the sky, climbing so high they were obscured by mangrove branches almost instantly.

"Great." Tiora smoothed her golden-brown dress from her seat next to Lark. "Sounds like we're having sparling for dinner. Again."

The small brown and white spotted aquatic birds made their home in the Boglands. Muse called them easy pickings.

"At least it's better than fish," Fillan said, sporting mud-covered overalls in the back of the canoe. He jabbed a long pole into the murky water. "I'm usually so sick of fish on this run that by the time I make it back to Bogsmo—" His shoulders slumped, and he clamped his mouth closed, either unwilling or unable to complete the sentence.

Lark's stomach churned. It was still hard to recall the carnage they'd witnessed as they fled for their lives. When she closed her eyes at night, she could still hear the screams from the poor townspeople who'd been eaten alive. It must be even worse for Fillan. His whole life was changed forever when the scourge destroyed his hometown.

At least he still had his father, Dal. He steered the smaller canoe behind them. The pair agreed to ferry their group of performers through the Boglands before disaster struck. As far as they could tell, they'd been the only ones to make it out of Bogsmouth alive.

Lark tugged her dark-blue dress, the cotton sticky in the humidity. Muse had saved them all. Without her warning, they wouldn't be here. She wouldn't have the chance to find a teacher, someone who could show her how to control her powers.

Just one more day.

A blur of movement set her heart racing. Muse dove through the air, dropping on an unsuspecting sparling in a flash. The poor thing didn't see it coming; it was over in an instant. Muse lifted the sparling in the air, triumphant. Then she dropped the dead bird with a splash.

"Oops. That was a fat one." Muse chuckled. *"Grab that one, will ya? I'll catch another."* She lifted back into the sky, and was soon gone from sight.

Lark grinned. Then a second splash sounded, this one close enough to spray her skin with warm water. Her stomach dropped to her feet. "Sunny. Get back here!" She stood in the wobbly canoe, hands on her hips.

The old mutt didn't listen. She was already halfway to the spot where the sparling bobbed on the water's surface. She swam until she reached the bird, then scooped it up in her jaws and turned, swimming back to the boat.

That was when Lark saw it. A shadowy form beneath the water stalking Sunny. Lark's eyes popped wide, her heart thudding madly. She couldn't tell what the creature was, but it was big and fast—really fast. Sunny wasn't going to make it.

"Fillan," she screamed, pointing to the shadow racing beneath the water.

"I see it." Fillan shoved the stick into the bog with renewed vigor. "Sit down, we'll get her."

Lark wobbled as the canoe lurched, coming dangerously close to falling in. Tiora grabbed her legs, steadying her.

She sank down to the wooden boat's floor, reaching out the side, preparing to scoop up Sunny as soon as they pulled alongside her. Aren held tight to her hips, ready to pull her in should she need help.

"C'mon, girl," she pleaded.

Sunny was just out of reach, her tail weaving back and forth through the water blissfully, when the creature surfaced.

Lark's jaw dropped. The beast was massive, at least five times as big as Sunny. It was a monstrous reptile with brown scales and a long, thin snout that opened to reveal a set of jagged teeth. Teeth aimed straight at her dog.

Not on her watch.

She shot forward, heaving her torso free of the boat, trusting Aren to keep her out of the water. Pain stabbed her stomach as the canoe's side rammed into her, but she ignored it, straining forward. She wrapped her arms around Sunny's neck, her fingers closing on the wet fur on her back. She grabbed Sunny and hauled her forward as the beast's jaw snapped closed on the spot she'd been at an instant before.

They weren't safe yet. "Pull us in," she yelled, as its jaw snapped open again. Her heart thundered. The creature drew so close she could smell its rank breath.

It was so fast. In a heartbeat it was even closer, the bottom of its jaw diving below the water, directly beneath them. The shadow of its jagged maw hovered above her head. They were too late! She screamed.

Thunk. She landed back in the boat, atop Aren. Squirming fur drenched them both instantly. The boat careened sideways, coming dangerously close to dumping them all in the bog until Fillan stabbed his pole down to steady them.

Sunny dropped the sparling. It smacked Lark in the face before rolling to the side. Great.

Then Sunny proceeded to cover her face with slobbery kisses. She should've been gagging—Sunny did just spit out a dead bird after all—but she was too happy to care. She grabbed her neck, clutching her tightly. "Never do that again."

As she hugged her close, Sunny saw an opportunity to reach Aren where he lay beneath them and exploited it.

"Blech." He twisted his face sideways but couldn't avoid her slobbering tongue.

"Guys..." Tiora's panicked voice halted the laughter bubbling inside Lark's chest. "It's turning around."

Lark's breath caught. The beast sped through the water, heading straight for them. It was easily as big as the canoe. If it rammed them, they didn't stand a chance. But her hands were full of squirming dog, and she was not about to release Sunny when she was in the mood to swim. She gulped. What were they going to do?

"Ti, the sparling. Throw the sparling!" Aren yelled.

Tiora's eyes widened, but she was already in motion. She snatched the bird off the canoe floor and tossed it directly on the beast's snout. The sparling landed with a *thunk*, then splashed into the water beside the beast. The shock of the hit must have startled it. It halted its advance, dunking its head beneath the water, surfacing a moment later and seizing the bobbing carcass with a sickening *crunch*.

Lark sighed as the creature turned, slipped under the water, and swam away slowly, satisfied with the free meal. She climbed free of Aren, sending him a sheepish grin, and deposited Sunny on the canoe's floor as Muse and Whisper reappeared. They both landed on their perches and dropped a pair of sparlings on the wooden boards.

"Ha, what did I miss?" Muse's head jerked back and forth merrily.

"Don't ask," Lark replied, wringing out her sopping, brown curls.

"I didn't realize we'd get a show before dinner tonight," called a voice behind them.

Lark spun around, sending a wry smile to Dausius in the second canoe.

"Everyone all right?" he asked, his beaded hair clinking as he shifted his gaze over them.

The second boat pulled up alongside their canoe. The twins, Mazen and Meital, smirked from the back as they caught sight of the others' sodden clothes.

"We're good," Aren said. "What was that thing?"

"Bogbeast," Dal answered from the rear of the smaller canoe, tugging the front of his mud-splattered overalls. "There'll be plenty more this close to the mainland. No more dips in the bog if you want to make it to Raimire in one piece, ya hear?"

Sunny picked that moment to shake the water from her fur, splattering everyone with droplets.

Lark laughed and tussled her wet, yellow fur. "I hope you heard that, girl. No more swimming."

Sunny stared back, her tongue dangling happily and tail wagging. Lark sighed. Too bad she could only speak to one animal.

Aren reached down and grabbed a sparling. "Here, Daus, catch." The bird sailed through the air. Dausius caught it with his lanky brown arms.

"Great, more sparling." Mazen's multicolored shirt glimmered in the sun as he leaned forward, frowning.

Meital slapped his back, her matching shirt shining just as brightly. "One more day, and we'll be home stealing fruit from tree monkeys like when we were kids." She shot him a cheeky grin.

Lark smiled, too. She was looking forward to reaching the mainland. And not just to leave this creepy place behind her. It had always been one of her dreams to travel. Next to becoming a mage, there was nothing that would bring her more pleasure. Now that she was traveling the world with the Wandering Bards, she was living the life of adventure she'd always dreamed of.

If only there wasn't a horde of vicious, blood-thirsty *ichneumon* ravaging her homeland to worry about, it would be practically perfect. A shiver raced down her spine. At least they would be safe in Raimire. There was no way those creatures could make it through the Boglands. She'd watched one drown to death before her eyes. The twisted water-logged maze they'd traversed would keep them safe long enough for her to find a teacher. And once she learned to control her earth talent, she would return and help set her country free.

Slap. Another bug, on her ankle this time. She grimaced and flicked the squashed bug off her palm, resisting the urge to scratch.

As she lifted her gaze from her leg, a small movement caught her eye in a gap between the tree cover. She spun sideways, peering at the mangroves curiously. They grew so thick that once they sailed past the small hole it was impossible to see anything but wood and vegetation.

"Something wrong?" Aren joined in her examination of their surroundings, tilting his hat back.

"I thought I saw something beyond those trees just now," she replied.

"Probably just a bogbeast or some other animal," Fillan said. "They won't bother us so long as we stay in the canoe."

She gasped. There it was again. A flash of bright color, there and gone in an instant. What was it?

She squeezed Aren's knee. "Did you see that?"

He shook his head. His gaze flicked to her and then back, squinting into the trees. "No."

"Whatever it was, it was bright pink. Are there any creatures or flowers that color in the bog?" she asked.

Fillan leaned down and scrutinized the crooked trees. "None that I've ever seen."

A pit formed in her stomach. She spun forward, realizing the path they were on would soon curve around, landing them directly in front of—whatever it was.

"Muse, there's something ahead of us on our path through the bog. Can you fly ahead and scout for us?" Lark's brow furrowed as she met her bondmate's gaze.

"All right, boss. Hm, that's too plain, I think. Cross boss? Ha, that's better. Just look at your face."

She scowled. *"Very funny. Just go see what's out there."*

Muse lifted into the air and hovered over the treetops. *"Lark... we have a problem."* She circled, flying above the next turn.

"What is it?"

"There's a bunch of boats blocking the way ahead. Lots of strangely dressed people on board. And weapons."

Lark stiffened. "We're about to have company," she announced. "Muse says there's a group of people in boats blocking the way up ahead."

They all stared at Muse circling the sky, frozen, their mouths hanging open, eyes wide.

"That doesn't make any sense." Dal pinched the bridge of his nose. "I've been this way hundreds of times. It's never been blocked once. You sure she's seeing it straight?"

The question had just escaped his lips when an arrow soared through the sky, heading directly for Muse.

Lark's heart skipped a beat. *"Look out!"*

"I see it." Muse sank like a stone in the bog, dodging the arrow then weaving between tree branches until she landed deftly back on her perch in the center of their canoe.

"Well, I guess that answers my question." Dal rubbed the back of his neck.

Lark gulped, her gaze flitting between the faces of her friends. What were they going to do?

Chapter 4

"What do we do?" Lark asked. "Can we turn back? Find another route?"

Dal shook his head. "This is the only path to the mainland. Unless we want to head back the way we came, or out to sea."

She swallowed, her heart sinking. The way back only led to death, fire, and ash. And she didn't need to be a sailor to understand these canoes were built for sailing the Boglands' shallow waters, not the open ocean.

"We can't just sail straight for them—they tried to shoot Muse out of the sky." Mazen's hand curled into a fist. "What if we're next?"

"Don't fret, my boy." Dausius squeezed Mazen's shoulder. "We just need to show them we're not a threat."

Lark raised a brow as they drifted closer to the turn. Although Dal and Fillan were not actively polling, the current was determined to see them forward, toward the blockade. "How exactly do we do that, Daus?"

"Easy." Dausius' grin widened. "By doing what we do best. Aren, your lute, please. Lark, hit them with our opener. Loud as you can until we make the turn, then cut to silence so I can make introductions."

"What's happening?" Muse shifted on her perch. *"We turning around?"*

Lark shifted on the bench as Aren strummed the lively tune's opening chords. *"Not exactly. We're going to show them we're no threat with a song."*

"Bold plan. I like it," Muse said.

Lark exhaled, shoving aside her nervousness. Then she opened her mouth and sang like her life depended on it. Her voice sprang free, bouncing off the water, joining the lute in perfect harmony.

She had to admit the song choice was inspired. It was energetic and catchy. The type of tune that always had everybody itching to dance. Dausius clapped and stomped in time with the beat. The music bubbled up in the air, infecting everyone with a smile. For one blissful moment, Lark forgot all about the danger ahead and the destruction behind them. Then they turned.

The boats appeared before them, exactly where Muse said they'd be, breaking the trance. The lyrics caught in her throat. Silence enveloped them as Aren halted his strumming and Dausius stopped clapping.

They all stared with trepidation at the strangers, half of them glaring back at them behind nocked arrows. There was a mix of men and women, their skin varied hues of tans, olives, and browns, on shocking display beneath the sheer green fabric they used to fashion their clothes.

They were practically naked. Lark's cheeks burned, and she tore her gaze away from all that flesh, examining the boats instead. The canoes these people sailed looked much the same as their own, only slightly larger, with polers on the forward and aft ends. They were positioned diagonally, all in a row, leaving no room for Lark's or Dausius' craft to slip past on the narrow waterway.

Dausius broke the silence, his voice merry and full of welcome. "Hello, friends! What a delightful surprise. We weren't expecting an audience until tomorrow." He stood, managing a graceful bow despite the wobbly canoe. "We are the Wandering Bards. It's a pleasure to meet you all."

A tense moment of silence followed until the clunk of boots on wood echoed across the water. Prowling forward to the aft poler, in the boat in the center of the bog, strode a tall, statuesque woman with a square jaw and her short brown hair braided tightly to her scalp. Around her neck hung a necklace adorned with a small, bright pink stone.

Lark stifled a gasp. Was that tiny stone the pink flash of color she'd seen? It didn't seem possible. How had she glimpsed something so small from so far away?

All eyes swung to the woman as she stopped beside the poler. She raised her hand as if to wave, but she did not smile, only slapped her hand on her thigh.

Lark's heart leapt into her throat. Was she signaling for an attack? But the next instant, she blew out a sigh. The archers dropped their bows, and the tension in the air subsided.

"Greetings, wanderers," the woman called out across the water, her voice strong and thick with command. She nodded to the polers in her boat, and they stabbed down at the bog, pushing the center canoe closer. "You come from Dracwood?"

Dausius cleared his throat. "Yes, we've spent the last season traveling and performing across Dracwood. Now we've returned to delight the villages of Raimire."

Swiftly, the canoe approached until they pulled in front of them. Lark's cheeks heated further. How could they walk around like that, with their whole bodies on display? She was no stranger to the human body, and had seen more than most with her work as a healer, but that was always behind closed doors, in private. She couldn't imagine wearing something so revealing out in broad daylight.

As she worked up the courage to look more closely, she noted they wore tiny opaque shorts underneath the gauzy green fabric, but they were so short and tightly fitted they left little to the imagination.

None of the folk in the boats seemed to register any discomfort with their attire. The aft poler even sent a smirk in her direction when he spotted her blush and shoved his chest out with pride. Lark tore her gaze away, glancing down at her lap and wrapping her arms around her chest.

The tall woman spoke again, her tone and bearing marking her as the group's leader. "Have you news from the north? We've seen smoke on the horizon. Great clouds of haze drifting through the sky." She pitched her voice softly and leaned toward them with gleaming brown eyes.

Dausius nodded, opening his mouth to explain, but the leader jumped in before he said a word.

"I can see that you do. The Matas sent us to bring any travelers with news to the village conclave. Come, we'll escort you."

Lark's belly fluttered. Village conclave? Matas? The words meant nothing to her but smacked of importance.

As the stranger's boat slipped forward through the hole left in the bog's center where they'd recently been stationed, and Dal and Fillan moved to follow, she realized she wouldn't have long to wonder.

Soon, they passed the line of boats, which spread out after they sailed by, blocking the bog once more. When Lark judged them far enough behind to be out of earshot, she leaned forward and poked Tiora's side. "You might've warned me the people here walk around half-naked."

Tiora had the audacity to giggle, dragging a hand through her short brown curls. "I believe I once told you modesty was not something they worry about here."

"They call that stuff luct fabric. It's made from some jungle plant. I think it helps keep the insects from biting." Fillan tilted his head and grimaced as he examined the folk in the boat ahead of them. "Ya still won't catch me wearing it, though," he added with a chuckle.

Lark shook her head, gazing at the boat of Raimish folk leading the way. She wasn't planning to don any of that fabric, either.

The lead boat took a sharp turn, steering toward a section of the bog that looked impassable. But the aft poler lifted his pole and nudged aside a section of branches, revealing a small channel, just wide enough for a single canoe to squeeze through.

"I've never been this way before." Fillan stared at the passage with bulging eyes. They sailed through, one after the other, the polemen crouching to avoid the low-hanging branches of mangroves until the waterway opened up again. "This is amazing. I bet this path will cut half a day's travel, at least."

It was soon apparent Fillan's guess was correct. Off in the distance, the first glimpses of the jungle rose beyond the mangroves.

Lark sighed and stroked Sunny's back. She couldn't wait to set foot on solid land. Except for the little marshy islands they'd stopped on through the bog to stretch their legs, it had been weeks since they'd left these canoes. She would be happy not to sail again for a good long time.

The jungle brimmed with life and color. It was a welcome change from the dreary swamp of the bog. Brightly colored flowers and birds teemed in the lush green canopy.

As they drew closer, the water echoed with sounds of wildlife. They sailed past a troop of small, orange tree monkeys. Some of the group trailed their boat and chittered excitedly as they leapt from tree to tree. Lark and Tiora giggled at their antics.

"Hm, I wonder what those taste like," Muse said.

Lark spared her bondmate a glance, raising a brow. *"Surely, they're too cute to eat."*

Muse bristled, her feathers shaking. *"Too cute to eat? Ha. Nothing is too cute to eat."*

The waterway curved around a bend, revealing sturdy wooden docks along the shore of a massive bay. A handful of people strolled along the banks, seeming to regard their appearance with little interest. Even the children wore the same flimsy green fabric. A few played on the shore, splashing rocks into the water and laughing.

The bay was dotted with half a dozen canoes. The people on board relaxed, occasionally flicking out and reeling in the lines of their fishing poles. Even more empty canoes neatly lined the docks, looking well cared for despite a few dents and dings.

Fillan followed the Raimish boat to an empty dock on the bay's far side and hopped off to tie them fast as they slowed.

Aren clambered out next. Fillan reached down, lending a hand to Tiora. That left Aren to help Lark. She slipped on her leather gauntlet before standing, then accepted Aren's hand and bounded up onto the dock, clicking her tongue at Sunny to follow.

"C'mon, Muse, you're with me." She held her arm out stiffly.

Aren whistled for Whisper at the same instant, and both birds flew forward, abandoning their wooden perches on the canoe. Then all of them plodded forward on the wobbly docks, joining the rest of their group on the shore. Lark breathed a sigh of relief when her boots sank into the spongy soil.

The tall woman was the last to climb out of the Raimish canoe. She strode toward their group, nodding backward to the water. "My people will carry your things into the village. Come, the Matas will want to speak with you right away." She started down a path leading into the jungle, beckoning them to follow. "My name's Gia. What are your names?"

Dausius fell in beside her, introducing them each by name. Lark nodded and smiled as he named her, then pulled Tiora toward the back of the group, while keeping pace with the others through the winding footpath. "Do you know where they're taking us? What's a village conclave? Who are these Matas?" she asked quietly.

Meital must have overheard her question from where she hiked behind them. "The Matas are the leaders of Raimire." She leaned forward, her voice soft and laced with pride. "Most of the time, the Matas stay in their own villages. A conclave is called when something big happens. Then a wise woman from each village is chosen to represent their people at the conclave."

Lark's eyes widened. "The Matas are all women?"

"Yes. Women have always led in Raimire. The men are always too busy hunting and getting into trouble, so women take care of things in the villages."

Things certainly were different here. Lark breathed in deep, bright notes of flowers and fruit mingling with the fresh scent of moist earth. Chittering, buzzing, and chirping echoed from all sides. She smiled as she picked out new birdsongs among all the sound. The jungle was so much louder, so much more alive than the forests back home.

But would the people who lived here welcome them after they shared the events they'd witnessed? The question sent a shiver down her spine as the path curved again. A village of bright green huts appeared before them, crowded closely together in a cleared valley within the jungle.

"I was expecting it to be bigger. There's hardly enough space for a hundred people here," Tiora said.

"There are likely more clearings like this nearby. A half dozen or more," Meital explained. "The jungle is allowed space to thrive in between. You won't find vast swaths of forest cleared here, like in Dracwood. No one here farms or raises livestock. There's no need. The jungle provides more than enough to feed everyone."

"As long as you can find it without getting yourself killed," Mazen chimed in with a grin.

Lark gulped, following Gia as she wove between buildings. "Is it really that dangerous?"

"Sure. There's poisonous plants, venomous snakes, and all manner of creatures happy to eat you for breakfast." Mazen's brown eyes sparkled, and his smile widened. "It's no wonder the women rule when half the men meet their end in the jungle."

Meital gave her brother a gentle push. "Stop teasing, Maz." She turned back to them, flicking her long, brown braid behind her shoulder. "It's true there are dangers in the jungle. But as long as you know what to watch for, you'll be fine. Don't worry, me and Maz will look out for you."

They stopped before a hut twice the size of all the rest. Gia pulled back the covering over the door—a slightly thicker sheet of the same sheer material the people here wore—and ushered them inside. They piled into a small room, which was empty except for shallow wooden benches lining the walls.

"Have a seat." Gia walked past them, headed for a set of wooden doors leading deeper into the building. "I'll be right back."

Everyone found a seat on one of the benches, except for Sunny, who circled the dirt floor by Lark's feet before lying down. Lark leaned forward, letting Muse hop down off her arm. Then she sat beside her on the hard bench, tugging the moist cloth of her dress.

She'd hoped Raimire would be less humid than the Boglands, but it was just as bad, if not worse. Perhaps that was why the people here were happy to stroll around all day in such flimsy clothes.

Gia returned, carrying a large ceramic bottle and a stack of wooden cups. She closed the door behind her with her foot before placing the cups and bottle on a bench beside the door. "The Matas will see you now. But they only wish to speak to two of you. They asked me to bring the elders among you."

Dausius and Dal rose and joined Gia by the door. "The rest of you, help yourselves to some refreshment while you wait. We'll be back in a moment." With that, Gia reopened the door, and all three disappeared within.

Mazen hopped to his feet and grabbed the bottle. "Figures. I've never met a Mata who didn't treat anyone under forty like a child." He lifted it to his nose and twisted off the lid, giving the contents a sniff. A mischievous smile lit his face. "At least they left us the good stuff."

After setting the bottle back down, he lined the wooden cups up on the bench and poured a measure within each before handing them out to everyone.

"What is it?" Lark cradled the wooden cup Mazen offered and gazed down at the burgundy liquid he'd filled to the brim.

"Fruit wine." He took a long swig from his cup with a grin and sighed. "Nothing like a taste of home, eh, sis?"

Meital smiled then drank deeply from her own cup. "Mm-hm."

Lark's stomach turned, and she glanced at Tiora. She was staring into her cup as well, her brows drawn and a tiny frown on her lips. Would either of them ever be able to stomach the idea of drinking after all they went through with Rasmus and Pax?

She sucked in a deep breath through her nose and sat up straight. *No. It stops now.* She was done letting the memory of those evil men rule her life.

Lark lifted the cup and took a sip. The sweet liquid danced on her tongue. She grinned and took another. It wasn't long before she drained it.

She sat there on the bench, a pleasant warmth spreading through her veins, listening with half an ear to the chatter of her friends in this little hut, halfway around the world from everything she'd ever known. Maybe it was the wine, but suddenly it didn't seem so strange to think everything would all work out in the end.

She sent Muse a wobbly grin. The bird cocked her head sideways, studying her. "What?" Lark asked aloud, then hiccupped, covering her mouth and giggling.

Yeah... It was definitely the wine.

"I ought to have a joke for this," Muse said. *"Give me a moment. I'll think of something."*

She laughed even harder at that, earning a chorus of raised brows and side-eyed glances from the rest of the group. Waving a hand, she snapped her mouth shut, holding her breath to still the hiccups just as Sunny padded over and rested her head on her lap.

Suddenly, all of her mirth disappeared. She cradled the mutt's head in her hands. Her chin wobbled.

Sunny was only here with her because Conall wasn't. Her brother, her mother... They were dead, and she'd never see them again. The grief she'd been tamping down for so long sprang to the surface, and she let out a weary sob.

Aren slid closer, grabbing her empty cup and settling it on the floor so he could wrap an arm around her shoulders. "It's all right," he whispered.

"I got it," Muse exclaimed. *"Laugh, cry,* wine—*don't keep your feelings* bottled *up."*

Lark shook her head where it rested on Aren's shoulder, a tiny smile curving her lips. The absurdity of the situation hit her full force. She was in a hut in the jungle, crying on a Dolnman's shoulder while a falcon cracked awful jokes only she could hear. Life had certainly thrown a few surprises her way... No wonder she was a mess.

The door opened. Dausius and Dal returned, followed by Gia. Lark sat up straight, drying her eyes on her sleeve.

"Good news," Dausius said. "We're free to perform throughout Raimire. The Matas have just advised us to keep quiet about the recent events in Dracwood as we travel."

"Keep quiet?" Fillan jumped to his feet. "Do they mean to act like nothing ever happened? We have to do something!"

"We are doing something," a weathered voice declared, as a brightly colored walking stick slammed down on the ground.

An old woman stepped out of the interior doorway. She was all skin and bones, her gray hair tied up in a knot, eyes almost the exact same charcoal shade. "Hm, this must be the son you mentioned, Dal." She eyed Fillan up and down, frowning. "Don't be so quick to judge, boy. Your father volunteered the both of you to join the people we're sending to keep watch over the Boglands for any sign of the foul vermin. We don't need the rest of you lot causing a panic in the villages."

"This is Mata Moyra," Dausius explained. "She and Gia have graciously agreed to accompany us to the western coast, where we'll find a healer who may be able to help

Lark. Thank you again, my ladies," he added with a bow. "We are most appreciative of your assistance."

Moyra nodded and made her way swiftly to the outer door, slamming the stick with every step, though she seemed nimble enough she had little need for it. "Yes, yes. See that you are ready bright and early on the morrow," she called over her shoulder as she exited.

A healer. The pieces were finally falling into place. Maybe her earlier intuition had been right. Everything would work out... It had to.

She smiled. Tomorrow couldn't come soon enough.

Chapter 5

So, this was what it felt like to blend in.

For the first time in her life, Kayda was surrounded by people who looked much the same as herself. Jorians crowded the city streets, most dark-skinned or various hues of brown, much like her own light brown freckled skin. Their clothes and hair were dyed all shades of the rainbow, a dazzling kaleidoscope of brilliant variety. Her auburn hair, so rare in Dracwood, was common here, though whether dyed or natural she couldn't be sure.

Sand crunched under Kayda's boots. Wyll steered her through the city, past countless shops and cramped-looking houses built of yellow brick and clay tiles. Everywhere they turned, people made way for him. Not even the boldest shopkeeps yelled out for him to sample their wares. Was it fear keeping them silent, or respect?

"You would think him a prince," Kayda mumbled under her breath.

"Pardon?" Wyll dipped his head from where he strolled beside her, quirking a manicured brow.

"Nothing. Just wondering why the people here are so keen to avoid you." She lifted a brow of her own. "Should I be worried?"

He barked out a laugh. His voice was so loud and deep a child ahead of them jumped at the sound and clutched his mother's leg before the woman ushered him inside a nearby store. Wyll frowned, watching them disappear into the darkened interior. Then he shrugged, his frown disappearing so quickly she could've almost missed it.

"Trade is king here in Joria. And my family—our family"—he added with a smile—"we're responsible for nearly half of it. No one wants to anger the people who put bread on their table."

It was fear, then. Strange. She hadn't known Wyll long, but for some reason, she had a hard time picturing him angry. During their interaction on the docks, she'd said much that might drive a man into a rage, but he had remained cool and calm. Was it Wyll these people feared, or someone in the family she'd yet to meet?

She was still struggling to get a read on the man. There was still the problem of the destruction in Dracwood and her promise to find aid for her people. Would she be able to find allies with her family? Would she even want to be allied with them once she knew them more closely?

She tried to erase the thought from her mind. There was much to see. Kayda had never traveled outside of Dracwood. It sparked an odd thrill in her chest.

Her own mother might have explored these same streets. She could picture her as a young girl, baking in the heat. Smelling the roasting meat and nuts from street vendors. Marveling at the decadent lengths of silk displayed in the store windows. Kayda had read all about Joria and listened to her nurse Izora's stories over the years, but there was nothing quite like seeing it all with her own eyes.

A flash of metallic shimmer caught her eye. She stopped before a shop window and gaped at the gorgeous dress on display. The fabric reminded her vaguely of her ceremonial gown, but it was a dazzling shade of gold instead of red and cut in a much slimmer silhouette.

"You have a good eye, Princess." Wyll joined her at the glass. "That's one of our newest dyes, cultivated from a flower recently discovered in the depths of the Raimire jungle. Aurelia predicts the shade will be all the rage before long."

She glanced sideways, curving a brow in question. "Aurelia?"

"My great aunt. She's rarely wrong about these things."

"If she's your great aunt, that would make her my...?"

"Your grandmother. You'll meet her later, at Oasis Manse."

Kayda straightened and rolled her shoulders back, trying not to let the shock that rocked her with those words show on her face. She stole a last look at the lovely dress and turned to follow Wyll again.

She had a grandmother... Why was this the first she'd learned of it? How much more family did she have in this strange land? Why hadn't they ever tried to contact her? It was a long journey, for sure, but these people were obviously wealthy. In the shipping business, no less. And they couldn't even be bothered to send her a letter all these years?

She'd come here searching for her family, but the part of her that ached for a connection to the mother she'd never known bristled at the news. Deep down, she'd been expecting to find nothing, or at the least, having to look much harder. Discovering they'd been here all along, happily living their lives without feeling the deep longing—the loneliness—she'd lived with her whole life, stung more than she wanted to admit.

A breeze blew in with the promise of moisture ahead. The murmur of running water filled her ears. They must be approaching the large river she'd seen cutting through the city. Kayda gasped as they rounded a corner and her guess was proven true.

The river was massive, with at least a dozen bridges spanning the channel. Children splashed in the water or crawled along the banks, searching the long grass covering the riverbank on both sides.

All of that she noticed in passing, for something much more wondrous hovered in the air all along the river's length. Thousands of butterflies fluttered over the water, a shimmering curtain reflecting the sun in shades of silver, white, and copper.

"Jorian butterflies." Wyll strolled toward a large wooden footbridge to the north. "They live along the Peat River's banks. Without their cocoons, there wouldn't be any silk to trade."

"They're beautiful." Kayda held out her hand as a silver butterfly floated beside her, its gossamer wings sending warm air shivering over her skin.

"Yes... beautiful." Wyll smiled at her. Then he reached the footbridge and turned, beckoning her to follow. "Here it is. Oasis Manse."

Kayda's breath hitched, her mouth falling open. She'd been so charmed with the butterflies she hadn't yet looked across the water. The home they headed toward was equally captivating. It sat on a hill of lush grass overlooking the riverbank. One would think a girl who'd grown up in a castle wouldn't be so easily impressed, but the large mansion made her home seem garish and cold in comparison.

Oasis Manse was beautifully constructed, sporting circular spires and peaked roofs. Ivy and flowers crawled over the yellow brick. It must cost a fortune to maintain the all that greenery in this arid country.

Her boots thumped along the wooden footbridge. They crossed the river quickly and stepped onto the long, winding path to the house. Sweet jasmine and rose drifted through the air, courtesy of the immaculate gardens. There was a large stable in the distance, no doubt filled with the finest mounts.

No wonder Wyll didn't bat an eye at handing over an entire ship to her. If this was how they kept things outside of their house, what would the inside look like?

Kayda clenched her hands together. "Is there anything I should know before I meet your family?"

She glanced sideways. Wyll had no reason to confide in her. They'd only just met, after all—and she had swindled him out of a ship—but she hoped he might say something, anything, to set her mind at ease.

"Well, I've already told you about Auntie Aurelia. She'll be eager to meet you, no doubt. I have a brother, but he won't be at home. Just Auntie and Father." His face tightened at the mention of his father, but he quickly smoothed his features with a smile. "We don't have a huge family, I'm afraid, but we make up for it with big personalities." He laughed again at that, his smile spreading. "I think you shall fit in nicely."

Well, that was something. His words didn't fully banish the sinking feeling in her stomach, but it helped to know she wouldn't be bombarded with a dozen faces and names all at once. She took a deep breath as they approached the front entrance, and Wyll opened the door, ushering her inside.

The entranceway led to a room featuring a winding marble staircase with halls leading off into the wings on the top floor. Skylights let in the sun, brightening walls painted a glossy cream.

Wyll turned from the stairs, his boots tapping on the tiled floor, and opened a door to the left. Kayda followed, stepping inside a sitting room decorated in emerald and ivory. Sunlight filtered in through floor-to-ceiling windows along the far wall, the forest-green silk curtains pulled back to let in the afternoon sun.

They weren't alone. An old woman reclined on a white silk settee by the window, her sharp brown eyes lifting to inspect them as they entered. Her hair was pinned up in a tight bun and dyed the same lovely golden shade of the dress she'd spotted in the store window. The color brought out the warm tones of her brown skin as she bathed in sunlight.

"Auntie." Wyll crossed the room. "You're looking particularly ravishing today." He pulled her hand from her lap and placed a kiss on the back of her wrinkled skin, then sank down beside her.

"I look like death warmed over, and don't you forget it." Aurelia snatched her hand back and smoothed her bright orange silk dress. "What are you in here sweet-talking me for, boy? What's the trouble?" Her gaze lit on Kayda then, where she lingered inside the doorway. "Who's your friend? Come in and have a seat, child. I won't bite." She smiled warmly.

Kayda crept forward, studying the woman before her. So, this was her grandmother. She returned her smile as she took a seat on an emerald settee opposite the pair.

Despite Aurelia's abrupt tone with Wyll, Kayda could sense affection and warmth behind their interaction. If Aurelia could care so deeply for her nephew's son, then why not her own daughter's? Kayda opened her mouth to introduce herself, but the crack of a door slamming open made the words die on her lips.

"Wyll! Where are you, boy?" yelled the gruff voice of a man from the entranceway.

"In here, Father," Wyll replied, lounging back on the sofa.

Kayda craned her neck back to the sitting room's door in time to see a hefty man, the dark skin on his forehead glistening with sweat, burst into the room. His short, dark brown hair was disheveled, his bright green suit stained with perspiration. He stopped in the doorway, and crossed his arms, glowering at Wyll.

"What's this I hear about the *Sea Silk* being back in port? And you giving it away to some charlatan?" His deep voice boomed through the room.

Kayda fought the urge to shrink back on the settee. This must be the reason for the townsfolk's avoidant behavior toward Wyll. She frowned, picturing him laying into some poor shopkeep with that temper.

Wyll wasn't fazed by his father's anger. He remained relaxed, lounging as if he were listening to a gentle ballad and not an irritated accusation. "I suppose you missed the part where the *charlatan* brought a real-life dragon into port with her?"

Aurelia sat up straight, her eyes twinkling. "A dragon! Then the rumors are true?"

"I don't care if they flew in on a damned cloud of dust or a sea serpent." Wyll's father—her uncle—jabbed a finger at Wyll. "You've got a lot of nerve making decisions about my business without even consulting me."

Wyll leaned forward. "The *family business*, you mean. We agreed everyone in the family would have a part to play. Or are you forgetting about Saltcliff?"

He said the last word as casually as the rest, but it must have held some deeper meaning she couldn't decipher. Her uncle's shoulders slumped, and some of the tension in his face evaporated.

"Yes, yes. You're right on that count. The family business," he conceded.

"Well, now that we're agreed on that, let me introduce you to our long-lost relation." Wyll smirked. "May I present Princess Kayda of Dracwood." He stood and lifted his hand, palm outstretched toward her.

That statement earned her shocked stares from her grandmother and uncle. She rose to her feet, positioning herself so she could look at each of them with a glance. Aurelia blinked rapidly, her palm raised to cover her mouth.

Her uncle was a different story. He'd ignored her in his rage at Wyll, but now that his incredulous stare flashed on her, sweat moistened her skin. He swayed slightly where he stood and huffed out a series of shaky breaths, a fist pressed to his chest.

"Aurelia." He directed his stare on his aunt, his voice steady and cold, tinged with carefully leashed anger. "You told me I'd never have to deal with this. Take care of it, or I will." With that, he spun on his heel and fled the room, slamming the door behind him.

Kayda flinched as the door banged closed, rattling the candlesticks on the walls. What was that all about? She turned to Aurelia—her grandmother. Would her welcome be just as hospitable?

"Sit back down, child." Aurelia sighed. "I suspected this day would come before long. You, too, Wyll. It's time you both learned the truth."

Wyll seated himself across from Aurelia on the emerald settee. Kayda sat beside him, perching on the cushion's edge. Aurelia drew in a deep breath, reaching for a silver bell on a side table. "Perhaps we should call for refreshments. It's a long story—"

"We're not hungry, Auntie." Wyll snatched the bell from the table and silenced it in his fist. "Let's hear it."

Aurelia narrowed her eyes at Wyll, frowning. Then she folded her hands in her lap and shifted her sharp brown gaze to her as she spoke. "You are not our kin, Kayda. It was all a lie. I'm sorry."

Kayda leaned back, her thoughts swirling around like a storm. "What do you mean? My mother was Solenne of Joria, daughter of traders. Are you saying she wasn't your daughter?"

Aurelia's eyes softened. "Solenne was my daughter. But she wasn't your mother."

Wyll rubbed his chin with his knuckles. "Let me get this straight... Our family—we built a reputation over the years, partly on the fact that we share blood with royalty. That was all a lie?"

"Yes," Aurelia said.

"Well, if she's not my mother, then who is?" Kayda asked.

"I don't know, child."

Kayda sagged in the seat, her limbs feeling too heavy to move. The certainty behind the words twisted her stomach in knots. It was all too much. First the mystery of her father, and now her mother as well? She thought she'd finally found a link to her past, only to have it snatched away before it was fully in her grasp.

"Tell us everything, Auntie," Wyll demanded. But when the old woman shot him a steely glare, he added, "Please."

"Solenne was a delicate girl. Sweet, biddable. And talented." Aurelia glanced at the ceiling before looking back at them. "It was a fluke. We've never had talent in the family before, and Solenne wanted nothing to do with being a mage. But her father insisted she be sent to Mage Keep for training. Before she was sent away, we were surprised with another offer—her hand in marriage to Prince Gideon. She only said yes out of fear. Fear and a healthy dose of guilt from her father and uncle, insisting she do what's best for the family."

Aurelia sneered at the memory, her fists clenching around the silk of her dress. "So, when the offer came to save her from the marriage, I took it. And I don't regret it for a second after I learned what happened to that poor girl who replaced her. All those mysterious deaths happening to royal wives in Kings Keep. It would've been her dead instead."

The girl who took her place... that was her real mother, then. Whoever she was.

"What offer?" Wyll asked.

"A mage approached me the week before Solenne was set to sail off to Dracwood for her wedding day. They said they could make a trade. Solenne for a girl of their choosing. She would have to disappear, but would be free to live her life as she chose."

Kayda's heart sped up. The mages were behind this? Who had they switched for Solenne, and why?

"So, Solenne is out there somewhere? Living her life with none the wiser?" Wyll leaned back and crossed his arms.

"No." Aurelia sighed. "She died a few years back." A bittersweet smile crossed her lips. "But for a long time, yes, she lived. Carved out a place for herself as a singer in a traveling show, if you'd believe it. I snuck off to see her every chance I could get. That's how your father found out, Wyll. He agreed to keep it all a secret. Please, you two must keep it to yourselves as well." Her gaze darted between them, full of urgency.

"Yes, yes, of course." Wyll waved a hand. He turned to her. "What do you say, Kayda? I gather you have as much to lose if this information became known as we would."

She nodded. "Yes, I agree. On one condition. Please, Aurelia, can you tell me anything more about my mother or the mage who made this deal with you? Anything at all?"

"I never learned the mage's name. But she was dark-skinned like me, average height and build, with white hair. Jorian by her accent."

Her stomach lurched, confirming the suspicion floating in the back of her mind, which she was too scared to voice. That sounded just like Izora.

"What about my mother?" Kayda asked. "Did you ever meet her?"

"Just once. I only saw her in passing. Long enough to know she could be mistaken for Solenne if you didn't look too closely." She closed her eyes, her brow furrowing. "I'm afraid she looked much the same as any number of young women who hail from these parts. But there was one thing that set her apart."

"What?" Kayda leaned forward again.

The old woman's eyes shot open. "She had her hair plaited in dozens of tiny braids."

Wyll stared at her curiously. "Sounds like your mother was a Sul. They all wear their hair like that. Some tradition of theirs."

A Sul... Blazes. Of course, her mother belonged to the most reclusive group of people in the whole southern continent. At least she had a clue. It was a start.

Kayda drew in a deep breath and stood. "Thank you, Aurelia. Wyll. You've been very kind. It's a shame we aren't kin. I would've enjoyed getting to know you both better." She strode forward, straight for the door.

"Wait, Kayda." Aurelia's plea made her pause. "You don't have to leave so soon. Stay for dinner."

She considered the offer for a brief moment. There was still the problem of finding aid for Dracwood. But it was probably best to wait for Wyll's father's temper to cool before broaching the subject. There would be time for that later, after she solved the mystery of who her real mother was.

She sent the old woman a grin. "Thank you for the offer, but I have a desert trip to prepare for." Then she opened the door and was soon gone from Oasis Manse.

Chapter 6

"Concentrate," Delyth said.

Conall stared at the sack of flour perched atop a hard slab of rock across from him on the Turney Mountains' lower slopes. Dim dusk light surrounded them, the chill air biting his cheeks. He sucked in a deep breath and held it, willing the sack to topple over. The hair on the back of his neck prickled.

Thunk.

"Excellent, Quent." Delyth smiled warmly at the boy, her cheeks rosy.

Conall glared beside him, but his expression softened upon seeing the boy's face lit with joy over his success. He blew out the breath and returned his attention to his sack of flour, still stubbornly standing on the rock and not flat in the snow like Quent's.

Blazes. It wasn't enough that a boy who hadn't yet finished growing had shown him up; he was growing, too. Growing soft. He had to concentrate.

They'd been at this every day since the avalanche. Delyth took every opportunity to train her newest recruits whenever they stopped to rest. But though their journey into

Doln had almost ended, he was still struggling. Even with the simplest and most abundant of the elements.

"Empty your mind," Delyth repeated the instructions he'd listened to so many times. "Feel the air flowing through you as you breathe. Shape it to your will."

Conall sucked in another breath, his gaze glued to the brown sack. He watched the blasted thing fall in his mind. He felt the wind rushing forward and heard that satisfying *thunk* echo through the air. All this he imagined while he held his breath until little dots formed in the corners of his eyes. He exhaled.

Nothing.

He clenched his jaw. "It's no use. I'm not meant to be a mage."

Delyth strode closer, the blue of her eyes piercing from within the hood of her gray fur. "It will come with time and practice." She didn't appear flustered in the least by his lack of progress. She turned and addressed them both. "That's all for tonight. It's getting late. Get some rest." Then she made her way across the small plateau, disappearing beneath the flap of her tent.

"Maybe you have a block," Quent said.

Conall raised a brow. "What's that?"

"Something stopping you from summoning, even when you ought to be able to." The boy strode over to the rock slab, retrieved his sack of flour where it rested in the snow, and hefted it up in scrawny arms with a huff. "You heard what Delyth said. We ought to be the strongest mages in centuries, since the Palisade didn't use our power." He glanced down, his gaze shifting rapidly. "Well, it took some of yours, but... you know what I mean."

Conall lifted his sack and grunted. Not from the weight—he'd hefted much more working daily on his family farm—but at the reminder of the Palisade's fall and what it had cost him. Not just years of his life but a measure of his power, too. He shrugged off the sick feeling of regret. He'd lingered enough on those emotions.

"That happen often? Someone gets blocked?" he asked.

Quent hobbled across the plateau, lugging the sack between his legs. "No, not exactly. But I heard my mom talking about it once. It happened to one of her friends years ago." He hefted the bag higher in his arms. "He found a way to work around it, eventually."

"How'd he manage that?" Conall stopped before the supply pile, lifted the tarp, and set the bag of flour beneath it.

Quent plopped his bag down beside his, then stood and stretched. "Sorry, I don't remember. It was a long time ago."

Conall sighed, dropping the tarp and heading for his tent.

Figures.

Quent shuffled forward, rubbing his back. "Well, I guess I'll see you tomorrow."

Conall lifted the flap to his tent. "C'mon in, Quent. Have a bite to eat."

They'd both skipped dinner to train. There'd be no one awake in the children's tent after the day's travel. He couldn't send the lad to bed on an empty stomach.

"Really?" Quent's green eyes lit up, and his posture straightened. "Thanks." He rushed forward, all signs of his earlier sluggishness disappearing with the invitation.

Shadow rested inside, atop a bedroll. He lifted his head lazily as they both crowded in, his tail wagging. *"Any progress?"*

"'Fraid not." He left the flap lifted while he pulled out his tinderbox, using it to light a stumpy candle within a glass and metal lantern the mages had provided him, before sealing the tent against the wind. The small tent he and Shadow called home the last few weeks was too small for a fire, but with the flap closed against the worst of the wind and bundled together beneath piled furs, it was cozy enough they slept soundly most nights.

"So, what've ya got to eat?" Quent plopped down beside Shadow.

Conall fought the urge to scowl, seeing the boy sitting so closely with his bondmate. Most of the children still kept a wary eye on the large gray wolf, especially after watching him stalk and slaughter peaceful mountain goats.

Not Quent. Ever since the day Shadow saved their lives, he'd treated the wolf like a treasured friend, no matter how many times he came back to camp covered in blood, dragging a fresh kill behind him.

Conall grabbed his pack and pulled out his waterskin and enough dried meat for all of them. "Here." He handed the boy his share and tossed a portion to Shadow.

They all chewed in silence for a time.

"Can I ask you something?" Conall handed the boy the waterskin.

Quent swallowed his mouthful of meat. "Sure." He lifted the skin to his lips and took a long drink.

"You mentioned your mother tonight. I'm not sure if you remember, but you brought her up before. When we were trapped under all that snow, before Shadow found us."

Quent nodded and handed the skin back. "I remember," he said solemnly.

"Why'd you want me to tell her you're sorry?" Conall grabbed the skin, took a quick gulp, and waited for the boy's reply.

Quent's gaze dropped to the tent floor, and he absentmindedly shredded the last of his meat between his fingers. "They sent her on assignment a few days before the Palisade fell. When she left, she asked me to keep an eye on my sister."

Quent had a sister? The meat he'd just swallowed caught in Conall's throat. By now, he'd met everyone on the mountain. Whoever she was, she wasn't with them.

"Oriana is four years older than me, but she's always been the one more likely to end up in trouble. She should've been the one looking out for me... Funny how that works out." Quent looked up, a halfhearted smile curving his lips.

"She ran off with Ereni?"

Quent nodded again, shoving the shredded meat into his mouth. "I ought to be heading back," he mumbled. He moved to stand.

Conall shot out a hand to still him. "You can stay here tonight, with us. No sense in you blasting the rest of the kids with the cold breeze and waking all the babes."

"You sure?"

"Yeah, it's no problem. We've enough room for the three of us."

Shadow raised his head again as Quent settled down against his side. *Are we collecting strays now?*

"It's just for the night." Conall reclined on the opposite side of Shadow after snuffing out the lantern.

Shadow snorted.

So, maybe he was growing soft. But it was hard not to feel for the lad. His mother had been thoughtless to leave a boy so young with so much responsibility.

His own father's last words to him had been much the same before the fateful sea voyage that led to his death. "Watch over your mother and the new babe," he'd said. Now, all these years later, hearing news of his father's supposed return from the dead, the heedless request burned him anew.

How could he have asked that of him—a mere boy of six—knowing he was destined never to return? All these years Conall had struggled with guilt and inadequacy over that request. His father should've been the one taking care of his family. Not pushing the responsibility off on a child.

Why had he left? What could have made his father turn his back on his family, fake his own death, and start a new life?

The questions nagged at him as he lay there on the mountainside. Sleep was slow to find him that evening, but eventually, his body's weariness overrode the swirling thoughts in his mind.

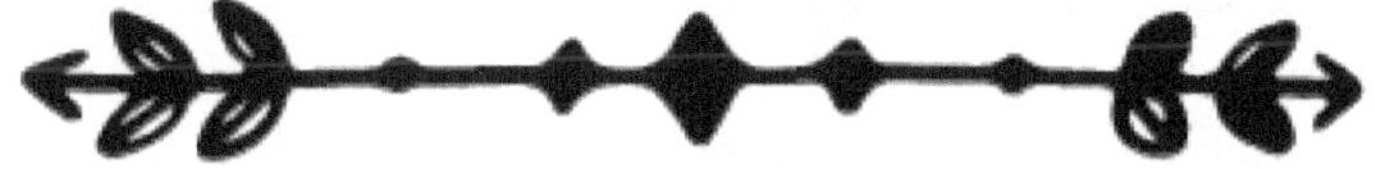

Riders from Gransea found them early the next afternoon. They'd just stepped down on the first level land they'd seen since setting out on the mountain passes weeks ago when two burly men galloped astride them. They dressed in dark furs, their thick beards obscuring the bottom halves of their pale faces.

"Ho, Dracians. We're charged with escorting you to Chief Aundrea," said the taller man as he pulled his chestnut mount to a halt.

Delyth swept forward from the center of the group. "Thank you. That would be most helpful."

The riders silently moved into position, one at the group's head, and the other bringing up the rear. Conall drifted among the mages and children, trying not to feel like a stray lamb being herded toward the city.

The air was slightly warmer at the lower elevation but still held a chill, unlike what he was used to this time of the fall. A thin layer of snow lay on most of the ground and covered the evergreens with a dusting of white. The rider led their group down a wide trail cutting through the forested countryside. At first glance, the path and surrounding woods appeared deserted, but the sight of several footprints the size of his head in the snow was enough to keep him from falling behind.

Conall lengthened his stride, the snow crunching beneath his boots. Soon, he reached Delyth's side, where she trekked behind the tall Dolnman and his mount.

"So, who's Chief Aundrea?" he asked.

Delyth cocked her head sideways. "He's the leader of these people. Well, one of them."

"And you think he'll help us?"

"I expect so. Doln differs from Dracwood in many ways, but Chief Aundrea is a good man. Just be sure to keep your opinions to yourself, if they're not favorable."

"What do you mean by that?"

"The chief is not the sharpest knife, but he is the rustiest. If you give him cause to cut you, you'll regret it."

"He has a bit of a temper, I take it?"

"Yes. And you'd do well to steer clear of it while we're in Gransea. I expect we won't be there long. Only a few days to make sure our people have settled in, then the three of us..." She glanced at him and Shadow in turn, "Will head out to meet the Winter Witch."

Conall's stomach clenched at the reminder. He'd not forgotten the reason for his journey into this frosty foreign land. He had to know, once and for all, what had happened to his sister. The journey to meet the Winter Witch couldn't come fast enough.

The forest path curved around a bend and opened to reveal a large valley. A walled city sat at the bottom, nestled along the coast. In the distance, the ocean sparkled in the afternoon sun, dotted with ships spanning the coastline and harbored along the shore.

The rider led them through wide swaths of farmland encircling the city, fallow now, so late in the season, and on a course straight for the massive gate standing at the trail's end. They passed without issue through the entrance onto the cobblestone streets. Except for the curious glances of a few pale-faced Dolnmen and women, no one made a move to greet or speak to them.

Port cities were used to foreign visitors. Still, it seemed strange to be met with so little fanfare after all they'd been through to reach this land. Back home, in Greenvale, there were a handful of busybodies that couldn't stand to let a traveler pass by without badgering them for details about their lives.

It was odd so many on the crowded streets of this great city would watch such a large group of mages and children—obviously worse for the wear—pass by with no remark. Perhaps this lack of curiosity was one of the differences Delyth had been referring to?

Even the shopkeeps kept quiet, content to sit silently over their wares, not hawking their goods to any who passed. The buildings, at least, bore a resemblance to the cramped houses and shops of Flamesmoat. Only these were built out of the silver and white mountain stones instead of the red brick prevalent further south.

They traveled long enough the smallest children began to tire, tugging the adults and older kids' sleeves, whining for a break. Then the tall rider pulled to a stop before an immense stone wall somewhere in the city center. He hopped down from his horse and rapped on a wooden gate in an elaborate pattern. It was likely some coded response, for the door slid open immediately. The man strode in without a word, and their group followed.

Inside, they found a large courtyard surrounding a stately square keep built of silver and white stone. A handful of burly, bearded men, dressed in the same dark furs as the riders, encircled the yard. Their stares locked on a pair of men fighting with blunted swords in the center of a dirt ring. The two fighters had doffed their furs and fought in similar garb—brown wool trousers, plain shirts, and calf-length leather boots.

At first glance, the shorter and older of the pair appeared to be faring worse. His white shirt was stained with sweat and his long golden hair hung lank, an odd contrast next to his neatly trimmed beard.

The second man stood nearly a head taller and was at least two decades younger, gauging by his pale, unwrinkled face. Though his fiery red beard was more unkempt, his bald head barely glistened. His muscles rippled beneath his tan tunic as he lunged and parried. His incredible speed and massive reach caused the smaller man to dodge and spin like a frenzied dancer to avoid his blows.

Conall did his best not to gawk, but it was a hard feat to accomplish. He'd never seen such a mesmerizing display. The clash of their blows and grunts of exertion rang out, their feet kicking dirt into the air. The mages and children drew closer, everyone craning their necks to watch.

It went on for ages with neither man gaining ground, though sweat continued to pour off the blond man as he whirled to evade blow after blow.

Then a child screamed. One of theirs, no doubt, for it was a sound Conall had become so accustomed to during their mountain trek it barely registered. But that was not the case for the red-bearded man. He flinched at the scream, and that single moment of distraction was all the blond fighter needed. He darted in quicker than a hare, sweeping his foe's leg, crashing the larger man to the ground and pointing his blunt sword at his neck.

"I yield," said the man on the ground, dropping his blade and holding his hands up flat in surrender.

The blond fighter only laughed, an airy chuckle full of pleasure. He speared his sword in the dirt at his side and reached down to help his opponent to his feet. Then he nodded to the larger man with a smile as his gaze zeroed in on their group.

The smile dropped from his face, replaced with a flat stare. He strode purposefully past the circled men, directly for Delyth.

"Well, it's not every day the Sade Prim comes for a visit." He slid a hand through his sweat-soaked locks, slicking his long hair out of his blue eyes. "What do I owe the pleasure?"

"We've come seeking aid, Chief Aundrea," Delyth replied. "The Palisade has fallen."

Aundrea showed no surprise at the announcement, only nodded his head somberly. "So, the rumors out of Minsport are true then. Dark days are ahead for us all." He took a deep breath, then turned his attention to the rest of the group, his gaze sliding over everyone until he caught sight of Shadow. His lips quirked up in a smile. "Son of a slushstorm. Is that a wolf? There haven't been wolves this far north in centuries."

"I think the chief likes you," Conall said.

Aundrea dropped to one knee, holding out his hand and clicking his tongue, as if inviting a pup over for a sniff.

Shadow snorted from where he stood at Conall's side. He stared straight at the chief and sat flat on his haunches. *"No thanks. I can smell him from here."*

Delyth jumped in. "That's Shadow. And this is Conall of Greenvale, his bondmate."

Conall stepped forward, holding his hand out. "Nice to meet you."

Aundrea clutched his hand and shook, his grip crushing in its intensity. "Bonded to a wolf. I'd love to pick your brain, Conall of Greenvale." He let go first, the wrinkles around his eyes crinkling as he smiled.

Conall resisted the urge to rub his hand after the brutal shake, forcing a tight smile.

Aundrea directed his attention back to the crowd, opening his arms wide and raising his voice. "You all must've had a rough journey through the mountains. Where are my manners? Come into the keep. We'll have a hot meal prepared and find a spot for the little ones to rest."

The gathered men had already begun heading inside. Upon hearing their chief's announcement, a pair of them threw the doors open wide, using a couple of large gray stones as doorstops. Children and mages streamed forward eagerly, likely excited about the promise of an actual roof over their heads for a change.

Conall moved to follow, but Delyth stopped him with a hand on his arm. Within a few moments, nearly everyone filed inside.

Not quite everyone. There was an old man, his olive skin standing out starkly among all the pale-faced northerners. He leaned down in the dirt pit, struggling to pull free the blunted sword Aundrea had stabbed into the ground. The red-bearded fellow approached him with a gruff, "Hey," and a pit formed in Conall's stomach.

Everyone knew the Doln kept slaves, but this was the first evidence he'd seen of it. He inhaled sharply as the bearded fighter approached the man, ready to rush over should he harm the poor fellow. But the fighter only shooed the man aside with a wave and pulled the sword free on his own, leaving the old man to shuffle inside the keep.

Despite the calm interaction, Conall had half a mind to say something. Slavery just didn't sit right in his mind. No man should be forced to work for another. But he took one look at Delyth's face and remembered her warning. His gaze slid to the chief. Perhaps now was not the time to debate the evils of slavery.

The red-bearded fighter tossed the sword into a nearby box, then made his way to the keep and knocked the rocks free. He closed the doors and strode over to stand at his chief's side. That left the four of them, and Shadow, standing out in the courtyard.

"This is my son, Taul." Aundrea nodded to the red-bearded fellow and make introductions.

Delyth spoke up as soon as they exchanged pleasantries. "I'll get straight to it, Chief. The scourge have returned." She strolled back toward the stone wall, where their group had stacked their various supplies and baggage once they entered the courtyard. She stopped beside a blanket-shrouded oval.

He'd seen beneath that blanket once before. Back then it had shuddered and swayed, the creature within shrieking and snarling. Not today. It sat silent and still.

Delyth lifted the blanket, revealing the carcass of one of the scourge. It appeared her prediction that the ferocious rodent wouldn't survive the Turney Mountains' extreme cold was correct.

In death, the silver and brown-striped creature seemed much less of a threat. But Conall remembered its viciousness. The wild, fearless way it strained at the metal cage bars, snapping and scratching to be free. He shuddered at the reminder that thousands of those beasts were roaming unchecked across his homeland, feasting on anything that moved.

"They don't look so fearsome." Taul crouched beside the cage and peered within.

"If it were just one, then I might agree." Delyth dropped the brown blanket to the ground, letting the men look their fill. "But there are thousands more where that one came from. Hundreds of thousands before long."

Aundrea jostled the cage, flipping the creature on its side. "Look at the teeth and claws on that thing." He stood and addressed Delyth. "We've already begun to assist the refugees from Dracwood pouring through Minsport. Your people are welcome, too, of course. When the time comes that we must battle these foul vermin, we'll add our steel to the fray. I have only one condition."

Delyth sent a shrewd glance to the chief. "Which is what?"

"Some of the mages you've brought with you must stay, both here and in Minsport, to defend our lands against the inevitable invasion, should we fail."

"That's reasonable." Delyth nodded. "Done." She lifted the blanket and covered the cage once more. "I have a favor to ask, in exchange."

Aundrea laughed again, an incredulous bark this time. "Have I not offered enough in exchange already?"

She ignored the question and tossed her long gray braid over her shoulder, extending her arm toward him and Shadow. "We've need of a guide. We have to see the Winter Witch."

All the humor drained from his face at the request. "That... I can't do. In the spring, certainly. Now?" He shook his head. "It would be suicide."

Conall's chest tightened, and he schooled his features, forcing his face to remain still instead of sending a heated glare in Delyth's direction.

Suicide... Why was this the first mention he'd heard of the dangers of this journey? What would they face that even this incredible fighter balked at the thought of undertaking this trip?

"The guide need not travel all the way to her hut. We just need someone to take us as far north as Norwich." She clutched Aundrea's forearm and gazed up into his face. "Please, Chief. This is of the utmost importance."

Taul sauntered forward. "I'll take you."

Aundrea frowned, opening his mouth, only to close it a heartbeat later and nod, his jaw clenched tightly. "Well, you have your guide, Sade Prim," he said, a lightness to his tone that sounded forced. "I wish you fair weather and good luck for your journey. You're gonna need it."

Chapter 7

Lark's body swayed in the warm early morning breeze. A cacophony of noise that never ceased pervaded the air.

The jungle never rested, but the Wandering Bards did. Each of them cocooned within a hammock strung in between the trees, high in the dense canopy. It was the only way to sleep safely in the deep jungle. Nocturnal hunters stalked the forest floor in the dark. And out here, between villages, they were all alone, with no one to call on, should disaster strike.

The first night had been the worst. The thought of sleeping high above the ground, one wrong move away from plummeting into the dirt in the black of night, sent goosebumps all over her flesh. But after watching ancient Mata Moyra climb one of the spindly jungle trees and hoist herself into a hammock, Lark had felt compelled to follow. Truth be told, it was quite relaxing once she got the hang of it.

A yawn rose from her lips, followed by a smile as her gaze drifted to her attire. She'd had more than her share of getting used to new things over the last few weeks of travel.

All of their group now wore the sheer green luct fabric so popular in the jungle. She'd balked at trying it on when Moyra presented the outfits on the first morning of their trek. But she'd relented once offered a thin sleeveless top to wear along with the tiny shorts beneath the transparent fabric.

Fillan's explanation on their journey through the bog proved correct. Since donning the garb, the multitude of biting insects swarming the jungle had ignored her. That alone was enough reason to keep her wearing it, even if it hadn't been a thousand times more comfortable in the thick humidity than the dresses and skirts she'd packed from home.

"Morning, Muse." Lark spotted her bondmate perched next to her on the branches of a massive diquat tree.

"Morning." Muse shook her feathers and stretched her wings.

Lark stretched, too. Then, balancing carefully, she left Sunny where she lay by her feet and crawled across the hammock. She climbed to the jungle floor, plucking one of the diquat fruits on her way down.

Her boots sunk into the spongy soil as she picked her way silently through the trees to the banks of the stream they'd camped next to. She leaned down and rinsed the diquat in the warm water before taking a bite of the sweet pink fruit. Diquats were smaller than the apples of Dracwood, and their flesh softer, but they were just as delicious.

"I thought I told you not to wander off on your own?"

Moyra's booming voice startled her, and she almost lost her balance on the slick rock she perched on.

"I'm not alone, Mata." She stepped back from the stream's edge, nodding to Muse in the branches above her head. They had taken to doing everything in pairs. With so many dangers in the jungle, it made sense to have a second set of eyes on alert for any trouble. "I might say the same to you..." she added with a smile, taking another bite of her breakfast.

The old woman huffed and inched past her, slamming her walking stick in the dirt before filling her waterskin from the stream. "The jungle hasn't killed me yet. Today will be no exception. Come, let's wake the others. If I'm right, which I usually am, we'll reach Stoneshore this afternoon."

Lark swallowed. She chucked the pit of her fruit into the water and followed Moyra back through the trees. "Really? That's great news."

Stoneshore was the coastal village where they'd meet the healer, who she hoped would become her teacher. After weeks of travel, and stopping to perform in a handful of tiny villages along the way, they were finally about to reach their destination. A tingle of excitement stirred in her breast.

They roused the others, packed camp, and set out, heading west. Lark hefted the pack on her back, her shoulders already protesting the familiar weight. Each of them carried all their belongings with them. There were no beasts of burden that could survive the dangers of Raimire.

But though the constant hiking was not ideal for her comfort, the constant activity strengthened her muscles and boosted her endurance, leaving her fitter than at any other point in her life. Hopefully, her physical transformation would be beneficial in the days to come, as she learned to control her talent.

Soon, the warm morning yielded to another sweltering day. Sweat trickled down her back underneath the heavy pack. When Gia called for a stop at the top of a tree-covered ridge that was home to an enormous waterfall, Lark sighed with relief. She shucked off her pack and slumped down on the roots of a massive diquat tree to rest in the shade.

"That's the Shore River." Gia pointed north at the waterfall. "Stoneshore rests along the river's southern banks, just west of this waterfall. We'll rest for a bit, then all that's left is to climb down the ridge, and we're home."

Tiora collapsed next to Lark on the diquat roots, gazing down the ridge's edge. "We have to climb down there?"

Mata Moyra scoffed. "If my old bones can handle the climb, then you shall, too, child."

Dausius stopped beside Gia. "I'm sure our guide will know the easiest way to the bottom."

Gia only smiled in response, her tanned cheeks reddening. She and Dausius had become rather cozy during their trek through the jungle.

Tiora leaned closer to Lark. "Hey, I need to make a stop in the woods. Care to join me?"

Lark nodded, pushing to her feet and leaving her pack on the ground. She followed Tiora through the trees the way they'd come, far enough from the main group they could be afforded a bit of privacy. She waited with her back turned for Tiora to take care of her business, scanning the trees for any sign of danger.

For all Mazen's teasing about snakes, jagoths, and the many other predators rumored to inhabit Raimire, they'd trekked across the jungle without trouble. There'd been a few times she'd spotted a scaled tail slithering through the underbrush or dangling from a tree, but the snakes seemed happy to allow their group to pass through their territory unmolested, preferring to hunt smaller game.

The jagoths—the creatures that made the hammocks a necessity—they'd not seen, but they'd heard their unmistakable growling mating calls countless times in the night. Luckily, the beasts rested most of the day. And so far, they'd been lucky enough not to run into any of the vicious cats sleeping in their dens. Still, she kept a wary eye on the jungle, not willing to press her luck by being less than vigilant.

"I'm done." Tiora popped up beside her. "Did you need to go?"

"No, I'm al—" The word snagged in her throat as she glimpsed something moving in the jungle ahead of them. She grabbed Tiora's luct sleeve. "Did you see that?"

Tiora frowned, peering into the distance. "No. Maybe we should head back, just in case."

Visions of jagoths flashed in Lark's mind. Could that be one of their dens?

She nodded, and was about to turn back when she spied another glimpse of movement. This time, the image appeared from within a small break in the foliage, close to the ground.

She gasped. It was a little girl, her long brown braid dangling in the dirt as she scrambled backward on her hands and knees, her face full of terror.

"What is that?" Tiora squinted into the distance, her lips pursed.

Lark heard the question, but as if from a distance. Her breath hitched, then flooded her chest, quick and shallow, her hands shaking. Then her feet flew forward as if they had a life of their own.

"Get the others, now," she yelled, not bothering to look back to check if Tiora was listening.

"Muse. I need you!"

"I'm coming," Muse replied, without hesitation.

Lark hurtled through the jungle. The glimpse she'd caught of the girl had quickly vanished, but she shot straight for the spot she'd last seen her scuttling through the underbrush. The fear on her face was branded in her mind's eye.

What was she running from? She had to save her. There was no way she was going to watch another child die. Not today. Never again.

She ran for so long. It didn't make sense... She should be there. How had she even seen this far?

She shoved the thought aside. Her lungs burned, and her legs wobbled like jelly when she finally arrived at the break in the foliage. She dove between bushes, adrenaline raging within her as she took stock of the scene.

The girl was there, cowering back against the gargantuan roots of a massive kapok tree. And there before her, poised to strike, was a red and black-striped snake.

The snake was huge—at least as long as the girl—and a thousand times more vicious. Its mouth opened, emitting a toe-curling hiss. Its head spun in Lark's direction as she stood there, fighting to catch her breath, soaked in sweat and dizzy with terror.

For a heartbeat she paused, eyes widening as she fought the panic and fear racing through her body. Then the serpent swung back to the girl, raising its head high off the ground, coiling back to strike.

Lark didn't think. She jumped, kicking the snake as she leapt, and rolled to a stop in front of the girl. Pain shot up her leg.

The snake slithered back from her strike, hissing louder than ever.

She gulped and positioned herself between the child and the snake as it recoiled, ignoring the pain stabbing her leg when she placed her weight on it.

The snake was angry now. Even angrier than before. Its scales rippled, and venom dripped from within its open jaw as it hissed.

Lark's heart hammered. She couldn't see a way out of this. It was her and a child against a pissed off predator, and she was out of ideas.

Wait. She dug her fingers into the soft soil, praying she could use the magic the same way she had to stop Gael.

Sink, snake. Blazes. Sink!

She waited for the vibration to fill her the way it always did when she used her talent, but all she could feel was panic, pain, and fear. It was too late. The snake drew back to strike.

Muse tore into sight, flashing down from the sky. She dove with expert precision, aiming for the massive snake's neck and latching onto its throat, tearing at its skin.

Worry swamped Lark for her bondmate, but she seized her chance. She pulled the girl to her feet and raced away. Lark shoved her through the hole in the underbrush and spun back to where Muse and the snake grappled.

"I got her. We're safe," she screamed in her mind.

Muse pulled free, abandoning her attempt to attack the back of the massive beast's neck and rose into the air.

The snake looked dazed for an instant. Then it bolted into a hole in the same kapok tree the girl had cowered under. Lark's lips quirked up in a crooked smile as she backed away through the underbrush.

So, the girl had been blocking the snake's den. Wonderful.

Now that the adrenaline and fear had passed, the pain in her leg started screaming. She glanced down, examining the wound on her leg for the first time. She had two lines of blood leaking down her right calf, topped with a pair of circular puncture marks. It was the same leg she'd used to kick the snake out of the way. The wound burned and was already starting to swell.

Had the snake bitten her as she kicked? Her stomach clenched with dread. She remembered Mazen's warnings of how quickly Raimish snakes' venom could kill.

Was she going to die?

She collapsed to the ground, a wave of dizziness washing over her.

"Lady, are you all right?"

A pair of curious brown eyes stared down at her. It was the girl. She was thin, wide-eyed, and dressed in the typical luct outfit, minus the undershirt. Now that she hovered above her, her brows knitted together with worry, Lark could see she wasn't a child at all. She was a girl on the cusp of womanhood, perhaps twelve or thirteen years old. Still, Lark's heart warmed all the same, seeing the young girl perched above her whole and unharmed, not bitten by that awful snake.

Muse landed beside her, and the girl hopped back in alarm. *"Lark. What's wrong?"*

"The snake, it got me." Her head swam with fuzziness as the pain radiated up her leg.

The girl snatched a stick off the ground and swung it at Muse. "Get away from her," she yelled.

It was Muse's turn to hop back. She screeched angrily, lifting off the ground and landing on a branch of a nearby tree, out of the girl's reach.

Footsteps pounded on the ground. A moment later, the faces of Lark's friends appeared in the jungle behind them.

"Ravenna?" Gia was the first to arrive, the name tumbling off her lips as she spotted them.

"Gia? Thank the Mother!" The girl—Ravenna—shot up from where she crouched beside Lark and dropped the stick. "A snake had me cornered. This lady saved me, but I think she got bit." She grimaced, glancing back at Lark. "It was a hexer."

"Rot and decay." Gia pressed a hand to her chest. "Find Mika. Have him meet us on the ridge. We'll carry her down the trail. Run!"

Ravenna sped off without another word, quickly disappearing in the distance.

Lark tried to speak. She tried to stand. But her body wouldn't listen. Panic struck her again, spreading through muscles as limp as old lettuce. Tiora knelt beside her and grabbed her slack hand. Aren and Dausius crowded around her. Mazen and Meital paced on the trail, gazing at her from a distance. All of their faces mirrored the shock and disbelief raging within her.

Aren turned to Gia, his voice wobbling. "What's happening? Tell me what to do."

Out of all of them, Gia was the only one who held her cool. She strode forward, grabbing Lark's brown leather boots and lifting her legs. "Grab her shoulders. We'll all take turns carrying her. We have to bring her to the healer, now."

Aren nodded, and soon Lark found herself lifted in his strong arms. They hurried through the jungle in silence until they reached the spot where Mata Moyra and Sunny awaited them.

"I saw Ravenna tear through. What's happened?" the old woman called out in question.

Gia didn't slow, only grunted out a single word as she hustled forward, struggling under Lark's dead weight. "Hexer."

Moyra gasped and grabbed Sunny's collar, holding her steady. "Go. I'll bring the dog so she's not underfoot. Don't wait for me if I fall behind. I know the way."

The urgency in Moyra's tone sent another wave of panic through Lark. She did her best to stay calm, but her mind was screaming. Why couldn't she move? Why couldn't she speak? Tears leaked out of her eyes, the only physical sign of distress in a body out of her control.

"Muse? Blazes, I'm in trouble. Please, tell me you can still hear me."

"Yes, yes, I'm here. Lark, you're going to be all right. The healer from the village will come." Muse hopped from tree to tree, shadowing their movements.

Hearing Muse's voice in her mind calmed some part deep within Lark. Her heart still raced, but the comfort of her bondmate swept over her, soothing the voice inside that screamed until it was merely a whimper.

Muse was right. She would survive this. Her friends would save her.

They reached the ridge. Gia barked out orders, having each of them climb a little lower and stand in a line so they could pass her down the hill. It was the same method the people in her village used to haul buckets of water to battle the flames of a house fire. Lark found she didn't enjoy being the bucket. Her body was constantly jostled, and the pain exploded within her leg and radiated up her thigh every time her leg was bumped.

Worse still, she had to glimpse the worry and fear painting each of her friends' faces as they shuffled her between them. Though they tried their best to disguise it, there was no mistaking their pallid complexions, shaky hands, and trembling lips. Her heart broke seeing the pain and anxiety behind their eyes. If only she hadn't been so impulsive... but no, then the girl would be dead.

They arrived at a craggy spot on the ridge. Gia's method wouldn't work here; the ground was far too steep. The group paused, each of them breathing hard.

Then the clatter of rocks falling greeted them from below as the heads of two people emerged. It was Ravenna and a handsome young man with wild brown locks carrying a satchel.

"There she is, Mika." Ravenna pointed up at where Lark rested, cradled within Dausius' lanky brown arms.

Mika sprang forward, closing the remaining distance in an instant. "Toss her down," he yelled, staring up at Dausius and holding out his muscular olive arms. "Do it! I'll catch her."

Aren's voice rang out from behind her, full of alarm. "Wait, are you mad?"

Lark couldn't see him. She only saw Dausius gaze down into her face and whisper, "Help her fly..." He winked at her. The next thing she knew, she was soaring through the sky, weightless.

She landed in Mika's arms. He wasted no time setting her on the ground and reaching inside his satchel. He pulled out something small, spindly and brown. It looked an awful lot like the plant roots she'd tended in the herb garden with her mother. He pressed the roots to her leg, his brows lifting slightly as he stared down at her calf.

A tremor whispered over her skin. The pain receded, and she almost cried out with relief, but—she couldn't.

The pain surged back. Mika let out a heavy sigh and shook his head. "I'm sorry," he whispered, lifting his hand. "It's too late. I don't have the strength to save you."

Aren jumped down beside her and cradled her head in his arms. "No... no, you have to save her. Please." Tears streaked his face.

The rest of the group climbed down more slowly, but within moments, they all crowded around where she lay on the ridge side.

Mika's shoulders slumped. "It's too late. The venom's spread too far. I haven't the talent to pull it all free."

"No." Dausius moaned and clutched onto Gia, shaking his head back and forth slowly.

Tiora started wailing. Mazen and Meital pulled Tiora close, their backs shuddering. From the air, Muse and Whisper both circled, Muse's shrieking cries ringing through the air.

"Please." Aren lifted bloodshot eyes to Mika. "We brought her here to meet you, so you could teach her. You have to do something!"

Mika's shoulders lifted and his eyes brightened. "She has talent? Why didn't you say so?" He slapped the hand with the roots back on her calf, his gaze zeroing in on her hazel eyes. He snapped at Aren with his other hand. "Her name. What's her name?"

"Lark."

"Listen to me, Lark." Mika leaned so close to her face her world narrowed down to his golden-brown eyes. "I need your help. Call on your talent. Lend it to me, so I can heal you."

Damn it! That was the problem. She would've cried if she had any control over the muscles in her face.

"What's happening? Is he healing you?" Muse asked.

"He needs me to use magic. But I don't know how. What am I going to do, Muse?"

A scoff sounded in her mind. *"That's all? Ha. That's nothing. You got this. You can do this!"*

She could do this. She would do this.

Lark stared back into those warm golden eyes, and she wished. But she didn't wish for herself. She wished with all her heart she could wipe the sorrow and pain off her friends' faces.

She felt it then. First, a spreading warmth on her calf where Mika's hand rested. Then the magic rumbled through her blood, shaking her from her very core.

Mika sucked in a breath. His eyes bulged. And Lark shot up from Aren's arms, gasping and nearly slamming her head into Mika's chin.

Then a wave of exhaustion crashed into her. She slumped back, and the world went black.

Chapter 8

The horizon slowly brightened in the dawn sky, pale blush and amber streaks banishing the inky black night. Kayda climbed above deck and made her way to where her bondmate rested.

"You ready, Dru?" she asked.

He cocked his head sideways, crimson eyes shooting open. *"Are you?"* he asked in return, his gaze lingering on her attire. She wore the same plain cotton trousers and a white shirt, much the same as the yellow she wore yesterday.

"Just about. I only have one more thing to take care of."

Druturion's eyelids drooped closed again. *"Wake me when you're really ready."*

Kayda rolled her eyes. One would think someone who spent the better part of a millennium sleeping would want to rise with the dawn.

Her boots tapped on the wooden boards as she strolled across the deck. She shuffled around a handful of sleeping forms. The former slaves were all still on board. Most had slept out here in the open air rather than roasting in the stifling rooms below deck.

Finally, she found the man she was looking for. Jayan stared beyond the back rail at the open ocean. His feet were still bare beneath his cotton shorts, but he wore a tan shirt this morning. Half the buttons were undone, allowing the warm breeze to blow through, billowing the fabric like a sail.

She joined Jayan at the rail and gazed down into the dark water. "Morning."

"Morning, Princess." He sent her a bemused smile.

"I've a journey I need to make. I'm not sure how long I'll be gone… a few days, maybe a week. Can you keep a handle on things here while I'm gone? Make sure the others know they're free to leave if they wish or free to stay."

"Aye, Princess. I can do that." He sighed.

She cocked a brow, shifting to look at him closely. "You miss the sea?"

"Yes, and no. I love sailing. Even as a slave, being out on the ocean, one with the waves and the sky, brought me such peace. But another part of me misses home. I never thought I'd have the chance to go back… now, thanks to you, I do." He pursed his lips and stared at the sea.

"Who says you can't have both?" She squeezed his arm. "Go, find your family. I'll leave someone else in charge. Come back when you're ready. Or never. The choice is yours to make."

He finally turned from the ocean, his brown eyes glossy in the dawn light. "It's a funny thing. I've spent so long without a choice, now that I have the chance to make one of my own, I can't make up my mind." He chuckled, rubbing the wooden rail.

"Hello," called out a familiar deep voice, as steps pounded on the gangplank.

Kayda and Jayan spun around, ambling toward the center of the ship to meet their early morning visitor.

It was Wyll, wearing a cream-colored suit and a bright smile. He carried a rolled parchment and a paper-wrapped package.

"Good morning," Kayda said.

"I told you I'd have the papers drawn up. Here they are." He handed the parchment to her and pulled a charcoal writing stick from his pocket. "I figured I'd get your signature before you headed off on your search."

Kayda smiled. "That's very thoughtful of you, Wyll." She scanned the pages quickly, and seeing all in order, she adjusted the charcoal in her hand, motioned for Jayan to spin around, leaned the parchment against his back, and signed.

She rolled the parchment back up and handed it to Wyll. "I wonder, could I trouble you for a favor, *cousin*?"

Wyll lifted a brow, clearly not mistaking the emphasis she put on the final word. "What might that be?"

"Could you keep an eye on my ship and my crew while I'm out of town?"

"I can handle that for you." He smiled. "So, you're all set to search for the elusive Sul, then?"

"As ready as I can be. Though I can't help but feel like I'm forgetting something."

"Perhaps this will help." Wyll handed her the paper-wrapped bundle. "Just a little gift. From one cousin to another."

Kayda blinked in surprise. He'd gotten her a gift? She tore open the delicate tissue, revealing a flash of gold. It was the beautiful golden gown she'd spotted in the store window yesterday. Blood rushed to her cheeks. "Thank you, it's lovely. Though this might not be what I need for a trek through the Suland Waste."

Jayan cleared his throat loudly. "I know exactly what you're missing, Princess."

She raised a brow. "You do?"

He took a step forward, wedging his way between her and Wyll. "You need a guide. Someone who's been there before."

Wyll scoffed. "Good luck with that."

Jayan's jaw clenched, but he didn't respond to Wyll. He kept his focus on her and her alone. "I'm ready to go home, Princess. I'll take you."

Jayan was Sul? Kayda smiled, pleased with this stroke of luck. Maybe now she wouldn't have to spend days flying over sand dunes, searching for the hidden people who were rumored to be as hard to find as a shard of glass in the shifting sands.

"Dru?" From the corner of her eye, she saw him lift his head again. *"How many people can you carry?"*

"I've never had cause to test my limits, but I expect I can handle you and the captain just fine." He dropped his head again. *"Wake me when you both are* actually *ready,"* he grumbled.

Kayda slapped Jayan's shoulder, her smile widening. "That sounds like a wonderful idea, Jayan. Why don't you go gather your things below deck? Would you drop this in my room while you're down there?"

Jayan grinned, taking the bundled dress and heading for the stairs.

"Oh, don't forget your shoes," she called after him.

He stopped in his tracks and swung a sheepish grin her way. "That's gonna be a problem. I don't have any."

His admission needled her heart. What kind of beast forced a man to captain his ship for years without even providing him with a simple pair of shoes?

She waved him off, shaking her head. "I'll take care of it. Go, grab whatever else you need."

Wyll remained at her side, casually leaning against the rail as Jayan disappeared below deck.

She bit the inside of her lip, an idea forming. Jayan had not belonged to Wyll. He'd been the *Sea Silk* captain's personal slave. But Wyll had employed that monster for years. He'd watched countless slaves be loaded and unloaded from within his ship's holds. She wasn't foolish enough to imagine she could balance the scales between them, but maybe she could tip them in the right direction. Her gaze lit on Wyll's expensive brown boots.

"Care to do me another favor, *cuz*?"

***

Hot, dry air flew through her long red hair from her perch upon Druturion's back. Sand spread out below them in all directions, as far as the eye could see.

Despite the heat and the desolate landscape, Kayda breathed in deeply and smiled. She was at home in the sky. Floating through the air like one of those delicate, shimmering, Jorian butterflies.

It would've been relaxing, if not for the set of shuddering arms latched around her waist like a child afraid of being torn from its mother's arms. She suppressed a smirk as Dru picked up speed, and Jayan's hands clenched even tighter. It was safe to say he wasn't a fan of flying.

"There," he yelled in her ear.

She swiveled her neck around but saw nothing out of the ordinary. Just an endless expanse of dunes. "Where?"

Jayan lifted his hand from her stomach, enough to point his finger slightly to the left. "Over there, on the horizon. Those rocky hills. That's home."

Kayda squinted. He called those hills? A handful of specks rose in the distance, barely distinguishable from the surrounding sand.

Druturion must've heard him, too. He banked to the left, and soon, they hovered above the rocky outcrop that was barely big enough to be called a hill and made of a stone the exact shade of burnt-orange as the ever-changing dunes.

No wonder the Sul were so hard to find.

Druturion swooped down for a landing. Kayda's nose twitched as sand sprayed up to greet them with each beat of his huge black wings. Then she gently pried Jayan's hands off her waist and hopped down from Dru's neck onto the hard sandstone.

Shading her eyes from the hot midday sun, she spun in a slow circle. A frown tugged at the corners of her mouth. "You sure this is the place?"

Jayan's new, expensive brown boots smacked down on the sandstone. "Yes. Home sweet home." He laughed. His voice boomed in the arid wasteland, loud and wild.

Kayda's stomach turned at the hint of madness in his laughter. Was she destined to be surrounded by people who were half-mad?

She stole another long look at the barren landscape. There was no sign of civilization. No village. No people. Was her intuition wrong to follow this man she'd only recently met into the middle of nowhere?

Then she heard something. A skittering murmur below her feet. A heartbeat later came the scrape of rock on rock and a dozen holes appeared in the craggy hillside. Countless people poured out, all of them dark-skinned, their hair braided in hundreds of tiny, neat braids wreathed around their heads like dark halos. The Sul.

It only took moments for them to be surrounded. The Sul circled them with weapons drawn. Most held long staffs with curved blades latched at the tips; a few bows and knives were sprinkled in. All of them wore the same rust-orange attire, long-sleeved tunics, and pants that matched the sand's color perfectly.

Despite their battle-ready stance, she couldn't mistake their amazed reactions when they gazed upon Druturion. They crowded around him, openly staring, glancing at each other as if confirming to themselves what they were seeing was actually there before them. He sat upon the rock in a relaxed stance, his neck and wings spread out, his eyes closed, soaking up the heat like a kitten lounging in a sunbeam.

She resisted the urge to roll her eyes. *"A greeting for our new friends might be in order. Maybe you could look a touch more menacing?"*

Druturion's crimson eyes snapped open, and he shot up on his hind legs, unfurling his wings to their full length before tucking them close to his body and sitting once more. His scaled tail flew around, curling before him like a whip.

The display made the Sul fall back in unison, their boots skidding on the rock, each of them staring in awe at the massive black dragon.

A man broke free from the pack, striding forward and targeting Jayan. "Who are you interlopers? Why do you pound upon our roof, uninvited?" The man was no larger than most present, but something about his bearing, the way his shoulders stood tall and strong, marked him as a leader among these people. His brown eyes bored a hole through Jayan, his full lips set in a grim line.

"Lazar, it's me, Jayan, son of Akilt. I've come home."

Lazar sneered. He circled around Jayan, scanning him up and down with undisguised disgust. "Lies. I knew Jayan, son of Akilt. He was a warrior. A Sandspear. Not this braidless, scrawny bag of bones I see before me."

Laughs rose from the gathered Sul. The sound sent a pang of sympathy through Kayda's chest as Jayan's shoulders slumped with the weight of their mockery.

What was happening? Was Jayan lying? She didn't think so. She'd watched recognition light on several faces in the crowd when he'd supplied his name. Was this the start of some strange ritual these people had for those who ventured out and returned? Or was something else going on underneath the surface she couldn't quite grasp?

Whatever it was, she didn't like it. Not one bit.

She stepped forward, pitching her voice loudly, not bothering to hide the anger tinging her words. "You're the liar. This man has battled more than you could imagine. He's a warrior in truth."

Jayan's eyes widened as Lazar swung to face her. "Still your tongue, dust eater. Your words hold no weight here. You're not sandborn. You're lucky we didn't skewer you on sight."

Kayda's skin thrummed with the force of the rancor behind the man's words, but she refused to cower. One of Lazar's words struck a chord within her. Sandborn. Hadn't Izora told her in that tower room her mother was born of the sand? "You're wrong there as well. My mother was Sul."

Gasps spilled into the air. Dozens of curious eyes lit on her, searching her features as they whispered among themselves.

Lazar's brows shot up in the air. The silver streaks in his dark brown braids glinted in the sun as he shook his head. He barked out a laugh, the deep boom echoing across the dunes. "It doesn't matter whose loins you sprang from. You're not one of the sandborn until you prove it."

A chill darted up her spine. Was that a threat? But no matter what these people asked of her, she would face it. She wasn't leaving the Waste until she uncovered the secrets of her mother's past.

Her hand clenched into a fist. "Then we'll prove it."

Jayan's face turned ashen as whoops rang out from the Sul. A flurry of motion began, some of the people already heading off in the distance, racing down the dunes in the opposite direction from which they'd come.

"After you," Lazar said, finally smiling. He held his hand out ahead of him in invitation. Then he frowned again and glanced back at Druturion. "The dragon stays."

Kayda nodded and strode forward. *I'll be back. Don't have too much fun without me.*

Druturion snorted, shaking out his wings and lounging back in the sun. *Don't go getting yourself killed, Princess.*

Kayda shrugged, catching up to Jayan. Whatever this test was, these *sandborn* could handle it. They'd handle it, too.

"Hey, Jayan. What did kind of trouble did I land us in?" she asked, her voice so quiet it could barely be heard over the sand shifting beneath their feet.

His face screwed up in a grimace. "It's all right. I'll walk you through it. The silk harvest—it's a two-person job." He rubbed his neck, gaze flicking to the ground. "It's been years since I've done it, but I still remember how... It's not something you'll ever forget."

Well, that sounded ominous.

"Wait, silk harvest? I thought the silk came from the river butterflies' cocoons?"

Jayan shook his head. "That's where most silk comes from. But the really fine stuff—like on that golden dress you were gifted this morning—that can only be found out here in the Waste."

Kayda scrutinized the scenery, her head tilting slightly. "There are no butterflies out here..."

"Butterflies aren't the only creatures that spin silk. Think bigger. Scarier."

Dread stole her breath, her stomach sinking like she'd swallowed a belly full of sand.

"Don't worry, Princess." He leaned close, sending her a wobbly grin. "You can be the bait."

Chapter 9

"Here we are." Taul guided his black stallion to the top of a small hill. "Norwich. It ain't much to look at, but at least there's an inn."

Conall led his white stallion to a stop beside him. Delyth's brown mare nickered behind him. He stared down at the tiny village perched on the Northern Depths' edge beside the mouth of the Gran River. The town couldn't have held more than a few dozen ramshackle wooden buildings, all of them dusted liberally with snow.

This far north, the snow never melted, and this late in the fall, blizzards were common. They'd been lucky to only encounter one so far. Taul shrugged it off, claiming it was milder than most, but the blistering wind and near blinding snowfall had been worse than the strongest winter storm in Dracwood. Still, they'd survived. Pressing on doggedly through the storm, hunkered down in their thick furs.

Even the horses were coated in furs. Bred for centuries to survive the harsh winters; they sported thick coats all over their bodies. They'd even adapted to accept an omnivorous diet, although given the choice, they still favored grain like the short-haired horses of his homeland.

They still had one thing in common with their southern cousins. An uneasy relationship with wolves. Shadow had trailed behind them for most of the journey north, only slinking into camp at night to avoid upsetting the skittish mounts.

"Brother. We've reached Norwich. How soon can you catch up?"

"Not long. I'm just behind you," Shadow replied.

Conall dismounted, his boots sinking into the soft snow. He handed Taul his reins. "I'll wait here for Shadow, and we'll meet you at the inn."

"All right." Taul pointed his gloved finger at a large building on the eastern edge of town. "That's the Hearth's Rest Inn. I'll see the mounts find a spot in the stable, and we'll all meet for a hot meal."

Delyth nodded in agreement, leading her mare to trot beside Taul down the hill into town. Soon, they disappeared between buildings, and Shadow materialized beside Conall, his gray fur crusted with white frost.

They headed into town silently. Conall trudged down the hillside, admiring his bondmate's nimbleness even when navigating the thick snow.

Frankly, he was sick of the cold. He kept his stare locked on the little inn as he stumbled through the snow and ice, images of a blazing fire and a warm bed playing in his mind.

Soon, they approached the Hearth's Rest Inn. Music and laughter leaked through the walls, bubbling up in the air as Conall shoved open the heavy wooden door and stepped inside. The heat from the enormous brick fireplace hit his face, and he sighed.

The place was crowded with people. The wooden tables were almost all occupied with rowdy villagers chugging ale and talking boisterously. In the far right corner, a bearded man plucked a lute, his long fingers dancing over the strings merrily. A smile pricked at Conall's lips as his cheeks tingled with warmth, and the delicious scent of hearty stew made his stomach rumble.

"Ho, Conall." Taul waved him over to a table near the hearth.

Conall stomped the snow from his boots, strode over, and sank down into a seat, removing his gloves. Shadow shook the snow from his fur and followed but turned at the last instant and curled up to rest beside the fire.

The innkeeper eyed Shadow as he hustled over to their table. "That a wolf?" The old man tugged his gray beard, blinking rapidly. "I don't need my patrons being hunted."

Delyth smiled and flicked a coin on the table before Conall had the chance to answer. "He's trained. You won't have to worry about Shadow. I imagine he's better behaved than half your patrons."

The innkeeper's blue eyes gleamed, a laugh falling from his lips. "I imagine you might be right on that count. What can I get you folks?"

"We'll need rooms for the night. Food and drink. Whatever you recommend, as long as it's hot." Delyth pulled more coins from her coin purse, and the innkeeper nodded readily. He pocketed the money and rushed off to arrange things.

Taul laughed. "He's going to wait on you hand and foot all night. That's likely more money than he sees in a month."

Delyth shrugged. "I won't be here long enough to be a bother to him. As soon as I eat and the rooms are ready, I'm heading up for a decent night's sleep. We leave on the morrow, Conall. There's no time to waste."

Conall nodded once, meeting Delyth's eyes.

"I still can't believe you're heading to the Witch this time of year." Taul leaned back in his chair. "The Depths are impassable after the frost sets in. Not even the bravest fishermen are willing to sail now. I mean, why'd ya think this place is so busy in the middle of the day? I bet in the spring and summer this inn doesn't get a lick of business until the sun goes down."

Delyth shook her head. "I'm afraid it can't wait that long. We'll make our way alone. All we need is someone willing to rent us a boat."

The innkeeper returned, carrying three flagons of ale. "You need to rent a boat? I've a row boat I can part with for another one of those coins."

"Thank you. That would be most helpful." Delyth smiled, handing off another coin.

Delyth was true to her word. She quickly ate the hot stew and disappeared into her room, leaving Conall alone at the table with Taul. They sat listening to the lutist for a time, slowly sipping their ale.

It was a strange feeling, to rest in an inn, enjoying a hearty meal and entertainment, surrounded by people chatting happily, and not running for their lives or on a mission to save the world. For so long, all he'd known was hardship and fear. First, the fear for his sister. That familiar wash of worry he'd been unable to quench. And now, fear for his country. For the entire world even, if what Delyth said about the *ichneumon*, the scourge, came to pass.

For once—for this one single moment in time—he pushed his fears aside and grabbed this tiny sliver of normalcy. After all, this was what he'd fought for. The chance to one day be one of those old men gathered around a table, his belly full and his heart filled with laughter. Those days would come again for the people in his country. He would make sure of it.

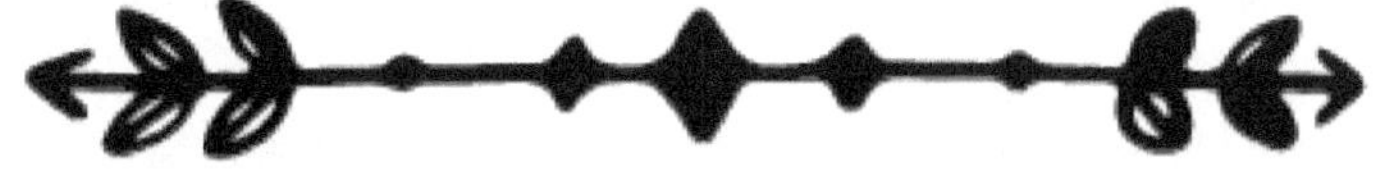

They departed the inn early the next morning. Conall's breath fogged the air as he trudged with Delyth and Shadow down the snow-covered streets to the docks.

Taul had agreed to wait in Norwich for two weeks, although the dubious way he rolled his eyes at their plans gave the impression he didn't hold out much hope of the two of them returning. When Conall took his first glance at the Northern Depths' waters, he could see why.

Ice floated everywhere on the shifting waves. Chunks as small as a grain of sand joined larger flat sheets that shined like glass in the morning sun. In the distance, dozens of gargantuan icebergs slammed about in the surf, twisting, tumbling, and occasionally smashing together with such force they cracked through the air like thunder.

Delyth led him to a tiny wooden rowboat tied to a rickety wooden dock. His stomach buckled as his gaze shifted between the small craft and the dark, frozen waters.

"You want to take that... out there?" His brows rose, and his chest tightened.

She chuckled, tossing her bag on the front bench and seating herself beside it. "Yes. You take care of rowing. I'll navigate."

Conall shrugged. It was too late to turn back now. He hopped in and seated himself in the back of the boat He stashed his bag on the floor and grabbed the oars.

"I don't like the looks of that water. Or that boat." Shadow backed up down the dock, his tail tucked between his legs.

"C'mon, Shadow. Delyth knows what she's doing. Hop on board."

Shadow crept forward slowly, for once looking less than fleet-footed on the shifting dock. *"Fine. But if we sink, I'm swimming back to shore without you."*

Shadow jumped aboard. He crouched on the boat's bottom by Conall's feet.

"Which way should I head?"

"You'll see. Just a moment." Delyth's hand slipped over the side of the boat and hovered above the water. She took a deep breath and closed her eyes.

When her lashes lifted a heartbeat later, the air flooded with moisture, and Conall's skin prickled like he'd fallen in a pricker bush. A path opened before them in the icy water, wide enough for three boats their size to slide through abreast.

So that's why Delyth didn't fear the Northern Depths.

"I didn't realize you had water talent as well as air," he said.

"I've a touch of earth talent, too." She smiled and stared off into the sea. "My family has been blessed. For generations, they've sought other talented folk to be their partners, and that's led to a generous inheritance."

"Huh." Conall rowed, steering through the hole Delyth made in the ice.

A quiet sigh escaped her.

Was she reminiscing about her daughter? Ereni's absence had affected both of them in different ways. He couldn't imagine what Delyth must be feeling, to have been betrayed by her own child.

At the same time, he was nursing his own wounds. Was that all he'd been to Ereni? A talented partner to add to the family inheritance?

He would be lying if he said he never thought of her. Though he wished it wasn't the case, her face was still fresh in his mind most nights when he closed his eyes. Was she out there somewhere, still fighting? Or had she been lost to the first wave of the creatures she'd helped to unleash on the world?

They sailed for ages. Conall's arms ached from rowing. Delyth's shoulders slumped, the energy she used to maintain their clear path through the water weighing on her. The width of the clear water before them slowly decreased until flecks of ice stuck to the oar's tips.

Thankfully, they arrived at a spot where the ice grew thick enough to walk on. They clambered out of the boat on top of the slick ice. He helped Delyth pull the boat free from the sea, and they dragged it behind them across the snowy wasteland.

It took them long hours to cross, each of them taking turns pulling the heavy wooden boat, only to arrive at more icy water. They crawled back into the boat, setting sail once more as the sun sank down in the sky.

Conall's fingers twitched beneath his thick gloves as he rowed. Would they reach their destination before nightfall? His toes had long ago gone numb with cold. The temperature continued to sink the farther they traveled. Even Shadow shivered, curling into a tiny ball on the chilled wooden boards. How long could they last in this bitter water once night fell?

Of the three of them, Delyth fared the worst. She'd started to cough as they'd trudged across the ice. Now that they sailed again, she'd begun to shiver violently, her teeth chattering and her whole body quaking every so often from a rattling cough.

The path before them through the water was so narrow tiny specks of ice jostled the boat's sides with every stroke. Conall's shoulders ached, and his nerves jolted every time they came close to the larger chunks of ice floating just out of reach.

Blazes. If only he'd not been so stubborn, maybe he'd have already figured out how to overcome his block and he could've helped to clear the way instead of just rowing blindly.

As the sun dipped down below the waves, painting the sky in shades of pink, purple, and orange, a spit of land emerged on the horizon. On it, a tiny shack sat, lit from inside with a warm glow seeping out the windows. Conall breathed a sigh of relief, rowing with renewed vigor toward the succor of the single spot of civilization on the frozen island.

The sky darkened, turning the water pitch black. By the time they trudged to the shack, stars twinkled, and the full moon shone down on the ice.

Delyth strode to the door and knocked firmly on it.

Conall's heart sped up as tapping footsteps drew closer, and the doorknob slowly spun.

Warmth and light escaped the building. He shielded his eyes from the sudden glare. A young woman stuck her head out, her sharp blue eyes sliding over each of them before she threw the door wide open and disappeared inside without a word.

Delyth didn't waste any time following her inside. Shadow bounded in on her tail, leaving Conall to slip in last and pull the door closed behind him.

He inhaled as he entered. The pungent scents of wood smoke and fish filled the tiny shack. The wooden walls were unadorned and the room practically bare. Stacked beside the door, a few sacks and boxes burst at the seams with all manner of things. Aside from the hearth, which Shadow had already curled up next to, and a small wooden table and single chair, the only other thing of note in the shack was its lone occupant.

The woman wasn't at all what he'd been picturing. She sat by the far wall, on a bed piled with furs, her legs tucked beneath a plain brown dress. Long golden curls spilled down her shoulders, framing a face of staggering beauty.

This was the Winter Witch? She appeared barely older than he was. Rather, how he would look had he not been prematurely aged. Yet Delyth claimed to have met her before, many years ago. How was that possible?

Delyth was the first to break the silence. She sighed as she sank down on the lone chair, her eyelids drooping with fatigue. "Freya has awakened, I take it?"

Conall cocked a brow at the odd question.

The young woman nodded solemnly. "Yes, Freya dreamed her last dream this past spring. I am Halynn. The new dreamer."

"I am—"

"I know who you are, Sade Prim. That you travel with shadows and trapped boys." Her gaze flicked to him.

He stared into the icy blue depths of her eyes. Something strange glittered back at him. An ageless wisdom that belied her youthful features. His breath caught until she looked away.

She patted the furs beside her in invitation, a smile spreading across her lips. "Come. Sit."

He crossed the room and sank down on the soft mattress beside her. Delyth, her head resting on her hands on the table, softly snored. The exhaustion of clearing their path through the ice had caught up to her.

It left the two of them, essentially, alone. Not many beautiful young women would be keen to have a strange man on their bed. But Halynn did not cower. She leaned forward, closing the distance between them, and peered straight into his face.

She laughed. It wasn't a girlish giggle or a simple chuckle, but an explosion of mirth, like his face was the most amusing thing she'd seen in her entire life.

Conall's ears heated as he stared back at her.

"I'm sorry," she said finally, wiping a tear from the corner of her eye. "It's bizarre, is all, seeing someone in the flesh you've only seen before in your dreams." She patted his knee, her eyes twinkling. "Don't worry. Soon, you'll understand."

Chapter 10

Lark awoke slowly, lying flat on a soft mattress. A wooden roof shaded her head, and all around her, green fabric floated. She groaned, stretching. Relief flooded her as her muscles complied. All except for her right hand.

She twisted away from the ceiling and spotted why. "Aren?"

He perched on a wooden stool, gripping her hand tightly, his eyes closed. At the sound of her voice, he jolted, eyes shooting open, a smile lighting his face. "Lark, you're awake." He leaned forward and squeezed her fingers. "How're you feeling?"

She met his gaze, her cheeks heating. "I can move, at least."

What about her leg? The pain was gone, but she was covered with a thin sheet. She started to sit, easing up on her elbows.

"Here, let me help you." Aren dropped her hand and slid an arm around her shoulders to lever her up.

She sucked in a breath, peeking at him from beneath her lashes. "Thanks." Then she flicked the sheet off her legs, certain she would see a bloody mark where the snake bit her, but there was nothing. Just perfect, intact skin. If it wasn't for the jagged hole torn into her sheer pants, she could almost convince herself it had all been a dream.

Incredible.

"Muse?" she reached out with her thoughts. *"Where are you?"*

"Good, you're awake. I'm outside. That rude healer wouldn't let me follow you in. If he hadn't just saved you, I would've clawed his eyes out."

She resisted the urge to giggle at her bondmate's indignant tone. *"I'm glad you didn't before I got the chance to thank him. I'm feeling much better, Muse. I'll come find you soon."*

She smiled and took another look around. Except for the cot she lay on, and the stool, she couldn't see anything beyond the curtains except for the occasional shadowy movement somewhere beyond their little private bubble. "Where are we?"

Aren stood right next to her, his strong arm wrapped around her shoulders. She leaned against him, taking comfort in his strength.

"We're in the healing hut, in Stoneshore." He gave her shoulder a squeeze. "The others are with Mata Moyra. She offered to show them where we'll be staying while we're here."

"Oh. You didn't go with them?" She stole another look at him. Her heart sped up. He was so close.

He met her gaze and slowly shook his head. "No, I—"

The rattle of hooks sliding and the swoosh of fabric interrupted him. Light streamed in as the curtains were drawn back. The man from the mountain glided in—the mage she'd come here to meet—her savior, Mika.

"Hello, Lark." Mika offered her a polite smile. "I thought I heard you two talking. I'm happy to see you're awake. How are you feeling?"

Aren kept his arm wrapped around her, a tiny frown flashing for an instant before he smoothed his features.

She swallowed and turned to Mika. "I'm great, thanks to you." She grinned, sticking out a hand. "Thank you for saving me."

He shook her hand, nodding perfunctorily. "Yes, of course. It's what I do." He dropped her hand and strode closer. "Let me just check a few things." He slid a glance at Aren, nodding toward the stool. "Do you mind?"

Aren's arm tensed slightly, but he released her shoulders and sat on the stool without a word.

Mika drew closer and stared into her eyes. He placed two fingers gently on her neck. "Are you experiencing any dizziness?"

"No."

He nodded, moving to examine her leg. He skimmed his fingers over her calf, firmly prodding her flesh. "Do you feel any pain?"

She shook her head. "Nothing." She smiled.

Mika nodded again, seeming satisfied. "You need to take it easy for the rest of the day. Get plenty to eat and a good night's sleep. You're going to be just fine." He turned to leave.

"Wait." She grabbed his sleeve. "I came here to learn how to be a better healer. Mata Moyra said you—"

He shook free of her hold. "Yes, we've spoken. I'll teach you, but not until you've rested." He grinned and turned to leave again. "I'm here every morning just after dawn. Don't be late." He grabbed the curtain, and instead of pulling it closed, he slid it open fully. "Go. You don't need to stay here any longer."

Aren rose to his feet. The wooden stool clattered across the floor as he rushed to grab her arm. "Let me help you."

She hopped down off the cot. "I'm all right, Aren." She let him steady her all the same, then linked their arms together.

She half expected her leg to buckle when she shifted her weight onto it, but it held her with no pain. She let out a sigh and glanced around as Aren led her across the room. The healing hut was a large rectangular building, lined with cots and filled with a multitude of potted plants.

She only gave it a quick look, pleased she'd have the chance to examine it more tomorrow. Finally, she'd found the teacher she'd been searching for. The thought had her smile widening as they opened the screened door and slipped out into the late afternoon sunshine.

The village looked much the same as all the others they'd passed through during their time in Raimire. The jungle loomed on all sides, shading the wooden huts crowded inside the town clearing. There were people all over, gathered together chatting in small groups. An air of excitement pervaded the village, no doubt due to their group's arrival and the promise of live performances.

"Lark." Tiora rushed to her side. "You're all better?" She tilted her head, examining her leg beneath the torn green fabric.

"Yeah, I'm all right." Lark sent a smile to Tiora and a nod to Mazen and Meital as they joined them.

Tiora grabbed her arm and tugged, pulling her away from Aren. "C'mon, you've got to see where we're staying. It's so cute."

Mazen fell in beside Aren. "I'll take you to our hut, Aren. It's this way."

"Don't let her do anything strenuous, Ti. She's supposed to be resting," Aren called out.

Tiora waved him off. "I won't, I promise."

Tiora led the way to the village's center. Meital trailed just behind them. Muse shadowed their movements, hopping from hut to hut. Soon, they found themselves in front of a small hut, practically identical to all the others from the outside, except for a dagger sticking out of the wooden door frame.

Lark raised a brow at Meital.

"What? These huts all look the same to me." Meital chuckled, making no effort to hide her smug smile.

Lark held back the screen so Muse could fly in, then followed the others inside. Sunny hopped up off the dirt floor and bustled over to greet her, tail wagging. Lark leaned down to tussle her ears as she took her first look around the wooden structure.

This hut was smaller than the healing hut, with three cots and a wide wooden bench serving as furniture. Brightly colored sheets and pillows adorned the beds, and the sun shone through green-screened windows, giving the space an earthy feel.

"Here, Lark. I put your things over here." Tiora pointed to the cot that sat beside the bench.

Lark sank down on the bed with a smile. The short hike across the village had her more worn out than she should be. Maybe Mika had it right when he said she still needed to rest.

Muse settled on the bench beside her. *"You got anything to eat?"*

Lark didn't bother holding back the giggle that bubbled up. When Tiora and Meital peered at her in question, she sent them a crooked smile and dug in her pack. "Sometimes I think Muse just sticks around me for the snacks."

She pulled out a pouch full of dried meat and placed a handful on the bench. *"Here, have at it."*

"Ha. That'll do till I get my claws on one of those monkeys in the morning."

Lark rolled her eyes, grabbing a piece of jerky for herself. "This is kinda cute." She popped the bite in her mouth, then tossed the pouch to Tiora.

"Yeah, real cozy." Meital lounged back on her cot and kicked off her boots.

Tiora pulled out a piece of jerky and lifted the pouch to toss it to Meital, but Meital shook her head and leaned further back on the bright pillows.

"I bet you lived somewhere like this when you and Mazen were kids." Lark caught the pouch and stuffed it back in her pack.

Meital sighed. "Not as long as I would've liked."

"What do you mean, Mei? Isn't all of Raimire like this?" Tiora asked.

"Not Slinas, the port city to the east. That's where our father brought us to live after our mother died." She wrapped an arm around her chest. "He was a seeker. Spent all his time trekking through the jungle, searching for rare flowers and exotic creatures to fill the menageries of foreign buyers. We were eight when Ma got sick." She scowled. "Da couldn't be bothered to travel all the way north to our little village after she passed, even though some of the villagers would've been happy to take us in. He stuck us in a boarding house in Slinas instead, with a bunch of other kids of seekers."

Her admission tore at Lark's heart. "I'm so sorry. You lost your mother and your home all at once."

"I'm sorry, too." Tiora spun the meat in her hands, her brows drawing together and features softening.

Meital forced a smile. "I had Mazen there with me. It wasn't so bad. At least, not at first. They left us alone, mostly. That's where me and Maz got so good with our knives. Da gifted us each a set before he dumped us there." She flashed a crooked grin. "We had a lot of time to practice."

Lark sat silently, not pushing, waiting to see if Meital would finally share the whole of their story. She and Mazen had shared dozens of stories about their pasts in the time they'd spent together, but they were always lighthearted and adventurous. This was the first time either of them had opened up about the hard times they'd had to face.

Dausius always introduced the twins during the show by spinning a tale of how he found them, living by their wits, dodging jungle cats and venomous snakes in Raimire. Neither of them refuted his claims. Was it just an exaggeration played out for the crowd, or was there a kernel of truth to his tale?

Meital sat up and folded her legs, gripping her knees tightly. "Me and Maz kept to ourselves. It was a few years before we noticed what was happening there. That the people who ran the place weren't the gentle caretakers they made themselves out to be to Da."

Lark's eyes widened. "What was happening?"

"Being a seeker is a dangerous job. Lots of kids lost their fathers. To make up for it, they demanded a premium. The contract our father signed, and the huge down payment he made, provided we wouldn't be tossed out on the streets should he not make payments, for whatever reason." She pulled her knees closer, her head tilting down. "We began to notice something strange happening to the kids whose parents disappeared. After a few missed payments, they suddenly had an endless stream of uncles appearing for late night visits. Uncles that usually looked nothing like them."

Lark's stomach turned. She could guess what was happening. To poor kids with no one there to look out for them, no less. It was sickening.

Tiora's face blanched. "That's awful."

Meital nodded, staring blankly out the screened window. "We were fifteen the last time we saw Da. By then, we didn't just suspect what was happening. We knew." She grimaced and shook her head. "We didn't stick around to meet our long-lost uncles."

"Where did you go?" Lark asked.

"We spent a few months living on the streets in Slinas. It's a whole different world there. Slinas is the one place in Raimire the Matas hold no power. The city's overrun with rough men and women who only care about coin." She turned from the window, a wry smile on her lips. "We had nothing. Just each other and our knives. We ended up doing whatever odd jobs we could find to survive. Picked a few pockets when we had to."

Tiora frowned. "That sounds terrible. Why didn't you go back to the village you were born in?"

"That was our plan." Meital shrugged. "But you've been in the jungle. If you go anywhere without a guide and the proper supplies, you won't last the night. We saved every spare coin we could scrape together, but it was never enough."

"And that's when Dausius found you?" Lark asked.

"Yep." Meital wrinkled her nose, tilting her head sideways. "He saved us, really. Caught Mazen red-handed, lifting his coin purse. He could've turned us in, but he offered us a job instead." She grinned. "The rest is history."

Lark smiled and rose off her cot, plunking down next to Meital. "I'm glad he found you." She slung an arm around her and pulled her close.

The bed sank an instant later as Tiora joined them. "Me too." Tiora joined in the hug, and they all started giggling.

"I think they put me in the wrong hut," Mazen announced as he slipped in the screened door, his arms loaded with bowls filled with something steaming and fragrant. He offloaded the bowls onto the bench next to Muse and approached his sister's cot as the girls pulled apart. "Hey, no fair! I missed cuddle time?"

Aren popped in behind him, a smile lighting his face, carrying more bowls. "Don't worry, you can cuddle with me and Whisper later," he offered with a wink. That set off another round of laughter.

Mazen shrugged, his smile mischievous. "Can't blame a guy for trying." Then he scooped up a bowl and handed it to his sister. "We brought stew. Smells pretty good."

Lark stood and grabbed one of the bowls Aren carried, then sat back down on her cot and patted the mattress next to her. "Have a seat."

Aren sat beside her. Mazen with Meital and Tiora. The stew melted in her mouth, and laughter filled her ears, warming a place in Lark's heart that lived for times like these. There was nothing like sharing a meal with friends.

Once again, she found herself marveling at the amazing friends she'd found. She wasn't sure what she would've done without them. At every turn, they'd been there to support her in her mission to learn more about her earth talent.

As much as she loved spending time with them, a small part of her was worried about what would happen now. After all, her journey had ended, for now at least. She'd found the mage she'd been searching for and would need to stay here to train. What would happen to her friends? Would they stay, or would they move on?

Lark sighed, finishing her stew and forcing the thought aside. There would be time for those worries later. She planned to enjoy every moment she had with her friends and save the questions for another day.

Chapter 11

Kayda had sand everywhere. A fine layer dusted her entire body, chafing her sweat-slicked skin. It snuck into her boots, crunching between her toes as she followed the crowd of Sul across the Waste's dunes.

"Not much farther now," Jayan said at her side.

She shaded her eyes, blocking the setting sun's glare. "How can you tell? There's just dunes and more dunes."

Jayan pointed to the sand. "Look, tracks. We're getting close to the mountains if we can see azaros prints."

"Azaros?"

"They're small lizards, no bigger than your forearm. They come down from the mountains at dusk to feed on the sandflies."

Sandflies... could they be the creatures whose cocoons they'd come to harvest? Kayda frowned. "I haven't seen any flies."

"You wouldn't have." Jayan grabbed her elbow as she struggled to climb an especially steep dune. "They're nocturnal. Most creatures of the Waste are." His eyes lit up as he reached the dune's top. "What did I tell ya? There they are. The Anaraine Mountains."

Kayda shaded her eyes again as she clambered atop the shifting sand. As she crested the rise, the sun sank below the mountains, and her hand dropped slack at her side.

The Anariane Mountains stretched out diagonally across the horizon in all their majestic glory. Now this was what she thought of when someone said mountain, not the sorry excuse for hills the Sul called home. The range spanned the horizon and rose high in the air, taller than the highest trees of her homeland.

Kayda sucked in a breath, gaping at the colossal jagged peaks. Much of the rock was the same burnt orange as the dunes they'd just traversed, but layered in between were a myriad of other colors. Copper, rust-red, and even hints of pearl and silver abounded, sparkling in the places where the sun's dying rays peeked through the multitude of holes in the rock.

Some of the Sul had already mounted the mountain's lower slopes and prodded the ground with the bottoms of their wooden staffs, searching within the craggy landscape for—something.

"Is that where we're headed?" she asked.

"Yes. Quickly now, we don't want to be out on the dunes unprepared after dusk."

Kayda gulped, then half running, half sliding, she followed Jayan down the dune and scrambled atop the rock wall before her. Luckily, the slope was modest this close to the ground, and it was an easy climb. Still, she was out of breath by the time Jayan bid her stop and turn, not used to such physical activity in the heat.

Kayda tugged the neck of her billowy white tunic, attempting to cool her heated skin. Whoops echoed from somewhere further up the slope, followed by an animal shrieking and hissing. "What was that?"

"Sounds like they found a duncoon."

Her brow furrowing, she opened her mouth to ask for further explanation, but snapped it closed as Lazar vaulted over a rock and landed beside Jayan.

"Will you be the harvester?" the Sul leader asked, his stare locked on Jayan's face.

"Aye." Jayan replied.

Lazar tilted his head, glancing at her face before flicking his gaze lower, down her torso. "Do you bleed?"

"Excuse me?" she asked, unable to hide the hint of incredulity in her tone or the blush warming her cheeks.

Jayan squeezed her forearm, leaning close, his voice soft. "It's important we know, Princess. You have to answer, truthfully."

She glared at Lazar, meeting his dark brown eyes. She could feel her cheeks burning but refused to drop her gaze. "No."

Lazar grunted, then reached down on his belt, pulled free a dented metal flask, and thrust it toward her. "Drink this."

Kayda backed up a pace and grabbed her own belt, jiggling her waterskin. "I brought my own water."

Jayan jumped in. "It's not water. You're gonna want to drink it."

Kayda frowned, her gaze flicking from the flask back to Lazar's face.

Lazar stared back at her, his expression flat, making no move to retract his hand. "Drink."

She plucked the smooth metal from his fingers, twisted off the lid, and took a sniff. The liquid sloshed within, giving off an odd metallic scent, no doubt from the container. If Jayan hadn't said otherwise, she would've guessed it water, but it was clear from the way they both watched her expectantly it was anything but.

She lifted it to her lips and took a tentative sip. When the liquid touched her tongue, she grimaced, wanting nothing more than to spit out the bitter brew. But she resisted the urge and swallowed. "Ugh, what is that?"

Lazar stared back at her, stone-faced. "More."

She glanced at Jayan. He nodded to the flask.

She scowled but lifted the liquid to her lips and took another swallow. The fluid was thicker than water, coating her tongue with a layer of foul, syrupy goo. She gulped it down hastily, praying the man wouldn't insist she drink more. But that amount seemed to satisfy Lazar. He jerked the flask from her hands and hopped upon a nearby rock, vanishing as quickly as he'd arrived.

Kayda spun to face Jayan, hands on her hips. "What was that vile drink? Why did he ask me *that*? What's going on here, Jayan?"

The scrape of a thousand claws on rock interrupted his answer. A sudden symphony of scratching and scrambling assaulted her ears as the sun slipped down below the horizon and the azaros emerged. The small orange lizards climbed free from the holes in the ground in the hundreds and raced for the dunes.

Jayan slid up beside her. They stared at the dunes as the cacophonous scratching died down. "Watch. The sandflies will be next."

Kayda squinted in the dimming light. "I don't see any—"

She gasped. Thousands—no, more like hundreds of thousands—of tiny specks broke free from the sand. They shot into the air, forming a cloud of glittering dust and fluttering wings. The azaros went crazy, their tongues flicking out, stabbing into the cloud and crunching down flies like starving children let loose in a sweets shop.

The sky brightened behind her. She started to turn, but Jayan shook his head and clasped her arm.

"Don't look at the torches. You'll want your eyes adjusted to the dark."

She stared down at the dunes again, watching the cloud of tiny flies thicken. "I thought you said the silk spinners would be bigger?"

"Oh, they are." He pointed to the dunes' edge. "Look, here comes a duncoon."

A hound-sized creature crept across the mountain's bottom edge. It was short-haired, similar in build to the foxes of Dracwood but longer and wider, with dark brown fur, pointed ears, and a long, skinny tail.

"The azaros come for the sandflies. The duncoons, for the azaros," Jayan explained, as the duncoon leapt forward, snatching a lizard off the sand and lifting it to its mouth with its clawed fists. "The creatures we're here for, they hunt the duncoons." He pointed, just behind the furred creature. "Look, in the dune."

The sand on the dune shifted, unbeknownst to the duncoon who'd viciously snapped off the lizard's head. Something was preparing to break free from the dune. Something massive. The pointed tip of a hairy brown leg poked free from the sand.

Kayda's eyes widened so much they ached within her skull. There was something familiar about that appendage. A cold sweat broke out on her neck.

The sand stopped shifting, with just that one leg peeking out. Then it blasted outward in all directions as the creature within burst free.

Blazes. Bloody blazes! Kayda stared in horror as goosebumps spread across her skin. It had to be a spider. Of course, it was.

The massive beast attacked from the air. Spiny hairs shot free from its abdomen and pummeled the sand like a hail of nettles. The duncoon only had time to look up and squeal before it was stabbed with the barbs and dropped on its face, motionless. Dozens of the lizards were caught in the crossfire. A few escaped and scampered away across the dunes, but a handful were impaled with barbs and fell down to the sand.

All of this happened in the fraction of an instant the spider flew through the air, scattering flies in every direction. It landed in a slide, then it clambered across the sand straight for the poor duncoon.

It swept it up with its spindly legs and twisted and twirled the creature, covering it in layer upon layer of the sticky silk that it exuded from the bottom of its abdomen.

"The tetrela. They're ambush predators. The spider silk is fine enough the duncoon can breathe, even while buried under the sand, but strong enough to keep it trapped after the barbs' poison wears off in a few hours. The tetrela will pull it underground and keep it alive for a few days, slowly sipping on its blood until it drains it."

Dread coiled in Kayda's belly as the helpless duncoon disappeared under layers of sheer silk. "Those things were under the sand the whole time we walked here?"

"Yes. But they only attack at night. Look at their eyes."

Kayda lifted her gaze to the creature's face. It had four pairs of huge black orbs.

"They're made for hunting in the dark," Jayan explained. "The sunlight can blind them."

Movement caught her eye near the tetrela's feet. An azaros, pierced in the back with the tetrela's spiky barb, struggled up on shaky legs and scampered off.

"I thought you said the barb's poison lasted for hours?" Even more of the impaled lizards lurched to their feet and bolted away from the tetrela as fast as their wobbly legs would carry them.

"The azaros have something in their blood. It counteracts the barbs toxin." Jayan smiled.

Kayda's hand rose to her lips, recalling that viscous liquid on her tongue. "Please tell me that's not what I just drank..." She shuddered, revulsion mingling with fear in the pit of her stomach. He'd said she would be the bait. "Jayan, how exactly do we harvest spider silk?"

"The tetrela prefer to drag their prey beneath the sand." As if on cue, the giant spider stopped spinning and dropped the silk-shrouded duncoon to the sand. Holding onto a length of silk like a rope, it dove back into a dune. Submerging itself beneath the dune, it tugged the bundled creature behind it. "It will climb back to the top of the dune and wait for more prey. The only time they break this cycle is if their prey is injured during their fight. If it smells blood spilling on the sand, it will drain the duncoon dry then and there."

"That's why you had to know..." Her cheeks warmed again.

"Yes. But we use this knowledge to our advantage. One of the Sul will march out on the sand. Let the tetrela cover them in silk. The harvester will follow, carrying a duncoon."

Kayda's eyes widened, recalling the Sul stabbing the rocks as they arrived. The animal shrieking she'd heard soon after.

"The harvester slices the duncoon and drops it nearby on the sand. When the tetrela scents the blood in the air, it abandons spinning, and heads for the quick meal, content to finish spinning its prisoner after. Then the harvester can sneak in and rescue their partner, silk and all."

Kayda trembled. "I'm just supposed to go out there and let that thing smother me?" Her voice rose, ending on a shrill note. She narrowed her eyes. "Why am I the bait?"

Jayan rubbed the back of his neck. "A successful harvest is a matter of timing—precision. There's only a short moment for the harvester to drag his partner away from the dunes. You're much smaller than me, Princess."

Kayda exhaled and clenched her hands together. He was right, of course. She'd struggle to pull him across the dunes, whereas he'd have little trouble lifting her scant weight. But the fact didn't help calm the tingling sensation swarming across her skin when she imagined that disgusting spider having her within its grasp.

She drew a deep breath and did her best to ignore the visceral terror quaking through her body. She had to pass this test. It was the only way to uncover the secrets of her mother's past.

Lazar appeared with a squirming duncoon slung under his arm. The Sul had tied a length of rope around its muzzle and each of its legs. But though the creature couldn't snap its jaws or scratch with its claws, it continued to buck and moan. Its short fur bristled and quaked with fury.

Lazar dropped the critter by Jayan's feet. Then he targeted his glare on her. "It's time."

Jayan grabbed her hand and slipped something small and hard into her palm. He pulled her close, his breath whispering over her ear, sending a tingle down her spine. "Just in case."

Enclosing the tiny object within her fist, she met his eyes one last time and fought the urge to scowl at the gleam of excitement she spied within their depths. Then she turned and climbed down the rocks toward the dunes.

It wasn't until she'd almost arrived at the sand that she unclenched her hand and took a peek at her mystery gift. It was a tiny switchblade. She'd seen Jayan use it countless times onboard *Nova's Champion* when handling repairs to the rigging. She shoved the small blade into her pants pocket, but it didn't bring her much relief. It would barely be enough to scratch the behemoth tetrela.

She paused on the sand's edge and squinted into the darkness that had only grown thicker since she'd reached the bottom of the mountain. Her skin itched as sweat trickled down her back, her mouth dry as she swallowed for the hundredth time.

Was she really about to do this? Allow herself to be struck with a barb, imprisoned by that monster, and wait to be rescued?

Yes. She had to.

Kayda blew out a steadying breath and lifted her foot, striking out across the dune. Raising a hand to her face, she swatted the air, trying to clear the space in front of her of the tiny sandflies.

Now that she was within the cloud, the reason for the insect's strange frenzy became clear. Hundreds upon hundreds of the bugs were clasped together as they floated, copulating in mid-air. Even more flew in erratic patterns, attempting to attract the attention of a mate, no doubt.

Kayda shuddered, pushing down her disgust. It was not bad enough she was about to be manhandled by a mammoth arachnid; she was barging into the middle of a fly orgy as well. Yuck.

She stared at her feet, watching her boots sinking into the sand, and tried to ignore the countless fluttering wings jostling her skin as she barreled through the cloud of randy insects.

Before long, the shifting sand on the dune caught her attention. She gulped and crouched down on the sand, making herself as small a target as possible, preparing for the fall to the ground.

Even though she knew it was coming, nothing prepared her for the blast of sand and the tetrela's emergence. Her heart hammered against her ribs, her arms instinctively covering her head against the rain of barbs streaking through the sky. A barb pierced her in each of her arms, and a third stabbed into the back of her neck.

The effect was instant. A sharp, fleeting pain, followed immediately by her limbs shooting out, suddenly as stiff and unyielding as the stone mountains she'd just stood on. She slammed into the sand face-first. All of her muscles contracted painfully, and her body locked up.

With her face pressed into the ground, she didn't see the tetrela approaching. But she heard the sand skittering in her ears. She felt the vibrations surrounding her as its huge hairy legs pummeled toward her.

Revulsion and fear swamped her. She fought to cope with the panic ricocheting within her chest as the beast lifted her prone body from the dune and spun her with its gargantuan legs. Her chest was tight, and her breath hitched, her throat suddenly locking up like she was choking.

Her eyes bulged as the beast flipped her, and she got her first close look at it. It was easily twice her size, covered in thick brown hairs all over its body. From where she lay beneath it, she couldn't see its face, but it had a set of sharp black fangs that curved underneath its chin, which sent shivers of ice through her veins.

Though she tried with every fiber of her body to move, she was paralyzed, forced to hang on while the hairy behemoth twirled her. The urge to summon was palpable. If it wasn't for the promise of answers, she'd have called forth the flames; consequences be damned. But she resisted the urge and ignored the voice within screaming at her to burn this massive beast to the ground.

Silk clouded her vision as it spun her. The tetrela moved incredibly fast. Lark's head swam with dizziness, her tense limbs quaked with vertigo. She was swathed in layer after layer of silk, confined in sticky softness. She felt the tension in her muscles subside, the azaros blood working its magic, but by then she'd been so tightly wrapped in the spider silk she could do little more than quiver within the cocoon's confines.

Her breath volleyed in and out in great gasping spurts. Where was Jayan? What if something slowed him, or he stumbled, or he dropped that squirming duncoon? Fear settled deep in her bones. She held on for the ride, twisting and twirling beneath the massive spider.

At long last, the tetrela stilled its spinning. It stopped twirling, and without warning, dropped her. The entire left side of her body slammed into the dune. Her cheek and shoulder took the brunt of the drop. Both throbbed dully as she sank further into the sand, unable to move.

Her heartbeat pounded in her ears. The spider hustled off, bounding away from her. Time slowed to a crawl as she waited for something—anything—to happen.

Was the tetrela preparing to dive into the dune and pull her with it? Her mind flashed back to that underground tunnel in Dracwood, where she was forced to wriggle like a worm through the earth. Lying on the hot sand, blind and defenseless, was so much worse. Would she be buried alive, helpless to do anything as the spider slowly drained her dry? Or had Jayan distracted the beast like they'd planned?

The sand beneath her shifted. Something smacked into the ground by her side.

"I've got you," Jayan whispered.

Relief flooded her. She drew in a sharp breath as the silk covering her face lifted and a blade pierced the cocoon above her brows.

Jayan slit the silk and pulled, ripping a hole large enough for him to peek in at her. He sighed when she locked eyes with him, and winked. Then he hopped away and pointed his blade at the silk near her feet. Another quick cut, and she was severed from the rope-like length of silk tying her to the tetrela.

Her gaze sought the beast. It was halfway across the dune, clutching the bound duncoon within its grasp. Those massive black fangs sunk deep in its belly as blood spilled from the critter's neck and splattered on the sand.

Jayan was already back at her shoulders. He lifted her, still shrouded within the silken cocoon, and hefted her in his arms like she was a sack of grain he was hauling onboard his ship. He sprinted across the dune. Grains of sand sprayed up from his footfalls and pelted her face.

With only the small hole for her to look out of, and her position within Jayan's arms, all she could see was the sand rushing by as he sped away. She held her breath as he slowed, praying the change in speed meant they were approaching the bottom of the mountain range and safety.

Finally, she spotted the first sign of rock beneath them. Jayan hefted her within his arms, twisting her upward, adjusting his grip that had gradually began slipping as they ran.

Slam. She hit the ground hard. Her back smashed into the hard packed sand. The wind knocked out of her lungs and her chest spasmed. Eyes bulging, she spotted the cause of her fall. The tetrela held fast to the bottom of her cocoon, stabbing down on the edge with one spindly leg.

The beast emitted a horrible chirping hiss. Blood dripped down from its fangs. Its gigantic eyes connected with hers and she quaked with fear. She struggled within the cocoon, her arms and legs shoving against the silk but barely moving.

From behind her, an angry roar rent the air. Jayan swung around and leaped forward, tugging her shoulders, trying to pull her free.

The tetrela swiped out a leg and smacked Jayan to the sand like a rag-doll. The tetrela spun to face where he landed and leaned forward, shooting out another batch of barbs. Jayan rolled through the sand, barely avoiding being skewered.

Metal flashed in the sky. The Sul. They sent arrows and spears sailing toward them. Kayda gasped. Didn't they care that she and Jayan might be caught in the crossfire?

She had to do something. But what?

The switchblade! She squirmed and wriggled, sliding her hand into her pants pocket. Even as she seized the blade, the tetrela grabbed her again, hefting her within its grasp, its body tensing, ready to race away back across the dunes.

Jayan lurched back to his feet. This time, he'd picked up one of the Sul pole-knives. He screamed and raced forward, stabbing the tetrela in one of its eight giant eyes.

The beast dropped her and screeched in pain, its head shaking and limbs shooting out to shove the weapon aside.

Kayda's head slammed into the ground, yet again. Stars flashed in her eyes, and her skull throbbed, but she ignored the pain. She flicked open the tiny blade and tore a hole in the cocoon, just big enough to snake her hand and forearm free.

Her arm was free, but the tetrela rounded on Jayan, hissing and dripping blood on the sand. His weapon was nowhere to be seen. No doubt flung far away by the beast's scrambling legs. It pounced atop him and shoved him onto the dune, grains of sand flinging in every direction.

Something flashed above her head and dropped onto the sand beside her free hand. A torch. Yes!

She reached out, the flame's heat kissing the skin of her palm. She pulled at the flames with her talent, faster than she'd ever done. Ice crackled in her veins.

"Hey," she screamed.

The tetrela paused, its fangs a hairsbreadth away from sinking into Jayan's stomach. It swiveled its black eyes toward her, and she shoved out her hand. She lit up the sky with a white-hot wall of flame. The fire burned so bright in the dark. Blindingly bright.

The tetrela hissed and scrambled off Jayan, shaking its head, swinging away from the light. Kayda didn't relent, using the magic to follow the beast wherever it turned, the dazzling fire inescapable.

Jayan hopped up, his gait wobbly. With an arm lifted to shield him from the blinding light, he staggered and slid, but pressed on until he grasped her shoulders and dragged her across the sand. She kept her hand outstretched, her concentration never wavering while they raced away from the tetrela.

Suddenly, a wave of exhaustion slammed into her. The torch. Her source. They'd moved too far from it and she was left with only her own talent feeding the flames. She shuddered and dropped her hand, extinguishing the light. Were they far enough from the beast they could escape this time?

Even as the thought crossed her mind, she was lifted off the sand, pulled into a pair of strong arms. The Sul quickly surrounded them and helped them up the lower slopes of rock, to the mountain's safety.

Within moments, torches blazed all around them, and a tall, dark-skinned woman worked to deftly slice her free from the silken cocoon. Kayda shivered as the silk peeled away by small degrees, all those eyes watching her revealed to the night sky. It was like she'd been reborn in truth; born of the sand.

Jayan sat by her side, holding tight to her free hand. His breath still hadn't calmed, his chest rising and falling erratically, his clothes askew from his tangle with the tetrela. But his eyes glittered nonetheless. He smiled. "What did I tell you, Princess? That was fun, wasn't it?"

She shot him a sideways glare. "Does fun mean something different in the Waste?" She curled a hand through her hair and sighed.

Lazar approached and knelt down beside them. His stony expression was gone, and his eyes had lost their hard edge, shining like dark gems in the night sky. "Welcome home, sandborn." He grinned.

Chapter 12

A rattling cough broke the cabin's silence. Conall's eyes shot open. He groaned from his spot on the wooden floor, stretching his stiff body.

He and Shadow had spent the night curled up beside the fire. His shoulders still ached from all the rowing he'd done yesterday, and the night's rest on the hard floor only worsened the soreness lingering deep in his muscles.

The coughing sounded again. A harsh bark in the quiet morning. Conall grimaced and rolled up to sit, staring across the room to where Delyth lay, shuddering beneath the blankets in Halynn's bed.

"She doesn't sound good." Shadow lifted his head and joined Conall in staring across the room.

"No, she doesn't."

He'd helped Halynn lay Delyth to rest on the large fur-swathed mattress last night. She hadn't stirred as they stripped off her snow-caked fur coat. Nor when he'd lifted her thin frame off the wooden chair and carried her across the room. He shuddered, recalling how frail she'd seemed then.

For as long as he'd known her, she'd always been so strong. She stood by, stolid and unwavering, as she led her people through the mountain passes. Those sharp blue eyes seeing all, always ready with an answer to everyone's questions. Last night, for the first time, he'd glimpsed the fragile soul beneath the force of nature.

He rose to his feet and crossed the room, laying the back of his hand across Delyth's forehead. *"She's burning up."*

A hard pit coalesced in his stomach. He was no healer. If only Lark was here, instead of him. She'd know what to do.

A flash of his own fever, back in that cave in Dracwood, rose in his mind. Hour after hour, he'd lain shaking and shuddering, his mind plagued with unrelenting nightmares. It had been awful. But it hadn't lasted forever. He'd made it through that; surely Delyth would, too.

At least she had them here to help. He strode across the room again. A few short steps and he was at the table. He found a pitcher of water, poured a measure into a wooden cup, then brought it back to the bed.

"Sade Prim. I've brought you some water." He knelt beside her and lifted the cup to her lips. Sweat poured off her brow, soaking the pillow and the wispy gray hairs that snuck out of her braid to frame her face. "Delyth. Wake up and take a drink, then you can go back to sleep."

Her eyes cracked open. Her blue irises were bloodshot and murky, but she stared straight at him before flicking her gaze to Shadow as he padded across the room to his side.

"Bitch whisperer." She laughed. A mirthless cackle that set off another round of coughing.

Conall's brow furrowed. Setting the cup down on the floor beside him, he rubbed her back as her coughing died down, then maneuvered a second pillow beneath her head and lifted her into a reclined position.

"What's she saying?" Shadow asked.

He shook his head. *"Nothing that makes any sense."*

Conall raised the cup again. "Have some water."

She grabbed the cup and drank greedily. He plucked the cup from her fingers after she drained it and rose to refill it.

"Won't have me groveling at your feet like that wicked bitch," she mumbled as he returned.

Conall frowned, ignoring her fevered rambling. "It's all right. You just need to drink." He placed the cup back in her hands. "Then get some rest. You'll feel better soon."

Delyth drained the second cup and sank back into the pillows. She scrubbed her brow and twisted sideways, grumbling under her breath.

Conall sighed, feeling utterly helpless. Where was Halynn? She wasn't inside. There was nowhere to hide in the tiny cabin. She should be in here, helping.

"I'm going outside to look for Halynn. Will you stay with her while I'm gone?" Conall nodded to Delyth as her coughing spilled out again from beneath the covers.

"I'll watch over her." Shadow curled up on the ground by the foot of the bed.

Throwing on his fur and slipping into his boots, Conall cracked open the door and stole outside into the cold. He shivered and pulled his hood up around his unruly gray-streaked brown locks.

He took his first look at the snow-blanketed island in the bright morning light. It looked much the same as it had swathed in moonlight. Barren and cold. The only thing of note was Halynn's tiny shack, and the even smaller outhouse sitting behind it. A massive ice-crusted pile of firewood rested between the two buildings, and beyond that, a set of footprints, leading north.

Conall set off, following Halynn's tracks. It wasn't long before he spotted her, crouched down on the ground at the island's edge, staring down into the sea. She was humming, wrapped in a heavy black fur coat over her simple brown dress and boots. Just out of arm's reach, a wooden bucket floated on the icy water.

He made no effort to walk stealthily. But though she must've heard him approaching, she didn't look up from her task; her stare locked on the floating bucket. Conall watched silently as he strode up beside her.

What was she doing?

Splash. A silver fish emerged from the sea and jumped directly into the bucket.

"Blazes," he exclaimed. "How did you do that?"

She stopped humming and tugged on a thin string, sliding the bucket across the water toward her. Turning from her task, she peeked up at him and smiled. "I asked her to come, so she did."

Conall gaped, his round eyes darting between her and the bucket as she pulled it into her hands. "You talk to fish?"

"Yes." She tsked and dipped the bucket into the water, filling it before lugging it up on the ice beside her. "Surely you understand. It's much the same as you and your Shadow."

"That fish is your bondmate?"

"Not exactly. But we are bonded nonetheless."

"I don't follow..."

She stood and brushed the snow from her skirt. "Carry that back for me. I'll explain while we walk."

Conall grabbed the wooden bucket, gripping the handles carved on either side of the top rim. The fat silver fish popped to the surface and glared up at him with its bulbous black eyes before disappearing back down to the bottom of the bucket.

He lifted, ignoring the twinge in his lower back and the reawakening soreness in his shoulders and arms. He hobbled across the snow, quickening his pace to catch up with Halynn, who'd already started tromping her way back.

"Have you heard of laumarles?" Halynn asked.

"Laumarles?" The word sparked a memory of the bright white oil lamps in the Church of the Dragon back in Flamesmoat. "Do you mean laumarle oil?"

"That's it. Laumarle aren't only useful for their oil. They're the bread and butter for the people of Norwich. They eat their meat and make their living trading their oil and horns."

"Wait, so laumarle oil comes from a creature?"

"A sea creature, yes. They're massive, elusive beasts that live in the Northern Depths."

"I see... but what does that have to do with a fish jumping into your bucket?"

"There are few creatures who can survive these waters." She nodded to the bucket. "The siltreak fish are one of them. Many years ago, they were close to extinction. Their numbers were decimated by a sudden explosion of laumarle. That all changed when the first Winter Witch arrived in Norwich."

How bizarre. The winter witches had the power to save an entire species from extinction? He tilted his head, listening closely as he followed Halynn across the snowy island.

"No one knows for sure how, but she made a discovery that saved the siltreak and opened up a whole new world for those of us who dream." She turned before the cabin and rounded the woodpile's side, stopping in the space between the cabin and outhouse. "Set the bucket down here." She pointed to a spot beside a large flat stump with an old rusty ax leaning against it.

"Isn't that what you said you were last night? The new dreamer. You see things in your dreams?"

She nodded. "It's the siltreak that make it possible. Here, I'll show you."

Halynn knelt down, the breeze blowing her long blond curls as she peered inside the wooden bucket at the siltreak. It floated back up to the water's surface. Those bulging eyes locked on her with an intelligence he'd rarely seen in a land animal, much less a lowly fish.

Shucking off her thick wool gloves, Halynn's hands slid into the water and reverently caressed the siltreak, her touch as gentle as if she were stroking a newborn babe. Then she twisted, sharp and sudden, cracking its neck in a single swift motion. She pulled it from the bucket and slapped it on the log, still twitching.

Conall reared back, swaying slightly. "Blazes! I thought you shared a bond with that fish?"

She pulled a switchblade from within the folds of her skirt, along with an empty glass vial. "I do. Not just with this one individual, but with all of them." Setting the vial down on the log, she flicked the blade open, the metal glittering in the sunlight. She sliced through the fish's neck, cutting its head cleanly off its body with one practiced stroke.

Conall's stomach gurgled as she picked up the head, using her fingers to probe around the viscera within.

"Ah, there it is." She pulled her hand free, withdrawing a small fleshy sack. "This, right here, is what we need. The elixir of dreams." Grabbing the vial, she used the knife to poke a hole in the fish's organ and carefully tipped it over, draining its contents.

Conall did his best not to gag as the thick green goo pooled at the bottom of the vial. "So that stuff lets you communicate with the fish?"

Halynn nodded and stoppered the vial before slipping it back into her skirt pocket. "I told you the laumarle were elusive. They have a knack for hiding from the fishing boats of Norwich. Without a guide using the dream elixir, finding and capturing one is as difficult as catching a solitary snowflake in a blizzard." She got to work again with the switchblade, slicing into the fish's body this time, cutting its flesh into neat even fillets. "An adult laumarle eats hundreds of fish every day. The siltreak help us locate them through the connection, and we keep the laurmarle numbers in check."

"And the fish just come when you ask them to?" He grimaced, recalling the intelligence in the fish's stare. "Do they know what awaits them?"

"They do. It's always a mother who answers the call. It's a sacrifice they are willing to make to ensure the survival of their young."

"I think I understand. But what does that have to do with dreams?"

Halynn rinsed her hands in the bucket, then dumped the water on the ground. "It's a secondary effect of the elixir. Depending who you ask, it's either a happy accident or a curse." She used her knife to slide the fillets into the bucket, then cleaned the blade on the snow and slipped it back into her pocket.

By now, her pale hands were bright pink from the cold. She rubbed them together as she stood, then shoved them back into her gloves. "Do you mind?" She nodded at the bucket.

Conall hefted the bucket once more, the weight much lighter with the water drained. They rounded the cabin as the sound of muffled coughing escaped the wooden structure.

He cringed. Damn. He'd been so caught up with the stupid fish he'd forgotten what he came outside for.

He stopped Halynn on the side of the cabin. "Wait, Delyth isn't doing so good. Can you help her?"

"I saw her state this morning." She cleared her throat, her eyebrows drawing together. "I'm afraid I've no talent for healing. I'll keep her fed and warm, but she'll have to fight off whatever ails her on her own."

Conall scowled and his shoulders slumped. "Can't you get help? Go to the mainland?"

Halynn stared at the sea, eyes narrowing, her voice quiet and laced with a wistful note. "I can't go back to the mainland anymore. My place is here." She turned to him. "Even if I could, the ice is too thick to travel through this time of year. The only people crazy enough to chance it are you mages."

His stomach sank. Delyth had to survive, or he and Shadow would have no choice but to wait for the ice to thaw in the spring. He cursed inwardly, lamenting the block keeping him from accessing his talent. If only he'd started training earlier, he might have some options. For now, it looked like they were stuck on this frozen island until Delyth got well enough to clear a path through the ice with her magic.

They reentered the cabin. Conall sat on the single wooden chair while Halynn busied herself by the fire, and the scent of roasted fish filled the air. His nerves rattled every time Delyth's coughs shook the walls.

Halynn slid a plate of steaming meat before him and rested a hand on his shoulder, giving him a gentle squeeze. "She brought you here like she was meant to. It's time you fulfill your part in coming here. Eat up. We'll begin when you've finished." She left his side and placed a second plate on the ground beside Shadow.

Conall's stomach growled, but even as Shadow began chomping, he made no move to eat. He couldn't stop picturing that fish's bulbous eyes glaring at him from within the bucket. He was no stranger to skinning and eating fresh game, but this felt different. Had she known he was about to eat her when she scowled up at him?

Halynn held no such qualms. She returned to the hearth and speared a serving of fish on a plate, only taking time to blow on the hot meat before taking a bite.

Conall shook his head. "Both of you talk like this was always meant to happen. But you can't possibly know that... It's only by pure chance I even met Delyth. How can you be so sure I'm meant to be here?"

"The dream connects us all. Each person's experience with the dream elixir is unique, but there are things every person, since the days of the first Winter Witch, has reported seeing. Delyth's seen it. I've seen it. You'll see it, too."

He stilled, his muscles tensing. "What is it? What will I see that's so important?"

She pulled the vial from her skirt pocket. She placed it on the table next to the plate of fish. "You want to know? Drink."

He lifted the vial in front of his eyes, the viscous fluid swirling against the glass. Then his gaze slid to his own hands. The deep lines on his knuckles he was still getting used to seeing demanded his attention.

"What about the cost?" He closed his fist around the vial, his gaze flicking to Halynn. "If I've learned anything about magic, there's always a cost."

Her shoulders stiffened. She set her unfinished plate down on the floor beside her, where she sat next to the hearth. "The things you see, you'll never unsee them. But the costs will be minimal for you. It's only with repeated use the effects become binding."

He tilted his head and pursed his lips. "Is that why you can't leave?"

She nodded slowly, her gaze downcast. "It is." She pulled her knees against her chest, wrapping her arms around them. "After so long communing with the siltreak it becomes… painful to be away from the sea. Those who serve as guides for the hunts are careful not to dream too often. But sometimes, mistakes happen." She sighed.

Conall's heart twisted. Was that what happened to Halynn? She dreamed one too many dreams as a guide and now she was stuck out here in this desolate hut, all alone?

Halynn shook herself out of her reverie. She marched over to the table. "It's nothing for you to worry about. One dream or even a handful won't be enough to affect you in such a way." Her voice was firm. She stopped before him with her feet planted and her shoulders pushed back. "If you aren't planning to eat, then let's begin."

She jolted slightly as Delyth, who'd been silent while they ate, coughed again, the wheezing abrupt and harsh, like her throat was full of wet sand.

Conall opened his fist, lifted the vial to his lips, and drank.

Chapter 13

"You're late." Mika glowered at Lark as she slid inside the luct screen of the healing hut.

"Sorry." She smiled and handed a diquat to her new teacher. "Did I miss any new arrivals?"

Mika dropped the fruit into a bowl on top of the large wooden desk near the door. This hut was the largest of all the huts in Stoneshore, even bigger than Mata Moyra's.

Lark peered behind Mika. The rows of cots were empty, the bedding folded neatly and turned down, ready for patients to arrive. A single spot was occupied, the patient within silent, a long green curtain shrouding the cot to block out the bright sunlight filtering in through the luct-screened windows. A pair of young men worked silently in the back corner, sorting through a box of bandages and stacking a variety of bottles and jars filled with unknown liquids atop some shelves on the wall.

"The morning's been quiet so far." Mika leaned back against the table and crossed his arms over his muscular chest, which was visible beneath his sheer luct top. "But that's no excuse to tarry. I've plenty I can teach you while we don't have a whole jungle's worth of sick and injured scrambling for help."

Lark nodded and rocked back on her heels on the dirt floor. "It won't happen again."

It was Muse's fault. Silly bird got tangled in a luct screen trying to fly out the window of their hut at dawn. The corner of her mouth lifted in a smile as she recalled the picture the falcon made, a tangle of feathers and squawking outrage.

Then she caught Mika sending her a scowl, and she pressed her lips into a thin line. "I'm ready to learn. I promise." She glanced back at the young men in the back. "Should we call the others over for the lesson?"

Mika waved a hand. "No. There are a handful of villagers who come help here each day. They're skilled enough to deal with all the minor injuries, allowing me to conserve my magic for the few that need the extra help. They've had all the training they need already."

"Oh. I see."

"All right. So, how much do you know about the art of healing?"

"Not enough." She glanced down at her feet. "I've just got my mother's spell book, really. She was skilled at herbal healing, but she didn't have talent like you and I."

"I'd love to take a look at that book."

"Sure, I can go grab it," she offered.

He shook his head. "Bring it tomorrow. I'm not surprised about your mother. My parents didn't have talent either. Everything I learned came from my Geema."

"Your Geema?"

"My grandmother. Talent skips a generation in our family. We aren't as blessed as you are, either. Talent like you have... I've never felt anything so strong."

"I've been meaning to ask you about that." Lark rubbed her arm, cocking her head sideways. "How did you borrow my talent out on the cliffside? I didn't even know that was possible."

"My Geema taught me. We'd often have to share our talent to heal patients we couldn't handle on our own. I'll teach you how. It's quite simple, only you must be sure to use it sparingly. The person sharing their talent is often exhausted in the process."

That explained why she'd passed out after helping Mika heal her snake bite. "I have a lot to learn." She grinned. "What else is there?"

He smiled and marched away from the desk, further into the hut. He stopped beside a row of shelves lined on the wall, overflowing with pots of plants of all different varieties. Fragrant flowers and herbs sat beside decorative ferns, prickly cacti, and a few ugly, bulbous blooms that looked garish and grotesque next to the rest.

"My Geema taught me everything she knew about tending to jungle plants. Healing with the earth is not just about utilizing the raw talent in your blood. There's knowledge behind it that takes a lifetime to master." He picked up a watering pot and tipped the slender clay vessel among the shelves, watering some and skipping others in a dizzying pattern that had no rhyme or reason she could discern.

A lifetime of knowledge? Her stomach clenched. She didn't have a lifetime. The scourge were already wreaking havoc in her homeland.

Mika continued, "Specific types of plants must be used to heal certain injuries. You can have all the talent in the world at your disposal, but if you don't know what kind of plant to use, it'll be about as useful as slapping a bandage on a sore throat."

"That makes sense. You wouldn't use the same herbs in a poultice to heal a flesh wound as you would for a sprain. Why would this be any different?"

Mika nodded and set the watering pot back on the ground. "I'm sure the herb lore you learned from your mother will serve you well. I expect many of the plants will overlap."

Lark crinkled her nose, a twinge in her right leg reminding her of her own injury. "So, when you healed the snake venom from my leg, you used roots?"

"Roots are amazing for absorbing things from the body. Venom, pus, infection. But roots would be useless for knitting flesh back together. For that, you want something fresh and green. The more alive, the better."

Lark stepped back a pace. Her gaze fell to her hands and flicked back and forth across the surface of her palms. Not so long ago, they were filled with mud and a child's blood. If only she'd known. If only she'd thought to grab a handful of the fresh green grass on the riverside instead.

Mika closed the distance between them and tipped her chin up with a long, tan finger. He stared down into her face, concern flooding his warm brown eyes. "Hey, what is it?"

She gulped, licking her lips. Should she tell him? Would he understand the devastation tainting her soul when she thought of the people she'd failed to save?

A swish of fabric at the door made the question moot. Mika dropped his hand from her chin and backed up a pace, sending a smile to the middle-aged woman and boy on the cusp of adolescence who entered. "Esmar, Nox. What brings you by today? Is your leg paining you again?"

"Mika. Thank the Mother," the woman exclaimed, shoving her way past the screen and tugging the boy behind her. "No, my leg is the same. It's Nox."

Esmar hobbled in, her pace stilted, favoring her left leg. She clutched Nox's hand, her brown eyes wide and panicked. She was slim and tall, her thick brows and sharp nose shared by the boy. Lark suspected the two were mother and son. But the similarities ended there. The woman was jumpy, flushed, and shrill; the boy, calm and silent.

"I woke up this morning and found him like this." Esmar dropped Nox's hand. Her arms flew all over as she spoke, running through her long brown hair, tugging her clothes. "Nox won't speak. Won't move unless you make him. Just keeps staring off into space like there's nothing there inside his mind."

Nox didn't say a word in his defense. He stood there, standing like a statue, giving further weight to Esmar's concern.

How strange. Lark peered at him closely, tapping her fist against her lips. What could cause someone to end up in such a state?

Mika strode forward and bent down, staring into Nox's brown eyes. He looked for a long while, silent and unmoving, then straightened and focused on Esmar. "What of his bondmate? Where is he?"

Lark's hand fell slack at her side, her mouth dropping open. This boy had bonding magic? It figured the first person she'd met that shared the rare ability with her couldn't speak.

Esmar gasped. "I—I don't know. I haven't seen him at all. The two of them are usually tied at the hip. Do you think that has anything to do with this?"

Mika nodded solemnly. "I'm afraid so. Bonding magic can have strange effects on the mind." Mika's gaze lit on Lark briefly before turning back to Esmar. "I'm going to assume something has happened to the poor creature. How many was that now?"

Lark's eyes widened. Questions swirled in her mind, each one louder than the last. He had more than one bondmate? Bonding magic could alter someone's mind? Bonding magic had caused—whatever this was—to happen?

Esmar rubbed her brow. "First there was the pengeen, then the geklit, now the meekrous. So, three?"

He had three bondmates? And different species, too. Meekrous were the cute little orange tree monkeys. As for the other two creatures, she'd no clue.

Lark exhaled, shaking her head. Whenever she thought she had a handle on all this magic stuff, something new came along to shake her understanding.

Mika didn't seem surprised. He sauntered back to the shelf of plants. His finger lifted and traced a line through the air as he scanned the greenery. "Ah ha." He strode forward and plucked a bloom from a light blue flower. He bent down and tore a few thin green leaves from another plant. Then he strode across the room to the front desk, opened a drawer, and plucked free a hairy white mushroom.

Esmar watched Mika's movements, her foot tapping against the dirt floor, arms crossed. "So, you can help him? Nox's father left a few weeks ago for Slinas. I don't know if I can do this all alone." She wrung her hands together, shifting from foot to foot.

"You're not alone, Esmar. I'll do my best to help." Mika set the plants on the desktop and dug into another drawer, his head disappearing as he crouched and rummaged around. "Lark, have Nox sit on one of the cots, please?"

"Sure." Lark hurried to the boy's side.

Esmar grimaced as Lark led him to the bed by the elbow, seeming to notice her for the first time. "I'm sorry, I should've introduced myself. I'm Esmar, and this is my son, Nox." She attempted a smile, but the corners of her mouth wouldn't cooperate.

"I'm Lark of Greenvale. Pleased to meet you. Mika is teaching me about healing."

"Oh. You're the singer who came with the traveling show, aren't you?" She frowned. "Nox came rushing home last night, going on and on about a girl at Stoneshore with a bonded falcon. He was so excited to meet you. I told him he had to wait until morning to make the trek. We live a few clearings away, you see. I've got this damn limp from a bad break I suffered in childhood that healed wrong. I wanted to come with him... now I wish I hadn't made him wait. Maybe he could've made it without me." A heavy sigh escaped her, her lower lip trembling.

Lark finished helping the boy sit on the cot and turned to his mother. "You made the right call. You couldn't have known this would happen. Besides, no one should be out traveling between clearings in the dark." She squeezed Esmar's arm, offering a small smile.

Mika reappeared, holding a wooden cup. Steam escaped from the top and curled through the air. "Lark's right, Esmar. Nox would be worse off than he is now in the belly of a jagoth."

He walked to the cot and held the cup to Nox's lips. "I've brought you some tea, Nox." But though Mika spoke loudly and stared straight at him, Nox made no move to drink.

"Here, let me help you." Lark placed one hand on Nox's chin and the other on his forehead, tilting his head back gently. Mika slid a finger on his lower lip and opened his mouth, spilling a few drops of tea on his tongue.

She was certain the clear brew would come leaking out the corners of his mouth. But then he swallowed, the muscles in his throat working reflexively. That seemed to give his body some signal. His lips clasped onto the cup, and he took slow sip after slow sip until it was drained.

Lark and Mika stepped back after he emptied the cup. All three of them watched the boy silently. Nothing changed. He kept staring blankly off into the distance, his eyes dull and unfocused.

Esmar frowned, her voice shaky. "I don't think it's working."

Mika returned to the desk and swept more of the plants he'd used for the tea into his hand. "We have a few more things we can try." He moved back to the cot. "Help me lay him down, please."

Lark rushed to comply. She rounded the back of the cot and helped Mika gently swing the boy down to lie flat, his brown eyes open and staring at the ceiling of the wooden hut.

Mika laid his hand on the boy's forehead. Crinkling escaped from the plants hidden beneath his palm. He closed his eyes, standing perfectly still.

A tremor spread across her skin. She watched Nox's face, holding her breath.

Still nothing.

Mika opened his eyes and sighed.

"Can I help?" She reached across the cot.

Mika nodded and clasped her hand firmly within his own. "Call on your talent, Lark. I'll do the rest."

Lark inhaled deeply. Having Mika here, guiding her, his hand warm and steady on her own, calmed the panicked part of her mind that always shouted at her when she tried to summon. She closed her eyes, and she wished. She wished for Nox to wake up. To emerge from whatever strange cloud clogged his mind.

A pleasant warmth spread over her palm. Then the tremor returned. Stronger this time. So forceful the cot quaked beneath the boy, swaying side to side like a leaf in the breeze.

Exhaustion came with it. Rolling over her like a wave, pressing her limbs to the ground. It wasn't long before she was swaying, too. Before the weariness consumed her, Mika lifted his hand from Nox's head, breaking the spell.

Her eyes shot open. She studied the boy, praying his eyes would find their focus. That he'd raise his voice and speak. But Nox remained unchanged.

Esmar wailed. "No. No! What am I gonna do? Will he stay like this forever?"

Mika turned to the older woman and wrapped his muscular arms around her thin frame, holding her while she wept.

Lark backed away, leaning against the empty cot behind her. The exhaustion lifted slowly, but she didn't feel any better for it. This poor boy... there had to be something they could do to save him. Her stomach churned with regret and worry. And if she were being perfectly honest, a bit of fear, too.

Was this something she should be worried about in her own future? The thought of Muse dying was enough to make her heart shudder, but having three creatures bonded to her so closely and losing them all? It would be soul-shattering. No wonder Nox was lost.

Mika unwrapped his arms from Esmar and held her at arm's length, gazing down into her face. "I'm not done trying yet. There's a blossom on the spoolwood tree that might help. Stay here with Nox. I'll trek out and retrieve some. There's a few of them growing at the top of the waterfall, a short hike from here."

"I'll go with you." He shook his head and opened his mouth, but Lark spoke up again before he could tell her to stay. "No one should travel alone, right?"

Mika narrowed his eyes but nodded once. "All right. Gather what supplies you need and meet me at the village's eastern edge. We'll be back by midday."

Lark sent a sympathetic smile to Esmar, spun on her heel, and left the healing hut. She rushed past a dozen huts crafted of wood and luct netting. The humidity clung around her like a moist hug. Her ears rang with the noises of jungle creatures and the buzz of insects as she spotted Meital's dagger, still piercing the wooden doorframe.

She slid behind the luct netting into the hut she shared with Tiora and Meital.

"Muse? You in the mood for a little excursion?" Muse wasn't in the hut, just Tiora and Meital, still lounging on their cots. And Sunny, sprawled on the edge of her own cot, her tail waving half-heartedly as she rolled over and went back to sleep. Lark grabbed her knapsack and started scrounging around for what she needed while doing her best to not wake them.

"Hm?" Muse answered. *"Sounds like fun."*

"Meet me back at the hut. I'm almost ready."

"Lark?" Tiora rose on her elbow, her voice groggy from sleep. "What's going on?"

"Hey," she whispered. Lark cinched her sack closed and crouched down beside Tiora's cot. "Nothing to worry about. I'm just taking a hike with Mika to find a flower he needs to heal someone."

"Oh. All right." Tiora sat up fully, swinging her legs off the cot. She sighed.

Lark frowned, squeezing Tiora's knee. "Ti, I know you're dying to see your family in Joria. Just because I have to stay here with Mika doesn't mean the rest of you do. If you and the others feel like it's time to move on, I understand."

Tiora yawned, rubbing the sleep from her eyes. "What? I—"

"Just think about it. Talk it over with the others. I'll be back in a few hours." Lark stood and strode outside.

She squinted and lifted her gaze to the sky, looking for Muse and trying to ignore the twinge in her chest.

She didn't want her friends to leave. Not truly. But she couldn't expect them to put their lives on hold for her. It might take weeks for her to learn all she needed from Mika. And after that, she would return to Dracwood.

She hadn't forgotten the destruction in Bogsmouth or the vow she'd made as she watched the village burn to the ground. But she wouldn't ask her friends to put themselves in danger for a promise she'd made to herself. They weren't even from Dracwood, after all.

She was still planning to defend her home from those vicious creatures. She had to believe she was given her talent for a reason. And she couldn't run from her destiny. At least, not forever.

Muse dropped from the sky and landed on the hut's roof.

"Took you long enough," Lark said. *"C'mon, Mika's waiting."*

"All right, all right. Ha. We don't want to enrage the mage."

She rolled her eyes and started walking. Something told her it was going to be a long day.

Chapter 14

"Wow," Kayda exclaimed.

She stood inside a large underground cavern beneath the Suland Waste. Light shone in from hundreds of holes in the rock above them; the sunbeams bent, ricocheting around the massive chamber between a series of mirrors. Light flashed everywhere. Mirrors angled this way and that to catch the strong desert sun and bend it to the Sul's will.

"Welcome to Sul Hollow," Lazar said. "The jewel of the desert."

People and animals crowded the massive rust-red cavern. There were no tents, houses, or even curtains she could see to separate the folk. Just blankets and pillows spread out on the ground and pens for the animals lining the far wall. Small groups of people gathered together, here and there, none seemingly bothered by the lack of privacy.

Of course, all eyes turned to stare in their direction as they entered. Kayda swallowed. That old familiar tinge of discomfort rose in her chest at being on display. It seemed she would have no choice but to get used to it here.

At least it was cooler down here, shaded from the blistering desert sun. She breathed deeply, sensing a hint of humidity. As they strode further into the cavern, she spotted the reason for the moisture in the air. A slow-moving stream cut through the rocky cavern floor.

Lazar stopped near the stream and hopped up on a rock, raising his fist. "Two new souls join the sandborn this day. Step forward, Jayan, son of Akilt."

A few of the Sul who'd accompanied them on the hunt cheered, shoving Jayan forward. The rest of the room erupted with hoots and applause. Jayan grinned. A young woman burst forward through the crowd, rushing up to him with tears streaming down her face.

"Brother. I thought you were dead," she cried out between sobs. She clutched him tightly, weeping with undisguised relief. Kayda's heart lifted. That must be the sister Jayan spoke of so often, Nova.

Then Lazar's deep voice boomed out again. "Step forward, Kayda, daughter of Chanti." The applause died as the true name of her mother spilled from Lazar's lips, replaced with gasps.

Chanti. Her mother's name was Chanti! At long last, she was on the cusp of discovering the truth of her past. The realization left her feeling buoyant, and for once, the hundreds of eyes on her didn't send unease squirming across her skin. Kayda drew in a deep breath, her pulse thumping beneath her skin, and stepped forward.

Silence reigned. Even Nova quieted her sobs, peeking up at her from within Jayan's embrace. Only the gentle trickling water at her back and the sheep and goat's soft braying at the cave wall remained as evidence that anyone populated the massive cavern. It was as if all the Sul held a shared breath, staring at her in disbelief.

A single clap rang out beside her. Jayan took another step forward, clapping again, even louder this time. It was enough to break the spell of silence. The Sul joined in, clapping, hooting, and hollering, the sound so loud and cacophonous it rattled the stone walls.

A huge mountain of a man hustled through the crowd, dark brown arms wide open as he approached. On his face, he wore a toothy-grin. Tears shone in the corners of his dark brown eyes. "Kayda. You look so much like your mother. My niece, welcome home!"

The man pulled her into a crushing hug. Kayda endured the tight squeeze, her hands trapped at her side.

"You're my uncle?" She tugged the hem of her white silk shirt after the large man set her aside.

"I am. My name is Bamzan. Chanti, she was my sister." A shadow crossed his eyes, but he blinked it aside, shaking his head, his long braids swaying with the motion. "Come, you shall sleep in my circle tonight. I can't wait for you to meet your cousins." He planted a hand on her lower back and steered her through the crowd, toward the cave's far wall.

Kayda peered up at her uncle, keeping pace with him as he barreled through the gathered Sul. "Cousins? I've more than one?"

"Yes, three." He chuckled. "My wife and I, we were very blessed. We have two daughters and a son."

"Will I meet your wife as well?"

The shadow was back, and a frown tipped down the corners of his mouth before he banished it with a grave smile. "I'm afraid not. She was called back to the sands a few years back."

Back to the sands? Did that mean... "I'm so sorry."

"Not to worry, my dear. It was her time. After all, we're all just dust in the end."

Bamzan stopped at a set of brown and tan blankets and pillows strewn together in a large circle. "Here we are." Three children sat among the pillows, busy braiding strands of white thread. "My little sunbeams, come meet your cousin," he bellowed.

Three sets of brown eyes collided with her own. The girls were lovely. Both of them wore their dark brown hair tied up in a simple knot. They were clearly younger than her, perhaps only twelve or thirteen. The boy was younger still, his shoulder length hair unbraided and the exact shade of auburn as her own.

They dropped the threads in unison and rose to their feet.

"Cousin. I didn't know we had a cousin," said the tallest girl. She paced forward, gazing at Kayda curiously.

"Yes, well." Bamzan scratched his chin. "I suppose you'll all like to hear the story. But introductions first, yes? Kayda, meet your cousins. This is Bani." The girl who'd spoken gave her a nod. "Adira." The younger girl nodded next. "And Kai." The boy stared up at her, his brown eyes round.

Kayda smiled. "It's lovely to meet you all. I've never known much of anything about my mother. If I'd known I had cousins... Well, this wouldn't be the first time we'd met, that's for sure."

Little Kai's face screwed up, and he stomped his foot. "Why didn't you tell us, Papa-sun?"

Banzam bristled, pursing his lips and huffing out a sigh. "It's a long story. Come, let's sit."

Her cousins quickly settled back on their pillows. Banzam plopped down on the largest pillow opposite the children. Kayda chose a smaller brown pillow next to Kai. The plush cushion sank as she settled upon it, cross-legged.

Though there were people all around, no one paid them any mind. All were busy greeting the returning sandborn. A breath of excitement and revelry filled the air, reminiscent of the Harvest Festivals back in Flamesmoat. Delicious scents wafted toward them, and laughter rang out, boisterous and carefree.

She spotted Jayan talking animatedly with his sister halfway across the cavern. In fact, everyone was talking. The Sul's constant chatter and the animal murmurings bounced off the walls, forming a gentle background noise that made their small family circle seem more intimate.

"We're waiting, Papasun," Bani said.

Bamzan cleared his throat, pointedly looking down at the piled thread in the circle's center. "First... idle hands."

Bani rolled her eyes, but she plucked one of the half-finished braids from the ground. Her siblings followed suit.

Kayda tilted her head, watching them spin and twist the thread expertly. She stifled a gasp. That wasn't thread. It was spider silk.

Bamzan chortled. "Thank you, my sunbeams." He pulled free a handful of silk as well, his hands busy. "To tell the story of my sister, you must first learn the story of my father. It all started one day out on the sands when he met a mirage."

Adira wrinkled her nose. "You can't meet a mirage, Papasun."

Bamzan clicked his tongue. "Do you want to hear me tell it or not?"

Adira nodded hastily, squirming on her pillow.

"So, my father. Back then, he was not yet my father but still a young man. Dechen he was called. He went on a hunt one afternoon and was caught in a sandstorm."

Kai gasped. "A sandstorm? Truly?"

Bamzan grinned, his gaze locked on the braid he threaded in his hands. "To hear him tell it, it was the storm of a century. Dechen was pummeled from all directions. His waterskin lost in the mayhem. All he could do was hunker down in a ball on the ground and pray the gods would see fit to spare him. When the storm blew over and he dug his way back to the dune's surface, he was half mad with dehydration. His sense of direction skewed. He wandered for hours, drifting through the Waste. But when he thought all hope was lost, he saw it. The mirage." His eyes lifted from his braid to glance at Adira. "What he thought at the time could only be a mirage. Only it wasn't. It was real, his savior."

"What was it?" Kayda asked.

"Not what." Bamzan smiled, his grin wistful. "Who. A beautiful young woman emerged from the Waste. She dragged him back to the modest home she shared with her mother. And though she and her mother had barely enough to get by, the young woman nursed him back to health. Dechen was smitten. Mira, he called her, for the mirage that brought them together. My mother."

Bani sighed. "How romantic."

"I imagine it was. For a time. Dechen made Mira his wife. Brought her here to live in Sul Hollow. They were eager to start a family. First came me. Then shortly after, my sister Chanti. It was during Chanti's birth that everything changed. A fire broke out in the middle of the delivery. It was chaos. Somehow, everyone survived. A few days later, Mira disappeared. My father searched for her everywhere, but she was never found. He spent the rest of his years assuming she'd suffered from the mother's melancholy and wandered off into the sands to meet her fate."

Bani's fingers paused. She sniffled. "That's so sad, Papasun. I can see why you don't like to talk about it."

"That's not the end of it, is it?" Kayda asked. "What of my mother?"

Bamzan took a deep breath. "My father died when Chanti and I were still young. He wasn't here on the day my mother returned."

Kai gasped. "So, she wasn't dead?"

Bamzan shook his head. "She wasn't. But she was changed. Aged far more than the lost years could account for."

Kayda's stomach churned. She had a suspicion she knew why.

"At first, the leaders here didn't want to let her in. A strange old woman claiming to be Mira, wife of Dechen? But she knew things. Things only a sandborn would. And when Chanti and I looked in her eyes, we just knew. She was our mother." A wistful smile crossed Bamzan's face. "She told us she'd come back for Chanti. That if she left with her, she would marry a prince in a foreign land. Her child would one day rule. That when the end times came, it would be our blood, one of the sandborn, who would save us all from the great storm to come." He lifted his gaze from his work, staring at her.

The children targeted their gazes on her, too.

Adira snorted. "A prince. Really? So, are you a princess, cousin?"

Kayda glanced down at the floor, then she raised her eyes and stared straight at Bamzan. "Your mother. Your father called her Mira, but that wasn't her real name, was it?"

Bamzan shook his head slowly. "No. Her name was Izora."

Kayda stood abruptly. "I have to get some air. Check on my bondmate. Please, excuse me." She fled from her circled family without another word, heading toward the tunnel to the dune's surface.

Izora. It all led back to Izora. Her grandmother.

All this time she'd spent searching for her family, only to find out her own grandmother had been there with her, hidden, all along. The knowledge sent a rush of conflicting emotions swirling through her. The relief was immediate and strong, to finally learn the truth. It gave the love she'd always felt for Izora new depth. Izora had stayed with her, watching over her and loving her for her whole life. How hard that must've been on her. Knowing she was her own kin but having to act as a simple nursemaid to her own granddaughter. Forced to love her from the sidelines, in secret.

Behind it all was a bone-deep sense of betrayal. Why keep her in the dark all these years? Why all the secrets and lies? She couldn't wait for the chance to confront Izora. To finally learn the full story behind everything.

She burst out of the cave, the hot sun bearing down like a dry blanket across her shoulders. Druturion was still sunbathing, his eyes closed atop the rocks.

"Dru." She came closer, but still, he didn't respond. *"Druturion."*

His eyelids lifted. Those red eyes connected with her own. *"Hm? What is it?"*

"My family. They're here."

"That's good news." He cocked his head sideways. *"Why don't you sound excited?"*

"My mother was Sul. I know that now." She sighed. *"But I still have so many questions I won't find the answer to here."*

"Shall we leave then?"

"No, not yet. The world won't end if I spend the day here, getting to know my uncle and cousins." She smiled. *"There's three of them, Dru. I've found my family."*

Druturion closed his eyes and settled back on the rocks. *"I'm pleased to hear it. Wake me when you're ready to leave."*

Kayda turned to leave. She paused, sending her bondmate a sideways glance. *"Dru, why are you always sleeping? What aren't you telling me?"*

His eyes popped back open, and his shoulders slumped. *"You're too observant for your own good."* He cocked his head, staring at her directly. *"I told you once before that having so many bonds wasn't a problem for my kind. Well, there's a bit more to that story."*

Kayda returned to Dru's side and rubbed the smooth scale on his cheek. *"Go on."*

"Dragons have been bonding creatures for millenniums. We long ago realized those of us who can bond more than one species could use the boons we receive to our advantage."

Her hand dropped from his cheek, and she bit her lip. *"Boons? You mean like how the scourge let you hibernate underground?"*

"Yes, exactly. Each species brings its own skills. Birds of prey sharpen the eyesight and enhance speed. Humans double their partner's lifespans. But the problems start when those bondmates die. The living partner is left alone with their grief, and the voices in their mind that never leave."

The image of her grandfather, his head in his hands, his room full of scattered disarray, rose in her memory. *"I imagine it's a hard burden to bear."*

"It can be very hard, especially for a species as long-lived as we dragons are. But there is one species that brings a boon that can lessen those effects."

"There is?"

"Yes. Jagoths, the jungle cats of the Raimire jungle. All dragons who could bond more than one species sought jagoths as bondmates. The skill they bring is the ability to block the voices of one's bondmates."

"So, one of your bondmates was a jagoth?"

"Long, long ago. Before even Algernon, I bonded a jagoth. Since then, I've been able to choose when to listen to the voices of my former bondmates and when to silence them."

"That's why the voices don't bother you the way they bother my grandfather."

It made so much sense now. She'd been so worried about Dru succumbing to madness without realizing he had a secret weapon to help him combat the magic's harmful effects.

"Yes." Druturion stiffened and stared off into the distance. *"Only not so much lately."*

She didn't like the sound of that. *"What do you mean?"* She tilted her head and crossed her arms.

Druturion inhaled deeply before answering, his chest rising and falling as he exhaled a deep sigh. *"Since the Palisade fell, the scourge's voice has been becoming harder and harder to ignore."*

"It has?" Kayda gulped.

"That's why I've been sleeping. It's... hard to explain. The intrusions are easier to manage when I don't focus on them with my conscious mind."

Kayda backed up a step, her brows furrowing. What did that mean for Dru? Would he be able to handle the weight of the evil voice in his mind? The voice he'd described as vicious, bloodthirsty, and full of unquenchable hunger?

No. He could handle it. She would help him.

"It's all right, Dru. Sleep if you have to. We'll figure out what to do together." She sucked in a breath, an idea forming. *"The other dragons... Maybe once we find the dragons you're searching for, they'll know how to help. I'm going to head back inside, spend the night with my family. Tomorrow, we'll go hunting for yours."*

Kayda struggled to breathe, suffocating under another crushing hug from her uncle.

"Are you sure you can't stay longer?" Bamzan asked as he released her.

Kayda nodded. "I'm sorry." She slid her gaze to her young cousins, lowering her voice. "There's the trouble back in my homeland. I have to help them."

She'd stayed up half the night, chatting and getting to know her cousins by the light of a laumarle oil lamp. Once the children went to bed, she'd called for Lazar. She'd told her uncle and the Sul leader about the devastation in Dracwood. Warned them to keep a wary eye on the horizon for the scourge.

But though she pleaded as sweetly as she could muster for the Sul to take up arms with her against the vermin terrorizing Dracwood, she could win no firm promise of support. At least, not yet. She had to hope, in time, the Sul would agree to join the fight.

Now it was time to leave. As much as she wanted to stay and spend more time with the family she'd discovered, she had to help her bondmate. Then, her country.

"Wait, Kayda, don't you at least want me to finish your braids?" Bani asked.

She'd insisted on braiding her hair in the Sul fashion last night. It was Kayda's right as a Sandspear, now that she'd proved her mettle with the silk harvest. But the Sul braids took a ridiculous amount of time on long hair like hers. Bani only completed half of her head before taking a break to sleep.

Kayda slid her hand across the left side of her head, running her fingers through the dozens of tiny neat braids. "No. I think I like it like this. I'm half Sul after all." She smiled.

After a few more hugs, she set off across the cavern to find Jayan. She tiptoed around countless blanket-shrouded forms. It was just after dawn, and many of the Sul still slept.

She made it to the spot where she'd seen Jayan last, circled together with his sister and a few other Sul. Standing on her toes, she peered around, trying to locate which of the heads peeking out of the blankets belonged to her friend.

She spotted him finally, wrapped in a thin blanket, softly snoring. She crept over, knelt down, and shook his shoulder.

"Princess?" His head popped up, his short hair transformed into shoulder length braids. It looked like the Sul had added some thread to create the extra length. From the way it glimmered in the early morning sunlight, she suspected it was spider silk dyed black.

"Morning. Dru and I are heading back to Joria."

He sat up fully, frowning. "So soon?"

"Yeah. Sorry to cut it short, but I have some things I need to take care of. Are you staying?"

Jayan stared at her, his brows furrowing. "I—"

"Is this her?" a high-pitched voice asked.

Kayda turned sideways and stood. Jayan's sister sat up on her blanket, watching them. She appeared to be in her late teens and was lovely, even with her braids tousled from sleep and the crust of drool on her dark cheek.

"Aye," Jayan said. "Princess Kayda, meet my sister, Nova."

Kayda sent her a smile and a wave.

Nova popped up off the ground, raced across the circle, and pulled her into a crushing embrace. For the second time that morning, Kayda struggled to breathe.

Nova whispered in her ear as she squeezed. "Jayan told me what you did. How you saved him. Made him captain. Named his boat after me. Thank you."

"It was no trouble," she forced out. The tiny girl's hold was even more crushing than her uncle's. "Your brother has been a great friend. He's helped me just as much as I've helped him."

Jayan appeared at their sides. "Nova, give the princess a chance to breathe."

The girl finally released her death grip around Kayda's waist and stepped back, smiling sheepishly up at Jayan. "Sorry. I'm just so grateful to have you back, brother."

Jayan slid a hand behind his new braids, rubbing the back of his neck. "About that..."

Nova's eyes darkened. "You're leaving? Already?"

"Aye." Jayan frowned. "There's evil brewing back in Dracwood. I mean to do my part to stop it."

Her brown eyes glistening with moisture, Nova blew out a breath between her teeth. "I'm coming with you."

Jayan shook his head. "You—you can't. It's far too dangerous."

Hands on her hips, Nova stared him down, stone-faced. "I'll not lose you again. Take me with you, or I'll hunt you down to the ends of the ocean. I swear it."

For a moment, they were locked in a stare, like two gamblers trying to catch their opponent in a bluff.

Jayan was the first to crack. He sighed, turning a quizzical look at Kayda. Kayda shrugged and nodded once.

"All right, all right. You can come," he said.

Nova squealed with delight. She hopped up and bustled about the circle, gathering her things excitedly. "Let me just wake up a friend of mine. I'm sure she won't mind watching Inky while I'm gone."

"Inky?" Kayda asked.

"My pet chumon. Would you like to meet her?" She lifted a small blanket-shrouded cage off the floor and pulled the blanket free, revealing the creature within.

Kayda drew back, her heart slamming against her chest, coming close to slipping on a pillow in her haste. "What are you doing with that thing?" Her voice was thready, quavering.

The creature lifted its head and stared up at her with black, beady eyes.

Nova held a caged scourge.

Jayan and Nova met her reaction with confused expressions. "Princess? What's wrong?" Jayan asked, eyeing her like a kitten needing coaxing off a tree branch.

"That thing. That's one of the scourge." Kayda's lips curled back with disgust.

Nova laughed, cradling the cage against her chest. "Surely not. Inky's a chumon. We Sul have kept chumon as pets for generations. They're excellent hunters, and the only thing keeping the tetrelas in check. Have you seen how many eggs a spider can lay?"

Kayda bit her lip and crept closer to the caged creature. The small rodent was brown and silver-striped with sharp claws. The edges of its sharp incisors rested atop its bottom lip as it lay calmly at the cage's bottom.

Nova might call it by a different name, but there was no question in Kayda's mind this was the same type of creature that was, at this very moment, terrorizing her homeland. She couldn't sleep at night without the malicious beasts haunting her dreams.

She leaned down and stared at the animal, eye-to-eye. Something was different. Absent. That strange feeling, the slithering discomfort she remembered so clearly when she first laid eyes on the vermin terrorizing her country, was no longer there.

What did that mean?

She straightened, still unsure what to think, but letting the matter rest for now. Perhaps Dru could help. Either way, they needed to start moving.

"My mistake," Kayda said. "I'll meet you two outside. The day's wasting."

Chapter 15

"Breathe," Halynn whispered for the hundredth time.

Conall cracked open an eyelid. He sat cross-legged on the wooden floor in the cabin, across from Halynn. She was the picture of cool concentration, her hands loose in her lap, eyes closed, taking slow even breaths.

Why was this taking so long? He closed his eyes again, trying to concentrate on his breathing. Trying not to wonder if this would end up another failure like all his attempts to summon.

"Breathe," Halynn said again. "In and out. Like the tide. Feel the waves lift you. Let them take you away."

Conall breathed. Again, and again, and again.

There was nothing. Just air flowing in and out of his chest.

Wait. There was something. A tickle on his cheek.

Conall's eyes snapped open. Blazes!

His mouth clamped shut even as his eyes opened wider. He was floating. Fully submerged in the near-black ocean, smack dab in the middle of a school of siltreak. The tickle he'd first felt on his face spread all across his skin, along with a frigid chill settling deep within his bones.

Panic filled him. The air trapped in his lungs burned.

"Breathe," a voice said.

No. He was underwater. If he breathed, he would drown. He would die.

A new sensation caressed his skin. Warmth. He turned toward it, and a face appeared in the shadowy ocean beside him. Halynn.

"Breathe," she said, again.

That's right. This was a dream. He wouldn't drown. Just a dream. He breathed.

Water flooded his lungs. The panic was alive now. Screaming he was wrong; he was going to die. But Halynn floated directly before him and met his gaze. She grabbed his hand and placed it over her heart. He felt the slow rise and fall of her chest as the water slipped in and out of her lungs. That was all it took for him to adjust to the strange sensation. He matched the rhythm of her chest with his own, and the panic slid away.

She smiled. "You're all right. See?"

How was she talking? They were underwater, weren't they?

Right. This was a dream. He had to keep reminding himself this wasn't real. Every one of his senses was convinced this was really happening. He shivered at the tickle of scaled fins, quavered with the teeth-chattering cold. His gaze flitted all around, searching the near-black abyss beyond the school. It all felt so *real*.

Even as he marveled at the wonder of being transported beneath the sea, he remembered his purpose. Lark. He had to find her.

"What are we doing here?" His voice rang out through the water, as loudly as ever, even though he shouldn't be able to speak. Shouldn't be able to breathe. He ignored the contradictions and spoke again. "I thought I was supposed to see my future?"

"You will," Halynn said simply. "Breathe."

Conall took a slow, deep breath. Ice-cold water flooded in and out.

A light appeared beneath them. He squinted, trying to see beyond the siltreak to what lay below. What could give off light so deep in the ocean depths?

"Do you see that?" he asked.

"Yes." Halynn dropped his hand. "Come, we must swim."

She pivoted and advanced through the school, swimming deeper down in the depths, toward the light. Conall followed.

After enduring the tickle of a thousand slippery scales on his skin, they emerged from the school. He found himself floating above a scene that played out like a moving painting where there should only be black water. Reflected in the ocean the same way the landscape could sometimes be seen in a lake on a windless day. Only this was not a simple reflection. This was moving. Alive.

It was a battle. A huge, bloody fight spread out before him in all its gory destruction. Humans and scourge locked in combat, fighting on a landscape he barely recognized but still knew all the same. He'd been there before, after all. Saw his fate changed there. The Abandoned Lands.

Amid all the devastation, three people emerged, clear as day. One of them, a young woman with fire flowing from her fingertips, her warm brown skin freckled, hair a red halo on one side and a tumble of braids on the other, he didn't recognize. But the other two, he knew instantly.

"Lark." There she was. Oh, how he'd missed her. And yet, there she was.

Her brown curls floated around her as she raced through the battle, faster than should be possible, her hazel eyes burning with fervor. She flung earth like daggers, felling scourge in every direction. A brown and gold falcon fought at her side, diving, swooping, and clawing like mad.

He wanted to reach out and grab her. Pull her into his arms and never let go. But she didn't see him. She fought on, oblivious to his presence and beyond his reach.

Beside her, fighting just as furiously, was Shadow—and himself.

He turned to Halynn. "Is this my future?"

She shrugged. "I've seen this vision hundreds of times. Everyone who dreams has. No matter what comes next, this one vision always remains. A constant."

"What do you mean, what comes next?"

Even as he asked the question, the picture below changed. The battle spread out before him disappeared, gone in the blink of an eye.

The scene shifted, morphing into a meadow filled with flowers. So many blooms, every color and shape imaginable. The floral aroma smacked him, even in the water—fresh, sweet, and so lovely. And in the middle of the field of vibrant flora, a single woman stood.

"Mother?" Warm tears joined the cold water spilling into his eyes. He felt that same powerful urge to pull her into his arms, but she was beyond his reach.

She spun at the sound of his voice, lifting her beautiful face toward him and smiling. She looked exactly the same, clothed in a simple white dress that stood out starkly among all the bright flowers. Her long brown curls looped behind her ears. Her green eyes shone with warmth and love. "Conall. My boy. I've missed you."

He gasped. She could hear him? Speak to him?

"Mother!" He flew through the water, swimming furiously, trying desperately to cross the boundary separating their dream worlds. Water rushed by, and his muscles ached from the effort, but he could make no headway.

"Conall." She made no attempt to move closer, seeming to understand she couldn't reach him. "Please. We don't have much time."

He stopped. His heart pounded, water flooding in and out of his chest as he floated there in the inky water above her. He nodded. "I'm listening."

"You'll find Lark off the western coast of Joria. There are a series of islands there. She will be on the largest of them."

His heart leapt at her words. Finally! Finally, he knew where to find his sister. Then suspicion crept in, and doubt. "How do you know this? Mother, how are you here?"

Halynn appeared at his elbow, catching up to him in the water. "That's not your mother, Conall. The dream shows you what you need to see. Tells you what you need to hear. Listen."

The dream. Yes. It was all just a dream.

"I love you, son." He turned back to the dream that was his mother. "Tell your sister I love her, too. I don't blame her for what happened when we got sick."

Lark didn't blame herself for their mother's illness, did she? Conall's brow furrowed. "I will. I'll tell her."

"The battle you saw will come to pass. Soon. Very soon. All three of you must be there, or there's no hope." She shuddered and twisted to look behind her shoulder and all around. Like she was afraid. Afraid someone or something was watching her.

He remembered that feeling. The itch slithering over his skin in the void while the Palisade fell. The presence he'd sensed in the back of his mind.

"Who's there?" he asked, his voice shaky.

"There's no time. No time." His mother's gaze shot back to him. It burned into him like a flame, shooting fire through his veins even among all the ice-cold water. "All three of you. Don't forget."

Halynn gasped beside him. He spun away from his mother and saw Halynn's face lit from the light reflecting off the vision, her features twisted in pain. She screamed, pulling her limbs close and dipping her head down to her chest.

He reached for her, but before he brushed her skin, she vanished. "Halynn? Halynn!" Where was she? He swiveled around, searching the dark waters.

The light below him shifted. He wasn't looking directly at it, but he sensed it in the corners of his vision. His skin prickled with gooseflesh. There it was again. The crawling itch. He swung his gaze down below.

He was shown a tunnel. A hovel dug into the ground. Moist brown earth and black decay stung his nostrils. A red light spilled from a tunnel off to the side. Heat came with it, roasting his skin and sending a cold sweat dripping down his back.

Unease swelled within him. What was this place? What was he meant to see?

From within the gloom, a form emerged. A man, his skin blackened and mottled, rose from a crouched position on the ground. His limbs moved awkwardly. Flopping bonelessly, then jerking, like a marionette in the hands of a child. He lurched closer, head lolling on his neck. Then his head jolted upright, and Conall held back a gasp.

"Tarquin?" Though he had only met the man once before, he recognized him. His pale skin was ghostly white beneath smeared dirt and char, but he would know that face anywhere, even before his blue gaze shot to Conall's, and his lips quirked up into a smirk.

"No. Not Tarquin." The words came out of Tarquin's lips, spoken in the haughty voice he remembered so clearly. But it wasn't him. No. The prickling unease swamping his skin confirmed it even without the denial from his lips. Whatever was speaking to him was not the prince. It was that same phantom presence he'd sensed as the Palisade fell.

Conall fought the urge to heave as the creature drew closer and its sickening effect spread. "You. You've been watching me. Who are you?"

"I am Unseen. The one who watches and waits. The giver of gifts and taker of lost dreams."

Dreams. Yes. This was a dream. The reminder made him bold in the face of certain danger.

"What do you want from me, Unseen?" Conall asked.

"A message. A warning. Heed me." He staggered closer, bobbing Tarquin's head side-to-side. "They don't tell it true. Those witches that caged me, they are the masters of secrets. The spreaders of lies. They can't be trusted."

Conall laughed. "So, I should trust you instead?" Even as the words escaped his lips, he knew he could never. Being in this thing's presence filled his whole body with revulsion. It was like swimming in an ocean full of bile. Like wrapping himself in a blanket of squirming maggots. How could anything that felt that way be trusted?

The thing that looked like Tarquin stilled at his laughter. "I've given you rotting flesh sacks everything!" he thundered, voice full of rage. "You don't know. You don't know the half of what I've given." He laughed, a nauseating chortle that gurgled up from Tarquin unnaturally. "One more gift shall I give to you. Three. Yes, three of you will come. I see that now. But only two will see the next day. Even that will not be enough. Not enough."

Did that mean... was one of them destined to die fighting this thing? He sensed with sudden certainty this Unseen was the true source behind the destruction of his homeland. This creature was responsible for unleashing the scourge to infest the world. Why should he believe a single word that left his lips? Wouldn't he say anything to stop the battle that had been foretold?

"Or perhaps we shall end things now, hm?" His voice was a promise of suffering, doled out slowly and with glee.

Unseen jerked into motion again. Stepping closer and closer to the edge of the vision Conall floated above.

Conall drew back. His stomach churned with disgust as the awful, revolting sensation grew stronger with every step it took. That thing couldn't reach him here. Or could it?

Fear paralyzed him. He should swim away. Fight back. Do something. But his limbs were locked. His stare glued to the jolting body creeping ever closer.

"Conall," a familiar voice whispered in his ear.

"Delyth?"

She appeared next to him, materializing in the water to his right. Confusion filled her face for a brief instant until she opened her mouth and breathed deeply. Then she spun toward the vision and gasped.

"You," she spat, the single word drenched with venom.

"Witch. You've returned." Unseen laughed again, the same sickening gurgle. "I told you you'd live to see me free. Only just." The force of his laughter slowed his advance, glee pouring off him like a torrent.

Conall shook his head, his chest tightening and thoughts freezing as surely as his body had. What did that mean?

Delyth turned to him, ignoring the thing wearing Tarquin's skin. "Conall, you have to wake. Wake from this dream."

A dream. This was a dream. The reminder broke the frozen cage around his thoughts. "How?" he asked.

"Summon. We must summon. Send this beast back to the darkness that spawned him."

Conall nodded. He tried to clear his mind the way Delyth had taught him. To picture the water surrounding him taking shape in his hands. Nothing. He wanted to scream.

Luckily, Delyth had no such problems. She formed a sphere of water and shoved it at the vision.

Conall gasped.

It crossed the barrier, coalescing around puppet Tarquin in a ball that encompassed him entirely. Unseen jerked within the floating sphere, his body convulsing as water swamped his lungs. He swelled with the force of the water pummeling him, his skin ballooning like a beached whale until it stretched around him unnaturally.

Conall's eyes widened with horror. Tarquin exploded outward in a disgusting eruption of flesh, blood, and bone. But that wasn't the end of it. His flesh molted and transformed with sickening speed into dozens of vicious snarling rodents. The scourge.

Delyth threw more water at the vision. The beasts squirmed, attempting to burst out of the sphere and reach the air, but liquid continued to fill the chamber, flooding in relentlessly until the entire space was filled to the brim with the dark ocean water.

Beside him, Delyth slumped where she floated. Black circles shadowed her eyes, her energy spent. "Rest. I need rest."

Conall lifted a hand, but before he could even reach out, she vanished. Gone as swiftly as Halynn, leaving him alone once more in the darkened sea.

What was he still doing here? The question filled his mind, but deep down he knew. That repulsive itch. It was still there. What Delyth had done wasn't enough.

He whirled around. The scene below him was much the same. The underground hovel still flooded with drowned vermin. Slowly, they coalesced. Turning into something new before his eyes. Something truly terrifying. A dragon.

An ice-white dragon formed beneath him, its scales glittering pink in the red light. Conall squirmed as it grew, sucking up everything in its wake like a whirlpool. Soon, its growing mass forced the dirt to move. The dragon shoved its colossal head through the ground and burst out into a night black sky.

He gawked at the vision as the beast rocketed up. Terror still paralyzed him. He begged his muscles to move, but they wouldn't listen. Then the dragon faced him as it flew past in the moonlight. It stared straight at him and opened its mouth, spewing forth a geyser of molten ice.

Horror speared him as the ice broke through the vision. At the last instant, he dodged. The ice came so close to his skin he shivered uncontrollably as it passed. Two more times he rolled through the water, barely managing to stay out of the path of the creature's blasts. Finally, it circled, racing through the sky, turning around for another pass.

He was done for. Nothing would save him now. He could dodge all day, but eventually, one of those bolts of ice would kill him.

No. He hadn't come all this way, and finally learned his sister's location, only to be destroyed. He would save himself. He had to.

Lark. He had to see her in the flesh. He focused on her face. The picture of her fiercely fighting rose in his mind, and he latched on to it. He would find her. He must.

The next bolt of ice barreled toward him. He stood his ground and lifted his hand. The water around him swirled and danced. The ice slowed. Halted. Then it shot back, slamming into the dragon with such force it screeched and dropped out of the air, careening in a circle and smacking into the ground.

Conall laughed. He'd done it. He'd summoned!

Then the world went black.

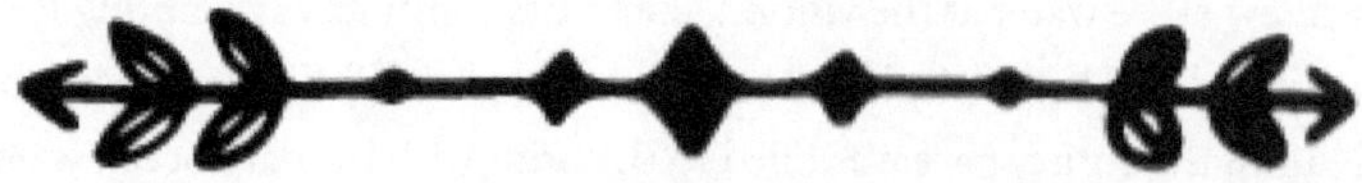

Conall's eyes shot open in Halynn's cabin. He lurched forward and coughed, falling out of his cross-legged position. Water spewed from his lungs and splattered across the wooden floor. He landed face-first in the puddle, his muscles like jelly.

"Brother." Shadow bounded over and leaned over his front paws, scrutinizing him with his golden eyes. *"Are you all right?"*

He groaned and forced a shaky hand beneath him, pushing his aching cheek off the wet floor. *"I think so."*

He rolled up to sit, his strength slowly returning, along with a feeling he'd not felt in ages. Triumph. He'd summoned! Alone in that strange ocean dream, he'd found the key to unlocking the talent sealed within him. Clearing his mind didn't work. Not for him. He needed to focus on what he was fighting for.

A hacking cough split the air. Delyth.

Halynn perched on the bed's edge. All the color washed out of her cheeks as she stared down at the woman resting on the sheets.

Conall jolted to his feet. His legs wobbled but bore his weight. A few short steps saw him hovering beside the bed, and the sight that met him made his stomach sink.

"What happened?" He drew closer to the bed, swallowing.

Halynn met his gaze with a blank stare. "I was supposed to be your guide. When that thing ejected me, she insisted on taking the elixir." Her chin trembled. "I shouldn't have allowed it. The water in her lungs... It was too much."

Delyth looked on the verge of death. Her face was drained of vitality, her eyes glassy. Her hair hung lank and stuck to her sweat-soaked skin. Another cough rattled her chest. Drops of blood joined the mucus staining the handkerchief Halynn held to her lips.

The Unseen's message reverberated in his ears. That vision, dream—whatever it was—was no normal dream. It didn't fade into his subconscious the way dreams always did. He remembered every image. Every sickening feeling. Every word.

He was eternally grateful for all Delyth had done. He'd stood silently while the Sade Prim fought that beast on her own, drowning it with the last of her strength. Yet, he couldn't let her fade into the next life without answers. She owed him that much.

Conall sat on the bed beside Delyth. "Tell me. Where is my father?"

She coughed again before she spoke. Her words escaped a throat raw with the scratches of a thousand thorns. "Raimire. Stoneshore."

Conall exhaled, a weight lifting off his shoulders. He had his answers. At long last, he could find his father and sister.

Another cough ripped from Delyth's chest.

He chewed on his lip until she stopped shuddering. "I broke my block in the dream. Let me heal you. Tell me what to do."

Delyth's clammy hand landed atop his own. She shook her head. "You can't. Healing is not so simple. We don't have the right pieces of earth on this barren island."

No. There had to be something he could do. He couldn't sit here and watch her die after the lengths she'd taken to save him.

"We'll head back to the mainland. I can clear—"

Delyth's grip turned crushing. Her eyes lit with fire, and her voice rang out strong and firm. "No." She stared straight at him. "Listen now. There's a book with my things; you must read it. All of it."

Conall gulped, nodding vigorously. "I will."

Her gaze softened. Her grip on his hand lost some of its strength. "I'm sorry. It had to be done. I could see no other option."

He leaned closer, his brow furrowing. "What had to be done?"

She coughed again. Halynn lifted the handkerchief to Delyth's lips, and the white cloth came back stained crimson.

"Ereni," she breathed, her eyes gone wild.

Conall started to pull away, but Delyth gripped him again, harder than before. He couldn't still the gasp that escaped him as her hand locked down on him like a vise.

"Don't blame her. It had to happen this way. You must see that."

Conall's heart skipped a beat. "No."

Delyth's hand fell slack, her voice a pained whisper. "It had to be you three. Now. The Palisade had to fall."

Conall stood, his blood racing through his veins. He held his head in his hands, dizziness washing over him. Had they planned this all along? Was Delyth not some unsuspecting victim of her daughter's betrayal but a willing participant?

He spun back to the bed to demand an explanation, but there would be none. Tears spilled down Halynn's cheeks as she lowered Delyth's eyelids. The Sade Prim's chest no longer rose and fell. She was gone.

Conall and Halynn built a pyre from the stack of firewood she kept behind her shack. As the sun dipped down low on the horizon, they set Delyth's body atop it.

He sighed and stepped back as the fire caught, watching one of the strongest women he'd ever known be consumed by flames. He rested a hand atop Shadow's head, standing as a silent witness while the pyre burned.

"Would you like to say a few words?" Halynn asked.

Conall rubbed his neck, blinking away the moisture filling his eyes from the smoke. He still hadn't wrapped his head around everything she'd revealed on her deathbed. Despite all her scheming, all her plotting and lies, Delyth deserved the honor of a true Dracian funeral.

He drew a deep breath and spoke. "Delyth was many things to many people. A patient teacher. Caring leader. Loving mother and friend. She will be missed."

They stayed out there in the cold, watching, adding wood to the pyre. Doing their best to ignore the sickening scent of charred flesh filling the air. The flame's heat warmed his skin even as the air grew colder and fought to sink deep in his bones.

Tomorrow, he and Shadow would return aboard the tiny rowboat to Norwich to begin their voyage to find his family. Tonight, he took the time to grieve. Not just for Delyth, but for all that he'd loved and lost. He'd lost a part of himself, his youth, his power. His hope for a normal life.

And his mother. She'd been there, too, in that strange underwater vision. The reminder of her loss tore at him anew. She'd been so kind. Such an amazing friend and neighbor to all who knew her. He would make her proud. He would do what needed to be done to destroy the unseen evil plaguing his country. No matter the danger. And not because destiny said so. He would do it for her.

Chapter 16

Lark stared up into the spoolwood tree's branches. A series of wooden stakes lined the trunk, forming a makeshift ladder Mika used to scale the thick tree. He dangled precariously on the highest stake, reaching out to grasp a gorgeous red blossom high in the tree's branches.

"Careful," she ordered, a hand held on her forehead to shade her eyes from the afternoon sunlight filtering in through the jungle canopy.

"Got it." Mika plucked the delicate bloom. "Here, catch." He dropped the blossom, watching it flutter through the air and land on her outstretched palm.

She grinned and lifted the flower to her nose to sample the sweet scent. "I got it. Come down now."

"We might need a few more." Mika pulled another stake from the satchel slung on his shoulder and quickly pounded it into the trunk.

Lark told her stomach to settle as she watched with apprehension. The spoolwood tree was massive, like most trees in the jungle, but its branches were skinny, brittle things, not suitable to hold the weight of a child, much less a full-grown man. Mika insisted the stakes would hold, but his words didn't stop her from picturing him falling and breaking a dozen bones every time the wind kicked up or he hopped from stake to stake.

Mika climbed higher, the added height allowing him to harvest a half dozen more of the colorful blossoms and stuff them into his satchel. Finally, he began the climb down. When his boots sank into the spongy soil, Lark breathed a sigh of relief.

"Ready to head back?" he asked.

"Sure." She tried to hand the spoolwood blossom to him, but he shook his head.

"Keep it. You should add it to your herb collection."

She twirled the lovely red bloom in her hand. "So, you really think this little flower can cure Nox?"

He nodded, starting back down the footpath to Stoneshore. "Spoolwood blossoms contain a powerful poison."

Lark's eyes widened as she followed him down the trail. Her fingers trembled. She'd sniffed poison?

"Don't worry." Mika's hand landed on her shoulder, a playful smile on his lips. "It's only poisonous when ingested."

She exhaled a shaky breath. "I don't understand. Why would a poison cure him?"

Mika dropped his hand from her shoulder. "Nox's problem is having too many bonds. There's only one way I know to break them."

Lark gasped. "You're gonna kill him?"

Mika sent her a crooked grin. "Just for a moment. I'll bring him back." Her face must have displayed her disapproval. "Look, I know it's extreme, but it's the only way I can think to cure him. I'll tell Esmar all about the risks involved first. Let her decide. But it'll work."

Lark frowned. "How did he end up with so many bonds in the first place? He can't be more than, what, twelve or thirteen?"

Mika's nose twitched. "Thirteen, I think. The poor lad's just unlucky. No one's quite sure how bonds are forged. Much less for someone as rare as Nox, who can bond more than one species. As far as I can tell, it has something to do with proximity and danger."

"Proximity and danger," she repeated, rolling the words around in her mind. It made sense, in a way. Muse had first spoken to her to warn her of the scourge. To save her.

"Nox fell into the Stone River two summers past. That was when his first bondmate found him. A pengreen fish saved him from drowning. He was brought to me after he pulled himself free of the river's banks. And I met with him a few weeks later when the pengreen met his untimely end. I helped him deal with the grief and depression that followed." Mika sighed, dragging a hand through his dark locks. "Such a heavy weight for a boy so young."

"That's so sad. The thought of losing Muse..." Her gaze flicked to the sky where she guessed Muse flew, though she couldn't see her with the thick jungle canopy blocking her view. "I don't know what I would do."

"Nox is a resilient boy. He grieved, long and deep, but eventually, he started spending time down by the river, seeking a new bondmate. We were all surprised when it was a lizard and not a fish who answered the bond next. But the jungle is a dangerous place. It's not been easy for Nox to find bondmates—or to keep them."

"I never knew bonding magic could have such a powerful effect on the mind."

Mika nodded. "All magic is intimately entwined in the minds and emotions of the people who wield them." He peered at her closely. "Tell me, Lark, what's your story? What's in your mind that is keeping you from summoning?"

She sighed. "That's the problem. I don't know what's stopping me from summoning. There are times when I call for my talent, and it's there right when I need it. Then sometimes, I try to summon and nothing happens. I don't know what I'm doing wrong."

He smiled, warmth pooling in his golden-brown eyes. "That's what I'm here to help you with. Can you tell me about the first time you tried to summon and couldn't?"

Dread and shame surfaced from the place deep in her belly where it lurked. A constant ache that she couldn't bury, no matter how hard she tried. She shook her head, not wanting to voice the terrible memory that tormented her.

Mika stopped on the path and trapped her hands in his own. "Lark. You have to face it. I can see from the look in your eyes—whatever it is—it haunts you. If you want to become the healer you were meant to be, you have to work through it."

Her mind fought to rebel at his words. To brush off his concern with a smile and a joke and bury the memory back deep inside. But she pushed the thought aside. He was right. It was past time for her to face it. To own up to the part she'd played in the death of the most important woman in the world. Her mother.

"There was a neighbor, back home in Greenvale. A boy, not much older than Nox. He had a sickness. A choking consumption in his lungs. My mother said he was too far gone. That nothing could be done. But I had to try. I'd just saved a babe with my talent, one on the verge of death." She sighed deeply, her gaze downcast. "I thought I could fix him." Her chin wobbled. "But I couldn't. And whatever it was he had... My mother and I caught it, too. I barely fought it off, but she—died."

Tears pooled in her eyes, her heart twisting. "If we hadn't spent so long trying to save him, we wouldn't have gotten sick. I tried to call on my talent, at the end. To save her. Nothing happened. I couldn't save her either." Her voice was thick with all the sorrow and anguish that burned in her gut. "It's all my fault. I killed her."

He pulled her close. Her cheek landed on the warm, hard plane of his chest. The tears splashed free, moistening his sheer luct top.

"You didn't kill her," he whispered. "The sickness did."

She shook her head, and he loosened his grip around her back, tipping her face up. He stared down into her teary eyes. "It's time to let it go, Lark. The pain you felt was real, but the fault was never yours. The guilt you're harboring will only hold you back."

She stared back up at him, breath hitching in her chest. "I-I don't know how."

Muse careened down from the sky, hovering briefly before landing on a branch to their right. *"I hate to break up—whatever this is—but something's happening back at Stoneshore. You two better hurry back."*

Lark shook off Mika's embrace, drying her eyes on her sleeve. "Muse says something's happening back at the village."

"What's happening?" Mika's feet were already in motion, picking up his pace on the footpath.

"What is it? Could you tell?"

"I'm not sure, but it looks like trouble. People running around, screaming."

Lark's stomach sank. "She's not sure, but it looks like trouble."

"We better get a move on then."

Lark nodded, and they took off running. They barreled through the jungle, racing along the path at breakneck speed.

Lark couldn't calm the worry rushing through her veins as speedily as she and Mika darted through the jungle. As they drew closer, the feeling intensified when she recognized that same strange sensation snaking across her skin that she'd first felt in the forest surrounding Mage Keep. The unshakable prickle of eyes on her back.

They'd been running full tilt for ages now, but the foreboding feeling sent her into overdrive. She swept past Mika, leaving him behind on the trail. She ignored her burning lungs and his calls to wait, and burst into the village with screams clogging her ears.

Chaos met her as she skidded to a stop. People lurched between huts, eyes wild and wide, their gazes flitting all over as if searching for something. Some invisible monsters hunting them from the shadows.

At first glance, she saw nothing. There were no enemies, or at least none she could see. Then a blur of fur and gnashing teeth hurtled into sight. It leapt from a tree with a high-pitched snarl, heading straight for a group of terror-struck villagers.

The scourge. They were here! Lark's stomach dropped to her feet. Before she could react, a trio of arrows speared into its back.

She drew in a series of gasping breaths, her chest aching from her run. She spun around in a slow circle, seeking the arrow's source. Finally, she spotted them. Archers—a dozen at least—stationed on rooftops, watched the jungle, eagle-eyed, ready to cut down the enemy.

They'd been ready. She sighed, her heartbeat slowing. Mata Moyra had heeded the warning they'd been given and prepared a plan of defense for the village.

Mika caught up to her at last. He stopped beside her and grasped her elbow. "What's happened?" he croaked out between gasping breaths.

"The scourge. They're here." She pointed to where the beast lay in a small pool of blood on the ground.

Lark's attention returned to the frightened villagers huddled in a group outside a small hut. They clutched each other and whimpered. Where were her friends? She had to find them. Make sure they were all right. She sped off, straight for the hut she shared with Tiora and Meital.

Images of the two of them, torn to shreds, blood spraying the hut's walls, played in her mind. *Please, no. Please let them be there, whole and unharmed.* If they'd been cut down while she was off picking flowers in the jungle, she'd never forgive herself.

Finally, she found herself outside the door. It was deathly quiet within. She tamped down the panic bellowing in her mind and drew a deep breath. Pushing past the luct screen, she peered inside.

Empty. Where could they be? Maybe they'd run to meet with the others?

Mika arrived on her heels. "C'mon, Lark." He tugged her elbow. "They'll need us at the healing hut."

She spared a glance in the direction of the hut Aren, Dausius, and Mazen shared. It was in the opposite direction of the healing hut. "I'll meet you there. I have to find my friends." She didn't wait for a reply, just took off like a shot.

"Muse, I need your help. I'm going to check the men's hut. Can you fly above the village, search for our friends?"

"All right. I'll find them." Muse lifted in the air, circling.

Lark weaved around buildings, her heart racing. Why did they have to house them so far apart? The men's hut sat on the village clearing's far side, close to the jungle's edge, whereas theirs was almost directly in the center.

In the back of her mind, she understood the logic. Keeping the women, the village's future leaders, protected in the center was sound. But right now, when she wanted to desperately know the fate of her friends, she cursed the convention that wouldn't allow the men to be housed more closely to her.

Adrenaline propelled her. She hopped from hut to hut, her gaze darting all around, searching for any sign of the vicious vermin. From somewhere far away, more screams resounded, sending ice through her veins.

Would her friends be there when she got there? The question nagged at her. She had just told Tiora she'd understand if they had to move on. They were a *traveling* show, after all. What if they'd taken their leave while she was gone? They might have set off to find another village to entertain before dark. Would they be caught unaware in a scourge ambush somewhere in the jungle?

Though it only took a moment to travel across the town, the journey seemed to last twice as long. Her mind raced, her nerves on edge at every sound, every scream. Was that her friends, crying out in pain? She had to find them.

At long last, the men's hut appeared. It was perched on the jungle's edge, shaded by a massive diquat tree's branches. No noise and no movement came from within. She burst through the luct screen, her heart pounding.

The hut was empty. She grasped her chest and cursed under her breath.

She spun on her toes and exited as quickly as she'd entered. Sweat poured off her body. With her back pressed against the outer hut wall, she shucked off her knapsack and gulped down a drink from her waterskin.

Had they really left her? Without saying goodbye? One thing was certain: she couldn't keep rushing around out in the open with no weapon. She grimaced. It was a miracle she'd made it this far.

A pair of scourge descended from the branches of the diquat tree shading the men's hut.

Blazes. Lark stood stock still, praying the vermin wouldn't see her.

They slinked down the bark, their sharp claws and lithe bodies working as well as the squirrels of her homeland to scale the rough trunks.

Her skin crawled as they crept closer. Those beady eyes darted all around, searching for prey. The leader reached the ground and shook his brown and silver-striped fur. It lifted its snout, scenting the air.

"Muse?" She fought to ignore the fear paralyzing her. *"Help! Scourge at the men's hut."* She replied instantly, *"I'm coming!"*

Of course, this had to happen when she had no weapon. If only Mika had taught her more, so she could call on her talent. If they spotted her, she was dead. They'd be on her in an instant, tearing at her skin and feasting on her flesh, just like those poor souls back in Bogsmouth.

Maybe if she froze, unmoving, they would miss her. Maybe they would move on.

For a moment, she thought it might actually work. The beasts made it to the ground and shifted, heading north, away from her. Then the second beast stopped in its tracks and swiveled its head directly at her.

Oh no. It saw her. Her eyes widened.

The beast bared its teeth and snarled. The leader turned at the sound and spotted her, too. Its lips curled back, flashing its wicked fangs. They leaned back on their hind legs, poised to leap at her.

Lark twirled the strings of her knapsack around her hands. She pulled her arms back, preparing to use the bag as a bludgeon to swat them away. If she could hold them off until Muse found her, she might stand a chance.

The scourge leapt. She watched with horror as the creatures sailed through the air, headed directly for her. They were so fast. They bounded off the ground with each leap, reaching the height of her chest easily.

An angry blur caught one of them mid-jump. Muse! The crack of the beast's neck breaking rang out clearly, even as the scourge struggled within her bondmate's grasp.

Lark didn't have time to celebrate. The second scourge lunged for her, its beady eyes locked onto her, mouth opening with a screech. She loosed her sack at the last instant, smacking the creature dead in the face, sending it flying backward, end over end.

Yes! But she swung so hard the bag flew free, leaving her hands empty and her weaponless.

Like a cat, it landed on its feet.

Bloody blazes. Her heart was a tidal wave, pulsing and slamming with the force of a storm.

The scourge turned. It sprang.

Then it fell to the ground, the blade of a knife lodged in its neck.

"Lark?" asked a familiar voice from above.

She lifted her face to the rooftops. "Mazen." She grinned. "Am I glad to see you! Where are the others?"

Mazen hopped down from the roof, joining her on the ground. "They're all back at the healing tent, except for me and Meital. We've been helping with pest control." He leaned down and pulled his knife free from the vermin's neck. "C'mon, I'll take you."

She nodded, grabbing her bag off the ground and following on his heels. *"You all right, Muse?"*

"Ha. Fine. Are you?" She hopped up on a tree branch, scanning their surroundings.

"Yes, thanks to you. You saved me."

Just then, a thought occurred to her and her stomach clenched. "Wait, Mazen. Why are they all at the healing hut? Was someone hurt?"

Mazen's brow furrowed. "Yeah, but not one of us. It was Fillan."

Lark gasped. "Fillan's back from the Boglands?"

Mazan nodded, twirling a knife in his hand. "He came racing into town to warn us just before the scourge arrived. If it wasn't for him, we might not have been so lucky."

They made it to the healing hut in record time. Mazen dropped her at the door, circling back to join the defense. Muse met her gaze and turned back, too.

It was crowded inside, every bed filled with villagers covered in scratches, bruises, and cuts. Mika and the young men from earlier flitted around the beds, applying salves and bandages.

Dausius, Tiora, and Aren were there, too, crowded around a cot in the back, which held the boy who'd guided them through the Boglands to safety. His face was weary, and he had bandages covering his chest and most of his right arm from view.

She raced back to join them. "Fillan. Are you all right?"

"Lark. I'm glad you made it back. When I got here to warn everyone and heard you were out in the jungle... Well, we all feared the worst."

She spared a glance at Sunny, who lounged beside the cot and clutched Fillan's left hand, her brows drawing together. "Don't worry about me. What about you? What happened?"

"The scourge. No one knew what good climbers they were. We had some unseasonable cold a few days back. It iced over a few of the bog passes near Dracwood. It was enough to give the beasts a foothold through the Boglands."

"Oh no," Lark said.

"We caught on in time. Burned and cut down enough trees that they can't pass any longer. But not before a dozen or so got through. That's why they sent me. I came to warn you."

"It's a good thing you did. We all owe you a great debt," Lark replied.

A scream rose behind the drawn curtain to their right. Mika crossed the room in a few quick steps and shoved the curtain aside.

Esmar stared down at an empty cot. Her words came rushing out, fast and frantic. "Where is he? Where is Nox? He was just sitting there, staring off into space. Then so many people came in with cuts and scratches. I left him to help with the bandages. Where is my boy?" She let out another wail, then her eyes lit with fire. "I'm going to find him." She took a quick step toward the door and landed on her bad leg with a startled sob.

Mika was there to catch her. He grabbed Esmar's shoulders, steadying her and spinning her to face him. "No, Esmar. You can't chase him with your leg. I'll find him. He'll be fine, you'll see."

Mika crossed the room, grabbed his pack where it rested by the door, and shoved aside the luct screen, disappearing outside.

Lark gave Fillan's hand a squeeze and moved to follow. Aren's eyes widened when she started walking, and he departed Fillan's bedside, joining her at the door.

"I'm coming with you." He grabbed a bow and quiver leaning against the wall by the door.

Lark quirked a brow. She'd never once seen Aren with a bow. "Do you even know how to use that thing?"

"Of course. You didn't think I spent my whole life laying around playing the lute, did you?" He spared her a quick half-smile as they burst out into the afternoon sunlight.

They were just in time to see Mika disappearing down a footpath that led west.

"Muse, with me," Lark called out.

Aren had the same idea. He whistled for Whisper to follow. Both birds circled the sky above them as they disappeared down the jungle path.

She'd yet to travel in this direction. She kept expecting an ambush to greet them. Or worse, for them to discover the poor boy being set upon by the scourge. But all they found was more jungle.

A new sound joined the jarring animal cries that never ceased. This was no animal. It hummed low in her ears, growing louder and louder the further they trekked. What was that sound? Then the scent of salt reached her, and her mind connected the dots. Waves.

They burst out of the jungle, finally catching up to Mika at the footpath's end. He stood atop a cliff, overlooking the sea.

Lark and Aren stopped beside him. She raised her gaze to the horizon and gasped.

Out on the ocean, a tiny row boat sailed toward a large island that she could just make out far off on the horizon. Sitting in the boat, his hands busy rowing, was Nox. And on his shoulder, perched there comfortably, like a baby bird in a nest, sat a scourge.

"No." She shook her head. "Tell me I'm not seeing what I think I'm seeing."

Mika sighed, and the words he spoke made her want to cry. "Looks like Nox just found a new bondmate."

Chapter 17

Honeyed shimmering silk slipped across Kayda's fingers. She was back on *Nova's Champion*, below deck in the former captain's study. She couldn't stand the thought of sleeping in that vile man's bed, so she'd made this room her quarters. She sighed, sliding her finger and thumb across the gorgeous dress resting within the paper wrapping.

Wyll had been true to his word while she'd been gone. He'd let no harm fall to the ship and the slaves it held that had once been his own. Now hers as well. She wrinkled her nose.

All was well as they sat docked on the wharf. Once again, she'd urged the people lingering on board to return to their lives. To leave. Except for a handful, they'd all remained. Jayan would welcome them as crew in truth. The *Nova's Champion* would join the fight to save her country. To save the world. As much as she didn't want the former slaves on board to remain out of duty to her, she wouldn't force them to leave. Dracwood needed all the help they could get.

That fact was what had her stroking the lovely silk dress. She frowned and lifted it from the packaging, holding it up in the late afternoon light spilling in the open window.

Would she ever again enjoy wearing this fine silk without her memory flashing back to the terror that was the tetrela silk harvest? Her head spun as she stared at the golden, glittering fabric. It wasn't so long ago she was wrapped in this same silk, quivering in fear beneath a predator's grasp, spinning, just spinning.

She blew out a breath and set her shoulders back. Then she settled the dress back on the huge wooden desk bolted to the floor and kicked off her boots.

Whether she liked it or not, she had to put on that dress. It was time to set aside the part of herself she'd found out there in the Waste. She would wash away the dirt, sand, and sweat and bury the part of her that was sandborn.

Tonight, she needed to be a princess again. She would wear that dress and finally secure the help her country needed. Then she could concentrate on helping Druturion.

She shucked off her filthy trousers and white silk shirt, dropping them onto the wooden boards. Then she got to work scrubbing herself with a bucket of water and a rag.

Dru was above deck, sprawled out on the midship deck, sleeping. How long would he be able to shut out the evil voices in his mind? The hair on her arms and neck stood on end as she scrubbed, giving her light brown skin a pinkish tinge from the force of her strokes.

No. He could handle it. She would make sure of it.

She grabbed a towel from the desk, drying her skin. Her hands slid over the braids covering half of her head. These she was resolved to keep. The corner of her mouth lifted into a grin. She might look a little strange with half of her head done, but the longer she wore them, the more she grew to love the braids. It felt right to have this one little reminder of the family she'd found in the Waste.

The towel joined the pile of clothes on the floor. Slipping into the golden silk, she shuddered as the smooth fabric slid across her skin. But this time it didn't squeeze her until she could scarcely move. She took a deep breath and forced aside the memory of the tetrela's spindly legs wrapping her so tightly.

After taking a moment to tidy her room, she slipped back into her boots and vacated the cabin, emerging into the bright sunlight above deck.

A whistle greeted her. She spun around, her cheeks heating as she spotted Jayan's gaze traveling down her body from her head to her toes. He was back at the helm in his causal state of undress, feet and chest once again bare.

"Princess—that dress—wow." He grinned.

She rolled her eyes. "Keep an eye on things, Captain. I'll be back later."

The smile fell from his face. His mouth opened. Closed. Opened again. "Be careful," he said, finally.

His quiet request sparked a feeling inside of her. One she didn't have time to turn over and examine. She smiled instead, a brash grin full of the confidence his reaction to her dress inspired, and nodded once before heading down the gangplank.

A warm breeze whispered across her bare arms and blew the sleek silk dress against her legs. Dozens of eyes shifted to watch her. She did her best to ignore the dockworker's stares and set her sights on the man who awaited her at the end of the wharf.

"My lady." Wyll offered a shallow bow as she approached, looking as handsome as ever in a dark brown silk suit. His eyes performed the same slow glide across her form as Jayan's had, but his gaze lingered on her head.

She stilled, waiting for him to mention her braids. He didn't disappoint.

"I take it your trip to find the Sul went well?"

She smiled. "It did. Thank you for keeping an eye on things for me while I was gone."

"It was no trouble. I'm so pleased you agreed to join me." He smiled, swiveled sideways, and held out an elbow. "Shall we?"

She slipped her hand into the crook of his arm and matched his steps. "Thank you for the invitation."

When they'd returned to the boat, she'd found a parchment resting atop her desk. A standing invitation from Wyll to join him for dinner upon her return. It was a stroke of luck, to be sure. She still needed to secure allies to defend her home from the scourge. This was the perfect opportunity to do that. She only hoped her efforts to convince Wyll would be more successful than her attempt to sway Lazar had been.

She exhaled, firming her resolve and sneaking a peek at her companion's face. He was still smiling, staring ahead as they strode away from the boat.

He would agree to help. She would make sure of it.

They arrived at a large building perched on the dock's outskirts. A signpost swung in the breeze above the door with a drawing of snake crashing through a wave and the words, the Salty Serpent Inn scrawled in red ink. She peeked in the window as they slowed, heading to the door. The bar was crowded, packed with dockworkers slugging back ale and laughing at bawdy jokes.

Interesting. This was not what she'd been expecting. She hadn't pictured Wyll as the type to frequent anywhere as common as a simple inn.

Wyll strode inside, leading her past the common room humming with raucous merriment. The delicious aroma of roasting meat followed them as they strolled further inside, toward a set of stairs leading up.

Kayda dropped Wyll's arm, cocking a brow. "Should I be concerned we're heading away from the dining room?" She stopped and peered up the carpeted stairs and into the shadowy hall above.

Wyll turned, one foot already on the bottom step, and offered her a hand. "The view's better up here. C'mon. Trust me." He grinned.

Kayda stared up at him, examining his smile in the dim candlelit hall. She'd already started on this course; she might as well see it to fruition. Besides, if he tried anything fresh, she could always scorch him. She smiled back and took his hand.

He led her to the third floor, pulled a key from his pocket, and opened the room's door. She steeled herself as the door swung open, preparing to enter a bedchamber, but she was met instead with a wooden chamber featuring a floor-to-ceiling glass window that overlooked the ocean with no bed in sight. Her jaw dropped as she strode inside to the simple table placed before the window. It was set for two.

"You're right. The view is lovely." The sun was beginning to set, throwing rose and lavender shades into the sky above the docks.

"You should see it at dawn."

She quirked a brow. "Should I?"

He pulled out the closest chair for her, his smile bright and mischievous. "The sun rises beyond the ocean every morning. It's spectacular."

Kayda slipped into the seat, dragging her gaze away from the window to look around the room. Shelves lined the walls, filled with hundreds of books. A worn wooden desk, covered in ink stains and neatly stacked piles of parchment, was wedged into a corner. "I take it this room is not always used for dining?"

Wyll seated himself across from her. "No. It's an office."

"Yours?"

"Yes. I enjoy being close to the action."

No wonder he'd shown up so quickly when they'd sailed into port. He must've been here all along.

Kayda's gaze slid along the bookshelves. There were several titles she recognized, and even more she'd love to examine more closely. "Are these all your books, too?"

Wyll nodded, leaning back on his chair. "Indeed. Are you a fan of the written word?"

It was her turn to nod. "I am."

His grin widened. "Feel free to borrow anything you'd like. My library is yours."

She smiled. "That's very kind of you to offer." Her smile drooped slightly. "I'm afraid I have little time for reading, presently. That's actually what I'd like to talk to—"

A knock on the door interrupted her.

"Come in," Wyll's deep voice boomed, full of command.

A pair of maids breezed in, carrying plates heaped full and fragrant. Kayda smiled pleasantly as they bustled about, dishing out food and pouring drinks.

There was stewed meat, potatoes, and a variety of fruits cut into bite-sized slices. Despite the delicious food on offer, she couldn't stomach the thought of eating. She had to know if Wyll could be persuaded into being an ally to Dracwood.

Soon the maids slipped out the door, closing it behind them.

Wyll lifted a wine glass, taking a tentative sip. "You were saying?"

She exhaled. "I'm sure you've heard what's happening in Dracwood."

He nodded once. "When the crew of the *Sea Sil*—pardon, the *Nova's Champion*—failed to return, we made inquiries."

"I didn't just come here searching for my family. I've come to seek allies as well. I'm sure you realize the scourge will not just be a problem for my country, but the entire world."

He took another sip of his wine. "We're traders, not fighters."

Kayda suppressed the urge to scowl. "You have a fleet of ships at your disposal. They would be indispensable. Ferrying those who will fight. Bringing weapons and supplies where they're needed."

Wyll leaned back, his gaze shifting to the widow before flicking back to hers. "I want to help you. But it won't be easy to convince my father."

She leaned forward, reaching across the table. "You know him well. What would sway him? Money? Trade rights? If it's in my power, I'll arrange it." Silence stretched between them. She held her breath, praying he would think of something. She couldn't return to Flamesmoat without the aid they needed.

Wyll leaned forward, matching her stance. He stared straight into her eyes. "We've enough money and trade already. There's only one thing that might work. Something he once had within his grasp before it was stolen from him."

Kayda's eyes widened. What could she give him that had been stolen from him?

Wyll's hand slid atop hers on the table. "Marry me."

She pulled her hand back, sitting upright in her chair. "What?"

Wyll stared down at his hand on the table before lifting his gaze to hers again. "My father thought he had royal connections when Solenne left to marry your father." He dropped his gaze and picked up a fork, poking at the food on his plate. "You can't imagine how much he used to brag when I was a boy. Practically every man he passed on the street heard all about how his niece married into royalty."

The fork stilled. "One day, he just stopped. I always wondered why. Now I'm sure that was when he found out the truth about where Solenne actually ended up." His gaze lifted to hers again. "I imagine he'd give just about anything to have that connection in truth."

Kayda's mind raced. He really wanted to marry her? "As far as anyone knows, we're family already. Won't it seem strange for us to be marrying each other? As cousins?"

"It's not so strange in Joria. Especially with large trade families like ours. No one here would bat an eye."

Kayda bit her lip. "It's not common in Dracwood but not unheard of, either."

Wyll leaned forward again. "And of course, we'll know we aren't actually cousins."

"True." She frowned. "You would marry me, for your father's sake?" She crossed her arms. "What do you gain out of this deal?"

"Besides the pleasure of a princess for a wife?" He sent her a crooked grin.

She cocked a brow, her lips pursed.

He sighed. "My brother and I have been making moves to bring the family business into the future. Trading more in goods and less in flesh. My father is... set in his ways. Not to mention his history of making rash decisions without consulting the rest of us." He grimaced, gaze flicking down. "That whole mess in the Abandoned Lands being one of them."

He met her eyes, sending her a rueful smile. "Frankly, we're getting a little tired of cleaning up his messes. But I have a feeling this might be what he needs to hand a bit more of the day-to-day decision making over to us."

It was commendable that Wyll was seeking to leave the slave trade. And learning it was his father who struck a deal with Tarquin and not him certainly lifted a weight off her shoulders. Kayda speared a piece of meat on her plate and popped it in her mouth, chewing slowly while she considered his proposition.

Could she marry him? She'd always been destined for a political match. Some arrangement that would benefit her country. And what was this if not a match that would benefit her country?

Would her grandfather and father allow her to take these matters into her own hands? Surely, they would see the logic and back her decision once all the facts were brought to light. It's not like she'd be running off with some stable boy, after all. She'd be marrying her way into a family that had the means to help their country stave off the enemies terrorizing their lands.

Truthfully, she hadn't expected to have to make such a decision so soon. Despite looking fully grown due to that minor mishap in the underground where she found Dru, she was only sixteen. Could she make a decision that would affect her entire life over dinner? Did he expect her to?

She swallowed, studying him. He was handsome. Though she didn't know him well, what she knew about him, she liked. But was it enough to bet a marriage on?

Wyll cleared his throat. "Perhaps this was a foolish idea." He rose and moved in front of the window, turning his back to her, his shoulders sinking.

Kayda's heart skipped a beat. Hadn't she just told herself she would do whatever it took to gain the aid her country needed?

She stood and joined him at the glass. "No. It's not foolish." She slipped her hand into his. "You understand, I must arrange this with my family first. We can't run off and marry today."

He spun to face her, grasping her other hand. "So, you agree?"

She nodded. "Yes, I'll marry you."

"Good." He beamed, his eyes twinkling, looking for all the world like a boy handed a massive sweet. Then his face shifted, darkening into an expression that sent a tingle down her spine as he drew closer.

He lifted a hand to her face, fingering a braid and sliding it behind her ear. "Kayda, I hope you know I'm not only interested in you for your title."

Her heart raced as his fingertips slid over the shell of her ear. She was suddenly very aware of the closed door. "You aren't?"

His dark brown eyes connected with hers. He shook his head, his stare sliding down to her lips.

Was he going to kiss her? She drew in a breath, her gaze flicking between his lips and his eyes as he dropped his head. His hand slid behind her neck, tracing the skin lightly, his fingertips smoothing the hair on the nape of her neck.

He drew closer, slowly, so slowly. Her eyelids fluttered closed as his lips brushed over hers, soft as a whisper.

And then he was gone. Her eyes shot open to find him an arm's length away, looking once more out the window.

She exhaled, blinking quickly. Had she done something wrong? Her stomach sank. Did he want out of their bargain?

Then he turned to her, his smile back in place. "So, after you speak to your family, we shall wed."

He didn't want out then. She gulped. Nodded.

"When will you return to Flamesmoat?"

She sat back down; her legs shaky after the kiss Wyll seemed happy to ignore. "Soon. I've something I have to do first."

Wyll joined her at the table. "And what's that?" He lifted his glass and took another sip.

Should she tell him about her promise to Dru? He was to be her husband. And he'd done nothing to suggest he couldn't be trusted. Once they wed, they would share everything. Perhaps she should begin trusting him now.

"Druturion believes there are more of his kind somewhere, sleeping underground like he was. I've promised to help him find them." She grabbed her fork and stabbed a potato. "The only problem is we don't know where to look."

Wyll's brow furrowed. "Wait there." He crossed the room to the desk and slid behind it. Fishing in his pocket, he retrieved a key ring and unlocked the top desk drawer. He pulled free something large, white, and oblong.

Was that a bone?

A moment later, he was back. He slid the bone across the table. "I just received this from one of my contacts in Raimire. It came from a massive beast that washed up on the beach in a little village called Stoneshore."

Kayda lifted the bone. Despite its size—it was nearly as long as her whole arm—the bone was surprisingly light. "It's hollow?" Her eyes widened.

Wyll smiled. "My contact believed the corpse originated from the largest of the Mido Islands."

Kayda placed the bone back on the table and leaned back in her chair. What were dragons doing washing up dead on the beach in Raimire? Whatever was happening, she was going to find out.

She aimed a smile at Wyll. Trusting him had already paid off. Perhaps this arrangement would be in her best interest. She could only hope that would continue to be the case. "Thank you for sharing that with me. Let's talk about your fleet."

Kayda knocked on the door to Jayan's chamber. The parchment in her hand crinkled as she awaited his answer.

She was back on-board *Nova's Champion,* below deck. She'd sat and talked with Wyll for hours, and then with Druturion, once she'd arrived back at the boat in the dead of night.

It was nearly morning. She ought to let the poor man sleep. But what she had to say couldn't wait until she returned. If she returned.

A *thump* sounded from within. Then the door slid open, and Jayan popped out. His braids were tousled, and he wore his customary pair of shorts and nothing else. He squinted in the dim candlelit hall. "Princess? Everything all right?"

She nodded and shoved the parchment into his hands.

"What's this?" He leaned closer, his gaze flicking across the words quickly. "I don't read, my lady."

Kayda hid the frown that fought to appear at his matter-of-fact statement. She smiled instead. "This is the deed of ownership for *Nova's Champion.* I want you to have it."

He shook his head and cleared his throat. "No, I can't accept this." He tried to hand the parchment back, but she took a step backward, clasping her hands behind her back.

"It's yours, Jayan."

He pulled the parchment close, eyeing it again. A smile crept across his face. "Thank you, Princess."

She nodded, her smile just as wide. "I hope you will consider joining the fleet of ships headed up the coast to Dracwood. Of course, the choice is yours to make, Captain." She turned to leave.

"Wait." He grasped her arm, stopping her. "Are you leaving?"

From the look in his eyes, she could tell he wasn't just asking about her leaving the hall. Somehow, he'd sensed she was leaving for good.

She nodded. "Druturion and I have business in Raimire, at a village called Stoneshore. We're leaving at dawn."

Jayan let go of her arm. He stared down at his feet before meeting her gaze and offering a small smile. "Good luck, Princess. I'll see you soon."

She quirked a brow. "Goodbye, Captain."

She returned to her room to pack her things. The first rays of dawn brightened the sky outside the open window.

The night had been a success. She'd finally secured the aid her country so desperately needed and found a clue that might lead her to her bondmate's brethren.

She stared out the window, breathing deeply of the salty sea air. In a perfect world, she would be happy to stay longer. To take her time getting to know her newfound family and her soon-to-be husband. But the world was far from perfect. At least she could leave Joria content that she'd uncovered some of the answers to the mystery of her past. One day, she would return. For now, she had a promise to keep.

It was time to discover what was happening on the Mido Islands.

Chapter 18

Conall made his way through another darkened forest. Snow stuck to his lashes and coated his stallion with a dusting of white atop his long brown fur. The wind was still this morning, making the cold seem less in its absence. It was an unexpected advantage in this frozen tundra, but he'd take all the good luck he could grab.

"Minsport is not far now," Taul said from his perch on the mount beside him. "Just on the other side of this wood."

Conall nodded, his fingers tensing beneath his gloves then tightly clutching the reins. A few more hours, and he would be on a boat sailing south. It was time to leave this frozen land behind and finally find his sister. "Thank you again for coming with me. I know you only agreed to venture to Norwich originally."

"It's no bother. Winters can be a bore in Gransea. I'm happy to have an excuse to venture about." Taul grinned, lifting his fur hat and scratching the stubbly red growth on his not-quite bald head. "Besides, Minsport is known for certain—how do I put this mildly—houses of ill-repute you won't find in Gransea. I've got plans for a nice long visit while I'm in the city."

He frowned. "Remind me to steer clear of those."

Taul chuckled. "You Dracians can be so stiff about these things."

Conall rolled his eyes. "I don't know why not wanting to pay a woman to—be nice to me—makes me stiff." He scoffed. "I don't understand how you Doln can be so casual about such things. Don't get me started on slavery."

Taul waved a hand. "I've been to your Flamesmoat. I've seen all the beggars and the poor in the slums. You don't see that around here. And do you know why?" He cocked a brow. "Everyone has a place."

Conall shook his head. "A place you can't leave isn't a place I want to be in."

"I guess we'll just have to agree to disagree, my friend."

They emerged from the wood and found Minsport spread out before them. Much like Gransea, it sprawled alongside the coast, only marginally smaller than the capital. Docks lined the ocean with boats of all sizes pulled into the harbor.

Conall dismounted, handing his reins off to Taul. "I don't know if I'll see you again, so I guess this is goodbye."

Taul smiled from atop his mount. "Well met, my friend. Pass on my goodbyes to Shadow." With a nod, he was off, leading the horses down the rise to Minsport.

"Brother. We're here. How long until you can catch up?"

Snow crunched behind him as his bondmate exited the wood, his tail wagging. *"Not long."*

Together, they began the trek to Minsport. The city itself was much the same as Gransea—buildings of gray stone laid out on neat streets. But the similarities ended there. This city was loud and brimming full of people. Chief Aundreas' claims about all the refugees flooding Minsport were no exaggeration.

Conall strolled through the throngs of folk crowding the streets, heading for the docks. Having a wolf at his side certainly had its perks. No one sought to stop him, and most seemed eager to stay a few paces away from where they tread.

It wasn't until he found himself a few streets away from the docks, the scent of saltwater and cawing of birds growing stronger with every step, he stopped. In the street ahead of him, he spotted a familiar face in the crowd, staggering away from the shadowy interior of an inn. Someone he had not expected to see.

"Aunt Brenna, is that you?" He jogged up the street to greet her. He wasn't about to miss this opportunity to sort out the strangled claims he'd overheard his stepfather crying about while he'd thought Conall dead at the bottom of a cliff.

Wild brown eyes turned to stare at him. She was dressed in a simple brown dress, her hair pulled up in a messy bun. She clutched a dark brown fur tightly against her chest, and a large sack bounced on her back. "Conall?" Her eyes bulged as she caught sight of him. "Is that you? You look different..."

Well, that wasn't much of a surprise. He certainly looked different these days. Not only from the aging but also from the thick brown and gray beard covering his chin when he'd always been clean shaven back in Dracwood. It was really more surprising that she recognized him at all.

Her jaw snapped shut, and she plastered a smile on her face, her gaze flitting between him and the building she'd just exited. "How fortunate I found you, nephew. I need your help. The people here, they're crooks and thieves, I tell you!"

A large blond man burst out of the building, his pale cheeks red. When he spotted Brenna on the street, he stalked forward, his lip curled back, jabbing a finger in her direction. "Stop, woman. You can't slink away without settling your debts." He skidded to a stop before her. "There are consequences around here for thieves."

Brenna grabbed the sleeve of Conall's fur, hiding behind him. "Please, Conall." Her voice was a thready whisper, thick with desperation. "You know me. I need your help with this *savage.*"

Conall breathed out a hard sigh. Who should he believe? The woman who sought to advise her brother into shooting him and leaving him for dead, or some random business owner, confident enough in his claims to follow a woman out in the street and shout about her debts? Despite his familiarity, or perhaps because of it, he was willing to bet on the latter.

He addressed the man first. "Sir, could you give me a moment to speak to this woman? I'll pay you for your time." He pulled a coin from his pocket and sent it sailing toward him.

The man snatched it out of the air and sent an angry glare his way. "I'll agree so long as you keep her here while I fetch the clan chief. I'll have this debt settled today."

Conall nodded. "Done."

The man whirled around to the crowd that had gathered to stare at the commotion in the street. "You all heard him. I've witnesses." He waited for several people to nod in agreement and form a loose circle around them before he sauntered off, his hurried pace taking him quickly down the street and out of sight.

Brenna glowered up at him. "What'd you do that for? I can't be brought before the clan chief. They'll have me turned into a slave after they side with that lying Dolnman."

Conall pulled his coin purse from within his fur. He hefted it in his fist and watched Brenna's eyes light up as the metal clinked. "If you answer my questions truthfully, then I'll settle your debts."

"All right. I'll tell you whatever you need to know."

Just then, the circle around them parted. Shadow ambled forward, joining Conall at his side.

Brenna swung wide eyes to him, and she backed away. "What is that beast doing here?"

Conall smiled. "This is Shadow. My bondmate."

"Your bondmate." She gasped. "You've a bondmate?"

He nodded. "I have your brother to thank for that. Shadow saved me in the woods when Gael shot me and left me for dead."

It was the crowd's turn to gasp. The sound echoed around him in a chorus as they leaned closer, their ears perked to bear witness to such a sordid tale.

But Conall wasn't focused on them. He kept his attention on Brenna, studying her reaction. "You wouldn't know anything about that, would you?"

She shook her head, her rosy cheeks jostling with the force of her shaking. "No, no. Not a word." She stopped her shaking, meeting his eyes. "I don't believe it, in fact. Gael would never!"

"Shadow, mind giving me a growl? I need this woman quaking in her boots."

Shadow didn't disappoint. He curled back his lips and flashed his teeth, growling deep in his throat.

Brenna jumped, taking a hurried step back, bumping into one of the men circled around them. He shoved her forward, indifferent to her ashen face and trembling limbs.

"I said to answer truthfully." He hefted the coin purse again.

Her gaze slid between his purse and Shadow. She drew a hand to her breast, tilting her head down to the ground. "All right. I knew. I knew he was after the farm. I advised him against it, of course, but I can't say I'm surprised. It's no fault of mine, I tell you!"

Conall shook his head slowly. "Lies after lies. Have you no shame, woman?"

"Again, brother."

Shadow opened his jaw, snapping and barking.

Brenna flinched, sweat beading on her forehead even in the bitter cold. "I-it was me. It was my idea." She cowered backward. "Is that what you want to hear? It's the truth, just like I promised you."

Conall sighed. There it was. The truth. This woman—this snake—turned her own brother against the only family he had left while he was battling the intense grief of losing his wife. Conall's shoulders stiffened, his fingers curling, his pulse rocketing through his veins.

The man reappeared, hustling down the street with a handful of burly bearded men on his heels. Brenna's eyes went wild, and she clutched his sleeve again. "You'll keep your part of the bargain, won't you?" she demanded.

He shook off her hold. "Why should I? When you'd have been happy to lie to my face if I hadn't pushed you for the truth?" He took a step away from her.

"I saved her. I saved your sister, that's why!"

He pivoted slowly. "You what?"

"Lark was on her way to Mage Keep. You know what happened there. You must've heard." She smiled, her words flooding out in a rush. "The scourge, they tore it all apart.

If she would've gone there like she wanted, she'd be dead. I convinced her to travel to Doln instead."

Conall's mind raced. A conversation he'd forgotten with his neighbor, Barrow, returned to plague him as she spoke. He'd said Lark departed for Flamesmoat *with Brenna*.

Blazes. He'd never even considered that she might stop Lark from traveling to Mage Keep. What could she want with her in Doln?

Oh no. A sick feeling spread in his stomach.

"What did you do?" His words came out short and clipped, his voice laced with anger. "Why would you send my sister to Doln?"

He didn't even have to ask Shadow to growl this time. Something in his tone must've startled him enough that he drew back his lips and roared.

From the crazed look in her eyes, he could tell Brenna realized the folly of her admission. She cowered beneath him, her throat working as she gulped. "I... I... You must know I—"

"Save it," he spat, as the man stepped back into the circle. A man with his shoulders back and a bearing of leadership, likely the Clan Chief of Minsport, walked at his side.

"There she is," the man proclaimed. "She owes me a fortune, and I caught her stealing away with no intention of paying. I've got witnesses and the unpaid receipts inside to prove it."

"Wait," Brenna said, the word a harsh croak. "My nephew here promised to pay my debt." She aimed her wild eyes at the crowd. "You all heard him. I have witnesses as well!"

The folk surrounding them all met her desperation with hard stares. It appeared none were willing to speak up for her after hearing her admit to her crimes.

The chief directed his gaze at him, raising a brow. "Is what this woman says true? Will you settle her debts?"

There was no question in his mind. He knew what he had to do.

"This woman is no kin of mine." His voice was cold. "She's a liar. I can vouch for this man and his claims. Don't believe a word that spills out of her rotten mouth. She poisons everything she touches."

Conall turned his back on her and shoved his way through the crowd with Shadow at his side. Brenna would get what she deserved. The Doln would ship her off to a workhouse, to spend the rest of her days as a slave. Maybe that made him a hypocrite for allowing it after all he'd said to Taul this morning, but if anyone deserved that fate, surely it was her.

She hadn't admitted it, but there was no doubt in his mind Brenna had sold his sister to a slaver. Trusting, sweet, innocent Lark. She must've followed her into Flamesmoat and stumbled right into a trap.

His nostrils flared, anger burning a hole inside of him. The only thing that had kept him from striking Brenna down where she stood was the vision he'd witnessed ensuring he would find Lark again. If he hadn't had that surety driving him, he would be the one in trouble right now, with a dozen witnesses accusing him of murder.

Conall marched on, his pace steady and his jaw set.

"What was that all about, little brother?" Shadow asked.

He halted outside a ramshackle tavern on the dock's outskirts. *"I'll tell you the whole of it soon. Not now. This is the place Taul told me about."*

A sign above the door sported a crudely drawn picture of a ship next to a flagon of ale. The Drunken Sailor. Taul had said this was the best place to seek passage south. It was a known haunt of captains waiting on the holds of their ships to be unloaded.

Conall shoved the door open. The hinge protested, letting out a grating *creak* that had him cringing and Shadow shaking his head.

All eyes swung to the door as they entered, but that wasn't saying much. The cramped shack was practically deserted. There were two men seated at the bar and a grizzled old barkeep behind a worn wooden counter that looked like it had survived a century of wear and tear.

"You lost, boy?" The barkeep kept a dubious eye on Shadow until he settled down on the floor near the small hearth in the corner.

Conall raised a brow. There weren't many people calling him boy these days. "I hope not." He strode up to the bar and took a seat on a wobbly wooden stool. "I heard this is the place to hire a captain."

The man closest to him, a tall fellow with a deep tan and a chiseled jaw, turned to him with a chuckle. "You might want to rethink that. Ships on this side of the continent only sail between here and Flamesmoat. You don't want any part of going there. Not now, anyway."

A pang of discomfort struck him at the warning. But he forced the thought aside. He would worry about the fate of his country later. "I don't want to go to Flamesmoat. I need to travel further south. To the Mido Islands."

"The Mido Islands?" The man scoffed, hefting up a flagon. Ale sloshed over the edge and wet his fingers. "Why in the world do you want to go there?" He took a long pull off his mug.

"There's someone there I have to meet."

Laughter spilled out of the man's lips. "No one's on the Mido Islands. They're uninhabitable."

"Just the same, that's where I need to go."

"Good luck with that." The man turned away.

Conall opened his pack and nudged aside his spare clothes and the book Delyth had gifted him. He dug deep down to the bottom and scooped up the heavy coin purse he'd found with the Sade Prim's things. He imagined she would approve of the expenditure. It was fate, after all.

He slapped the purse down on the bar, doing his best to amplify the clink of metal as it banged the wood. "I can pay."

But the man didn't turn back. "You'll be paying for your pyre. Or more like a watery grave. There's a reason none sail that far south."

The barkeep nodded. "Current's too strong. Even I know that, and you'll never catch me setting foot on one of the death traps these old dogs sail." The old man let out a raspy chuckle that shifted into a cough. He recovered quickly, grabbing a cloth to wipe up the spilled ale.

Conall caught his hand, stilling it atop the bar. His other hand hovered over the pooled liquid, and he sucked in a deep breath.

He needed a ship. It was the only way to reach his sister. He lowered his lashes for the briefest instant, picturing her face in his mind.

The air crackled with electricity while simultaneously filling with moisture. A cloud of liquid sprang out of nowhere, hovering above the bar. Then it spun, the wind whipping through the wooden shack, shaking the walls and blowing the hair across the men's faces. They gasped, each of them leaning back in their chairs, or in the barkeep's case, falling out of it and slamming into the floorboards.

As quickly as it started, it stopped. The liquid vanished without a trace. The wind, once again, still.

"The current won't be a problem." Conall opened the bag and spilled the coins atop the bar. Most of them fell neatly into a mound, gleaming even within the dim light inside the shack. One of them landed on its side, rolled down the bar, and spun before clattering to rest in front of the second man. The one who'd been silent the whole time.

This man was shorter than the one who'd spoken, but just as darkly tanned, with a short-shorn beard and long brown locks that came down to his shoulders. He lifted the coin off the bar between his finger and thumb, then turned to Conall with a grin. "You've got yourself a deal."

Conall grinned as well and scooped the coins back into the purse.

The taller man crossed his arms, frowning. He opened his mouth, then snapped it closed and nodded. "Fine. Your greed'll be the death of us one day, Captain."

Conall plunked the bag on the bar in front of the captain. "When do we leave?"

"On the tide. My first mate, Kris, will see you to the ship." He gestured to the tall man. "Kris, I'm Conall and this is Shadow."

Kris only glowered, then chugged the rest of his ale. "C'mon then." He stood. "Follow me."

They exited the little shack and turned left, heading to the far side of the port.

"Hey, you mentioned Flamesmoat earlier. What's been happening there?" Conall hurried to keep step with the long-legged sailor.

Kris scoffed. "It's a madhouse. The entire city is surrounded with a horde of those scourge. Nasty little critters, like something out of a nightmare. You don't want any part of that place. I can tell you that much." He tilted his head, eyeing him sideways. "Why do you ask? You got kin there or something?"

"Something like that," Conall admitted, his stomach clenching. All those people. His friends in Greenvale. He hoped they were faring all right.

"I'm sorry to hear that." Kris stopped in front of an aged wooden sailing ship sitting at the docks' end. "This is it. *The Lady Luck.*"

"She's not much to look at, is she?" Conall stared at the dented wood and chipped paint visible on the outer hull. The sails didn't look much nicer. Even rolled up at port he could spot countless stains and dozens of patches.

"You're one to talk." Kris grinned, rubbing a loving hand over the wooden rail as he made his way onboard. "She'll get you where you need to go. That's all that matters."

Conall sighed and settled his bag on the deck, nodding hello to the handful of deckhands who stared at him and Shadow curiously. Kris was right. All that mattered was finding Lark. Flamesmoat would have to wait.

Chapter 19

Lark's stomach churned. "Ugh, more sailing," she mumbled beneath her breath. They were back on another tiny boat, a few moments away from landing on the large island's shore.

By the time the three of them climbed down the cliffside and located a rowboat that was barely larger than the canoe they'd traversed the Boglands in, Nox had almost reached shore. Then the tide changed direction, leaving them to fight the current that had worked to swiftly carry Nox across the ocean. That left them hours behind him.

The island loomed large before them, filled with scraggly trees and rocky, mountainous terrain. It looked like an excellent place for a boy to get lost. She sighed, craning her neck to scan up and down the coastline. Wherever Nox was, he was already out of sight.

"Don't worry. We'll find him." Mika sat at the back of the boat, rowing in time with Aren, who sat up front. Whisper perched before her, his talons clasped tightly on one of the middle seats.

The sun slipped behind the highest mountain peak on the island as they rowed close to shore. Aren hopped out of the boat first. The water soaked the bottoms of his luct trousers instantly, and the surf splashed waves up to his waist before he tugged them ashore.

The three of them dragged the boat far onto the beach, well away from where the highest tide lines rested. Rocky sand crunched beneath their boots. Chirping sea birds competed with the surf's roar.

Lark spun in a slow circle, looking for signs of anything that might lead them to Nox. *"Muse, where are you? Have you found him?"* She'd sent her bondmate to search for the boy when it became apparent they would end up onshore so far behind him.

"I've been flying low, but I still haven't spotted him."

"Keep looking."

Mika started trudging in a northerly direction up the shoreline. "C'mon. If we find where his boat landed, then it'll be easier to track him."

"How do you know he went this way?" Aren asked. "Maybe we should split up."

"I was watching when he landed. It's this way, I'm sure of it." Mika shook his head. "Go south if you want. But you'll be wasting your time."

Aren's pale skin had slowly taken on a reddish tinge as they'd sailed across the channel in the rowboat, but his cheeks reddened to scarlet at Mika's clipped tone.

Lark rested a hand on Aren's arm. "I think he's right. Let's stick together. I don't like the looks of this place."

Aren met her eyes, and his expression softened. "North it is." He tightened his grip on the bow in his fist and set off, following Mika across the sand. "At least there's a little shade now that the sun's setting."

She stole another look at his skin. "You forgot your hat with all the commotion back in Stoneshore, I take it?"

Aren nodded. "I'll be all right. Sunburn won't kill me."

"I might have something in my pack that will help," she offered.

He waved her off. "It's not so bad at the moment. But I might take you up on that later."

They rounded a curve on the beach, and Mika took off. "Here it is." He skidded to a stop beside the small boat, peering within.

"Look, tracks leading inland." Aren pointed to the ground.

Muse's voice rose in her mind. *"Lark. I found something."*

Lark stopped, tilting her head. *"Is it Nox? You found him?"*

"Not him. Someone else. Two people. They're hurt, bad."

Aren was watching her. "What is it?"

"Muse. She's found some injured people."

Mika turned from his inspection of the boat. "Who could that be? No one lives here." He eyed the footprints in the sand. "We have to find Nox."

Lark stepped forward. "We can't just leave them to die. Not when we can heal them."

"You're right." Mika sighed. "Where are they?"

"Muse, can you fly straight up in the air so we can see your position?"

"On it."

Lark tipped her neck up and searched the sky. "There." Muse hovered above the base of the mountain, further inland and a little further to the north.

Aren squeezed her arm. "Go, find those people. Whisper and I will follow Nox's tracks."

Lark frowned. "I thought we were going to stick together?"

Mika jumped in. "It's a good plan. Look at the clouds, Lark. If it rains, we'll lose any sign of Nox's tracks."

Gray clouds hovered in the air to the south. She sighed, seeing the truth in his statement, her heart sinking all the same. "Be careful."

"We will." Aren sent her a smile and disappeared beneath the scraggly trees.

Mika and Lark started forward, heading further up the beach toward Muse's position. She circled high in the air like a beacon.

"Can you tell me more about the people you found?" Lark broke into a jog. It was strange indeed to find anyone on this desolate beach. The trees bore no fruit, and besides the seabirds perched high in the branches, she'd seen no wildlife. She understood why no one would be interested in settling here with all the variety and abundance in Raimire.

"Ha. I'm no human expert."

Lark rolled her eyes. *"Try, please."*

"There's a man and a woman. Young, like you. They're wrapped in bandages and curled up in the dirt near a stream."

Lark's stomach sank. What were they doing out here all alone?

Clues began to emerge, half buried in the sand and scattered along the rocky terrain bordering the beach. Debris and splintered wood, coated with a thick lacquer that was clearly not natural, littered the coastline. Had those poor souls survived a shipwreck?

They came abreast of Muse's position and turned inland. It was tough going. The vegetation grew thick, and there was no sign of any trails, forcing them to take careful steps through the underbrush. Just as the sky darkened, from a combination of approaching rain and impending night, they found them.

It was just as Muse described, only worse. They were curled up together on the ground, their clothing torn to shreds and wrapped around their thin limbs as makeshift bandages. Though she and Mika didn't try to move quietly through the underbrush, neither of them stirred as they approached.

Lark hurried forward as Muse settled on the riverbank beside her. She knelt beside the girl, and Mika, the boy, inspecting them both and wincing in sympathy.

The girl had her right leg exposed, wrapped tightly in fabric dyed a dark brownish-red and still moist to the touch. Her features were slack, her lips covered in dried skin with dark circles ringing her eyes.

The boy appeared to be in slightly better shape. He had a bandage wrapped around his head, but from the fabric's color, it looked to be well on its way to healing, even before Mika gently lifted the bandage to peer at the swollen flesh within.

That action was enough to wake him. His blue eyes shot open, and he gasped, jolting upright to sit. "Who are you? What's going on?" Then his startled gaze fell on his companion and some of the confusion lifted. "Help! We need help. We've been shipwrecked for days."

Mika shushed him. "It's all right, we're healers. We've come to help you."

Relief washed over his features. His shoulders slumped, and he closed his eyes, breathing out a deep sigh.

Mika turned to her. "He can wait. Let's take care of the girl first."

The sky chose that moment to split. Rain drenched them, and lightning flashed across the sky to the south, followed by the loud crack of thunder. Lark shivered, the cold rain soaking her luct outfit and moistening her skin.

"Her name is Oriana," the boy said, watching them work from his spot on the streambed.

Lark met the boy's gaze and raked her wet brown curls out of her face. "We'll take care of your friend. Don't worry." She smiled reassuringly as Mika joined her beside the girl and began untying the wet cloth from her leg.

"Be careful. She's still bleeding. The gash in her leg—" His chin quivered. "I did my best, but it just won't stop bleeding."

Mika loosened the cloth enough to peek under it. Lark watched him work, even as the rain spilled over the girl's bandage, soaking the cloth and making the dirt below her turn red. He clenched his jaw tightly and pulled the bandage closed after a brief peek. "You did well. She wouldn't still be living without your care. Let us take care of the rest."

He dug in his satchel and pulled free a handful of roots and some vibrant green leaves. "Lark, I need your help. Will you lend me your talent again?"

She nodded and held out her hand. Lightning flashed again, the rain pelting her fingers and pooling in her palm.

But Mika shook his head. "Grab my shoulder. I'll need both hands for this."

She did as requested, holding Mika's shoulder and closing her eyes to concentrate. She wished to help him. To heal this poor girl of the brutal bleed slowly draining her.

Warmth spread across her palm. The tremor came next, shaking her to her core. A wave of exhaustion rose with it. Her thighs wobbled, and her head drooped, swinging lightly on her neck as dizziness swamped her.

Just as she was sure she would collapse, it was over. Her eyelids slid open in time to catch the girl raising her head off the ground, her bright green eyes flitting all around, a hand flying to her chest.

"Who are you? Where's Edrik?" she asked.

"Here. I'm here, Ori," the boy answered. He reached past Mika, grabbing her hand. "These people are healers. We're saved." He smiled.

Mika focused on her and placed a steadying hand on her shoulder. "Are you all right, Lark?"

Muse hopped up on a tree branch, chirping noisily. *Kak-kak-kak.*

She sent Mika a wobbly grin. "Yeah, I'm fine. Just a little tired."

Mika frowned. "That's what has me worried. Sharing talent can be draining on the giver. You need to rest."

She leaned back on her heels. The rain continued to fall around them. Lighting shot through the air to the north. This time, the thunder took a moment to echo around her. She shivered, hoping the storm would pass quickly. "What about Edrik?"

Mika squeezed her shoulder and dropped his hand to his side. "I can handle him on my own. His body has already done much of the healing." He turned to others. "You'll both be fine after some food and rest."

Oriana's face lit up. "You have food?"

Edrik grinned. "We've had plenty of water here, but nothing to eat for days except for bugs." He shuddered.

Oriana grimaced. "That was what you made me eat?" She gave Edrik a gentle push. "Gross!"

Mika chuckled. He dug in his satchel and handed the girl a pouch filled with dried strips of meat and fruit. "Eat slowly. Your stomachs will need time to adjust after so long empty."

The pair crowded around the pouch, stuffing food into their mouths. The rainfall slowed, and Lark sighed. It seemed her prayers would be answered after all.

The crunch of footsteps sounded in the woods. Lark stilled, her eyes widening.

"Ha. Don't worry. It's just lover boy and the old snoozer," Muse assured her, just as Lark spotted Aren's blond head peeking out from behind some trees. Whisper rested on his gauntleted arm.

"Aren." She smiled and rose to her feet. She wobbled, her gait unsteady from the exhaustion lingering in her limbs.

Aren rushed forward and grabbed her arm before she tumbled sideways. "Lark, are you all right? What happened?"

She waved him off but let him maneuver her to sit on a large stump close to the streambed. "I'm fine. How about you? Did you find any sign of Nox?"

He nodded. "I followed his tracks into the woods, not far from here. Then that storm started, and I lost the trail. I figured I might as well try to find you. Whisper must have heard Muse calling. I was able to follow his lead and find you."

Lark smiled, remembering Muse's cawing from the trees.

"I left a trail we can follow in the morning to where I lost Nox's tracks. He must've stopped for the night, too. We'll find him tomorrow."

She nodded and wrapped her arms around herself tightly. The rain had fully stopped, but with the sun hidden behind the mountain spanning the island's center, it would be a long time before she was warm again. Too bad she hadn't thought to bring a change of clothes in her pack.

Aren frowned, watching her shiver. "I passed a cave on the way here. It's not far." He turned to Mika and the others, pointing back the way he came. "It looked dry inside. We should head there for the night."

Mika nodded. "Good plan. Take Lark and set up camp. I'll wait until these two finish eating. By then, I'll have the strength to heal Edrik, and we'll meet you there."

Aren bristled. She could tell he wasn't fond of taking orders from Mika. But Aren held his tongue and extended a hand to help her to her feet. Then he turned back to Mika. "I left a trail of luct string tied to the trees. Follow that, and you'll find us." He started to walk away but paused. "Don't wait too long. The sun's not long from setting."

"Yes, yes. We won't." Mika waved a hand dismissively.

Aren set his shoulders and pushed forward through the underbrush. "C'mon, Lark. It's this way."

She followed, her gaze landing on a dangling string of sheer green fabric tied on a branch at eye level off in the distance. "That was quick thinking, leaving a trail to follow. But where did you find the string?"

Aren grinned, lifting his pants and showing her the torn edges stuffed into his boots. "I'll have to sleep with my boots on if I don't want my feet covered in bites, but it was worth it to not get lost." The Raimish trousers were long enough to roll down and cover their bare feet at night, but Aren had torn the bottom of each pant leg, leaving him with trousers that barely hit at his ankles.

She smiled, admiring his ingenuity even as her stomach filled with knots. Except for the few moments they'd spent together behind the curtains in the healing hut, this was the first time since leaving Dracwood that she'd been alone with Aren.

Traveling with the group was amazing, but it left little time for privacy. Especially when they'd been trapped in a canoe or traversing a jungle crawling with predators.

For the first time in weeks, she'd have a chance to speak to him privately. A part of her wanted that more than anything. But the larger part was suspiciously tongue-tied, only able to sneak glances in his direction as they trudged through the woods.

It didn't take long for them to locate the cave. The mouth was set into a large rocky hillside a bit farther inland from the little stream.

They stepped cautiously into the shadowed interior. The cave was empty, with a high ceiling that allowed even Aren to stand without threat of smacking his head on the rocky roof. In truth, it was not a full cave at all, but more of a rocky outcropping open to the air on three sides.

The dirt and patchy grass beneath were dry at least. Lark curled up on the ground as Whisper and Muse flew up to the top of the rock, finding perches quickly.

"Hey, there's a bunch of old nests up here." Muse hopped along the ceiling's edge.

"Are they empty?"

"Yep. Looks like it."

"Can you knock them loose? We can use them to start a fire."

"Can I? Ha. Easy."

Scratching sounded as Muse got to work. Soon a rain of sticks and twigs came tumbling down upon them.

"Hey, watch it," Aren exclaimed, brushing his face and sputtering.

"Sorry. I asked Muse to knock those down. Can you help me start a fire? I have a tinderbox in my pack."

Aren smiled. "Good idea."

Working together, they got a small fire blazing. Lark sighed as the flames danced, holding out her hands to warm them.

Aren backed away a few paces.

"Aren't you cold?" she asked.

He grimaced. "The sunburn."

She smiled gently. "I can help you with that." She dug into her pack and pulled out a little metal tin filled with a green herbal ointment. "Sit down." She patted the dirt beside her.

"Thanks." He sat with his back to the fire, extending his legs in front of him.

She grabbed a palmful of the slick cream and began applying it to the red skin on his forehead. He closed his eyes, letting out a sigh when the cool ointment swept over his heated flesh. "That feels amazing." A smile spread across his face.

She gulped. The green ointment blended in with his skin as she gently massaged, relieving much of the redness. She reminded herself it was only the ointment making him smile as her fingers slid over his nose and the prickly skin on his cheeks.

This she could do. This was what she was meant to do. Healing people was her calling.

She tried repeating that in her mind as her hands slid lower over his neck. And again, when the rapid pulse beating under his skin thrummed beneath her fingertips.

"Take off your shirt." Her eyes widened. Did that raspy voice belong to her?

Aren's eyes shot open. Ice-blue orbs full of questions connected with hers. Her stomach fluttered.

She cleared her throat. "Your shoulders are burned, too. The luct fabric doesn't stop sunb—"

He pulled off the shirt, and the words died on her lips. Lark's mouth went dry. The sheer clothes didn't leave much to the imagination, but being so close, and so alone, with *this* man... It was enough to set her heart racing. He was exceedingly well made. Strong and broad, covered in muscle and a smattering of light hair. And so much *sunburn.*

She shook her head and blew out a breath, quickly scooting behind his back. Without his gaze on her, she could concentrate on the task at hand. She could pretend this was some random villager in need of healing. She grabbed another handful of ointment and gently smoothed it across his back and shoulders.

"Lark?" he asked.

"Hm?"

"Tiora told us what you said to her this morning." Aren's back muscles tensed beneath her palms. "Do you really expect us to leave you here alone? With Mika?"

Her fingers stilled on his back. She dipped back into the tin, scooping up more ointment. She moved onto the back of his neck, the short hair at the nape flicking across her fingertips. "I can't ask you to put your lives on hold for me. To face danger and death. If any of you were hurt because of me..." Her insides twisted with pain at the thought.

Aren whirled around so quickly her hands landed on his chest. "Do you think any of us would leave now? After everything we've been through together?" He met her gaze again, his blue eyes reflecting the dancing flames. She could see something there. Something that scared her more than the scourge ever had.

She dropped her gaze to her hands, both flat on his warm skin. The slick ointment between them did nothing to disguise the rise and fall of his chest beneath her palms. The ebb and flow was hypnotic, like the tide, ready to pull her out to sea.

He lifted a single finger and tipped up her chin, compelling her to meet his eyes again. "I won't leave you, Lark," he whispered.

Her heart squeezed. She rose on her knees and pressed her lips to his, her eyes closing.

There was no hesitation. He met her instantly, with just as much pressure. Just as much desperation. Then his tongue was in her mouth. His fingers tangled in her curls, and she was melting right there on that tiny island in the middle of nowhere.

Aren hissed, breaking the spell. Her eyes shot open and she realized she was clutching his shoulders so hard her nails left little half-moons in his reddened flesh.

She gasped and lifted her hands, backing away. "Your sunburn, I'm sor—"

"No, don't be sorry." He seized her hands before she could get far and pressed them back on his chest, his voice deep and husky. "Don't be sorry." He dipped his head and kissed her.

Lark trembled, skimming her fingers across his chest. His touch drifted down her back, rocking her up off her knees, pulling her closer.

"I hate to be the breaker of close embraces—again—*but the others are coming,"* Muse warned.

Lark pulled away. She sucked in a deep breath, lifted Aren's shirt off the ground, and handed it to him. "The others..."

She didn't need to finish. The crunch of footsteps in the underbrush sounded, and excited chatter followed. Aren slipped his shirt back on before the trio emerged from the darkened forest and joined them under the overhang.

Lark snapped the lid back on the little metal tin and slipped it back into her pack. Her cheeks burned and her heart still quivered wildly. She forced a smile and turned to greet the others.

The newcomers seemed oblivious to any tension in the air, but Mika's gaze flitted between the two of them before landing on her. He raised a brow. "Any trouble while we were away?"

She shook her head, still smiling. She glanced at him quickly before staring into the fire. "No. No trouble at all."

"Hm." He spared Aren a glance before seating himself beside her. "I learned something interesting about our new friends here while you two were setting up camp. We're not the only ones with talent on this island."

Lark's smile dropped, her mouth falling open. She spun to Edrik and Oriana. "You two can summon?"

Edrik nodded. The bandage on his head was gone, revealing a tangled mess of dirty blond hair. "I'm a water mage, and Oriana summons wind. We were sent here to request aid for Flamesmoat. Mika tells us you already know about the scourge. That a few of them even made it as far south as Raimire already."

Lark shuddered. "Yes, just this afternoon."

"We've been dealing with them for weeks." Edrik sighed, crossing his arms. "They've got the whole city surrounded. Our leader sent us to bring whatever help we could find."

"And then you were shipwrecked," Aren added.

"Yeah. We're lucky you found us when you did." He grimaced. "Between starving and all the crazy sounds we've been hearing, I didn't hold out hope for lasting much longer."

Lark raised a brow. "What sounds?"

Edrik shrugged. "I don't know for sure. It was like nothing I've ever heard in my life. Like there was some huge monster somewhere on this island screaming, over and over again every night." He grimaced again. "At first, I was scared witless, certain the thing was dying to find and slaughter us. But the longer I listened, the stranger it became."

Edrik's brow furrowed, and he shook his head sadly. "It sounded like a mother crying out in anguish over her lost child. Whatever was making those cries wasn't angry. It was heartbroken." He scooted closer to the fire and stretched out his hands, shivering. "But we haven't heard the screams for the last few days. Hopefully, whatever was making them is gone now."

Mika stiffened as he listened to the tale, eyes round.

Lark elbowed him in the side. "You all right?"

Mika scrubbed a hand over his face, and for a moment, she was certain he would keep whatever was bothering him to himself. Then he let out a deep sigh and spoke, his voice heavy with frustration and tinged with fear. "I found a carcass washed up on the shore not long ago. It was huge. Easily the size of a whale. That's what I told the townsfolk it was, so no one would panic, but it was no whale."

Aren leaned closer, his brows sinking. "What was it?"

"You're gonna think I'm crazy, but—it was a dragon."

Lark raised a hand to her mouth, blinking repeatedly. "You think it came from here?" She clutched her legs to her chest, peering into the darkened trees beyond their little cave. Her mind flashed back to that massive black dragon tearing through the sky above Bogsmouth, setting the scourge ablaze. It wasn't too much of a leap for her to imagine finding dragons here, too.

Mika quirked a grin, looking pleased no one thought to question his sanity before dropping the smile and nodding solemnly. "It makes sense. The direction of the tides. The noises Edrik and Oriana have been hearing." He shrugged. "Why else would Nox head here with the scourge if they're not searching for something?"

Lark bit her lip and stared off into the dark. Had Nox come here searching for a dragon? Wherever he was, she hoped he was safe and warm for the night at least. Tomorrow, they would find him. She would make sure of it.

Chapter 20

Wind blew in Kayda's face, whipping through her braids. She perched atop Druturion, flying above an endless expanse of greenery dotted with bright flashes of color. The scent of flowers and sounds of teeming life reached her even with the wind rushing past.

They'd been flying for most of the morning. First through the Waste's dry air, the burnt-orange sand reminding her of her time spent finding her family. Reawakening the hopeful feeling that had washed over her as she began her search. She would help Dru locate his family. She could sense it.

Eventually, they'd left the desert behind, crossing high over the Anaraine Mountains she'd only seen on foot. From above, they were even more majestic, stretching out across the horizon in all their glimmering glory. It took them ages to pass, but once they made it to the other side, the jungle spread out before them, green and lush, a stark contrast to the barren sands and rocky cliffs they'd just passed.

The humidity hit them then. Kayda's white silk tunic and cotton trousers stuck to her skin, even with the wind cooling her. They had to be getting close to the coast. Blue flashed on the horizon to the west, exactly where Stoneshore should be, based on the maps she'd studied in Wyll's office.

The thought of Wyll had her stomach churning. Had she done the right thing trusting him? Would he follow through with his promise to help her people fight back against the scourge? Time would tell, and she could only hope he'd be true to his word. She pushed her worries aside as Druturion flew lower, skirting the top of the jungle canopy and gliding up alongside the coast.

As they hovered above the beach, Kayda saw the name *Stoneshore* was fitting. The beach was littered with pebbles and what appeared to be broken shards of shells worn smooth by the crushing waves. The tide was out as they approached, revealing a low beach bordered by a high cliffside, the jungle hovering close to the cliff's edge and shading the rocks below.

Off in the distance, Kayda spotted the first of the string of islands bordering the western shore of Raimire. That was where they needed to go. The Mido Islands.

"There they are, Dru. We have to head for the largest of those islands." She raised a brow as Druturion kept straight on his course up the coast, making no effort to turn west across the sea channel. *"Where are you going, Dru? We've got to fly to the island."*

"I have to see... there." He blasted down to the ground, his claws skittering rocks as they landed. Kayda hopped down off his back, stretching. Dragon riding was incredible, but it was as tough on the legs and hips as a long ride in a horse's saddle.

Druturion bounded up the beach and started digging.

"What are you looking for?" Kayda veered off near the cliffside, avoiding the rain of pebbles Dru sent flying as he dug. He must have found something.

He stilled, his whole body slouching as he stared down at the beach.

Kayda rounded his side and gulped. His digging had revealed a massive bone sticking up from the rocky soil. She placed a hand on his neck as he shuddered. *"I'm so sorry, Dru."*

"I'm too late. All that time I spent underground. I should have sensed this was happening. I should have known." His grief was palpable. Anguish colored his words, his body thrumming as he stared down at the massive bone.

"Don't blame yourself. There's no way you could have known this was happening. How could you?"

Druturion shook even more strongly. Then he stilled. He raised his head skyward and let out a deafening roar.

Kayda drew back, her heart hammering.

"I'll find who's responsible for this." Dru's voice was a promise of retribution. *"I won't rest until their bones are charred and buried for what they've done to my kin."*

Kayda returned to Dru, placing her hand on the hard smooth scale on his jaw. *"I'll help you, Dru. We'll make them pay together."*

Dru snorted, cocking his head sideways and staring out across the ocean at the Mido Islands. *"Hop on. Let's discover what's been happening on those islands."*

Kayda nodded and vaulted up on Dru's back, clasping his neck. Two running steps, and he was up in the air, the blue sea spread out below them. The chain of islands slowly grew larger on the horizon.

Druturion aimed for the largest northernmost of the isles. It was covered with thin tangled trees, their leaves less vibrant and the covering more meager than the lush greenery of Raimire. Above the treetops, a rocky gray mountain rose, the cliffs reaching at least twice higher than even the tallest of the trees. It was here they slowed and circled the island, peering down at the landscape below them.

"What are you looking for?" Kayda asked.

"I'm not sure." He continued to circle, his head bobbing all around. *"I'll know it when I see it."*

Kayda leaned over his neck, seeking something, anything, that looked out of sorts. She wasn't sure what she was looking for. Certainly, it wouldn't be as simple as finding a valley full of dragons lounging in the sun.

The third time they circled, she spotted something on the island's far side. There was a spot on the mountainside that had a few trees toppled over on their sides. Had a storm caused that damage, or could it be from something else?

"Dru, look, do you see that flat plateau? And those trees below it?"

Druturion pivoted in the air, spinning toward the area she'd mentioned. *"What about it?"*

"If a dragon fell off the cliff side there, they'd splash right down into the sea, wouldn't they? Maybe smash a few trees on the way down?"

She could feel her bondmate stiffen at the mention of a dragon falling into the sea, but he flew toward the spot. *"Let's check it out."*

He slammed down on the plateau a moment later. Kayda released her death grip on his neck and slid down, her boots slapping against the hard rock. Upon closer inspection, she was even more sure something happened here recently. Grass was torn up in the few places it grew, and faint scratch marks marred many of the rocks.

She trekked to the cliff's edge, vertigo causing her head to spin as she stared down at the sheer drop to the sea. It was even more apparent from up close that the tree damage below was not natural. Only here were the thin trees snapped and broken; all the greenery up and down the coast grew undisturbed. No storm destroyed only trees in such a short space.

She backed away from the cliffside and veered across the plateau to Dru. *"What do you think, Dru?"* She nodded to the ground where he sat studying the scratch marks. *"Looks to me like a scuffle happened here."*

"I think you're right." He lifted his head and surveyed their surroundings. *"But where are they now?"*

The landscape was dominated by rock at this height on the mountain. She could see no sign of life. Even the sea birds she'd caught glimpses of on the rest of the island appeared unwilling to venture here. It seemed an unlikely place to house a dragon.

"I don't see how a dragon could have survived up here. When you lived underground, you still had to eat and drink, didn't you? I remember the bones in that underground cavern. The trickle of water in the distance." She took a closer look at the rocks surrounding them. *"Wouldn't the dragons here need something to eat as well? A source of water?"*

"Yes, you're right. Algernon arranged it all when I decided to hibernate. He founded the order that kept me fed, bringing me a goat on the same day every year." He chuckled. *"The same group of people that morphed into your Church of the Dragon."*

Kayda frowned. *"There are no people here to help. There must be something in place already that would allow the dragons to keep themselves fed all these years. I wager they're somewhere within this mountain, below our feet."*

Druturion shook out his wings. *"How will we find them? I can dig on the beach, but this is solid rock."*

Kayda strolled around the plateau, searching. She withdrew from the plateau's edge and made for the center, where the mountain rose again, so steeply they would have trouble climbing. She set her hand on the rock wall and traced her fingers along the gray stone, gliding along the edge. Suddenly she gasped. Her hand slipped right into the rock, vanishing as if it had been sucked in.

"Kayda, are you all right?" Druturion paced closer, his red eyes bulging as her fingers disappeared into the wall.

"Yes, I'm fine." She pulled her hand free and waved it in the air. It was whole and uninjured. *"It's an illusion, like the Palisade, only different. Weaker somehow."*

Druturion gasped. *"You're a genius! This must've been made long ago. There's no way it could be a true barrier without the constant sacrifice required of the Palisade, but a simple illusion. Yes, it could surely last this long."*

Kayda stuck her hand back inside the illusion, marveling at the way her fingers disappeared as if they weren't there. She could feel them wiggling, but it looked like only rock existed beneath her palm.

A muffled roar blared, rising from within the illusion. Kayda startled and backed away, her hand dropping at her side. *"Did you hear that?"*

"Hear what?"

She turned to her bondmate. *"There's something in there."* Maybe she could hear it because she was touching the barrier when it sounded?

She stretched out her arm and stepped forward to place her hand through the illusion once more, but before her fingers grazed the rock that wasn't rock, she slammed into the ground.

"Oof." Her head crashed into the hard ground; her body shoved sideways. She rolled up to sit, groaning and clutching the back of her head. It throbbed beneath her fingers. Her sight was fuzzy, the world a spinning blur. It took a few heartbeats for the spinning to stop. When it did, her breath caught, and she scrambled backward, her shoulders banging into the rock wall at her back.

An ice-white dragon sat before Druturion, staring him down. Shimmering white scales glittered in the sun, strikingly bright, shining with flecks of silver and gold.

"Belstasia! Is that you?" Druturion's voice sounded clearly through their bond, then he paused, tilting his head as if listening to a response she couldn't hear. It appeared Kayda would only be privy to half of this conversation.

Kayda peered at the new dragon curiously. She had a feeling from the sound of the name and the white dragon's slimmer, smaller build, she was female.

"What do you mean, something's after you?" Dru backed up, making room for Belstasia on the plateau as she paced nervously. She unfurled her wings, looking for all the world like she wanted nothing more than to fly off and escape.

"Slow down, Bela, you're not making sense." Dru paced closer, only to retreat when the white dragon cowered beneath him as if she were terrified. *"We heard word of dragon bones washing up on the coast close to here. Tell me, who's hunting you? Where are the others? We need all the help we can muster. The scourge have returned. The Palisade has fallen."*

Dru stopped talking, his body still as he stared intently at the white dragon, still cowering before him. She slumped on the ground, her wings curled around herself protectively, quivering visibly.

Dru lifted his head and roared. Kayda cringed at the deafening blare, her head hammering even more as the blast of sound compounded with the pain from her fall.

"You did what?" he bellowed, rising up to his full height, his wings unfurling, teeth bared.

Faced with his anger, Kayda shrank, instinctively tucking her chin to her chest and hugging her torso. What could make her bondmate react so strongly? What had Bela done?

Belstasia continued to cower, lowering herself even closer to the ground. Then she stuck her neck out of her wings, eyes closed, reminding Kayda of a lamb ready for slaughter.

What was happening? Was she begging Dru to kill her? Kayda lurched to her feet, ignoring the wave of dizziness slamming into her.

Dru was seething. She could sense it through the bond, anger flooding off him like a wave. He opened his mouth. The fire deep within his throat burned bright and hot. He rose on his hind legs, towering above Bela's prone form.

Kayda slid in between the dragons, cursing herself all the while for the dangerous decision. She couldn't stand by and watch her bondmate slaughter one of his kind—maybe the only one left. She had to do something to cool his anger. She knew him. If she allowed him to give into the anger boiling in his veins, he would never forgive himself.

"Stop, Dru," She barreled between the two behemoth beasts. *"You can't hurt her. I don't care what she's done. It's not right."*

"Move out of the way, Kayda," he ordered, his voice steely and sharp.

"No."

She stood her ground, hands on her hips, chin in the air. Maybe she was crazy. Maybe this was the start of the madness that haunted her future. She didn't care. There was no way she was going to let Dru go through with this. She planted herself on the plateau, staring down an angry dragon with another at her back. She wasn't even afraid. Not truly.

But that was when the trouble started.

Chapter 21

Lark stood in front of a small stream, less than an hour's walk from the cave they'd slept in. It was early morning, just after sunrise. Each of them stared off into the woods, searching for signs of the boy they'd come to rescue.

Aren pulled off a piece of luct string hanging from a tree branch. "This is where I stopped when the storm broke and I lost Nox's trail. From what I could gather from his trail yesterday, he seemed to be headed inland, on a northwesterly track."

Mika spun in a slow circle. "We should spread out in a line headed northwest, keep our eyes peeled for any clues."

It was as good a plan as any. Whisper and Muse rose in the sky, and the five of them spread out on the ground, advancing slowly and making their way inland. They weaved between the scraggly trees, sidestepping pricker bushes, their steps crunching in the sandy soil. It wasn't long before someone shouted that they'd found something.

Lark raced to her left and spotted Oriana kneeling next to a pricker bush.

"This looks like the sheer cloth you all are wearing." Oriana pointed at a shredded piece of luct fabric dangling from one of the branches.

"You're right." Lark grinned. "We're on the right track."

They spread out again, using the bush as the center of their search grid, moving further inland.

Though Lark tried to keep her mind on the search, her thoughts kept drifting back to Aren and that kiss. They'd had no time to discuss it last night or this morning. Even now, she shouldn't be thinking about it. Not when there was a boy that needed saving. But as she trudged through the island forest, she couldn't stop herself from replaying the moment in her mind, wondering what would've happened if they'd not been interrupted. She sighed. Would the timing ever be right for the two of them?

Then it was her turn to yell out she'd found something.

She halted before the entrance to a cave much smaller and darker than the outcropping they'd slept under the night before. The mouth was barely big enough to fit a person, the blackness within so complete it made her shudder. It appeared to lead into the gray mountains rising beyond their path. As the others crowded around her, they all gazed inside with trepidation.

Lark slipped the leather gauntlet out of her pack as Aren whistled for the birds to return. Muse landed on her outstretched arm soon after.

"He must've gone inside." Aren glanced upward, holding Whisper on his gauntlet. "The cliff is far too steep here to climb."

"How can we know for sure?" Edrik leaned forward and squinted into the dark hole. "What if he turned and ventured around the mountain instead?"

Lark placed her free hand on the gray stone next to the cave entrance. Deep in her belly, that prickle of unease rose again. "He's in there. I can feel it."

Mika shrugged. "That's good enough for me." He paced around in a circuit, selecting a trio of sticks from the ground. Then he reached into his pack and pulled out a roll of bandages. "Edrik, Oriana, help me, please." He handed a stick and a length of cloth to each of them. "Wrap the tops of these in bandages, like so." He twirled the top of his stick to demonstrate. "Then slather them with some of this." Reaching into his pack again, he pulled free a vial of oil and tipped a bit onto the cloth. "We're sure to need torches to navigate inside that cave."

Lark stood stiffly, tapping her foot while they finished crafting and lighting the makeshift torches. Then all five of them ducked down and crept inside the cave, one by one.

Lark hiked at the head of the group, behind Mika. He strode forward confidently, lighting the way with his torch. Oriana was behind her, then Aren and Edrik bringing up the rear.

The flickering torchlight sent shadows spreading on the walls, casting them in an eerie gloom. They found themselves in a wide, low tunnel, carved into the rock. It appeared to be natural, full of jagged, rocky outcroppings sticking out in all directions that they were forced to maneuver around. Water dripped down the walls, wetting a floor littered with rock and spotted with holes soaked in black.

They ducked and weaved their way through for ages. Lark's neck and shoulders began protesting after so long crouched down in the cramped tunnel. Her legs ached from all the walking, much of it on a tilted pitch that made her certain they weren't only traveling inward, but upward as well.

At long last, the way ahead opened up. The ceiling lifted, and they stepped inside a large chamber, the walls glittering with sparkling rocks.

It was here they spotted movement across the cavern on the far wall. It was him.

"Nox," Mika yelled.

Nox jerked around at the sound, the scourge still dangling from his shoulder like a sinister scarf. But he didn't stick around to greet them. He disappeared into another tunnel, leading further into the mountain.

Mika raced after him for a few paces, then fell, a shriek on his lips as he walloped the ground. His torch skittered across the floor, staying lit but falling out of his reach.

Lark started toward Mika, but he held up a hand.

"Careful," Mika said through gritted teeth. "It's slipperier than it looks."

She heeded his warning, making her way to him carefully. Her boots slid on the slick rock, but though she wobbled, she kept her balance until she was at his side. "Are you all right?" She crouched beside him.

"Rot and decay." He hissed with pain, lifting his pant leg and untying his boot to reveal his ankle, already swollen. "I'll live."

Soon the others crowded around them, everyone careful not to make the same mistake of moving too fast. Their torches lit his wound. His skin continued to swell before her eyes.

Lark winced in sympathy. "Let me help you."

Mika waved her away. "No. I can heal myself. Nox is just ahead. You all go on without me. I'll catch up soon."

Her heart squeezed at the thought of leaving Mika all alone. "Are you sure?"

"Yes, go. Find Nox. Keep him from doing something stupid until I catch up to you."

"I'll leave a trail if the tunnel splits." Aren grabbed her arm, turning to leave.

Edrik handed Mika his fallen torch, and the rest of them hustled off after the boy.

Lark squinted into the darkness ahead of them. It was another tunnel, much like the first, only this one pitched at an even steeper incline. Nox was already out of sight, somehow able to navigate the black tunnel with ease.

She shuddered, struggling to imagine what it must be like in these tunnels in the total black without a light source. She'd have fallen a hundred times over, with all the ducking and weaving around rocks. But the scourge lived below ground. Perhaps the creature granted him an advantage when traveling through the earth?

It seemed they wouldn't have much further to travel. The first sign was the sound of rushing water, somewhere close. Then the ground leveled, and a dim light seeped into the tunnel from up ahead. The first light they'd seen since entering, except for their torches.

Lark's breath caught as she spotted movement again, momentarily blocking the light before disappearing. Was that Nox? She wondered for the hundredth time how he'd ended up bonded to one of the scourge… It must be so awful to have the voice of such a destructive beast whispering inside his mind.

She shared a look with Aren in the dim tunnel. Both of them hastened forward. They had to save the poor boy from the creature that had latched on to him.

They crept into another large chamber. This one was ten times the size of the last, lit from a massive entrance shrouded by a sheer covering that glimmered strangely in the sunlight. A wide, fast-moving stream gurgled along the far wall. As she stood staring, a fish leapt through the air, its scales a flash of glittering gold before it splashed back down in the water.

The cave floor was covered with more jagged rocks. They shone in the sun, sparkling in shades of gold, silver, and white. She tilted her head, searching for any sign of movement. With all these rocks, Nox could be hiding anywhere.

There. She spotted something. She squinted, craning her neck sideways to peek behind a huge white rock.

Then her jaw dropped.

It was the rock moving, not something behind it. And it was not a rock at all, but a massive beast, the size of a small house, curled up in a ball on the ground. A dragon!

The creature lay still except for the slow rise and fall of its chest, wings wrapped around its body, eyes closed in slumber. White scales glittered with flecks of silver and gold. A long sinuous tail curved along the cave floor, twitching slightly.

Her heart hammered in her chest. Nox and the scourge *had* come here seeking a dragon. But why?

It was then she spotted them. Nox rose behind a rock, creeping toward the slumbering beast. Suddenly he stopped and clutched his neck, falling to the ground.

The four of them raced forward in unison, the cause of his fall apparent as they drew closer. The scourge was on him, tearing at his neck.

Blazes. His own bondmate turned on him? It made no sense.

Lark shoved the mystery aside, flicking her arm in the air. *"Muse, go!"*

Muse shot forward and snatched the beast off the boy's neck, lifting it up into the air. The scourge fought back, scratching and clawing, trying to force Muse to drop it. It wasn't long before she lost hold and it fell. The scourge slammed into the hard rock then sprang back to its feet and leaped toward the dragon.

By this time, Lark had made it to Nox's side. She shucked off her gauntlet in record time, dug through her pack and slapped a wad of bandages on the boy's wound, applying pressure.

It was Whisper's turn to grab the scourge. He lasted only an instant longer before the beast struck the ground once more. Aren was behind Lark, his fingers flying as he readied the bow, but before he could take aim, a ball of water slammed into the scourge, completely covering the beast.

Edrik sat by the stream's edge, one hand in the water, the other outstretched as the vile rodent struggled. And for the second time in her life, Lark saw fear and panic fill the beady eyes of one of the scourge as it drowned.

Nox let out a gurgling cry as the beast died.

"Shh." Lark kept pressure on his neck. "You're going to be all right."

Aren dropped his bow on the ground and crouched beside her.

A sudden shriek stole Lark's attention. The dragon was awake, staring at all of them.

Her stomach jumped into her throat. Were they all done for now? What would that enormous monster do after finding them inside its home?

After a heartbeat, it turned and raced away and through the cave entrance.

Lark couldn't relax yet. She still had a boy bleeding out beneath her hands. The bandage was already soaked; the blood poured out, gushing between her fingers even as she fought to apply pressure without crushing his windpipe.

Oriana approached and peered down at Nox's neck. Her face blanched.

She met her eyes. "Go. Get Mika. Now!"

Oriana sped off at a run, back into the tunnel they came from.

Aren grabbed her shoulder. "I don't think Nox can wait. Lark, you have to heal him."

She stared back at him, tears wetting her lashes. "I don't know if I can." Her mind flashed back to the last boy she'd tried to save. The bloody laceration on his scalp had bled just the same, the hot spill of fluid drenching her fingers.

Aren squeezed. "Yes, you can. I believe in you, Lark." He held her stare, his blue eyes full of all the determination and confidence she couldn't muster. "Tell me what you need. I'm right here."

She blew out a breath. He was right. She could do this. She would do this. Now she knew what to do. This boy wouldn't die, not here. Not now.

"In my bag," she ordered. "Grab me the freshest, greenest plants you can find."

Aren nodded. He dumped her pack on the ground and snatched up a handful of fresh herbs, offering them to her on his open palm.

"Yes, that should work." She lifted one hand, the fingers stained red, and grabbed the leaves. She took a deep breath. This would work. It had to.

She pulled free the wad of bloody bandages. She slapped the herbs down over the wound. Nox's eyes were closed, his features slack as blood spurted against her palm. She could sense a change in the pressure of blood flooding through her fingers. His heartbeat was erratic, sluggish. Aren was right, he wouldn't last much longer.

Lark closed her eyes and wished. She wished with everything in her for this boy to live. For the bloody jagged gash beneath her hands to knit itself back together.

There it was. Her talent rushed through her, rattling the earth beneath her, knocking a handful of stones loose. A rain of pebbles crashed to the ground from the cave ceiling.

She cracked open an eye and slowly lifted her hand. Her jaw dropped. It worked. She'd done it. She'd saved him!

As she stared down at the blood-soaked but no longer bleeding flesh before her, Nox's eyes fluttered open. Mika arrived, then Oriana fast on his heels.

"Nox," Mika yelled. He skidded to a stop and crouched beside them. "Nox... you're all right?"

Aren chimed in, a wide smile on his face, "Lark healed him."

The simple statement left her feeling euphoric. Lark smiled. The tension drained from her, replaced with warmth infusing her chest and spreading slowly through her limbs. "I did, didn't I?"

Nox blinked rapidly, his stare flitting between all of them crowded around him, his face the picture of confusion. "Where am I? What's happening?"

Mika's brow furrowed. He helped Nox sit up on the stone floor. "What exactly do you remember?"

The boy bit his lip and shook his head. "A lot, but it's all out of order. All jumbled up like a puzzle." He gasped. "My bondmates. Mika, I can't hear them anymore. Any of them."

Mika turned to her. "How close did he come to dying?"

Lark shuddered, recalling all that blood rushing between her fingers. "Very."

Mika nodded solemnly, giving Nox a gentle squeeze. "Don't worry about that now, Nox. We've got to get you out of here. Do you think you can stand?"

Suddenly, an ear-shattering roar blasted, coming from the cave mouth. Lark flinched, muscles rigid, her heart racing.

"What was that?" Nox's eyes bulged.

Lark shuffled sideways and scooped her things back into her pack. "I don't know, but I'm going to find out."

Aren jumped up beside her, lifting his bow off the ground.

They turned to the mouth of the cave. Lark lifted her foot, but before she could take a single step, Nox gasped again. She shifted at the sound and found him staring at the scourge's drowned carcass on the cave floor.

"Chumy." His chin wobbled. He lurched on his knees to reach the beast and cradled it in his arms.

Lark drew back in disgust. "That thing just tried to kill you, Nox. How can you hold any affection for it?"

Nox lifted tear-filled eyes to her. "No, you don't understand. I remember now. Chumy didn't want to hurt me. None of them do. There's something else—something evil—behind it all. He was there with us, too. I could feel him through the bond. *He's* the one that made Chumy attack me."

Lark rubbed her brow. Could any of that be true? Were the scourge not the villains she'd believed them to be but victims of some hidden evil? It was too much to wrap her head around. Nox already admitted to being confused; how could he possibly be sure of this?

A second sound rent the air. This one was more familiar to her, but just as portentous. The howl of a wolf.

She shook herself free of her reverie and turned back to the cave's entrance. There'd be time to mull over those questions later. Something was happening out there. It was time to find out what.

Chapter 22

Conall drug the rowboat ashore with a sigh. The pebbly sand crunched beneath his boots as he walked with his bondmate toward a mountainous cliffside. They'd made it just north of the Mido Islands before the captain he'd hired refused to go any farther. The row boat made swift work of the remaining distance, but the spot they'd landed on the northern beach left them with no other option but to go up.

"What is it with mountains, Shadow? Everywhere I go there's always a damn rock to climb."

"You have seen your fair share of trouble on cliffs." An amused noise followed, reverberating in his mind.

"Snicker all you want, brother." Conall grinned, staring up at the cliff face. It was steep, for sure, but no worse than what he'd faced in the Turney Mountains on the way to Doln. *"But haven't you heard? This is fate."*

"Just try not to fall down this one. I'm getting tired of finding you at the bottom of a ridge, close to death." Shadow vaulted up on the rock, his step sure.

"Neither of those falls were my fault." He found a spot that looked promising and took his first step up on the gray stone. *"You try keeping your balance when you've just been shot. Or jumping out of the way of an avalanche."*

"If I remember correctly, you jumped into *the avalanche."*

Conall grimaced. *"All right, all right. There won't be any jumping today. Let's just climb up there so we can have a look around. See if there's any sign of Lark on this island."*

The thought of his sister made his steps lighter. He could feel it. She was here. He was moments away from reuniting with Lark. The realization buoyed him so much he had little trouble keeping up with Shadow on the cliffside, even though his bondmate was far fleeter-footed.

He'd decided not to listen to the tiny voice in the back of his mind. The one telling him Lark wouldn't want to see him. That she would blame him for not watching out for her. That she'd be so put off by his changed appearance she wouldn't want anything to do with him. Maybe even refuse to recognize him.

No. He buried those thoughts deep inside. All that mattered was that he find her. Whatever came after, he would deal with it, happily. If she wanted to hate him for the rest of her days, then so be it. He would be satisfied just seeing she was alive. He had to find her.

By the time they made it about halfway up, sweat poured down his back. He paused and gazed out to sea while he gulped from his waterskin. From this height, he could make out a tiny blip on the horizon, already high-tailing back north.

He sighed. No turning back now.

They continued to climb. The gray rock glistened in the sun. Conall basked in the warmth, amazed that only days before he'd been shivering, stuffed into furs. It was a welcome change to be clothed in a pair of brown trousers; his tan, long-sleeved tunic rolled up, a gentle breeze tickling the hairs on his arms. He'd even shaved off the thick beard he'd grown in Doln, leaving him feeling even more like his old self. It would almost be relaxing if it weren't for the climbing.

They'd made it about three quarters of the way up to the summit when a thunderous roar tore through the air. His body jerked, and his heart jolted to life, his step slipping. Conall clutched the rock before him, his feet skidding against the stone. His palms scratched and bled, but he managed to right his balance.

He turned to Shadow, shaking his stinging palms. *"What the blazes was that?"*

"I don't know, but it was coming from up there." Shadow raised his snout and scented the air. *"Smells... strange. Do we turn back?"*

Conall followed suit, lifting his nose and breathing deeply. Whatever was up there smelled musky, smokey, and sharp, unlike anything he'd ever encountered. But that changed nothing.

"No." Conall shook his head. *"What if Lark's up there? Let's climb. Fast."*

They climbed with renewed vigor, racing up the steep slope as fast as they could manage. Shadow made it to the top first, and an instant later, Conall joined him, his breath harsh in lungs worn out from exertion.

He gasped, blinking furiously. They found themselves on a flat plateau, staring at a pair of dragons locked in a stalemate.

A huge black dragon stood on its hind legs, wings spread, mouth open, red light spilling out its throat behind sharp teeth. Conall quaked, the reaction visceral and immediate at seeing such a powerful beast in the flesh. A beast poised to strike.

Cowering on the ground below it lay a white dragon. A dragon he recognized.

It was the same ice white dragon he fought in his dream! Seeing it here, alive and oh so real, reawakened the terror that had filled him as he'd dodged for his life in that black abyss. Did the Unseen infect it still? What if this was his chance to stop the evil plaguing his country?

Conall sucked in a deep breath and pulled his waterskin from his belt. The black dragon appeared to have the upper hand, but he wasn't taking any chances. If this was fate, then there was a reason he was here. He had to believe he was meant to help. And if a blast of ice had stopped the beast beneath the sea, then maybe it would now.

Cupping his hand, he spilled a drop of water on his outstretched palm. He brought forth the memory of his sister's face in his mind. He had to protect Lark. A ball of ice formed on his palm as moisture surrounded him, humming across his skin.

He sent the ice soaring. It sailed through the air, glittering and so cold it left behind a trail of mist in its wake. Then it smashed into the white dragon's back and shattered into millions of pieces like tiny shards of glass.

The white dragon's head spun. Its long elegant neck extended, gaze shifting wildly. The black dragon's gaze zeroed in on him, and it shuffled sideways, even as he spilled another drop of water in his hand, a second ball of ice coalescing just as quickly.

A girl charged out from between the dragons. It was the girl with the braids. The same freckled redhead he remembered from his vision.

Her eyes were wide, her mouth falling open as she caught sight of the ice growing larger on his palm. She screamed, "No!"

It was too late. The ball of ice had already left his fingers, sailing straight for the white dragon.

The girl called forth flames out of nowhere and sent a blast of fire at the ball of ice. But the ice only sailed through, losing a portion of its mass to the fire, dripping water through the air on course for its target. Conall smiled, certain the ice would shatter directly across the dragon's face. At the last instant, the dragon opened its wicked jaw and snatched the ice ball out of the sky. It swallowed.

He didn't have time to wonder what that meant. The fire was headed straight for him. Conall dodged, falling to the ground on the ridge's edge, his shoulder alive with pain.

Shadow lifted his muzzle and howled.

Conall rolled, desperate to put out the flames burning his tunic. He twisted and slapped his sleeve, finally extinguishing the burning cloth, a hiss escaping from his clenched teeth.

He sat up to view the scene. Shadow barreled toward the girl, his teeth bared, growling viciously.

"Shadow. No," he screamed in his mind.

What was he thinking? She would burn him to a crisp.

But the girl just stared at the white dragon with horror on her face, making no attempt to cut down the predator tearing toward her.

The black dragon's front legs smashed into the ground. The whole plateau vibrated as its tail whipped into Shadow and knocked him off course, away from the girl. Conall stood, racing to the spot where his bondmate had fallen.

"Shadow!"

He skidded to a stop beside him as Shadow righted himself, his fur bristling. His lips curled back in a snarl.

"Brother, stop. It was a mistake." He jumped directly in front of Shadow, blocking his view of the girl and the dragons. *"We're meant to be allies."*

Shadow shook his head. The growl died in his throat. *"Little brother, are you all right?"*

"I'm fine. Are you?"

His bondmate didn't answer. They both dropped to the ground instead. The white dragon raced toward them, but before they could do anything more than fall to the rock, it rocketed over their heads and blasted into the sky.

The black dragon hesitated, staring at the girl. Then it took two leaping steps and bounded into the sky.

The girl fell to her knees, her arm outstretched, an anguished bellow escaping her lips. "Dru!"

Conall lifted himself off the rock. His palms stung, but that was nothing next to his shoulder. The pain was alive, throbbing, and so hot. Little shreds of his tunic stuck into the wound, his skin red and swollen. The sickening scent of charred flesh filled his nostrils, reminding him of the pyre he'd stood witness at just days ago. Reminding him it could've been worse.

He scowled at the damage. Damn good for nothing mountains.

"Conall?" A new voice rose to greet him. A voice he would recognize anywhere.

He spun to the sound. The glorious sound. "Lark," he breathed.

There she was, emerging from within the rock wall like a dream. Like an answered prayer. Her hair was a wild tangle of curls, her eyes shining. "Conall!" She raced to him and thudded into his chest, her arms latching around his waist so tightly. Her voice was strangled. "I thought you were dead. I thought you were gone."

"I'm not. I'm here. I found you." He clutched her just as tightly, all the pain forgotten. "Lark, I found you."

He closed his eyes and held his sister in his arms. Her slight frame shuddered and shook, her tears wetting the front of his shirt.

Finally. All his fears slid away. He should've known she'd recognize him instantly. That she'd fall right back into his life without pause. Without question.

Blazes, he'd found her! He clutched her tightly and silently thanked fate. Thanking even the cursed circumstances he'd been forced to endure. All the pain and hardship. The suffering and sacrifice. It had all been worth it. But the blissful moment couldn't last forever.

She pulled back but stayed close enough to touch, staring up at his face. She raised a hand to his hair, twining her fingers in brown locks shot through with silver. "How?"

He chewed on the inside of his lip. "It's a long story."

Her gaze lit on his shoulder, and she gasped. "Why didn't you tell me you were hurt?" She frowned and pushed out of his arms, digging into her pack.

Why hadn't he? Probably because nothing mattered as much as assuring himself she was alive. His shoulder still burned, but the pain was a dull ache in the back of his mind. A trifling nothing compared to having her back. Finally, having her back.

"I'm fine." He tilted his head, smiling down at her. At the tiny wrinkle between her brows. The same one she'd had even as a newborn babe.

The little wrinkle deepened. "No, you're not." She held up a tin, opened it, and scooped out a handful of green goo. She slicked her palm over his wound, and he yelped in pain. "See?" She lifted a brow. "Not fine. Don't worry, this should help."

Lark gently removed the shreds of fabric sticking to his wound and rested her hand atop the reddened flesh. Then her eyelids fluttered closed. A tremor spread across his skin, centered around her palm.

He gasped. The pain—it was gone.

She lifted her hand, revealing smooth, perfect flesh.

She'd come into her own in their time apart. There was so much he needed to ask her. So much he wanted to know. He grinned, his smile so wide his cheeks ached. "Thanks."

He couldn't stop staring at her. His sister was here.

Then movement behind her drew his attention. More people had emerged from the rock while they'd been busy reuniting. A blond man, clothed in the same sheer fabric Lark wore, was watching them from nearby. Two teens, both clothed in tattered, torn garb, stood by his side. As he watched, a second man—this one brown-haired and deeply tanned—emerged, his arm wrapped around a sullen boy, his face drawn, gaze downcast.

Conall flicked a glance at Lark. "How many more of you are there?" He squinted, staring at the rock. "Where did you come from?"

"We were in a massive cave system." She turned to look at the rock, her eyes sparkling. "Crazy, isn't it? The wall isn't really there. It's an illusion." Then her smile widened as her gaze shifted to her friends. "This is all of us." Lark pointed to each, making introductions. As she finished naming everyone, a gold and white falcon spread its wings, shaking its feathers from a perch on the cliffside. He recognized it as the same bird that fiercely fought at Lark's side in the dream vision. "And this is Muse, my bondmate."

Conall grinned, gazing at the majestic bird of prey. After seeing the vision, he'd assumed Lark would be bonded like he was, but hearing the confirmation from her own lips warmed his heart. It made perfect sense. As a child she was always staring out the window, watching birds in flight, drawn to them just as he'd been drawn to dogs.

"I've a bondmate as well. Meet Shadow."

Shadow wagged his tail, his golden eyes meeting Lark's for the first time. *"She looks just like you, little brother. I knew we'd find her."* His tail picked up speed, and joy radiated off of him, flowing through their bond.

Lark smiled widely and gave Shadow a little wave. Then her smile slipped, and her brow furrowed. "Who's your friend?" Lark nodded to the redhead. She was curled up in a ball on the ground, her head in her hands, seemingly oblivious to the world around her.

"Actually, we haven't met." Conall strolled to her. He tapped her on the shoulder.

She lifted tear-filled brown eyes to stare up at him. "He cut me off," she whispered.

"Pardon?" Conall asked.

Lark's mouth flew open, and she pointed, shaking her finger at the girl. "I saw you! I saw you at Bogsmouth flying a dragon. The scourge... you burned them all." Her gaze drifted to Conall's shirt. The healed flesh stuck out from his blackened and scorched tunic. She stepped back, a hand flying to her mouth as her gaze flitted between them.

"It's all right," Conall said hurriedly. "It was an accident." He knelt down and grabbed the girl's shoulder, staring into her face. "I'm Conall, and this is my sister, Lark. What's your name?"

Chapter 23

"*Dru? Where are you?*" Kayda sat on the mountain plateau, cradling her head in her hands.

He was gone. Druturion was gone. Not just gone from her side, but from her thoughts. He'd taken off after that white dragon, Belstasia, and used whatever strange boon he possessed to block her thoughts from reaching him.

Her stomach churned, and her head throbbed. How could he do that to her? Leave her here all on her own? The bond they shared had become so comfortable, so familiar. Now that he was gone, it was like she was missing a piece of herself, leaving an aching hole in her heart and mind.

It hurt. Blazes. It hurt so much to reach out to him, only to be ignored. Where was he? Why couldn't he take her with him? Why?

She felt something. A tapping on her shoulder.

She lifted her head and found a pair of people before her, but she couldn't fully focus on them. Her head was still pounding, her heart still shattering. Her voice was a broken whisper. "He cut me off."

Then they were both talking, fuzzy murmurs sliding through her ears. The girl pointed at her and backed up, gasping.

Whatever they were going on about, it didn't matter. How could it? She was alone. All alone. Dru was gone. She should've just let him cut Belstasia down. But no. She'd had to step in, and now he was gone, chasing Bela who knew where.

When would he be back? Her breath hitched. Would he ever come back?

The pressure on her arm returned, firmer than before. There was a man crouching down before her. "I'm Conall, and this is my sister, Lark." His words were slow and measured, like he was speaking to a frightened child. "What's your name?"

Kayda drew a deep breath. She tamped down the hurt Dru's abandonment had caused and forced her eyes to focus. She focused on the man. His hazel eyes were soft, the skin at the edges of his lids crinkled, his dark brows drawn down with worry. Wild brown locks shot through with gray curled around his face. Wait...

She drew back and tugged her arm free from his hold. "You!" Her voice was louder now, but just as broken. "Why would you hit her with ice? That's exactly what she needed!"

It was him! The man who'd interrupted them on the plateau. The man who'd freed Bela.

"I don't understand." He sat back on his heels and rubbed his temple. "This is gonna sound crazy, but I saw that dragon before. In a dream. A vision. I fought it off with a blast of ice."

Kayda frowned. "What are you talking about? Dragons need to consume the elements they summon. You just gave her exactly what she needed to regain her strength and escape."

Conall's jaw clenched tightly. "Oh." His eyes widened and he stood, pacing. "I didn't know. I'm sorry, I didn't know."

The girl, Lark, shook her head, her brown curls bobbing around her shoulders. She stepped in the path of her brother's pacing and halted him. "It's all right, Conall. It's clear we don't have all the pieces of this puzzle laid out yet. We'll figure it out, together." Lark shifted closer, her eyes the exact shade of hazel as her brother's, though she looked two decades younger. "You still haven't told us your name."

Kayda shook off the anger bubbling up in her chest. It wouldn't change anything. Dru was still gone. She wrapped her arms around her knees. "I'm Kayda."

A gasp rose from behind the pair, where more people gathered. A green-eyed girl with tattered clothes stepped forward. "Princess Kayda? Everyone in Flamesmoat's been looking for you."

Conall turned to look at her again. "You're the Princess of Dracwood?" Then the side of his mouth quirked up in a crooked smile. "Of course, you are. Who else would be dragon bonded?"

A pang struck her at the mention of Dru. She sighed. "I might be dragon bonded, but thanks to you, I'm dragonless."

The girl spoke up again. "Princess, please." She gestured to a young man beside her, his clothes tattered and torn as well. "We've been sent to seek aid for Flamesmoat. The scourge have the city surrounded."

The news unleashed a gnawing pain in her stomach. What of Izora? Her father and grandfather? Were they all right? She rose to her feet, her legs stable despite the heavy weight on her shoulders.

Conall spoke up, his hand on his chest. "How long ago did you leave for aid?"

The boy in the tattered clothes answered, "I'm not sure. Two weeks maybe? The days since the shipwreck are mostly a blur."

Shipwreck? That would explain the torn clothes and how the pair ended up on this desolate island. What of the rest? Lark and most of the others wore the luct clothing favored by the Raimish, but Conall was clothed like a Dracian. How had they all ended up here at the exact moment she and Dru had? Lark had the right of it when she likened the situation to a puzzle.

But one thing was certain. She had to save her country from its plight. "I have to go back to Flamesmoat." she shifted her gaze across all of them. "Please tell me one of you has a way off of this island?"

"We have a boat, down the mountain and a bit to the south," offered a tanned man with his arm slung around a glowering youth.

"I have one as well," Conall said. "Kayda and Lark, I'd like you to come with me. There's much we must discuss."

"All right," the tan man said. "Sail around the coast of this island until you see our boat on the shore. We can head back to Stoneshore together to regroup. I'm sure once the Matas hear about the situation in Flamesmoat, they'll be willing to send aid."

They split up, heading for their respective boats. The tall blond man joined them—Lark introduced him as Aren—along with two birds and the wolf.

Kayda stole a closer look at all of them with their animal companions. "Do you all have bonding magic?"

Aren shook his head. "I'm just a falconer."

But the other two nodded.

Kayda's stomach fluttered as she took her first look down the steep slope. The wooden boat sat propped up on its side, leaning against the cliff, seeming incredibly small when viewed from above. "I've yet to meet anyone besides my grandfather with bondmates, and now, I've met two in the same day."

"Three actually," Lark added. "That young boy back there, Nox, he's had four bonds already."

"Four bonds?" Kayda's eyes widened, the warning she'd been given not to bond more than one replaying in her ears. "And he's not mad?"

"Well, he was." Lark grimaced. "That's why we were out here." She sent her falcon into the sky, using both hands to balance as she started down the steep slope. "It's a long story."

Conall grinned, looking up at them. "Good to hear I'm not the only one with one of those." His foot slipped, and he scowled, shaking his hand after using it to stop himself from falling. "Let's just concentrate on the climb for now. We'll have plenty of time to talk in the boat. Plus, I've got something I need to show you both."

Kayda nodded and carefully took her first step down. Her heart pounded. Despite watching Conall and Lark descend successfully below her, she kept expecting to slip, sending them all tumbling to the sand with broken necks.

Damn it, Dru. If he were here, they'd be down there in an instant, or better yet, on the way to Flamesmoat already. She sighed and forced the thought aside. She couldn't afford to let her attention slip, lest she lose her footing.

The wind kicked up and slapped her braids in her face. What had Conall meant, he had something to show them? She didn't like the way he looked at her—like he knew her. Like he had some knowledge she was missing.

Her stomach clenched, even as she descended far enough a fall would only leave her with scratches instead of an untimely death. She was all alone, forced to rely on these strangers to get home. They seemed friendly enough, but could she trust any of them?

Soon Kayda descended to the beach. She sighed deeply as her boots sank into the sand. Together, they tilted the boat back on its side and carried it into the surf.

Kayda hopped in, settling next to Lark in the front of the boat. Conall seated himself before them with his wolf curled up by his feet. Aren took charge of the paddles in the back of the small vessel while the birds flew overhead.

Lark clutched her stomach, her face taking on a greenish tinge. She mumbled something under her breath about sailing, then swallowed, raising her voice. "What did you want to show us, brother?"

Conall tugged on a bag stashed below the bench he sat upon. "This isn't easy to say. Nor will it be easy to hear." He settled the sack in his lap but made no move to open it. He stared at her and Lark instead. "I've spent the last weeks traveling through Doln with the Sade Prim, Delyth. She and I traveled to the Winter Witch of the North. There, I was shown a vision of the future, among other things." He grimaced, his gaze downcast, as if the memory pained him. "I saw the three of us, locked in a great battle in the Abandoned Lands."

"You saw us in a vision?" Lark cocked her head, raising a brow.

"Yes. It's how I knew where to find you. But that's not all of it." He frowned, his fingers clenching in the sack's fabric. "I felt a sickly presence there, watching me. It appeared to me and spoke. Named itself as the Unseen. That is the true enemy we're facing. The scourge, they're merely puppets for this thing. A means to an end to satisfy its need for destruction."

Kayda's hand flew to her chest, his words bringing back the memory of that creeping, slithering wrongness she'd felt while battling the scourge. But his admission made sense of another mystery she'd been struggling to wrap her mind around. "The Sul. I've met with them recently. They've kept creatures they call chumon as pets for centuries. They're one and the same as the vile beasts terrorizing our land, only these pets of theirs are biddable, with none of the scourge's unquenchable hunger."

Lark sucked in a sharp breath. "That boy, Nox, he bonded a scourge. It tried to kill him. He claimed something was controlling it. I didn't believe him, but now it all makes sense."

Kayda stared at her feet. "If there's something out there controlling the scourge, then can it control other beings, too?" A pang of fear stabbed her. She swung her head up, meeting Conall's hazel eyes. "You said you saw the white dragon in your vision... We found dragon bones on the beach in Stoneshore. Evidence that something big fell from the cliffside back there. But all we found when we got there was..." She trailed off, slowly connecting the dots.

Was that why Druturion was so mad at Belstasia? Had the Unseen driven her to do the unthinkable to her own kind?

Conall gulped and nodded slowly. "You may be right." He leaned forward, his nostrils flaring. "There's something else. That first vision—the one with the three of us battling—I learned that vision has remained constant. Every single person who's met with the Winter Witch for hundreds of years has seen it."

"What does that mean?" Lark asked, voicing the question reverberating in her own mind.

"I don't know," Conall answered. "That it's fate we'll fight the Unseen? Delyth certainly seemed to believe it. It led her to make some destructive choices."

"What choices?" Kayda asked.

He lifted his gaze to the sky and studied the fluffy clouds overhead. The water sloshed against the boat, the spirited cawing of seabirds seeming far too cheery for such a tense moment.

When his gaze dropped, it was colder, his throat working as he swallowed. "The mages arranged it all. They believed it was the only way to stop the Unseen for good. The Palisade's fall was planned."

Kayda rocked back in her seat, her eyes bulging. No. She shook her head. That couldn't be true.

"Here." He handed her a crumpled parchment. "This letter is by no means fully conclusive, but it alludes to what I heard from the Sade Prim's own lips before she died. The mages were pulling strings behind the scenes all along."

She stared down at the yellow paper. Her heart skipped a beat. She recognized the handwriting. Lark leaned over her shoulder, and Kayda angled the letter between them so they could both read its contents.

Delyth,

Please, I must beg of you more time. Things here are progressing but not as quickly as we'd hoped. I fear she will not be prepared, should the inevitable occur so soon.

My contacts in Greenvale report the disappearance of the others, on the same day, no less. The falcon flies to you at Mage Keep, but the wolf is presumed dead. Should that be the case, then all our careful planning would be for naught. Ereni expects to head there next to investigate.

Your daughter has laid the trap admirably. The bait has been taken. Please, do what you can to slow the results. I will do my part, as always.

Izora

Kayda closed her eyes, her stomach roiling. Tarquin. She'd been convinced her stepbrother's greed caused the Palisade's fall, but now she could see he'd only been a pawn to the mages and their scheming.

What of the attack on the king? Had that been part of their plan, too?

For the second time, she felt the full force of Izora's betrayal. How could she have kept her in the dark for so long? She'd not just been lying about her family history but about her very identity. Her supposed future in this twisted game they'd been staging.

But no matter the shock of the revelations, it still didn't change what she needed to do. Flamesmoat was in trouble, and she'd be damned if she wasn't going to do something to stop it.

She opened her eyes. Conall held Lark's hand, her stare still fixed on the parchment clutched tightly within her fingers. Kayda loosened her hold and handed the paper back to Conall.

"None of that changes anything. Flamesmoat still needs saving. The Abandoned Lands, and this Unseen, will have to wait." She spoke with confidence, but inside, she was a quivering mess of uncertainty.

All the help she'd secured from Wyll was weeks away and headed up the wrong side of the continent. Would she be able to make a difference without Druturion by her side?

Conall dropped his sister's hand and stuck the parchment back in his pack. "We're coming with you," he said, voice just as firm.

Lark nodded. "I'm not sure why, or how, but we were meant to find each other. Why else would we all end up on this tiny island at the same time? We're in this together, Princess." She smiled and squeezed her knee.

"I might have something that can help." Conall pulled a second item from his pack and carefully unwrapped it from a waxed cloth covering. It was a small brown book, the leather cover worn, the pages' edges yellowed and dappled with age. "Delyth made me promise to read this on her deathbed. I think this book may hold the key to defeating the Unseen. Maybe something inside can help us save Flamesmoat." He passed it to Kayda.

Kayda flipped the smooth leather over in her hands and squinted at the handwritten title on the spine. But the words were faded beyond recognition, whether from age or heavy handling, she couldn't be sure. She gingerly lifted the cover to peek within.

Eyes widening, she realized the book was ancient, perhaps the oldest book she'd ever held. Then she spied the author's name on the title page and stifled a gasp. "Afton. Was this penned by the first Sade Prim? Truly?" She shook her head, lifting the corner of a page carefully. "I've never known a book to last that long. How is this not crumbling to dust in my fingers?"

Conall shrugged. "Magic? That's the whole point of the book, you see." He reached forward, as if to flip the pages, but Kayda pulled it closer instinctively, cradling it on her lap. He raised a brow but retracted his hand without comment, with barely a pause before continuing, "The mages of old had far greater powers than anything we've seen in many generations. Delyth hinted as much to me, but this book explains it in great detail. I haven't read it all yet, but what I've seen so far..." His smile spread slowly. "It's incredible."

So, the fate of the world might come down to a book? A smile crept across Kayda's lips. "Do you mind if I take a closer look at this?"

"Go ahead. I imagine you're a faster reader than I am. And Lark and I still have plenty to discuss." He smiled warmly at his sister.

Kayda wasn't listening. As the boat slowly progressed across the channel to Stoneshore, she flipped page after page. When they pulled up on the rocky beach, the sun sinking down in the sky behind them, she closed the cover and smiled. Maybe they stood a chance after all.

Chapter 24

The boat skidded against the rocks of Stoneshore beach. Lark breathed a sigh as her boots sank down into the pebbly surf. The sailing was over. For today, at least.

Her gaze was drawn to her brother and his wolf as they hopped out of the small canoe. She still couldn't believe it. Conall was alive! She'd spent so long certain he was dead. She'd cried so many tears, accepting the fact that she'd never see him again, but now her heart was so full she could almost burst.

When she'd first seen him, standing there on the mountaintop on that tiny island in the middle of nowhere, she'd had the shock of her life. Before he'd met her gaze, a battle raged inside of her mind. Confusion and disbelief swirled around her like a tempest. But when his gaze connected with hers from across that plateau, she'd known. Even though he was irreparably changed. Even though she'd been *sure* he was dead. One look in his eyes swept the storm of doubt aside like it had never existed. Her brother was there. He was alive!

The second boat skidded to the shore next to them. They were all back on the mainland. Soon, they'd all piled out onto the beach and tied the canoes fast.

Conall stared up at the steep cliffside. The rock was eroded down to a vertical slope, with carved footholds forming a makeshift ladder. "Shadow can't make that climb."

Mika pointed south down the beach. "There's a gentler slope just around the bend. Shouldn't take long to reach. You'll find a footpath leading to the village at the top."

Lark slid her arm in Conall's, linking their elbows. "I'll walk with you. No one travels alone in the jungle."

"We're taking the long way back. You coming with us?" she asked.

"I'll catch up with you later. Ha. I've got a craving for monkey that can't be denied." Muse lifted into the sky and quickly disappeared.

Before they turned to leave, she spotted a familiar face peeking down at them from the top of the cliff. "Nox! Nox, you're back." It was Esmar, tears shining in the corners of her eyes as she caught sight of her son shuffling forward on the beach.

Mika glared up at her and raised his voice. "What are you doing out here alone with the scourge on the loose?"

"The scourge are dead. The archers took care of them all yesterday." She waved, grinning from ear to ear. "I couldn't just sit around waiting. I knew you'd be back."

She looked like she was ready to climb down, but Mika held out a hand and called up to her, "Esmar, stay there. We'll be right up."

Esmar nodded, the relief on her face apparent. Then her gaze slid along the rest of them, and her brows sank. "Jett?" She squinted, her stare locked on Conall.

Conall lifted a hand to shade his brow, looking up at Esmar curiously.

Mika shook his head. "No, Esmar. The sun must be in your eyes. That's not Jett." He leaned closer to them, pitching his voice low. "Poor woman must be overwrought; she's mistaking you for Nox's father. Don't worry, I'll take them both back to the healing tent." He nodded to Conall's hands. "You should head there as well. Let someone clean those scratches."

Then Mika turned to the rest of the group. "Climb on up. This is the quickest way to the village." He nodded toward Kayda and the two mages. "Aren, would you mind taking these three to Mata Moyra's while I get Nox settled in the healing hut?"

Aren agreed, then sent Lark a smile. "I'll see you back in the village."

Lark met Aren's gaze, trying to silently communicate the gratitude she felt for his steady support as she reunited with her brother. Then she nodded once and turned with Conall to stroll down the rocky coastline.

Her brother stared down at her, his hazel eyes shining as the waves crashed into the beach. The sun setting over the water provided a panoramic backdrop of brilliant pink and orange clouds.

"I still can't believe it." She laughed and clutched his arm. "I'm so happy you found me."

As the boat sailed to Stoneshore, he'd shared much of his story with her. How Shadow saved him from Gael's betrayal in the woods. The part he'd played in the Palisade's fall and how it changed him. His trip across Doln to find her. It was nothing short of amazing.

"I'm glad, too." His smile matched hers briefly, but it wasn't long before it slipped. "There are a few things I've been waiting to tell you until we had a moment alone."

She gazed up at him, her smile dropping. "What is it?"

He looked down at her and exhaled deeply. "Our father's alive."

She tugged her ear, her pace slowing. "Our father's alive? Are you sure?"

He shrugged and shook his head slightly. "Delyth told me I would find him here. Raimire, Stoneshore."

"I don't understand... Why would he be in Raimire? Why would he let us think he was dead all these years?"

Conall grimaced. "I wish I knew. If we find him, I'll be sure to ask him myself."

Her hand flew to her chest, feeling a sudden urge to sit down. She paused instead and planted her feet in the rocks, closing her eyes.

Their father was alive? So many emotions bombarded her. Joy, confusion, anger. How? Why?

"There's something else I have to tell you."

Her eyes shot open, her brow furrowing at his serious tone. "What is it?"

"I told you about my vision on the boat, but I didn't tell you all of it. I didn't just talk to the Unseen." He drew in a deep breath. "Mother was there, too."

Lark's heart twisted. "She was?"

Conall nodded. "She wanted me to tell you something, Lark." He squeezed her hand. "She loves you. And she doesn't blame you for what happened when she got sick." He peered down at her closely, his hazel eyes full of warmth. "You don't blame yourself for her death, do you?"

Her chest burning, she spun to stare at the sunset. "She would've never gotten sick if it wasn't for me. I thought I could heal that boy." She closed her eyes, the boy's wet gurgling cough echoing in her ears. "Mother heard him coughing, and she knew he was too far gone. But I insisted she let me try. I was wrong."

Her brother's arms wrapped around her, and he pulled her close. "And you've been hating yourself for it all this time?" His chin rubbed across her forehead as he shook his head. "You're not to blame. Mother doesn't think so, and neither do I." He pulled back slightly, and she opened her eyes, staring up at his face. "You can't keep punishing yourself for things that happened you couldn't control. After the Palisade fell, I spent so long being angry and resentful. Cursing the twist of fate that stole years of my life and a piece of the power I'd only just learned I possessed. That made me look like this." He lifted a curly gray-streaked lock and twirled it in his fingers. "It wasn't until I decided to let go of the past that I could move on with the future."

Lark swallowed, her throat dry, her chest hollow. "You make it sound so easy." She sniffled. "You really saw her?"

He smiled and nodded. "She was right there—only for a moment—but she was there, and just as beautiful as ever."

Lark sighed and leaned on his chest, staring at the sunset once more. Of all the things she could've said in the short time she'd appeared to her brother, her mother had talked about her? It took a moment to sink in, but the words slowly twined within her, like an invisible thread repairing the frayed seams of her tattered heart.

Conall was right. It was time to let go of the guilt. A small part of her would always wonder what would've happened if she'd never tried to save that boy, but it was time to stop letting the question rule her thoughts and the shame lurk in her belly.

"Thank you for telling me." She squeezed her brother's hand and gave him a little tug, starting back down the beach. They walked in silence, the crashing waves competing with the raucous chirping and squawking jungle animals.

They circled around a bend, revealing a gently sloped ramp carved into the cliffside. Canoes lined the beach, tied to thick wooden stakes impaled into the rocky soil. A lone boat lingered on the water beyond the crashing surf, a pair of Raimish sailors dangling fishing poles over the sides. They detoured around the canoes and headed straight for the ramp.

Soon, they were back under the jungle canopy. The wind died as they started down the worn footpath, the humidity swamping them.

Conall's gaze darted all around, taking in the scenery. "We've sure come a long way from home."

"Speaking of home. I've got something to show you." Lark grinned.

"You do?" Conall laughed. His laughter glided around her, so warm and welcome. A sound she'd thought lost to her forever.

"C'mon. You're gonna flip out." Her smile widened. She grabbed his hand and started jogging. Her mind raced even faster than her feet, wondering where she'd find her friends when she got back to the village. No sooner had they picked up their pace than the noise of travel greeted them on the path before them.

Her friends appeared from the trees, racing toward them. But in that moment, Lark turned to Conall. The joy spreading over his face was dazzling in its intensity.

"Sunny!" He let go of Lark's hand and knelt just in time for the yellow mutt to barrel into his chest. Sunny's body hummed with excitement, her tail swinging so forcefully her entire body shook and swayed. Conall laughed again, his voice muffled by his dog's sloppy kisses.

Lark crouched beside him and rubbed Sunny's back. Conall lifted his head, his eyes filled with tears. "You've had Sunny with you all this time?"

She nodded, her heart radiating warmth and her limbs feeling weightless. For once in her life, she was sure she'd done right. There'd been hundreds of times she'd cursed her sanity for dragging a dog halfway around the world with her. Saving her from predators in the Boglands. Making poor Aren haul her up and down to her treetop hammock while they trekked across the jungle. But seeing the joy on her brother's face at this moment made it all worth it.

Conall petted the top of Sunny's head and stared down into the face of the dog he'd always loved like a child, his eyes shining. Then he directed his gaze at Lark, and the smile he sent her was nothing short of radiant. "Thank you for taking care of her."

Lark smiled, recalling all the nights she'd spent curled up beside the yellow mutt, petting her soft fur, the comfort she'd brought her. She ruffled Sunny's fur one more time before standing. "We took care of each other."

She turned to greet the others who crowded around her. Tiora, Mazen, Meital, and Dausius were all there, watching the two of them petting Sunny.

Tiora was the first to speak. "Aren told us where to find you. I'm so glad you're back!" She pulled her in for a hug. An instant later, Lark found herself smothered as everyone joined in, laughing and squeezing. They all started talking at once, a flurry of admonitions and praise heaped atop her from all sides.

Finally, they released her. She took a deep breath, a sheepish smile on her face. Conall chuckled as he watched them, and Lark quickly made introductions.

They all stared with astonishment when she introduced Conall as her brother.

Dausius was the first to overcome his surprise. He grabbed Conall's hand and shook it vigorously, smiling widely. "It's a pleasure to meet you, Conall. I'm dying to hear the story behind how you two found each other. We all thought you were dead." He chuckled. "I'm sure glad to learn that's not the case. Why, you ought to have seen how torn up our Lark was after she got back from that farmhouse." He released his hand finally, but only exchanged the motion for a slap on his back. "I'm sure she'll tell you all about it, if she hasn't already."

Conall turned to her, his brows rising. "I'm sure *our* Lark will get around to it, eventually."

Her stomach twitched, and she cringed. There hadn't been time to spill all the details of her journey with how much Conall had shared. Still, she should've at least tried to tell him more of her story beyond just the barest details.

But Conall sent her a smile, and she sighed. There'd be time for more talking later. She'd tell him everything. She'd just got her brother back. She wouldn't waste the second chance they'd been given.

Conall allowed Dausius to usher him down the trail toward the village, an arm slung around his shoulder. Shadow and Sunny trailed the pair. Lark smiled, watching Sunny's tail wagging like crazy, her tongue lolling from her mouth, her gait infused with all the pep of a puppy as she danced down the footpath.

The rest of them followed closely behind. Tiora linked their arms together and tilted her head sideways, leaning close. "Remember what you asked me to do in the hut yesterday morning?"

Lark gulped, nodding slowly. How could she forget? It wasn't every day she told her friends it was all right if they left without her.

"We talked it over," Tiora said. "We're staying, Lark."

Mazen piped in, "Can't let you have all the fun, can we?" He tossed a knife in the air, causally flipping and catching it. "I've gotta say, the show's a lot more exciting since you two joined up."

Lark's stomach churned. Could she really let them follow her into danger?

Meital grinned. "We're in this together." She squeezed her shoulder.

The simple statement sparked a memory. Hadn't she said the same thing to Kayda in the canoe? No one forced her to say those words then, and she wasn't forcing her friends to make their choice now. And she had to admit, she was beyond grateful they'd chosen to stay with her.

She smiled, blinking quickly and rubbing her chest. "I'm glad we're staying together." She squeezed Tiora's arm. "But you might want to change your mind when you learn where we're headed next."

"Where is that?" Meital asked.

"Flamesmoat," Lark said.

Mazen tossed his knife again, the silver glittering as it sailed through the sky. "Flamesmoat's always good for tips." He caught the dagger between his fingers and winked. "When we leaving?"

Lark grinned, then her smile fell, her voice serious. "I'm not sure. Soon, I expect. Flamesmoat is surrounded with the scourge. It won't be fun and games this time."

Mazen sheathed his blade and leaned forward with a grin. "We can handle it."

Meital nodded. "We will, together."

Tiora squeezed her arm, nodding, too, even though her face blanched at the news.

Lark smiled, her heart bursting with gratitude. Even with all the risks that would come with fighting the scourge, they were determined to face their fears and stick together. She wasn't sure what she'd done to deserve such amazing friends, but she was so relieved to have them at her side. And now she had Conall back, too.

For the first time in ages, things were going right. She'd made a breakthrough with her talent when she healed Nox. And Conall's words—her mother's words to him in his vision—had given her the sense of closure she'd never realized she'd been missing. Now it finally felt possible for her to let go of the guilt she'd harbored over her mother's death.

Despite all the danger they would soon face, and the battle looming on the horizon, she was finally hopeful. Surely, together they would prevail. They would destroy the evil being threatening their country and set things right.

It was time for her to fulfill the promise she made to herself so long ago as she watched Bogsmouth's destruction. She was going back to Dracwood. It was time to fight.

Chapter 25

"*Can you tell your mutt to settle down already?*" Shadow paced beside Conall as they entered the village, letting out a loud snort that sent Sunny halfway across the path with her tail between her legs. Only an instant later, she was back, weaving around both of them, her tail whipping through the air.

Conall smiled indulgently. The pure delight emanating off Sunny sent warmth radiating throughout his body. *"She's only excited. Can you believe it? Lark had her all this time."*

He couldn't wipe the grin off his face. But for Shadow's sake, he said, "Sit, Sunny," as they stopped in front of a large hut.

He gazed in wonder at the village nestled within the wild jungle. Trees shaded the huts, the overgrowth tamed enough to allow the wooden structures room to crowd together in the clearing. People ambled about, wearing sheer green clothing and chatting as they went about their daily tasks.

It all seemed so ordinary and right. Almost like he was back in his hometown on the streets of Greenvale. Conall sighed. Would anywhere in Dracwood be like this again?

A place where people felt confident enough to walk outside without looking over their shoulder. Where they didn't worry about letting their children out to play.

He spotted a group of youngsters ahead, running and chasing each other, laughter spilling into the air. Suddenly, they scattered, abandoning their game of tag and darting off without a word. Conall lifted a brow and peered behind the kids to see what had them spooked.

In the short time they'd spent hiking to the village, Dausius regaled him with the tale of the scourge attack on the village yesterday. According to him, the beasts had all been slain, their path to Raimire blocked, all thanks to the Raimish folk's diligent work keeping watch over the Boglands. But maybe one of the foul vermin managed to sneak through? Or perhaps one was missed?

A colorful cane slammed into the ground, appearing from within the doorway of a large hut in the clearing's center. An old woman followed, gray-eyed and gray-haired. Was she what had the children disappearing? Surely not...

"Finally gracing us with your presence, are we?" She lifted a gray brow, a scowl on her face that didn't quite match the twinkle in her eye.

"Mata Moyra, lovely to see you, as always." Dausius bowed, his beaded hair clinking gently as he swayed.

"Humph." She frowned. Her gaze swung to him, trailing up and down his body before landing on his face. "I've been chatting with the others for nearly an hour. You surely took your time. Have a relaxing stroll into the village?"

An hour? She was clearly exaggerating. He opened his mouth, but only managed to stammer before Lark jumped in to save him. She appeared at his side, a wide smile on her face.

"Mata, this is my brother, Conall." She held out a hand to Shadow. "We had to bring his bondmate, Shadow, the long way. He couldn't climb the cliffside."

Moyra's frown deepened. She tilted her head sideways and stared at his face. "You look familiar. Have we met before?"

Conall finally found his voice. "I don't think so. This is my first time in Raimire."

She whirled around and beckoned him and Lark to follow. "C'mon then, the princess insists you two are included in our discussions."

Lark turned to the others and quickly bade everyone farewell.

Conall smiled as he stood at her side. Although she still hadn't shared all the details of her adventures with him, it was clear she'd made friends on her journey who cared for her deeply. Whatever trials she'd faced, she'd found a way through them with the help of her friends.

They were a motley crew, for sure, but he liked them all instantly. He'd be forever grateful to them for sticking with her and taking care of her when he couldn't.

He ducked his head as he entered the hut, slipping behind a screen of sheer green fabric. It was surprisingly spacious inside. Wide wooden benches strewn with blankets and pillows lined the walls in the front room, the walls painted a cheery yellow.

He nodded to Kayda and the mages, then seated himself on a bench beside Lark. Edrik and Oriana had washed up in their absence and traded their tattered clothing for some of the transparent Raimish garb.

He had to admit to being shocked at all the flesh on display. Even the ancient Mata wore the sheer clothing, and none seemed bothered by their lack of decency. He tried his hardest to not let it bother him, but he was certainly glad he wouldn't be here long enough to need to change out of his clothes. Only he and Kayda still wore normal, opaque shirts and trousers. He found his gaze drawn to her, if only for a break from all the sheer green-clad skin.

The princess' nose was still stuck in Delyth's book. As the Mata cleared her throat loudly, Kayda snapped the ancient tome shut and returned her attention to the group. "Mata Moyra," Kayda said, wasting no time. "We're leaving on the morrow to return to Flamesmoat. We could use all the help we can get. Can we count on your support?"

Mata Moyra was the only one not seated. She paced in the center of the room, her cane tapping loudly with each step. "What would you have me do? We've sent all we can spare to man the bog. We can't leave our villages undefended. And by the morrow, no less?" Moyra snorted, stabbing her walking stick onto the wooden floor. "You want the impossible."

Kayda inhaled, her brows drawing together. "We don't need fighters. At least, not on the morrow. What we need is boats. How many canoes can you spare?"

Conall frowned. What was she planning? Surely, she couldn't mean to sail those small canoes all the way back to Flamesmoat?

Moyra halted and directed her glare at Kayda. "You can have the boats. But they're not fit for long-distance sailing. The waters between here and Flamesmoat best even the bravest sailors and the finest boats." She waved a hand. "Better yet, wait here a week. I'll call a few of the bog ferrymen back—"

"No. We can't wait a week." Kayda clenched the book on her lap and shook her head. "We'll take the canoes."

Oriana beamed, grabbing Edrik's hand. "I knew we'd do it! Ereni will be so excited when we bring the princess back with us." Edrik offered a half smile, looking less than excited at the prospect of sailing up the coast.

Conall's mind reeled. "Ereni's in Flamesmoat?"

Oriana nodded, her smile wide and eager. "Yes, Ereni organized everything, what with the king still out of sorts." She lifted a hand, ticking off the tasks she listed on her fingers. "She got the fire moat lit, arranged housing for the displaced villagers, and convinced

Prince Gideon to start sending refugees to Doln." She turned to Kayda. "They'll all be so glad to have you back, Princess."

Conall's ears were ringing, his stomach roiling. He flipped his hands over in his lap and stared down at his empty palms. The scratches stared back at him, angry and red. He jolted to his feet. "If you'll excuse me. I need to have these scratches seen to."

Lark bounced up beside him, tilting her head. "I'll walk with you." She sent Kayda a nod as Conall rushed past her out of the hut. "We'll be ready to leave tomorrow."

Conall pushed past the netting and drew a deep breath in the humid air outside.

Ereni. She was alive. He closed his eyes, listening to the jungle's noise echo around him.

What would he say when he saw her? What was there to say? *Thanks for lying to me. Tricking me. Forcing me to take part in this strange play you arranged with your mother. Oh, and by the way, she's dead. Burned to ashes on a tiny island in the Northern Depths.*

Blazes. Bloody blazes.

Someone grabbed his arm. He opened his eyes and found Lark, right there, her hazel eyes wide, full of concern.

"Are you all right?" she asked.

He forced a smile. "I'm fine, really." He lifted his hands, showing her his palms. "Just forgot I needed to have these washed and bandaged."

She stared up at him, her gaze turning shrewd, but she didn't push. She linked their arms together. "The healing hut is this way."

Conall sighed as they weaved between huts. He wasn't ready to talk about Ereni with Lark. Not with anyone. Only Shadow knew the whole of what happened between the two of them. Her betrayal still burned like an open wound, even after Delyth's admission and his dream vision.

Had what they had ever been real? All those nights they'd spent together in each other's arms with the stars winking down at them. He could still recall the contentment he'd glimpsed in her eyes that resonated in his soul. He'd never felt so close to anyone. Not even Shadow.

He couldn't help but wonder if she'd had any feelings for him at all, or if it had all been a lie. A clever orchestration to keep him close and draw him into the plans they'd so carefully plotted. Forced to follow the fate that was his destiny.

At least now that he knew she was alive, maybe he'd finally discover some answers. Even if the thought of seeing her again had his stomach churning and his throat stinging with bile. He would find her and demand the facts. For all that he'd suffered, he deserved the truth. She owed him that much, at least.

Lark led him to a large hut on the opposite side of the village. "I'm glad I got the chance to bring you here. In the few days I've been here, I've already learned so much about healing." Her eyes sparkled, her smile banishing some of the clouds lingering in his mind.

"I never thought I'd have to travel all the way to Stoneshore to learn how to be a better healer."

They entered as Mika lit tall tapers hanging along the walls in the large wooden hut. The interior was one big, rectangular room, lined with rows of cots along the walls. About half were occupied with curtains dangling from the ceiling, shrouding the patients within.

Lark waved to Mika and led him to an empty cot in the room's center. "I'll be right back." She smiled.

He perched on the foot of the bed as she hustled off, busying herself clipping herbs from a wall of potted plants, then digging through a drawer in a wide wooden desk at the front of the room.

Her arms were laden when she returned. She dropped everything on the cot beside him, grabbed his hands, and gently *tsked* as she examined the assorted gashes on his palms. He watched the little wrinkle between her brows deepen and smiled.

"What are you grinning at?" she asked.

"Nothing." He flinched as she prodded the wound with a wet cloth. "Can't you just heal me like you did on the island?"

"Your hands are filthy. I've got to clean them first. It won't do you any good to have the flesh knitted back with sand and grit inside."

He supposed that made sense. But knowing that didn't make the cloth sting any less. He lifted his gaze from his hands, seeking a distraction.

Mika had just finished lighting the last candle on the wall, washing the room in a warm glow despite the darkening sky outside. He drew open a curtain toward the back of the room and slid inside.

Conall caught a glimpse of the people within before the curtain closed behind him. It was the sullen boy from the island mountain top, Nox, and his mother, Esmar. Their voices rose in the air distinctly.

"When can I take Nox home?" Esmar asked.

"Not until the morning. It's far too late now. You'd never make it before nightfall," Mika said. "I want you back in a few days to check in. All right, Nox?"

Silence followed. He imagined the boy might have nodded. How strange it must be for him to have lost so many bondmates in such a short time. It was no surprise his mood was so dour.

If he lost Shadow… Conall shuddered and forced the thought aside. With any luck, he wouldn't have to worry about that for a good long while.

Lark set the cloth down, finally satisfied with the results of her cleaning. "I'll have you all fixed up in a moment." She grabbed the bright green herb clippings off the bed and flattened them against his palms, pressing them firmly with her hands.

He winced at the pressure, patiently awaiting the tremor that would accompany her healing magic.

Lark didn't disappoint. The vibration thrummed through him, and suddenly, the stinging weight on his palms lifted as if it had never been there. When she raised her hands and removed the herbs, she revealed perfect tanned skin, completely unmarred, with no sign of the scratches that had just been present.

"You've gotta teach me how to do that." He laughed.

She leaned closer, eyes twinkling. "I—"

"Nox!" The luct netting at the entrance swished as a man shoved his way into the hut. "Where is he? Where's my boy?" His head darted around, searching each bed.

Conall's heart seized at the exact instant the man's hazel eyes met his.

Father. Delyth had been right. There he was, in the flesh. A part of him still hadn't believed it, but now there was no denying it. Their father was alive.

Lark took one look at his face and spun forward, her hand flying to her mouth as she spotted their father inside the doorway. His gray-streaked brown hair curled around his shoulders in disarray. Except for the dusting of whiskers on his jaw and a small scar cutting through his left eyebrow, he was exactly the same as Conall remembered him.

Their father's step faltered. His stare locked on both of them, and his expression shifted. The panic that had just been so apparent slid away as his mouth fell open, eyes blinking furiously.

At the same time, the curtain shrouding Nox tore aside, the ceiling hooks clattering. Esmar bolted across the room. "Jett." She slammed into his chest, clutching him tightly.

Lark's hand slipped, revealing a tentative smile.

Conall's nostrils flared. "A new name for a new life. I suppose that's fitting." He hopped off the cot, standing to his full height and marching down the aisle toward the man who'd once shared his name.

A cold chill spread through his veins. They might look like kin—blazes, since the Palisade aged him, they could easily be mistaken for brothers—but the father he'd been named after was little more than a stranger now.

Esmar pulled free from Jett's arms. Eyes narrowing, she set her hands on her hips. "What's going on, love? Do you know this man?"

Conall had half a mind to blurt out the sordid tale, right then and there. To scream out to the entire room—to the whole damn village even—about the man who'd abandoned him as a child. The cad who'd ditched his pregnant wife and son and disappeared. Let them believe he was dead and started a new life. A new family.

But he didn't. It was clear from the confusion on Esmar's face she had no idea about his father's checkered past. And as much as he wanted to hurt the man who'd abandoned him, he wouldn't heap that pain on the boy. He couldn't do that to Nox, not after all he'd suffered.

He took a deep breath, instead, and swept past his father. "C'mon, Lark. Jett can find us after he's spoken to his family. Seems they have a great deal to discuss."

Once again, he stood alone outside a jungle hut, the world spinning off its axis. He breathed in the moist jungle air and closed his eyes. Anger and shame burned in his belly as he grappled with the news.

Deep down, he'd been hoping Delyth was wrong. That he'd search this little village and find no sign of the father he'd long believed dead. Surely, she'd only used his father as another carrot to make him follow her. A false lead to ensure he would comply with her request to travel to Doln.

He should've known better. The Sade Prim had been happy to withhold information from him, but she'd never lied to him once.

Now he saw the evidence with his own eyes. His heart ached as he stood there, swaying on his feet.

It was true, all of it. He was alive. Why hadn't his father returned home? He racked his brain, trying to remember the days leading up to his father's departure. Was it something he'd done?

A hand slipped into his own and squeezed. Lark. He stared down at her and offered a crooked smile. Shadow and Sunny bounded into sight, appearing from the jungle, their tails wagging. He squeezed back and shoved aside the pain threatening to overwhelm him.

It wouldn't do to wallow in the past. He'd learned that lesson over and over again. He would hear the truth from his father's own lips. For now, he took comfort in everything that he had.

He had his bondmate. His beloved dog. And he had his sister back. The vow he'd made so long ago, broken and bleeding on the forest floor, had finally been fulfilled. No matter what else he did, he could rest easy knowing she was safe. Alive and well, clutching his hand. Whatever came next, they'd face it together.

Chapter 26

Kayda's eyes shot open in the darkened hut.

"Druturion?" She silently prayed for a response that never came. She lay there, curled up on a cot beneath a thin sheet, listening to the women's gentle snores in the hut and the warbling cries of birds leaking in the screened windows. How long would it be before he answered?

She'd spent long hours in bed last night, puzzling over the new information she'd learned from Conall and Lark. Now she wasn't just worried about Druturion never returning; she was plagued by visions of Belstatsia turning on him, forced by the Unseen to destroy him. Or of Druturion succumbing to the whispers of that evil presence. And worse of all, the possibility that she might have to take up arms against her own bondmate to save her country. She lay there that morning, trying to banish the lingering memory of those nightmares and wishing with everything in her that he would just return.

But she couldn't wait forever. She sighed and sat up. The gentle light of dawn seeped into the shadowy building. She threw off the sheet, scooped up her things, and left, emerging into the cool morning shade.

She lingered there for a moment, not moving, not thinking. Just being—alone.

Then footsteps crunched behind her. She wheeled around and spotted Conall approaching, his pack slung against his back. His wolf paced calmly at his side, a yellow mutt bouncing around his legs.

"Good morning, Princess," Conall said.

"Please, call me Kayda." She dropped her gaze to the ground, shifting her stance. They stood in silence, the awkwardness between them unspoken but palpable.

"Kayda, I really am sorry for what happened on the island." He rubbed the back of his neck. "If I'd known attacking that dragon would cause you to lose your bondmate, I would've never struck him."

"Her."

"Sorry, what?"

"The white dragon was a female. Belstasia." She shook her head. "Not that it matters now." She grimaced and met his eyes. "I'm sorry, too. I didn't intend on burning you. I've never burned a person before. Only the scourge." She shifted again, clenching her hands together.

He sent her a lopsided smile, moving his hand from his neck to rub his shoulder. He'd changed into a new tunic. Brown fabric covered the flesh that had gotten singed. "It's all right. No harm done. I'm good as new, thanks to Lark."

She nodded, a pang of jealousy striking her. She'd never know what it was like to have a sibling that loved her so completely. Though she spent much of the boat ride scanning the book Delyth had given Conall, she couldn't block out the whole of his conversation with Lark. The lengths he went through to see himself reunited with her... it was worthy of a minstrel's ballad.

Her own brother had only ever treated her with scorn and veiled derision when he wasn't ignoring her completely. And now, after the Palisade's fall and Tarquin's demise, she didn't even have that left. It was long past time to admit she would have to count on herself and herself alone. Strong familial bonds were not in the cards for her.

She shook off the thought. None of that mattered now. The only thing she needed to focus on was getting back to Flamesmoat.

"Are you ready for sailing, then?" she asked.

"Actually, there's someone I need to talk with first. I was just heading to the healing hut to speak with him."

"That won't be necessary," exclaimed a man who appeared from behind a nearby hut, a well-worn pack slung over his shoulders.

Kayda did a double take. This man wore the typical Raimish garb, but he shared such a close resemblance with Conall it was striking.

"I heard about your voyage. I'm coming with you," he continued.

Conall stiffened as he approached. She thought it had been awkward before, but now the air practically seethed with tension. Something lay unspoken between these two that had Conall positively thorny and the unnamed man quavering with discomfort.

She jumped in. "Thank you. The citizens of Flamesmoat will be grateful for your help. I'm Kayda." She stuck out her hand.

"Jett." He glanced at her quickly, his gaze flying back to Conall as he grabbed her hand and shook. Then he looked down at her light brown freckled wrist bobbing up and down in his grasp, and his gaze shot back to her face.

She saw the recognition light in his eyes. She waited for the question that inevitably followed when someone realized she wasn't just Kayda, but *Princess* Kayda of Dracwood—only it never came.

Instead, they were interrupted by the crunch of footsteps and the murmur of voices. Jett dropped her hand and backed up, his head craning toward the sound.

Within moments, the village came to life as dozens of people crowded the earthen streets. There were the folk she recognized from the island, along with many others she'd yet to meet, all carrying bags and assorted weapons.

Then came the rhythmic tapping of wood in the dirt. Mata Moyra appeared, her scowl as firmly in place as it had been the night before. "Well, Princess. I've done what I could. These brave souls have agreed to answer your call."

Kayda's heart lifted to see so many strangers ready to stand by her side. Ready to fight.

"Do you really mean to take canoes all the way to Flamesmoat, my lady?" a young man asked.

She gulped, blinking at the boy who couldn't be more than a year older than she was. Was she really going to take his life—all of their lives—in her hands? She drew a deep breath, readying her response.

The slap of boots on the path stilled the words in her throat.

A youthful girl skidded to a stop a moment later. "Mika. There you are." Her long brown braid swung as she took in the crowd, her breath coming in fast from her run. "You're not gonna believe this! C'mon, to the cliffs."

Mika rolled his eyes. "What is it now, Ravenna?"

But the girl spun on her heel and took off, obviously expecting the flustered healer to follow. "C'mon. You're *all* gonna want to see this," she called over her shoulder as she disappeared the way she came, rushing down a footpath heading west, toward the cliffside bordering the ocean.

Mika offered a lopsided shrug. "She's usually right about these things." He started down the trail, following the excited girl's tracks.

Kayda grinned, matching his pace. They needed to head to the cliffs, anyway. What could have the girl in such an uproar?

Her heart skipped a beat. Could it be?

"Dru?" she tried again.

Still nothing. She tried not to let the disappointment strangle her, but her shoulders sank and her step slowed all the same.

How could she do this—any of this—all on her own? With Druturion by her side, she felt so strong. Practically invincible. Now, she was just another girl with delusions of grandeur. How could she lead these people into battle when she barely had a clue what she was doing half the time?

The roar of the rolling ocean waves soon overpowered the jungle's noise. Kayda approached the cliff's edge and stared out at the ocean. It was a gorgeous day; the blue waves capped with fluffy white clouds, the sea, calm and tranquil.

Kayda took a slight step back. Nothing appeared worthy of Ravenna's hasty declaration. Then she turned south and squinted. She spotted a tiny set of sails far off on the horizon.

Lark stopped beside her, gasping. "It's a proper sailboat, heading right for us."

Kayda's jaw dropped. There was something very familiar about that vessel.

"I didn't think any captains sailed around the southern tip of Joria?" Conall mused, stopping on her other side.

Kayda grinned. "Just the crazy ones." Jayan's last words came back to her, ringing in her ears. He hadn't said goodbye. He'd said, "See you soon." She laughed, long and loud.

"A friend of yours, I take it?" Lark crossed her arms, raising a brow.

"Yeah." She wiped a tear from the corner of her eye. "The best."

Kayda stood there, Lark on her right, Conall on her left, and watched *Nova's Champion* slowly float up the coast. She might not have any family she could count on, or a dragon, but at least she had this. She had friends, old and new, who would stand by her side and vow to do whatever it took to help her win this fight. Together, they would free her country from the evil that plagued it.

Epilogue

Warmth shrouded him. He awoke in the dark, heart thumping, ears reverberating with the scratching of clawed feet on rock.

Where was he? And why was his blanket moving?

Panic swarmed across his skin. He was encased in a cocoon of fur. The musk of a hundred squirming vermin filled his nostrils. He screamed, tearing at them. Shoving them aside.

The creatures scattered, leaving him alone in the dusky black. He gagged, the scream dying on his lips as he leaned over to spill bile in the dirt. The smell—the horrid, disgusting stench—hadn't abated. He shuddered as he realized why. His clothing, blazes—even his skin—was coated in a thick layer of feces.

How long had those things been on him? He reached for his memory, and the panic spread. His mind was like a pile of books thrown on the ground with no order; a jumble of facts and feelings, none of which could explain this. His memory was a crudely drawn map riddled with gaps.

What was happening? Where was he? *Who* was he?

His stomach, still stinging from his retching, twisted, his head pounding. He should know who he was, shouldn't he?

He stared down at his filth-encrusted hands as his eyes adjusted to the light. It wasn't fully dark, after all. A red glow spilled into the room, lighting the underground chamber he found himself in.

How did he know enough to deduce he was underground but not know *who* he was? The question nagged at him, and he cursed under his breath.

"Hello?" He stood. His head slammed into the ceiling, and he cursed again as dirt rained around him in a cloud.

Crouching, he hobbled toward the light. "Hello?" he asked again.

No answer. What was he expecting? The vermin to talk back?

The thought struck a chord within him. Talking animals... Bonding magic. A memory jarred him, and he stopped in his tracks.

He sat in a chair, legs dangling, a toy soldier clasped in his fist, watching a white-robed man talk to his father. His father clutched a flagon in his hand, a wide smile across his lips.

"You're sure she's the one?" his father asked. "The babe inherited the family talent?"

The mage glanced his way, his weathered face filled with concern. "Perhaps we should have this conversation in private, sire?"

"Nonsense, man. Tell it to me straight. Is the princess talented or not?"

"She is." The man sighed. "My condolences on the death of your wife. Such a tragedy."

His father chugged from his flagon. "Yes, of course." He waved a hand. "And the boy?"

The mage glanced at him again, his brow furrowed, voice soft. "I'm sorry, sire. It's as I told you before. He's been skipped."

His father looked at him. Sneered at him. Disappointment seeped out of him as surely as the foul stench of stale ale wafted out of his pores.

He shook off the memory and took another step in the near dark. Why was he remembering that day now? He cleared his throat, blinking rapidly as he walked. Something else happened that day... Something important. What was it?

The feeling lashed him first. A wave of devastation. The crushing weight of his father's disappointment was nothing compared to his own. And on top of it all, there was an anger so intense it stole his breath. He raged at the mages who anointed him as "lesser." At the father who made no effort to hide his scorn.

Then he saw it all in his mind's eye. The child he once was, curled up in a ball in a closet in the dark. He felt the hot tears spill down his cheeks, his throat thick with mucus. No mother to comfort him. No father that cared enough to seek him out. He was all alone with his grief. His desolation.

He clutched his head as the memory washed over him. His heart shattered all over again, his blood boiling.

Then he remembered. Of course. This day—this moment—was when his life changed. He heard it again. The voice in his mind.

"I've been searching for you, my son."

The boy he used to be raised his head and swiveled his neck, finding nothing but clothing and dust. *"Who are you? You're not my father."* He clutched tightly to his knees, curling up even tighter on the ground.

"You cannot see me, but I am with you." He felt it then. The prickle of eyes on his back. *"You're not alone, son. I'm with you."*

Confusion had pierced him, and disbelief. Beneath that, another feeling rose to the surface. One that made a smirk spread across his face.

Blazes. The mages were wrong. Those lying witches told him he wasn't talented. What was this if not talent?

"Yes, son. You won't be alone any longer. There's so much I have to give you."

He'd laughed then, in that closet in the dark. The mirth and triumph of that moment infected him once more, and he laughed again.

The memory vanished, and with it, came a new realization. He was where he was meant to be. He was finally home.

"Hello?" he asked again. This time, the reply came instantly.

"Ah, you've awakened, my son. Come to me." It was the same voice. The voice that had whispered to him so long ago.

He nodded, creeping closer, searching for the light. The red glow around him deepened as he trod through the earth.

"You've done well. Now it's time. Come claim your reward."

As he shuffled along, his memory came flooding back. The map in his mind sharpened and came into focus, the gaps filled with all the pieces of his life.

A life of leisure, yes. But beneath the picturesque facade, it was a life filled with unspoken pain. With the shattered remnants of what could've been, had he only had that one little missing thing—bonding magic.

But he had something else. Something different. Secret, but just as powerful. He had the whispers in his thoughts. His true father, who was always there for him, so much more than the drunken fool that had spread his seed and sneered at his existence. The voice that guided him through life. That led him here.

Another memory pushed to the forefront of his mind. He was fighting for his life, protected beneath a shield of magic, slaughtering thousands of the same vermin that had covered him upon waking. The scourge.

Yes, he remembered this day. He'd fought long and hard, his men flanking him. Like he was supposed to.

Then she came. The bane of his existence. Red hair flowing in the wind, atop a *dragon*, no less. She'd sneered at him then. Just like his father. They were much the same, those two. It wasn't his fault he'd been born without that tiny insignificant thing she had in abundance. He would prove himself her equal—no, her superior.

That was why he'd stayed when those cowardly mages fled. That and the voice whispering once again.

"*Stay,*" it had said. "*I'll protect you, son.*"

So, he'd stayed, and he'd fought. And when the scourge rose up and consumed his men, he'd not fallen. Not truly. Instead, he found himself dragged down into the earth whence they'd come. Down into the dark.

He remembered everything now. Everything.

"*I want what you promised me, Father,*" he said. "*I want it all.*"

"*And you shall have it, son. I've so much to give you. Come to me.*"

Tarquin took another step forward and smiled.

AMBER L. WERNER

LINES THAT DREW US

PALISADE TRILOGY

Prologue

Ereni doubled over and retched, praying her breakfast wouldn't make a reappearance splattered across the fine silk carpet. The moment passed. The nausea retreated.

She lifted a steaming cup of ginger tea and took a tentative sip. The hot fluid slid down her throat, banishing the sting of bile. Every day had become a ghost of the same in Flamesmoat. All spent waiting.

She leaned back on the plush feather bed, lifting her brown cotton tunic for a peek at the vibrant purple glow emanating from her belly.

At least some things were worth waiting for.

A knock at her door chased away her smile. She slipped her tunic down and cleared her throat. "Come in."

"Sade Pr—"

The icy glare she sent across the room stilled the young mage's lips.

"Sorry, Ereni. Old habits die hard." Baris sheepishly raked a hand through his curly brown locks. The blue aura around him blazed bright against the floral wallpaper.

"It's all right. Have a seat." Ereni's gaze softened, her blue eyes meeting Baris' directly. She stood, leaving the bed and taking a seat at the tea table.

"Thanks." He pulled out a chair, the wooden feet sliding soundlessly, courtesy of felt pads wrapped around the bottoms.

Nothing but the best furnishings adorned the home she found herself in. The family who'd once lived here no doubt spent many lifetimes and a massive fortune to surround themselves with all the trappings of wealth. All abandoned now. They were likely among the first to hightail it out of the city when the scourge came knocking.

"What brings you by?" Ereni quirked a brow and lifted the teapot in invitation.

Baris shook his head, sliding forward the delicate, intricately painted teacup and saucer in front of him. "It's the tunnels. We're doing all we can, but they won't hold much longer."

"Show me." Ereni tied her long brown hair up in a quick ponytail and pulled her thick fur cloak from the closet. In a matter of moments, they found themselves on the streets of Northgate, surrounded by a wall of flame.

She hadn't chosen her opulent house for comfort but for proximity to the flame moat that kept the scourge at bay. Here, the mages worked around the clock, shoring up the magic that stood between them all and certain death. But that was not where she was needed today.

Ereni followed Baris through the empty streets, the echo of their boots clattering loudly on the cobblestones.

In the time they'd spent here, the crowded city had dwindled to a meager population of mages, castle guards, and a handful of stubborn fools too stupid or set in their ways to flee. The empty houses and shops were left to greet them, their bright painted facades garish and laughable in light of the demise they faced.

Baris stopped in front of an abandoned bakery. He threw open the front door. Ereni breathed deeply as they entered, greeted not with the aroma of fresh baked bread but the dank scent of the deep earth. They hurried past an array of tables and chairs, which once held patrons gathered around a pot of tea and delectable scones, all empty now, covered in dust and pushed to the sides of the cheery yellow room.

Behind the counter, a hole in the ground beckoned, lit with a warm glow.

Baris grabbed an oil lamp from the counter and held out a hand. "Watch your step."

Ereni followed him down a set of steep steps to a narrow underground passage. Her skin came alive with the hum of vibration that signaled the use of earth talent.

The tunnel was lit with a series of torches, the flickering flames sending shadows dancing across the dirt walls. She passed by a handful of harried faces, all covered in a fine layer of grime that did nothing to dampen the blue glow surrounding them. A few spared her a smile, but most just kept at their task, tirelessly bracing the tunnels with layer upon layer of dirt and mud.

Baris led her further east until the tunnel dead-ended. Three mages furiously flung mud and chunks of rock at the end of the tunnel.

Baris cleared his throat loudly. "Any change?"

The weary mages lifted their heads in unison, their hands still moving as they worked.

"No. Still the same," the closest woman replied, her blond hair pulled back in a tight bun, the yellow strands doused in a liberal dusting of brown.

"Why don't you three take a quick break?" Baris asked.

"Are you sure?" The woman eyed the tunnel wall dubiously.

Baris patted her shoulder. "Just for a moment. Grab a drink. Ereni needs to hear it."

All three nodded, their hands falling slack at their sides. The heavy vibration in the tunnel faded, but it didn't evaporate entirely with the rest of the earth mages still working nearby. The trio retreated a few steps, talking in hushed tones and sipping from a pile of waterskins stacked on the ground.

Ereni strode to the end of the tunnel. She bent sideways and set her ear directly against the freshly packed earth. Her eyes widened. The scratching was the loudest it had ever been. Baris was right. There wasn't much time.

She turned to the mages, smiling at each of them. "Thank you all for your hard work. Do you think you can handle a few more hours?"

They all nodded quickly, moving back into position. Vibrations hummed to life in the air. Ereni's skin tingled with the force of it as she grabbed Baris's arm and tugged him back toward the entrance. "Have everyone stop just before dusk. Don't waste any time crossing the bridge."

Baris left with a parting wave and circled back, no doubt on his way to spread the news throughout the entire network of tunnels beneath Northmoat.

Ereni made her way to the surface. She walked a circuit of the empty city, calling out to everyone she saw. Her breath clouded in the chill air as the day rolled on, yet still she searched, tugging her cloak tighter and ignoring her sore feet. No one could be missed. She had to be certain.

Before she knew it, she stood on the wide wooden bridge spanning the Riddle River that cut the city of Flamesmoat in two. The river churned beneath her as she waited. As the final stragglers arrived, the sun sank down, leaving the gathered mages awaiting her on the Southmoat streets swathed in the light of dozens of torches.

"Is that everyone?" Ereni peered behind Baris as he approached, bringing up the rear of a small group of mages she recognized from earlier in the tunnels.

His brown curls bobbed inside the hood of his dark cloak. "Yes. I'm the last."

They hurried together across the icy bridge, careful not to slip. Within moments, they arrived safely on the other side. They joined the group of huddled mages standing on the dirt road in Southmoat.

Ereni smiled at them. All of them glowed blue so strongly. "Is everyone in position?"

A chorus of nods answered her.

"Let's begin."

Two fire mages approached the edge of the Riddle Bridge, each holding a torch. The air, already cold enough to force Ereni to stuff her hands into her pockets, grew even colder as the pair called forth the flames. Fire lit the night, flowing from the mage's hands. The scent of charred wood filled her nose.

"Wait!" a familiar voice called out. One she was not expecting to hear tonight.

"Izora?" Ereni whirled on her heel just as the elderly mage burst through the crowd of young mages, her cloak buttons done up askew, leaving it halfway open, showcasing her gray castle servant's uniform beneath.

"The king. The king is missing!" Izora sucked in a gasp, her breathing harsh and labored. "We have to find him!" Her gaze finally fell on the burning bridge, and her brows shot up, disappearing beneath the white curls that covered her forehead. "Are you mad? What are you fools up to?"

A white-haired mage plowed through the crowd, one Ereni didn't recognize, wearing the signature white robes of the Palisade Mages. "Izora." He grabbed the blustering woman's elbow. "What's happened? You tore by like you saw a ghost."

Izora turned to the mage, her face lighting with what looked to Ereni like recognition, even as she continued to shake her head, inching closer to the bridge. "The king. I have to find him."

Ereni frowned, stepping into her path. "Wait, you can't charge over there now. It would be suicide. Surely the king is somewhere in Southmoat. I watched him cross the bridge earlier this afternoon."

"No. No, I heard it from his own lips. He's headed to the stables."

Ereni pressed a hand to her chest. "The king is speaking?"

Izora sucked in another gasp, trying to push past her again. "That's what I said, isn't it?"

"Look." The white-robed mage's arm shot out, pointing across the river.

There, on Northmoat's cobblestone streets—where no one was supposed to be—strolled King Quinton in a bright red bathrobe and a pair of red silk pajamas. His gray-streaked blond head was unmistakable as he passed beneath a torch someone left behind.

"Blazes!" Ereni exclaimed.

Izora was back in motion, heading for the burning bridge.

Ereni caught her cloak sleeve, her stomach sinking. "You can't."

But the old mage shook free, her mouth set in a grim line. "I told Kayda I would keep him safe. I've never broken a promise to her before, and I don't plan to start today just because you fools feel like burning the place down."

Izora swept past, setting her hand down as she reached the bridge, banishing the flames in a line down the center. She turned back. For a moment, Ereni was sure she'd changed her mind. But a smile crossed her dark face, and she lifted a brow at the white cloaked mage. "You mind?"

The man strode forward and leaned down to lift a handful of soil from the dirt road. He closed his eyes briefly, and when he opened them, a tremor whispered over Ereni's skin. The dirt flew from his hand, forming a flat disk before his feet, the size and shape of a stepping stone. He grabbed Izora around the waist with a wink. "Hop on."

All the young mages crowded behind Ereni, and everyone watched the pair hover across the burning bridge, the flames reforming in their wake to swallow the wooden boards behind them.

"That was either incredibly brave, or incredibly stupid," Baris said as the old mages reached Northmoat and hopped down onto the cobblestone road.

Ereni sighed, meeting Izora's gaze just before she disappeared behind a building, following the king. "A bit of both, I'd say."

"Should we follow them?" Baris asked.

As if to punctuate his question, Riddle Bridge chose that moment to crumble, breaking in two with a deafening *crack*, followed by a massive splash as it slammed into the icy water below.

"No." Ereni raised her voice to be heard over the din. "We go ahead with the plan. Maybe it will buy them time to find the king and get to shelter."

They all stood in silence, watching, waiting for the signal. Waiting. Always waiting.

Finally, it came. A whistle split the night. The earth and water mages strode forward to the river's edge, twisted the lids of their vial necklaces open, and linked hands.

A vibration thrummed through the earth, shaking Ereni's feet. A massive chunk of the riverbed on the riverbank's northern side broke off and splashed into the churning water.

Moisture flooded the air, making Ereni shiver. But her gaze locked on the dark river below. Slowly, the roiling waters stilled. Then the flow reversed, forced by the water mages to flood into the gaping hole revealed by the fallen earth.

The mages stood in deep concentration beside the riverside for so long the cold numbed Ereni's toes. Then they stepped back, weary and spent, clutching at each other and falling to their knees.

Ereni didn't move from her spot. Not even to shake the feeling back into her feet. She stared down as the water reversed course, rushing back to the river. Rushing back filled with countless drowned scourge corpses floating in its wake.

Baris whooped beside her, pumping his fist in the air. "It worked! Ha, drowned like rats, the ugly bastards."

Ereni smiled sadly. The victory didn't feel so great now that they had a stranded king and rogue mages to rescue.

Even as the river below bobbed with the dark corpses of an uncountable number of scourge, she knew there would be more. She didn't delude herself into thinking they'd slayed even a tenth of their ranks.

As she stood there staring, the light of the flame moat surrounding Northmoat flickered and faded. The last of the laumarle oil they'd used to light the moat in place of the fire mages had finally died out. Almost instantly, the snarling and screeching across the river intensified as hundreds upon hundreds of vermin flooded the streets of Northmoat.

"Hang on, Izora." Ereni whispered. She turned toward the docks and closed her eyes. "Help will come."

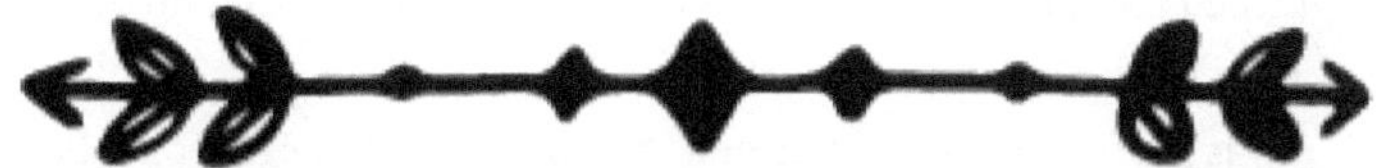

Tarquin pulled himself free of the earth, breathing deep the chill afternoon air.

"Bloody blazes those vermin are rank," he murmured. He shook himself and stood to his full height for the first time in ages, the bones in his neck and back cracking.

"How you can stand it down there in that hovel, I'll never understand."

A chuckle sounded in his mind, reverberating darkly. *"I'm where I need to be."*

The stench of the scourge clung to his nostrils, covering him like when he'd awoken underground. Tarquin shuddered, shoving aside the memory of the darkened tunnels where he'd found his savior. He buried the memory of the unspeakable things he'd suffered in the red gloom. He needn't go back there again. It had been a necessary evil. A means to an end. And now, it was time to take back what was his.

"Soon, my son," the voice whispered.

His gaze flicked over the desolate landscape. He recognized it instantly. The Eastern coast of Dracwood, in the Abandoned Lands.

He bit back a chuckle. It almost felt like yesterday when he'd stood with that traitorous bitch mage surveying the lush fields and rolling hills that dominated the coastal plain. Now the place was completely unrecognizable. Charred plants, torn up earth, and the bones of thousands littered the ground, crunching beneath his boots as he strode forward.

He headed for the river, passing the bare skeletons of metal and charred wood that were all that remained of Mage Keep's ugly buildings. The mages were all gone, scattered in the wind like so many flakes of ash.

Soon he approached the slow-moving Palisade River's banks. He shucked off his soiled clothing, all of it covered in layers of dirt and shit. Then he plunged himself into the icy water, frantically scrubbing his skin. The water clouded, hazy with all the grime of his weeks underground.

After scrubbing his skin till it was practically raw, and washing the filth from his clothes, he emerged from the river, shivering, flushed pink and totally spent. He collapsed on the riverbank, the hard ground ice cold against his naked flesh.

"My boy, you do too much. What good will it do you to freeze to death?"

"I'd rather be dead than forced to smell that filth," he retorted, his chattering teeth not affecting the conversation in his mind.

"No matter. Take what you need. You must keep up your strength."

Tarquin raised his head from the ground as the skittering of claws approached. Another of those damned scourge came, bringing with it its foul, musky stench, its beady eyes staring blankly ahead.

"Take it," the voice demanded.

Tarquin grasped the quivering beast. His hands closed around its throat. He watched the life fade from those beady black orbs and felt a change come over him. His skin warmed, all of his muscles infused with new strength. And beneath it all, he sensed the whisper of something *more*. Something he'd been chasing all his life. The power he'd been promised.

Tarquin smiled, sitting up on the cold ground. *"Send me another."*

Chapter 1

Lark reached into the bucket at her feet and lifted another handful of soil into her hand. She gazed off *Nova's Champion's* port side as they sailed up the western coast toward Flamesmoat.

She closed her eyes, visualizing the shape of a dart in her mind. A tremor whooshed over her skin. Then she lifted her eyelids and let loose. A clump of soil flew from her hands and splashed into the sea below.

"Ha, keep it up. Maybe you can nab us a fish for dinner."

Lark shot her bondmate Muse a glare where she sat preening on the midship deck but didn't bother with a response. Silly falcon. One would think she was training to be a jester with all her jokes.

"That's it. You're getting the hang of it," Kayda said, at her side. The sea breeze tousled her flowing white silk shirt and brown trousers, whipping at her braids and tangling her long red hair.

Lark frowned and dumped the dirt back into the bucket and leaned over to stare at the dark sea. "I was picturing a dart. That looked more like a marble."

Kayda patted her shoulder. "Don't be so hard on yourself. I'd say that's pretty impressive for your first training session."

Mika dumped out another handful of soil. "You'd think after a lifetime spent healing, this would be child's play, but I don't seem to have the knack for it." He brushed his hands over the bucket, then curled his dark brown locks out of his eyes.

Kayda turned to him, the freckles on her light brown skin illuminated by the afternoon sun. "Don't give up. It gets easier with practice."

Lark sent Mika a smile and squeezed his arm. "We can practice together."

Conall strolled to the side rail, leaving his bonded wolf, Shadow, curled with his mutt Sunny on the midship deck. "Need any help training?" he asked with a grin, the sun's rays glinting off the silver streaks in his curly brown hair.

"No, I've got it," Kayda said, her tone a touch more abrupt than it needed to be.

Lark sighed as her brother's shoulders sank. It wasn't entirely his fault. His actions may have chased Kayda's dragon away back on that lonely island in the sea, but he'd only been doing what he thought was right, at the time. Yet it seemed that Kayda still hadn't forgiven him for that mistake.

She opened her mouth to say something, to break the tension, but snapped it closed at the tapping of booted feet approaching. The tension thickened so much it was almost tangible, hanging in the air like a cloud of smoke, dense and choking.

"Jett," Conall said through clenched teeth.

The older man strode forward, his hazel eyes and gray-streaked brown hair a perfect match for his son's. Now that all the folk from Raimire donned cotton and wool in preparation for the colder climes they sailed toward, the familial resemblance was even more striking, leaving little doubt in Lark's mind that what Conall had said about the stranger was true.

Lark still couldn't wrap her head around it. How had their father returned from the dead?

"Conall, Lark. I'd like to talk to you now, if you have a moment." Jett cautiously stopped beside them at the side rail.

Mika took that as his cue to leave. He disappeared into the depths of the ship without a word. The squeak of a wooden door swinging on its hinge sounded over the breaking waves and wind.

Kayda's brow furrowed, her brown gaze flicking between the three of them before she let go of the rail. "I'll leave you to it then."

"Wait, Princess." Jett held up a hand, tilting his head back to the rail. "I have a feeling you'll want to hear my tale, too."

Lark frowned. What did the princess have to do with their father faking his death and disappearing to Raimire for the entirety of her life? Was that a crime in Dracwood? Maybe he was planning to ask her to put in a good word for him with the magistrate...

Jett sighed deeply, angling his face into the wind. "I'm sure you're all wondering how I ended up in Raimire." His gaze darted between her and Conall. "Does Kayda know who I am?"

Lark crossed her arms and shook her head.

Conall's stare dropped to the wooden boards. "He's our father."

Kayda's lips pursed, her brow wrinkling. "Are you sure I should be here for this?"

"Yes," Jett blurted as Kayda moved to leave. "Stay. This concerns you, too."

Kayda stopped and turned. "All right."

Jett stared at the sea, his knuckles turning white as he gripped the rail. "Before I moved to Raimire, I lived in Southmoat. I was born and raised in the slums." He swallowed, his Adam's apple bobbing up and down. "You weren't yet born, Lark." His gaze flicked to Conall. "But I'm sure you remember those years back in Southmoat. There was never quite enough to eat. And no matter how hard I tried, my hunting and trapping was never enough to get ahead like I would've liked. Your mother even needed to keep her job in that shit tavern just to make ends meet."

Conall's face screwed up. "It wasn't that bad... was it?"

Jett smiled sadly. "I'm glad you remember it that way, son. Your mother and I did our best to make your childhood normal. To shelter you from the hardships we faced. It was the least I could do, after the way I was raised."

"Is that why you left? You couldn't stand a life lived in the slums?" Conall asked.

"Wait, that doesn't make sense." Lark clasped her brother's forearm. "What about the farm?" She pivoted to Jett. "You inherited the plot in Greenvale just before I was born, didn't you? You already had your ticket out of Southmoat."

"I'm getting to that." Jett rolled his neck, his gaze shifting nervously between the three of them. "I don't want you to feel sorry for me, or to forgive me even. I just wish I could make you understand... leaving you and your mother was the hardest decision I ever made."

Lark leaned forward, angling her head so he'd meet her gaze. "Then why did you?"

His hazel eyes met hers, glossy with unshed tears. "It all started when a mage came to see me."

Conall stiffened. He gripped the back of his head, his hand clenching in his unruly locks. "Always the damn mages," he muttered.

But though the announcement seemed to unsettle her brother to no end, Kayda drew closer, quirking a brow. "What happened?"

"It was strange. Some old man in white robes found me one day. Offered me a sack of coins to answer some questions." Jett tugged his collar. "Well, times were tight. Of course, I accepted. I would've been an idiot not to."

Lark crossed her arms. "What did he ask you?"

"At first, he asked me a million and one questions about my mother." Jett rubbed the back of his neck, eyeing the deck again before his gaze lifted. "I never got around to telling you, Conall, what with you being so young. My mother wasn't your typical moral citizen. There's no easy way to say this..." He grimaced. "She was a whore."

Her grandmother—Lark shook her head, fighting to reconcile the facts with the picture she'd created in her mind. She'd never met the woman, never even known her name, but it hadn't stopped her from imagining what her father's mother might've been like. Never in a million years would she have pictured this.

Conall appeared to struggle with the news as well. His tanned skin took on a white pallor, and he leaned back against the rail and gripped the wood tightly with both hands.

"She wasn't a bad sort, your grandma," Jett hurried to say. "Just a bit absent. She never confided in me the reasons why she did what she did." He shrugged. "Southmoat... it's a rough life. Hunger and poverty will drive folk to do desperate things."

Kayda splayed a hand on her chest. "I had no idea."

Lark lifted a brow, glancing at the princess dubiously. Had they kept her so sheltered she had no clue what happened in the city she ruled?

"In any case," Jett rambled on, "that was just the start of the questions. After he finished asking about my ma, they tried to locate my whole family tree. I told him the truth—I never met my father, and as far as I know, I don't have any siblings. If my mother even knew who sired me, she took the secret to her grave."

He turned again to stare at the sea. "Then he started asking about my wife and children. That's when I stopped answering. I was so angry, so disappointed in myself that I might've gotten us all tangled in some mage's scheme. I ran out of there. I left that old geezer without even bothering to ask for the coin he promised me."

Jett laughed, a single bitter scoff. "I didn't hear from them again for some time. Not until Rhea had a run in with a group of local thugs on her way home from the pub one night. If that was even what they were, and not puppets of the damned mages."

Lark's stomach dropped. "What happened?"

"They beat her bloody. Stole her wages for the week." His jaw tightened, and his eyes narrowed. "Happens in the slums every day."

"Then why do you think the mages were behind it?" Kayda asked.

"I didn't at the time. It's only looking back that I start to wonder, because of what happened next." Jett's gaze flicked to Conall. "Your mother was in bad shape. We didn't have the coin for a healer. Rhea did what she could with her herbs and tinctures, but she was in so much pain. We'd only just learned we were expecting a new baby." He sent Lark a sad smile before returning his gaze to Conall. "I brought you with me the next morning to search for work so your mother could rest. That's when the mage came back."

Jett wrinkled his nose. "He wasn't alone this time. He brought a woman with him. She did all the talking."

"Did you learn their names?" Kayda asked.

Jett shook his head. "I likely did, but it's been so long now. Can't say I remember."

Kayda frowned. Nodded.

"They found me at a local pub, begging for work in the kitchen. The woman invited me to sit down with her to chat."

"And I was there?" Conall asked. "I don't remember any of this."

"They brought a hound in for you to play with, Conall. You know how you always used to light up around dogs. It was like the whole world stopped every time you met a mangy old mutt in the street."

Conall gaze darted to where his bondmate and mutt lounged on the deck before he waved a hand and nodded.

"The woman offered me a job. They needed me to complete one week of work, and after that, I would be free to go on my way. In exchange, they offered me the plot in Greenvale. Said they'd set it up to look like I just inherited it from some distant relation."

Lark gasped. "You're kidding!"

"'Fraid not. Of course, I was suspicious. Especially when she wouldn't explain what I'd be doing." Jett grimaced. "And even more so when they named their conditions."

"What conditions?" Lark asked.

"After the job, I had to leave Dracwood for good. She didn't seem to care where I went, only that I never returned."

Conall scoffed. "And you agreed? Just like that?"

Jett sighed heavily. "It took some convincing. She said they would make it look like I'd died at sea. Rhea would receive a widow's stipend to help the three of you get on your feet at the farm. And they offered to send your mother a healer, too."

Lark's heart twisted. Who would turn down a deal like that? Certainly not a man on the brink of poverty, whose only desire was to protect his family. To gift them the kind of life he'd tried, and failed, to give them.

"I took the deal. I left you all behind. I'm sorry."

Conall bowed his head beside her, his hands clenched into fists.

"What was the job?" Kayda shifted, leaning closer to Jett. "What did the mages have you do?"

Jett, his hand outstretched toward Conall, stilled. He turned to Kayda with a pained grimace. "We sailed down the coast. We met a Jorian shipping vessel on its way north. They introduced me to a girl on board. Her name was Chanti."

Kayda's face paled. "What did she look like?"

"She looked an awful lot like you, Princess," Jett replied somberly.

Kayda blinked repeatedly. "Another mystery solved." She muttered something under her breath so quietly it was unintelligible.

Lark's brows furrowed. "You mind filling me in?"

"I only had one task on board that ship. They wanted me to lie with her. An easy enough task for the son of a whore. At first, I refused. But the mages can be persuasive when they need to be. And Chanti convinced me she was willing." Jett shrugged. "We did what they asked."

Lark's stomach churned. It was so strange. Why would the mages go to such desperate lengths to make their father sleep with some woman from Joria?

Her mind racing, her gaze flitted between everyone. Jett was looking sheepish. Conall murderous. And Kayda, like she'd just been told someone drowned her kitten.

"How could you do that to our mother?" Conall asked through clenched teeth. "She was back in Dracwood, pregnant with your child!"

Lark swallowed hard and stared at her father. "The better question is why? Why would the mages ask that of you?"

"Because of me. Chanti was my mother." Kayda twisted to face Jett. "And you're my father. The timing fits. She must've already been with child when she married the prince."

Lark rocked back on her heels and steadied herself against the railing. "You're our sister, Kayda?" They certainly didn't share much of a resemblance. In fact... "Wait, that would make you slightly younger than me." She set a hand on her hip, eyeing the princess up and down. "You're only sixteen?"

"Yes, I am." Kayda reddened slightly, rubbing her arm. "I summoned without a source once."

"Oh." Lark cringed, her gaze darting to her brother, who'd also suffered the effects of premature aging, although on a much greater scale. "Sorry."

"No, I'm the only one who should be apologizing," Jett jumped in. "I should've told those mages they could take their deal and shove it. But I didn't. I'm sorry for all the pain I've caused you. All of you."

"Did Mother know?" Conall asked. "Or did you let her believe all the lies?"

Jett shook his head. "I never told her. After that week, I left the boat and never looked back. I figured that was the least I could do for Rhea, after what I'd done."

Conall sighed. "I guess that was for the best. She went to her grave thinking her husband loved her, instead of knowing you'd betrayed her." He pushed off the railing and charged away.

Jett moved to follow, but Lark grabbed his arm. "Give him some space. Conall's always been one to work through things on his own time."

"I need some time to think, too. Thank you for telling me the truth." Kayda flashed them both a half-smile then strolled away in the opposite direction Conall went.

Lark's stomach rolled and swayed, and for once, she was sure it wasn't the ship's motion upsetting it. It was all so much to take in.

"I'll give you some time, too, I guess." Jett started to leave.

"Thanks, Father," Lark blurted out on a whim.

The smile he sent her looked so much like her brother's it made her heart ache. "You're welcome, Daughter."

He left her standing there, staring at the sea, wondering if her life would ever be the same.

Chapter 2

C onall stomped past Shadow and Sunny, heading for the bow of the ship.

"You all right, little brother?" Shadow lifted his head from the deck and gazed at him curiously as he strode by.

Conall paused. *"Not really, but not much I can do about it,"* he grumbled in his mind.

"What's wrong?" Shadow rose on his front paws and shook out his gray fur. Sunny perked up, her yellow tail wagging.

"Don't get up." He waved them off. *"I'll explain everything later. I just need some time to think."*

Shadow lay back down. *"I'm here when you need me."*

Conall reached down to pat Sunny between the ears and resumed his walk.

Nova's Champion was a fine boat. A welcome change from the rickety mess that was *The Lady Luck*. Instead of warped, dented boards and tattered sails patched in a hundred places, this ship was practically new.

The fresh scent of spruce and oak lingered beneath the tang of salt air. The deck gleamed in the midday sun, shaded by huge yellow sails. Deckhands scampered about, handling their tasks with smiling faces and ribald jokes on their tongues.

Conall wasn't in the mood to appreciate any jokes today. He stormed off, passing the wild Sul captain Jayan at the helm, and he didn't stop until he'd reached the bow's rail.

His thoughts swirled as he tried to piece together the crazy tale his father spun and the fragmented memories from his childhood. Had it really been that bad?

It was true a home in Southmoat wasn't something anyone yearned for. The lower section of Flamesmoat was cramped and dirty, inhabited by all kinds of riffraff. Not just regular, honest, poor folk, but thugs and thieves—whores. He grimaced.

His grandmother... that'd been an unpleasant surprise. A part of him wished he'd been told of his family's humble origins, but he couldn't say it surprised him that they'd sheltered him from the truth. It's not exactly the type of profession people bragged about.

But a rotten childhood didn't give his father the right to abandon them for a new life. Even if he secured them a ticket out of Southmoat in the deal. They were family. They were supposed to stick together.

"Conall?"

He turned and found one of the mages his sister had rescued on the Mido Islands approaching. Her clothing was no longer tattered and torn, but he still recognized her, though at the moment her name escaped him. What could she want?

He didn't know if he could handle any idle chit-chat. "Yes? Can I help you?" he asked, trying to tamp down the hint of annoyance in his tone. He must not have managed it well enough.

The girl flinched and backed up a step. "I can come back later."

He shook his head, forcing his voice to soften further. "No, don't. I'm sorry. I didn't mean to snap at you." He raised an arm toward the empty rail beside him in invitation. "Would you care to join me?"

She nodded once and slid up to the rail. They stood in silence for a time. Long enough that he began to think she'd simply come to the bow for the view.

His mind wandered back to his childhood, before his father left. All those days spent together in the woods. He'd only been a boy, but his father had been so patient attempting to teach him all he knew about trapping and hunting, while all Conall had been interested in was goofing off. He'd probably scared away all the game with his antics, but he couldn't recall a single time his father raised his voice to scold him.

His father was always smiling, his hazel eyes filled with laughter. When Conall looked back on those days, that one image always stood out in his mind, crystal clear.

"I heard you traveled through Doln with the mages after the Palisade fell."

"Hm?" The girl's statement drew him out of his reverie. He cleared his throat. "Yes, I did."

She picked at a spot on the bow rail, rubbing at a tiny imperfection in the wood. "Did you happen to run into a boy named Quent while you were there?"

Conall spun to face the girl and surveyed her more closely. Those bright green eyes, that pale freckled skin. How had he missed it? "Oriana?"

Her gaze lifted from the rail and connected with his. "Yeah, that's me."

"I met your brother. He's alive and well—or at least he was when I left Gransea—if that's what you're wondering." Once again, he fought to keep the annoyance out of his tone.

That poor boy was so worried about his sister. Another family split up when they should've stuck together. His stomach clenched as he remembered how torn up Quent had been, thinking he'd failed his mother.

"Good," Oriana said quietly. A small smile flitted across her lips. "That's good."

"Did you know your mother asked him to look out for you before she left?"

Oriana's face fell, and her smile vanished. "She did?"

"Quent befriended me while we trekked through the mountains." The side of Conall's mouth lifted in a crooked grin. "More than that. He saved my life once. Used his air talent to build a cave in the snow during an avalanche. Your brother is a hero."

"He can summon? At his age? That's... it's incredible."

He crossed his arms. "How could you leave him? He's just a kid, all alone. You're his family."

"I know it was selfish." She sighed. "I believed in Ereni. I still do. I wanted to be part of it all. Saving the world."

"Is that what Ereni sold you?" Conall wanted to scream. "Mages and their damn fate. And we're all just puppets in their show."

Oriana seemed to sense his mood shifting. She backed away, rubbing her chest. "Thank you for telling me about Quent." Then the tapping of her boots faded as she disappeared.

Barely a moment passed before boots pounded again, headed toward him. What now?

The frown plastered to his face faded as he spotted the footfall's source. A white and gold-feathered falcon landed on the railing beside him, just before his sister marched into view.

"Lark."

"Were you just talking to Oriana?"

"Yeah. Why do you ask?"

Lark scowled. "Oh, no reason. She definitely wasn't just racing away from here in tears." She cocked a brow at him, hand on her hip.

"Maybe I was a little hard on her." Conall grimaced. "I met her little brother on the trek to Doln. I had a few choice words to say about how she shouldn't have abandoned him at Mage Keep."

Lark joined him at the rail. She tugged her long brown curls over her shoulder and stared down into the dark sea. "You expect so much from everyone. Sometimes people make mistakes."

He tilted his head to glare down at his sister. With her bent beside the railing, she barely made it up to his shoulder. "This isn't just about Oriana, is it?"

"Do you ever think you can forgive Jett?" Lark's hazel eyes shone up at him, the color a perfect match for his own. For their father's as well.

Conall shook his head. "I don't know. I'm just so angry with him."

"Yeah, I get that." She slid her hand over his where it rested on the rail. "There's nothing wrong with being angry about the whole situation. I am, too. But when I look at it from his point of view, I can see why he did what he did."

"That doesn't make it right."

"I know." She squeezed his hand. "I believe him, though. When he said he was sorry, I think he really meant it. And I don't want to waste this second chance. We already lost our mother."

Conall pulled his hand free. "He's nothing like Mother."

"He made a mistake."

"Why are you sticking up for him?"

"Maybe because I know what it's like to do something you regret." She wrapped her arms around her chest. "I never told you what happened at the farm."

Conall's heart twisted as he recalled standing outside the burned-out shell that had once been their home. "What do you mean? It burned down." But even as the words left his lips, the image of the half-sunken foundation returned to his mind, and a sick feeling settled in his gut.

"I returned there after I escaped from the slavers." Lark turned to him, her shoulders trembling. "I set the fire. Gael... I killed him."

Conall gulped. "You didn't."

"I did. I set the fire. I stood there and watched it burn. And when I heard that bastard drunkenly stumbling around, trying to escape, I sunk my fingers into the earth and used my talent to trap him there."

He closed his eyes, just for an instant. Then he opened them and pulled his sister into his arms. "It's all right. He deserved it."

Lark shuddered, and he wished he could take away all her pain. He should've been there for her in that moment. Instead, he'd been recovering in the woods from the arrow wound Gael inflicted on him. If anyone deserved a violent death, a man who would leave his own stepson for dead in the woods certainly qualified.

"If I could go back, I would've done things differently." She sighed. "I know he deserved it, but I still wish I wasn't the one to kill him. To have his death weighing on me." Her voice wobbled. "I'm supposed to be a healer, not a killer."

He rubbed her back, not saying anything. Just holding her close while she dried her tears.

Eventually, she eased out of his arms and looked up with a wobbly smile. "Thanks. I just hope you can forgive our father for his mistakes one day, like you have mine."

Conall barely resisted the urge to roll his eyes. "It's not the same."

"I know. Except, it kind of is." She shrugged. "Either way, Jett gave us one thing we can be thankful for."

Conall cocked a brow. "What's that?"

"More family. Kayda. Nox. We've got two new siblings now." Lark grinned. "That's pretty exciting, don't you think?"

He flashed her a half-smile. "I guess you're right. I forgot about that."

Lark beamed up at him, her eyes shining. Then she tilted her head sideways, her gaze landing on her bonded falcon, Muse. She gasped.

"What is it?" Conall asked.

"Flamesmoat." She squinted at the horizon beyond the bow. "We're here."

Chapter 3

Kayda paused on the midship deck of *Nova's Champion*, her gaze drawn to the spot where Druturion used to laze in the sun, as content as a cat with a bowl of cream. A bittersweet smile crossed her face.

Then the smile vanished just as quickly as her bondmate had when he chased after Belstasia into the unknown. No matter how many times she reached out to him through their bond, he never replied.

Where was he?

Kayda pushed her worry for her bondmate aside and resumed pacing. They'd be approaching Flamesmoat soon. She'd not forgotten the promise she'd made to herself. She wouldn't just stand by and allow the city she'd grown up in to be destroyed without doing something to help. Even though parts of it seemed to be less than worthy of salvation.

Her stomach churned, her mind still reeling from all she'd learned from Jett. Had she been so blind she'd not noticed the common people suffering? Looking back, she realized that even though she'd lived in Flamesmoat all her life, there were vast swaths of the city she'd never stepped foot in. Why hadn't she ever thought to ask for a tour of the rest of the city?

She was too comfortable in the keep. Too complacent. Too trusting that the loving faces she interacted with in church and at public feasts were all that the city had to offer.

She should've done more. Her heart had broken as she listened to Jett's tale. All of that suffering going on right under her nose. As princess, she could've helped them.

Not that she even deserved to be princess. That fact was blatantly obvious now. She didn't share any blood with the king. All her life, she'd been an unwitting imposter. A product of the mages' schemes.

Her chest burned. Just one more thing for Izora to explain, once she found her.

Kayda's pacing brought her within shouting distance of the helm. Jayan waved her over.

She sighed and headed over to chat. "Captain. How's the sailing?"

"Smooth as silk." He sent her one of his signature toothy grins, his teeth gleaming against his dark skin and his chest on display beneath his wide open cloak. Even the steadily decreasing temperatures as they made their way north couldn't convince him to button his shirt. Although, he appeared to have taken a shine to his new, expensive boots. "How's your day treating you, Princess?"

She bristled and wrinkled her nose. "Kayda," she blurted, holding back a wince at her own clipped tone. "After all we've been through together, you can call me Kayda, Jayan."

"Aye, Kayda." He peered at her more closely. His smile slipped. "Everything all right with you?"

She waved him off. "Yeah, it's nothing." She patted his arm. "Just nervous about what we'll find when we arrive at Flamesmoat."

"Well, you won't have to wonder much longer." He nodded in the bow's direction. "Flamesmoat, ahoy," he said with a playful smirk.

"Already?" Kayda left Jayan at the helm and strode forward toward the bow. Conall and Lark were already there, staring up in the air and shading their eyes.

"What are we watching?" Kayda asked as she reached the rail.

Lark spared her a glance, then went right back to craning her neck up at the sky. "Muse. I sent her ahead to scout."

"Good plan," Kayda admitted. She joined the pair in their staring, finally glimpsing a bird high in the air and closing in on the far-off city.

It would likely still take the boat the better part of an hour to arrive at the docks in Southmoat. Her heart fluttered, and she tapped her foot on the wooden deck. If only Druturion were here, she might be the one flying ahead. More likely, she'd have arrived days ago.

Lark gasped.

"What is it?" Conall asked.

Kayda's heart dropped to her feet as Lark's normally tan face lightened to a ghostly white.

"We're too late," Lark whispered.

Kayda gripped the railing with both hands, her knees wobbling.

"Wait." Lark splayed a hand on her chest and bowed her head. "It's only half." She laughed. "Damn bird had me scared out of my wits."

Kayda frowned. "What's only half?"

Lark twisted sideways to face her, looking sheepish. "Sorry. Muse overshot the city, then swung down on it from the north. She thought the whole place was overrun with the scourge. But it's only Northmoat. Southmoat still stands."

Lark was smiling, obviously elated with the fact that half of the city still stood, but Kayda's blood turned to ice. Kings Keep was in Northmoat. Her home was lost. What of her family? The king and prince? Izora?

"Northmoat is gone?" Kayda gulped and stared down at her boots. "How could that happen?"

Lark's hand landed on her shoulder. "I'm sorry, Kayda. It looks like the fire moat was breached. The scourge are running rampant on the streets."

Conall loosed a loud sigh. "How does Southmoat fare? Can Muse see any people there, still?"

Lark was silent for a moment, then she nodded. "Yeah, there are people there, scattered all over. There're a few ships at the docks, taking on passengers. The fire moat is still lit. But Muse says the streets are practically deserted." She grinned. "Sounds like the mages have been busy."

Kayda's heart lifted, if only for an instant. She sucked in a breath and said a silent prayer that all of those she loved were on one of those boats already.

The mages had accomplished at least one task they could be thankful for. Emptying a city of tens of thousands was no small feat. But had they evacuated everyone out of Northmoat before it fell?

They spent the next hour rousing everyone from below deck and preparing to dock. The Raimish warriors they'd brought with them readied their bows and knives. Everyone watched as Flamesmoat loomed larger on the horizon.

From their southern approach, the devastation Muse reported in Northmoat remained largely hidden. Only the smoke of some smoldering blaze, left to burn unchecked in the distance, rose as evidence that anything was happening in the city's northern section.

The docks were alive with activity as they pulled into port. Jayan parked them on one of the innermost docks in the bay. All the while, Kayda felt that same crawling itch creeping up her back, the sensation becoming nearly overwhelming when she spotted the scourge prowling the Riddle River's banks on the city's Northmoat side.

Kayda was one of the first to hop off the gangplank. She strode down the dock, heading for a group of young people who appeared to be directing foot traffic onto a rickety old wooden ship. Dozens of people rushed about, young and old, loaded down with bags and whatever valuables they could carry.

A man who looked to be in charge whirled around to greet them. But instead of addressing her, he brushed his curly brown locks aside and his brown eyes lit on the young mages behind her. "Oriana, Edrik. You're back!"

"Baris!" Oriana rushed forward and clasped the man in a hug. "We've brought help from Raimire."

"Good, this boat is almost full. We still have some stragglers we need to evacuate." He turned and shaded his eyes, scanning *Nova's Champion* up and down. He whistled. "That's some ship. We'll be able to fit a lot of refugees on that."

Conall strolled up beside her with a smile. "Well, I'll be damned."

Kayda raised a brow. "What is it?"

He pointed at the old, beat-up ship being loaded. "*The Lady Luck*. I hired them to sail me from Doln to the Mido Islands." He chuckled. "I guess the captain couldn't turn down a second payday ferrying refugees."

Kayda spared the ship another glance. It didn't look like much, but—she gasped. "Father?"

She raced forward, her boots slapping loudly against the wooden docks. Prince Gideon wheeled around at the sound of her voice, his brow furrowing until he spotted her racing toward him. Then his face lit with joy.

"Kayda!" He stumbled down the gangplank, reversing course so quickly his round belly nearly knocked the man beside him into the bay.

She hadn't given it much thought at first. Her reaction had been purely instinctual, calling out for the man she'd always considered her father and running to greet him. But as he met her gaze and pulled her into a hug, all the knowledge she'd learned over the last few weeks rushed to the forefront of her mind.

This man was *not* her father. He'd never been her father. She was a sham princess.

As he squeezed her, embracing her so tightly she struggled to breathe, she had to tamp down the desire to scream out the truth. But if she knew anything, she knew now was not the time. She couldn't have that conversation on a crowded dock with the city crumbling beneath them.

"I'm so glad you're back." Gideon held her at arm's length and smiled down at her, his blue eyes misty.

She sent him a tremulous smile, then shifted up on her toes to peek behind him. "Are you the last to leave? Where are Grandfather and Izora?"

The prince sucked in a shaky breath. "I—about that..." He dropped her arms and frowned down at the docks.

"What?" Kayda couldn't keep the hint of anger from her voice.

"I know I promised you I'd look after him. And I did. I swear I did." Gideon curved a hand through his blond hair. "But just before the bridge burned down, Father took off into Northmoat."

Kayda's heart dropped. "He's out there, all alone?"

"Not exactly. Izora followed him."

She turned from her father, doubling over and gripping her knees.

"Kayda, what's wrong?" Lark rushed up the dock toward her, followed by a gaggle of her friends from the boat. She reached Kayda and rubbed her back. "Hey, it's all right."

Kayda allowed Lark to soothe her for a moment, her mind racing. Then she straightened, spinning to face her father.

"How long have they been stranded in there?"

He shook his head. "Not long. Northmoat only fell last night."

Kayda nodded. "Then there's still a chance they're alive." She scanned the city. "I have to find them." She started walking.

"Wait, where are you going?" Lark called out. "Slow down."

Conall jogged up to their group and grabbed her arm before she got far. "Hey, what's wrong?"

Kayda shrugged off his hand. "The king is in Northmoat. I'm going to find him," she announced again.

"You can't," Prince Gideon said. "They burned the bridge down."

"I don't care. I'll find a way."

"Wait, Princess," Conall said.

She glared at him but halted.

"We just got here. Let's get some more information and piece together a plan before we do anything."

Kayda inhaled through her nose, forcing her body to stay still when all she wanted was to move. How long could they last there, surrounded by the scourge?

Conall turned to the prince. "What exactly happened? How did the king end up stuck there?"

Prince Gideon's brow furrowed. "I wasn't there at the time. I can't tell you exactly."

By now, a small group had gathered around them, including several young mages. The brown-haired man who'd greeted them, Baris, stepped forward. "I was there. We gathered everyone in Southmoat before we set fire to the bridge. Somehow, the king snuck back into Northmoat. A couple of mages followed him before the bridge collapsed. After that, we just moved ahead with the plan, hoping they managed to make it to shelter. With how many scourge we killed, they might've had time to hole up somewhere before the fire moat ran out of fuel."

Kayda clenched her fists. It didn't make any sense. "The king just wandered off with no one noticing? The last time I saw him, he would only move if you led him somewhere."

Baris shook his head. "Izora said he'd spoken to her before he left. Told her he was going to the stables."

Lark perked up. "Where are they? Tell me how to get there from here, and I'll send Muse to scout from above."

Baris started detailing directions but Kayda wasn't listening. She stared up at the sky, her mind reeling.

The king had broken free of his stupor! After those days they'd spent together, locked up in the tower room, she'd believed he'd never be the same again. But now he was back! She *had* to save him.

As Muse rose into the sky and disappeared across the river, Mika approached Kayda. "The king, his condition, was he that way from having too many bonds?"

Kayda met his gaze. "He was attacked at the Harvest Festival, but ever since his second bondmate passed, he'd been acting differently. Do you think bonding magic had something to do with why he wouldn't recover?"

"I believe so," Mika said. "I've had some experience with healing his condition. I'd like to come with you. I think I can help."

Baris jumped in. "That's all well and good. I mean, someone ought to save the king, but we've got a host of problems to solve on this side of the city."

"What problems?" Conall asked.

"The fire moat and the tunnels are close to failing. We just don't have enough mages to keep up with the scourge. Now that they've realized there isn't anyone left in Northmoat, they've redoubled their efforts to tunnel in over here."

Kayda stared across the river. He was right. The crowd of scourge snarling at them from the riverbank had already thinned in the time they'd been standing here.

Baris continued, "It's insane, the way they act. I've never seen another animal so coordinated, except maybe a hive of bees when they've been attacked. Like they're all connected, or under orders or something."

"What do you mean?" Kayda asked, a sick sense of dread settling in her stomach.

"They all swarmed Northmoat last night. But after only a few hours, they started retreating. We didn't know where they were going, but this morning a huge crowd of them arrived on this side of the river. They must've doubled back, found a bridge outside of the city to cross. What kind of animal does that?"

Kayda's stomach churned. More evidence of the Unseen at work. But maybe the scourges' cohesion could work to their advantage. It certainly helped that there were a lot less of them in their way of finding the king.

"How close are they to breaking through Southmoat's defenses?" Conall asked.

Baris rubbed his chin. "I'm not sure. I know they can use all the help they can get in the tunnels and moat. I'd be there myself if I hadn't used all the magic I could handle already today."

"I'll go," Edrik offered.

"Me, too," Oriana said.

Conall turned to Lark. "We should head there, too. You can help in the tunnels, and I'll lend a hand at the moat."

Lark nodded. "Agreed, just as soon as I hear back from—wait, Muse reached the stables." A wide grin split her face. "Sounds like they made it. She says all the doors are barred and there's a white flag hanging from a window."

Kayda's heart lifted, and she sighed. There was still a chance.

"How can the rest of us help?" asked Dausius, the leader of Lark's gang of traveling entertainers.

"There are still pockets of citizens refusing to leave. We could use help finding them and convincing them to evacuate," Baris said. "I'm afraid we don't have much time."

All around Kayda, the others discussed plans to split up—who would head where and when to return—but the conversation slid around her, unheard. She was busy trying to think of a way to cross the river. The churning waters were full of rapids and scattered rocks, making boat travel unlikely. But there must be another way. How else had the king crossed with no one seeing?

But though she racked her brain, she just couldn't—unless...

Kayda smiled, a snippet of a conversation from long ago in the king's chambers flashing in her mind. She'd thought it was just more of his mad rambling, but maybe it wasn't. Maybe it was the answer she was searching for.

Mika turned to her. He pointed across the river. "Looks like the path is clear, for now. How are we getting across?"

"I know how to get us there; it's getting back that will be a problem," she admitted.

Prince Gideon leaned forward. "I might have the solution for that."

Kayda turned to her father and lifted a brow. Her entire life, she'd never been able to count on him. Even after he'd apologized for ignoring her, he couldn't handle watching the king like he promised. Could she really trust him to help?

Maybe she could give him another chance. Besides, it wasn't like she had many choices. "I'm listening."

Chapter 4

Lark sighed and shook her head. No wonder her father wanted out of this place. Southmoat was a dump.

Conall, Oriana, and Edrik weaved through the empty streets with her, hurrying to reach the underground tunnels and fire moat. The dilapidated houses loomed over them, just as shabby and run-down as she remembered them from her last trip through the slums.

Back then, she'd been forced to view them from the cramped confines of the back of a horse cart, smashed together with Tiora on her way to becoming a slave in Doln. She shivered, shoving aside the memory of the terror that'd overcome her that night.

Things were different now. No one would force her to do anything ever again.

Edrik stopped at a fork in the road. "Here's where we need to split up. The fire moat is this way." He pointed at the eastern road. "Ori, you should head there with Conall. Your wind talent can help fan the flames. Me and Lark need to go this way." He pointed south. "The closest tunnel entrance is over here."

Lark responded with a curt nod, but inside, her heart thudded wildly. Was she really about to split up with Conall again, after everything he'd gone through to find her?

Conall seemed to sense the uncertainty warring within her. "Hey." He grabbed her arms and stared down at her face. "Don't worry. We'll meet up back at the ship. I won't lose you again."

"All right." She offered him a wobbly smile. "Keep him safe, Shadow," she said to the gray wolf at his side. Maybe it was her imagination, but her brother's bondmate looked like he understood, even inclining his head in her direction.

"What, do you speak to wolves now?" Muse asked from her perch on a ramshackle roof of a nearby house. *"Should I be jealous?"*

Lark rolled her eyes, setting off on the road beside Edrik. *"Don't be silly. You know you're my tweetheart."*

"Ha! Was that a joke? I'm finally rubbing off on you."

Lark cringed inwardly. Yeah, maybe she was. After so long listening to awful puns from her bondmate, it was no wonder she was coming up with a few of her own.

Edrik turned a corner, revealing another street just as run-down as all the rest. But unlike the others they'd passed, this one was occupied. A woman sprawled in the middle of the road, a bevy of sacks loaded full to bursting scattered in the dirt beside her. Two filthy, raggedly clothed children glanced up as they approached, tears painting clean tracks down their dirt-encrusted cheeks.

"Help!" the larger of the two exclaimed. He hopped up and raced toward them. Lark guessed he was likely around ten-years-old, and the little girl who stayed crouched by the woman's side, probably only around five.

"Please, you've gotta help us!" he pleaded. "My momma fell down on our way to the docks. She hurt her leg."

"It's all right," Lark said with a gentle smile. "I'm a healer. I'll take a look at her leg."

"Thank you! Thank you so much," the little boy gushed, rushing back to his mother's side.

Lark knelt down beside the woman's face. "Hello, my name is Lark."

The woman's brown eyes shot open. A sheen of sweat covered her forehead, even though her threadbare cloak appeared far too thin for the chill in the air. Her teeth gritted shut, and her brows pinched tightly together. "My ankle." She moaned. "We were rushing, and I tripped over something in the road. I felt something snap. I think I broke it."

"Do you mind if I take a look? I'm a healer."

The woman nodded, wincing.

Lark moved beside the woman's leg, gently lifting her wool pants. She scowled at the swollen flesh she found underneath. "I'm afraid you're right. It's either broken or badly sprained."

"Oh, what am I going to do?"

"Hey, don't worry." Lark kept her voice as soothing as possible. "Did I mention I'm a mage?" She quirked a brow, aiming a smile at the boy and little girl—who hadn't yet said a word, only sat clutching her mother's hand with trembling fingers. "I'll get you all fixed up in just a moment."

She shucked her bag off her back and dug inside. To heal bones, she needed greens or beans, and for the swelling she'd need—

An explosion of sound blasted through the air, followed by a vibration in the ground so strong it shook the earth where they sat.

"What was that?" the little boy asked, his voice thready and quavering.

Edrik, the only one still standing, wobbled beside her. He stared at a brick building at the end of the road—one that had a cloud of dust escaping from the open door and windows.

"Lark, that's where we're headed," he said after he caught his balance. "I don't know what that was, but I should probably go check it out."

"Go," she waved a hand, shooing him toward the dust-clouded building. "This will only take a moment, then I'll meet you there."

"Are you sure?" he asked, but he was already in motion, turning backward for a final glance in her direction.

"Yes. Go. I'm right behind you."

Edrik took off at a jog, and within moments, he ducked inside the doorway and out of sight.

"Where were we?" Lark said, more to herself than the confused faces crowded around her. That's right—swelling. She rummaged in her pack again, found what she needed, and exhaled, then met the woman's wide eyes. "I just need to press this to your injury. It will hurt for a moment, but then you'll be good as new."

The woman set her jaw. "Yes. I'm ready. Just get it over with."

Lark pressed her hand against the wound, ignoring the woman's yelp of pain. She closed her eyes and wished. The earth trembled again, much fainter than before, but still enough to be discernible. The vibration flowed through her, coalescing on her palm and flooding into the wound beneath her. When she lifted her hand, the flesh was no longer swollen.

"Try moving your ankle, please," she instructed.

The woman complied, her eyes widening even further as her ankle twisted and turned. "It's like I never hurt it. Bless you!"

Lark's cheeks warmed as she cinched her bag closed and brushed the dirt off her knees. She stood, glancing at the overloaded bags once more. "You should be able to make it to the docks now, but you might consider leaving some of this stuff behind. I'd hate for you to fall again."

The woman flushed, nodding sheepishly. "That's good advice. I promise I'll heed it. Thank you!"

"You're welcome." Lark flashed the kids a smile and set off after Edrik.

Her heart lifted. Just a few weeks ago, she would've been helpless in that same situation. She couldn't be thankful enough for all the knowledge Mika had taught her. Not to mention the confidence he'd helped instill in her.

Of course, she had someone else to thank for that as well. After all, it's not every day her mother sent her a message from the grave.

"Muse, I'm going underground, you better stay—"

Noise from somewhere close by halted her. A pained voice, crying out.

"Did you hear that?" She swiveled her head around, looking for the source but finding nothing.

Muse darted off. *"Yeah. Let me see what I can find."*

Lark stopped just outside the doorway to the brick building. Whatever explosion happened inside hadn't repeated itself, but dust still swirled in the doorway, motes catching in the sun's rays and dancing in the air. She leaned closer, listening carefully for any sign of distress coming from within. After a moment, she heard a male voice speaking calmly and someone else chuckled gently in response, though they were too far away for her to make out their words.

"I found something," Muse said.

"What is it?"

"A tall building, just up the road from where you are. There are people on the top floor. I think they're trapped."

Lark gulped, sparing a glance at the doorway. But her feet were already moving. *"I'm coming."*

She broke into a run, her boots pounding on the dirt road, ignoring the twinge of guilt in her stomach and the tiny voice in her mind that told her to return to the tunnels.

There were people—her friends among them—out here searching for stragglers. She was supposed to be helping the mages underground. But she couldn't just leave those people there to die. What if they weren't discovered in time? Surely, she could free them quickly and return before the mages realized she was missing.

As she drew closer, the voice reached her ears, clear as day. "Help!" he cried, over and over, the voice hoarse and distinctly masculine.

She arrived in front of a circular tower built of stone and mortar and spotted Muse circling it. It had to be at least four stories tall, far larger than any of the buildings surrounding it. The scent of decay hung heavy in the air. One she recognized intimately from her time in the Boglands. The road ended beyond the stone tower, and the tops of mangrove trees rose on the horizon behind it.

"Are we back at the bog?" she asked.

"Yep, this building is built right on the border. It's all water on the other side."

"I didn't realize we'd made it that far south." She slowed down and climbed the steps to the doorway. The door was barred, a wooden bar nailed down over the entrance.

"What in the world?" she said aloud, all thought of the Boglands driven from her mind.

"The door's barred with a wooden beam," she explained to Muse. *"Why would someone lock people inside of here when everyone is supposed to be evacuating?"*

She craned her neck up and shaded her eyes. The unmistakable shape of a hand slipped out of a top floor window and waved down at her. "Help! Please, help! We're in here."

"Are you going in there? I've got a bad feeling about this," Muse said.

"I'll be all right. I can't leave those people in there to die." She scanned the doorway, searching for a way in. The door looked like it was made to swing outward, but maybe with a little magical push, she could knock it off the hinges and slip inside.

Lark hopped down the stone steps and scooped up a handful of dirt. She rose to her feet and turned, but then she swiveled back around and leaned over again, slipping a few handfuls of dirt in her cloak pockets—just in case.

Then she returned to the door, exhaling a deep breath and slipping her hand beneath the beam on the wooden door next to the lower hinges. She closed her eyes, visualizing the door breaking. A tremor filled her, rattling her jaw and thrumming through her blood.

Crack. She opened her eyes and smiled. The door still hung there, but the lower half tilted ajar, the hinge blasted to nothing. She knelt down and pushed. The heavy door protested, but with a shove of her shoulder, it opened just wide enough for her to shimmy inside.

Lark's eyes took a moment to adjust inside the dimly lit interior. The room looked curiously more like a dock than the inside of a building.

Brick shelving lined the wall next to the door, with piles of neatly stacked poles, rope, and tackle resting next to buckets full of dirt that likely held live bait. Skinny canoes hung on the rest of the walls, smaller than the ones Fillan and Dal had ferried them through the bog on. Half of the back wall was open, and a hole in the floor on the far side even allowed some of the sulfuric water to creep inside, providing a second entrance to the building. One that led directly to the bog.

A shadow darted inside the opening, setting Lark's heart racing. She shrieked.

"It's just me." Muse landed gracefully on a rafter crisscrossing the high ceiling.

"You scared me half to death," Lark admitted with a chuckle, a hand clutched to her chest as her racing heart slowed.

She spun in a slow circle, scanning the building's interior. In here, the lapping water and the distant croaks of bog life dominated her ears. The cries from upstairs were so muffled she could barely hear their echo.

At first glance, she didn't see any way to climb to the top floors. But as her eyes fully adjusted to the dim light flowing in from the hole in the wall, she spotted a rope dangling down, and the shape of a wooden rectangle set in the ceiling.

Walking beneath it, she raised up on her tip-toes, reaching for the rope. It dangled just out of her reach.

"Of all the times to be short," she grumbled under her breath.

"Ha, you need a hand there, runt?"

"Very funny." She crossed her arms. *"See if you can pull that down for me, would ya?"*

Muse flew down from her perch, clasping the rope in her beak and flapping her wings furiously. But after a few moments, she dropped the rope and returned to her perch. *"It's too heavy. Too bad. It looks like those folks upstairs are out of luck."*

Lark's heart sank. She couldn't just give up. *"Can you fly out of here and find Aren or Daus, bring them back with you?"*

"You don't quit, do you? Fine, I'll be back."

"Thanks, Muse."

Lark sighed, watching her bondmate disappear outside. So much for being back before the mages noticed she was missing. She tapped her foot, scanning the walls again. All those canoes. They must use this place for fishing.

A smile crept across Lark's face as a thought crossed her mind. She approached the closest canoe, and bending her knees, hefted the small vessel off the wall. It almost knocked her over, but she managed to slide the craft onto the stone floor, upside down. Then it was only a matter of scooting it across the floor, and she stepped atop the bottom of the boat, and grabbed the rough rope in her hands.

She pulled. The wooden hatch door swung down, and a folded wooden staircase came with it, unfolding so quickly she had to jump down off the boat to avoid being struck. It smashed into the canoe with a loud *crack*.

Lark wobbled on her feet, her heart slamming to life. She came dangerously close to falling into the bog before she righted herself. Blowing out a shaky breath, she shoved the boat sideways so that the ladder could completely unfold.

The cries returned, louder than before. She could hear not just one, but dozens of voices screaming for release.

She mounted the stairs, taking her time, the rickety stair swaying with every footfall. The second floor was even dimmer than the first, and she cursed herself for not bringing a torch. The only light filtered in through the barred windows.

As her eyes adjusted, she gasped. She stood in a hall surrounded by dozens of cells, all of them empty, the metal doors shut tightly. On the wall beside the door, dozens of weapons hung. Cudgels and staves mostly, many of them covered in dark brown stains.

A sick feeling rose in her gut. She was in a prison.

The scared little girl inside of her screamed to turn around and leave. To abandon these criminals to their fate.

But beneath the fear, a different voice was there, convincing her to stay. Telling her that these men were someone's father. Someone's brother. Did they really deserve to be left here to die? Starving to death, locked up in a cell, alone and forgotten while the rest of the city fled. Or worse yet, torn to shreds and eaten alive by the scourge.

Lark remembered the woman on the docks in Bogsmouth. She'd watched helplessly as a horde of the vicious beasts ravaged her.

She shook her head. No one deserved that death. No one.

Lark found a stairwell leading up. She passed another floor, opened the door from the stair, and peered within. All the cells were just as quiet and empty as on the last. In a matter of moments, she found herself on the top floor. Here the voices of men greeted her as she pushed open the stairwell door.

"Help, please help us!" called out the voice she recognized hearing outside.

She strode over to the nearest cell. Inside, there was a man, bearded and clothed in tattered rags, his right arm torn to shreds. Dried blood encrusted the sleeve of his gray prison coveralls. The cold wind whistled through his window. He clearly used his bare hands to smash a hole in the glass between the metal bars.

A chorus of pleas surrounded her, all the men shouting and screaming at her.

"Help!"

"Free us!"

"I don't want to die," one cried out, voice thick with fear and desperation.

Lark shuddered, her heart breaking for these poor, abandoned men. Who could leave someone here, alone, to die?

She grabbed the metal bars of the man's cell by the broken window, tugging with all her might. It was no use. The door was locked. She reached into her cloak pocket, the cool soil sliding in her fingers.

The man within raced over and shoved his face against the bars just beside her. His eyes were wide, cheeks streaked with tears.

Lark gasped, backing up a pace.

"Hey, you're here. Thank the Lord Dragon!" His chin wobbled, and his hands trembled. His voice choked with emotion. "The keys!" He pointed behind her to a set of keys dangling from a hook on the wall beside the doorway. "There, grab the keys!"

Lark nodded, strode back to the doorway, and removed the key ring. Then she slid the key into the man's cell door.

The door swung open, and the man stepped out. His face, which only moments ago had been the picture of suffering, morphed before her eyes. His gaze landed on her, and he licked his lips, smirking. "Well, well, well. Looks like my prayers have been answered. What do you say, boys?" Hand moving lightning quick, he snatched the keys from her grasp. "It's time to have some fun."

As the pleas for help died down, replaced with raucous laughter, Lark gulped.

Blazes. She just made a terrible mistake.

Chapter 5

Conall followed Oriana through the ramshackle streets of Southmoat. Silence surrounded them. And not just from the empty buildings and deserted streets.

Shadow strolled beside him, just as quiet as Oriana. He'd left Sunny back on *Nova's Champion*, sleeping peacefully on the deck. But even the presence of his bondmate and the thought of his beloved mutt couldn't calm the discomfort roiling in his belly every time he glanced over at the silent girl beside him.

He cleared his throat, slowing as the first flicker of flame rose in the air beyond their path. "I'm sorry for the things I said earlier."

Oriana's step faltered, and she nearly fell face-first on the dirt road before she righted herself. "What?"

Conall winced, watching her wobble. Even apologizing, he still managed to frighten the girl. "You just wanted to know about your brother. I shouldn't have chewed your head off."

Oriana's chin quivered, and she sniffed.

Blazes. What did he do now? He didn't want to make her cry—again.

But then she flashed him a smile and shook her head. "No, I'm glad you didn't hold back." And the next words she uttered made him certain the moisture in her eyes were tears of pride, not sadness. "Our Quent—a hero. I'm glad he had you for a friend, Conall."

He rubbed the back of his neck, his own eyes feeling a tad teary. Surely it was just from the fire moat they were fast approaching. "He's a good lad. I'm glad to know him, too."

Oriana sent him one last bright grin, then faced forward, her step quickening. "C'mon, we're almost there."

As they passed the last buildings, the road ended. Instead of more city spread out before them, a chest-high wall of flame burned, forming half of a semicircle and shielding the city's lower section.

The flame's warmth kissed his cheeks. Conall turned his head slowly, gazing in awe at the incredible display of magic.

He'd been to Flamesmoat countless times in his life. Before now, the ancient moat had been barely discernible; a shallow depression ringing the city, overgrown with grass and weeds. Now, the moat stood out starkly against the surrounding ground, the dirt freshly dug, so deep that even without the flames, the average man would likely struggle to climb out.

The mages had been busy. The lengths they took to protect the common folk of Dracwood were impressive, to say the least. If only they hadn't been the ones responsible for the Palisade's fall, he might think them all heroes.

A petite young woman noticed them approaching and cut off the stream of fire flowing from her hands to turn and greet them. She rubbed the sweat-slicked brown hair off her brow. Even in the chilly air this far north in the late fall, she sweated, clothed only in a short-sleeved tunic and what appeared to be light cotton trousers.

"Oriana, is that you?" she asked.

"Karina, I'm back from Raimire. We've come to help man the moat."

Karina drew closer and shivered. She chuckled, rubbing her bare arms. "You tend to forget it's almost winter when you spend half the day roasting next to the moat." She smiled crookedly. "Forgive my rambling. You've come to help, you said?" Karina flicked a glance at Conall and Shadow, her brows lifting, face lighting with what might be curiosity. "Both of you?"

Oriana nodded. "This is Conall. He can summon fire."

"Conall. I remember you from Mage Keep." She stuck out a pale hand expectantly.

Conall grasped her hand and shook firmly. "Can't say I can admit the same."

Karina released his hand. "You wouldn't. We weren't properly introduced." Her gaze flicked down, and she crossed her arms. "I was there, watching, when the Palisade fell. I'm sorry for what happened to you."

Conall tilted his head, examining Karina. This was the first time anyone who'd sided with Ereni had apologized for the trial they forced him to undertake.

Karina stared at the ground for a long moment before lifting her gaze to meet his. He could sense her apology was sincere. This girl, who didn't know him beyond watching him age before her eyes, seemed to be the picture of remorse. Could it be that the mages who had followed Ereni had as little say in what had happened to him as he had?

Conall flashed her a tiny smile. "It's ancient history. How can I help?"

Karina pointed south. "The two mages stationed next to the Boglands are due for a break. If you follow the moat until you hit the bog, you'll find them."

He and Oriana headed south. They passed several pairs of mages stationed alongside the moat, directing streams of fire and air. Most paid them no mind, their stares locked on the moat, intent on their task, keeping the city safe.

It wasn't long before twisted mangroves appeared on the horizon, and the distinctive stench of decay filled his nostrils. The walkway ended at the edge of a small cliff, and beyond that, the bog stretched out far as the eye could see. Murky water was dotted with so many mangroves it looked more like a maze than a proper waterway.

They stopped. Oriana spoke briefly with the two mages they'd been sent to replace. The hum of their pleasantries buzzed around him, but he was too distracted to focus on the words spoken.

They were so close to the fire moat now that the flames, which only provided a pleasant warmth on their walk, blazed with enough heat that he had the urge to remove his thick wool cloak.

But more than that, the scourge were finally visible, sending a chill through his veins that lessened the effect of the heat before him. Their musky scent competed with the stench of the bog for dominance, and their snarls roared in his ears. And underneath it all, the faint scratch of digging reverberated, causing the pit in his stomach to grow.

Worry swamped him for his sister, sudden and sharp. Would she be all right in the tunnels?

Shadow stopped beside him. His lips curled back in a snarl as he spotted the vermin crawling all over the ground beyond the moat. *"Ugly little beasts, aren't they?"*

"Yeah." Conall bit back a grimace.

The creatures they'd feared for so long were small—barely bigger than squirrels—but much more vicious. Covered in black and silver striped fur, their teeth snapped as they crawled atop each other, each of them vying to reach the moat. Their beady black eyes roved all around, and their wicked claws dug at the dirt or slashed through the air in a constant show of aggression.

He squinted, trying to see as far beyond the moat as he could. The entirety of Flamesmoat was bordered by large swaths of farm and pasture land, which would normally be used to feed the city, either with crops or livestock.

Now, as far as he could see, stretching back to the beginnings of the thick forests that rose beyond the fields, the scourge swarmed. They covered the ground like a living blanket, squirming and snarling, altering the landscape from the unrelieved browns and greens of fallow fall fields to a scene from a nightmare.

"Be careful, and good luck," one of the retreating mages called over his shoulder with a wave as he hustled off.

"What was that about?" Conall glanced briefly at Oriana.

"Weren't you listening to anything they said?"

Conall grimaced, sending her a half-hearted shrug. "I got a little distracted," he admitted, his gaze returning to the scourge beyond the flames.

"They said the scourge have been acting strangely today. Even more so than usual."

"Oh?" He turned to look at her, his curiosity piqued. "How so?"

It was her turn to shrug. "They couldn't put their finger on it exactly. But they both agreed they seem less combative today. Almost like they're working in unison."

Conall's skin prickled with gooseflesh. The Unseen. Was that phantom here, now? Pulling the strings on the scourge like so many puppets, there to do its bidding?

The fire before them wobbled, the chest-high flame guttering and fading to merely waist-high. Oriana lifted her hands. A tingle of static flashed across Conall's skin before the wind whipped to life, fanning the flames before them.

"C'mon." She stopped beside a lit torch the retreating mages left half-planted into the ground. "We've got a job to do."

Conall stepped beside her. His lashes fluttered closed for an instant as he visualized the flames he wanted. Then he brought forth the image of Lark's face. He needed to do his part to keep the city safe. To keep her safe. A chill settled over his skin and sank into his chest. Then twin flames shot from his palms, flowing freely, joining with the massive fire wall before him. Within moments, the two of them returned the wall to its former height.

Conall grinned. This wasn't so hard.

But then the moment stretched out, time passing slowly. Fatigue set in. The cost of summoning so much magic weighed on him. His back and legs ached. Not for the first time, he cursed the changes that had aged his body far more than his mind. If he didn't have these old bones, he might not be so wiped already.

Finally, Oriana dropped her hands and stepped back. "Time for a quick break. You, too." She set a hand on his shoulder. "We have to pace ourselves. If we don't rest every now and then, we'll be worn out too quickly."

The flames shooting from Conall's hands disappeared. His arms fell slack at his side, and he slumped to the ground, resting on his knees.

"Are you all right, little brother?" Shadow asked, sidling up beside him.

"Yeah. Just a need a moment to rest." He pulled out his waterskin and gulped down a long swig. *"You thirsty?"*

Shadow's tail wagged. *"Yes."*

"Here." Conall cupped his hand and filled it with the cool water, which Shadow lapped up quickly.

As he refilled his palm, Oriana chuckled. "Sometimes I forget Shadow isn't a dog, with how he acts. I can't believe you trained a *wolf* to eat out of your hand."

Conall smiled. "I didn't train him at all. Shadow's my bondmate."

Oriana settled down next to him cross-legged, quirking a brow. "What's the difference?"

"It's hard to describe. He's more like a brother to me than an animal. We share our thoughts. Our hopes and fears. He's always there for me, and me for him."

"That sounds incredible."

"It is. I wish more people could know what it's like. But from what I've seen, the talent is extremely rare. Much rarer than summoning the elements." It was strange to think that all the people he'd met so far with bonding magic were actually his siblings. But he'd met mages who hailed from all over the world.

"You're lucky to have both talents, then."

"Yeah, really lucky."

He sighed. Sometimes it didn't feel that way. Especially when the only people he knew who possessed both talents were the same people who'd been embroiled in the mage's schemes: Kayda, Lark, and himself.

"We better get back to it." Oriana rose to her feet and stretched.

Conall shoved his waterskin back into his pack and set it on the ground beside Shadow. He rose to return, then turned back. He shucked off his thick cloak, folded it, and rested it atop his bag. The fire moat would keep him warm enough.

Then he was back beside Oriana, fire once again flowing from his hands. The work was tiring physically, but he found once he started summoning, continuing didn't require much mental concentration. It wasn't long before his mind began to wander.

He couldn't help but see the irony in his situation. Here he was, with the same mages that'd brought down the Palisade, working to keep a different wall standing. It was funny how things happened like that; everything repeating, coming around full circle. He hated to say it, but it felt—fated.

He kept telling himself it was ridiculous to believe his future was preordained. But he'd drunk the dream elixir. He saw the battle in his vision. His stomach clenched. Was his future really set in stone, or could things change?

His gaze was drawn to the scourge, the lot of them, blanketing the earth with fur and claws and teeth. Their numbers were daunting. How could they hope to defeat them? Especially now that they knew the beast's vicious nature was not controlled by instinct alone. They would never give up. Never surrender. Not with the Unseen driving them.

What did the Unseen want? Why did he seek to destroy them? It was all so strange and confusing, trying to predict the motivations of something so unknown.

From across the fire, one of the scourge opposite him stilled, its beady eyes locking onto his. He gazed into the black depths of its stare and thought he spied something there. A hint of intelligence the rest of its brethren lacked.

He tried to shake the thought from his mind but couldn't. It stuck there like a thorn caught on his trousers. He went to move his gaze instead, to break the stare he held with the beast, but found his gaze just as fixed. Panic gripped him, and his muscles tensed, his heart pounding out of control.

"You've returned," boomed a harsh, gravelly voice in his mind. And though he'd never heard the voice before, instinctively he knew who it was. The Unseen.

Fear joined the panic slithering up his spine. That sick feeling he remembered so well crawled up with it, making his stomach spin.

"What do you want?" he spat.

"Conall?" Shadow paced to his side, backing away from the heat still streaming from his hands. *"What's wrong?"*

But he couldn't answer. Not while that vile voice infected his mind. He wouldn't let the Unseen hear him speak to his bondmate.

"Who is that?" The Unseen asked, curiosity clear in his tone. *"Who's speaking to you?"*

"That's none of your concern."

"Ah. I see." Laughter filled his mind. A gurgling chortle that made his skin crawl. *"We have more in common than you'd like to admit."*

"I have nothing in common with you."

"That's not true. We're cut from the same cloth. One day soon, you shall see."

Conall shuddered, trying with all his might to break free from the hypnotic stare he was locked in. To break the hold that allowed this thing to pollute his mind. Shadow circled him, ducking beneath the flames flowing from his hands, whining and shoving at his legs.

"You will come to me," the Unseen said, voice thick with glee.

Oriana's head spun to him, no doubt alerted by Shadow's strange behavior. She frowned. "Conall?"

Shadow rammed into him again, harder than ever. But though the blow would've been enough to topple him at any other time, he stood fast, his stance just as locked as the rest of his body and mind.

"You'll join me," the Unseen said.

"Never!" Conall shouted.

That laughter reverberated in his mind. Madness echoed inside his head. He wanted to claw his eyes out to break the stare. To silence that sickening voice.

Oriana's brows furrowed. Her gaze locked on Shadow as he reared back for another shove. Just as he connected, she turned her hands on Conall, blasting him with a wall of wind.

Slam. He landed in the dirt, hard on his back. The fire flowing from his hands halted, his chest heaved. Without the scourge's stare, he broke free from the Unseen's hold. The laughter cut off in his mind, and the sick crawling itch dissipated from his skin, vanishing as quickly as it had come over him.

Oriana and Shadow appeared at his side and tugged on his legs. He peeked behind him, and his heart skipped a beat. He'd fallen a mere handbreadth away from the cliff leading to the bog. Scrambling away from the edge, he rolled onto his knees and met Oriana's and Shadow's gazes.

"Thank you," he said.

"Thanks, brother," he thought.

"What was that?" Oriana asked.

"Was that the Unseen?" Shadow asked in unison.

Conall held up a hand, still reeling from the unexpected invasion. After a few deep breaths, he answered his bondmate first. *"Yes, I don't know how, but he used one of the scourge to connect with me."*

"Are you all right, little brother?"

"Yes. I am. Thanks to you." He reached over and pet Shadow behind the ears, the simple action bringing him a measure of comfort.

He turned to Oriana and scrubbed his face. "I don't even know where to begin. It's a long story, one I don't have the energy to dredge up at the moment. Just... thank you for what you did. It was the right call."

He spotted the mages they'd replaced earlier returning. They were chatting among themselves, smiling and laughing. But then one mage—the same man who'd warned them to be careful—flicked his gaze away from his companion and at the wall of flame. His eyes widened, his tanned face blanching. He raised a hand, finger pointed at the wall, a wordless scream forming on his lips.

Conall's gaze shot from the mages to the moat. At first, he noted nothing out of sorts. The fire still burned, just as strongly as before. But then he looked beyond the fire, and his stomach sank.

The scourge piled atop each other, forming a massive mound of creatures that reached high in the air. High enough he could see a tiny sliver of shining silver fur peek out above the chest-high wall of flame. Before he could do anything other than gasp, the top creature leaped straight for the fire.

It slammed into the fire moat, lighting up instantly, its dying screech pained and shrill.

"What are they doing?" Oriana yelled, bouncing to her feet.

Conall scrambled up as well, his stare locked on the climbing vermin as the scent of burning hair and roasting flesh clogged the air.

The pile beyond the flames steadily grew. More *ichneumon* ran to join their brethren, stacking atop each other higher and higher. In the space of a few heartbeats, the pile grew so tall he could clearly see the top few rows of beasts above the flames.

When the next beast jumped, it cleared the flames and landed on the ground at their feet. Shadow jumped for it in a flash, and the beast zeroed in on him, the two animals quickly turning into a snarling blur of ferocity.

"Breach!" one of the approaching mages screamed. "Quick, make the wall higher!"

All four of them summoned. The flames appeared in Conall's hands, quicker than ever before, with his fear for his bondmate at the forefront of his mind. He had to protect him.

The moat roared to life, the flames rising to reach the height of the pile. But not before a half dozen beasts cleared the wall and landed on the ground beside them. Three of them tore off straight for Shadow, but the other three bolted toward Conall and the mages.

Conall turned from the wall, still summoning fire. He aimed his hands at the scourge. A smile lit his lips as they burst into flames and shrieked, screaming in pain.

That still left the rest of them on his bondmate. While they'd been focused on the wall, he'd managed to latch his teeth around the first of the vermin. He clamped the beast in his powerful jaws, blood gushing out from his mouth as he shook his head wildly.

But with three more after him, Shadow struggled. He ducked and weaved, inching ever closer to the cliffside that bordered the bog. He dodged two of the beasts, but the third vaulted atop his back, digging its wicked claws in an instant before it bit the nape of Shadow's neck.

He dropped the carcass in his jaw, letting out an ear-splitting howl.

"Shadow!" Conall raced closer, shooting a ball of flame at one beast as it reared back for a second leap at his bondmate. The satisfying sound of its shriek filled the air as the flames roasted its face, and the beast dropped to the ground. He sent a second blast engulfing the vermin's body.

Another growl tore from his bondmate. The second scourge leaped on Shadow, its claws dug into his flank, teeth latched onto his hind leg.

He couldn't strike them with fire now. Not with them on Shadow. He'd hit him, too. He could run back and grab a waterskin, but that would waste too much time. Even the air, always present, might end in a disaster with Shadow so close to the cliff. If he pushed him off with a blast of air, Shadow would tumble down to the bog.

The mages furiously flung magic at the fire moat, fanning the flames ever higher. He'd have no help there. What could he do?

Desperate, he lunged, intending to rip the bastards off with his bare hands if he had to. No one messed with his bondmate.

He saw what was happening an instant too late. The beast on Shadow's leg bit down harder, just as he attempted to shake it off. His leg buckled. Shadow dropped sideways and fell off the cliff, splashing into the bog below with the beasts still latched onto him.

Conall screamed, "Shadow, no!" He landed on his stomach on the cliff's edge, right where Shadow had just been. He stared down with wide eyes, watching the current tug him away.

He didn't give his decision a second thought. He scrambled up on his feet and jumped. *"Brother, I'm coming!"*

Chapter 6

Lark shuddered as the man's smirk spread. His chapped lips cracked and bled, but he didn't even wince, only grinned ever wider, giving her a glimpse of his rotten teeth.

Immediately, her mind flashed back to the last man who'd looked at her like that. To that tiny warehouse room in Southmoat, where two vile men kept her against her will. She stood frozen, staring, her heart beating like a caged bird desperate to escape.

Then the man turned from her, his head and shoulders thrust back, reveling in the laughter and hoots of his cellmates.

Her gaze locked on that sickening grin, she started to back away.

"Hey," he crowed, his head swinging around to watch her, "don't leave so soon. The fun's just getting started."

He grabbed her cloak—just as fast as he'd snatched the keys from her hands—and shoved her into the cell she'd freed him from. He seized her pack while she staggered on her feet and ripped it off her back. Before she could right her balance, the door slammed closed behind her. The man sent her an evil smirk as she spun around, and he dropped her bag on the wall hook where the keyring had once hung.

"Hey, what'd you do that for?" called out a dark-skinned man a few cells down. "I want a taste of that little morsel."

The freed man laughed. "Can't have the first few ruining the meal while I free the rest of you blokes, now, can we?" He twirled the key ring on his fingers. "This way, we all get a taste."

More laughter and cheers met that statement as the man moved to the first cell door, and then went about methodically opening them, one by one.

Terror threatened to immobilize Lark. Her breath came hard and fast, her gaze darting across the men's faces. They stared back at her with violence and something more sinister in their eyes.

No. No! She stared down at the hard stone floor, forcing herself to take a calming breath.

She was not the same powerless girl who'd been tricked into bondage all those months ago. These men would not get what they wanted from her. She'd rather die fighting.

"Muse? I'm in a bit of a tough spot here... Please tell me you've found someone."

"I've got Daus. We're headed back. What's the trouble?"

"Remember that bad feeling you had?"

"Yeah..."

"You were right. I get the feeling these people were left here for a good reason."

"Bird brains! You went up alone?"

"Yes, just hurry back with Daus. I'm seriously outnumbered here, and I'm gonna need your help."

Lark slipped her hands into her cloak pockets, sinking her fingers into the smooth soil she'd picked up outside. The echoes of laughter and the squeals of the rusty metal doors swinging open reverberated in the air.

Let them come. They were in for a big surprise.

Moments ticked by. Her stomach roiled, but she set her stance, boots firm and hands clenched around the cool dirt. Except for a pair of men who only spared her a quick glance before they hustled to the stairwell door then quickly disappeared, all the freed men gathered around her cell. They yelled out taunts, licking their lips and tugging at their groins.

Lark waited.

Finally, the first man returned, the key ring swinging. Flecks of dried blood flicked off his sleeve, and his smirk spread wide. "Fellas. I'm sure you'll all agree, seeing as it was my plan that saw us free, first turn goes to me."

"Aww, there's plenty to go around, Ulric. You really gonna make us all wait?" yelled out a man in the back of the crowd. There had to be at least twenty, probably closer to thirty men in front of her cell. The sight of so many sent a spike of fear up Lark's spine.

Ulric's grin turned feral. He shouldered through the crowd to the front of the cell. "You blokes can divvy up the spoils how you like once I'm done. I won't be long."

Lark's stomach turned at the undisguised glee on their faces. And the way they spoke about her—like she was a thing and not a person—was sickening.

Ulric slid the key inside the door. The dark-skinned man grabbed his elbow before he could swing the door open, and Ulric turned a menacing stare his way. The man dropped his arm immediately and retreated a step. "You sure you don't want a few of us in there? Lass looks like a fighter."

The smirk was back, and a cruel glint lit Ulric's eyes. "Perfect. Just the way I like it."

Then the door swung open, and Ulric slid in, then pulled the door firmly closed behind him. He stalked closer, the key ring enclosed within his fist with the sharp ends sticking out menacingly.

"What's your name, Pretty?" he asked.

Lark panicked. Her mind raced as she tried to plan something to say that would make this vile man think twice about laying a finger on her. An image of Meital flashed in her mind. The way she'd dealt with those creeps back in that little inn. Fierce and fearless.

Lark stared Ulric in the eyes and channeled Meital, her voice just as sharp and sweet as hers had been. A dagger drenched in honey. "Call me Death."

The fiend laughed in her face and circled around her, the keys pointed at her neck. "Lady Death. Do you hear that, fellas?" He rounded her back, his gaze roaming over her body with overt lust. "Won't be the first time I screwed death."

Lark swallowed a grimace as laughter exploded from the men. Not quite the effect she was going for there. Maybe she could try another tactic.

"Is that right?" Lark purred. "Or has Death been waiting to screw you?" She forced a coy smile across her lips as Ulric turned to face her. She ignored the cold metal key poking into her neck and spread her hand over his chest, caressing him softly.

"Ha, she ain't a fighter, boys. She's a whore," yelled one of the men.

"We're almost there, Lark. Hold on!" Muse called out through their bond.

"We'll see about that," Ulric smirked again, his lips aimed at her own.

She closed her eyes and wished. A vibration thrummed through her body, racing into Ulric's chest through her palm before his vile lips descended on her. She threw everything she had into it, and her eyes flew open as Ulric slammed into the metal bars, grasping his chest, a look of horror on his face.

"Mage! The bitch is mage!" someone screamed. A few men scattered, but the dark-skinned man reached his hand into the bars, swiping the key ring from Ulric's dying grasp. Before they could get far, the stairwell door swung open.

Dausius and Muse! They'd come to—

A stranger leaped through the doorway. It was a young woman, her long brown hair pulled back in a ponytail. Her blue eyes were cold as steel, and in her hands, she wielded a swirling ball of vapor.

She took one glance inside and sent air blasting into the crowd. Chaos ensued. Lark used it to her advantage, flinging darts of dirt at the men still crowded around the bars of her cell. Cries of pain rang out, and bodies fell, smashing into the cold stone floor.

The dark-skinned man still grasped the key, clamping it tight to his chest. But with the bodies tumbling around him, he tripped, and the ring went flying. It skittered across the stone toward the brunette. Lark's heart skipped a beat. She needed those keys!

The brunette spotted the ring hurtling toward her and caught it with a blast of air, sending it flying back into the cell. "Get out of there, quick!" she ordered.

Lark scrambled to grab the key ring. By now, all the prisoners either sprawled on the ground or had been blasted deeper into the hall, held immobile by the mage's constant stream of wind. Lark's shaking hands slipped the key in the lock. It turned. She stepped over Ulric's dead body and out of the cell. She was free!

Then the same heavy wind keeping the prisoners back caught her. If she hadn't still clutched the cell door, she would've surely lost her footing and slammed back into the crowd of prisoners.

But then the mage cut off the wind. "Let's go!" she screamed, frantically waving her arms.

Lark didn't need to be told twice. She raced to the stairwell, only pausing to swipe her bag off the wall.

The mage slammed the door closed behind them. She sent another blast of air at the door. "Do you have more earth? Jam the door, quick!"

Lark dug in her pocket and flung earth at the door's seams, picturing it caked fast with mud.

A moment later, the brunette tugged her elbow. She pulled her away from the door and down the stairs. "That won't hold them forever. Hurry."

They raced down the stairs, taking them two at a time. Lark bit back a gasp as they passed the two men who'd fled on the stairwell, lying in matching pools of blood, their throats slit.

The brunette stepped over their slack bodies without a word. Had she killed them?

Soon they descended down the rickety wooden staircase to the bottom floor. As they hopped off and the girl turned around to send the folding stair back up into the ceiling, Lark spotted a problem.

The racks of shelves she'd noticed when she'd entered had been smashed to pieces. The supplies that had once been neatly stacked, lay scattered and broken. Piles of brick littered the floor in front of the door, blocking the bottom section she'd knocked askew. She reached into her pocket again, preparing to call on her talent to move the bricks.

"No." The brunette grabbed her arm. "We can't let those men into Southmoat. There's not enough time for us to climb out and barricade the door again."

The pounding of footsteps echoed above them. She was right. The men had already broken the door holding them upstairs. It wouldn't be long before they made it downstairs.

"What are we going to do?" Lark eyed the canoes on the wall, seeing only one other viable exit. "The Boglands are a maze. We'll be lost if we try to escape that way. Do you mean to stay and fight?"

Her stomach churned. They'd barely fought them off upstairs, and that was before the men spotted the weapons hanging on the first-floor walls. Thirty armed men against two tired mages were not great odds.

The girl lifted her hand, using the wind to send the canoe she'd used as a footstool earlier into the murky water. Then she shucked off her cloak, nodding for Lark to do the same. "We'll hide underneath that canoe. Let's hope the prisoners leave out the docks. Let them be the ones to get lost. If we hear them moving the stones to escape into the city, we'll need to take our chances fighting them off."

The brunette grabbed Lark's cloak and pack and marched to the chamber's wall. She pressed on a stone, one that looked just the same as all the rest.

Lark gasped. A hidden chamber popped open. Lark peered inside, hopeful they could hide inside it instead of jumping in what would no doubt be freezing water, but the stone drawer was far too small, barely large enough to fit their cloaks and her bag inside. The girl shoved them inside, then shucked off her boots, too. Lark's boots joined hers atop the piled clothes a moment later.

"C'mon." The girl shoved the drawer closed. She hopped into the water with a splash, winced, then quickly smiled. "It's not even cold. Jump in."

Lark sensed she was lying about the cold. But the footsteps above were only getting louder. She took a deep breath and jumped.

The breath gushed out of her lungs as the freezing water surrounded her. Definitely lying.

"C'mon," the brunette demanded, then she ducked beneath the overturned canoe.

Lark wondered—not for the first time—who *was* this girl? Obviously, she was a mage. That much she could be certain of. One with an intimate knowledge of the city and this building. Whoever she was, Lark owed her life to her. That fact made it easy to duck her head beneath the water and follow her beneath the canoe, even when she didn't yet know her name.

The cold was like a slap to the face, sapping her energy. When she resurfaced under the overturned canoe, her teeth-chattered, and she gripped her chest tightly beneath the water. Luckily, the depth was shallow, and she could hold herself up on her tiptoes so that her mouth and nose cleared the murky water's surface.

The brunette, being taller, was steadier on her feet. She held the canoe in place around them as the water swayed.

"Who are you? How did you know I was in trouble?" Lark wasted no time asking, her voice a harried whisper.

"My name is Ereni. I'll explain later. They won't be long now." She cocked her head sideways, listening intently to the footfalls above as they grew louder.

A prickle of recognition came over Lark at the name. She could swear she'd heard it before, but where and when she couldn't put her finger on.

Lark couldn't waste time racking her brain for where she'd learned the girl's name. Instead, she took the opportunity to update her bondmate. *Muse? I'm safe for now. I'm hidden beneath an overturned canoe in the bog. You better stay hidden, too. The prisoners are on their way to the bottom level.*

"Hidden? Prisoners? Oh no."

"What's wrong?"

"Daus, he's at the entrance trying to move the rocks and make his way inside."

Lark's stomach sank. *"Get him to stop! He has to hide!"*

"I'm trying!"

She started to explain, "My bondmate—"

But Ereni slapped a hand over her mouth, her gaze darting sideways.

An instant later, the folding stairs crashed down.

Blazes! Dausius came running to help, and she was about to get him killed.

"Is Daus still out there?" she asked, her own voice in her mind panicked.

"I can't get him to stop digging! Damn humans, the whole lot of you don't know when to quit!"

Lark clutched her chest beneath the icy water. She prayed for the men to leave through the bog. Ereni said they needed to fight if they made for the city... The odds were certainly stacked against them, but she wouldn't leave Daus to die. Never.

Time to change strategy. *"Can you find somewhere to watch the men in here without being seen? I need you to be my eyes. If Daus is in trouble, I have to know right away."*

"On it," Muse replied.

In the room beyond their little hidden shelter, the lumbering thuds of the prisoner's footfalls reverberated on the creaking wooden ladder, making it impossible to hear any of their conversation. Were they already attempting to dig their way out into the city streets?

"I can see them. Looks like they're all just standing around, arguing."

Lark blew out a heavy sigh. Just then, the ladder's creaking stopped, and the door slammed heavily. They must've sent the trapdoor back up into the ceiling. The men's conversation finally became intelligible. Muse was right. They were definitely arguing.

"We should escape to the bog. There are plenty of canoes," one man said, his voice firm.

"The bog is a deathtrap. We'll be lost or eaten alive. I'm taking my chances in the city," another insisted, his voice deeper than the first.

Ereni tensed beside her at that.

"Are they digging at the door?" she asked Muse.

"No... wait. The man who just spoke is headed there. A few of the men are following him."

Lark shuddered. She stared at Ereni, tilting her head sideways. The mage's stare bored into hers and spoke volumes without having to say a word. She gripped the canoe's edge, ready to flip it aside and fight.

"Wait!" A third voice yelled from further away. "I can hear something on the other side. Shut up and listen!"

Lark stilled and forced her teeth to stop chattering, listening just as intently.

"Someone is digging out there." A pause. "Shit! It's the guard!"

Deep voice spoke up again, "How do you know that? It could be anyone!"

"Listen, you ass! I can hear the man bellowing out there. It's the Guard Captain! He says there's an entire contingent surrounding us."

A chorus of shouts and chatter exploded at that announcement, with everyone talking over each other. Lark couldn't make heads or tails of it until she heard the far away voice frantically shushing the lot, and they quieted down again.

"How do we know it's not a trick?" a new voice asked.

"Shh, you idiots," the far voice demanded. "I hear horses nickering. And a horn blow. It's them. It's the guard!"

"Is the guard out there with Dausius?" she asked Muse.

"No, I would've heard or seen them. It's just Daus out there."

Lark almost laughed. That old showman. He was out there putting on the performance of a lifetime.

"That settles it. Out through the bog if you want to stay free," someone yelled.

"Pull down the canoes. Quick!"

Grunting and noise resounded as the men got to work. Lark's heartbeat slowed a tiny fraction. Daus was going to be all right.

"Lark, one of the men is heading for your canoe!"

Shit! Her eyes widened as booted footsteps came closer and the canoe rocked around them. What were they going to do?

Ereni caught her attention. She sucked in a deep breath and pointed a finger down an instant before her head disappeared beneath the water.

Lark gulped down a breath and followed. Not a moment too soon. The water above her head splashed and heaved as the canoe they'd hidden under flipped over.

"Lark, where are you?" Muse asked frantically. *"Are you all right?"*

"Yes. I'm underwater. I'm fine," she insisted. But even as the thought left her mind, she couldn't escape the panic. How long could they last under here? Surely not long enough for all those men to clamber into boats and set sail.

Her bondmate wasn't buying it either. *"How long can humans hold their breath?"* Muse asked.

Lark's mind raced. She struggled to come up with a reply. Her lungs were already burning. Daus was safe, but she was about to drown. The canoe above her sank in the water, no doubt with the weight of the man jumping in, forcing her to sink down to the very bottom of the bog.

Something grabbed her beneath the water. Lark's heart skittered and her eyes popped open.

Ereni. It was hard to see in the murky water, but she could make out her outline as she lifted a hand. A sphere formed, floating in the water between them. Ereni shoved her face toward it and the bubble shrank.

That's right—Ereni could summon air. Lark pushed her face to the bubble and breathed deep, sucking air into her lungs.

"Muse, I'm all right. There's an air mage here with me." Her voice was almost giddy. *"I need you to keep watching. Tell me when the coast is clear."*

"Sure. I can do that."

Time passed by excruciatingly slow. She and Ereni drained a bubble of air with a few breaths, and then the mage formed another one. The cold seeped into Lark's skin, deep down into her bones. Her body shuddered so much she worried the men atop the water would notice the ripples she made.

As Ereni formed another bubble, Lark saw her shuddering just as strongly. How much longer could they stand the cold?

"They're almost all gone." Muse announced. *"When this pair of canoes leave, you'll be safe to resurface."*

"Thanks, Muse." Lark sighed internally. She couldn't wait to escape the bog. This day had certainly taken a turn on the strange side, but thankfully, the danger was almost over.

Finally, the water above them stopped echoing with splashes.

"They're gone," Muse confirmed.

Lark grabbed Ereni's arm and tugged. They burst out on the water's surface and took deep gulping breaths of air.

Lark turned to Ereni, a smile on her lips. "That was clos—"

The word caught in her throat as Ereni's eyelids fluttered shut and her head slipped under the water.

"No!" She dove under, frantically searching for the mage in the murky water. There! She grabbed her and hauled her to the surface.

Ereni was unconscious but breathing normally. Her dead weight was such a burden Lark struggled to hold them both above the water. How in the world would she pull them both out when she could barely keep them floating?

Then the skittering of rock sounded.

"Daus, help, we're over here."

A few moments later, Dausius peered down at them, the beads in his braids clacking together as he shook his head. "How did you end up here?" He reached out, frowning. "Here, hand her to me."

"Thanks."

He hauled up Ereni's motionless form, then reappeared a moment later, his hands slipping beneath the water and under her armpits, to help lug her out of the bog.

She slapped onto the stone floor. Her chest heaved, her entire body shuddering violently with cold.

"You've got to get out of those wet clothes," Dausius said. He swiveled his head, scanning the room. Then he made his way to a bin with crumpled cloth sticking out the top. Reaching inside, he pulled out a set of prison coveralls.

Lark wrinkled her nose. The thought of wearing the same garb as the men who'd nearly attacked her didn't sit right. But it was that, or staying in her wet dress. There wasn't much of a choice.

Dausius tossed her a coverall and grabbed another, heading for Ereni. "I'm sorry for this, whoever you are," he muttered as he peeled off her soaked trousers.

Lark finished changing quickly. The cold still clung tightly to her, but without the soaked clothing, her teeth finally stopped chattering. She let out a sigh as she buttoned the last button on her chest.

"Um, Lark. We have a problem," Daus announced.

She turned, her eyes bulging as she spotted where his gaze was locked. Ereni slumped on the ground, still unconscious. Dausius had stripped her of the wet clothing but hadn't yet reclothed her in the coveralls. Her stomach curved up into the air, the skin stretched taut around her huge belly.

How had she missed that before? Lark scrubbed at her eyelids. The mage was heavily pregnant. From the looks of it, she was due any day.

Dausius spoke up again, his voice filled with panic. "I'm no expert now, but I think her water just broke."

Chapter 7

Kayda scanned the riverbank beside the docks, her eyes peeled for any sign of the conveyance that would see them across the Riddle River. Where was it?

"What exactly are we searching for?" Beside her, Mika adjusted his brown cloak's collar.

Kayda spared the Raimish healer a glance. He and a handful of castle guard trailed after her, their faces painted with a mixture of curiosity, annoyance, and fear.

"If you're looking for a boat, we're heading in the wrong direction," the Guard Captain grumbled, scrubbing at his sweat-slicked forehead. He was one of those portly men who perpetually sweated, even with the chilled breeze blowing up from the fast-moving river to cool them.

Kayda spotted it finally. "We're not sailing across." She crept closer to the riverbank's edge and brushed aside a row of weeds overgrown around a huge stone boulder, revealing an old rope tied around it. A rope that stretched taut across the river, from one bank to the other. "We're flying."

"Blazes," exclaimed a young guard with a stubbly chin and shaved head. "You expect us to cross the river on that old thing? It'll never hold!"

Kayda smiled. "It held the king. It's the only way he could've made it across with no one noticing."

The Guard Captain scoffed. "How would he even know this rope was here?"

"Because he used to slide across the river on this supply line as a youth, for the thrill of it. He told me the story, once. Said the dockmaster ruined all his fun when he found out and told his father."

Well, those weren't the exact words he'd used, but close enough. If she explained how he blurted out the story to her in his wreck of a room—dressed in his underclothes no less—her reasoning might start to sound a little crazy.

Mika crouched beside the line and scanned the rope. "Is that what this is used for? Moving supplies?"

Kayda nodded. "It's the quickest way to move goods from the docks to the castle. They don't use it much anymore."

"Why is that?" Mika rose to his feet.

Kayda shrugged. "I'm not sure."

The Guard Captain spoke up. "I know why. Goods tend to *disappear* more often when they're sent this way. The dockworkers claim some are lost in the process, falling into the river, but more often than not they end up in the same workers' pockets." He shook his head. "The king would rather wait longer for his goods to be carted over the bridge than send a handful of workers who can't handle the temptation to prison every year."

Kayda's heart stirred at the reminder of her grandfather's inherent goodness. He was one of the kindest, most caring people she knew. Just one more reason she *had* to find him.

She exhaled, eyeing the rope. The ground on this side of the river was a great deal higher than the opposite bank on the Northmoat side. It should be a simple matter to slide across. Kayda knelt down and shucked off her bag, pulling out the supplies she'd brought with her.

"Here." She pulled free a stack of handkerchiefs she'd pilfered from an abandoned clothing shop bordering the docks. She handed one to each of the men with her, then stuffed the rest down the top of her blouse beneath her thick wool cloak. "We can wrap these around the rope and slide across."

Kneeling back down, she pulled out the second item she'd insisted on finding before heading for the riverbank. This one she'd located in a Jorian antique shop. The little can of oil she'd filled it with, she'd borrowed from the hold on board *Nova's Champion*.

Mika peered over her shoulder. "What's that?"

"We're bound to run into the scourge in Northmoat. I need my source readily available." Kayda finished pouring the oil inside and lifted the delicate glass oil lamp aloft. She'd wrapped a length of cord around it, to enable her to wear it around her neck. Standing, she walked to the closest guard holding a torch and stuck a dried twig into the fire then used it to light the lamp.

"Isn't that going to get hot?" Mika asked.

Kayda patted her chest, her palm denting the stack of handkerchiefs. "That's what the extra padding is for." Kayda pointed to the rope. "Once I make it across, I can take it off my neck if it starts to burn."

Mika grinned. "Very impressive. I see you've got this all thought out."

"Thanks." She ducked her head, hoping no one noticed the blush she felt warming her cheeks. Pacing to the edge, she started to slip a handkerchief over the rope.

"Nope. No way are you sliding over there first, Princess," the Guard Captain said. "Let me do the honors."

Kayda backed away, watching as the burly man slung his handkerchief over the rope. Then he drew a deep breath and leaped off the edge.

"Ahh!" he screamed, his voice surprisingly high pitched for a man his size.

She bit back the tiny smile that fought to appear. The guards surrounding her had no such qualms. Hearty laughter rang out, rising in volume when the Guard Captain slammed onto the ground on the Northmoat riverbank.

He walloped into the dirt, luckily landing on the side of his body that didn't have an enormous sword strapped to it. The other side of the rope was attached to a thick limb on a huge oak. He'd hopped off before crashing into the tree trunk, but his landing had certainly been less than graceful.

Kayda winced as she watched the man lumber up off the ground. She started to second guess her plan to wear the lamp around her neck. What if she landed on it? She'd end up with a chest full of glass, not to mention, covered in oil and potentially set on fire...

Kayda gulped. No. She had to be prepared. If the scourge showed up and she didn't have a flame, she'd be utterly defenseless.

Well—not quite—but if she was forced to summon without a source, she'd be trading years of her life for the magic. Lighting a torch with her tinderbox would take time. Time she might not have if the scourge arrived.

It appeared Mika held similar reservations. Frowning, he shot the lamp on her chest another glance before heading for the rope. "Let me go next. The captain and I can help steady you when you land."

She nodded her assent.

Mika slid across silently, and even landed on his feet, though he wobbled a good deal and would've likely lost his balance if not for a helping hand from the captain.

She stepped up to the rope next, her mind and heart racing. Despite seeing the two men make it over successfully, the thought of sliding across the rope still raised the hair on the back of her neck. If she lost her hold on the handkerchief, she'd tumble into the river below, swept away out to sea in the strong current, battered between boulders and drowned in the rapids.

Kayda sucked in a deep breath and shoved aside her fear. She needed to do this. For her grandfather. And her grandmother.

She clutched the handkerchief tightly and jumped.

Sliding through the air brought back a tiny sliver of the thrill that ignited within her every time she rode atop her bondmate's back. The wind surrounded her, and she raced across the river.

A smile flashed across her face. Why had she been so scared of this? It was exhilarating.

Before she knew it, she was barreling toward the riverbank. That's right. The landing.

Fear returned, slamming into her as the first sign of dirt appeared beneath her feet. She jumped, her heart hammering, and landed with a jarring thump on her feet. She tilted forward, eyes bulging.

Two pairs of strong hands caught her, steadying her before she landed face-first on the ground. "Thanks," she exclaimed as she found her balance.

Snarling cut through the air. The scourge had found them! The sound had them all tensing, their heads swinging to find the source.

Kayda was the first to spot them. The sight sent a cold chill through her veins. A half dozen at least, climbed the big oak. They were headed right for the rope.

"There!" she pointed up in the branches.

"They can't cross that? Can they?" Mika asked.

Kayda gulped, watching as the leader gripped the rope with its claws, swinging its sleek little body atop the thick rope.

"We can't let them climb across," the captain yelled. He unsheathed his sword and swung, severing the rope with a single stroke. The beast attached to the rope tumbled down with it, screeching.

A second scream came from behind them, and a splash. Kayda's stomach dropped. With the scourge ahead of them, she didn't dare turn around, but she was certain that scream belonged to one of the guards. The captain didn't just send one of the scourge tumbling down when he severed the rope, he'd sent one of his own men to his death.

The thought was sobering, but there was nothing she could do for the poor fellow. And with the rope cut, there would be no more help from the rest of the guard. The three of them had to complete their mission alone.

They'd be enough. She'd make sure of it.

With that thought echoing in her mind, Kayda inhaled, concentrating on the flame on her chest. A chill spread over her skin as a ball of fire appeared, hovering above her open palm. She sent it soaring, catching the scourge on the ground before it could leap up and attack.

The satisfying sound of its dying scream flooded her ears. In another heartbeat, she shot a ball of fire at another. Then another. Soon all the little beasts were roasting. They littered the ground, tiny scattered piles of flame and writhing, screeching bodies.

"Wow, that was fast," Mika said. He rose from a crouch, his hand full of dirt. "I didn't even have time to visualize yet."

Kayda shrugged. "I've had a lot of practice." She swung her head around, looking for more vermin. The coast appeared clear for now, but with the sound of the burning scourge's death throes inundating the air, it wouldn't be long before more came. "C'mon, let's go."

They jogged off, quickly traversing the deserted streets of Northmoat. The shops and homes all stood empty, except for the occasional scourge who sprang at them from the shadows. Fortunately, they seemed to have mostly cleared out. The few that ran at them were all swiftly dispatched, either on the captain's blade or to a ball of flame.

They turned a corner and Kings Keep appeared. The sight of the stately stone castle—the home she'd lived in practically every day of her life—stirred warmth in her heart. This place held so many memories, some wonderful—others, not so much. But even though she'd never felt entirely comfortable there, it was still her home. A small part of her rejoiced over knowing it still stood, as permanent a fixture of the city as it had always been.

As they approached the entrance to the Royal Grounds, Kayda's stomach churned. It was all going so smoothly. Too smoothly. She kept waiting for them to encounter a huge crowd of scourge. One that would actually prove a problem for the three of them.

Rounding the massive square keep, the Royal Stables came into view, and her prediction proved true. Surrounding the stables, hundreds of scourge gathered. They rammed the building, scratching at the ground beneath the thick wooden doors, attempting to tunnel underneath.

Kayda's hand flew to her mouth, and she stopped in her tracks.

"Damn." The Guard Captain halted beside her, his breath coming hard and fast. "We're too late."

"Or we're just in time," Mika retorted. He alone continued jogging, calling over his shoulder, "They wouldn't be trying to dig in if there wasn't someone alive inside."

He was right. They had to be alive. Kayda dropped the oil lamp back around her neck and closed her eyes, embracing the icy chill rushing through her veins. Then her brown eyes flashed open, and twin flames hovered over her hands.

"Hurry," she yelled to the Guard Captain as she broke back into a jog. Within a few moments, she'd caught up to Mika. The slight vibration humming across her skin told her he'd summoned too, even before she spotted the chunks of dirt and rock hovering above his hands.

Dodging immaculately trimmed bushes, and hopping over flower beds bursting with zinnias and mums in the gardens, they quickly closed in on the stables.

Kings Keep featured one of the finest stables in the kingdom. Due to the king's condition—even before he'd been stabbed and nearly died—the building remained largely unused, only housing the mounts of visiting dignitaries and guests. None of the royals kept horses, not since the king lost his second bondmate a decade ago.

But clearly that had all changed now. What drove Grandfather to risk everything to hole up in the stables with the scourge on the loose? Had he truly found another bondmate?

Kayda shoved the thought aside as they drew closer, and the first of the scourge turned toward them. A scream tore out of her throat, and she flung fireballs in every direction. The sick stench of burning fur filled the air.

Beside her, Mika scattered dirt and rock into the crowd. Being practically untrained in combat, he missed as many hits as he landed. But the flying debris caught in the scourges' faces, confusing and infuriating them. The guard captain stayed close by Mika's side, his sword swiping through the throng, felling all the beasts who came close enough for his blade to reach.

Though it had seemed impossible when viewed from a distance, the three of them pushed through the crowd, unleashing death on all sides. The door was within reach.

"Grandfather! Izora!" Kayda yelled. "We've come to save you!"

A heartbeat passed. Then two. Three. No movement came from the door. No sound. Kayda's heart twisted.

Instead, something flew at her from above. A scourge descended from the roof in a desperate leap. She reacted an instant too late. The beast caught in flame, but not before its claws connected with the cord around her neck, slicing it clean in two. Her eyes widened with horror, and she jumped back just in time to avoid the splash of oil as the glass shattered on the ground in front of her.

"Blazes!" The dirt and grass lit up everywhere the oil spread, catching a few scourge who'd been unlucky enough to get in the way. But Kayda's stomach dropped. When those flames on the ground died out, her source would be gone.

She sucked in a deep breath, determined to make every moment count. She screamed again. Her battle cry rang out, echoing loudly above the screeching vermin. Fire flew from her hands furiously, a constant stream of death aimed at the crowd. But still the scourge came. More and more appeared on the horizon, no doubt attracted to the spot by the sounds of battle.

For a few moments, she held them off. But then the fire on the ground guttered out, and exhaustion slammed into her hard. Kayda staggered on her feet, letting go of the flames.

Instantly, her strength returned. The heavy weight on her limbs lifted. But terror pummeled her instead. Her source was gone. And the scourge still pressed in all around them.

The Guard Captain yelped in pain as he darted forward to block her. One of the scourge raked its claws through his leg. He sliced it clean down the middle before it could leap atop him, but more pressed forward to take its place.

Mika still flung dirt, but his face had paled, shoulders slumped.

How long could they last out here? Kayda's stomach sank. She didn't like the answer.

The stable door burst open, scattering the scourge in every direction. A wall of earth and straw appeared, encircling the three of them.

Izora's dark face popped out of the doorway, and a blast of fire flew from her hands, landing on one of the scourge who'd been close enough to the doorway to be included inside the protective barrier of earth. "Get in! Now!"

Kayda grabbed the Guard Captain's arm, helping him hobble forward. Mika raced inside before them, throwing the remaining dirt in his hands at the trio of scourge left. Izora shot fire at the group, all of them bursting into flaming piles of fur and gnashing teeth.

"Hurry!" called another voice from inside.

Kayda turned, staring behind them as she crossed the threshold. The scourge outside threw themselves at the barrier, then bounced off covered in dirt and straw. None of them made it through, but the top of the wall slowly dissipated with every strike. Soon, they would be able to leap over the crumbling barrier.

It didn't matter. The door slammed shut, shielding them within the dimly lit stable house. The slight chill and hum of vibration in the air halted as all the mages let go of the elements. She dropped the Guard Captain in a pile of hay, and Mika crouched beside him, attending to his slashed leg.

Her breath coming hard and fast, Kayda swiveled around. She spotted the king slamming a wood bar down into place on the heavy door.

"Grandfather!" Tears blurred her vision. She ran to him, clasping him in a tight embrace. He clutched her back just as tightly. As his warm arms connected around her, the tears spilled free, running down her cheeks and wetting the king's silk tunic.

He was hugging her back! All those days spent together in the tower, he'd never hugged her back. It was true. Her soul rejoiced. She didn't need to hear him speak to feel it. He was back. Her grandfather was back!

"Little Red." Hearing his special nickname for her caused her heart to practically burst. He pulled free from her arms, and his blue eyes connected with hers, the hazy clouds that'd once filled them gone. "What are you doing here?"

Kayda laughed and scrubbed her face with her sleeve. "We came to save you, Grandfather."

The king's eyes grew misty. "I've been a bit of a fool, haven't I?"

She shook her head. "No, don't say th—"

Izora scoffed. "Don't sugarcoat it for him. He's a blazing fool, if I've ever seen one."

"And you haven't let me hear the end of it since you followed me out here, you old witch," the king retorted.

Kayda's brows shot up, but despite his harsh words, Quinton's voice was filled with humor and not malice.

Kayda turned, her gaze connecting with Izora's across the dim room. So many conflicting feelings slammed into her. All the lies her nurse had been party to, all the deception—everything she'd discovered on her journey to find out her true parentage rose in her mind. But underneath the anger, the hurt, and the confusion, something stronger lived—love.

She raced across the room and collided with Izora. Their arms clasped around each other. And for the second time that day, her heart felt full enough to burst.

"My princess," Izora whispered, her voice thick with emotion. "I've missed you so much."

"I've missed you, too," Kayda choked out, her voice a strangled whisper. "Grandmother."

Izora pulled back far enough to meet her gaze. She gently grasped one of the tiny braids framing the left side of her face, her brown eyes full of love and warmth but shadowed with the ghost of all that lay unspoken between them.

"I hate to break up this touching reunion, but we don't have much longer before they break in," announced another voice. One she vaguely recognized.

Kayda eased free of Izora's arms and turned to the white-cloaked mage behind her. She found a kind face she'd never forget. One that had saved the king in his time of greatest need and led her through a rain of arrows to find her bondmate.

"Vespen?" She stepped closer to him, her eyes filling with tears again. "I thought I'd lost you!"

"Not forever, it seems. I'm glad to see you again, Princess." He reached out, clasping her shoulder gently.

Kayda smiled up at him.

The wooden door, which had been pounding constantly since it slammed shut, shuddered on its hinges. All eyes turned to it, and everyone present held a collective breath. But the door stood. For the moment.

"I'm afraid we can't stay here much longer." Vespen frowned at the door.

"Don't worry." Kayda grinned. "We have a plan."

Chapter 8

Lark knelt beside the naked, unconscious mage, examining her swollen belly. The water continued to gush out between her thighs. She sniffed. Definitely not urine. Lark gently stuck a hand on Ereni's belly. She could feel a contraction tensing her muscles.

Dausius was right. Ereni was in labor. Lark's heart hammered. She had to wake her up.

She leaned over, slapping Ereni's face gently. "Wake up. Your baby is coming."

Nothing. The mage still slept. Through the slapping and the contractions.

Lark wrung her hands, staring down at the motionless young woman. What was she going to do? She couldn't deliver this baby *here*, could she?

Mothers died in childbirth every day. Was Ereni destined to do the same, after using so much of her talent to keep them alive while the prisoners fled?

No. Ereni had saved her life. She wasn't about to quit on her now. She would save her and the baby.

She tilted her head up, catching her bondmate's eye where she perched in the ceiling rafters. *"I need your help again."*

"What can I do?" Muse sounded alarmed. *"My kind lay eggs!"*

Lark bit back a chuckle. *"Nothing like that, silly. Can you find Aren? Or Tiora, or Meital, or even Mazen? If things here go sideways, I might need another set of hands."*

"That I can handle." Muse lifted into the air. *"Be back soon."*

Lark turned to Dausius. His brown eyes were wide, his mouth hanging open. "You have to help me deliver the baby, Daus. Can you do that?"

Daus shook himself, blinking repeatedly. "What do you need?"

"Bring me more of those coveralls. And my pack! There's a hidden drawer, set into the wall. She hid our cloaks and my pack inside." She pointed in the general direction she remembered the drawer being, though she couldn't pinpoint the exact spot. With the drawer closed, it blended into the wall so perfectly she would've never known it was there if she hadn't seen it opened with her own eyes. "Just start pushing on the stones until it pops open. One of them triggers the drawer."

Dausius nodded, then he stood and got to work. Soon he dumped a huge armload of coveralls beside her and started prodding at the stone wall.

Lark shoved the coveralls around Ereni, using them like she would normally use blankets. This wasn't her first birth. Her mother had worked as a midwife and a healer. She'd witnessed and assisted with dozens of births in her lifetime. Even so, this situation made her stomach churn. Never once had she birthed a child with the mother unconscious. She needed to find some way to wake Ereni.

Lark took a peek between Ereni's legs, and her stomach clenched even tighter. The baby was crowning! It didn't seem possible. How had things progressed so fast? Had Ereni been in active labor the entire time they were escaping? No, that couldn't be. She'd shown no signs of contractions while they were underwater or running from the prisoners. And besides, her water just broke a few moments ago.

"I could really use my pack," she said, hoping Dausius didn't notice the fear tinging her words.

"I'm working on it," Daus grumbled. "You sure it was over here?"

"Yes, I'm sure."

"Well, I'm moving as fast as I—"

The drawer popped open, nearly catching Daus in the shins. He hopped back, then bent down and pulled everything out. He returned with a victorious smile painting his lips. But when he met her gaze, the smile dropped.

"What else can I do?" he asked.

"My pack." Lark thrust out a hand expectantly. "I need to wake her. Hold her shoulders so she doesn't jolt up and hurt herself." She grabbed the bag, breathing out a sigh as the reassuring weight of her supplies settled in her grasp. She dug inside and pulled out a tiny glass vial.

"What's that?" Daus asked.

"Smelling salts." Lark twisted off the stopper. "If this doesn't wake her, I'm out of ideas."

Lark slid the little jar beneath Ereni's nose. She held her breath, waiting, the sound of the water lapping against the bog and her own heartbeat pounding loudly in her ears.

No reaction. She started to despair. Would this baby lose its mother before it even drew its first breath? Would it even be born at all without Ereni pushing?

But just as she pulled her hand away, her heart full of defeat, Ereni's blue eyes snapped open, and she cried out in pain. Dausius gripped her shoulders, keeping her firmly pressed into the pile of coveralls Lark had slid beneath her head.

Gaze flitting around, Ereni's breathing quickened, a groan tearing out of her throat. "What's happening? Ah, it hurts! Am I dying?"

Lark leaned closer, staring Ereni straight in the eyes. "No, you're not dying. Your baby is coming."

She expected the statement to calm the panic flooding the mage's face, but it did the opposite. Her eyes widened as she stared down at her stomach, shaking her head. "No. It's too soon. It's months too soon." She gasped. "The air. No source..."

Lark's stomach dropped. Did she mean... Blazes! The pieces finally clicked together. That's why she didn't appear pregnant before she resurfaced from beneath the bog. Why the baby was coming so quickly.

"You've been aged." Lark held back a gasp. What did that mean for the baby? She'd never heard of a mage aging while pregnant...

Ereni screamed again. Lark grabbed her hand, wincing as Ereni's grip turned crushing. It seemed she wouldn't have long to wonder.

Soon, the contraction passed. But Lark knew from experience another would come, right on its heels. "Daus, hold her hand, please." Lark moved back down into position between Ereni's legs.

"I can't do this. I can't have a baby *now*. The fire moat, the tunnels... the blazing scourge!" Ereni moaned, her eyes wild.

"Don't worry," Lark said, adopting the most calming voice she could muster under the circumstances. "I've delivered lots of babies. The mothers always think they can't do it, but they can. You will, too. And I'll be right here with you, every step of the way."

Ereni locked gazes with her. She sucked in a deep breath through her nose. "All right. All right, let's do it."

Lark smiled, then took another peek between Ereni's thighs. It was good she was ready. The baby was coming, whether she liked it or not.

"The next time you feel a pain, I need you to push."

Ereni nodded, her jaw set. They didn't have to wait long. A few heartbeats later, Ereni screamed. Dausius looked like he wanted to scream with her, his teeth gritted and eyes pinched closed. But Lark couldn't concentrate on them. She reached down, preparing to catch the baby.

"Good. You're doing so good," she said as the screaming died down, and Ereni sucked in a series of gasps. "One more push. The baby's almost here."

Lark stared down at the baby in her hands. Its head was already out, covered in flecks of blood and wispy little blond hairs. She'd never witnessed a birth progress so fast.

Her stomach churned as she waited for another contraction to come over Ereni. Was it just luck? Or was something wrong? Was some effect of the magic that'd aged her so unnaturally fast contributing to the super speed birth?

Lark shoved her misgivings aside. As far as she could tell, the birth was going smoothly. The baby was in the proper position and just moments away from letting out its first cry. She had to concentrate.

Ereni let out another scream.

"It's time to push," Lark instructed. "That's it."

The baby's shoulders popped free, and then the whole torso. Ereni bore down, her teeth gritted. And then the baby was out. Lark pulled her free, a huge grin on her face.

"You have a daughter." Lark quickly checked her over, scanning her little body for any issues. She was tiny. Far smaller than most babies born full term. In fact, she reminded Lark of the litter of piglets she'd helped Gael birth last year on the farm in Greenvale. The infant was closer in weight to one of those tiny piglets than most of the babies she'd birthed.

But the girl's lungs certainly weren't affected. As Lark reached into her mouth to clear her airway, the babe let out a loud wail. With the supplies in her pack, she took care of the cord. Then she grabbed a coverall, wrapped the baby quickly, and handed her to her mother.

"She's small, but she looks healthy. Congratulations, you're a mother," she said.

Ereni's eyes filled with tears as she gazed down at the tiny babe, her cries still ringing out through the air. "She's so beautiful. My Violet."

"Is that her name?" Dausius asked.

Ereni flashed a grin at him. Nodded. "Yes. Violet." Her nose crinkled, her smile luminous as she cradled the infant in her arms.

"It's a wonderful name," Daus said, teary-eyed. He turned to her. "We did it, didn't we? We birthed a baby!"

"Well, Ereni did most of the work." Lark chuckled. "You were great, Daus."

But Dausius' expression of wonder shifted to one of confusion. "I've heard that name before..."

Suddenly Ereni cried out, another contraction hitting her. "What was that? Is there another?" Her brows nearly disappeared into her hairline.

Lark frowned, taking a peek. "No, It's just the babe's birth sack. You need to push that out, too. It's all very normal, don't fret." Even as she finished speaking, the sack began to slide out.

Lark's frown deepened. There shouldn't be so much blood.

"Dausius, why don't you take a turn holding little Violet?" Lark said, forcing a smile. "Ereni has a bit more work to do."

Dausius kneeled, grabbing the bundle. Violet had quieted and appeared to be content, her tiny fist shoved inside her mouth.

Ereni surrendered her reluctantly. Then she craned her head down and stared at the mess between her legs. "I think I might be sick." She shook her head. "There's so much blood. Is there supposed to be that much blood?"

"It's all right," Lark lied, her chest twinging briefly at the words. But she needed her to stay calm while she worked. "Don't worry, I have everything well in hand." Lark dug in her pack searching for what she needed to stop the bleeding.

Ereni didn't look like she was buying it. Her breathing was labored, her stare still locked on all the blood flooding between her legs. She needed a distraction.

"You still haven't explained who those men were or how you found me," Lark said. "Tell me, please."

"What?" Ereni asked. "You want to know that *now*?"

Lark nodded. "Yes. Were those men meant to stay locked up in here while everyone fled and left for the scourge? What did they do to deserve that?"

Ereni leaned back on the pile of coveralls, closing her eyes. "This is a prison. I take it you figured that much out already. When it became obvious the city would fall, we had to decide what to do with the men and women inside. With the king incapacitated, the decision fell to Prince Gideon. From what I gather, he and the Guard Captain reviewed all the prisoner's cases individually. Anyone who'd committed minor crimes was set free. That's why most of the cells were empty."

Lark finished gathering what she needed from her pack. "And the men who were left?"

"Repeat offenders and violent criminals. Those they deemed irredeemable or who'd committed the most heinous crimes."

Lark gulped. She set the handful of fresh green herbs beside her and opened a jar of her mother's ointment, and slathered some on Ereni's stomach. She'd just released murderers and worse into the world... The thought was unsettling, to say the least.

Ereni's eyes popped open as the cream touched her belly. "What's that?" Her gaze slid back down, and she caught another glimpse of the blood soaking the coveralls stuffed there, her chest heaving.

"This will heal you," Lark insisted, infusing her voice with all the confidence she wasn't feeling. She'd certainly never had to contend with a birth under such strange circumstances. She wasn't entirely sure this would work, but she wasn't about to tell Ereni that when she was already acting panicked. "What about me? How did you know I was in here?"

Ereni's brows furrowed, but she tore her gaze away from her torso and leaned back again, closing her eyes. "It was just pure chance. I was walking outside when I heard a loud bang. Then I spotted the door ajar. Once I ducked inside and saw the stair hanging down, I knew someone was upstairs."

She must've heard the stairs clattering when they'd descended from the ceiling. That'd been extremely lucky for her. Without Ereni's help, she might've met her end on the top floor at the hands of those prisoners. She owed her a great debt.

Lark drew a deep breath, smoothing the fresh green herbs against Ereni's flesh. It was time to repay the favor. She would not let her bleed out here.

She closed her eyes and wished. Her talent flowed through her, the vibration humming to life. A tremor rattled the bones in her arms, then shot through her palms into Ereni. Lark opened her eyes.

Ereni's stomach shrank beneath her fingers. Lark removed the bloody coveralls between her legs. Lark blew out a sigh. "The bleeding stopped. You're going to be all right."

"I am?" Ereni laughed. "You had me worried for a moment there."

Lark knelt beside the bog and washed the blood from her hands. Ereni grabbed a pair of clean coveralls and blushed, seeming to notice for the first time that she was lying on the ground practically naked.

Just then, a series of splashes sounded. Lark's heart skipped a beat. "What was that?" she whispered, peering into the bog but seeing nothing. "Do you think the criminals have returned?"

"Hey," Dausius said. "Could you give me a hand with little Violet?"

Ereni looked torn, her gaze flitting between the bog and the babe. But after a few heartbeats she set her stare on the bog. "Go," she said, "Take care of my girl. I'll keep watch."

Lark crossed the room to Dausius. "What's wrong?" She peered down at the tiny babe in his arms. Her eyes were closed, her hand still shoved in her mouth as she sucked on her fingers furiously.

"I'm not sure if it's wrong, exactly. But it's strange." Dausius frowned. "It's her eyes. I always thought babies were born with dark eyes. Hers..." He glanced up at her, then gently tugged Violet's fist free. Her eyelids popped open.

Lark's brows lifted. Violet's eyes were different. They were a far lighter blue than any newborn she'd ever birthed, and her irises even had a slight red tinge. She took a closer look at the babe. At the light blond tuft of hair on her head. Her pale, creamy skin. In contrast, Ereni's hair was dark brown, her skin tanned.

"She's albino. It's rare, but sometimes children and even animals are born this way." She smiled down at the tiny infant as she found her fist again with her mouth, her eyes closing as she started sucking. "It's not life threatening or something I need to heal, but thank you for telling me, Daus."

Another splash sounded, this one much louder. Lark whipped around, her mouth dropping open.

"Where are you going?" she demanded.

Ereni had pulled the last canoe from the wall and was already halfway out the opening to the bog. "No time to explain," she yelled. "Take care of Violet. Keep her safe. I'll be back. I'll find you. I trust you, Lark!"

Lark stared at the retreating canoe as it rounded a bend in the bog and out of sight. Where was Ereni headed? And what in the world was she going to do with a newborn baby?

Dausius' mouth was agape, too. "Did that just happen? Why would she leave?"

Lark shook her head. "I don't know." She glanced around, scanning the mess of bloody coveralls on the ground. "Hey, she stole my cloak," she said, incredulous.

Dausius peered around, frowning. "My pack is missing, too."

Then a thought struck her, and she rocked back on her feet, her knees feeling weak.

"What is it?" Daus asked.

"I never told her my name. How did she know my name? This day just keeps getting stranger."

"Lark, we're back. I found lover boy," Muse announced.

"Muse! Do you see a canoe nearby?"

"Hold on, let me look."

Aren's blond head poked through the opening Daus had dug at the entrance. "Lark." His voice cracked. "You're all right! When Muse showed up without you, I feared the worst."

Lark smiled gently, her heart fluttering as Aren's blue eyes met her own, filled with concern.

"Thanks for coming, Aren." Lark gestured to the baby Dausius cradled in his arms. "I thought we might need help to deliver baby Violet, but her birth went much faster than I expected."

"Good thing you're finished." Aren scanned the room as he finished crawling into the building. "We need to leave. Now. They're saying the moat is about to fall." He offered her a hand, his brow furrowing when he ran his gaze down her prison coveralls.

Lark's cheeks warmed under his scrutiny, but thankfully, Aren chose not to pepper her with questions. He grasped her hand and silently led her back to the doorway to Southmoat.

"Did you find it yet, Muse?"

"No, it must be hidden beneath the mangroves. Should I keep searching?"

"No. We have to return to the docks." Lark's stomach sank. As much as she hated to leave Ereni, it looked like she had no choice. Without a canoe, following her wasn't happening, and she couldn't stand around waiting and put Violet in danger. Ereni would have to take her chances in the bog on her own.

Chapter 9

Conall smacked into the water. Cold enveloped him. The shock would've stolen his breath, if it wasn't for what came next.

He slammed into the bog bottom and screamed, the sound muffled by the water flooding his mouth. Pain flared up his leg. He didn't have to look down to realize that something was very wrong. He didn't have to look—but he did, regretting the decision instantly.

Blood clouded the murky water. His right foot stuck out at an unnatural angle, bent at the ankle. Broken. Definitely broken.

It didn't matter. He was alive. He was alive, and he had to save Shadow.

Conall burst to the bog's surface and spit out the bitter water, searching frantically. There. He swam for the flash of gray fur disappearing in the distance.

Swam was a generous description for the flailing half-hop, half-stroke he maintained in the shallow bog. The water was low enough he could reach the bottom in most places, but being forced to keep his weight off his injured leg, he couldn't swim or walk properly.

It could've been worse. It was a miracle he hadn't broken his neck instead.

"Shadow," he called out through their bond. *"I'm just behind you. Hang on!"*

"Hurry, brother," came his reply.

A spike of fear lodged in his gut. Conall picked up his pace, rounding a bend. A thrashing, snapping scourge was there to greet him. Its beady eyes locked onto him, and it lunged through the water like a starving child grasping for food.

Conall pushed off the river bottom with his good leg, launching himself forward. He would not be that vermin's life raft. Leaving it behind to drown, he swam onward.

Shadow floated in the waterway's center, just ahead. Clearly, he'd dislodged one of the scourge, but the last held on, its foreclaws sunk into Shadow's jaw.

Shadow was not faring well. His head hovered above the surface, but most of his body remained submerged, the water surrounding him tinged red. As Conall approached, even his head began to bob.

"Hang on, brother," he ordered.

Conall lunged again, desperate to reach him. Pain was his reward. He screamed, locked in place. His injured leg exploded with agony, like a thousand daggers stabbed into his muscles. Something clutched him in its grasp, beneath the water.

Conall grabbed the top of his thigh with both hands and tugged. Another flash of pain shot up his leg. Dizziness washed over him. He gritted his teeth, shaking his head. He couldn't pass out. Not now.

Shadow had just been almost within reach. In the few heartbeats he'd been trapped, the current pulled his bondmate halfway to the next bend in the stream. He needed to free himself, fast.

Sucking in a deep breath, he dove beneath the water. The cold smacked his face, banishing the last of the dizziness. He held still, waiting for the murky water to clear enough that he could see what had him trapped. After a moment, he realized it would take too long. He contorted himself under the water instead, using his hands to feel what gripped him in its grasp.

The silky length of a plant wrapped around his injured foot like a tourniquet. His first thought was to slip the boot off. He tugged and pain shot up his leg again. When the boot refused to budge—his ankle no doubt swollen fast around it—he pulled out his crafting knife.

By now, his lungs burned, the need for air hard to ignore. But swimming back to the surface would only waste more time. He needed to pull his leg free now.

He sawed at the plant, slicing through the tendrils in a few harried strokes. This time, when he tugged his leg, it pulled free.

Conall burst out on the water's surface, sucking in a grateful breath. He thrust off of the river bottom with his good leg, only to be met with a set of angry beady eyes—again.

The beast he'd left to drown floated directly in front of him, holding fast to a piece of driftwood. When it spotted him bursting free of the water, it sprang, shrieking and aiming for his face.

Conall reacted too slowly. He barely had time to dodge, and with his feet still flying out behind him after his last push off the river bottom, he couldn't propel himself out of the beast's path like last time. Claws sank into his shoulder. He screamed.

Blazes! He slammed back under the water, taking the scourge with him.

How long would it take to drown it? Too long. And he still clutched the knife in his fist.

Conall resurfaced, stabbing, catching the beast in the side. He tugged and twisted, not stopping until the vermin's entrails spilled out into the water and its claws detached from his shoulder.

He didn't have time to celebrate. The river rushed past him, blood pouring from his body in two places now. The cold, the pain, both worked together to sap his strength, but he shoved them aside.

Shadow. He had to save Shadow.

By now he was out of sight again. He had to make it around the next bend in the river. Avoid the vines. Catch up. Kill the vermin and pull Shadow to the bank.

Slow push by slow push, he forced his body to move. With one arm and one leg screaming in agony with every flailing stroke, it was slower than he'd like. But when he made it around the next bend, he spotted Shadow, caught against a mangrove tree's twisted roots.

Finally, some luck! He closed in quickly. But he spotted a new problem that made his stomach sink. The scourge had abandoned Shadow in the water, and climbed up in the mangrove's branches. But it didn't appear content to escape to the relative safety of the treetops. It flipped around, poised to leap on Shadow from above.

Dropping his knife, Conall lifted his hand and shot a blast of water at the beast as it leaped. He caught it in midair, enclosing the vermin in a bubble of water that he suspended, immobile, floating above his bondmate's head.

The beast didn't give up easily. It squirmed in the bubble, limbs flailing, claws slicing through the water and teeth snapping. But it was no use. He held the creature aloft until it drowned, then let go. Its limp body slapped onto the bog's surface and floated off in the current.

Finally, he reached his bondmate. He slid his good arm beneath his chest, helping hold him afloat. While he could stand, Shadow had been forced to tread water, and his weariness was evident.

"Little brother, you came for me." Shadow's tail wagged weakly on the water's surface.

"Of course, I did. I'll always come for you, brother. Always." He met his golden eyes and smiled, the pain in his ankle and shoulder fading in the moment of triumph. *"Hey, at least this time it wasn't me doing the falling, huh?"*

The sound of his bondmate's laughter echoed quietly in Conall's mind. Shadow was all right. For now, at least. Blood still seeped out into the water, far too much to be coming from only his injuries.

Conall allowed himself a moment to rejoice, but then he broke eye contact with Shadow and set his gaze on his surroundings. *"We need to find dry land before we both bleed out. How badly were you injured by the scourge?"*

"I... It's hard to say. It feels like my whole body is aflame," Shadow admitted.

Conall's stomach churned. That didn't sound good. *"Don't worry. I'll get us both out of this."*

The mangrove they rested against was one of many lining one side of the river in a scraggly line. But the mangroves didn't need dirt to grow. Their twisted roots plunged into the murky water, taking root far below. They wouldn't find what they needed on this side, unless they lucked into one of the marshy islands scattered somewhere further down the river.

The far bank, the one that bordered Dracwood, sported a high cliff. It appeared just as high from down here as the spot where he'd been forced to jump in, and equally steep. There was little chance he could haul both himself and Shadow up the cliff with his injuries.

With any luck, the river they found themselves in would flow toward the ocean. At least there, he might have a chance of someone on the docks spotting him and Shadow and lending them a hand.

He could only see two choices: try their chances at finding dry land and help further down the riverside, or try to use magic to save them. Maybe he could do both? He didn't know if he had enough strength left to force the air to lift them that high up the cliffside. And if he dropped them halfway, he might actually break his neck this time. But the water might be easy enough to manipulate... the current already wanted to sweep them forward, after all.

"C'mon. We need to find a spot that's easier to scale and make our way back into the city. I'll help you float, all right?"

"I trust you, little brother," Shadow said.

Keeping his good arm slung beneath Shadow's torso, Conall pulled them away from the mangrove and out into the waterway's center.

Then he closed his eyes, picturing what he wanted, the image of Shadow at the forefront of his mind. This had better work. He could feel his strength ebbing. They didn't have much time.

Conall bent the water flowing around him to his will. He lifted his foot from the river bottom and used the current swirling around him to carry Shadow and himself through the water. They picked up speed quickly.

He grinned. It was working. The water lifted them, and the current tugged them forward. Without him constantly jerking his limbs, the pain faded to a dull ache. But even as the agony of his injuries lessened, his body grew weary. He kept a close watch on both sides of the river, searching for any people, or somewhere he might be able to pull them free.

The waterway wound and twisted, and they lost sight of the cliffside and Dracwood several times in the bog's maze. Conall began to despair. Would they ever find a way out of this blazing swamp?

The magic propelling them was a blessing and a curse. Keeping still, the constant cold wore on him. His teeth chattered, his entire body wracked with shivers. It certainly didn't help that he kept bleeding, his injuries and Shadow's painting the murky water red.

Shadow wasn't faring any better. His body soon went limp in Conall's arms. He shook him awake each time it happened, but eventually he lost the strength to do even that, barely keeping them both aloft and the magic flowing around them.

Within a few moments of Shadow passing out for the last time, even that strength faded. Conall's grip on his talent slipped. The water slowed around them. The current stopped holding them aloft. Using the last of his strength, he scrambled to keep both of their heads above water.

As he bobbed and splashed, he glimpsed a building sitting on the riverbank's far side, on the Dracwood border. Was that a dock?

Hope erupted in his chest. He turned toward it, managing a single stroke in its direction before Shadow's head dipped underneath the water.

No.

He ducked under the water, searching. He spotted Shadow and grabbed hold, hauling them both to the surface.

It was all he could do to keep them both afloat. Despite the water helping boost him, Shadow's weight was a heavy burden. Conall refused to drop him, even as the dock disappeared from sight and his last shred of hope that he'd be able to reach the shore evaporated.

The current towed them into the waterway's center, where the depth increased slightly. His good foot barely grazed the river bottom. The lack of footing and his increasing exhaustion did not bode well for them. His shoulder and ankle screamed with agony as he flailed in the water, but he welcomed it. The pain was likely the only thing keeping him awake.

Even so, he could sense the exhaustion winning. It was just too much.

Curiously, he thought he heard his sister's name. His heart clenched, his body overcome with a different kind of pain. He should've never left her. He'd promised he'd make it back to her, but now his death would just be another unanswered question. Another mistake weighing on her soul.

With that morose thought ringing in his ears, his hold on Shadow slipped. Shadow sank without warning, his gray snout the last thing to disappear.

Not again.

Conall sucked in a breath, preparing to dive and find him. But the next instant, his breath flew out in a gasp and his eyes bulged. Static crackled around him, the air above the river's surface suddenly dense, like he was floating through a cloud of mist.

Shadow reversed course all on his own, his snout emerging from the water first, then his head. But it didn't stop there. His body quickly followed until he floated above the water's surface. Conall scrubbed at his eyelids with his good hand, his body whipping around as his bondmate floated over his head.

A canoe!

Shadow drifted down inside the wooden vessel, his body landing with a gentle *thunk*. And as soon as he landed, Conall began rising from the water. The tingle of electricity intensified, thrumming all over his skin. The water pushed him up from below, the pressure on his bad ankle causing a pain so intense he closed his eyes and bit his tongue, lest he cry out and break the spell.

Then he was out of the water. A blast of air took over and lifted him, gliding him toward the canoe. The pressure on his ankle subsided, and he opened his eyes just in time to see himself hovering over the small boat. Then the air cut off. He dropped onto the canoe, much less gently than his bondmate had. His back flared with pain. He landed half off, half on a wooden bench before sliding off onto the bottom of the boat. The fall to the bottom jarred his shoulder, and the deep gash there screamed again.

He groaned, but popped up off the floor, crawling for Shadow.

Please, be all right...

Conall collapsed beside him, resting his hand on the soaked fur on his chest. The slow rise and fall of Shadow's breathing pressed against his palm. Conall's eyelids fluttered shut, the exhaustion and the pain too strong to ignore.

A tiny smile tugged at his lips. They were alive.

Something warm landed on him. From somewhere far away, he heard a woman's voice—the same voice he heard all too frequently in his dreams—whispering, "It's all right, I've got you. I'll keep you safe."

Chapter 10

"What's the plan, Princess?" Vespen asked.

"There's a cliff behind the tower that overlooks the ocean. We need to make it there."

The thudding on the stable door intensified. It wouldn't be easy, but with two more mages to help, they should be able to make a run for it.

Kayda shifted to look at Mika. He was crouched beside the Guard Captain with his hand on his calf. "How's he doing?"

Mika rose and lifted his hands from the gash, revealing smooth, unmarred flesh. "He's healed. We can leave when you're ready."

The Guard Captain hopped up. He brushed the straw from his backside and tested out his leg, stomping his foot and swiveling his knee. "Thanks." He grinned.

A screech rang out. Kayda jumped, and her hand flew to her chest. She turned in time to see Vespen slam a pile of dirt in the face of a scourge who'd dug far enough beneath the wooden doors to stick its snout in the crack.

"Better go sooner than later." Vespen sighed. "Are we ready?"

"Wait," the king shouted. "We can't leave without Valiant."

"Who's that?" Kayda asked, peering around the darkened stable. The light of a handful of torches illuminated the interior. Stalls lined the walls, most of them empty. But just to her right, a chestnut stallion stuck its head free of a stall and whinnied loudly. His muzzle sported a long scar on the right side. As she drew close enough to peer within the stall, more appeared, dotting his hide all over. It was clear Valiant was not some horse of leisure; he was a seasoned fighter.

"This is Valiant." King Quinton strolled to the beast's side, a proud smile lighting his face. "My new bondmate."

Kayda's heart lifted. She couldn't remember the last time she'd seen her grandfather so happy. "Hello, Valiant." She walked directly in front of him, meeting his dark brown eyes, grinning just as widely. She glanced at the king. "How did you find him?"

"It was only when the bridge was about to fall, and the scourge descend upon Northmoat, that his voice reached me. The bond did what no magic, no healer, could. It gave me a new reason to live. And a way to escape from the strange prison trapping me within my mind. I owe Valiant everything." His eyes shone with unshed tears, his smile turning tender but just as radiant.

"Well, then we'd better bring him along," she said, squeezing her grandfather's shoulder. But then she tilted her head, frowning.

"What is it?" Izora appeared at her side, her brow furrowed and the corners of her eyes crinkled.

"The escape route, I don't know if—"

A hole burst open in the ground in the back of the stables.

"Hurry!" Vespen yelled, throwing dirt at the breach. "I can't keep this up, forever."

The king threw open the stall door, and in a fluid leap, he bounded atop the horse's back. Kayda's eyes widened momentarily at the incredible jump from a man who, until yesterday, had been one step away from being bedbound. But then she remembered the boons. Perhaps sharing a bond with horses awarded increased jumping capabilities?

She raced toward the doors and pulled a torch from the wall. Izora grabbed another while Mika and Vespen frantically scooped dirt into their pockets and the Guard Captain drew his sword.

"Rally around the king and his steed," he ordered, holding his blade aloft like a talisman. "On to the tower!" Then he lifted the wooden beam and shoved the door open with his shoulder.

A cold chill spread through Kayda's veins, and vibration hummed to life around her. The scourge were quick to jump into the gap as soon as the door sprang open, but they were ready for them. Fire and earth flew, and steel shredded fur and flesh. They forced the horde to fall back, laying waste to any that pressed too close.

The five of them formed a loose circle around the king. He alone remained unarmed. He made a peculiar sight, riding bareback on a horse in his robe and pajamas. But though he lacked a means to fight, he helped as he could, yelling out encouragement and a word of warning when any of the crowd attempted to sneak up on one of them from behind.

The tower loomed large on the horizon. It perched on the Royal Grounds' northwest corner and would normally only take a few moments to reach from the stables. But with the scourge pressing in around them, they had to fight for every step.

They fought for what felt like hours. More and more scourge came, flooding in from every direction. It seemed like with every one they slew, two more rose to take their place. By the time they reached the tower door, all of them showed signs of exhaustion. Izora nearly stumbled as she sent a wave of fire into the crowd. Mika drew a hand across his forehead, smearing sweat and dirt across his brow. They couldn't keep this up much longer.

The Guard Captain pivoted, heading for the cliffside that stretched out behind the tower as planned. But then, the scourge surged forward.

"Izora, behind you!" King Quinton yelled.

The old mage reacted an instant too late. A scourge jumped onto her back, sinking its claws into her flesh. She screamed, her knees buckled, and she fell to the ground. Her torch spilled from her hands and rolled into the crowd, guttering out almost instantly.

"Izora." Kayda leaped into action, rushing to her side.

Vespen beat her there. He jammed a dart of dirt into the scourge on her back, flinging it aside. Kayda reached her the next instant and threw an arm under her shoulder, pulling her to her feet as Vespen threw down a barrage of dirt for cover.

"Quick, into the tower to regroup," King Quinton yelled. He'd already dismounted beside the wide wooden doors and ushered his mount inside. The Guard Captain hovered at his side, his teeth gritted and sword slashing furiously.

They all piled inside. Mika barred the door after the Guard Captain rushed in. Kayda gently set Izora down on the cold stone floor in the entranceway, then rose to her feet and hung her lit torch on the wall.

She turned back to find Vespen pulling Izora's cloak off her back and examining her wound. "I'll fix you right up," he murmured. Mika hovered beside him, but Vespen waved him off, determined to heal Izora despite his obvious exhaustion.

Kayda sighed, scanning the tower. The last time she'd entered these doors, the building had been full of activity. Now, it was cold and empty, only the brightly painted murals of battles left as a reminder of the men who once worked and lived in these halls. Even the weapons that festooned the walls had been removed, leaving brighter spots of paint below the bare hooks and nails; shadows of what once was.

The Guard Captain mounted the first flight of stairs curling around the circular tower. He stopped when he reached the height of the high glass windows and peered outside. "Where do all the bastards keep coming from? I thought they'd all headed for Southmoat?"

Kayda's stomach sank. The tower was the most secure building in the entire keep. Originally built as a prison, the stone walls stood strong and sound. But given enough time, the scourge would undoubtedly find a way in. And with more beasts arriving every moment, they would have just as hard of a time advancing through the horde to reach the cliffside.

"How much farther do we have to go?" Mika leaned against the wall, his breath heavy.

Kayda gulped. "At least triple the distance we just traveled."

Mika's face paled.

The king patted his bondmate's hide, his gaze locked on Izora's back. She hissed as Vespen pulled down her gray servant's dress low enough to attend to the wound on her back.

King Quinton frowned. "Kayda, I think I know what you're planning." He turned to her. "I'm not coming."

"What? No, you can't, Grandfather." Tears prickled the corners of her eyes.

"I can't leave Valiant behind." A sad smile painted his lips as his fingers trailed down Valiant's mane. "I've heard about your bondmate. A dragon." He shook his head. "Incredible. But I can't help noticing you're alone."

Kayda took a deep breath, the reminder of her bondmate's absence wrenching her chest. She nodded.

Her grandfather clutched her hand. "Then you understand, don't you? I can't go through it again. I won't."

Mika pushed off of the wall. "Sir? I can help. Back in Raimire, I have a patient who's lost four bondmates. There is a way to remove their voices from your mind. It's risky, but I've seen it wo—"

The king held up a hand. "No. I'm not leaving Valiant. Absolutely not."

Kayda's eyes swam with tears. The pain that welled within her from Druturion's absence—she wouldn't wish that on anyone. But she didn't want her grandfather to die. If he stayed behind, with no one to protect him, it would only be a matter of time before the scourge found him.

"Please, Grandfather. We're so close. I can't go back without you."

"You can and you will." Quinton squeezed her hand, his blue eyes soft, but his voice hard as steel. "I'm so proud of you. Everything that you've done for this country—for our family—I couldn't have asked for more." He beamed, his eyes shining. "You're going to make a marvelous queen one day."

Kayda shook her head, her gaze downcast. "I'm not who you think I am—"

He reached up, cradling her cheek. "Stop. You are everything and more, Little Red. I've watched you your whole life. I might not have been around as much as I would've liked, but I wasn't blind. You have a kind heart, you're bloody smart, and tough as nails." He laughed. "Just look at you, now. You fought your way through a mountain of monsters to save us. You are a wonder, Kayda."

Her heart warmed at his words. But they sounded too much like goodbye. The tears were spilling now, flowing down her cheeks, splashing on her grandfather's wrinkled hand. "Maybe we can slow his fall. Mika and Vespen can—"

"No. You'll never make it with the two of us slowing you down." His gaze shifted to Valiant. "We've already discussed it. We'll leave first, lead the beasts away. Give the rest of you a chance." He brushed away her tears. "Take it, Little Red."

Kayda gasped, backing away. "You're going out there all alone?" The door they'd entered slammed for the hundredth time as the vicious beasts fought to break in. How could he even consider it? The scourge would tear them to pieces.

"My king." The Guard Captain hopped off the bottom step, then bowed before them. "I would be honored to stay behind and protect you."

King Quinton waited until he stood to his full height. Then he focused on the captain, peering straight into his eyes. "Gawain, your service has been exemplary. The depth of your loyalty, sacrifice, and courage is beyond compare. I would ask you to use those qualities now to protect my granddaughter." The Guard Captain looked like he wanted to argue, but Quinton grasped his shoulder and continued, "Not as your king. I'm asking as a friend. Protect Kayda for me, Gawain. Please."

Kayda pressed her fingers to her temples, watching the Guard Captain—Gawain—nodding in agreement. She'd never even learned his name. How could her grandfather expect her to make a good queen?

Inside, she seethed, sorrow and disbelief warring in her chest. She couldn't let him go through with this. But the one thing that might make him change his mind could ruin her forever.

"I'm not your kin," she blurted out. "Don't throw your life away for me."

King Quinton turned from Gawain. Kayda steeled herself, preparing to greet his shock and anger. But when he met her gaze, a soft smile lit his face. Her brows knitted together.

"I told you, Little Red. I'm not blind. You were still in the womb when I learned the truth. Your grandmother isn't the only one in Kings Keep who can keep a secret."

Kayda bit her lip, her gaze flitting between Izora and Quinton. He already knew? He'd allowed an imposter to be princess all these years? It didn't make sense.

"I wager I even know more than you think you do. But none of that matters. This is my choice. Valiant and I, we've both had long lives already. And both of us are itching for a good gallop." He sighed. "Oh, it's been so long." A wistful smile flashed on his face. He spun back to his bondmate, caressing his mane once more. Then he leaped atop his back and set his shoulders straight and his gaze forward. Valiant trotted up to the vibrating door.

"You can't, Grandfather! Please, see reason," Kayda tried again, her heart breaking.

"This is happening, Little Red. You won't sway me."

"No, she's right," Gawain said.

Kayda's heart jerked. Was someone finally going to stop this mad plan?

But Gawain only beckoned the king away from the front door. "There's too many out there. You won't make it more than five steps before they're all on you. Leave out the back door instead."

Izora, now healed, her clothes back in place, rose from the floor and wrapped an arm around Kayda's shoulders.

The king met Izora's gaze. "Keep our girl safe."

Izora lifted her chin. "You know I will." Something unspoken passed between them. An understanding that Kayda was not privy to.

Kayda sucked in a breath, ready to demand an explanation, but then the king guided Valiant toward the back door. She raced over to his side and stared up at him. "I love you, Grandfather. Please don't do this. We'll find a way... I—"

Valiant halted, and King Quinton leaned down. "I love you, too, Little Red. I'm sorry I wasn't there for you when you needed me. I wish I could stay with you forever. But I can't." He caressed her cheek, staring down at her. All signs of that far away longing that always filled his eyes had vanished, leaving them shining—radiant. "Let me go. I need to feel the wind in my hair while I ride, one last time. You wouldn't deny an old fool one final wish, would you?"

Izora caught up to her again and pulled her into her embrace. Kayda sank into it, allowing herself a moment to weep. But when the door slammed open, she pushed free of Izora's arms and raced to the back window.

Valiant burst free from the back door and tore off like a shot. King Quinton rode atop his back, his head held high, a laugh bursting free of his chest. They bowled through the few scourge gathered around the back of the tower with ease and pulled up to a stop after galloping back toward the stables.

"Try to catch us, you bastards!" The king's shout was loud enough to reach her ears through the stone walls, though barely above a whisper. "I dare you." Then they tore off again, galloping into the distance.

Kayda pressed her hand to the glass, chin quivering, tears flooding her cheeks. She watched the scourge take off after them. Dozens of the beasts zipped through the grass, slowly gaining ground.

"It's working." Gawain peered through the glass behind her shoulder. "C'mon, Princess. Now's our chance. We need to leave."

She let herself be pulled from the window, numbly following the others to the front door.

Izora grabbed the torch from the wall and shook her hard. "Kayda, listen to me. You have to fight now. He made that sacrifice for you. For us. Don't let it be wasted."

Kayda met her gaze. Nodded. She was right. It was time to fight.

The front door slammed open. She burst out first. Cold swam through Kayda's veins. She welcomed it, lifting her hands. And for the first time, the fire didn't just flow from her hands in a stream; it burst out in a wide semi-circle, incinerating everything in front of her.

She reveled in the flames, the power. The cold grew so intense she shivered, even as the fire before her blazed so hot the scourge's carcasses melted before her eyes. It felt like she lived in that moment forever, but before she knew it, it ended, and she fell to her knees.

"Blazes." Gawain knelt beside her. "That was incredible."

Kayda smiled weakly, allowing him to slide an arm underneath her and tug her to her feet.

"C'mon." Izora turned around. "Keep close to me, Captain. The princess needs to stay close to the torch."

Slowly, Kayda's strength returned. What was that blast? She'd read about something similar in the ancient book Conall brought back with him, but she'd never experienced anything like it. Whatever it was, she didn't have the strength to repeat it.

It was good then that most of the scourge had taken off after the king. The five of them ran, making much better time with only a few beasts leaping out at them instead of a vast crowd surrounding them. Kayda allowed the others to dispatch them, focusing on moving one foot in front of the other.

Finally, they made it to the cliff. Kayda stepped up to the edge and stared down at the sea below.

"You want us to dive down there?" Mika asked. "Are you sure?"

Gawain grinned and thumped Mika on the back. "Oh, it looks scarier than it is. The guard jump in from this spot during training. A test of courage. And fortitude as well." He frowned at Izora. She was doubled over, her chest heaving after the short run. "The swim to the docks tests even the most seasoned of men. Are you sure *all* of us are up for it, Princess?"

"We won't be swimming to the docks." She hoped they wouldn't, at least. Kayda shaded her eyes, staring past the setting sun. "There." She pointed, a tiny smile creeping across her face. Her father could be counted on after all. There on the horizon sailed the rickety old ship, *The Lady Luck*, ready to scoop them up like promised.

There was nothing left to do but leap. She took one last look at Northmoat. Already the scourge were regrouping. More of them barreled up the path from the tower, chasing after them.

Tears welled in her eyes as her thoughts drifted to her grandfather. Was he still alive? But she shook her head, biting them back. He'd believed in her enough to sacrifice himself to ensure her survival. She would not let him down.

Kayda turned her back on Northmoat and jumped.

Chapter 11

Lark mounted the gangplank to *Nova's Champion* as the sun sank down over the sea. Jett and Jayan were there to greet them. Her father lent her a hand as she struggled up the swaying boards.

"Thanks," she wheezed out around a sigh, still fighting to catch her breath. They'd sped through the streets of Southmoat to make it back. From how crowded the huge boat appeared, with folk peering over the sides of every rail, they'd come none too soon.

Jayan assisted Aren, then rose on his tiptoes to peer within the makeshift carrier Lark had fashioned out of a pair of coveralls strapped to Dausius' chest. His dark brown eyes widened before a grin spread across his face. "So that's what has you folks arriving so late. I've never seen a babe so small." After a moment his gaze lifted, and his smile fell. "What of the mother?"

Dausius shook his head sadly. "Gone."

"Oh, that's a shame," Jayan said.

"It's not what you're thinking," Lark hurried to say. "She took off on a canoe into the bog."

Jett's brows shot up. "Into the bog? Whatever for?"

Lark shrugged, then grabbed hold of Jayan's cloak sleeve. "Have you watched everyone boarding?" At Jayan's nod, she continued. "Are there any mothers with infants on board?"

Jayan's gaze flicked back to the babe, and he raked a hand through his braids. "I don't think there are..."

Lark's stomach dropped. What were they going to do with a newborn on a boat at sea with no milk to speak of?

Aren rubbed her back, pointing toward the city. "Look, there are more people arriving. We might get lucky."

Lark bit her lip, standing by the rail to watch the group approaching. Jett joined her, frowning as he stared into the city.

As the people drew closer, Lark's heart sank. No one carried a babe in their arms. In fact, they all appeared worse for the wear, their hair and faces dusted with dirt and their boots caked in mud. But it wasn't until they began making their way up the gangplank that she recognized one of them.

"Edrik." She waved him over as he boarded. "I'm glad to see you."

"Lark, oh thank goodness." He pulled her into an embrace, and a cloud of dust rose from his clothing, tickling her nose. "I was so worried when you didn't show up in the tunnels."

"Sorry about that." She grimaced. "I ran into some surprises. It's a long story."

Edrik opened his mouth, but then shut it again, swiveling to view a commotion headed their way from the city. A crowd of young people raced toward them, flinging blasts of air and fire behind them.

Lark gaped, her keen eyes spotting the beasts chasing after them, teeth snapping. "Pull up the gangplank and shove off!" she yelled.

Jayan turned to her, his eyes widening. "What of the young mages? They won't be able to board."

"Yes, they will. Trust me."

Jayan stared at her. For a moment, she feared he would ignore her command, but he must've seen something in her face that convinced him. He spun on his heel after only an instant, barking out orders to his crew.

Lark whirled around and shouted across the deck, "Any mage who still has the strength to summon, gather around. Now."

Soon a crowd of harried young folk joined the dirt-dusted mages already nearby. They all aimed curious looks in her direction, their jaws dropping as they spotted the mages rushing toward them, and the gangplank disappearing.

When the ship slowly began to move, a burly mage rushed to the front of the crowd. "What are you doing? We can't just leave them there to die. Put the gangplank back!"

Lark patted the mage's shoulder reassuringly. "Don't worry. We'll make a new gang-plank. Everyone, gather around. Link hands."

She blew out a steadying breath and stuck her hand in her pocket, then removed a handful of fresh soil from her coveralls. This had better work or those mages would be stranded.

She reached out, clasping hands with Edrik, squashing the handful of earth between them. "Everyone, call forth your talent, please."

Lark closed her eyes, reaching for the magic all around her. Her palm warmed as she connected to the linked mage's pooled energy. Then she snapped open her eyes and held out her free hand. The boat shook and swayed, the wooden deck vibrating. Slowly, a wide curved bridge formed between the dock and the ship.

It appeared not a moment too soon. The first of the running mages arrived, and wasted no time leaping atop the dirt bridge and up onto the ship. Lark kept a constant watch on the bridge, adding more length to the ends as the ship slowly drifted away from the dock.

Before long, a half dozen boarded, but there was still a pair lagging behind. A crowd of scourge—a few dozen, at the least—trailed at their heels, and they kept twisting back to throw blasts of air and fire behind them.

"Hurry," Jett yelled.

The folk at the rails joined in, shouting encouragement. A few of the guards on board picked up bows. Arrows sailed through the sky, skewering the vermin, their dying shrieks setting off whoops of glee from the watching townspeople.

Even with all the mages lending her their strength, Lark could sense her hold on the magic fading. The bridge stretched the length of half a city block, and with every passing moment, she was forced to add more dirt to the end. Her shoulders trembled, and her knees buckled. She would've surely smacked down atop the deck if it weren't for Edrik's tight grip on her hand and Aren throwing a hand around her waist when he spotted her staggering.

Still, she kept the bridge going, until Edrik's grip slackened. She chanced a glance behind at the mages, and spotted several of them wobbling on their feet. Mika's words echoed in her mind and she recalled the weariness washing over her after linking—the same weariness all the mages linked with her must be feeling now.

But when she flicked her glance back to the docks, her heart lifted. The pair finally made it to the bridge. As soon as they both jumped upon it, she breathed out a sigh. Carefully, she shifted the dirt from the far end to the end resting against the boat. Soon a gap appeared, so large not a single scourge took the chance of leaping after the racing mages.

As soon as the last mage's boots smacked down on the wood, Lark dropped Edrik's hand, and the last of the dirt splashed into the sea. All the linked mages sagged in relief. A few of them dropped to the deck, holding hands to their stomachs and heads.

Lark winced. Had she held on too long? But soon, they all lurched back up on their feet, and she loosed another sigh, turning to greet the newcomers.

She'd been so completely focused on holding onto the bridge she hadn't bothered to examine the mage's faces closely. As she approached, she scanned the crowd, and when she recognized one of them, her heart skipped a beat.

"Oriana?" She pushed through the throng to reach her, frantically searching the newcomers, again and again. "Where's Conall? He was supposed to be with you."

When Oriana's face fell, Lark's heart twisted. "Lark, I'm so sorry. There was a breach at the moat. Shadow fell into the bog, and Conall leaped in after him. We were so busy keeping the fire lit I didn't have a chance to search for him."

Lark's gaze connected with Jett's across the deck. She watched her father's face sag at Oriana's announcement. Then he strode away, weaving through the gathered townspeople, his shoulders slumped.

Lark pressed a hand to her chest. Not again. Blazes. They should've never split up.

She paced back to the side rail and turned to stare at the city growing small as they headed out to sea. Would Conall be all right? Would she ever see him again?

The shrill cry of a newborn broke her trance. Dausius strode up to her, gently rocking the baby against his chest. "What do I do? She won't quiet."

"Hand her to me." Lark stretched out her arms. She stared down at Violet as she wailed, then cradled her tiny body against her chest. Violet's face immediately sought out her breast, instinct driving her movements. But she wouldn't find any succor there.

Lark crossed the deck, shouting to be heard above the infant's wails. "Are there any wet nurses on board?" She walked to the aft rail, repeating her question every time she reached another group of huddled townsfolk. Every time, she was met with shaking heads and grave stares.

After reaching the stern, she veered toward the bow. With every group she approached, and every denial, her heart sank lower, until she found herself with no one left to ask, the crying child silent again. The walk had lulled her to sleep, but it wouldn't be long before she awakened again, even hungrier than before.

She found Tiora, Mazen, and Meital standing at the bow rail with Aren. Her friends and fellow performers had been true to their word, sticking with her as she left Raimire. She exhaled a deep sigh. At least they'd all made it back on the boat in one piece after the madness in Flamesmoat.

"Lark." A soft smile lit Tiora's beautiful face as her brown cloak billowed around her curvy frame. "I hear you had quite the adventure without us."

Lark's cheeks heated. "I seem to have a knack for finding trouble."

Mazen grinned, knife in hand, hard at practice balancing the sharp blade atop his knuckles. "You don't say?" His multi-colored tunic flashed beneath his cloak in the fading afternoon sunlight.

Meital elbowed her twin, nearly making him drop his knife into the sea. "Who do we have here?" She flicked her long brown braid over her shoulder and peered at the bundle wrapped in Lark's arms.

"This is Violet. I'm stuck playing nursemaid until her mother returns." Her shoulders sank. "I'm making a real muck of it already."

"What's wrong?" Tiora asked.

"I need to find her a wet nurse. I've already asked everyone on deck with no luck."

"Have you gone down below?" Meital asked.

Lark shook her head, a seed of hope taking root within her. "Below deck—of course. Maybe I'll find someone down there."

Tiora took a turn peering at the sleeping babe, and her golden-brown eyes shone with warmth. "Let us ask around. You don't want to wake the little doll."

"You don't mind?"

Her friends all insisted they didn't, then disappeared into the bowels of the ship, leaving her alone at the bow.

She didn't stay alone for long. The light taps of paws on the deck sounded. Lark whipped around, praying for the gray fur of her brother's bondmate to appear with Conall beside him. But it was only her brother's mutt, Sunny, approaching. She wagged her tail when she spotted Lark, rushing over to greet her. A small smile graced her lips in the face of Sunny's enthusiastic welcome, but it didn't stick around for long.

The flapping of wings alerted her an instant before her bondmate touched down beside her, digging her talons into the deck railing.

"I didn't see your brother and his wolf make it back on board. Are you all right?" Muse asked.

Lark quickly relayed Oriana's story. *"He found me once before. He'll find me again."*

Muse was silent for a long moment before she finally responded. *"Hey, what if that mage went after him? She could've seen them splashing out there and left to save them."*

"Yeah, wouldn't that be crazy?" She stared down at the baby sleeping in her arms. She still couldn't wrap her head around Ereni's motivations. Why would anyone leave their newborn in the care of a stranger?

Could she be just that selfless that she saw a man drowning and rushed off to save him? Surely stranger things had happened, but it all seemed so farfetched. Then again, what other reason could she have to disappear into the bog only moments after giving birth?

But was it too much to hope that Ereni had found Conall? Something tickled her mind at the sound of both their names in the same sentence.

Of course. That was where she'd heard the name Ereni before... Conall asked if she was in Flamesmoat right before he raced out of the Mata's hut on the night they'd arrived in Stoneshore.

If they knew each other already, maybe it wasn't such a crazy idea after all...

The inner hatch swung open, and Aren climbed back above deck. Lark's heart picked up speed when his gaze zeroed in on hers, but she did her best to ignore it. Now was not the time for flirting, no matter how handsome he might be or how much she wanted to sink into his embrace.

"Any luck?" she asked.

He shook his head. "Speaking of luck…" He pointed ahead, beyond the bow's rail. *The Lady Luck* was fast approaching, readying to pull alongside their boat. "Maybe we'll have better luck among the townsfolk over there."

"Good thinking, Aren." She rushed over to the side rail where sailors flung ropes between the two vessels, latching them together in the water. Soon, long wooden boards joined the ropes, and chaos ensued as people began hopping from one ship to the other.

"Everyone headed to Doln, make your way on board *The Lady Luck*," Jayan called out. "*Nova's Champion* sails for Joria."

Lark stepped closer to the barrier, but Aren squeezed her arm before she made it to the side rail. "Why don't you stay here? Let me hop over there and ask among the folk who're on board. You can ask all the newcomers on our boat."

She watched him hurry across, then got to work, asking the handful of people who came aboard the same question. She asked so many times the words *wet nurse* felt like they lost all meaning. But it was no use. The people joining them on the journey to Joria were young and fit for the most part, or grizzled old men. All of them carted weapons and fierce expressions, ready to partake in the fight to come.

Lark sighed, taking another look at the folk gathered on deck. Most of the families and almost all the children had departed, boarding *The Lady Luck* to join the other refugees fleeing to Doln.

"Lark?" a familiar voice called out behind her.

She turned and spotted Kayda returning across the makeshift plank bridge. Mika and a handful of other people trailed in her wake.

"Kayda, you made it." She smiled, walking up to greet her.

Kayda's answering smile was not as bright as she'd expected.

"What's wrong?" Lark asked.

Kayda bit her lip. "The king… I couldn't save him."

"Oh. I'm so sorry." She reached briefly before remembering the baby cradled against her chest. "I would give you a hug, but my hands are a little full at the moment."

Kayda quirked a brow, looping her braids behind her ear and smiling down at the baby. "Who do we have here?"

"Her name is Violet. I'm in desperate need of a wet nurse for her. You didn't see any nursing mothers on *The Lady Luck* by chance?"

Kayda shook her head sadly. "Can't say that I did."

Just then, Lark spotted Aren making his way back across the planks. He met her gaze and shook his head. Her heart sank. The future appeared bleak for little Violet. What was she going to do?

"She's so tiny. How did you end up with a newborn in your care?" Kayda asked.

"I helped birth her, actually. It's a bit of a crazy story. Violet's mother saved my life. She and I hid below water in the bog to avoid a bunch of armed criminals. She summoned enough air to keep us alive while we were below water, but because she didn't have a source, little Violet made an early appearance."

"Wow. That is pretty crazy." Kayda stared at Violet again. "What happened to the mother? Did she..."

Lark frowned as Kayda trailed off. "No, that's even stranger. She took off on a boat into the bog. Left the baby behind. Told me to take care of her until she could find us again."

Baris, the mage they'd met on the docks earlier that day, approached them. "I'm sorry. I couldn't help but overhear your tale. Tell me, what was that mage's name?"

Lark glanced at him. "Oh, it's all right. Her name was Ereni. Do you know her?"

Baris' eyes widened. He nodded. "Yes. She's missing." He rubbed a hand across his face. "That explains why she was always holed up in her chambers every morning. And that awful ginger tea she'd offer me when I'd come to her with a question." He peeked at the sleeping child. "This is her daughter? You're certain?"

It was Lark's turn to nod. "Absolutely. I witnessed the birth."

"Well, I'll be." Baris smiled. "I wonder who the father is?" Then his eyes widened again, and he shot a glance at Kayda before flicking his gaze back to the baby. "Exactly how early was her appearance, do you think?"

Lark shrugged. "I'm not sure. She said something about it being months too soon, but how many, I have no idea. Why do you ask?"

Baris gulped, his Adam's apple bobbing in his throat. "It's just, I've only ever seen one man who looked like more than a friend to Ereni. When the Palisade fell, her and Prince Tarquin were acting awfully cozy."

Kayda's brows shot up at that. "Is she the brunette with the ponytail I remember from the fight back in the Abandoned Lands?" Baris nodded, and she flashed a grin at the baby. "It would be kind of nice, knowing a part of him lived on."

Lark sighed, shaking her head. "I guess I better change ships before they pull apart."

"Wait." Kayda frowned. "I thought you were coming with us?"

"I was, but Violet will never make it to Joria without a wet nurse. Even Midsport..." Her stomach twisted. "I just don't know. But I need to give her a chance."

"Lark, there you are." Tiora bustled up to her, a wide smile on her face. "We found someone."

"You did?" Her heart lit with joy. "Below deck? What took you so long?"

"That's the thing." Tiora drew closer, speaking softly. "She's not a normal wet nurse. She's just a mother who lost her baby yesterday."

Lark's brows pinched together. "Oh."

"She had some reservations at first, as you could imagine. But she finally agreed to help our little Violet out," Tiora said. "Her name is Elmena. C'mon, I'll show you where she's holed up below deck with her other kids. They have family in Joria, so they were already planning to stay on board."

Lark waved goodbye to Kayda, Aren, and the others, and followed. Tiora pulled back a curtain a few moments later, revealing a small corner of the hold where several families gathered, seated on the floor, the adults chatting quietly together while the children played. When Lark's gaze landed on the woman seated next to Meital, a wide grin broke out across her face.

"Hello. It's nice to see you made it," she said to the woman whose ankle she'd healed on the road in Southmoat.

Elmena smiled back, hers much more tentative. "Lark, was it? It's nice to see you again as well." She rose to her feet, cooing at Violet, her expression turning bittersweet. "Look at you, what a tiny little gorgeous girl you are." Elmena met Lark's gaze, her brown eyes swimming with tears. "I'll take her, now." She held out her arms.

"Thank you, so much." Lark handed Violet to Elmena. "I can take her when she's fed, if you need to tend to your children."

Elmena shook her head, settling back down, already tugging her breast free from her tunic. Violet clasped on instantly, not even bothering to open her eyes. "Oh, she'll be no bother. What a beauty." She rocked her gently, staring at Violet, tears falling soundlessly down her cheeks.

Lark's heart squeezed. Was she doing the right thing, or was she only traumatizing this poor woman who'd just lost her own child?

But then Elmena lifted her head and smiled up at her. "When your friends first asked me to do this, I didn't want any part of it. But now..." She gazed down at Violet again. "It feels right. Even though my Landra isn't here anymore, I can still help this little one. Landra was only three months old. She was never well, her entire life. It's a miracle she lived as long as she did; all the healers thought so. They told me she'd be lucky to live a few days when she was born. But she was a fighter. I did everything I could to make her comfortable. To make her short life one filled with love. Even when having her at home, too ill to travel, meant that we had to stay in Southmoat while all our neighbors fled. Now, I have to believe she held on for this. So that her milk could save another. Isn't that beautiful, in a way?"

Tiora knelt down beside her. "It is. It's wonderful." Her voice was choked, tears in her eyes.

Lark had tears in her eyes, too. Her brother might be missing, and the whole world faced with war, but here on this boat, she was witnessing something to be grateful for. People banding together to survive against all odds. In her eyes, that was the most beautiful thing of all.

Chapter 12

Kayda pushed open the door to the former captain's study on board *Nova's Champion*. The sight of her hammock swaying invitingly with the motion of the surf sent a wave of weariness washing over her. But she couldn't sleep. Not yet.

She held the door wide open. "Come in, we can speak privately in here."

Prince—no—King Gideon strode in, his nose wrinkling at the modest room. "This is what they expect a princess to use on board?" he grumbled under his breath, scanning the chamber with undisguised disdain.

Kayda pinched the bridge of her nose, seating herself atop the large desk by the window. She hadn't come here to discuss the quality of the housing arrangements. She had much bigger problems to discuss. Like the fact that she was an imposter. She could only hope her father would be as understanding as her grandfather had been. With him gone... She couldn't have the lie weighing on her with everything else happening. She needed to come clean to her father and accept the consequences, whatever they may be.

"Take a seat," she offered, easing the single chair away from the desk with the toe of her boot.

King Gideon lifted a brow, but he sat in the chair, groaning as his large girth settled atop the cushion. "I'm pleased you asked to speak with me. We have much to discuss."

Kayda gulped. "We do?" A pit coalesced in her belly.

Had the Guard Captain spoken with him already? He'd been privy to her conversation with the king before his... sacrifice. Did he confess the truth to his commander immediately?

But the next words out of her father's mouth made her shoulders sag. "Tarquin. Tell me, how did he meet his end?"

Kayda pursed her lips. She still had conflicting feelings about that day. Her half-brother had been so confident he could destroy the scourge—the evil that an entire order of mages dedicated their lives to caging for hundreds of years—in a single afternoon, leading dozens of men to their deaths. But looking into her father's eyes, seeing the pain that lurked there at the memory of his lost son, perhaps it was best to spare the man all the gory details.

"He and his men fought valiantly until they were overwhelmed. The vast number of scourge was simply too much. I'm sorry I couldn't save him."

Gideon closed his eyes and drew a deep breath through his nose. Then his eyes snapped opened, and he nodded once. "Don't blame yourself, my dear." He patted her knee. "No one holds you responsible for your brother's foolish decisions."

Kayda flinched. She'd expected a bit more sadness, but perhaps he'd cried all his tears already in private. "I—"

"Have you heard what they're saying about that little albino brat on board?" The king rolled his eyes. "It's Tarquin's bastard, apparently."

Kayda stifled a gasp. "Yes, I've met *her*. Violet. She's a lovely child."

The king scoffed, shifting in his chair. "Lovely or not, she could become a problem for us. For you. I've half a mind to arrange a little swim for the brat before we dock in Joria."

Kayda saw red. She hopped to her feet, her nostrils flaring. "I'm going to assume you aren't thinking straight after hearing the news of Tarquin's death. That innocent little *baby* will not be touched. Is that clear?"

The king bristled, blubbering incoherently, his face flushing.

Kayda turned her back on him, fighting not to lose her cool. How could he even suggest that? It was beyond the pale. About his own grandchild, if the rumors proved true. If he was willing to murder an innocent baby just for being born a royal bastard, what would he say to her confession?

All thought of coming clean fled her mind, replaced with a rage that burned as hot as the flame in Druturion's throat. She had to send him away before she said something she would regret.

She spun to face him, forcing a smile. "I'm feeling very tired, Father. Can we continue this conversation later?"

King Gideon heaved off the desk chair and smoothed the front of his tunic. "I see my joke was in poor taste. Of course, I wouldn't dream of harming that child. I'm simply frustrated, is all. We don't need her growing up and staking claim to the crown. A child of a mage, no less." He shook his head. "I'll leave you to your rest, my dear."

"Goodnight." Kayda walked him to the door, feeling marginally better after his parting words. Still, she knew so little about her father. Was his *joke* really that, or was he just saving face after how she'd reacted?

She closed the door, paced back to the desk, and leaned against the top, staring down at the jagged holes dotting the surface. The former captain had the habit of stabbing his knife into the wood like a pincushion. Kayda rolled her neck, suddenly understanding the compulsion. If she owned a knife, she would've added a few marks of her own.

Grandfather. He would've known what to do. But he was gone, and she was even more alone than she'd ever been before.

A knock drew her from her grief. "Come in."

The door opened, and Izora slid in. "Kayda, I thought you might want to talk."

She took a deep breath and perched atop the desk again. "I do." She inclined her head to the chair her father had just vacated. "Have a seat."

Izora's boots tapped across the floor. She smoothed her skirt and settled down on the chair, cocking her head sideways, her gaze landing on the tiny braids covering the left side of Kayda's head. "You've been to Sul Hollow."

Kayda grinned. "I have. I met my uncle. Your son. You have three grandchildren out there in the desert."

A wistful smile lit Izora's face. "That's good. I'm glad to hear it."

"Don't you want to meet them?" She ran her gaze down the gray castle servant's dress Izora still wore. "How could you do it for so long? How could you spend so much of your life living a lie?" Her voice cracked. "Lying to me?"

"Oh, Kayda." Izora stretched out her arm, her brow wrinkled, but Kayda folded her legs beneath her and shifted out of reach before Izora's hand landed.

Izora curled her fingers in her lap instead and let out a weary sigh. "There were so many times over the years I wanted to tell you. Every time your father ignored you to drown himself in his cups, or that brat brother played another dirty trick on you, I wished I could scoop you up and secret you away with me back to Sul Hollow. But don't you see? You had to grow up at Kings Keep."

Kayda sent her a glare. "No, I don't see. I never belonged there at all. My mother was an imposter, and so am I."

Izora met her gaze, smiling warmly. "That's not true. Not entirely, at least. Let me explain."

"I'm listening."

"I'm sure Bazman told you the story of how I disappeared from Sul Hollow after Chanti's birth."

Kayda nodded.

"What he couldn't have told you was why. After I set that fire, I was terrified. My grandfather had been talented, too. But instead of going to the mages for training, he hid his talent, refusing to leave my grandmother and his children." She shook her head sadly. "It was a decision that eventually led to his demise and took my grandmother with him. They both died in a massive fire he set unintentionally. My mother was the only survivor out of her entire family of eight. When I discovered I'd inherited the same power, I knew I couldn't make the same mistake."

"So, you went to Mage Keep."

"Yes. Even though it broke my heart to leave my family, I left. I refused to do what my father had done. Leaving them was the hardest choice I ever made, but if I hurt them by staying there... that would've been so much worse."

Kayda chewed her lip. Another family driven apart, just like Lark and Conall with their father.

Izora continued, "At Mage Keep, I discovered so much more than just how to control my powers. I learned about the mission that drove the mages to keep watch over the Abandoned Lands. I befriended a young mage named Delyth and joined the future Sade Prim on her voyage to the Northern Depths. There I witnessed a glimpse of my own future. I learned the role I would play in the battle to come. The role you would play."

Kayda wrinkled her nose. More of that damned prophecy.

"It might sound odd to you, but there is a power in that knowledge that is hard to escape. I spent many years trying to hide from it. But when news reached Mage Keep of Tarquin's talent being skipped, Delyth pulled me aside. She knew, the same as I did, that if the Palisade fell with no one left of the first king's bloodline in power, then the whole world would be doomed."

"But I don't understand. I'm not—"

"Oh, but Kayda, you are." Izora smiled. "Let me finish, dear, you'll see."

Kayda crossed her arms, frowning.

"It was apparent something fishy was happening with the royal bloodlines. The rumors flew about Tarquin's mother. Everyone assumed the fault lay with her. But she was innocent. Tarquin was the true son of Prince Gideon. The bloodlines were broken before that."

Kayda gasped. "It wasn't Father's wife who'd been untrue. It was his mother." Her brows drew together. "I would've never suspected—the resemblance all three of them share—how can they not be kin?"

Izora shifted on the chair. "It's because they are still kin, in a way. King Quinton's wife fell in love with someone very close to him."

A portrait flashed in Kayda's mind. Her grandfather smiling with one arm wrapped around his lovely wife—and the other around his beloved brother. "My great uncle." Her eyes widened. "Tarquin wasn't King Quinton's grandson. He was his grandnephew."

"Yes. Luckily, the mages had enough eyes and ears within Kings Keep that we figured it out before it was too late to fix. You see, the king had not been entirely faithful either."

Kayda cringed inwardly. It was all so sordid—her own grandfather—learning the ins and outs of his sex life made her skin crawl.

"We knew he frequented a few working girls. Delyth sent seers through Southmoat, searching for anyone who showed signs of bonding talent."

"And you found Jett."

Everything clicked into place. He said himself he was the son of a whore. That his father could've been anyone.

"I gather you've met him as well." Izora sighed. "Tales had spread about the little boy who could charm any dog. Delyth went personally to make sure. Brought the meanest, most vicious dog she could find with her." One side of her mouth quirked up at the memory. "Apparently, the hound was snapping and barking like mad, but the instant she caught sight of Conall, she ran over, tail wagging and begging for belly rubs. She didn't even need the seers' confirmation after that."

The lengths they'd gone to... it was insane. How far had they gone to ensure those prophetic visions came to pass? "What about their mother? Did you arrange her beating as well? And Grandfather. Did you have a hand in arranging his attack?"

Izora frowned. "No. We would never harm the king. And Delyth wouldn't condone injuring an innocent woman. But she certainly took it as evidence of fate in play and used it to her advantage. Can't say that I blame her when it led to your birth."

Kayda rubbed her brow. "Why didn't you just make Conall the prince, then? If what you say is true, then he and Lark are of the king's blood, too."

Izora shook her head. "We considered it. But King Quinton wouldn't allow it."

Her jaw dropped. "He knew? The whole time, he knew?"

"Yes. Delyth approached him after the seer first spoke to Jett. The news only confirmed the suspicions he'd long harbored." Izora twisted her hands in her lap. "But he'd also raised Gideon as a son. He loved him dearly and insisted on keeping the truth from him. That's why we switched Chanti for that trader's daughter the prince had agreed to marry. We needed to ensure she was pregnant before the wedding, to set the bloodline straight."

Kayda hopped off the desk and strolled to the window. She stared down into the dark sea, glistening in the moonlight.

So, she was the king's true granddaughter, after all. She almost laughed. To think, only moments ago she'd been about to tell her father she was an imposter... All the while, he was the one who didn't belong.

"What do I do now?" she mused aloud.

The chair creaked, and boots tapped lightly behind her. Izora joined her at the window. "That, I leave entirely up to you. I've spoken to everyone who was with us when you came to save your grandfather. They've agreed to keep silent about what was discussed. Tell everyone, tell no one—the choice is yours."

Kayda closed her eyes, breathing deeply. She wasn't sure what to do. At the very least, Lark and Conall deserved the truth. But with Conall missing, now didn't seem like the right time.

And her father—now her king. Did he even deserve to rule? For that matter, did she? Should she seek to dethrone him, or should she honor her grandfather's decision to keep the secrets of Gideon's birthright hidden? The whole situation was mind-boggling.

"Why her?" Kayda shifted to meet her grandmother's gaze. "Why did you pick your own daughter when any young mage would've surely been willing to step in as the prince's wife?"

"The vision. I saw you fighting, Kayda. I never truly returned to see my family until the day I came to take Chanti, but I kept tabs on them, watching in secret whenever I could. You do look so much like your mother..." Izora smiled sadly.

A sudden thought struck her. "You told me she was a mage, but she wasn't, was she? If you inherited talent from your grandfather... she would've been skipped."

"You're right. Chanti was never a mage. I couldn't exactly tell you it was me who you'd gotten your talent from back when you were training, now could I?" Izora chuckled, then her face turned serious. "She might not have had talent, but your mother was an incredible woman. Fierce and strong, just like you."

Kayda sighed. "I wish I could've known her."

"She would've been so proud of you."

A wave of exhaustion hit her right between the eyes. She yawned.

Izora took that as a sign to depart. "Get some rest, Princess. Things will look clearer in the morning."

As Kayda closed the door to her room and climbed into her hammock, she hoped Izora's words would prove true. But for once she didn't fall asleep with a thousand questions plaguing her. Only one remained, repeating in her mind like the strangest of lullabies.

"Dru—where are you?"

Chapter 13

“Conall,” a voice called to him.

He ignored it. He was having the most wonderful dream.

The summer sun's golden rays kissed his face. Warmth flooded him from above and within as he watched Sunny zip around the grazing field on his farm in Greenvale, happily nipping at the goats' heels to herd them inside the barn.

Shadow trotted out of the woods, a fresh kill dangling from his jaws. And in the distance, his home stood as it once was, whole, not the burned-out shell he'd last seen. Someone stepped out of the door, calling his name.

“Conall.”

It was a woman with a babe in her arms. Blue eyes met his. She smiled.

“Conall, wake up.”

He jerked awake, groaning. The blissful dream evaporated, chased away by the awakening agony in his limbs. Every muscle in his body ached. Sharp needles stabbed at his shoulder. But worse of all was the constant throbbing of his ankle.

Where was he? Why was his bed swaying?

He rubbed the sleep from his eyes as the memory of his swim through the bog surged back.

The scourge—Shadow.

He shifted so fast he jostled his broken foot and hissed in pain. But he spotted Shadow beside him, his chest rising and falling beneath the cloak draped atop them, and he heaved out a sigh.

"I've stopped the bleeding, but I'm afraid that's the extent of what I can accomplish with my earth talent. I'll need your help to heal you both fully."

Conall's heart seized. He knew that voice.

As if they had a mind of their own, the fingers of his good hand rose and tugged down the wool cloak covering his face.

"Ereni?"

She stood at the front of the canoe, securing a rope around the mangled roots of a mangrove tree in the fading light of sunset.

"What... how?" A thousand words were on the tip of his tongue, but all he could manage was the strangled questions before his throat locked up. She'd saved them? Alone?

"I happened to be on the docks when the two of you floated by. I could see you were in need of assistance." She turned and met his eyes for the first time since she'd ripped the bindings from his wrists and ordered him to place his hands on the Palisade, setting into motion the chain of events that brought him here. That unleashed the Unseen on the world.

He wasn't sure what he was expecting. Did he want her to break down in tears and beg for his forgiveness? Maybe some small part of him had. But it looked like that wouldn't be happening. Not now, at least.

Ereni's eyes were clear, direct, and so blue. Her gaze pierced him, setting off a ricochet of conflicting feelings. Anger and hurt quickly rose to the surface, but deep underneath, there was the shadow of something softer. Something he was quick to bury before it could fully surface.

There were so many things he needed to say. But seeing her there, dressed in a ridiculous, oversized set of coveralls, it was as if he'd been transported back to that moment when she crested the hillside before the wall fell and grabbed another man's arm. Struck dumb, waiting for the next words to escape her mouth.

"Do you think you're up for it?" she asked finally.

He blinked. "What?"

Her gaze flicked between him and Shadow. "Healing. I only have a small affinity for earth talent, I'm afraid. But if you lend me your strength, we should be able to take care of both of your injuries."

He had half a mind to tell her where she could shove her talent. To demand they return to Southmoat and find another healer.

Conall stole a look at his bondmate. He slept uneasily, twitching, his gray fur caked with blood in more places than he could count. If Shadow didn't make it because he'd delayed healing over a grudge...

The thought of sharing his talent with the woman who'd betrayed him had his palms sweating, even with the still damp clothing chilling his skin. But for Shadow, he would do anything. Even put his trust in the woman who'd shattered him so completely.

"What do you need me to do?" he asked.

Ereni slinked closer, her step slow and measured, like a cat stalking its prey. She settled down beside him and dug into a pack resting on the canoe bottom. Leaning over Shadow, she placed her palm over one of his wounds, a flash of bright green peeking out from the edges of her hand. Shadow twitched at the pressure but didn't awaken.

Ereni extended her empty hand to him. Conall stared at it, wanting nothing more than to slap it away like he would a snake coiling to strike.

He heaved a deep breath and grasped her hand. For an instant, he could've sworn she shivered at the simple touch, but then her gaze snapped to his. "Call on your talent," she said flatly.

He nodded and broke eye contact, staring at Shadow. This was for him. Warmth tingled across his palm, seeping up his wrist and through his arm. Then the boat shuddered, shaking in the water far more than it should have. A whisper of exhaustion slunk up his spine. But then, Ereni removed her hand from Shadow's hide, and the weariness lifted.

Conall peered down at the spot. Just moments before a jagged gash puckered the skin, now it was healed. He tugged gently on Ereni's hand, but she tightened her grasp. His gaze shot to her face. She scanned Shadow's body, her palm slipping down to another wicked gash.

"We're not done." She met his gaze. "Again. Please."

His breath caught. A memory rose, unbidden, of that last word on her lips, so long ago. They'd been touching then, too. Staring into each other's eyes.

He shook his head, shoving the memory aside. Shadow. He had to help Shadow.

He called forth his talent, again and again. Every tremor struck him with a fresh wave of fatigue. By the time they finished healing his bondmate, he felt as if he could sleep for a hundred years. His breath came shallow and quick. His shoulders slumped, the weariness in his body compounding with the pain of his injuries until he was ready to welcome death, if only for a moment of relief.

Ereni pursed her lips, eyeing him closely. "You'd better get some rest before we heal your wounds." She perched atop the forward seat of the little canoe, wrapping her arms around her torso. "I'll keep watch. Sleep."

Conall thought to protest, but it was a fleeting urge that vanished as soon as his head hit the canoe's cold wooden boards. He slept.

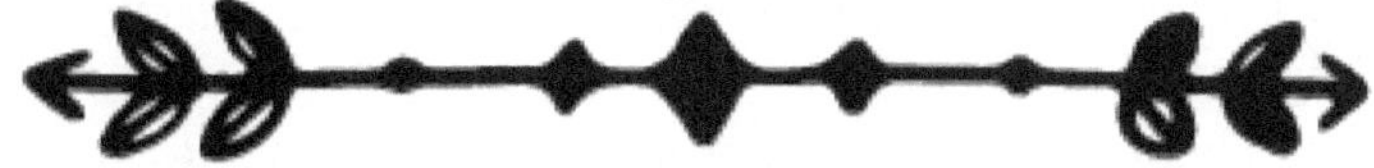

Growling woke Conall in the middle of the night. His eyes shot open, pain exploding as he jolted up. *"Shadow, what is it?"*

His eyes quickly adjusted to the moonlight. Shadow had left his side and stood in the center of the canoe, his teeth pulled back, and his golden eyes shining in the dark. But he'd not spotted some far-off danger, like Conall had first suspected. He stared at the bow, his nose twitching, a growl reverberating deep in his throat, his gaze locked on Ereni.

"Brother, calm down." Conall shuffled closer, scooting across the boat bottom using his one good leg and arm. *"She's not here to hurt us. She pulled us from the bog and healed you. She's going to heal me soon, too."*

Shadow snapped his jaw closed, his growl quieting. *"How long have I been asleep?"*

Conall sighed, sinking his fingers into the fur atop Shadow's head. *"I'm not sure. Since before we were pulled from the bog."* He looked up at the sky, scanning the moon's position. *"Half the night, maybe?"*

His gaze drifted back to Ereni. She hadn't said a peep, even with a huge wolf growling at her menacingly. It was soon apparent why. She was fast asleep, curled up in a ball atop the bow seat.

Something wasn't right. Her color was off. He could see her pallor clearly, even in the moonlight. The shudders wracking her thin frame.

He glanced to the side. Not one, but two cloaks rested on the boat bottom where he and Shadow had slept. She'd given them both, and slept alone, with nothing but those ridiculous coveralls.

Conall frowned. *"She's freezing. We need to get her warm."*

He scooted closer, wincing as his broken foot dragged on the canoe's bottom.

"Don't hurt yourself for her, little brother. Not after what she's done."

Conall shook off the words. *"We still need her to heal me. I never learned how to do it on my own."* Of course, that was all. It wasn't like his stomach was turning at the thought of her freezing to death. He reached out with his good arm and slid her off the seat into his lap. *"The cloaks, brother. Bring them over here, please."*

The sweet scent of lavender tickled his nose. He breathed in deeply. There was something else. The metallic tang of blood. Was she injured? Or was it just his and Shadow's blood on her hands?

He scanned her carefully but didn't see any injuries. Just her chattering teeth and blue lips. He grabbed the first cloak from Shadow, doing his best with one arm to wrap it around her before setting her gently on the boat floor beside him. Then he draped the second cloak around them both and stretched out behind her, pulling her back against his chest. Trying to ignore the memories that fought to surface.

How many times had they lain like this? Curled up together, laughing, spent, contentment bubbling up inside, overflowing.

He pushed the thought aside. This was not the same. It would likely never be like that between them again. He just had to keep her alive. Keep her alive so she could return the favor.

"C'mon, you, too. She needs the body heat."

Shadow settled down in front of her, and Conall lifted the cloak again, draping it over all three of them the best he could. Another scent drifted toward him through the fabric. Something familiar, but with the pain in his limbs screaming at him and exhaustion making his eyelids droop, he couldn't place it. Maybe in the morning, it would come to him.

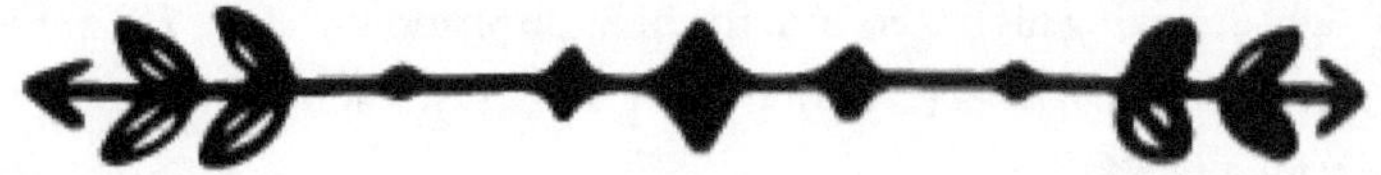

Conall woke with the dawn. Waves lapped against the hull. The croak of some distant reptiles and nearby birds trilled in his ears. Lavender lingered in his nose. The canoe's gentle swaying and the warm weight pressed against his chest sought to lull him back to sleep. But the pain, ever present, decided for him.

He yawned, stretching his sore muscles. His good arm tingled as he rolled it out from underneath his neck.

When he flexed the fingers on his wounded arm, his cheeks heated. At some point in the night, his hand had slipped beneath the cloak wrapped around Ereni's waist, and he found himself holding a handful of warm flesh. He gently removed his hand, careful not to wake her.

Wait—why was his hand wet? His stomach dropped.

The memory of that metallic scent last night made him jerk his hand back, much too sharply for his wounded shoulder. He bit back the cry that rose in his throat and prepared himself for the sight of crimson staining his fingers. But his brows rose instead. His hand glistened with moisture, his fingers slightly pruned, but not a hint of pink painted his skin.

He blew out a shaky exhale. She must be sweating. It wasn't that surprising; she had just spent half the night penned in with a man at her back, a furred wolf on her chest, and two cloaks draped atop her.

He sat up gingerly, flinging the top cloak aside.

"Shadow, wake up. We did our job too well. Ereni's sweating through her coveralls."

Conall paused. That scent he couldn't quite place last night drifted through the air. It was so familiar. He grabbed the cloak and pulled it to his nose, breathing deep.

"Little brother?"

"Hold on a moment." He closed his eyes, bunching the fabric in his hands, sniffing it all over. This was definitely where it was coming from. Herbs of all kinds and hints of flowers, just like when his sister opened up that pack she always carried with her. His eyes widened, his fingers slipping into the pockets. Tiny specks of dirt crumpled beneath his fingers. *"This is Lark's cloak. What is Ereni doing with Lark's cloak?"*

Shadow met his gaze, his nose twitching. *"That's not the only question you should be asking. Human sweat rarely smells this"*—he dipped his snout down, taking another long sniff of Ereni's torso— *"sweet."*

Conall blinked repeatedly, shaking his head. Ereni still slept, oblivious, her back facing him. He gently grabbed her shoulder and rolled her onto her back. Shaking fingers peeled back the cloak wrapped around her chest. The entire front of her coveralls was soaked down to her belly, staining the light gray fabric to a deep charcoal.

"What the blazes?" he said aloud.

Ereni's eyes popped open. Her gaze flicked between him and Shadow, both practically atop her, staring down at her intently. Then she shot up, scrambling away, her legs catching in the cloak and knocking her to her hands and knees before she got far. The boat rocked precariously in the water, and she groaned.

"Calm down." Conall gripped a bench as the water sloshed up along the sides. "You'll knock us into the bog if you're not careful."

"What happened? The last thing I remember I was on watch..." She rolled to face him and shuddered, tugging the cloak higher on her body.

"You fell asleep. Shadow and I woke in the night and found you half frozen. We warmed you with body heat."

Her brows furrowed an instant before her head bowed. "Thank you."

He scoffed. "Sure. Tell me, though." He held the cloak aloft. "What are you doing with my sister's cloak?"

She met his gaze, lips pursed. "It's a long story."

"We've got time." He opened his arms wide to illustrate his point, but the motion set off a shooting pain in his wounded shoulder, and he winced.

"At least let me heal you first," she insisted. She scooted closer on the boat bottom and settled down beside his broken ankle. In the bright morning light, the wound looked even more painful than it felt. His leg throbbed and stuck out at an unnatural angle.

She stared at him, a brow arched. He nodded his assent. She was right. He'd dealt with the pain long enough.

She started digging in a pack. He peered at it curiously, opening his mouth to ask if that was Lark's bag, but he closed it again when he got a close look at it. Lark's bag was plain brown; this one was dyed with bright stripes of rainbow shades.

"I'm afraid this will hurt. I need to set the bones straight before the healing." She thrust something in his direction. "Here, you can bite down on this."

Smooth leather slid across his hands. A knife sheath. The thought of her with a knife set off a momentary jolt of panic before it dissipated. He slipped the sheath between his lips and bit down, closing his eyes.

If Ereni had wanted him dead, she could've simply let the bog carry him away. She certainly wouldn't be going to all this trouble to heal him, just to turn around and stab him in the back. But why? He still hadn't figured her out. Had she only saved him so he could live to see through the battle to come? Or was there another reason—

Snap.

He screamed around the leather, the pain so sharp and strong he fell back, slapping his wounded shoulder against the hard boat bottom. But even that was nothing compared to the agony that tore up his leg, radiating from his ankle all the way up his thigh like a bolt of lightning.

He opened his eyes and spat out the sheath, breathing hard. His leg was straight once again, but now fresh blood gushed out from his boot, the throbbing so intense he could barely keep his eyes open.

Ereni slid her hand beneath his boot, sending another jolt of pain up his leg. "Call on your talent."

Conall sucked in a series of deep breaths, trying to concentrate.

"Now, please."

"I'm trying," he bit out between clenched teeth.

"Sorry, take your time." Ereni's cheeks flushed.

Conall closed his eyes. Lark. He focused on her image in his mind.

Warmth spread along his leg an instant before the boat trembled. The vibration worked its way through his skin, deep in his muscles, rattling his bones. A wave of weariness washed over him just before the pain in his leg vanished.

He forced his eyelids open as Ereni's hand slid out of his boot. He twisted his ankle experimentally. No pain. Normal range of motion. His mouth quirked up in a crooked grin.

Ereni scooted closer. Her breath warmed his cheek as she reached across his chest and lifted his tunic gently, placing her hand on his wounded shoulder. She met his gaze. "Once more."

Again, he closed his eyes. The warmth, the tremor, the weariness, each washed over him again until the pain receded.

He opened his eyes to find Ereni slipping her hand away. He clasped her wrist before she could retreat. Something wasn't right. Her face was pallid, her body trembling. The cloak wrapped around her slipped down, showcasing the darkened stain spread across her front.

"What's wrong? Are you hurt, too?" He stared down at her chest.

She tugged her arm. He loosened his hold, only to watch her wrap her arms around her middle, bowing her head. She shook even harder, saying nothing.

"Ereni," he gripped her shoulders, "tell me. We can heal you, too."

"There's no need." Her voice was a fragile, thready thing, like a single string of silk stretched taut. "Lark already healed me."

Conall frowned at his sister's name. Is that how Ereni came across her cloak? But why did Ereni end up with *it* and not his sister? If it wasn't pain wracking her... He sucked in a breath, his gut clenching. What had she done?

"Then what's wrong? Tell me what happened." He tilted her chin until she met his gaze. Her eyes were flooded with tears, her lips quivering. Conall bit back a gasp, his eyes widening at the guilt and shame writ across her features.

"I-I left her." It was as if she'd erected a dam around her emotions that suddenly collapsed. Tears spilled down her cheeks, her breath heaving in and out in great gasps.

Conall dropped her shoulders, backing away. "What did you do to my sister, Ereni? Where is Lark?"

Ereni shot him a glare, eyes like knives. "Your sister is fine. I'm not talking about *her*." The indignation slipped, replaced with another wave of sorrow engulfing her so strongly it was palpable. "Violet. I-I left her behind."

Conall rubbed his temples, his thoughts spinning. Whoever Violet was, she was obviously important if she was causing this reaction from Ereni. He'd never seen her cry. Just like her mother, she was always so strong. Fierce.

He scooted closer and pulled her into his arms. Ereni tensed for an instant, but then she melted into his embrace, her body wracked with silent shudders.

"It's all right," he said, even though he wasn't sure it was or ever would be.

Lavender drifted up to his nose from her hair. And beneath that, another scent rose. Sweet and subtle but nonetheless distinct. A scent he couldn't remember smelling for many years. Not since his mother held his newborn sister to her breast.

"Ereni." He drew back, holding her at arm's length. "Who is Violet?"

Her answer shattered his heart. "Our daughter."

Chapter 14

"What?" Conall backed away further, until his back rammed into the wooden seat behind him. He must not have heard her right. "How could that be?"

"Do you think I would lie about this?" Ereni hissed. She tugged down the cloak and pulled the soaked coveralls away from her heaving chest. "Is this a lie, too?"

"Forgive me if I don't take every word of yours as gospel," he muttered, crossing his arms.

Ereni stared back at him, the red in her cheeks fading, her eyes turning glassy. She pulled her knees against her chest and curled into a ball on the canoe's floor, her shoulders shuddering.

Conall had to stop himself from pulling her close again. Growing up without a father, with a mother and sister to protect, he couldn't stand the sight of a woman crying. But he needed space. He had to think.

It just didn't add up. It was true they'd lain together. She'd even admitted she wanted his child. But the timing was off. This was months too soon.

Had she been pregnant already when they'd first met?

No, even that timing made no sense. Her belly would've been heavy already, not flat like he remembered.

A strangled sob broke his line of thought. It certainly would explain the way she was acting now. Having a midwife for a mother, he'd heard stories about women reacting strangely after birth, all their emotions worn on their sleeve. Sometimes even making them act irrationally. Harming themselves.

His gaze landed on the empty sheaf sitting on the canoe floor. Then at the sack curled up by her feet.

Whatever he did, he needed to tread carefully.

Conall inched closer. The canoe swayed.

"Don't touch me." She curled up even more, her voice thick with anguish.

He halted. "I won't," he whispered. Then he snatched the bag away from her, smiling triumphantly.

She peeked at him and rolled her bloodshot eyes before her head sank to her knees again. "Have it. It's not even mine."

Conall shoved the bag behind him, not bothering to open it. "Can you just explain it to me?" He winced at his tone. Forced his voice to soften. "Please?"

"Isn't it obvious?" she said. "I summoned without a source."

Conall rocked back, his hand flying to his chest. Of course. How hadn't he seen it? It was the only explanation that made any sense.

"We have a child," he stated flatly. "Are you sure she's mine?"

That was obviously the wrong thing to say. She glared at him, venomous. "Yes."

Conall bristled. "The prince—"

"He never touched me," she bit out, practically seething. She turned away from him again, hiding her face.

Shadow had been so quiet while all this was happening that Conall had almost forgotten he was there. But as silence descended on the canoe again, broken by the occasional sob from Ereni, he spoke. *"What's happening?"*

Conall flinched, his gaze shooting to Shadow. *"I-I—Sh-she."* He drew a deep breath. It was all so bizarre he was stuttering in his thoughts. *"She had a baby. A little girl.* My *little girl."*

"A cub? That's good news." Shadow's tail wagged. He tilted his head. *"Did you not want a cub?"*

Conall shook his head. *"It's not that simple."* He closed his eyes. Was that even true? Or was he just being stubborn and too quick to believe the worst? First with his father, and now Ereni.

Lark's words on the boat rang in his ears. "People make mistakes," she'd said. From where he was sitting, Ereni's mistakes were myriad. He'd not even had the chance to question her about her betrayal at the Palisade, and here she was admitting to another.

"Why did you leave her?" His voice came out surprisingly even for how much the question weighed on his shoulders.

Ereni sniffed. She was silent for so long he started to believe she wasn't planning to answer. But then she lifted her head and met his gaze. "I didn't want her to grow up without her father."

Her words hit like a punch to the gut. She'd left their daughter to save him?

He opened his mouth.

"Little brother, someone's here."

He snapped his mouth shut, his head swiveling around, searching.

"Wh—" Ereni began.

He thrust out a hand to cut her off as the sound of chattering men rose in the distance.

"Get down," Ereni mouthed, barely audible, catching his eye and slinking down against the boat's bottom.

Conall frowned, following her lead. Shadow lay down, too, without having to be told.

He hadn't given their location much thought, what with everything happening within their canoe, but as he crouched unmoving on the boat's bottom, he took a closer look around.

It appeared that Ereni had chosen the mangrove she'd tied them to carefully. Their canoe sheltered within a pocket of water between two massive trees. They would need to maneuver backward to make their way out to the main waterway, but the spot had one advantage: they were practically hidden. With all three of them crouched down, only a small amount of the hull would be visible to anyone floating by.

His gaze flicked to Ereni. The sadness that had been so evident in her features had been pushed aside. She was on alert; her face pressed to the boat's side, gaze lifted just high enough to peek over the edge.

She'd been expecting this... What else wasn't she telling him?

He slid beside her as the voices came closer. Soon they drew near enough he could make out much of what they were saying, though he still couldn't see anyone between the twisted branches they hid behind.

"Are you sure we're headed the right way?" asked a man with a deep baritone.

"Do I look like an idiot to you?" a different voice answered, this one nasal and edged with steel. "This'll lead us back to the docks."

"I still don't know why we're going back," a third voice piped in. "I'm not gonna let them lock me up again."

Conall's stomach sank. He shot Ereni a sideways glare, but she didn't deign to meet his eye, her gaze still locked on the water beyond their hiding spot.

"We won't let 'em catch us. Besides, you heard the guards before they ditched us. The city is about to be overrun by monsters." Steel Voice chuckled. "Pathetic scared fools, the lot of 'em. We'll have the city to ourselves, I bet."

The waterway rippled, waves spreading down the stream and gently swaying their boat side to side. Out in the waterway, a canoe appeared around a corner, and Conall's throat went dry.

A muscular man stood, shoving a long pole down into the bog, a cudgel strapped to his back. Two more men sat inside, loaded down with more weapons, looking just as menacing. All three sported matching gray coveralls, just like the ones Ereni wore.

What was he to think of that? Had she been locked up, too?

"I wouldn't mind running into Lady Death again," one of the seated men mused, licking his lips. "That was one nice piece of ass."

Another canoe turned the corner, with three more men inside. And then a third and fourth. All of them shared a laugh and murmured agreements while a sick feeling spread in Conall's gut. He clenched his fist so hard his nails dug into his palm, lest he send a wave of water spilling them all into the bog.

But then Steel Voice spoke up again. Conall could put a face to the voice. He was a hulking, balding fellow with a crooked nose and a bevy of scars covering his skin beneath the rolled-up sleeves of his coveralls. "You have fun with that. Won't catch me inviting a mage into my bed. If I see either of those witches again, I'll slit their throats."

Conall held in a breath, his burning lungs a welcome distraction from the images swirling through his mind. From the way Ereni stiffened at the statement, he had no doubt that she was one of the mages they were currently laughing at and plotting to slaughter. Was Lark the other? What had happened? It took everything in him to stay still and silent, his body thrumming with rage.

Conall released the breath as the boats slid away. The echoes of the men's cruel laughter bounced off the water and burned inside his ears.

Once the laughter faded, he grabbed Ereni's shoulder, twisted her to face him, and lifted a brow. "Who are they? What aren't you telling me?"

She only swallowed and lifted a shaky finger to her lips. Then she brushed his hand off her shoulder and stood, making her way to the boat's bow and untying the rope that tied them to the mangrove.

Conall snatched the long pole off the side holder and readied to push as soon as she detached the rope. Ereni met his gaze and frantically pointed in the opposite direction the men had headed.

Soon they were out in the open waterway, gliding away from their hiding spot. It wasn't until they'd turned at least half a dozen times that Ereni finally spoke, her voice barely louder than a whisper.

"They're prisoners. The worst of the worst. The prince left them locked in Southmoat Prison rather than evacuate them with all the other citizens." She sighed. "I guess no one told your sister that. I happened to be walking by the prison and heard something. It's lucky I decided to investigate. The two of us barely made it out of there."

He sucked in a shaky breath. "Did they hurt you?" He exhaled, the lust in the one fiend's voice clear in his mind. "Did they *touch* you? My sister—"

Ereni shook her head quickly. "No. From the looks of it, Lark made them regret trying."

Conall jabbed the pole into the murky water again. Why would Lark try to free criminals? Yet again, it wasn't too surprising. "Lark has always been the type to rush in to save anyone who needs help."

Ereni nodded. "I gathered as much." A tiny smile curved the corners of her lips. "That's why I left Violet with her."

Conall stiffened. "You brought a baby into a prison?"

"No," Ereni replied woodenly. "I didn't have her yet."

"Wait, what?"

"We hid underwater while the prisoners fled through the docks." She shrugged. "We needed to breathe."

Conall almost dropped the pole. "You *just* had a baby. Yesterday?"

Ereni's gaze turned murderous. "Yes."

Conall stopped poling. "If Lark and Violet are back there, then why are we going in the opposite direction?"

"Keep pushing, Conall."

"Not until you answer my question."

"I already tried returning after I pulled you and Shadow out of the bog." Her voice was quiet, filled with a note of defeat. "There's nothing to go back to. Southmoat has fallen. Those men will be heading back this way eventually, and I'd rather not get my throat slit."

Conall's mind raced. What should they do now? "What about the ocean? Shouldn't we be heading for the ocean docks to meet up with the others?"

Ereni shook her head. "The bog doesn't lead to the Eprora Ocean near Flamesmoat. Only the Orddon Ocean to the east and south to Raimire."

If that was true, then his plan to reach the docks last night had never had any chance of success. If Ereni hadn't gone after them...

Conall thrust down on the pole, and the boat picked up speed. "And you know where you're going?"

"Not exactly." She grimaced. "But what other choice do we have? Dracwood is crawling with scourge now."

"No, you're right," he conceded. "Lark and Kayda will head to Joria next, and then north up the coast to the Abandoned Lands. If we can make it to the Orddon, we might have a chance of catching up with them."

"Princess Kayda was with you?" Ereni asked, a single brow arching.

Conall shot her a glare. "Happy to see all your schemes falling into place?"

Ereni frowned. "It's not like that."

"Isn't it?" He scoffed. "Seems to me that all of you mages have been itching for the three of us to fight in the Abandoned Lands for centuries now."

Ereni wrapped her arms around her legs.

"Did you see it, too? Have you met the Winter Witch?"

The startled look in her eyes was enough of an answer. A thought jumped out at him, one that hadn't crossed his mind before, and it settled in his gut like a sunken stone.

"Did you know who I was from the very start? Did you recognize me back in the *Greenvale Inn*?" He drew in a deep breath, his brow wrinkling. "Did your mother send you to seduce me?"

Her gaze burned into his again. "What? Don't be ridiculous, she would never ask that of me."

He didn't miss that she hadn't denied his first accusation. "What do you expect me to believe after what happened? After what you did?"

"I'm sorry for that. Truly, I am. But the wall had to fall. And you couldn't follow me. You *had* to journey north with Mother. Can't you see that now?"

"Why didn't you just tell me that? You lied to me, Ereni. You threatened Shadow. You killed those mages who helped me bring down the Palisade. Am I just supposed to forget about that?"

Ereni shook her head. "I don't expect you to understand." She sighed.

Conall turned another bend and spotted a small, marshy island stretching out between a dense thicket of mangroves to their left. He directed the canoe toward it.

"Where are you going?" Ereni asked.

"I need to stretch my legs." Really, he desperately needed to relieve his bladder, but he was hoping she'd read between the lines.

She seemed to understand, and after scanning behind them, she nodded, gripping her legs tightly. "Me too," she admitted.

He pushed up to the island, and Ereni hopped up to tie the canoe to a mangrove's roots. "I'll be right back," he called over his shoulder, hopping out, Shadow at his heels. Maybe he should've offered to let her go first, but he wasn't feeling particularly generous at the moment.

His stomach churned. Ever since he'd brought up the Palisade falling, he couldn't stop picturing it in his mind. Remembering the agony and betrayal he'd grappled with in that moment, like she'd torn out his heart and stomped on it.

She didn't expect him to understand? That's all she had to say?

He took care of his business quickly and strode back to the water. Shadow stayed behind on the island, digging at a corner of the marshy soil.

"Your turn." He seated himself back inside the canoe.

Ereni stood, meeting his gaze. She looked like she wanted to say something, but after a moment, she dropped her gaze and wordlessly climbed out and onto the island.

Conall kept his stare trained on the water, watching for signs of the men behind them. How had he gotten into this mess? Running from criminals and separated from all of his friends. Stuck on a tiny boat with the woman who'd betrayed him. He sure had the best luck these days.

Shadow returned a few moments later, licking his chops.

"What did you find?" Conall asked, his stomach rumbling at the thought of food.

"Frog. You want me to find another?"

Conall grimaced. *"I'll pass."*

His gaze lit on the rainbow-colored pack he'd stashed beneath the aft seat. He opened it up and dug inside, finding a full waterskin and a pouch stuffed full of jerky. After quickly cramming a mouthful of jerky into his mouth and taking a swig of the water, he continued to dig.

His blood went cold. There was no knife. The sheaf still sat empty on the boat's bottom, but the knife...

Why wasn't Ereni back yet? Conall jumped up, swallowing. Panic made his feet feel like they were encased in rock, every step a struggle.

She wouldn't do something stupid... would she?

He raced behind a pair of mangroves, his boots slipping in the marshy soil. Then he spotted her, an arm's length away, her back turned to him, just lifting the coveralls back over her shoulders.

She spun at the sound of his approach. Her cheeks flushed, and she quickly wrenched the front of the coveralls closed. But not before he glimpsed the dark purple lines snaking across her stomach.

She sputtered, indignation flashing across her face, but before she could say a word, Conall grabbed her and slapped a hand over her mouth. Her eyes widened as he shook his head slowly, staring pointedly behind her.

"Did you hear something?" a hushed voice said an instant later.

Conall stood still, angling him and Ereni behind the mangrove as best he could, praying whoever the voice belonged to would leave them in peace. A moment later, a boat slid by, filled with more rough men dressed in coveralls. None of these he recognized from earlier. How many of them were on the loose?

"I don't hear nothing. Probably just some wild animal," a different man replied. "Keep pushing. If we don't find a way out of this maze soon, I'm gonna go crazy."

Conall held his breath, waiting. Luckily, their boat was heading away from where they'd tied their canoe, so they didn't need to worry about this group catching them—for now. Finally, he judged the boat far enough away to be out of earshot. He released Ereni and backed away, his gaze slipping down the front of her shirt, still gaping open.

She was quick to tug it closed again. "Do you mind?"

"Blazes," he snapped back. "Did you want me to let them find you?"

She finished forcing the buttons back in place and threw up her hands. "Don't do me any more favors. I can take care of myself." Then she stormed off, back to the canoe.

Conall followed behind her, rolling his eyes. This was shaping up to be a fun voyage.

Chapter 15

Lark stared at the blue sea, the tingle of static and moisture in the air surrounding her. Mages at the bow took turns coaxing the water and air currents to their will, leaving a constant grin on Captain Jayan's face, even in the face of shallow waters that few dared sail.

"Incredible, isn't it?" Mika said, stopping beside her. "Here I thought I'd only ever see magic used for healing."

"Yeah, it's pretty amazing." She met his gaze. "How are you doing? We haven't talked since you got back from Northmoat."

It had been two days since they departed the waters off the coast of Dracwood. Mika had been keeping to himself, barely even interacting with the people he'd come with from Raimire.

She'd seen how failing to save the king had affected Kayda. Was it weighing on Mika, too?

He curled a hand through his wild brown hair. A slanted smile crossed his lips. "Have you been looking for me, then?"

"Sure. We were going to train together, weren't we?" Maybe if she could convince him to a join her for a training session, he would open up about what was bothering him.

He chuckled. "Well, if the story of the babe's birth that Dausius has been telling is true, you might have a few things to teach me."

Lark's cheeks warmed. "Oh, you know Daus. He could watch someone washing dirty socks and spin it into a grand adventure."

Mika leaned closer, his golden-brown eyes meeting hers. So close she noticed little flecks of copper in his irises sparkling in the sun. "Is that all it was?" His smile widened. "Somehow, I doubt that."

Mika straightened, breaking eye contact and glancing over her shoulder. "Ah, here's the little one now."

Lark sucked in a breath, strangely jittery all of a sudden. Must be all the magic in the air.

She turned and waved to her approaching friends, Tiora, Meital, and Mazen. Violet cooed in Mazen's arms, her eyes wide open and a tiny line of drool hanging out of her mouth.

"Lark, I've been looking for you." Tiora stopped beside her, brow furrowing. "Actually, it's the princess who's looking for you. She stopped me on the way up from Violet's nap to ask me to send you and Aren her way when we saw you."

Lark sighed. "I guess I better go see what she needs."

"We haven't spotted Aren yet." Meital tilted her head, her gaze flicking to Mika.

"I'll get him. He's with Muse." Lark rubbed Violet's tiny hand. "Do you mind watching Violet a little longer?"

"No, not at all," Mazen chimed in, a mischievous grin on his face. "Meital and I are planning on making her part of our act." He feigned tossing her, earning a set of gasps from Tiora and Meital.

Lark rolled her eyes, spinning on her heel to leave. "I'll be back soon," she called over her shoulder.

Her boots tapped on the deck, a pleasant breeze blowing through her long brown curls. But a thread of tension spooled in Lark's belly as she made her way closer to the aft rail where she knew Aren would be, keeping watch over Whisper and Muse as they soared through the sky, hunting for seabirds.

What could Kayda want? She wasn't surprised she'd asked to speak to her. After all, they had shared history now. And with everything happening in Flamesmoat, there'd been little time to discuss Jett or how they were suddenly related in a very real way.

But Aren... Why would she be asking for him, too?

Soon she caught sight of Aren, leaning against the rail, a wide brimmed hat shading his face, and his gaze on the sky. In the distance, two little specks circled high in the clouds. Lark's breath caught as he turned at the sound of her boots and graced her with a smile.

"Hey." Aren tilted his hat up slightly, his blue eyes meeting hers. "Have you come to watch Muse?"

Lark smiled back, placing a steadying hand on the rail beside him. "No, I came for you."

She cringed inwardly, her cheeks warming. She hadn't meant that to sound so forward.

"Oh?" He grinned. "Did you need my help with something?"

"Yes." She brushed her brown curls out of her face. "Kayda wants to see both of us for some reason. Tiora just told me." She shot a glance at her boots. "I was about to head to her room now..."

"Well, I'll come with you. Let me just signal for the birds." He raised his arm high in the air, and soon, the birds swooped down to land gracefully on the railing.

"Good flying today," Muse said as she landed. *"Not enough seabirds this far off the coast, though."*

"Sorry to cut your session short. I need to borrow Aren for a moment."

"Borrow him? Is that what you're calling it now? Ha."

Lark clicked her tongue. What was that supposed to mean?

But then Aren reached into his pack and pulled out some meat. Muse's gaze zeroed in on the morsel.

Lark shook her head, letting the matter rest. There was no use talking to her when she was eating. Gluttonous little thing.

Aren turned to her. "Ready?"

She nodded and followed him to the closest hatch leading into the inner part of the boat. *Nova's Champion* was a large vessel, originally used for trade before being commandeered by Kayda off the coast of Dracwood. A multitude of rooms spread out below deck, some filled with rows of hammocks, many occupied as the night shift rested. Even more rooms lay empty or were filled with stacked crates and boxes.

It wasn't until they neared the forward hull that they reached the hall that led to Kayda's room. The hallways here were lined with oil lamps instead of the stubby candles affixed in place on the other parts of the ship. Threadbare tapestries were tacked to the wooden walls, showcasing scenes of sea serpents and lush, green islands floating in the sea.

"This is it." Lark stopped beside a closed door. She knocked.

"Come in."

Lark opened the door and stepped inside. The room was small but brightly lit from glass windows along the far wall, the dark blue curtains tied back. A wide wooden desk, scarred with countless gouges, sat front and center. A single hammock hung suspended from the ceiling in the corner.

As they entered, Kayda rose from a wooden chair behind the desk and closed the cover of the book she'd been reading. It was the same ancient book Conall had brought back with him from his adventures in Doln with the Sade Prim.

Lark's curiosity grew. Had Kayda found something in the old tome she wanted to discuss?

But Kayda left the book behind, circling around the desk to greet them. "Lark, Aren, thank you for coming so quickly. I have a problem I'm hoping you can help me with."

Aren clutched his hat in his hands. He shared a glance with Lark before meeting the princess' eyes. "How can we help?"

"We'll be reaching Joria in a few days. I've been planning to send a fast-sailing ship to Doln, to request aid meet us on the Abandoned Land's coast. But Izora told me the tale of how they knew I'd survived the last battle there, and it got me thinking."

Lark nodded, wondering where she was going with this. Did she want the two of them on that ship?

"Apparently there was a pair of cousins passing notes between Flamesmoat and Joria with trained doves. We don't have any doves on board, but I wonder if maybe Muse or Whisper would be up for the task."

Lark's eyes widened. "You want Muse to deliver a message to Doln?" She shook her head, her stomach clenching at the thought of sending her off on her own. "She's never been to Doln."

Aren leaned forward and captured her gaze. "Whisper has. He grew up in the mews in Clan Chief Aundrea's household, in Gransea. The two of them together could make it there, I expect."

Lark frowned. "Are you sure they'll be all right?"

"Sure, why wouldn't they? And they'll arrive there and return back much faster than any sailboat." Aren smiled at Kayda. "It's a clever plan, Princess."

Kayda rubbed her arm and grinned back at Aren before turning to Lark and meeting her gaze with a look of concern. "I know it's a lot to ask, separating you from your bondmate, Lark. I wouldn't ask if it wasn't so important. If the warriors from Doln don't meet us in time..."

Lark bit her lip. "No, you're right. We need all the help we can get."

"Good." Kayda's face lit up. "I'll prepare a parchment for Chief Aundrea and have it ready by morning. Thank you."

Lark forced a smile. "Happy to help." She whirled around to leave. "I better go check on Violet."

"Goodbye, Princess." Aren followed, closing the door behind him.

Lark shuffled a few paces away before Aren caught up to her. He slipped a hand around her elbow, stopping her in the empty hall. "Hey, they'll be all right. Muse and Whisper are a formidable pair."

Lark peeked up at him, blinking quickly. "I know. It's just hard knowing we'll be apart for so long." She sighed.

"But that's not all, is it?"

She grimaced. "No." All the events of the last few days swirled around her mind, pressing down on her shoulders. "Conall's gone again, and I have Violet to care for, and the battle looming. Everything's changing so fast. I just wish I could slow it all down. Get a chance to breathe." She wrinkled her nose, straightening her back. "But I'll be all right."

Aren stared down at her, brow furrowed. Then he let go of her elbow, smiling widely. "Follow me." He beckoned her down the hall.

Lark watched curiously as he stopped in front of a doorway a few feet away, sticking his ear to the door. He listened for a few heartbeats, then shook his head and strode to the next doorway, repeating the action there.

"What are you doing?" Lark quirked a brow and crossed her arms as he stopped beside a third door.

"Shh." He propped his ear on it and must've found what he was searching for. His smile widened, and he fitted his hand on the knob, slowly opening the door and peering within. Then he grabbed her hand and tugged, and they both spilled inside the room, the door banging closed behind them.

Lark giggled, scanning the room. Pots and pans hung on the walls. A hearty stew bubbled nearby, and knives and various half-cut vegetables decorated a nearby countertop.

"What are we doing in here?" She strode to the counter and lifted a carrot. "Did you need a snack?"

"No. I'm just stealing you a moment to think." He grinned, leaning back against the door. "No one ought to come looking for you here."

Lark's heart was like that stew, full and bubbling. She spent all her time taking care of everyone else. It was so nice to have someone worried about her for a change. And not just anyone.

Her mind flashed back to the kiss they'd shared. She could see from the casual way Aren stood, his back pressed to the door, giving her all the space to do whatever she wanted, he'd not brought her in here intending to repeat that kiss. But they were alone. And she found she couldn't think about anything else.

She glanced up at him and glided away from the counter, back toward the door. Back to Aren.

"I've been meaning to ask, how is your sunburn healing?" She reached up tentatively, gently tugging at the collar of his shirt. "Do you want me to take another look at it for you?"

He met her gaze, and his smile brightened. His chest rose as her fingers grazed his skin. But the words he said next had a hard edge. "I didn't bring you here for more work, Lark." He enclosed her hand within his.

"I know you didn't." She blushed, staring down at her feet. "But I don't want to think right now." She peeked up at him, meeting his gaze, her heart thrumming madly.

"No?" His gaze zeroed in on her lips, and her stomach clenched. "What do you want?"

For once, she didn't care a bit about being forward. "You."

That one word was all it took for his lips to descend on hers. She pushed up on her tiptoes, meeting him halfway. The swish of fabric fell to the floor, and then Aren spun her and pressed her against the wall next to the door, his hands tight on her waist.

Lark lost herself in his kiss. Her hands bunched in the silk of his shirt, and she pulled him closer, wedging herself against the hard plane of his chest. Her mind stopped spinning, all the fears and plans for the future slipping out of her mind.

Her world narrowed down to this moment with this man. The blood pounding through her veins. The giddy, wonderful rush of sensation she felt when she was in his arms.

A deafening clang shattered the air. Aren jumped back, breathing heavily. Lark's eyes popped open, and her jaw dropped as she spotted an angry man banging a pot just behind them, the door wide open.

Her face burned. When had he come in? She certainly hadn't noticed the door open or any sound until that awful clamor began.

The chef—she guessed, being as they were in the galley and this man wore a stained apron atop plain cotton clothes—was red faced as well. "Out! Out with you, ya randy buggers," he yelled, shooing them out the door. "Worse than the sailors, you are."

Aren bent down to scoop up his crumpled hat, and they wasted no time hustling out of the room and down the hall.

Lark laughed. "I wasn't expecting that today."

Aren stopped her before they reached the outer hatch. "Lark, I didn't want to..." He trailed off, shaking his head.

Lark frowned, her stomach sinking.

"Not that," he hurried to say. He straightened his hat in his hands. "I wanted to kiss you." He met her gaze, smiling gently. "I just don't want to be another thing that's changing too fast for you. You just finished telling me you needed to slow down, and then I—"

She squeezed his arm. "You're not. I wanted to kiss you, too." Warmth spread in her chest as she beamed back at him. She leaned closer, wetting her lips.

A door somewhere in the hall slammed open, and she flinched. Damn crowded ship. But the noise was another reminder of everything she had to accomplish. As much as she wanted to hide away with Aren, there were things to do. The world didn't stop just because someone wanted to kiss her.

She sighed, pushing open the hatch. "C'mon. We better go break the news to Muse and Whisper."

Chapter 16

Kayda approached Jayan at the helm. A cloud of haze drifted off the ocean in the early morning hours, thickening even more with the mages' constant stream of magic boosting their speed.

"Good morning, Jayan." She handed him a warm cup of tea. "Are we still on track for Port Joria this afternoon?"

"This morning, I expect. Those mages of yours really speed things up. I've never seen anything like it." He swigged from the cup and grimaced, squinting at the horizon. "Once all this mist clears, we should have a clear view of the coast."

Kayda took a deep breath. "I have a favor to ask you."

"Whatever it is, consider it done, Prin— er, Kayda." He grinned.

She raised a brow. "That so? And what if I asked you to throw yourself overboard?"

Jayan pursed his lips and set down his teacup on the deck, then shrugged. "I reckon I could stand a swim." He lifted a foot, untying the laces of his boot.

Kayda nudged his hand aside. "Stop." She laughed. "I'm only joking."

She shook her head. The fool man likely would do anything she asked. But just because his loyalty knew no bounds, she wouldn't take advantage of it.

Jayan straightened, running a hand through his braids. "So, what is it then, if I won't be swimming?"

"On our trip to Sul Hollow, I couldn't convince Lazar to join us. My nurse, Izora, has ties there. She's agreed to travel there to speak with him on my behalf."

"And you want me to tag along?"

Kayda nodded. "I wish I could go with you, but there's too much to do in Joria and not enough time. Do you min—"

"Aye, like I said, consider it done." Jayan grinned again.

Kayda smiled back, then let out a sigh. That's one less task she needed to worry about. Hopefully Izora and Jayan could convince the Sul to fight at their sides.

"Thank you, Jayan. I'll leave you to it, then." She turned to leave, but he caught her arm.

"You take care of yourself while I'm gone." His fingers slid down to her wrist, and he clasped her hand, leaning close. "The Jorians are a strange breed. Half of them would sell their own mother if it would make them a profit." He squeezed once, then dropped her hand and grabbed the helm. "Just be careful who you trust."

She flashed him a half-smile. "I will."

The warning didn't help to ease her anxiety as they sailed closer to port, but she knew she'd be wise to heed his words. Things had changed a great deal since her last visit.

Without Druturion by her side, would the people of Joria still be eager to come to their aid? It was one thing to follow a dragon rider into battle, but now, she was just a displaced princess whose country was under siege.

And she still had the deal with Wyll to solidify. Her father had grudgingly agreed to the terms—her hand in marriage for his family's fleet of ships—but she had a feeling that any wrong move could see the tentative agreement broken.

She wasn't worried about Wyll. Her future husband would likely charm her father easily. But his uncle might be a different story. She had to hope that Wyll's claim about his uncle's desire to have a royal connection at any cost was enough to calm his temper.

Kayda made her way to the forward rail as the mists dissipated, chased away by the bright dawn sun. The noisy hustle on deck was muted with most of the passengers still sleeping.

But not everyone rested. Lark stood at the rail beside a trio of mages at work directing the ocean currents in the sea below.

Lark turned as Kayda approached, no doubt alerted by the gentle tapping of Kayda's boots on the polished deck. She cradled Violet in her arms, bouncing the wide-awake little babe gently.

"I see I'm not the only one who likes to rise early." Kayda aimed a grin at the babe.

"Violet isn't much of a sleeper. Funny thing is, she quiets down every time she's near the summoning at the bow."

"I'm not surprised. Magic is in her blood." Kayda stared into Violet's distinctive reddish-blue eyes. "Huh, in the right light, her eyes almost look violet. I wonder if that's why her mother chose the name?"

Lark smiled crookedly, peering down at Violet. "Yeah, you're right. But I don't know if that's why Ereni picked the name." Her smile faded. "Hopefully one day we can ask her."

Kayda didn't say as much, but she had a sinking feeling that Violet's name might remain a mystery. "We'll be docked in Joria for a few days before we head north. Are you and the show planning to do any entertaining?"

"Not me. I have to hire a new wet nurse for Violet, now that Elmena's leaving. And then Aren and I are planning to accompany Tiora to visit her family." Lark sighed deeply, staring at the sky.

"You're missing your bondmate?" Kayda asked.

"Yes, and no." Lark chuckled. "She certainly hasn't stopped chattering away in my head, no matter how far north she gets. Muse is not a fan of snow, I can tell you that much."

"Really?" Kayda's stomach clenched. "I wish it was like that with me and Dru."

"You can't hear him at all?"

Kayda frowned. "Not since we fled that island mountain top. I don't even know if he's still alive."

Lark squeezed her shoulder. "He is. He'll be back. I just know it."

"I hope you're right."

Without her bondmate by her side, the city appeared so much wilder and foreign. They were one of the few ships to approach the port from the south. Curious children and adults stopped to watch them pass, likely surprised to see a ship so large sailing the southern waters, which usually only the bravest of fisherman dared venture.

The city's southern stretches added to the strangeness. All along the coast, tiny huts and hovels crowded together, more dilapidated than the worst of the brick and wood buildings in Southmoat or the modest tile and clay huts in Joria's northern section.

Kayda's heart broke for the throngs of weary-eyed, malnourished people they passed. With so much wealth and plenty brought in by the silk trade, it was criminal these people were left to suffer.

She clutched the railing, hardening her heart to their plight. This was not her country. She was coming here to beg for help in dealing with the terrible destruction of her own lands. But one day, she would do what she could to set things right here. One day.

As the first glimpse of Port Joria rose in the far distance, Kayda made her way below deck. It was time to shuck off the casual silk shirt and cotton pants she'd grown so accustomed to on board and don something more befitting a princess.

She settled on the lovely golden silk dress Wyll had gifted her. As the smooth fabric slid on, her chest fluttered. Was it from the reminder of the tetrela's silken embrace, or her future husband's kiss?

It still felt so strange, knowing she would soon be wed. In truth, she wasn't ready. Not at all. But it was a sacrifice she was prepared to make. When Izora and Jayan returned with the Sul, they would need ships to bring them all north. She smoothed her sweaty palms down the shimmering silk. This was the only way.

A knock interrupted her musing.

"Come in," she said, pulling a brush through the tangled mess of red heaped atop her right shoulder.

King Gideon entered, smiling as he noted her attire. "You look lovely, Kayda." He twisted his nose, closing the door firmly behind him. "I wish you would let the rest of your hair out of those ridiculous braids, though."

Kayda's stomach flipped. She'd still not explained the story behind her new hairstyle to her father. Could she trust him now?

"You know we're in desperate need of the Sul aid. I thought it wise to adopt some of their customs."

Gideon scoffed. "I don't think the way you wear your hair is liable to matter to those hermits." Then he shook his head, sending her a tentative smile. "But then again, I was never much of a statesman. We'll be pulling into port in just a moment. Shall we head up?" He offered her his elbow.

Kayda set down the brush and grabbed his arm. Soon they were back on deck, watching the city grow large as they docked.

It was just how she remembered it. Sun-drenched and sandy, packed with colorful buildings and people dressed in even more colorful silks, many with their hair dyed to match.

It appeared Wyll had been hard at work while she was gone. The port was much more crowded than their last visit, with rows of ships much like *Nova's Champion* docked. People hustled about the decks, no doubt making ready to set sail.

"Hm, those aren't the type of folk I'd expected to see joining the fight," said a voice at her side. Jett stood beside her at the rail, squinting at the large ships as they passed.

Kayda spun back, her brow furrowing as she spotted all the bright silks the people wore. "They are a bit more finely dressed than I'd expected." She shrugged. "But of course, we are in the silk capital of the world."

Gideon chuckled, patting her arm. "You're right, my dear." He leaned forward and thrust a hand out in front of her toward Jett. "We haven't met. I'm Kayda's father, Gideon."

Jett grasped his hand and shook. "Jett."

Kayda leaned back, her gaze flicking between them as they shook. Time seemed to stand still. Her heart squeezed as she realized she was watching two cousins unwittingly meeting. With their differences in coloring—Jett tanned and dark-haired and Gideon pale and dirty-blond—it was easy to miss the signs of shared heritage. But the more she looked, the more similarities stuck out. They were both tall with strong chins and similar facial features—straight noses and high cheekbones.

Finally, their hands unclamped. Gideon glanced between her and Jett. "How did you two meet?"

Kayda's eyes widened, and she stiffened.

Jett opened his mouth.

"My king." Gawain stepped up beside them, and Kayda's shoulders slumped at the interruption. "You must allow me to accompany you ashore."

Gideon waved off the Guard Captain's concern. "Don't be silly. We're meeting with family. The princess and I will be fine on our own."

Gideon was right—only not about the family part. But they'd risk infuriating Wyll's father by showing up with a contingent of guards surrounding them. And she needed this meeting to go off without a hitch.

Kayda smiled at Gawain. "He's right, Gawain. With Jayan leaving, someone needs to protect the ship. Are you up for the task?"

Gawain's frown deepened, but he nodded. "Yes, I understand. I'll keep watch. Be safe, sire. My lady."

As the gangplank touched down on the wooden wharf, a grin crept across Kayda's lips. There was already one face in the crowd she recognized.

Wyll strode purposefully toward their ship, wearing a green silk suit, his dark curly hair just as perfectly coiffed as always. He captured her gaze and sent her a wide smile. There was that flutter again, spreading through her belly this time.

He met her and her father at the bottom of the gangplank. "Princess, it's a pleasure to see you back so soon."

"Father, this is Wyll," Kayda said. "Wyll, King Gideon of Flamesmoat."

"King…" Wyll's brow furrowed. "That must mean King Quinton…" He shook his head, then gentled his voice. "I'm so sorry for your loss, my dear."

Kayda bowed her head, pushing back the rush of grief that swamped her at the reminder. "Thank you," she murmured.

Wyll turned to her father. "But I suppose congratulations are in order, too. It's not every day we have the pleasure of hosting royalty in our fair city. I would be honored to invite you to breakfast at Oasis Manse."

"That would be lovely," Kayda said.

"Yes," King Gideon agreed. "I would be grateful for the opportunity to get to know you and your family better, son."

Wyll's smile tightened a fraction, then slipped right back into place. "They'll be excited to get to know you better as well, sire. I understand you never traveled to Joria before your betrothal to my late aunt."

"That's right." Gideon rubbed his brow, curling a lank blond strand off his forehead. "I had too many pressing engagements at the time to travel."

Kayda bit back the frown that threatened to spread. She hadn't known that... her father hadn't even bothered to meet the family of the woman he was to wed? No wonder the mages' plot to swap his wives went off without a hitch.

Wyll spread out his arms, gesturing to the waiting city. "Well then, let me be the first to welcome you to Joria. I took the liberty of preparing transportation when I got word *Nova's Champion* was due to dock."

Wyll led the way to a fancy, open wooden carriage at the end of the dock. A pair of short-haired black horses sat at the ready, and a thin, dark-skinned boy of perhaps twelve perched on the driver's bench.

That wasn't the only thing perched on the carriage. Kayda tilted her head, locking eyes with a large black crow balanced on the roof. How strange... She was under the impression crows didn't live this far south. She opened her mouth to comment on the peculiar sight, but the bird lifted off as they drew close and fled, flying straight out to sea.

"Allow me to give you a hand, Princess." Wyll extended an arm beside the tall carriage steps.

Kayda slipped her hand in his. A gentle tingle spread up her arm and settled in her chest as she rose on the step and met his gaze before stepping into the carriage. His brown eyes twinkled, his smile never slipping as he assisted her up. Then he backed away, making room for the king to hop up, and took a moment to speak with the driver up front.

"He seems a pleasant fellow," Gideon said quietly as the plush silk cushion sank beside her with his weight. "I hope the rest of his family are as accommodating."

Kayda only had time for a smile before Wyll hopped up to join them and seated himself across from them. The carriage rolled off into the city, and Wyll pointed out many points of view along their route. But all the little anecdotes that made her father grin and chuckle slid in one ear and out the other for Kayda.

She clenched the golden fabric of her silk dress in her fingers, her stomach churning far more than it should have from a simple carriage ride over the sandy roads weaving through the city. So much was riding on their families meeting. She tried to bury her misgivings and enjoy the ride, but something inside of her just wouldn't settle.

"You're awfully quiet, my dear." King Gideon patted her knee. "Is anything amiss?"

Kayda forced a smile. "No. Not at all."

"It must be a big shock to lose your grandfather. How did it happen, if you don't mind my asking?" Wyll inquired.

"It was the scourge," Gideon said. "The blazing vermin must be stopped."

Kayda blinked, blowing out a hard sigh.

"I'm so sorry. I heard all about Flamesmoat's fall. I still can't believe the city was overrun." Wyll frowned briefly, but then his smile returned, just as bright as before. "But together, we'll be able to stop the vermin from spreading further." He tilted his head sideways and stared out the window. "Well, enough of that talk for now, yes? Here we are at Oasis Manse."

The beautiful mansion appeared, covered in ivy and bright vibrant blooms. The green grass on the lawn stood out starkly among all the sandy roads they'd traveled across in the dusty city.

"You have a beautiful home, son." Gideon ran an appreciative eye over the grounds.

"Thank you, sire. It's been in our family for many generations." Wyll hopped down after the carriage stopped. He held out a hand to help her down, and then she and the king followed Wyll inside.

Wyll led the way to the left, passing by the bright entranceway with the circular stair she remembered from her last visit, and heading inside a tiled room with massive bay windows. An enormous table sat in the center, heaped with dozens of platters. Fresh fruit, steaming cuts of meat, and fragrant loaves of bread and pastries had Kayda's stomach rumbling.

But the sight of Wyll's uncle, his frown firmly in place at the table's head, was enough to spoil her appetite. He stood as they approached, a hand out to greet King Gideon.

"I hear congratulations are in order for you, sire. It's *King* Gideon, now, I take it?"

"Yes, it is. I'm pleased to meet you finally, Egard." A rare smile spread across her father's face as he clasped Egard's hand and shook. "We spent so long corresponding back when I wed your cousin—it's nice to finally put a face to the letters."

Egard's brow rose, and his jaw clenched.

Kayda's heart sank. She still hadn't told her father that Egard's cousin wasn't her mother. But she should've expected Gideon to bring up his shared history with Wyll's family. Now that Gideon was the only one still in the dark about her true ancestry, she might be in trouble. What would she do if Egard took it upon himself to bring up the truth of the arrangement and revealed how the mages swapped his cousin out for Kayda's real mother?

But Egard's features smoothed, and he pulled out the chair beside him. "Yes, it's nice to meet you finally as well. Please, have a seat. Let's share a meal and discuss the future of our families, shall we?"

Kayda took a chair across from the older men beside Wyll. The meeting seemed to be progressing smoothly, but she still wasn't sure if the men's big personalities would get in the way. She'd been hoping Wyll's great aunt would be present to guide the conversation if it went off the rails.

She leaned closer to Wyll. "Where is Aurelia this morning?"

Wyll spread a bright white napkin across his lap. "Oh, she had some business to take care of in the city, I believe. I'm sure you'll see her later." He poured her a glass of something pink and fragrant. "Here, you must be parched after that long carriage ride. Have some diquat juice."

Kayda smiled and took a sip. The sweet liquid danced on her tongue. "Thank you. That's delicious."

"I'm glad you like it," he said with a grin.

Kayda glanced across the table and spotted her father draining a cup of juice and holding out his cup for a refill. She swallowed a chuckle. Neither of them were used to the southern heat. She turned back to Wyll and opened her mouth to ask something... but the question slipped out of her mind.

It was like she was swimming in an ocean of cotton, her head heavy and limbs shaky. "I'm feeling strange..." she murmured, lifting a hand to her brow.

Across the table, the king's head smacked on the wooden tabletop with a loud *thunk*.

Kayda's jaw dropped, and her hand fell slack in her lap. The last thing she saw before her eyes became too heavy to hold open was Wyll's face, still smiling.

Chapter 17

Lark waved goodbye to Dausius and stepped out of the *Salty Serpent Inn* into the bright afternoon sun in Port Joria. A bead of sweat rolled down her back. She sucked in the dusty air, happy to be back on solid ground for a change.

"Did you find someone?" Tiora stood from the stoop on the wide wooden front porch.

"Yeah," Lark said. "That was easier than I expected. Violet's new wet nurse will head to the ship directly."

"That's good news." Aren pushed off from where he leaned against the inn wall and crooked both his elbows. "Ready for the next stop?"

Lark smiled, taking Aren's right arm. She peeked around his tall frame and watched Tiora tentatively grasp his left, while releasing a deep sigh.

"Are you all right, Ti?" Lark asked as they strolled southward through the crowded docks.

"Yeah, I'm just nervous, I guess. It's been years since I've seen my family." She threaded a hand through her short brown curls. "Amilya and Cyrie ought to be nearly grown now."

"Don't be nervous." Aren flashed her a grin. "They'll be delighted to see their big sister. I just know it."

But Aren's optimism didn't seem to reach Tiora. She clutched his elbow, her steps carefully measured, sweat dripping down her brow.

Lark couldn't imagine what she was feeling. This would be the first time Tiora had seen her family since she'd sold herself into bondage to save her mother and sisters from sickness and ruin. She'd made that difficult choice all on her own, knowing it was the only way to keep her family safe. Now, she was returning to them, but whether she would be accepted with open arms or pushed out for her decision remained to be seen.

The situation brought back a wash of memories from her own forced separation from her family. Lark might not have the opportunity to reunite with her brother, but she was determined to be there for Tiora while she sought out her kin. And if they even thought to condemn her for the actions that saw her end up a slave, she would be the first to speak up for her friend.

Without Tiora, she would've never survived her own captivity. She would've gone mad locked up with those slavers all on her own and likely never mustered the courage to try using her talent to free them both.

Every step of the journey, Tiora stepped up. Brave beyond measure, always willing to help anyone who needed it. If her family didn't see that instantly, Lark would make them see it before the day was through.

"What's with your face, Lark?" Tiora asked with a giggle. "You look like you're thinking about punching someone."

Lark joined her laughing before quickly schooling her features. "It's nothing, just woolgathering." Time to change the subject. "So, tell me about the city. It's so big and crowded. Way bigger than Flamesmoat."

"It is. We're almost through the dock section. My family lives south of the city proper on the Peat River's eastern banks."

"That's the one you used to swim in practically every afternoon?" Lark fanned herself with her hand, understanding the need for a daily swim in this dry heat.

Tiora sighed. "Yep. We'd swim in the hottest hours and spend the rest of the day scouring the banks for river butterfly cocoons. Anyone who rounded up a basketful could trade them for a coin at the silk factories. Me and my sisters usually gathered a basketful every week."

"A week's worth of work for a single coin?" Aren frowned. "That's all?"

Tiora shrugged. "Yeah."

As they left the dock section behind and tread down the crowded streets to the south, more evidence of squalor appeared. Tiny huts made of mud and clay tiles crowded every block. Not a single person looked overweight. Many even had sunken cheeks and thin, frail limbs.

The beautiful dyed silk clothing worn by the fashionable folk wandering the docks was absent here. The people donned worn, patched rags and dull homespun attire. Everyone she passed was hard at work, stirring vats filled with bright liquid, or hanging dripping cloth to dry.

"Do all the people here work in the silk trade?" Lark asked.

"Most do," Tiora explained. "The dye houses north of the city handle all the fine fabric. They contract out the everyday stuff to workers like my mother, who bulk dye in vats like these."

"And I imagine they aren't paid much better than you were for gathering all those cocoons," Aren said.

Tiora shook her head. "No. No, they aren't."

"You'll never guess what I ate just now." Muse's voice in her mind made Lark flinch. *"It was delicious."*

"You mind filling me in on the details later? I'm a little busy," she replied.

"Fine," Muse grumbled. *"I'm just bored is all, with only the old snoozer for company. Ha, you're gonna owe me big time when I get back."*

"I'll have a big snack waiting. Something tasty, I promise."

"You better."

Despite her bondmate's playful banter, Lark's stomach churned. It was hard to walk past all these people, knowing they'd spent their whole lives toiling just to line some rich trader's pockets. No wonder Tiora had needed to take such desperate measures to save her family.

Tiora stopped suddenly, her golden-brown eyes open wide, staring at a woman stirring a huge vat of dark purple liquid in front of a tiny mud hut, which was identical to all the rest.

It didn't take Lark more than an instant to realize the woman was Tiora's mother. Her dark hair was long and streaked with white, braided into a tight plait resting on her shoulder. Except for the different hairstyle, she was practically identical to Tiora, with the same golden-brown eyes and beautiful features.

Tiora's mother stared down into the vat, absorbed with her task as Tiora blinked back tears, moving closer. It wasn't until they were directly in front of her that her brow furrowed and she glanced up.

She dropped the wooden pole. "Ti-ti? Is that you?"

"Mama." Tiora dropped Aren's arm and rushed around the vat. She thudded into her mother's open arms.

"My baby. I thought I'd never see you again. Oh, Ti-ti."

"Mama, I've missed you so much. I'm so sorry I left."

They clutched each other, laughter and tears bursting free. On the other side of the vat, Lark grasped Aren's arm, her heart so full it was practically overflowing. This was exactly the kind of homecoming her friend deserved.

Two heads popped out of the hut a moment later.

"What's all the noise out he—" the older girl began, only to stop short when she spotted Tiora still clutched tightly within her mother's arms. "Tiora? You're back!"

Then both of the girls jumped in, hugging their sister and mother, squealing and shouting questions so quickly Lark couldn't keep track of what they said. But one thing was immediately clear. There would be no need for her to stick up for her friend during this reunion. The love and relief washing through all the women was immediate. So palpable Lark brushed aside all the worries that any of them would be anything other than grateful for Tiora's return.

After a few moments of hugging, Tiora eased free from her mother's arms, wiping the tears off her face. "Mama, you have to meet my friends." Tiora beckoned them over, a wide smile on her face.

"This is Aren and Lark," she began. "This is my mama, Gisila."

Tiora pointed to the older girl, who looked to be in her late teens, with dark brown eyes and her dark brown hair tied up in a simple bun. "This is Amilya."

Then she turned to the youngest, who appeared to be twelve or thirteen, with her hair wreathed around her head in a mass of short curls much like Tiora wore hers. "And this is Cyrie."

Lark and Aren took turns shaking hands with all of them and exchanging pleasantries. Then they all piled into the little hut at Gisila's insistence.

The inside of the hut wasn't any more impressive than the outside. The single room was barely large enough to fit all of them, with three mats spread out on the dirt floor serving as beds for the women. A fire pit in the corner held a single, worn pot sitting empty atop it.

Lark sat on one of the mats beside Aren and listened quietly while Tiora's sisters and mother grilled her about the last years of her life. Tiora glossed over the details of much of the beginning of her time apart from them, but grew more animated when she shared the last few months of her journey, traveling with the Wandering Bards, and battling the scourge.

"And that's how we ended up back here in Joria. Princess Kayda was promised a fleet of ships from one of the silk traders in the city to help win the fight in the Abandoned Lands," Tiora finished.

"Wow," Amilya exclaimed, her brown eyes wide. "You've been on such an incredible adventure."

Tiora reached into her skirt pocket. "Mama, this is for you." She handed her mother a small coin purse, the metal within clinking noisily.

Gisila's eyes bulged, and she shook her head. "No, Ti-ti. That's yours. We'll get on just fine here on our own."

Tiora frowned. "Take it, Mama. I'll only make more. Performing with the show, it's a good, honest way to make a living." She closed the purse in her mother's hand and smiled at her sisters. "Now Cyrie and Amilya can pay for training in the mills. Or use the coin for a dowry."

Lark's stomach flipped, and she shared a dubious glance with Aren, though she didn't interrupt.

They had to pay to work a decent job, and even pay to marry, here in Joria? It seemed the system was designed to keep the poor from ever gaining ground.

Lark couldn't still the tiny grin that crossed her face. Tiora had found a way. After all her suffering and hard work, she would be the one in a million that broke her family free of the ties keeping them stuck in this trap. It nearly brought tears to her eyes.

Gisila was equally moved. Her cheeks shone with tears, and she clenched the coin purse to her chest, smiling radiantly.

Amilya crouched beside her, leaning forward next to her mother and slipping her hand around the bottom of the coin purse, her big brown eyes going round as she traced the coins inside. "Oh, thank you, Tiora. I can't believe it. I never imagined..." Her voice trailed off, choked with emotion.

Cyrie bit her lip, shaking her head, her legs wrapped tightly around her knees.

Gisila's brow rose. "Aren't you gonna thank your sister, too, Cyrie?"

Cyrie cleared her throat, then reluctantly nodded, glancing at Tiora. "Thank you."

Tiora scooted closer, wrapping an arm around her little sister's shoulders. "What's wrong? I thought you'd be happy?"

"I am, it's just..." A tear slid down her cheek and splattered atop the threadbare silk skirt wrapped around her knees. "There won't be any marriages or mills. Not after they leave."

"What?" Lark's heart thrummed to life.

Cyrie clamped her mouth shut, her eyes widening.

"You can tell us, Cyrie. Maybe we can help," Tiora insisted, rubbing Cyrie's back and staring in her eyes.

Cyrie sucked in a shuddering gasp. "Please, you can't tell anyone how I knew. If anyone finds out, Davit could be killed."

"What does Davit have to do with this?" Gisila demanded. She turned to them. "He's our neighbor's son." Then she glared back at her daughter, still sheltered in Tiora's arms. "What's that boy gone and got you wrapped up in now?"

"It's not like that, Mama." Cyrie scrubbed the tears off her cheeks. "He only told me what's gonna happen. Made me swear I'd keep it a secret. If he's hurt because of me..."

"I don't understand. Why would anyone hurt your neighbor?" Aren asked.

"Davit found a job as a driver at Oasis Manse," Cyrie said. "I guess that rich trader thought a young boy from the slums would be too stupid to piece together what he's been planning, but Davit's smart."

"Oasis Manse?" Lark's jaw dropped. "Isn't that where Kayda was headed?" She stared at Cyrie, her skin prickling with goose flesh.

Cyrie shook her head, sighing deeply. "They haven't been packing those ships in the harbor with fighters and supplies to join your fight. They're planning to run. They're gonna leave us all to die."

"But where will they go?" Aren turned to Lark. "What if it's true? Remember, I told you about how I wanted to sail out beyond the Orddon one day, to search for the island paradise with the clear water that I'd heard about?" He gulped, running a hand down his face. "With all the ships they have, I wouldn't be surprised if they've found it."

Lark frowned. "Are you sure, Cyrie? That trader promised Princess Kayda he'd aid us in our fight. They are to be wed."

Cyrie nodded sadly. "Davit wouldn't lie to me. He's been listening in on them plotting in that carriage for weeks. They aren't planning to help your princess. They're gonna betray her."

Lark's stomach dropped as she stared at her friends. What were they going to do?

Chapter 18

A hazy cloud encased Kayda's mind. Blearily, voices reached her through the fog clogging her ears.

"I think she's coming to," said a familiar voice, one she should be able to place, but couldn't in her current state.

A second voice replied, "Surely not so soon. A single sip of that juice had enough sleeping tonic to knock her out for hours."

She fought to open her eyes as her body jostled, but the task proved impossible. Her eyelids might as well have been glued shut for how much they refused to budge.

"Disgusting," the first voice said. "This pig won't stop throwing up."

"How should I have known he'd drain the whole cup in one swig? Fat bastard," answered the other.

"Leave him. He doesn't matter. All they want is the girl."

A spike of fear shot through her as retreating footsteps echoed in her ears. But even that could not force her eyes to open. Blackness reigned.

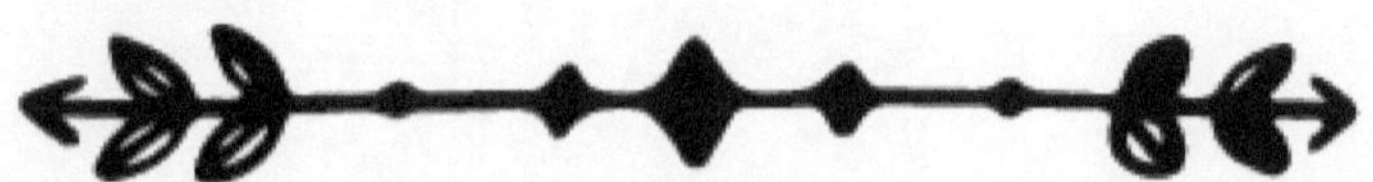

She came to sometime later. An hour, a day—how much time had passed was impossible to tell. Light shone in from high windows, revealing a basement room. Dirt walls and floors, bare except for herself and another occupant, sprawled in a heap beside her, his face resting in a pool of vomit.

"Father?" Her voice was hoarse. She reached out to him. Her hand stopped short, encircled by a metal shackle.

Kayda gasped, staring down at her torso for the first time since she awakened. Thick metal chains wrapped around her waist, wrists, and legs. The far end latched around a hook high on the wall. A period of frantic scrambling and tugging proved she was well and truly trapped, unable to move more than a few degrees in any direction.

The morning's events returned to her in a flash. That sweet juice. Wyll's traitorous smile.

Blazes. Why was this happening? What could he hope to gain by capturing her and her father like this? It made no sense.

An echo of the overheard conversation rose, like the hazy memory of a half-forgotten dream.

All they want is the girl.

Terror struck her, and the weight of the chains pressed against her unbearably, squeezing, constricting her limbs. Her breath came, harsh and labored. Who wanted her? Why?

Footsteps pounded just outside the door. Kayda fought to shake off the panic and school her features as the door swung open.

"Ah, finally awake I see." Wyll strode in, his smile still firmly in place, looking for all the world like he'd just happened upon her waking from a peaceful nap.

"What is the meaning of this, Wyll? Set me and my father free. Now."

"I'm afraid that won't be happening, my dear."

Kayda's heart seized. Whatever tiny sliver of hope she'd held that this was all some massive mistake evaporated with those words. That saccharine smile. "But we had a deal."

"Yes, we did. But it wasn't much of a deal now, was it?" He crouched in front of her, meeting her eye to eye. "Our entire fleet, for the hand of a single *bastard* princess?" He scoffed, shaking his head slowly. "Do you really think you're worth an entire fleet of ships?"

Kayda's stomach twinged, his words pummeling her like a gut punch. How could she have believed this snake wanted to marry her?

"Are you mad?" Her voice was surprisingly stable, considering how much her stomach churned with dread. "Don't you see, if I don't bring the fight to the scourge, they'll only spread? What good will your silk trade be with no one left to purchase?"

His smile shifted into a sneer. "You think you know everything, don't you, Princess? That just because you grew up in a castle, surrounded by gaggles of fools desperate enough to believe your family had some divine right to rule, that any of that nonsense was true? You couldn't stop the scourge from destroying Flamesmoat. I don't have any faith that you'll keep them from spreading here as well."

She met his stare, her jaw clenched. "Coward."

Wyll rolled his eyes. "Let all the brave fools keep their battles and their graves. I have other plans."

"What plans? There won't be anything left."

He scoffed. "Oh, you truly don't know, do you?" He stood, turning to leave. "I told you once, trade was king here. Someone offered me a better deal. It's nothing personal. I'm sure you understand."

Before he made it to the door, another set of footsteps sounded. Egard appeared in the doorway, carrying a lit candlestick.

Wyll shot him a murderous glare. "Blow that out, now. I thought I told you? No fire near this one."

Egard quickly snuffed out the flame, grumbling, "I didn't know she was awake."

Wyll smirked. "Can't have our little mage burning the place down, now, can we? Don't get any ideas about melting those chains, Princess. I have it on good authority that the talent it would take to manage that task would cost you more years than you have to spare." He laughed, turning to leave again.

"Wait. Please, at least help my father. Look at him, he's not well." The king hadn't moved since she'd awoken, his chest rising and falling in a labored pattern that did not bode well for his state. Surely, they would help him?

Egard set the candlestick down and strode into the room, sneering down at the king on the floor. "Yes, that is unfortunate, isn't it? Don't worry, Princess. I'll help him for you."

"Thank you." Kayda sighed.

Egard leaned over beside the king's head, reaching behind his back. His hand flashed forward, metal gleaming in the dim light. Before Kayda realized what was happening, the knife was at her father's throat, slicing through his neck. Red spurted through the air, the gush of blood pooling on the floor and mixing with the chunks of vomit in the dirt.

"No!" she screamed.

Egard laughed, wiping his blade on the back of the king's tunic as he bled out. "I've been waiting to do that for decades. He thought he could toss Solenne aside and take some dusty Sul for a wife behind my back." He paused, only to spit out a glob of mucus on her father's closed eyelid. "Good riddance."

Kayda's chest burned. "He didn't even know! He never knew. You just killed an innocent man."

Egard frowned for an instant, then shrugged. "Oops." He smiled at Wyll and slid the knife behind his back. "I wonder if we can get a bonus now? They asked for a princess, but we're bringing them a queen."

Wyll shook his head. He stood far back from the blood pooling on the floor, casually leaning against the dirt wall. "No. What is she queen of, after all? Queen of ruin isn't much of a prize."

They left her with her father's corpse. Slammed the door on her, and left her to watch the pool of red creep closer and closer to where she sat, chained and alone.

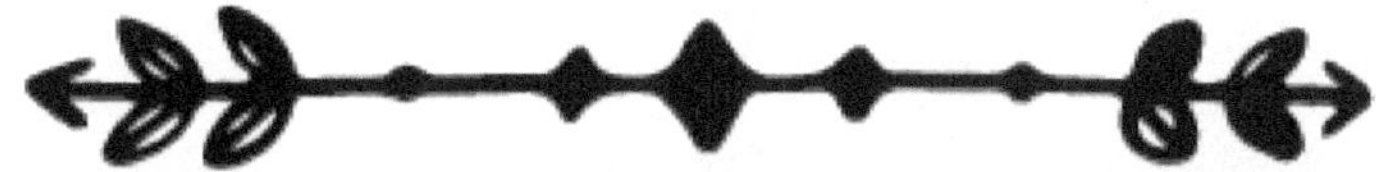

Long hours passed with nothing happening. Kayda sat, tied in place, watching her father's blood seep into the dirt floor and dry. Her mood shifted, alternatively turning from determination to be freed to despair that she'd never see a way out of this.

Bone-deep regret burned inside her every time she glanced at her father's corpse. If she'd only trusted him, maybe none of this would've happened. She'd been so suspicious of her father's motives. So worried he'd reject her when he learned of her true parentage that she kept him in the dark until this...

He'd taken the first step to repair their relationship when he apologized back in the tower, but she hadn't done the same. Now she'd never have the chance to make things right between them.

Wyll and Egard could not be allowed to get away with this. She needed to find some way out of this prison. She had to make them pay. But no matter how much she wracked her brain, she could see no path out of this basement room.

Was she even still at Oasis Manse, or had the villains moved her while she was unconscious? It was impossible to tell from where she sat. If she managed to escape somehow, could she even find a way back to the docks?

She needed to warn everyone on board *Nova's Champion*. Even now, Wyll and his father might be out there, betraying her friends like they'd betrayed her.

Footsteps clattered outside the door. But instead of the door opening, a harried whisper sounded from outside.

"Kayda? Kayda, are you all right in there?"

It was a new voice that spoke. One she remembered from her last visit. "Aurelia? Is that you?"

"Yes, it's me. I'm sorry, Princess. I didn't know Wyll and Egard were capable of this treachery."

"Aurelia, let me out of here. If you don't agree with what they're doing, then set me free."

"I wish I could. You're locked in, and I don't have the key. Even if I could, they'd never allow it. This is the first chance to get Ignace back."

"Ignace? Who is that?"

"Wyll's brother. He's been missing for over a year. Left on some mission to find a new trade route beyond Saltcliff. Only he's not really missing. He's been captured. By whom, I'm not sure. Wyll's been trying to find some way to trade for his freedom. But no amount of silk could sway these people. There was nothing they wanted. Not until now."

Kayda's stomach roiled. "Me. They want me."

"Yes. I'm so sorry. If I could—" Aurelia's voice abruptly cut off.

"What are you doing down here?" a deep voice boomed. It was that bastard, Egard.

"Nothing, I was only checking on her," Aurelia said.

"Well, come away from there. We need your help to get everything set for sailing in the morning."

"All right, I'm coming." Aurelia's voice faded, and the sound of footsteps trailed off into the distance.

Kayda's mind spun. Who were these mysterious people who wanted her badly enough to arrange all this? What could they possibly offer Wyll that he'd be willing to sell out his entire country? Surely it wouldn't help him to win his brother back, only to have his home destroyed.

Only... what if they offered him a place in this new trade land instead?

There'd long been rumors of islands past the Orddon Ocean. She'd come across plenty of tales in the books in the Royal Library back in Flamesmoat. But she'd always assumed they were tales of fancy. Or the exaggerations of sailors who'd happened upon the tiny string of islands that they knew for a fact did exist in the Orddon Ocean.

Saltcliff was one such island. A tiny isle resting off the coast of Joria in the midst of the Orddon Ocean, only remarkable for its natural salt deposits.

If what Aurelia said was true, then maybe there *was* something out there. But why would they want her?

Chapter 19

Conall pushed the stick into the bog, his shoulders and legs aching. A day and night had passed without another sighting of the armed men sharing the bog with them.

Ereni sat at the canoe's bow, her sharp blue eyes staring ahead. She'd overcome her heightened emotions, returning to the cool, collected woman he remembered so clearly.

"Are you ever going to talk to her?" Shadow asked.

Conall sighed inwardly. *"I don't know."*

They'd spent most of the ride in silence since their last run in with the men. He was beginning to think Ereni would rather ignore him than attempt to right things between them.

There was so much he needed to know. So much he wanted to say.

At first, he hadn't wanted to upset her further, seeing how emotional she was. But now, the silence wrapped around them like a physical thing. A barrier keeping things civil. Part of him wanted to leave it standing until they found a way out of this place.

Did he really want to tear down the wall and peer beyond the cracked foundation at the tormented souls within?

No. They couldn't keep this up forever. He had to think of something to say to break—

"My mother. Is she all right?" Ereni turned, her expression flat, back straight. But her fingers clenched around her coverall's sleeves, betraying the feelings she tried to hide.

Conall shook his head. "I'm sorry. She's gone."

"She told me she wouldn't be coming back. I didn't want to believe it…" Ereni trailed off, her fingers straightening, releasing her death grip on her sleeves. "How did it happen?"

"A fever on our journey to the Northern Depths." Conall frowned. "Wait, what do you mean? She told you she wouldn't be back?"

"It was one of the things she saw in her first vision." Ereni shifted on the bench. "All Sade Prims make the journey to the Northern Depths in their youth."

"You've been there, too," he stated flatly.

"I have."

"Were you meant to be the next Sade Prim, then?"

Ereni nodded. "If things had kept on like they had been, yes."

"But they didn't."

"No, they didn't."

Conall stared at her, so many questions bombarding his mind. He picked the loudest. "Why did it need to be now?"

Ereni shrugged. "The Palisade was weakening. It had been for years. If you hadn't brought it down, it would've fallen eventually."

"Then why didn't you let it?" The faces of Amora and the other mages who'd died at the Palisade's fall flashed in his mind. "You could've saved Amora. You could've spared them all."

"Perhaps. Or maybe more would've died when the wall fell without warning and caught us unawares."

Conall grimaced. He hadn't considered that. She could be right, but there was really no way of knowing that now. "Why them?"

"Mother chose the weakest among us who could still handle the task. And those who would balk when they learned of our plans."

"And me."

"She knew you would survive because of the vision she had of you two traveling to the witch. That you would be aged, but live. I'm sorry."

"How can you put so much stock into these visions? What if they're wrong?"

Ereni scoffed. "They aren't."

Conall glared at her, a single brow raising.

"I told you, all Sade Prims travel there. Sometimes they even bring others with them. Everyone who drinks the dream elixir witnesses things that one day come true; we had a ledger at Mage Keep to record it. Without fail, every vision comes true. It's hard to argue with hundreds of years of results."

"If that's the case, at least we know we'll make it out of this bog and back to the others. I saw myself fighting in the Abandoned Lands with Kayda and Lark."

Ereni flashed a sad half-smile. "That's true. I've seen it, too."

But if that was the case, then was what the Unseen said true as well? Was one of them destined to die fighting the scourge?

Conall's stomach churned, and he stared into the murky water, replaying the vision he'd witnessed beneath the ocean.

He'd seen a glimpse of the battle but not its end. Kayda and Lark were definitely there, and he was as well, but the rest of the battlefield was a blur of chaos in his memory. Except for Shadow and Muse, he couldn't be certain of any other face in the crowd. Not even...

His heart thudded, dropping to his stomach just as the stick dropped to the bog's bottom.

His gaze flicked to the front of the canoe. "Are you there at the battle? What did you see in your vision, Ereni?"

Ereni exhaled and stared at her hands as if gathering her thoughts. Then she met his gaze, her lips parting.

"Brother, I hear something." Shadow sat up straight, head cocked. *"It could be men, talking."*

Conall raised a finger to his lips before Ereni spoke. He pointed to Shadow and tugged his ear, then flicked his gaze to the bog.

Ereni's eyes widened, and she closed her mouth, pressing her lips into a thin line. She pointed at the mangroves looming around them.

Conall squinted, then shook his head.

Last night, just like the first night, they'd found a spot to cram their canoe behind some trees, hiding among the mangrove roots. But the trees here grew tightly together on the waterway's sides. He didn't see any space large enough where they could fit.

Until now, he'd heard nothing strange. Just the normal croaking and buzzing of the reptiles and insects that called this swampy land home. Shadow's ears were far keener than his, after all. But now, the echo of voices carried across the water.

The hair rose on the back of his neck. There was no question now. The sound Shadow heard was definitely men's voices. And if he could hear them, they must be coming closer.

Conall gulped. What were they going to do? If those men found them—which seemed likely, considering they had nowhere to hide—would they be able to fight them off? They were rested now, at least, but they'd be outnumbered. And if they carried ranged weapons with them instead of just cudgels and swords...

Ereni's hand slid out of the canoe and hovered outstretched above the water. Moisture whispered through the air, and a cloud of icicles materialized in front of the bow, sparkling in the late afternoon sunlight.

Conall gritted his teeth and stashed the pole on the canoe's side holder, careful to make as little noise as possible.

The voices grew louder. Someone must've just told a joke; laughter peeled out, rich and hearty, bouncing off the water and filling his ears even as a shiver slid down his spine. His stare locked on the bend ahead of them.

He snaked his hand out of the canoe, joining Ereni's hovering just above the bog. He reached for his talent, pushing the fear of the unknown aside. He had to fight. For Shadow. And Ereni. This would not be the end for them. They *would* join the others. They'd make it to the Abandoned Lands.

The air around their boat thickened so much it was like they slid through a cloud of fog. Ice crystalized, taking shape beside the canoe. He added dozens of ice shards to the ones Ereni summoned. When those prisoners rounded the bend, they'd be in for a wicked surprise.

The first glimpse of wood rounded the bend. Conall held his breath, waiting.

Laughter still rang out, but it was tapering off now. The bow of a second canoe appeared, right next to the first, and then a third, just behind it. Conall exhaled, readying his shards, preparing to send them flying to the unsuspecting men as soon as their faces were revealed.

Then the first man's smiling face appeared, and Ereni's icicles splashed into the water in front of their canoe.

Conall stared ahead, his gaze flicking between the rippling water and the men, all three visible now, each one poling a canoe, their smiles falling and jaws dropping as they spotted them in the water ahead of them.

Why wasn't Ereni attacking? They'd lose the element of surprise if they didn't act now.

But before he sent his ice shards sailing, he stole another look at the men. He didn't recognize any of them. And they weren't wearing the ugly coverall's either. Two of them dressed in dirty overalls and matching wool cloaks. The third sported a cloak as well, but beneath the cloak, sheer green fabric flashed. The same fabric that was so popular in Raimire.

These weren't the prisoners. They'd just stumbled upon a few of the Raimish sailors keeping watch over the bog.

Conall grinned, feeling as lucky as a hare who'd escaped a snare. Just as Ereni spun toward him, he let his ice drop into the bog, splashing the canoe again, tiny waves rippling outward.

"Friends of yours?" he asked.

Ereni shook her head, smiling. "Not exactly, but we've met."

She turned back to the newcomers, raising her voice. "Dal, Fillan, I'm pleased to see you."

The face of the older man wearing overalls screwed up, his gaze flitting up and down Ereni, as if he were not sure where to place her, but the younger man's face lit with recognition.

"Ereni? Is that you?" he asked, thrusting his pole down and gliding closer.

She beamed. "It is. I'm certainly glad to find you out here, Fillan. We could use a guide right about now."

Conall frowned. That must make the older fellow, Dal.

The older man spoke up, shaking his head, pushing his canoe behind Fillan's. "We're not guides. Not anymore. We've been keeping watch over the bog for those foul beasts." He gestured to the Raimish man in the final canoe, who stayed silent, letting the pair do all the talking. "There's more of us, spread out between here and Raimire."

"What are you doing out here?" Fillan slicked back his brown hair. "I thought all the mages fled after the scourge broke loose. Shouldn't you be with the Sade Prim?"

Ereni's smile dropped. "It's a long story. But what matters is my," she paused, glancing at him, "friend Conall and I got separated from the others when Flamesmoat fell. We need to find a way through the bog to meet up with the others on the eastern coast, in the Orddon Ocean."

Fillan exchanged a glance with Dal, and it looked like they held a silent conversation with only their eyes. It was the kind of familiarity that only existed between family or close friends. Conall suspected from the resemblance they shared, it was the former.

Fillan gave a small nod and stared back at Ereni. "You're a long way off track if that's where you're headed. We can guide you there."

Ereni beamed. "Thank you. That would be most kind."

"You haven't come across any other folks in these waters lately, have you?" Conall asked.

Dal shook his head. "Nope. Not a soul."

"About that..." Ereni grimaced. "A handful of prisoners escaped the Southmoat Prison into the bog."

"Prisoners?" Dal's eyes widened. "That changes things. We can't leave the rest of our people without warning."

Another one of those weighted looks passed between the men. Then it was Dal's turn to nod.

"We split up," he announced. "Fillan, you guide Ereni and her friend." Dal thrust his hand backward at his silent companion. "We'll spread the word to the others about this new threat."

With that, they took off. The men spun their canoes around and headed back the way they came, discussing the routes they planned to take and saying their goodbyes, while he caught Shadow up on the new plan. At the first fork in the bog, the Raimish man peeled off, his path leading south. A few moments later, Dal took another turn, headed southwest. That left their two canoes slowly poling eastward.

Moisture flooded the air again. Ereni lifted her hand above the bog, a trio of ice darts hovering before her face.

"What's that for?" Fillan asked, scratching his head.

Conall pointed to a group of small waterfowl floating just ahead of them, atop the murky water. "Watch."

Ereni sent the ice soaring. The darts slammed into three of the birds, striking each of them cleanly in their necks. The remaining birds scattered, squawking and flapping away as quick as their wings would carry them.

Fillan's face lit up, and he shifted his canoe, heading for the carcasses. "Yum, sparling. I've been eating too much fish lately."

Ereni glanced at Conall. "I'll take a turn with the pole if you can handle the plucking?"

Conall passed Shadow, lazing in the middle of the canoe, and handed Ereni the pole, then took a seat at the bow.

Fillan floated up beside them and tossed the birds into their canoe. "I thought watching a falcon and hawk hunt sparlings was impressive, but your method has them beat."

Falcon and hawk... "You must've met my sister Lark and her friends the Wandering Bards."

"You're Lark's brother?" Fillan eyed him up and down. "I see the resemblance now. But she told me her brother was dead."

Conall picked the first sparling off the boat bottom. "Yeah, that's another one of those long stories. She thought I was dead for a while, but we've reconnected." He glanced back at Ereni as she stabbed the long pole down into the bog, then back at Fillan. He seemed a nice enough fellow, and about the same age as Ereni. "How do you two know each other?"

"My father and I hail from Bogsmouth." Fillan clenched his stick so tightly his tanned knuckles turned white. "Well, we used to." He sighed. "Being so close to Mage Keep, we spent a fair amount of time ferrying mages about. I met Ereni a few years back, when we gave her and her mother a lift to Raimire."

Ereni nodded, smiling. "That was one of my first outings as a seer for the keep. I found five talented folks in Slinas on that trip."

Fillan grinned back at her, chuckling. "That's right. The boats were a lot more crowded on the trip back."

Conall's gaze flicked between the two of them, smiling at each other. A sliver of something uncomfortable took up space in his chest.

He tried to shake it off. She could smile at whoever she wanted. It didn't mean anything.

He concentrated on the birds, making quick work of the task with a hunting knife.

Ereni had surrendered the knife that belonged in that empty sheath yesterday. She'd stashed it underneath the forward seat. He'd kept a close eye on it since then, and she made no attempt to retrieve it.

Maybe it was silly—considering her talent, she could harm herself just as easily without it—but having the knife brought him a measure of comfort all the same.

"I suppose we should start hunting for a spot to pull over and cook those," Fillan said.

"No need." Ereni smiled again. "We can cook them on the go."

Fillan leaned back, brow raising. "You can? I've got to see this."

Ereni dug through the rainbow pack and pulled out a tinderbox. She sent a few sparks flying, as she lit a bundle of dried sticks aflame.

"Careful, now," Fillan said. "You don't want your canoe up in smoke."

"Don't worry. We only need it for a short while." She lifted the makeshift torch, holding it above the water, stomping out the few cinders that fell to the boat bottom.

Ereni drew in a deep breath, and Conall's skin prickled all over, like he'd rolled through a pile of evergreen needles. Then the naked birds rose in the air and hovered beside the boat, between their canoes.

She shifted her gaze to him, an expectant look on her face.

That was his cue. Conall closed his eyes briefly. He meant to call on Lark's image in his mind, but all he could picture was a pair of blue eyes instead of hazel. Nevertheless, his talent responded. The birds burst into flames, the fire so bright he flinched back from the heat. He kept the flames flowing until the bundle of sticks in Ereni's hand died out.

Then she sent a wave of air, gliding one of the charred birds into Fillan's canoe, and the others dropped on the boards of their boat, still sizzling.

Shadow popped up from where he'd been napping, licking his chops in anticipation. They settled down to eat, their poles stashed, canoes listing in the gentle current.

"I have to say, that was mighty impressive, too. I've got to travel with mages more often." Fillan chewed, a thoughtful expression replacing his grin. "How come you didn't cook like that the last time I ferried you?"

Ereni glanced his way, swallowing. "We didn't have anyone on board with fire talent then."

Fillan chuckled. "You're stronger together. Makes sense."

Conall glared down at his meat to avoid rolling his eyes.

"It's getting late. We should search for somewhere to tie up for the night, after we're done eating," Ereni said.

"There's a spot close to here that ought to do." Fillan licked his fingers, staring at Ereni. "You can sleep here with me, if you want. I've got extra blankets. Proper wool, even."

Conall chewed slowly. He watched the grin spread across Ereni's face, and his stomach churned.

"And why would I want wool when I have fur over here?" Ereni answered, nodding to Shadow.

"Would be more room is all." Fillan shrugged. "Suit yourself."

"I'm staying here." Ereni tossed the rest of her bird to Shadow. "Besides, you kept me up practically all night on our last trip through the bog."

Her words caught Conall mid-swallow. He coughed, grabbed the waterskin, and met Ereni's gaze. Mischief glinted back at him.

"I did nothing of the sort," Fillan declared.

"Yes, you did. You snore. Loud." She laughed, and Conall's heart squeezed.

He hadn't heard that sound in ages. Now this dirty ferryman had her laughing.

He used to be the one making her laugh. Putting that mischievous glint in her eyes. Now, all they had together was hurt and the shadow of betrayal. Would it ever be easy like that with them again? Did he even want it to be?

Fillan splayed a hand across his dirty overalls, feigning shock. "I never snored a night in my life."

Ereni laughed again and shook her head. "All the same, I'm staying here."

Fillan shrugged then hopped up and grabbed his pole. "Follow me. The spot I was talking about is just ahead."

Ereni manned the pole again, and soon, they were sheltered within a large hole in the bog, hidden by mangrove roots.

Fillan settled down to rest in his canoe without delay by unfolding a stack of wool blankets. "I'll see you guys in the morning."

Conall lounged beside Shadow and stared up at the crooked mangrove branches. Ereni plopped down behind Shadow, snuggling up against his back. Shadow allowed it, stretching and yawning.

Conall's eyelids drooped. The long day of travel and his full belly caused drowsiness to envelop him quickly. Until a loud, grating sound met his ears. His eyes shot open.

"Told you," Ereni said with a giggle.

Conall met her gaze in the dusk light. He cringed as Fillan snored again, the harsh rattle repeating without a discernable pattern. "Yeah, I see what you mean." He sighed, the weariness he'd just been feeling chased away by the obnoxious noise. It was going to be a long night.

"It'll be worth it not to get lost." Ereni tugged one of the cloaks against her back, shivering.

Conall scooted over, lifting the cloak draped atop him. "C'mon, climb in the middle."

"Are you sure?" she asked.

He nodded, and she rose from her spot.

"Roll over, brother. Ereni's cold."

Shadow snorted and cracked open one golden eye, meeting his gaze. Conall sensed he wanted to say something, but he must've decided against it. He simply rolled over and breathed deeply, settling back down to sleep.

Ereni slid in between them. She turned her back to him and draped an arm around Shadow's side.

Conall tucked the cloaks around them. Then he rested on his back and listened to Fillan snore, wide awake.

After a few moments, Ereni stopped shivering. "Do you still want to know what I saw?"

"Hm?" What she saw... Her vision. "Yes."

"It started with the battle. The same one everyone sees. I saw the three of you, all glowing purple." Her voice rose in pitch, sounding hopeful. "Until then, I didn't know it was possible."

Conall blinked. She could see them glowing with her seer sight, even within the vision?

She shifted to face him. Conall kept staring at the branches, but he could feel her stare on his face, her gaze landing on his cheek like a caress.

"Were you there at the battle, too?" he asked.

She shook her head gently. "I don't know. When I think back on it, everything except for you three is all a blur."

Conall inhaled. "Me, too." He exhaled. "What else?"

Ereni tugged the cloak higher on her shoulder. "I almost didn't make the journey to meet the witch. I was planning to leave Mage Keep. Cut ties, live a normal life somewhere."

Conall turned to her, raising a brow. "You were?"

He thought back to when they'd first met. She'd asked him what he planned to do with his life. When he'd told her about the farm, how he'd wanted to settle down and have a few kids, she'd said it sounded lovely. At the time, he'd assumed she'd just been humoring him. Was she envious instead?

"I was toying with the idea. But my mother convinced me to make the journey to the Winter Witch first. And what I saw after the battle changed my mind."

"What was it?"

"A man appeared. One I barely recognized. My father. He died when I was just a child."

Conall's brows pinched together. "I'm sorry."

Ereni smiled. "Actually, it was nice to see him. A relief, in fact."

He could understand that. After all, he'd seen his mother in his vision.

"It was nice until he started speaking. He told me the future depended on me. On my choices. That if I left Mage Keep like I'd planned, the world would be doomed."

Conall frowned, his heart aching for her. "That's awful. Don't the mages have other seers? Couldn't someone else have taken your place?"

"No, you don't understand. This isn't about the Palisade, or the Abandoned Lands. It's about her."

Conall met her gaze. "Who?"

Ereni's eyes were misty. "Violet. Our daughter is going to change the world."

Conall's heart skipped a beat as he realized they shared something much bigger than hurt feelings and betrayal. They had something binding them together, flesh and bone and beyond amazing. Their daughter.

"Tell me everything."

Chapter 20

The night passed slowly for Kayda. After Aurelia's visit, no one came. Not even to remove her father's body from the room. She was left to stare at him while the flies found him. And when night fell, to scream every time a rat slunk out from some hole in the wall to gnaw on his flesh. After the first few times, the wretched things ignored her, and she was forced to listen to them feasting in the darkened basement room.

She couldn't sleep. Not with the awful stench of death clogging her nose and the chains wrapped around her. The thick metal rested heavily on her skin, weighing her down just as surely as grief burdened her heart.

It was all her fault. Her father wouldn't be dead at her feet if she hadn't trusted Wyll and his family. And now he was threatening to steal her away before she could fulfill her plan to save her country. She couldn't let it stand. She wouldn't.

As the first hint of dawn washed over the sky outside, transforming the shadowy black inside her room to a chalky gray, the lock clicked open. The crowd of rats scattered, their claws skittering on rock.

Wyll strode in, nose wrinkling as his gaze flicked to her father's corpse. "My, it is rank in here. Can't believe we forgot to move that body yesterday." He shook his head slowly, meeting her gaze. "Sorry for that, my dear. I really had no idea what my father was planning. You understand he has a bit of a temper. Always one black sheep in the family, isn't there?"

She met his crooked smile with a hard glare. Did he actually think she'd laugh off her father's murder because Egard didn't know how to control his temper?

Wyll strolled closer, straightening his freshly pressed, cobalt-blue silk suit, detouring around the pooled blood that had darkened to a brownish-black stain on the dirt floor. "Let's get you out of here. We have a boat to catch."

A thread of hope unspooled in her chest. If the basement she was currently trapped in *was* in Wyll's house, then they'd need to travel through half of the city to return to the docks. Someone might see her and offer aid. Or better yet, she might sneak close enough to an open flame to burn these chains and free herself.

Wyll led her through the darkened house. The basement did belong to Oasis Manse. He'd made certain not to light any of the candles or lamps, leaving them to shuffle through the dim light filtering in through the drawn curtains.

Soon they made it outside. Kayda breathed deeply the warm dusty air, trying to banish the stench of decay that clung inside her nostrils. Wyll didn't grant her much time for the task. He tugged her behind him to a black carriage tied up in the courtyard. He opened the door, revealing the darkened interior of a closed carriage, much less fine than the one that had driven them here yesterday. And instead of holding out a gentle hand to help her up, he shoved her inside without a word and slammed the door closed.

Kayda's chest burned with rage as she surveyed the empty carriage. Black cloth blanketed the windows, leaving the dreary interior just as dark as her mood. She needed to think of some way out of this. A plan to break free of her chains and put these murdering snakes in their place.

"Kayda."

She was so wrapped up in thoughts of revenge, she almost ignored the voice in her mind.

"Kayda. Please answer me."

"Dru? Druturion, is that you?" Hope exploded, bright and wild, infusing her body with a lightness she'd almost forgotten. *"Where are you? I'm in trouble. I need your help."*

"It's good to hear your voice."

"You too. I've missed you so much. Where are you? Why did you leave me?"

"I'm sorry. There's so much to explain, and I'm afraid there's not much time. Even now, I can feel it trying to take over."

"What? I don't understand." Her eyes widened. *"The Unseen. He's trying to take over you like he has the scourge."*

"Is that what you're calling it? That voice, it's gotten worse. Belstasia and I, we've both been affected. We left the rest of you before it took full control."

Her stomach clenched, his words confirming her worst fears. *"How is that possible?"*

"I'm not certain. It happened already to Bela. She killed the others, but it wasn't her fault. You were right to stop me from harming her in my anger. I see that now. You've given us a chance at a future, Kayda."

"That's good. I'm glad it was the right thing." She sighed. *"But why did you leave?"*

"Distance is the only thing that helps. Bela and I returned home."

"Home? I thought Dracwood was your home?"

"Dracwood was never our home, only our breeding grounds. But much has changed while we've been underground. People swarm the lands that used to belong to only dragonkind."

Kayda gasped. *"There is a land out there with other people."*

"Yes. And I'm afraid our presence may have some men here eager to find you, so that they can get to me. I could feel your pain seeping through our bond. I had to warn you."

"You're too late, Dru. I've been betrayed. You have to help me."

"I'm sorry. If I return across the sea, the voice will take over. We might have a way to return, but we need something first. It will take time to procure."

Kayda's heart sank. *"So, I'm still on my own?"*

"For now. Do what you must to free yourself. You must. The Unseen cannot be allowed to flourish. We will be back to join the battle, but you need be there to start it, Kayda."

"Dru! Don't leave. Please. I can't do this all on my own."

"You're not alone. I'm with you, even when you can't hear me. Call on my strength." His voice faded, filled with a note of pain. *"I have to go. I can't hold it off any longer."*

Once again, she was alone. But the conversation with Dru had given her new hope. Even though she was still shackled, just as desperate as before, she had one thing to hold on to. Her bondmate was alive. She would see him again. These bastards keeping her hostage would not win.

Footsteps echoed outside. Kayda drew a calming breath and prepared for the carriage to start. Once it was in motion, she could shuffle sideways and peel back the cloth covering the wind—

The door swung open. Kayda squinted at the sudden light spilling in through the doorway. But it only stayed open long enough for Wyll to slide in and seat himself across from her. The lock outside clicked shut, and the carriage shook, no doubt from someone seating themselves in the front.

Kayda glared across the seat at her former intended. She'd never known a carriage that locked from the *outside*. How long had he been planning to betray her? Not that it mattered. Knowing the details wouldn't change anything. It wouldn't bring her father back.

And now with Wyll in the compartment with her, she'd need to come up with a different plan. There was no chance of him letting her wave for help from the window.

The carriage jolted forward without warning. Kayda's head bobbed against the hard seat back. It was a far cry from the thick cushions she'd traveled on just yesterday.

Wyll grimaced and pulled a small flask from his pocket. He unscrewed the top and took a sip. "Can't say I'm a fan of sailing. A little tipple helps." He offered the flask to her with a raised brow.

Kayda only stared back at him flatly. What was it with men, thinking alcohol could solve all the world's problems? Although…

"Sure, thanks," she leaned forward, opening her mouth slightly.

Wyll leaned forward, too, lifting the flask, only to snatch it back at the last instant. He jerked back in his seat, staring at her with scrunched brows and pursed lips. "No, I think not. I don't like that look in your eye." He twisted the stopper on the flask. "You're liable to spit it back in my face."

Damn. Another plan foiled. Kayda snapped her mouth shut and leaned back, annoyed he could read her so well. She scanned the darkened interior, searching for anything else that might help her break free of this carriage. There was nothing.

The liquor might still work. She'd caught a whiff of it when he held it out toward her. It had practically burned her nostrils. She just had to ensure he took another sip.

"It's funny you don't like sailing, being that you own a shipping company and all." Kayda forced an amused smile across her lips. "I can't get enough of sailing. The waves rolling under you. All that water stretching out as far as the eye can see. The way the water sways you, side to side. It's like being rocked in a mother's embrace."

"And what would you know about that?" A cruel grin lit Wyll's face.

Kayda resisted the urge to scowl, instead gazing to the side thoughtfully. "No, it's more like dancing, I think. Spinning around and around on the floor, the waves heaving merrily. Soft and slow like a ballad until a storm hits, then the water pounds like the drums in a country jig."

"Enough. I get the picture." Wyll grimaced, clutching his stomach. Then his hand slipped into his pocket, and he pulled the flask free.

Kayda set her stare on the carriage floor, feigning disinterest. She wouldn't give him the chance to glimpse anything in her gaze this time. But as he twisted the stopper free, she reached for her talent.

She would have to pay for this with no source. But for what she had planned, it would likely only be a wave of exhaustion and not years of her life.

He lifted the flask. Set it to his lips. And just as the liquid touched his tongue, Kayda struck.

Cold coursed through her body, like she'd been drenched in a vat of ice water. At the same time, she conjured a tiny flicker of flame and sent it right into Wyll's open mouth.

Dizziness washed over her limbs, and she trembled where she sat.

Wyll screamed as the flame whooshed to life using the alcohol as fuel. He dropped the flask, and the flame spread even farther, engulfing his chest and lap as he clutched his throat. Within moments, his screams turned ragged, his voice garbled. He pounded his feet and slapped at the fire coursing across his body.

The noise must've reached the driver. The carriage pulled to a halt, and the door swung open. Egard stared in, his eyes bulging as he spotted Wyll, groaning and slapping out the last of the flames. The scent of charred flesh and burnt silk wafted through the air.

"Healer," Wyll croaked, his voice distorted and raspy. "Now, healer!"

Kayda squinted against the bright daylight and wobbled in her seat. She shivered, fighting to keep her eyelids from closing with the exhaustion weighing her down.

"What did you do, you witch?" Egard spat, fists clenched.

Kayda forced her eyes open fully and met Egard's gaze. "Oops."

Egard's fist flew at her face, and the world went black.

Chapter 21

Lark and Aren arrived back at the *Salty Serpent Inn* just as Dausius wrapped up a long story to thundering applause. They slipped through the crowd, dodging sweaty sailors and silk clad villagers, until they made it to the table where Mazen and Meital sat.

"Hey, you two are back early. I thought you'd be gone for most of the day with Tiora," Mazen said.

"Where's Ti?" Meital tilted her head, scanning the crowd behind them. "How did it go with her family?"

Lark slid into a seat across from the twins. Aren sat down beside her. "It went well. But she left with her sister to find someone. We ran into a problem while we were there."

Dausius strolled up to the table. "Problem? What problem?"

Lark glanced around, well aware of all the eyes and ears present in the crowded inn. "We might want to discuss this in private."

Dausius' brow furrowed. "All right. I'll tell the owner we're taking an extended break. Let's head back to the ship."

Lark nodded. "Good idea. I have to check on Violet, make sure the new wet nurse has everything well in hand."

Soon, they were back outside, the scorching afternoon sun beating down on them. Lark made her way down the wharf, her step hurried.

Poor Kayda. Surely, she would be all right, wouldn't she? With her talent, she could take care of herself. Maybe she'd already figured out some way to turn the betrayal to her advantage.

As they drew closer to *Nova's Champion*, a familiar face hustled toward them.

Lark smiled. "Hello, Jett."

Jett reached her side and clutched her elbow, a wide smile plastered on his face. He spun her around and hurried back the way they'd come. "Hello, dear. I'm so glad you and your friends agreed to meet me for lunch," he bellowed, waving emphatically at the others. "Come, I've secured a private room at the inn, just over here."

Lark quirked a brow but kept step with Jett, allowing him to lead her into a nearby inn. This one was a degree shabbier than the *Salty Serpent*, with only a handful of patrons staring gloomily into their mugs of ale atop worn wooden stools.

Jett led them away from the common room to a side door. They all crowded inside quickly, without a word, until Jett pulled the door shut behind them.

The room was small, housing only a large wooden table and chairs. An untouched pitcher and a pair of glasses rested on the table, and a single man sat behind it. Lark vaguely recognized him as the large man she'd seen following Kayda back from *The Lady Luck* when they left Flamesmoat. Sweat glistened on his brow in the stuffy room, made even stuffier with all the windows shuttered.

"Jett, what is the meaning of this?" Lark asked. "I know I didn't forget any lunch plans with you."

The sweaty man stood. "Something is deeply wrong in this city."

Lark's stomach twisted. She crossed her arms and raised a brow.

Dausius strode forward, sticking out a hand. "We haven't met. I'm Dausius of the Wandering Bards. Who might you be?"

The man turned a glare on Jett. "I asked you to meet me back here with help, and you bring me a traveling show?"

Jett flushed. "At least I found someone, Gawain. I see you've returned alone."

"Gawain, is it?" Dausius withdrew his hand, unshaken. "Aren't you the Guard Captain? What's going on?"

Lark spun on her heel. "I have to check on Violet."

Jett grabbed her arm. "You can't return to the ship. They aren't letting anyone off."

"What?" Aren asked.

"A few hours after we docked, a group of men claiming to be with the Port Master ordered *Nova's Champion* surrounded and quarantined." Jett explained. "They're saying there's an illness on board. But of course, that's a load of horseshit."

"Are you sure?" Lark's heart skipped a beat. "Violet... I can't leave her on board with a sickness spreading."

Gawain shook his head. "It's not true. Jett and I left to take a closer look at the other boats on the wharf just before the quarantine. There wasn't a single word about sickness until the Port Master showed up with his invented claims."

Meital stepped closer, placing a gentle hand on Lark's shoulder. "Even if it were true, Mika's still there with Violet. She'll be all right."

That's right, Mika was there. He wouldn't let anything bad happen to Violet. Lark let out a deep sigh. "I guess this only confirms what we learned while we were with Tiora."

"That's right. You said there was trouble earlier but not what it was," Dausius said.

Lark nodded. "One of Ti's sisters knows someone who works as a driver at Oasis Manse. The boy told her that the trading family Kayda's meeting with is planning to betray her."

"That would explain all the rich layabouts on the ships that we saw," Jett said.

"Rich layabouts?" Mazen asked.

Gawain scoffed. "Princess Kayda was sure that Wyll fellow was prepping those ships to join us in the fight to save Dracwood. Instead, they're practically crawling with finely dressed folk dripping with gems—most looking like they've never worked a day in their lives or know what a sword or bow looked like—much less how to use it. That and a ton of armed men and women hovering over them like it's their job to keep the rich pigs breathing."

"Then it's true. They're not planning to join the fight. They're going to run." Lark's heart thrummed madly. "What are we going to do?"

"Tiora." Aren's eyes widened. "We told her to meet us back at the ship."

Meital stepped toward the door. "I'll find her. C'mon, Maz."

The twins slipped out the door, shutting it firmly behind them.

Dausius paced behind the head of the table, tapping his chin. "We need to find the princess. With everyone stuck on the ship, it's up to us to stop this foul trader's plan from succeeding."

Gawain scratched his sweaty brow. "How is the question? With all the mages stuck on board *Nova's Champion,* we don't stand much of a chance." He gestured to Jett. "The two of us, a few traveling entertainers, and a single mage against the whole of Jorian high society and all of their sell-swords? I'm not a betting man, but I doubt many would chance those odds."

"What choice do we have? Without Kayda, everything falls apart. We can't fight the scourge without her," Lark said.

The door creaked open. Tiora stepped inside.

"You're back." Lark smiled, giving her a quick hug.

"What's going on?" Tiora asked. "Maz and Mei rushed us in here before we could reach the ship."

"I'll tell you everything in a moment," she promised, turning to greet the skinny young boy cowering behind Tiora, next to her sister. "I see you found him. Hello, I'm Lark. It's nice to meet you, Davit."

The boy stared down at his threadbare boots. "Hello."

Lark smiled at him, though he didn't look up to meet her eyes. "Please, we're friends of Cyrie's. And friends of the princess' as well. Can you tell us what you know? We only want to help our friend."

Davit peeled off his dusty hat, wringing it in his hands. "I could lose my job for this."

Dausius dug into his pocket and lifted out a heavy coin purse. Davit's eyes lit up at the jingling.

"I'll pay you handsomely for the information," Dausius offered.

Davit glanced at Cyrie, and after she sent him a gentle nod, he spoke, "It's all true. Everything Cyrie told you. The trading families are planning to flee. I heard them laughing about it. Bits and snatches while they've been in the carriage."

Gawain's neck stiffened, the corded muscle there sticking out. "I knew it."

"Is there anything else?" Lark asked.

Davit nodded. "I drove them there this morning—the king and princess. After I took care of the horses, Sir Wyll ordered me to take the rest of the day off. He *never* gives me the day off."

"She must still be there." Gawain rose to his feet. "We have to save her."

Jett squeezed his shoulder. "Wait. We don't know that for sure. They could've easily moved her in a second carriage." He turned to Davit. "What's their security like at Oasis Manse?"

"They've got a dozen men, at least, keeping watch over the house at all times."

Lark's heart sank. That didn't sound like good odds. They'd have to fight their way inside, without the certainty that she was even there.

"There's more. Sir Wyll and Sir Egard are planning to take the princess with them when they leave on the morrow."

"Are you sure?" Aren asked.

Davit shuffled, his shoulders sagging. "Yes. I heard them say they needed her. What for, I don't know."

"So, they'll need to bring her here tomorrow or at some point in the night," Dausius mused, rubbing his chin. His face lit up. "I have a plan that could work." He spread out his arms, his smile spreading just as widely. "I hope you're all prepared to do what we do best."

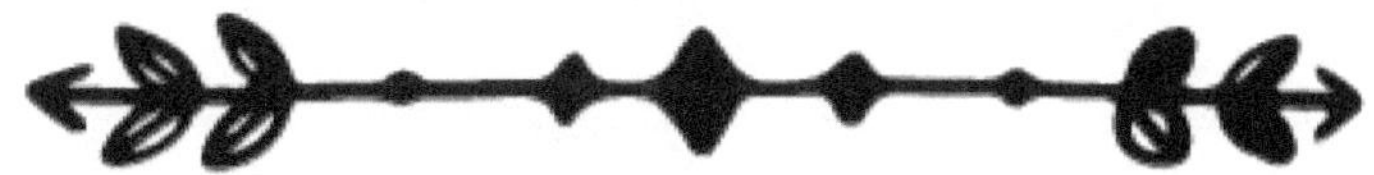

Lark stepped down from the tabletop in the *Salty Serpent Inn*, the roar of applause echoing throughout the common room. She displayed what she hoped was a radiant smile, all while exhaustion tugged on her shoulders and apprehension spread through her belly.

The thick crowd parted, allowing her and Aren to make their way to the long table they shared with the rest of the show members. With barely a pause for the clapping to subside, Dausius hopped up on the table and immediately launched into a tale filled with adventure and mystery.

Lark sank into a hard wooden chair, heaving out a sigh. "Any word?"

Meital's gaze flicked to the windows. "No sign of her yet. We might need to keep this up until morning."

Mazen groaned. "Much more of this and my knives are liable to start missing their target."

Tiora squeezed his shoulder, her smile a touch too bright. "Surely not... You're the best there is."

The grin he aimed at her was interrupted by a yawn. "Flattery doesn't work as well in the wee hours as it does when I'm well rested."

The inn door slammed open, and a group of three wobbly sailors stumbled outside into the dark.

"How many is that now?" Lark's stomach churned.

"Don't worry." Meital shook her head. "Did you see the way they were walking? They won't be in any condition for sailing anytime soon."

Lark couldn't stem the unease that swelled inside her chest every time the door opened. They'd arranged an evening of entertainment for the captains and sailors of the ships docked on the wharf. A grand send-off with ale flowing freely and non-stop acts that were supposed to keep all of the crew so enthralled they'd stay the entire night and be in no condition to sail on the morrow.

So far, the plan had been going smoothly, but as the hours passed, more men trickled out, back to their hammocks on their ships. If enough left... She didn't even want to think about what that would mean for the rest of the plan. They had to put on the show of their lives tonight. Kayda's life depended on it.

"What song should we do next, Aren?" Lark scanned the crowd, noting a handful of sleepy-eyed patrons. "I don't think we should chance another ballad. The last one sent that table out the door."

"Shall we do the opener again? We've played all the merry tunes once already," Aren replied.

Lark scrunched the hem of her multi-colored tunic. "Repeating sounds like a recipe for disaster, too." Lark missed her bondmate even more than usual. Without Muse and Whisper, they were down an act, making them rely much more on their songs.

Tiora bit her lip, then leaned over. "What about some new material? When I was at the *Joria Rose*, they hired a singer once a week. I have a feeling the songs she performed would be a big hit with this crowd. They're simple enough to learn. Just a repeating tune and rhyming lyrics."

Lark frowned. "Are you sure, Ti?" Surely remembering her time in that brothel was bound to dredge up some painful memories.

Tiora straightened in her seat and sucked in a deep breath. "I'm sure. I want to help."

Aren shrugged. "It can't hurt to try."

Lark smiled and squeezed Tiora's hand, impressed once again by her friend's incredible strength.

"Does anyone have a parchment? I'll tell you the lyrics, and you can write them down, Lark," Tiora said.

Mazen hopped up. "I'll see if the barkeep has a bit to lend."

"No, don't bother, Maz." Lark pulled her pack from the back of her chair. "I'll add them to the book Daus made me. There are a few blank pages at the end."

As Lark dug out the book and a charcoal, Tiora hummed the tune to Aren.

"Like this?" He thrummed his lute quietly with Tiora listening intently.

"Yes, that's it exactly," Tiora said. "Just keep that up on repeat."

Dausius finished his tale, and the crowd roared again.

Meital stood, clasping Mazen's shoulder. "C'mon, Maz. Ti can sit this one out to help Lark and Aren."

The twins wove through the crowd. The crush of sailors swallowed their multicolored tunics until they replaced Daus on the tabletop and sent their glittering daggers flying to a chorus of oohs and aahs.

Lark wasn't watching. She was too busy trying to keep her cool while her cheeks burned. But she kept writing, copying down the lyrics to some of the dirtiest limericks she'd ever heard. Dausius returned to the table and nearly choked on his water when he discovered what they were up to.

As Tiora finished the last of the verses, she leaned back in her seat and sipped her water. "That's all of them. The ones I can remember, at least."

"These are great, Ti." Lark grinned. "At least your time at that brothel will come in handy for something."

A gasp sounded behind them. Lark and Tiora spun in unison. Cyrie slowly backed away, her hand over her lips and her eyes wide.

"You were in a brothel, Ti-ti?" Cyrie's chin quivered, and her eyes filled with tears.

Lark scrubbed her face as the girl fled the room. "I'm so sorry. I should've never said—"

"I have to find her." Tiora jumped out of her chair and chased after her little sister.

Lark stood, but Daus stepped in front of her. "I'll go after them. Don't worry. It'll be all right. You two are up next."

Lark sighed as she watched him disappear into the crowd. She hoped Daus was right. She'd forgotten Cyrie had volunteered to keep a watch for Kayda's arrival at the docks with her friend Davit. If she'd only thought to peek over her shoulder, or just kept her mouth shut, then Tiora wouldn't be forced to spill all her secrets to her little sister. Lark's stomach knotted from knowing she'd been the cause of it all.

Just then, the applause rose, signaling the end of the twin's act.

Aren slung an arm around her shoulders. "That's us. You ready to try the new songs?"

She bit her lip, wanting nothing more than to tear out the pages from the book and forget these songs ever existed. Not only had they forced a wedge between her friend and her sister, they were definitely not the kind of song she was comfortable singing.

But as she debated internally, another table of sailors rose and headed for the door. Lark pushed aside her misgivings. She had to do this for Kayda. Surely a few moments of discomfort would be worth it to save the sister she'd only just discovered.

"Let's go."

Soon they arrived at the head of the room, and Aren helped her atop the table before hopping up beside her. He strummed the lute, and Lark took a deep breath and sang, choosing one of the milder lyrics to start with.

There once was a young lady of Flamesmoat
Who woke with a tickle in her throat
The healer said sure, I've got the cure
That panicked young lady of Flamesmoat

Lark cringed on the inside while forcing a brazen smile. Silence filled the common room for a heartbeat as all the sailors stared up at them, no doubt shocked at the bawdy innuendo that was much different from the grand ballads and lively dance numbers they'd performed so far.

But then the crowd erupted in laughter. The men who'd been on their way to the door joined in and spun around, heading back to the table they'd just abandoned.

Lark turned to Aren, shaking her head and smiling as she signaled for him to start up the tune again. The things she did for her friends...

The morning sunlight flickered inside the inn windows. Lark stepped down from the tabletop, yet again, and made her way to the table she shared with the Wandering Bards.

Exhaustion wasn't just prickling her shoulders anymore. It lay heavy on her limbs like a warm blanket, ready to lull her to sleep. But she couldn't succumb to the urge for slumber. There was still so much left to do.

Dausius hopped up on the table behind her, launching into a humorous story before she and Aren sank into their seats. Lark glanced at Tiora, sending her a wobbly grin.

Tiora smiled back warmly. "Those limericks Dausius thought up are even better than the ones from the brothel."

Lark chuckled and shook her head. "Yeah, who knew our Daus had such a dirty mind?"

Dausius had sat down with the charcoal after Lark's first round of bawdy songs and came up with a dozen of his own, each one filthier than the last. They'd certainly been a big hit with the crowd of sailors. Dozens of men had stayed the whole night. Even now, a few hours after dawn, the room was still full, with more than one group of sailors sleeping on their folded arms atop the tables or leaning back in their chairs, mouths wide open and snoring.

Tiora giggled before turning to gaze out the window.

Lark squeezed Tiora's hand. "I'm sorry again about your sister."

"Stop apologizing. I'm not mad. I'm relieved I got the chance to explain everything to Cyrie." Tiora smiled again, looking hopeful. "I have a feeling that after today, a lot of things around here will end up changing for the better."

Just then, the inn door slammed open, and Cyrie rushed in. She stopped at their table and leaned forward. "They're here. Davit confirmed it." She glanced at her sister and sent her a wide smile, her excitement evident.

Lark sat forward in her seat, the exhaustion that'd just been so heavy lifting with Cyrie's announcement. This was it. She exhaled, her palms moistening and her heart fluttering like a hummingbird's wings.

Meital stood, signaling Dausius at the front of the room.

"That's all for us, my fine friends. You've been a wonderful audience." He bowed hastily and jumped down from the tabletop, quickly joining them.

"We're on." Aren hopped up and strapped his lute to his back.

Dausius blew out a breath, turning to look each of them in the eye. "You all remember your places, yes?"

Tiora bit her lip. "Wait. My mother and sister did as you asked, but Jett and Gawain haven't checked in. Shouldn't we wait?"

Daus shook his head. "No. They were always a long shot. The show must go on without delay."

Lark rose to her feet and walked to Mazen's side. "Ready?"

"Do you need to ask?" He twirled a knife, cocking a brow.

Aren grabbed Lark's arm. "Good luck. Be safe."

"You, too." Lark flashed him a smile and strode to the door, where she waved goodbye to her friends.

Dausius called out to them as they opened the door. "Time to put on the show of a lifetime."

Chapter 22

Kayda woke to her body gently swaying. She groaned, opening her eyes to a world of black, her face swaddled in a layer of dark silk. Her heart pounded as confusion reigned. Images of the tetrela rose unbidden, and she shuddered, twisting where she lay. She flashed back to that dark desert night, her body immobile while being manhandled by the enormous spider. But the clatter of chains against the hard floor she sprawled on brought her back to the present.

What the blazes? What was on her head? And why was her face throbbing?

It all came back to her in a flash. The reek of charred flesh. Wyll's garbled screams. Egard's fist flying at her face. She smiled despite herself, hissing as the action tugged on her swollen jaw. But the pain was worth it to make that bastard pay for what he'd done to her father.

If only it had been Egard in the back seat instead... She clenched her fists, feeling the tug of the shackles attached to her wrists. She might still get the chance to make him regret what he'd done.

Kayda forced the thought aside. There were more important things to worry about now—like where she was and why she couldn't see. The sweat-soaked cloth on her face had to go. She reached up, but with her shackled wrists held close to her body with the metal chain, she couldn't quite make contact with the soft fabric.

She rubbed her head against the floor while taking stock of her body in the dark. She was lying flat on something hard. Maybe with enough wiggling she could… There. After scrunching her body into a ball, she caught a bit of the hem between her middle and ring finger. She pulled.

Kayda squinted, the dim light in the room setting off a cascade of thrashing in her skull. Well, that explained the swaying. She was on a boat. A glass window on a nearby wall provided a view of the waterline. She must be below deck on one of the ships.

Were they still parked at the wharf or already out to sea? With her head still swimming, she couldn't be sure.

One thing was certain—she was alone. The tiny window didn't let in much light, but it did a fair job of illuminating the room. The contents certainly didn't give her much to go by. It was completely bare, with only the darker wood and nail holes on the floor remaining as evidence that anything had once been here.

If she had to guess, she would bet this room was once a cabin. But now it might as well be a prison for all the good it would do her. All she had was bare wooden walls, the black silk shirt clutched in her hands, and what looked like a chamber pot in the far corner. Not much to use to escape.

Kayda sighed, rolling up to a seated position, though the motion made the throbbing in her head intensify so much that she groaned again. Now, to get to the door. It was probably too much to hope her captors had left the door unlocked, but she would be a fool not to che—

Footsteps pounded outside. Her stomach churned as the door swung open.

"Ah, you're awake." Wyll peeked in, an apple-red silk suit covering his tall frame, looking no worse for the wear after the scorching she'd delivered, though his voice was slightly raspy. He sent her a wide smile from the doorway. "You were hoping to see me burnt to a crisp, I expect. Sorry to disappoint."

Kayda glared at him. Guess he'd found a healer in time to avoid any permanent damage. Damn.

Wyll tossed a sack inside the room. "Now that I've seen my investment is intact, I'll be on my way." He chuckled. "We'll hand you over to your new *friends* in a few days."

"Wait," she said before he shut the door. "You don't have to do this. There's still time for you to free me. I can ensure that your father pays the price for his crimes and you're let off easy."

Wyll sneered at her. "It's adorable you think you still have anything left to bargain. Can't you see you've been outmaneuvered? Don't fret, my dear. Happens to the best of us, from time to time."

"That's where you're wrong. I *will* be at the battle in the Abandoned Lands. It's fated. Your plans will be foiled, and when they are, I won't go easy on you. This is your last chance, Wyll. Set me free. Now."

Riotous laughter met her statement. But after a moment, Wyll's laughter cut off, and he clutched his throat. Kayda bit back the smirk that fought to spread at the evidence of the damage her fire had wrought.

Wyll cleared his throat and narrowed his eyes. "You actually believe that dreck? Puh-lease. Let me break it down for you. You've lost your dragon. Every member of the royal family is dead. No one knows where you are, and even if they did, there's nothing they can do about it on your *stolen* ship, since it is currently under quarantine with all souls stuck on board for the foreseeable future. No one is coming for you, and your magic won't be any help without a source. You've been outplayed, Princess. The sooner you get used to the idea, the easier it will be for you. Now, if you'll excuse me, I have more important things to see to than delusional *former* royalty."

With that, he slammed the door, and the click of the lock reverberated in Kayda's ears.

Quarantine? *Nova's Champion* was quarantined? Kayda's heart sank. She couldn't expect any help from there.

What was she going to do?

She had to find some way to escape. There was no way she would let herself be carted across the sea to become some stranger's slave or used as leverage against Dru.

With that thought in mind, she slid across the floor toward the sack Wyll had tossed to her and grasped it with her shaking fingers. Was it too much to ask that he'd slipped up and gifted her something she could use to escape?

Apparently so. All the sack contained was a stale loaf of bread and a full waterskin, neither of which would be helpful. As unappealing as the loaf looked, it still made her stomach rumble. She tore off a corner and stuffed the hard bread into her mouth, considering while she chewed.

Jayan and Izora were still out there with the Sul. Surely, they would come to her aid. But how would they know she was in trouble? And could they make it to Joria from Sul Hollow before the ship set sail?

From what she'd overheard in the basement, it had sounded like they'd been planning to set sail straight away. But the longer she sat still on the floor, the more she suspected they were still at port. The boat was certainly not swaying the same way *Nova's Champion* did while they were at sea, and all the boats she'd seen on arrival appeared so similar; surely it would feel the same, too...

Perhaps her little trick in the carriage had slowed their timeline, but whether it would be enough, she had no idea. She needed to slow them further. If they set sail, all hope was lost.

Kayda swallowed the chalky lump in her mouth and cast her gaze about the room again. There was nothing. Absolutely nothing.

Wait—maybe the silk could be useful. She scrambled to her knees and across the room. She crammed the fabric beneath the door. All she needed was another small spark. If she was lucky, the door would catch.

Let's see how they deal with a fire on board.

But before she could call on her source, something clattered in the hall. Kayda stilled, listening intently. Were those footsteps? These were much softer than Wyll's had been, but after a moment, she was certain it was footsteps—and they were coming closer.

She snatched the silk from under the door and scrambled back. A few moments later, the sound halted, and something strange took its place. The gentle clinking and scraping of metal on metal.

She barely had time to wonder what the sound meant before the door popped open, and a wave of relief crashed into her so strongly she nearly squealed with glee. "Lark, thank the Lord Dragon! How did you find me? Wyll said the ship was quarantined."

Lark slipped into the room with one of the twins she performed with, both of them wearing multicolored tunics and wide smiles. "Kayda, it's good to see you. I'll explain everything in a moment. Let's get you out of those first." After eyeing the chains, Lark turned to her companion. "Maz, can you unlock these chains, too?"

That's right—Kayda remembered their names now. Mazen and Meital, the knife jugglers.

Mazen closed the door gently behind him, then crouched beside her and grabbed the lock on her chains. "Yeah, this one looks easy. I'm glad my years as a pickpocket and thief are coming in handy." He sent Lark a mischievous grin. "Never thought I'd be stealing a princess."

Kayda didn't have long to ponder over that. Lark knelt on her other side and gripped her jaw gently. Kayda winced as Lark's fingers prodded at the flesh on her chin.

Lark's brow furrowed. "Looks like someone clobbered you pretty hard. Don't worry, I can fix it." Lark released her chin, pulled the pack from her back, and dug inside. "Do you have any other injuries?"

"No. I'm all right." The lock on her chains clicked open, and Kayda sighed. "Forget about healing me. It can wait. Let's get out of here."

Lark nodded, replacing the bag on her back. With the three of them working, they removed the chains quickly, and Kayda breathed out her first deep breath since she woke with the heavy weight dragging her down. All the while, Lark kept up a steady stream of chatter, filling her in on everything that had happened while she'd been trapped by Wyll.

"So, you got all the crew too drunk to sail?" Kayda chuckled. "That was smart thinking."

Lark smiled. "Not quite all, but enough of them they won't be sailing anywhere for a few hours. We have a few surprises in store if we catch any trouble on the way out, too."

"Where is the king?" Mazen asked. "Do you know where they're keeping him? We can get him ou—"

"No, we can't." Kayda's voice shook. "He's dead."

Lark squeezed her shoulder. "I'm so sorry."

Kayda heaved out a deep breath and nodded once. "C'mon. Let's go."

They made their way through the barren room's door. The hall looked identical to the ones found on *Nova's Champion*, except all the candles and oil lamps that decorated the wall had been removed. Wyll clearly wasn't taking any chances that she'd get close to an open flame.

"Blazes. Where's a torch when you need one?" Kayda mused.

"I almost forgot. I brought you something." Lark pulled the pack from her back again and removed a metal tin and a long stick wrapped in cloth.

"Here, I'll light it while we walk." Kayda grabbed the supplies. She quickly opened the tinderbox and worked the flint and steel, thankful for Izora's instruction with the same materials back in the tunnels beneath Kings Keep. Within moments, she lit the torch, just before they opened the door to the outer deck.

The bright torchlight and near blinding sunlight made Kayda squint as they strode out on the deck. Then the door they'd just exited slammed, and a pair of women popped out from behind it. They tossed buckets of water on her, extinguishing her torch and drenching her golden silk dress. They moved so quickly Kayda only had time to gasp before she stood there soaking and stuttering.

"My, my. I hope you weren't planning on leaving already?" Wyll's deep voice greeted her as a circle of armed men and women surrounded them. Kayda spotted at least a dozen and knew there were likely more that she couldn't see, all with weapons trained in their direction, their faces locked in hard stares.

Wyll elbowed between a scowling, dark-skinned bald fellow with a bow pointed at Kayda's face and a pale long-haired man wearing a bored expression behind the longsword he aimed at Mazen's throat. Behind them, a crowd of finely dressed folks lounged on the deck, smirking and snickering at each other quietly.

"Did you think you'd escape so easily? Your little group of tricksters won't be enough to free you, my dear," Wyll said.

Lark stepped forward, ignoring the blade a grizzled, bearded man held at her throat, raising her voice far louder than was necessary. "Who said we were alone?"

A whistle rang out, and Kayda's eyes widened. A series of sharp whistles followed, each one fading in succession in such a way that she was certain each whistler was further away than the last. Then chaos erupted.

Several multicolored tunics flashed in the streets as the rest of Lark's performer friends emerged. With them, hundreds of people flooded the docks, pouring into the streets like a swarm of bees whose hive had been kicked. The buzz of all that angry humanity rose in the air and reached the armed men on the deck. Most stood strong, but some turned in astonishment, shifting on their feet.

"A few laborers with sticks won't stop us," Wyll announced with a scoff. "Will they, men?"

With that, even more armed people revealed themselves, stepping out from doorways and rounding the nooks and crannies they'd been hidden in.

Kayda gulped as her gaze flitted between the mercenaries on board and the crowd. Wyll was right about one thing—the caliber of fighters the performers brought definitely didn't match the men Wyll hired to protect the ships. The men and women on the docks carried rusty old knives and homemade weapons—some indeed held what looked like nothing more than sharpened sticks.

Kayda's heart thundered to life. She'd seen what could happen when a few trained men stood against the common folk. Would this be a repeat of the battle in Kings Keep on the night she found Dru?

She shook off the worry. No matter her misgivings, these people were here for her. To save her and stand up to the rich cowards who'd built a fortune with their labor, only to abandon them when their lives were on the line. They deserved a chance to stand up for what was right. And the gutless traders deserved to pay for their cowardice.

Kayda dropped the useless soaked torch and flicked her wet braids out of her eyes, stepping beside Lark. She projected her voice loudly, booming above the buzz of the commoners. "Your time as leaders of this city is over. The people have spoken."

The mob responded with hoots and cheers. Wyll backed away a step, scanning the crowd warily as it continued to increase in size. The other rich traders watching on deck edged away from the rails or hurried to the hatches leading inside the ship.

Kayda smiled brazenly. "These people might not be slaves in name, but what has their freedom earned them? Just a life lived in squalor and a ruling class that would abandon them at the first sign of trouble. Trade is *not* king here anymore. It stops today."

Wyll's eyes blazed with barely contained fury as he signaled for the fighters to spread out. "This mob doesn't stand a chance against these fine fighters. Let's see how long they stand when they start dying in droves. Men, it's time to do what you've been hired for."

Kayda's stomach clenched as the fighters stepped forward to the rails. Beyond them, she saw similar action happening on each ship on the dock. This would not be an easy win for the common people. She held her breath, waiting for the first arrow to fly and the blood to flow.

But then a new voice roared above the mayhem. "Interlopers! Remove yourselves from our ships."

Kayda's heart stalled. She knew that voice. Her jaw dropped for a heartbeat, and then a smile slowly spread across her face.

Lazar pushed through the crowd with Izora and Jayan at his side—and surprisingly—Jett and Guard Captain Gawain. Dozens of Sul, armed with pole knives and bows, followed at their backs.

"Your ships?" Wyll scoffed, his voice sounding equal parts incredulous and drenched with hate. "These ships are *mine*."

Lazar didn't balk at the enmity aimed at him. He strode forward, the silver streaks in his braided hair gleaming as the crowd parted in his wake, allowing even more Sul to filter into the streets. "No. These ships have been promised to the sandborn. They *will* ferry us to the great battle to come. Remove yourselves or prepare to return to dust."

The fighters who'd appeared only mildly wary of the commoners were clearly shaken now. They shot each other wide-eyed glances, hands shuddering on the hilts of their swords and quivering against their bowstrings. When a group of mages appeared from the direction of *Nova's Champion*, elements swirling in their outstretched hands, Kayda knew they would fold.

One by one, the fighters backed away from the rail and marched to the gangplank, sheathing their swords and shouldering their bows.

"What are you doing?" Wyll grabbed closest mercenary's arm, trying to tug him back to his spot at the rail. "I hired you to defend the ships. Do your jobs or you can forget your pay."

The man shook off his hold and pressed forward. "You can't pay the dead. I'm out of here."

Kayda strolled forward. "I'm afraid you've been outplayed, *my dear*. The sooner you accept it, the easier it will be for you."

Behind her, the door to the inner hull cracked open, and the traders inside filed out. They crowded around on the deck, gathering their things and scrambling to leave. Chaos flooded the streets and the boats. The common people, who'd been happy to let the sell-swords pass unmolested, were not so kind to the traders. Screams broke out on all sides.

Wyll backed away, blinking wildly. At that moment, Egard burst from the nearest porthole, rubbing the sleep from his eyes.

"What is the meaning of this?" Egard bellowed. Then he took stock of the scene, and his fat face blanched.

Wyll grabbed his father's arm, tugging him backward toward the gangplank.

"I hope you're not planning to leave already?" Kayda grinned, taking extreme pleasure in echoing Wyll's words back at him, yet again.

Wyll and Egard flinched in unison. They scanned the crowd as another trader screamed out in pain, trying unsuccessfully to escape the bloodthirsty mob. Egard's gaze locked on a trader just beyond the gangplank as a trio of youths with sticks wailed on him, the dull *thwack* of their hits beating in time with the surf against the hull.

The man spotted him looking, and he reached out, desperation shining in his eyes. Then one of the boys struck him hard across the jaw. His head jerked sideways, and blood sprayed in a fine mist. His golden chains swung as he crumpled, and the mob swallowed him.

"Please, Princess. M-my queen. Have mercy." Wyll fell to his knees in front of her, and in less than a heartbeat, Egard followed suit.

"Help us," Egard chimed in, his head bowed.

"And what price will you pay for my help?" Kayda smiled. She strode up to Mazen and grabbed one of the thin daggers strapped to his back, flicking the blade up and hiding it behind her wrist.

"Anything you want," Wyll rushed to offer. "Take all the ships. They're yours."

Kayda smirked, striding closer to the kneeling pair. "Perfect. Then of course I'll help."

Egard's shoulders sank, and his head bowed even further. "Thank you. Oh, thank the gods."

Kayda knelt beside him and sliced the blade across his throat. "Have all the help you gave my father."

Wyll scrambled back from Egard as blood spurted from his neck, painting the deck red. Wyll trembled, a stain quickly darkening the crimson trousers of his finely pressed silk suit. Then, like the coward he'd proven himself to be time and again, he ran. He made it to the aft rail and jumped, splashing into the bay's deep water.

Kayda rose to her feet, shook Egard's warm blood from her fingers, and strolled to the aft rail. She leaned over the side and spotted Wyll surface in the ocean. He spun back and stared up at the boat, a smirk on his face, before he lifted an arm to swim away.

The glint of silver flashed in the air just before a pole-knife lodged in Wyll's throat. Kayda smirked back at Wyll one last time before he slipped beneath the waves. Then she turned to the wharf, in the direction the pole-knife flew from. Jayan stared back at her and winked.

Kayda met his eyes and winked back.

Chapter 23

The days in the bog passed in a predictable routine. Each morning, Conall woke, bleary after a night spent tossing and turning, to spend countless hours slowly poling eastward through the maze.

But despite Fillan's snoring, Ereni proved all too right to trust him. It was soon apparent they'd had little hope of ever finding their way to the Orddon Ocean with how much the tangled waters weaved. Luckily, the young ferryman knew every twist and turn of the bog. Eventually, they grew close enough to the coast that a seabird's cawing joined the familiar croaking and buzzing of the Boglands' critters.

"How much longer until we reach a sea pass?" Ereni asked from her seat at the bow. Shadow's ears twitched at the sound of her voice, but he didn't glance up from where he napped in their canoe's center.

"Not long now." Fillan pushed on his pole, easing his canoe forward. "An hour or so, I expect."

Conall's heart lifted. It couldn't come too soon for him. Day after day spent penned up in a tiny boat with only a few short breaks to stretch his legs on solid ground wasn't exactly his idea of a good time.

Not to mention, they hadn't exactly been prepared for the journey to begin with. Fillan lent each of them a set of stained overalls so they hadn't been forced to spend the entire time in the same set of clothes, but rinsing out his shirt and trousers in the murky bog water hadn't exactly cleaned them properly. He was dying for a change of clothes and a chance to wash up with soap and clean water.

There would be all that and more on *Nova's Champion* once they met them on the coast. He smiled, picturing Lark's face when she spotted him and Shadow returning. He couldn't wait to reunite with her once again. And it wasn't just his sister waiting for him on board. There was someone else he was eager to meet.

He flicked a quick glance at Ereni, and his stomach fluttered. The time spent in her company had reminded him how much he once cared for her. It wasn't quite the same, yet, but he was beginning to think that in time, they might regain some of that ease. Perhaps even more. Especially now that they had Violet.

What would their daughter be like? Despite himself, a tiny spike of fear prickled his chest. Would Violet like him? She was only an infant—he knew it was silly to worry, but he couldn't help it. It was so strange knowing there was a piece of him out there, completely unaware that he even existed.

Would she cry when he held her? He tried to mentally prepare for the very real possibility that the babe would wail and treat him like a stranger for long after they first met.

He'd still not fully wrapped his mind around everything Ereni told him about their daughter's future. It was strange to think she would one day grow up and hold the fate of the world in her hands. But then again, there was no shortage of prophecies latched to the members of his family.

Conall sighed, thrusting the stick down from the back of the canoe. He may not have met her yet, but he was already determined to be a part of his daughter's life. If she was destined to change the world, then someone had better do a damn good job of raising her right.

He might not be the perfect man for the task, but he knew from experience there was plenty of evil out there. The least he could do was ensure that Violet grew up happy and healthy, with parents who'd love her and teach her everything she'd need to navigate a harsh world when the time came for her to fulfill whatever task fate demanded.

His stomach clenched as the Unseen's words returned to haunt him—*Three will come, but only two will see the next day.* He'd not forgotten that he might not have the chance to be a part of Violet's life. But if he was one of the two that survived, would that be any better? That meant either Kayda or Lark would be the one to fall. Could he live with that, if one of his sisters died instead of him?

Shadow's ears twitched again, and his head lifted. *"I hear voices."*

Not again. Conall had hoped they'd traveled far out of the escaped prisoners' path. "Fillan." He waved his arms, speaking barely above a whisper. "Shadow hears voices. Could it be your men?"

Fillan frowned. "It's possible, but we better take cover in case it isn't. Quick, follow me."

Fillan led them to a spot where the mangroves thinned and craned his neck behind the branches. He used his stick to brush a few wispy tendrils aside and beckoned them forward.

Ereni's brow furrowed as they slid inside. "Wait, there's not enough room."

Conall peered around the small hole behind the tree. She was right. Although the shrubbery hid them well enough that he couldn't see much of the waterway beyond the leaves, the space was far too narrow to fit more than one canoe inside.

"Don't worry. There's another spot just ahead." With that, Fillan dropped the branch and slipped away in the water just as the voices rose enough to become audible, although they were still far enough away that he couldn't make out what was said.

Conall squinted, bobbing his head to keep an eye on Fillan's canoe as it slid through the waterway. His heart raced as the voices grew louder and louder. Fillan still hadn't stopped, his head flitting frantically around the tree bank on the waterway's opposite side.

Conall gritted his teeth as he heard the first words clearly.

A loud smack rang out before a voice grumbled, "Blazing bugs are gonna be the death of me. At least back at the prison, we weren't getting eaten alive."

Oh no. Fillan had to hide now.

Conall crouched down in the canoe, making himself as small as possible, all the while keeping a watch as Fillan struggled to locate a spot on the other side of the bog.

Suddenly, a second voice rang out, clearly coming from a different direction. "Hey, is that you, Garnell? Where are you blokes?"

A chorus of voices answered, all of them louder than the last.

"Hey, over here!"

"Where've ya been?"

"We're over here."

There were so many. Fillan scrambled faster. He shoved his pole into the bog and brushed aside branch after branch, peering behind them. Conall sighed as the ferryman's canoe finally slipped behind a large mangrove close to the nearest bend in the bog.

He'd hidden not a moment too soon. Just as Fillan's boat disappeared completely, the water rippled around the bend. One boat appeared, then a second. Soon, five boats perched in the waterway outside of their hiding space, all the men hollering hello to a single canoe that approached from the opposite direction.

Conall's heart skipped a beat. Had that man been trailing them? They'd been lucky to happen upon the larger group when they had, or the single man might've snuck up behind them without notice. Unless he was in the habit of talking to himself, it would've been unlikely for them to hear him speaking in enough time to hide.

"So, did you find anything?" a bald man from the larger group asked.

The single fellow puffed out his chest, smirking. Conall recognized him as the same hulking man he and Ereni crossed paths with the first day, with the crooked nose and scarred arms. The same man who'd threatened to slit the girl's throats. "Wouldn't you all like to know?"

"C'mon, Reg. Don't be like that. We want a way out of this maze as much as you do," pleaded a short man with a cudgel strapped to his back. He slapped his wrist loudly and grumbled under his breath.

"Bah, he's just as full of shit as always," a new voice declared.

"He must've found something. Where else are the rest of the blokes he brought with him?" said the bald man.

"I found it all right—the answer to all our problems. If you joker's wise up, you'll come with me and see for yourselves." Reg sent them a wide grin full of confidence.

Conall watched the larger group as they circled together and argued among themselves in hushed tones, flicking occasional scowls in Reg's direction. Finally, they broke apart.

The bald man pushed his canoe to the front of the group. He lifted a worn bow from the bottom of his boat and slung it over his shoulder. "All right. We'll go see. But if shit goes sideways, you're gonna get an arrow in your back."

"C'mon, Garnell, would I do that to you?" Even from their hiding spot, Conall glimpsed the cruel glint in Reg's eyes that contrasted his affronted tone.

It seemed Garnell wasn't buying it either. His hand tightened on his bow, and he rolled his eyes. "Enough chatter. Lead the way to our *salvation*."

"Don't worry. You won't be disappointed." Reg chuckled. "You're gonna love him."

"What was that all about? Who could they be meeting?" Ereni whispered after the men's canoes disappeared down the waterway and around a bend.

Conall shrugged. "No idea. But at least they're heading in the opposite direction."

He backed out of their hiding spot, returning to the waterway's center. Fillan joined them and silently motioned them to follow. They slid further away from the prisoners until even the echo of their voices receded. When Shadow's ears finally fell and he rested on the canoe bottom, the last of the tension in Conall's limbs lifted.

Ereni leaned forward, pitching her voice softly and meeting Fillan's gaze. "Are you sure you'll be all right heading back into the bog? Why don't you come with us?"

Fillan shook his head. "Nah, I'll be fine. If I sail south when we split up, there's no way those men will catch me before I make it back to Raimire."

Conall frowned. "I'm sure you're right about the route, but how can you be sure there's no one else out there? Or what if those men turn back? Ereni's right. You should come with us."

"I can't leave my dad that long. He's the only family I've got left."

Conall sighed. He could certainly understand the need to be with family in these trying times.

"Don't worry. If there's anyone else, I'll hide like we did back there." Fillan flashed a lopsided smile. "And I'm not worried about the last group. They ought to have their hands full where they're headed."

"What do you mean?" Ereni asked.

"That bend they turned down leads to Bogsmouth. Nothing there these days except for the scourge."

Conall's brow furrowed. Strange. Why would Reg lead them there? Could he be leading those men into a trap?

He tamped down the questions. There was no way to find out without following them, and despite his curiosity, that wasn't a path he would be taking. All that mattered was finding the ocean and meeting the ships before the battle started.

They continued eastward as the sun sank slowly in the sky behind them. Little clues emerged that the ocean was close at hand. The few patches of dirt planted among the mangroves shifted from deep brown to a sandy tan, littered with chipped shell fragments. The cawing of seabirds intensified and was eventually joined by the gentle roar of the surf.

Fillan stopped in front of a fork in the bog and pointed down the path behind him. "Here's where we part ways. This will lead you to the ocean. Here. You're gonna need these." He scooped something out of his canoe and tossed it to Ereni.

Conall leaned forward, but before he got a look at the object, Fillan sent another one sailing at his face. He scrambled to catch the small oar.

"I noticed your canoe didn't have any. Be careful out there. The swells close to shore can be crushing. Even with the oars, you might struggle until you sail beyond them."

Ereni grinned. "We mages have our ways of handling the current. Thank you, Fillan. For everything."

"Yeah, thanks, Fillan." Conall lifted the oar and waved.

"It was no trouble. Tell Lark I said hello when you see her." With that, he pushed on his pole and slid away, heading south.

The mouth of the waterway widened as they sailed closer to the ocean. When Conall stuck the pole down and it didn't connect with the ground, he realized the water was growing deeper as well.

"Do you want to row, or handle the waves?" he asked as he stashed the pole on the side holder.

Ereni handed him her oar. "I'll summon."

She settled down in the front of the canoe and stuck her hand out the side, sucking in a deep breath.

Conall shivered as the air simultaneously clouded with moisture and crackled with electricity. He dipped the oars into the water, rowing them forward even as the wind and water sought to force them forward far quicker than he could accomplish with the oars alone.

Soon, they passed the last mangroves and burst out into the open sea. The waves jostled them fiercely, even with Ereni smoothing them with her talent. Beyond the mangroves, huge rocks littered the surf, sticking out high in the air like forgotten monuments to the earth. From far away, the surfaces appeared glossy and smooth, no doubt chipped away by the surf over countless days. But if the rocking waves smacked them into one of the monoliths, their boat would not survive the experience. Worse, there might be even more sharp peaks hidden below the surf's surface, ready to impale the bottom of their boat.

"Ereni." His voice wobbled as they approached a large rock formation. A tremor crawled up his spine as the waves crashed around them, splattering them with a fine mist of salt water. He pulled furiously at the oars, seeking to turn them sideways and around the behemoth.

"No, head straight."

Conall gulped, catching a glimpse of her blue eyes—normally so bright, clouded over—as she flicked a glance back at him, only to spin back and stare ahead blankly.

"What? We'll crash," he insisted.

"There are rocks below," she said simply. "I'll guide us through. Trust me."

Was she using her talent to sense the rocks below the surface?

"What's happening, little brother?" Shadow cowered on the boat bottom. The wet fur on his face matted against his skin, and when he aimed his wide golden eyes backward, Conall had to shake off the desire to pet him—Shadow looked miserable and adorable all at once.

Instead, Conall rowed, steering straight as directed. *"Don't worry, brother. We'll get out of this. Ereni knows what she's doing."*

He hoped the statement was not proven a lie as they sailed straight toward the colossal rock.

When they were only a boat length away, Ereni screamed, "Break right, now!"

Conall dug in with the oars, pounding the water. The left one bounced off the surface of something hard below the waves.

Ereni's hands flew through the air, directing the wind and sea, buoying their little canoe. They slipped past the huge boulder not a moment too soon, and Conall sighed.

But they weren't out of the woods yet. More rocks littered the water, and the surf still pounded, seeking to shove them back to shore. Each stroke of the oars was hard fought, and Conall's shoulders ached from the constant motion.

"Conall..." Shadow's panicked voice made him pause. He flicked a glance at the boat bottom and spotted his bondmate slinking backward from a puddle slowly growing larger. He gulped, realizing it was filling too quickly to be from water splashing over the sides, though he couldn't see a hole.

"We've sprung a leak," he yelled over the crashing waves.

Ereni shifted, her eyes still glazed over, before turning back to stare forward. "Call on your water talent, push the sea out. I can't spare the concentration now."

He flashed Shadow a crooked grin. *"Don't worry. I'll fix it."* He hoped.

Conall pulled at the ocean all around him, using it as his source. He closed his eyes briefly, picturing the puddle flowing back down the crack to join the sea. When he lifted his lashes, he smiled, watching the puddle slowly decrease in size until he could finally see the source of the problem. A small crack marred the wooden floor, almost directly in the center.

Great. But at least it was dealt with, for the moment. He kept the magic flowing, using a constant stream to keep the water from seeping back in. Now it wasn't just his shoulders aching, but his whole body, the exhaustion of summoning quickly compounding with the physical ache until he was ready for a nap.

At last, they wrestled free of the huge rocks and into the deeper water beyond the coastline. The hum of vibration in the air faded, and Ereni peered at them, her eyes back to their normal bright-blue. "You two all right, back there?"

Conall nodded. "That was intense."

"Which way should we head?"

"You're asking me?"

She craned her head sideways, gazing up and down the coast. "I was hoping when we made it to the ocean, the ships would be here to greet us, but it looks like we'll need to find them. Do you think they made it off the coast of the Abandoned Lands yet, or should we head south toward Joria? The way I see it, we have a fifty-fifty chance either way."

The ocean spread out before them, empty of ships in every direction. Worse still, the coastline was littered with more rocks. To the south, the mangled mangroves stretched far into the distance, and to the north lay high cliffs that even the strongest of climbers would likely struggle to scale.

Conall's stomach sank. The leak in their boat would require constant supervision from here on out. That, coupled with the summoning they'd need to navigate and avoid being driven back into shore, spelled exhaustion for them both. If he chose wrong here, it could be a death sentence.

Ereni spoke up, breaking the silence. "I trust you, Conall. You'll lead us the right way."

His heart stuttered. He met her gaze and saw the certainty there. After everything, all the harsh things he'd said, she still trusted him?

Conall closed his eyes. If it really was fate that he found them, he couldn't choose wrong now, could he?

Lark, where are you?

His eyes flicked open. "South. Let's go south."

Ereni turned forward, moisture and static flooding the air instantly.

Conall dipped the oars into the sea and prayed he hadn't just killed them.

Chapter 24

"L ark." Muse's voice woke Lark from a dead sleep.

"Ugh, what is it?"

"Ha, cranky much?"

"I was sleeping."

"In the afternoon? You've grown lazy while I've been gone, I see."

"You try being woken by a babe half a dozen times a night," Lark grumbled.

She rolled out of her hammock in the single room Kayda had arranged for her to share with little Violet and the wet nurse on board *Nova's Champion*. She crept over soundlessly and peered into the tiny bassinet in the corner. Lucky for her, their silent communication didn't bother the babe.

"Hm, remind me to spend the night with Aren when I get back. I don't need any noisy critters waking me all night long."

The reminder of her bondmate's return made Lark smile after she rolled her eyes. *"How far away are you?"*

"We're close to the Boglands' northern edge."

"Good. We've been passing the bog all day. You can't be far off now." Lark snuck over to the window and peeled back a corner of the curtain. Streaks of pink and purple painted the clouds. How long had she slept? *"Jayan will likely drop anchor soon. Maybe you and Whisper ought to stop for the night and meet us in the morning?"*

"We'll fly for a little while longer. If we don't spot sails on the horizon before dusk, we'll stop."

Violet stirred. Lark quickly let the curtain fall back into place, but it was too late. She was met with a hearty wail.

"Violet's awake. I'll talk to you later. Be safe."

"You, too."

"Hey, little one. I'm here." Lark cradled Violet in her arms, rocking and shushing until she quieted. "I bet you're hungry after that big nap, hm? Let's find Indra."

She found the new wetnurse in the mess hall, chatting up a table full of sailors. Her brown eyes twinkled, and the sailor's brash laughter filled the air.

"Hello, Miss Lark. Is our beauty ready for her dinner?" Indra called out as Lark entered the room. She flicked her long, black curls off her chest, unbuttoning her top.

Most of the men turned aside as Indra settled Violet on her breast, but one bold man stared unabashedly. Lark glared and stopped in front of him, blocking his view.

Indra only chuckled. "Go on, Miss Lark. Me and Violet will be just fine on our own. I'm sure you have plenty to tend to."

"You sure?"

"Of course. I've got this. Go."

Lark sent Indra a smile and the forward man a parting glare, then made her way to the top deck.

Lark passed Kayda, who chatted with a group of Sul warriors. Her golden dress was long gone, replaced with a simple shirt and trousers and a wool cloak, much like her own.

The Sul huddled in groups, clutching blankets around their shoulders or shrouded in thick furs. Lark pulled her own cloak closed as the chill air hit her. It was easy to forget it was early winter in Joria. She might be more used to these northern climes than the desert dwelling Sul, but the closer they sailed to Dracwood, the more the sea breeze bit.

"Hello." Aren greeted her with a grin, tipping back his wide-brimmed hat.

Lark smiled back. "Aren, hi."

"I'm glad I found you. I have a surprise."

"You do?"

"C'mon." He beckoned her to follow.

Lark's boots tapped on the wooden deck as Aren led her to the center mast. She stopped beside him, her gaze flitting all around but spotting nothing different.

"What did you want to show me?"

"Oh, it's not here." He tipped his hat up further, nodding to the crow's nest perched above them. "It's up there."

Lark's stomach dipped. "You left me a surprise in the crow's nest?"

"Yep. It's no different from climbing the diquats in Raimire." His brow furrowed. "If you don't want to climb, I can fetch it down."

She spared the rope ladder a dubious glance before turning to Aren. "Are you coming up with me?"

"Mm-hm. I'll be right behind you."

"All right." Lark grabbed the rough rope and scaled the shaky ladder. Then she clambered onto the circular wooden balcony, high above the midship deck. Aren arrived just behind her.

The boat's swaying intensified, but luckily the chest-high railing left little chance of her falling. Lark clutched the rail and peeked over the edge. Her stomach wobbled when she realized how far up they'd climbed, and she tore her gaze from the deck to look back at Aren.

He smiled at her before leaning down to grab a small covered basket off the nest's floor. He lifted the lid, revealing a loaf of bread and some cheese. "I saw you missed lunch, so I thought we might have a bite to eat and watch for the birds at the same time."

"What a great idea. Thank you." Lark grinned.

She reached inside the basket and broke off a small piece of cheese and a hunk of bread. Then she shifted to stare out at the northern horizon. The pinks and purples painting the clouds had only intensified since she'd first woken, making for a gorgeous sunset. A small flock of birds flew in a 'V' ahead of them, but they didn't come close to matching the grace of Muse and Whisper.

"Muse just told me they were closing in on the Boglands' northern edge. Do you think they'll reach us before dusk?"

Aren set the basket down again and joined her at the rail. "With how fast they fly? Yeah, I think they might." He popped a bite of cheese into his mouth and chewed thoughtfully. "I bet you're excited to see Muse again."

"It will be good to have her back. She certainly hasn't been quiet in my head while she's been gone, but it feels strange being apart from her all the same." She took a bite of the bread and cheese, savoring the sharp flavor.

They ate in companionable silence for a time. It was certainly lovely up here. And quiet. But the wind—she shivered and adjusted the collar of her brown wool cloak as the breeze picked up, whipping her curls against her face.

"Here." Aren grabbed a folded bundle off the nest floor, quickly shaking out the plaid wool blanket and wrapping it around her shoulders. "I thought the wind might kick up while we were waiting."

"Thank you. You thought of everything, didn't you?"

Aren shrugged. "When you grow up where it snows more than half the year, you learn to prepare for the cold."

Aren blew on his cupped hands, then stuffed them into his black cloak pockets.

Lark opened one side of the blanket and held it toward him. "There's plenty of room under here. We can share."

Aren grinned and wrapped the blanket around them both, tugging her tight against his side. Lark snuggled against his chest and sighed.

"I've been wondering something..." Aren started, pausing to gaze down at her face.

"What?"

"Have you decided what you'll do after the battle is over?"

Lark bit her lip. "I'm not sure. Honestly, I haven't given it much thought. I mean, I haven't had much time with a new problem popping up every other day."

"Yeah, I get that. I know it's hard to picture the future with this battle hanging over our heads." He stroked her shoulder gently.

"Why do you ask?"

Aren's hand stilled. "I haven't gone home to visit my family since I left. I want to travel back to Gransea. Maybe not right away, but in the spring or summer, for sure."

Lark blinked. "That's right. You told me the whole show was planning to travel to Doln in the spring, didn't you?"

"Yeah. They might still be planning to, but after that last show in Joria, the inn offered Daus a permanent spot. I'm still not sure if he'll take it, but either way, I want to go home—at least for a week or two. With everything that's happened, I feel like I need to see my mother and father again."

Lark nodded. She could understand that. It was only natural to want to spend time with family, especially now. If she were in his shoes, she'd likely be dying to know how her parents were holding up, and she'd want to make sure for herself, in person.

"I was hoping you'd come with me."

Lark's heart skipped a beat. She stared up into Aren's blue eyes.

He watched her intently, and his hand tightened slightly on her shoulder. "If you need time to think about it, I—"

"Yes." A grin stretched her face so wide her cheeks ached. "I'd love to."

Aren's answering smile was blindingly bright. "Really? Great—that's great." He pulled her closer, wrapping her in a tight hug. Then he pulled back to peer down at her face, his smile falling. "There's one more thing I've been wanting to tell you."

Lark met his gaze. Why had he turned so serious? "What?"

Before he could answer, the wind whipped to life, and a huge bird zipped behind Lark's head, making her jump.

"Blazes." She spun around, spying Whisper landing on the rail just behind her. She beamed at Aren. "They're back." She swiveled around, searching for Muse.

Aren let go of her shoulder and slipped out of the blanket to greet Whisper. "Hey, buddy. I missed you."

Whisper shifted on the railing, his head tilting and pupils dilating the same way Muse always did when she was excited about something. Lark might not be able to speak to Whisper, but she had a feeling he was happy to see his handler again.

She turned again to watch the sky for Muse's return. What was taking her so long?

"Whisper just showed up. Where are you?"

When she didn't answer immediately, Lark's stomach churned. Aren joined her, staring at the sky.

"I don't see Muse yet, do you?"

"I just called to her, and she didn't resp—"

"Hey, I'm here."

Lark gripped the railing, and her shoulders slumped. She sent Aren a half-smile. "She's there. Let me find out why she's so far behind."

"What's taking you so long? Whisper beat you here. I didn't realize you'd grown lazy in our time apart."

"Ha. Lazy, am I? I'm not lazy at all. Just for that, I don't think I'll tell you what I spotted."

"C'mon, don't be like that. I was only joking."

Aren squeezed her arm. "What is it?"

"She spotted something, but she's got her feathers all ruffled and won't tell me what."

Aren chuckled and shook his head. He carefully examined Whisper and began untying the folded parchment strapped to his leg.

"Oh, you're gonna love this," Muse exclaimed.

"You sure about that?"

"Hey, didn't you say Jayan was liable to drop anchor soon?"

"Yes, he always does at dusk."

"Yeah, you don't wanna do that. Make sure he keeps sailing."

"Muse—what is it already?"

"It's your brother. He's not far from you, on a tiny boat close to the shoreline."

Lark gasped. "Conall. Muse found Conall." She headed for the ladder. "I need to ask Jayan to keep sailing until we reach him."

"All right. I better bring this parchment to Kayda." Aren waited for her to mount the rope ladder, then followed just behind her.

Kayda was there to meet Lark as her boots thumped down on the deck.

"I saw one of the birds made it back. Did they bring news?" Kayda asked.

"Yes." Lark's words spilled out breathlessly. "Aren has a parchment for you. And Muse just spotted Conall ahead of us, near the coast. Where's Jayan? I have to make sure he doesn't drop anchor."

"He should be at the helm."

"Thanks." Lark sped off, her heart racing. Conall and Muse were both coming back. The news had her grinning like a fool as she spotted Jayan.

"Captain Jayan." She waved frantically and jogged up to the helm. "There's a boat just ahead we need to locate. My brother is on it."

Jayan glanced at the darkening sky, then turned to frown at her. For a heartbeat, Lark thought he might say no, but when Kayda ran up just behind her with Aren in tow, the parchment clasped in her hands, he said, "Aye. I reckon we can handle that."

"Thank you." Lark left the helm and raced to the bow railing. Where were they?

"I got the boat to keep sailing. Are you with Conall still? How is he?" she asked Muse as she reached the rail and stared out at the slowly darkening sea. She still didn't see any sign of either of them.

"I'm keeping an eye on them from above. He seems all right, if a little wet."

"Who's with him? Shadow?"

"Yep. Ha. He looks miserable." The humor in Muse's tone made Lark want to roll her eyes but reassured her they were safe. She knew her bondmate well enough to understand Muse wouldn't joke if they were injured or in serious distress.

"Good." Lark grimaced. *"Not that he's miserable. You know what I mean."*

"Guess what else?"

"What?"

"Remember when I said it would be weird if that wind mage found your brother?"

"Ereni, Violet's mother? Yes, I remember."

"Ha. I was right. She's here, too."

Lark sighed, and another weight lifted off her chest. Not only was she getting her brother and her bondmate back, she could finally reunite the child she'd cared for with her mother. Today was shaping up to be an amazing day.

Aren caught up to her, carrying a coiled rope in his hands. Kayda walked just behind him, the parchment unfurled and her gaze dancing across the page as she read.

"Have you spotted them yet?" Aren asked.

"No. Not yet." Lark bounced on her toes, her gaze flitting around ahead of them.

A crowd gathered, no doubt alerted by her shouting at Jayan. Soon the rail was crowded with dozens of people staring out at the sea, everyone murmuring excitedly and smiling.

Lark turned to Aren, her brow furrowing as a thought struck her. "I'm sorry. You were in the middle of telling me something earlier when Whisper landed. What was it?"

Aren opened his mouth, then glanced at the crowd around them and shook his head. "It's all right. It can wait." He squeezed her arm gently.

Lark flashed him a smile then stared off the bow. The sun was nearly fully set now. The clouds darkened to a deep blue-violet, the sky an ever darkening blue-black. A crescent moon rose in the sky, hovering over the eastern horizon further out to sea.

Lark's smile widened. "I can see them." A tiny dot appeared far off ahead in the sky, a slightly larger shape beneath it on the shifting waves.

A few of the folk gathered at the rail sent her dubious glances, then squinted into the shadowy dusk ahead. Of course, no one else could see them yet.

Lark had grown used to spotting far-off things much quicker than others. After meeting Kayda and learning a little more about the boons that bondmates brought to their pairing, she could only assume that was the reason for her advanced eyesight.

After a few moments of sailing, the little canoe grew nearer. The people sending her doubtful looks stopped, and everyone began pointing and waving. An air of excitement broke out, even more so when the few mages gathered at the bow spotted Ereni in the front of the canoe. Magic hummed to life on deck as wind and water mages sent gusts into the sky and surf to advance the ship forward more quickly.

Muse landed on the railing beside her. *"Told ya, you'd be excited. Now that I found your lost brother, I think you owe me a treat."*

Lark chuckled and grinned at her bondmate. *"Name it, and it's yours, my fine feathered friend."*

"Ha. I like the sound of that." Muse puffed up her chest, then turned to stare back at the ocean. *"Don't worry, I'll think of something."*

Finally, the canoe pulled up alongside them, and Aren tossed the rope down. Ereni was the first to climb on board. All of the mages crowded around her as soon as she touched down on the deck, still wearing the ugly gray coveralls they'd been forced to don back in Flamesmoat, her brown hair tied back in a ponytail, damp and askew.

Ereni only spared the mages a small smile before craning her neck around, as if searching intently for something—or someone. When Ereni's gaze locked on Lark, she pushed through the circle of mages and strode up to her.

"Violet. Where is she?" Ereni's eyes were wide, her jaw clenched tight.

"I left her below deck in the mess hall, with Indra, the wet nurse I hired," Lark replied.

Ereni pressed a hand to her chest, then sighed deeply. "Thank you, Lark. I can't thank you enough." Ereni strode off, heading for the closest hatch.

Lark smiled at her retreating back, then leaned over the bow railing. Aren had thrown the rope back down to Conall while she'd been talking with Ereni. Shadow was already wrapped in it and being hoisted into the air by Aren with the help of a trio of sailors, who gripped the rope behind him. They strained and groaned under the large wolf's weight, but soon, he thudded down on the deck.

Lark rushed forward to untie him after seeing no one else was brave enough for the task. Shadow met her gaze with his golden eyes, his sopping wet tail wagging, though he dutifully stood still to allow her to unknot the rope.

Sunny appeared out of nowhere, her tail spinning and her whole body thrumming with excitement. Once Shadow was released from the rope, he padded up beside her and they rubbed flanks. Lark watched on her knees, her chest tingling with warmth and her eyes filling with moisture.

Then it was Conall's turn to climb aboard. Lark rose to her feet as his boots hit the deck. "Brother. You're late." She only gave him enough time to grip the railing and right his balance before thudding into his chest and wrapping her arms around him.

"Lark. I told you I'd meet you on board." He squeezed her tightly, his voice filled with joy. But he only hugged her for a few heartbeats before pulling back and staring down at her.

His clothes and hair were soggy, but his smile was exactly the same as she remembered. The sight of it filled her heart with glee. But the next thing he said wiped the grin from her face and made her knees buckle.

"I hear I have to thank you for more than just waiting for my return. How's my daughter?"

Chapter 25

Kayda stuffed the crumpled parchment in her pocket and strode forward to greet Conall as he released Lark from a tight hug.

"...How's my daughter?" Conall said.

Kayda halted beside them. Lark's mouth dropped open, her eyes just as wide.

Kayda raised a brow. "I didn't know you had a daughter."

Conall flashed a crooked grin and rubbed the back of his neck. "Yeah, me either. Hey, Kayda, it's good to see you."

Kayda sent him a tentative smile in response. Should she hug him, too? Or maybe a handshake?

She was saved from deciding by Lark's gasp. "Don't tell me I've been taking care of my own niece all this time."

Kayda stifled a gasp of her own. "Violet's yours?"

Conall nodded. "Ereni and I traveled to Mage Keep together last summer."

For half an instant, Kayda's heart sank. That meant Tarquin... No. This was much better. Violet would grow up with her father by her side.

Lark squeezed Conall's arm. "Ereni already went below deck to find Violet. She's with the wet nurse. I'll show you."

"If you don't mind, I'll walk with you," Kayda said. "I have some news to share."

"All right, let me just tell Shadow." Conall flicked a glance at his wolf, who sat on his haunches while Sunny circled him whimpering, her tail whipping nonstop. Conall chuckled, then turned to them with a smile. "Let's go."

"What news do you have?" Lark led the way to the nearest hatch. "Are the Doln on their way to meet us?"

Kayda stepped into the candlelit hallway. "Yes. It seems they're not far. We should both arrive off the coast of the Abandoned Lands tomorrow afternoon."

Conall frowned. "So soon? I knew we were close, but I'd hoped we'd have more time…"

Kayda stopped outside the door to her room. "It appears so. I don't want to keep you from your family, but if you could both meet me back here. There's something we need to discuss. It won't take long."

Conall glanced at Lark and then back at Kayda. His brow furrowed, and he shifted his weight, then motioned Lark to follow. "If it won't take long, we can discuss it now. I have something I need to tell you both as well."

Kayda's brow rose. "Are you sure?"

"Yes. Ereni will be happy for a few more moments alone with Violet, anyway."

Kayda nodded once, then unlocked the door and slipped inside. She held the door wide for Conall and Lark to file in behind her.

The room was dim, lit with only a single oil lamp strapped down on the dinged desk. Kayda closed the door and strode to it, where she quickly worked the wick to brighten the room. She inhaled, gathering the courage to spill all the secrets she'd learned from Izora. Now that Conall and Lark were here together, and before the battle began, she had to tell them the whole of it. They deserved the truth.

She turned around, but before she spoke, Conall broke the silence.

"One of us is going to die."

"What?" Lark practically gasped out the single word.

Conall paced, his clunking boots echoing the thudding beat of Kayda's heart. "I'm sorry I didn't tell you sooner. I assumed the Unseen was just screwing with me. That he'd say anything to stop the battle from happening. But then Ereni told me it all comes true. Every single vision for hundreds of years."

"The Unseen predicted one of us would die in your vision?" Kayda rubbed her forehead.

"Yes. I didn't believe him, or I would've told you when we sailed to Stoneshore."

Lark stepped into her brother's path, halting his pacing. "It's all right, you're telling us now. The Unseen didn't say who?"

Conall shook his head, his face grave. Lark blanched and splayed a hand over her chest.

"It doesn't matter," Kayda said. "This changes nothing. There's always the chance of death when you engage in battle. At least now we know two of us will survive."

"You're right. There is that," Lark agreed.

Kayda drew in a deep breath. "In fact, this news makes me even more sure about the favor I have to ask of you both."

"Whatever you need, we'll help you, Princess," Conall insisted.

"Actually, it's *Queen* now," Lark said.

Conall's eyes widened. "What did I miss?"

Kayda sighed. "A lot, I'm afraid. Lark's right. Technically, I'm Queen of Dracwood. My father and grandfather are gone."

"I'm so sorry." Conall moved closer, his hand outstretched, but Kayda waved him off.

"Thank you. But I didn't ask you here for your condolences, as much as I appreciate them. The fact is, I'm alone now. Should I die, the kingdom would have no heir."

Lark bit her lip. "There isn't any other family to step in? A cousin, or uncle?"

"No. I'm afraid not." Kayda looked them both in the eyes. "Just a half-brother and half-sister."

Conall's jaw dropped.

Lark shook her head and backed up until her shoulders struck the wood-paneled wall. "No. You can't mean us? We aren't royal. And if you tell anyone we're related, they'll know you aren't royal either."

"I thought the same until after Flamesmoat," Kayda admitted. "Then Izora told me the truth about what happened with Jett and my mother all those years ago. All three of us have royal blood in our veins."

Lark's brow furrowed, and she stared down at her feet. "I don't get it. How could that be?"

Conall appeared just as confused, his lips pursed and brows sunken. But then he stiffened and inhaled sharply. "Jett didn't know who his father was."

"His father was King Quinton," Kayda explained. "My grandfather. *Our* grandfather. I'm sorry he never got the chance to meet you both. I know he would've loved you dearly if he had the chance."

"That must be why the mages made Jett leave. They didn't want him around to put two and two together." Conall bit his lip and stared at his feet.

Lark shook her head even more forcefully. "But Kayda, you can't possibly want us to rule. We don't know a thing about rul—"

"And you think I do?" Kayda waved a hand. "There will be plenty of people around to help with the minutia. What the country really needs is a figurehead. Someone they can rally around. Whoever survives this battle will certainly qualify. If I end up being one of them, then you two don't need to worry. But if I don't... Someone has to step up. After everything that's happened, we'll need to rebuild."

"What about Jett?" Lark asked. "If what you said is true, then he's just as royal as we are."

Kayda smiled gently. "I talked to him yesterday. He doesn't want any part of rul-ing—not that I planned to ask him. He agreed with me that both of you have proven your worth. Even before learning the Unseen's words, I was planning to ask you to be my heirs, should I fall. Before we met, you both fought to overcome the evil plaguing our lands. You stood by my side when I lost my bondmate. And we will stand together to put a stop to the Unseen. You deserve to reap the rewards, and I have every faith that you can handle the responsibilities that come with it."

Conall straightened. "All right. I agree. But on one condition."

Kayda met his gaze. "Name it."

"If it's me who falls, then I want Violet taken care of. Who knows what will happen tomorrow. Ereni could be hurt, too." He rubbed a hand across his chest. "Violet deserves a decent life, with family that loves her. If I'm not there, then I need—"

"Done." Kayda agreed. "She can live at Kings Keep."

Conall shook his head. "No." He grimaced. "No offense, Kayda, but she doesn't need a life of luxury. Violet—she just needs a normal life."

Kayda blinked, shifting on her feet. "I understand. I'll keep an eye on her from a distance, if that's what you'd prefer."

Conall nodded.

Lark wrapped her arms around her middle. "I don't like this. I don't want to think about either of you dying. It's not fair."

Conall pulled her into a hug. "What about you, Lark? Would you watch over Violet for me?"

Tears spilled down her cheeks. "Do you even have to ask? Of course I will." She sniffled. "And you, Kayda. I'll do whatever I can to help, if it comes to it."

Kayda blinked back tears of her own. "Good. So, that's settled." She turned to her desk and lifted the ancient book off the top. "Lark and I have already read this cover to cover. We have a few ideas that might come in handy for the battle. We should discuss it together before we arrive tomorrow, but that can wait. Go. Spend some time with your daughter, Conall." She handed the book to him. "You can have this back. Thank you for letting me borrow it."

Conall grabbed the book. "You're welcome—sister."

For a moment, she thought he would leave it at that, but the next instant, he pulled her into a tight hug. Lark thudded against them both a heartbeat later.

Kayda couldn't stop the smile that split her cheeks.

Just a few weeks ago, she'd been so certain this kind of love would never be hers. Tarquin had certainly never treated her like this. Like a treasured friend. Now she had a brother and sister who would stand with her and stare down the end of the world. It was more than she'd ever dreamed of.

She only hoped it would be enough.

Conall and Lark left with a parting goodbye. Kayda strolled to the window and stared out at the dark sea.

"Dru, are you there?"

No answer.

"We'll reach the Abandoned Lands soon. I really need you."

Still nothing. She sighed.

"Conall says one of us will die tomorrow. If you don't make it back, then this might be goodbye."

A tear slid down Kayda's cheek, and she brushed it away with the back of her fist. *"I'm sorry for what happened to your kind. I wouldn't blame you if you wanted to stay away. To stay in your home and build a new future with Bela."*

She exhaled, closing her eyes. *"I love you, Druturion. I only wish you could hear me."*

Chapter 26

Conall followed Lark down the dimly lit hall, clutching the ancient book in his hands. This was it. He was finally about to meet his daughter. They'd stopped in the mess hall, only to learn that Ereni had taken Violet back to her room.

"Almost there." Lark looked up at him with a grin. "Oh, I almost forgot. I don't want you to be alarmed when you first see Violet. She looks a bit different from other babes, but it's nothing to worry over."

Conall halted, grabbing Lark's elbow. "What do you mean, different?"

"I'm not sure if it's because of the nature of her birth, being fast tracked and all, but Violet was born albino."

"Albino." Conall's brow furrowed. "Like that goat we had the one year on the farm?"

"Exactly. Just like Snowy."

Conall chuckled and resumed walking. "You had me worried for a moment there."

Snowy had been a favorite of Lark's the year she'd been born. The nanny looked a bit peculiar compared to the other goats but was normal in every other way. Surely, it would be the same with Violet. And who knew, the pale hair and skin might even suit her.

"Yes, like I said, nothing to worry about. She is on the smaller side as well, but she's catching up quickly. She's thriving." Lark beamed up at him and turned a corner, then stopped. "Here we are." She pointed to a door in the middle of the hall. "I'll leave you to it then." She moved to leave.

"Lark, wait. Are you all right, after my news earlier?"

Lark's smile shifted, suddenly looking a touch too bright. "Yeah. I—yeah, I'm fine."

He grabbed her arm. "Really? Why don't you come with me? We'll talk some more."

She shook her head. "No. I just have someone I need to talk to, is all. And you need time alone with your little girl." She squeezed his hand. "I'm all right, I swear. I'll see you in the morning."

Conall frowned but let her go. Sometimes, it was still hard for him to not see the little girl that begged him to play dolls in her room. But Lark wasn't a little girl anymore. She'd grown so much in the time they'd been apart. He had to keep reminding himself she could take care of herself.

Conall turned and strode to the door. He stopped just outside, his palms moistening with sweat.

Footsteps thumped down the hall, and he spun toward them.

"Jett?"

The older man rushed forward and pulled him into a hug. "Son. I'm so glad you're back."

At first, Conall stiffened, but after a moment, he wrapped his arms around Jett and returned the embrace. Memories flooded back, unbidden, of so many other hugs. It wasn't the same—back then he'd barely reached his father's chest after all—but the feeling, the love, washed over him just like it had when he was a child.

"When you didn't come back to the docks, I didn't know if I'd ever see you again. I know we didn't have time to talk, but—"

Conall pulled back and met Jett's gaze. "Wait. I have something to say."

Jett's mouth snapped closed.

"I'm sorry for the way I reacted to your story. I—It was hard for me to wrap my head around it all, but I understand now."

"You do?"

"Have you met your granddaughter yet?" Conall inclined his head to the door beside them.

Jett's eyes widened. "Violet—she's yours?"

Conall nodded. "I still haven't met her, but as soon as I learned about her, I understood the choice you made. If I could guarantee Violet would have the kind of life she deserves, even if I would never get to be part of her life, I would take that deal in a heartbeat."

Conall flashed back to the conversation in Kayda's chambers. In a way, he'd already made that deal.

Jett's gaze darted between him and the closed door. "You haven't met her yet…" A wide grin split his face. "Go on then, son. I won't keep you." Jett squeezed his arm and stepped away.

"Thanks, Father." A rush of rightness spread through his chest as the words left his lips. He still wasn't happy about all the years they lost, but he could admit now that Lark was right. He refused to hold on to the anger and hurt when forgiving his father meant they'd have a chance at a future spent together.

Jett sent him a parting smile and disappeared down the hall.

Conall turned to the door. He knocked gently, then tried the knob. It twisted open, and he peeked inside.

Ereni perched on the edge of a hammock, her dirty coveralls replaced with a plain brown dress. She gently rocked a blanket-wrapped bundle in her arms. She glanced up, her eyes shining, as he slid inside and smiled.

Conall set the old book on an empty side table and strode over to the hammock.

Ereni stood as he approached and glided toward him. "Do you want to hold her?" she whispered.

Conall stretched out his arms. Then the slight weight of his daughter landed on his chest. He stared down at her face, her eyes closed in slumber, and his heart melted.

"Hello, Violet," he whispered. He hadn't meant to wake her, but either the low rumble of his words or the motion of being transferred made her eyelids pop open.

A pair of eyes the most beautiful blend of blue, red, and violet greeted him. As he gazed down at her, he was overwhelmed with love unlike anything he'd ever felt. This little girl had taken his heart and wrapped it around her finger so thoroughly with that one simple look. He would never be the same. He was a father now.

She opened her mouth and wailed.

Conall laughed. "Well, she has a good set of lungs. That's for sure." He rocked her gently. "Shush, little one. It's all right." After a moment, she quieted.

He flicked a glance at Ereni. Tears slid down her cheeks.

"Hey, what's—"

The door creaked open, halting his words. A voluptuous, dark-haired woman slipped in, heading straight for Violet. "I see I'm right on time for Little Miss' next meal. She's up like clockwork, this one." She stopped before him and lifted the hem of her dress, performing a shallow curtsy. "I'm Indra, Violet's wet nurse. You must be her father. It's nice to meet you, sir."

His heart squeezed at her simple statement. Her father—he was a father. "Please, call me Conall. It's nice to meet you as well."

Indra held out her arms. "I'll bring her back as soon as she's fed."

Conall's brow furrowed. So soon? He'd only just got her. But, of course, she needed to eat. He passed her over. "All right. Thank you."

Indra slipped back into the hall and pulled the door closed behind her.

Conall exhaled, then walked to Ereni's side. She'd stationed herself beside the window, staring out at the dark sea. Moonlight filtered in, making the tears on her cheeks shimmer.

"Hey, what's wrong?" he asked.

Ereni shook her head and forced a smile. "Nothing. It's nothing." She scrubbed her cheeks with the sleeve of her dress.

"You can tell me." He tilted his head to meet her gaze. "Aren't you happy to have Violet back?"

"I am. Of course, I am." Her chin wobbled. "She's so big already. When I saw her last, she was such a tiny thing. Now..." She waved a hand, then crossed her arms. "It's silly, I know. It's only been a few weeks, but I feel like I missed so much."

"I'm sorry for that. If you hadn't come after Shadow and I—"

Ereni squeezed his forearm. "No, I didn't mean that." She dropped her gaze and pulled back her hand. "I'm not sorry I saved you. I would do it again. And not because of the battle or even for Violet."

Ereni sighed and turned back to the window.

There was still one question he'd been wanting to ask her since she found him. For whatever reason, he'd kept it buried, but he found he couldn't bear having it unanswered any longer.

Conall took a deep breath. "Ereni?"

"Hm?"

"What was I to you, back then?"

She spun to face him, her brows sinking. "What are you asking?"

Conall stared down at his boots, gathering his thoughts. Why was this so hard? His heart raced, and his stomach knotted.

"You knew who I was when we first met. And you knew you were destined to have a talented daughter like me—to have Violet. When we were together, was it just because of fate? Did you ever care for me at all?"

Ereni didn't balk at the question or at the hint of accusation in his tone that he couldn't hide. She met his gaze and smiled gently. "Yes, I cared for you. I still do."

Conall bowed his head and closed his eyes. When her arms wrapped around him, he leaned into the embrace, the scent of lavender tickling his nose.

"Do you want to know what I was thinking when we first met?" she whispered.

He nodded wordlessly against the top of her head.

"I thought you were handsome and far too trusting. And a bit naïve."

He grunted. "Naïve?"

"Yes. Like when you tried to convince me and everyone else that Shadow was only a simple hound." She chuckled. "But the more I got to know you, the more I saw what a wonderful man you are. Walking across the country to find your sister. Treating a stranger you'd only just met like a true friend."

He pulled back and stared into her blue eyes. "So, you weren't thinking the whole time about the vision you had?" He cocked a brow. "I find that a bit hard to believe."

Ereni sighed. "There was that as well."

He tried to pull away fully, but she tightened her grasp on his waist.

"I won't lie to you. I knew from the start." She pursed her lips. "If I could go back in time, I would do things differently."

"What?" Conall shook free of her hold and backed away.

"No—you don't understand." She stepped toward him, but when he backed away further, she furrowed her brow and turned to the window. "I wouldn't change what happened. Not in a million years. Those days we spent traveling together—they were amazing. You were amazing."

Her words calmed his racing pulse, if only a little. "Then what do you mean? What do you wish you'd done differently?"

"I would tell you all of it from the start. The truth about the Palisade. The vision I had about Violet. I should've never lied to you. I'll regret that for the rest of my life, Conall. I'm sorry."

Conall stilled, watching Ereni closely. She didn't make another move to draw nearer, just remained staring forlornly out the window.

"You can't imagine the debate I held in my mind when we first met. I've never been one to accept my fate easily. I think we're alike in that." She glanced at him and smiled half-heartedly before gazing at the window. "I didn't want to be a mage. You would think growing up surrounded by them, I would want nothing more, but I didn't. I wanted a simple life. But fate had other plans for me, just like it did for you.

"After I visited the Winter Witch, it all changed. I stopped trying to fight becoming a mage. Especially when we were set upon by thieves and my talent was awakened. But then, when I first met you, it started up all over again. I didn't want to surrender to fate and bind myself to someone I barely knew, no matter that I felt something for you instantly. I spent so long fighting against it. Trying to convince myself that I wouldn't let fate control me."

Conall recalled those early days they'd spent together. All the mixed signals she'd sent him, flirting in one breath and then giving him the cold shoulder the next... Was this why? She'd been fighting to stop herself from caring about him? To avoid the fate that was meant to be her destiny.

He could certainly understand the feeling. All that time he'd followed Delyth, the weight of his fate had burdened him exactly the same. Like he'd been locked into a future he had no say in. Was that what he'd been like to Ereni?

"Do you know what I realized?" Ereni turned from the window. "When I stopped fighting, for just one instant, and really thought about it, there was no question. That first night under the stars, *I chose you*—not fate. I chose you then, and I would choose you again if you'd let me."

He stared back at her. He saw the question in her eyes that she left unspoken. Would he choose her, too?

Ereni held his gaze, her chin lifted, chest heaving. She made no move closer—she just stood still, waiting.

The moment stretched out. He stayed there, glued to the spot, his mind reeling and his tongue tied just like it had been the night the Palisade fell. Back then, he'd cursed himself for a fool. But as he stared back at her tonight, he felt far from foolish.

Finally, he moved.

Ereni's head dipped, and she silently shuddered as he left her side and strode across the room to the door.

Conall slid the lock closed with a *click*.

The sound was deafening in his ears, but Ereni didn't seem to register it. She wrapped her arms around herself and sank to the floor. It wasn't until he stopped directly in front of her that she lifted her tearstained face to look at him, her eyes widening.

Conall knelt beside her and pulled her into his arms. She climbed atop his lap and buried her face in his neck, her body trembling.

"I'm sorry," he said.

Ereni stilled in his arms and pulled back to peer at his face, shaking her head. "You don't have anythin—"

"No, listen. Please."

She nodded gravely.

"All my life, I've been so certain about what was right and wrong. But I've come to realize things aren't always so simple. Sometimes people do the wrong thing for the right reasons." He grimaced, recalling how he'd lied to make sure Brenna received the punishment she deserved. "I've even done the same. I can't keep blaming you, Ereni. I won't."

Her lashes lowered, and she nodded again.

"Just promise me one thing. We can't keep each other in the dark anymore. Never again. We have Violet now. We have to be on the same page if we're going to raise her together."

Her blue eyes collided with his. "Never again. I promise."

Conall lifted his hand and caught the teardrop that slid down her cheek. Ereni tilted her head, leaning into his touch. But then she exhaled and sat up straight, wrapping her legs around his back.

"Is Violet the only reason you want to be together?" She traced her fingers across his chest, the shadow of a seductive smile on her lips.

But when he looked into her eyes, he saw the vulnerability she tried to hide. The wounded heart that craved the answer to the question she'd been too scared to voice.

"No, she's not." He caught her hand in his and stilled its exploration, making sure her gaze stayed glued to his. "I choose you, too."

He watched the last flicker of doubt fade from her eyes, and a smile slowly spread across her lips. Then he kissed her like it was the last thing he'd ever do. Like this was the last time he'd ever get the chance.

Who knew, maybe it was? In the back of his mind, he realized he had to tell her. They'd just promised not to keep each other in the dark. He needed to tell her he might die tomorrow.

But then her fingers tangled in his hair, and she did that thing with her hips that drove him crazy.

Later. He'd tell her later.

Chapter 27

Lark strode away, leaving her brother to meet his daughter. She grinned alone in the dimly lit hall.

Conall was a father. And to the sweet little girl she'd just spent so long taking care of. It was all so strange—but in the absolute best way.

If only all of his news had been so pleasant. She shuddered, pushing the thought from her mind before tears filled her eyes again.

Not now. She had other plans for tonight.

"Have you seen Aren?"

Muse's scoff reverberated through Lark's mind. *"I've been gone for ages, and all you want to ask me about on my return is lover boy?"*

Lark shook her head. *"You're right. How are you? What's happened that you haven't reported back to me in excruciating detail? How about your lunch? Did it make a reappearance like you thought it would, or did you manage to keep it down?"*

"Ha. You've got jokes now. Nice. Aren's out here with me and the old snoozer, up top."

"Thanks." Lark opened the nearest hatch.

The cold night air rushed forward to greet her. She shivered and pulled her cloak closed, then strolled toward the ship's center. It didn't take her long to find Aren. He stood next to Whisper and Muse, tossing them little tidbits from a pouch he wore around his waist.

"There you are. Let me guess. You want to borrow *him again? Ha."*

Lark rolled her eyes. *"So what if I do?"*

Muse cocked her head. *"Fine, just let him finish feeding me first."*

Aren turned, following Muse's gaze. He smiled when he spotted her approaching. "Lark. Everything go all right with Conall?"

She stopped in front of him. "Yes, and no. I need to talk to you about something."

Aren's brow furrowed, and he cinched his waist pouch closed. "Sure, what is it?"

"Hey," Muse squeaked.

Lark giggled. "Do you mind doing me a favor first and leaving my gluttonous bondmate a pile of whatever it is you've got in there?"

Aren chuckled. "Sure." He opened the pouch again and dumped a handful of dried meat on the deck in front of each bird.

"That's better." Muse hopped down and gobbled at the meat greedily.

"So, what do you want to talk about?"

Lark grabbed his elbow. "Not here. Come with me." She pulled him back through the hatchway to the inner deck.

She grabbed a candle holder off the closest wall, then set her ear to the nearest door. When the muted sound of chatter reached her ears, she lifted her head and moved on.

"Don't try the galley this time. I don't think the cook will be too happy to see us again," Aren whispered, his eyes twinkling.

At the next door, she found what she was hunting for—silence. She cracked open the door and peeked in. Perfect.

She turned to Aren. "In here." She grabbed his hand and tugged him inside.

They entered a wooden chamber filled with piled cloth. What at first glance looked like the perfect spot for a little privacy lost a bit of the appeal upon closer inspection. The musky scent of sweat lingered in the air. Lark wrinkled her nose. This must be the crew's laundry room.

Aren coughed as she shut the door behind her and set the candleholder on a wall hook. "So what—"

Lark silenced his question with a kiss. Aren stiffened for half a heartbeat, but then his lips parted, and his arms wrapped around her waist.

Lark closed her eyes and leaned into him, sliding her hands up his back. This was what she needed. If tomorrow might be her last day, then she would make every moment count until then. She trailed her hands around to Aren's chest, her shaking fingers working the buttons at the neck of his tunic.

Aren pulled back, his chest heaving as her hands slid off his neck. "Lark, wait. What's wrong? You're trembling."

She met his gaze in the dim candlelight and shook her head. "Nothing." Her voice cracked, and his eyes narrowed. She reached for him again, tipping her face up. "Please, I don't want to talk."

Aren didn't take the bait. He traced his thumb over her bottom lip and pressed their foreheads together. "What aren't you telling me?" he whispered.

Lark shuddered and sank into his arms. "What if we die tomorrow? I just wanted to..." Lark's cheeks heated, and she started to pull away, but Aren squeezed her tighter.

"You're not going to die."

"There's a good chance I will."

Aren stepped back, raising a brow. "What are you talking about?"

"Conall told me and Kayda one of us would die during the battle. That out of the three of us, only two would survive."

"How could he know that?"

"The Unseen told him, during his vision. The same visions that always come true."

Aren bit his lip and stared at the ground. But then his face lit up, and he smiled. "It won't be you."

Lark barely resisted rolling her eyes. "You can't know that for sure."

"I do. Don't you remember what Daus said?"

"Daus says a lot of things. You're going to have to be more specific."

Aren snorted. "Yeah, he does." Then all the humor faded from his face, and he stared at her intently. "I'm talking about in the boat outside of Bogsmouth. The girl who saw his future. She said we would save the world—together. Together means you're there, Lark. You're *not* going to die."

He said the words with such confidence, such unwavering belief, she almost believed it, too.

"But—what if you're wrong? I don't want to have any regrets."

"Neither do I."

Her heart fluttered, and she stepped closer. "Good."

"That's why this is a bad idea."

Lark halted, her stomach sinking. "Oh." She turned to the door.

"W-wait, I don't mean it like that." Aren grabbed her wrist and spun her around. "It's just this room. The smell. The door that doesn't lock." He flashed a lopsided smile. "I have a feeling if we do what you're thinking here, we'll have a whole heap of regrets. It's not a bad idea—just bad timing."

Blazing timing. Lark sighed.

Aren tipped up her chin, and she met his eyes. "I want you, Lark."

Her heart thundered, and she gulped.

"I don't think I've ever wanted anything more. But I can wait until we have a proper bed and the specter of death isn't forcing our hand."

"It's not force—"

"Are you sure about that?" He reached past her and lifted a dirty pair of trousers by the bottom hem, wrinkling his nose.

Lark laughed. "Put those down."

Aren dropped the pants and grinned down at her.

Lark smiled back, but she must've let something slip on her face.

"Something's still bothering you, isn't it?" he asked.

Lark frowned and stared down at her boots. How could he read her so well?

Aren grabbed her hand. "Tell me."

"Conall has Violet now. And Kayda's the queen. They both have people depending on them." Her voice wobbled. "I can't help feeling like it should be me."

"It should be—no. No." Aren shook his head. "That's just not true."

Lark glanced into his eyes. She saw the certainty there but couldn't find it in herself to agree.

Aren squeezed her hand—hard. "You're a healer, Lark. Think of all the people you've saved. All the people you'll save in the future. The world needs you."

"I suppose that's true."

"And it's not just that. I need you, too."

Her heart beat frantically. "You do?"

He nodded, loosening his grip and stroking the back of her hand. "Remember, I wanted to tell you something earlier?"

She met his gaze, her lips parting. "Yes."

"I love you, Lark. I fell in love with you the first moment we locked eyes back in that clearing in the middle of nowhere."

"Really?"

Aren stepped closer. So close she could see the flicker of the candlelight reflected in his irises. He swallowed. "You don't have—"

"I love you, too."

He chuckled and pulled her close, grinning like a fool. "Good."

She rose on her tiptoes, meeting his lips. The kiss they shared was different from all the rest. It still sent a jolt through her body, weakening her knees, but the desperation from before was gone, replaced with a warmth in her chest that resonated deep within her soul.

Lark hummed with contentment. This kiss was everything. This kiss felt like home.

Then the door popped open, and a shadow darkened the entrance. Lark and Aren pulled apart, turning wide eyes toward the new arrival.

"You again," the chef blubbered as he hustled in, his arms loaded with a stack of dirty white aprons. "Get out, you randy buggers. Out, I tell ya!"

They spilled into the hall, laughing and rushing away from the cook's continued verbal assault.

"What is it with that guy?" Aren leaned in conspiratorially, lifting his brows. "Do you think he's following us?"

Lark chuckled and linked their hands. "I think he might be."

They rounded a corner and bumped right into Tiora. "There you two are. I've been looking all over for you."

"You have?" Lark asked.

Tiora flicked a glance between the two of them, lingering on their linked hands before smiling widely. "Mm-hm. I see you've been busy."

Lark's cheeks warmed, but she couldn't wipe the grin off her face. "I guess you could say that. What's going on?"

"Daus offered to put on a bit of a show for the sailors before everyone turned in for the night. Are you two coming?"

Aren quirked a brow. "Duty calls."

Lark squeezed his hand. "Let's go."

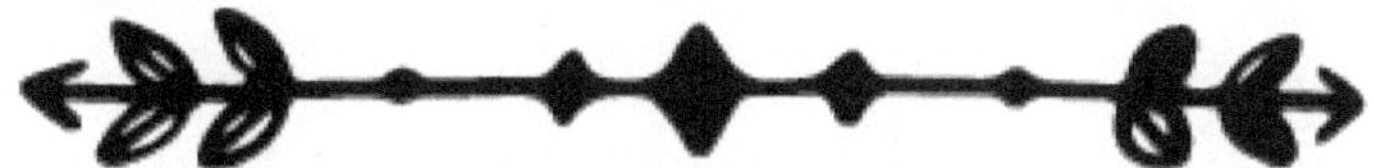

Lark opened the hatch and shivered. Her breath clouded in the afternoon air like a fine white mist.

She walked to the bow railing, a smile on her lips as the swaying boat sparked a memory of last night. Singing and dancing. Laughing with her friends. The night might not have turned out as she'd first envisioned, but they certainly made every moment count.

"Good morning," she said around a yawn.

Conall whirled around, his wide-eyed daughter resting in his arms. "Don't you mean good afternoon?" He chuckled. "I would ask if you'd slept well, but it looks like you did."

Lark grinned. "It was quite nice to have my slumber uninterrupted for a change." She leaned closer, cooing at Violet until she met her gaze and gurgled happily in response.

Lark straightened and stared off the bow. "Did I miss anything?"

"Not yet." Conall pointed ahead of them. "You're just in time."

Lark's eyes widened as she spotted a fleet of ships approaching from the north. "Yeah, it looks like I am."

At least a dozen sets of sails approached their position. When added to the handful they'd brought with them from Joria, they'd make an impressive force. Still, Lark's stomach churned as her gaze drifted to the west, and she spotted the coastline. They'd left the bog behind and sailed beside a charred wasteland she'd been told was once a gorgeous coastal plain.

The Abandoned Lands. They'd arrived.

A whisper of the creeping shiver she'd grown to associate with the scourge crept up her spine.

They hadn't even landed, and already she could sense it. This place felt off. Wrong on a visceral level that made her stomach roil more than the motion of a ship ever had.

Kayda strolled up beside them, frowning. "That place gives me the creeps. Every time I get close to the scourge, I have the strangest feeling. Like someone's watching me."

Lark shuddered. "I do, too."

Conall nodded. "Me, too."

The three of them exchanged a look, their faces grave and unsmiling.

"Are you ready to talk strategy yet?" Lark asked.

Kayda shook her head and gestured to the ships fast approaching. "We might as well wait on the Doln. I'm sure they'll wish to be included in our discussions."

Ereni appeared from a nearby hatch with Indra in tow. Conall turned, a wide smile lighting his face.

Lark's gaze darted between her brother and Ereni as they drew closer. She could practically feel the air thicken with the force of their undisguised attraction.

So, her brother was in love. That much was plain to see. And from the way Ereni's eyes lit up as she stared back at him, she could only assume the feeling was mutual.

Conall had a fling or two with girls back in Greenvale, but she'd never seen him look at anyone like this. It warmed her heart to know that he'd found someone he cared about so deeply.

"Ereni. It's good to see you again," Lark piped up with a smile.

Ereni glanced at her and nodded. "You too, Lark." Then her gaze swung back to Conall in a flash. He'd still not taken his eyes off her.

"Hello." Conall's grin widened as Ereni stopped in front of him.

Ereni's cheeks flushed a deep red. Lark had a suspicion it wasn't just from the chill air. "I brought Indra to collect Violet for her next feeding."

Conall's smile slipped, and his fingers tightened around his daughter. Then he sighed and planted a gentle kiss on Violet's forehead and handed her over to Indra.

The wet nurse disappeared without a word, just as the lead Doln ship pulled alongside them. Within moments, the crew on both ships tied the boats in place, and boards slammed down, forming a makeshift walkway between the two vessels. Lark followed Kayda toward the ship's center, watching silently as the sailors gave the all-clear that the bridge was ready.

A flurry of motion began. Lark expected a bevy of pale-skinned blondes to come rushing over—and granted, there were plenty of them included—but just as many white-robed elders pounded across the wood, clasping hands and hugging the young mages that crowded around on deck.

Two beefy men in thick fur coats brought up the rear. The leader was a head shorter than the second man, but he swaggered forward with an air of confidence, his shoulders thrust back and a wide smile on his lined face. He halted midway across the planks and peered around until his gaze lit on where Conall stood between Lark and Ereni.

In a few short steps, the Dolnman stopped in front of her brother and thrust out his hand. "Conall of Greenvale. Why am I not surprised to find you here?"

Conall clasped his hand, wincing slightly as they shook. "Clan Chief Aundrea. I'm glad to see you're well." He peered behind him at a younger, red-bearded man. "Taul. How are you?"

Taul stepped forward, clasping Conall in a quick hug. "Mighty fine, now that we've a battle to begin."

Conall held out his hand and quickly made introductions. Lark smiled politely when he introduced her but kept quiet. The men nodded in response but seemed to dismiss her in favor of staring at Kayda once Conall introduced her as queen.

"Perhaps we should adjourn below deck to talk strategy?" Kayda offered.

They all followed her inside the cramped halls and down to her room.

Kayda closed the door and turned to the clan chief with a grateful smile. "I must thank you again for coming to our aid, Clan Chief Aundrea. I know I said as much in my letter, but—"

"Think nothing of it, my lady. The scourge—and this Unseen that's controlling them—are a problem for us all, not just you Dracians. And we Doln have never been ones to back down from a fight."

"I'm glad to hear it," Kayda replied. "Should we talk timing? I expect everyone is itching to begin the battle, but I wonder if it would not be more prudent to wait until morning to sail ashore." She strolled across the room to the window, gesturing outside. "It's fairly late in the day already."

"I'm afraid that may not be wise, my lady." Taul frowned. "We brought a weather seer with us. He predicts a storm is not far off. A big one."

A weather seer? Lark lifted a brow. She'd never heard of any such thing. But perhaps she could help.

"I could ask Muse to take a look," she offered.

Kayda nodded. "That would be helpful."

Lark reached out to Muse in her mind. *"Hey, are you busy?"*

"Nope, unless you count napping as being busy."

"Would you mind taking a quick flight and checking the weather headed our way? The Doln seem to think we're due a storm soon."

"All right. Give me a moment."

Lark turned her attention back to the conversation that had kept up while she chatted with Muse. Ereni, Kayda and the Clan Chief crowded around a map, debating where to send which forces.

"If the battle is anything like the last time we fought in the Abandoned Lands, then we'll need to keep an eye out for the scourge swarming up from the ground," Ereni said.

"Speaking of underground." Conall stepped forward and exhaled a deep breath. "That's where I have to go. That's where the Unseen will be."

Lark's brow furrowed. "Underground. Are you certain?"

Conall nodded. "Yes. In my vision, I was shown a tunnel. I saw it all so clearly. That's where he'll be."

"We'll form a party to go with you. Will you need soldiers? Mages? How will you get there?" Kayda asked.

Conall shook his head. "I took another look at that book Delyth gave me last night. I found something that should work, but it's not without risk. It's best if I go alone. In case I fail, the rest of you will need to find a way below ground."

"Lark, they're right. Snow and ice is on the way. A few hours, tops. It's a big one."

"Thanks, Muse," Lark replied, even as her stomach sank.

"Muse confirms it. There's a storm coming. A big one," she said.

Kayda stood straight, speaking with an air of command. "Then we better hurry. We can't wait until after the storm, or the bog might ice over and allow the scourge to spread south. We need to stop them now."

"That's what I like to hear. To battle." Taul hefted his axe with a wide grin.

The young man's smile was infectious, but Lark's stomach churned. This was it. The day she or one of her siblings would die.

She couldn't help worrying it would be her.

Chapter 28

Conall stared at the coast. It was even more devoid of activity than the last time he'd been here. But where last time it looked like a paradise of untouched fields and trickling streams, today, the surface echoed the ugliness that dwelled below.

The ground was charred and littered with bones. The cold wind blew across the landscape, flicking motes of dust and the first glittering sprinkles of snow.

There was no time to waste. Even now, a handful of small boats filled with fighters were on track to land ashore. The ships' captains pulled as close to shore as they could, but without a proper port, they were forced to drop anchor in the bay. But they couldn't rely on the dinghies for everyone. With all the fighters they had, it would take a full day to transfer them all.

Luckily, they had other plans.

Everyone remaining on board gathered on deck, shouldering weapons and stretching. They hugged their friends and family, whispering harried goodbyes before the chaos began.

Beside him, Ereni slid her hand into his and squeezed. He met her gaze.

They'd spent long hours last night curled in each other's arms, alternately making love and scouring the ancient spell book, searching for answers. Just before dawn, he'd happened upon a page that made his lips quirk with a grin. But when he'd shown the passage to Ereni, she'd been less than enthusiastic about his plans.

Now he could see the echo of that conversation shadowed in the blue depths of her eyes. But before she left to rally the mages, Conall tugged her hand and pulled her into an embrace. Their lips met, and a spark hummed through his veins.

After only a moment, he ended the kiss and stared down into her face. "Stay safe," he whispered. His stomach churned as she nodded and silently walked away.

She had to live. Violet would remain on board with the wet nurse, but Ereni was determined to stand and fight. And though a part of him wanted to plead for Ereni to stand aside for Violet's sake, he knew his pleas would fall on deaf ears.

This battle was as much Ereni's as anyone's. More so, since she could trace her ancestry back to the first mages who'd built the Palisade. She'd admitted to him last night that the ancient book Delyth had gifted him was a family heirloom. Generation upon generation of her family had stood guard over the Abandoned Lands, waiting for this day. Waiting for their chance to destroy the evil that plagued them.

"Time to link," Ereni's voice rang out behind him.

The mages hustled to comply. Conall watched from his spot at the rail. The forces in each boat pulled alongside mirrored the movements on theirs. Young mages stood shoulder to shoulder with white-robed elders, linking hands.

On each ship, one mage strode to the front of the pack. Onboard their ship, the task fell to his sister, Lark.

Lark lifted her hand. A bucket full of dirt sat on the deck next to her. She closed her eyes, and a vibration hummed through the ship, tickling the soles of his feet.

The next instant, soil flew into the air, forming a wide plank-like shape hovering beside the ship. The rattling vibration intensified as the other boats lined up in the water beside them followed suit.

"Hurry, now. Everyone on," Ereni ordered.

Conall was one of the first to hop on the dirt platform. Shadow bounded on beside him.

"You all right?" Conall asked as Shadow wobbled precariously atop the floating dirt.

"Yes. It's strange, is all."

It seemed Shadow was not the only one who held reservations about traveling in this fashion. Though some warriors hopped off the boat readily, others had to be coaxed. The linked mages were the worst of all, requiring a helping hand, their step wobbly and faces flushed. The exhaustion of linking appeared to be already taking its toll.

Kayda hopped onto the platform beside him, a glowing oil lamp strung around her neck. In her hands, she carried another, already lit. "I've been looking for you." She thrust the lamp toward him. "Here, you're gonna need this, I wager." She pulled a stack of handkerchiefs from the pocket of her black cloak. "Stuff it down your tunic, and the heat won't be a problem."

"Thanks." He took the supplies and arranged them as she'd suggested. He had a full waterskin on his belt, dirt stuffed in every pocket, and now this.

But although he had all the elements at his disposal, he still couldn't fully banish the tiny voice in his mind that screamed it wouldn't be enough. That this battle was doomed before it even began.

No. Conall shoved the doubt aside. He crushed it with the staggering weight of his determination. He would make sure they won this fight. Even if he wasn't around to see the battle's end, he would ensure they succeeded, one way or the other. He had to. For Violet.

Before long, the deck emptied. Conall wobbled as the dirt beneath him began to move. The icy breeze rushed past, stinging his cheeks. Lark kept their platform moving, swiftly dragging dozens of people with it, closer to the shoreline and lower in the air until they floated just above the rolling surf.

Somewhere beside them, a massive splash sounded. Conall gulped. Another group had failed, the linked mages unable to keep their boatload of fighters afloat. He swiveled his head and watched as they surfaced, their heads bobbing in the dark water.

From across the platform, Ereni met his eye and shook her head. Conall's stomach clenched, but he nodded once. They'd known this might happen. It was why they'd chosen to split the mages into groups on each ship rather than risk everyone falling together. The few sailors left on the boats would fish the unlucky folks out of the sea.

Conall sighed, setting his sights back on the coast. Perhaps they were the lucky ones, after all.

Ahead, the first of the dinghies ferrying fighters arrived on the sandy shore. They'd barely stepped foot on dry land before the scourge emerged, bursting out of the ground in the thousands. Steel flew and shrieks of the dying vermin rose in the air, joined in time by grunts and screams of wounded fighters.

Before long, the fighters were massively outnumbered. Sul pole knives sliced into the crowd of vermin, and the Doln axes and swords cracked and whistled, painting the surf red with blood. But even so, many among them faltered, falling to the ground with ravenous beasts gnawing and slashing at their throats.

There were too many for the few men who'd arrived to handle. They had to do something.

Lark seemed to have the same thought. They soared above the surf, picking up pace. Within moments, their earthen raft reached the shore and disintegrated, dropping them all into the sand behind the first wave. The linked mages collapsed, panting, their energy spent.

"Form up," Ereni shouted, blasting a wave of air ahead and displacing a manic group of beasts that leaped for them immediately. "We need a shield, now."

Conall rushed to comply, joining Lark at the head of their group. He called on his talent, the image of his daughter fresh in his mind. The vibration thrummed in his blood as a massive semi-circle of dirt coalesced in the air before them.

The formerly linked mages were protected, for now, along with a large number of the struggling fighters who'd been close by. With the shield in place, they would have enough time to recover from the weariness washing over them.

"Archers," Ereni shouted, even as the first of the bowmen burst forward.

Lark's friend Aren was among them. His bowstring twanged as his first arrow flew over the shield into the ever-growing crowd of scourge.

With every passing moment, the scourge came, throwing themselves upon the shield relentlessly. By now, the shield was half the size it had been when it started. The weakened mages staggered to their feet behind him, slowly catching their breath.

They just needed a few more moments. Conall dug deep, throwing more magic at the shield, desperately seeking to shore up the holes. But with every hole he patched, two more appeared, until he was certain the thing would fall at any instant.

Lark staggered beside him, her hands flying furiously. They held on for one heartbeat, two. Then the shield crumbled to dust, and chaos ensued.

Snarling filled the air. Conall strode forward with static coursing across his skin, flinging blasts of air in all directions, shoving the beasts back. All around him, steel rang out. Shadow leaped forward, snatching a scourge mid-jump and crunching down on its neck.

Kayda appeared at his side, the oil lamp bouncing against her chest. Fire blasted from her hands, and the stench of roasting flesh and singed hair enveloped him, making him want to gag.

"C'mon," she yelled, as she carved a clear path ahead of them.

Conall followed, grateful for her help. He had to trek further inland for his plan to work. Lark and Ereni closed in on either side of him, and they all moved together through the chaos, sending blasts of magic in every direction.

The further inland they fought, the more that strange, lingering sensation grew, until he felt certain someone was watching him. When the prickle of eyes on his back became unbearable, he halted. "Here," he shouted over the roar of battle.

Lark knelt in the dirt, her arms spread wide. A smaller shield coalesced around them in a tight circle. Ereni and Kayda stood watch, tossing balls of fire and air over the shoulder-high dirt wall to push back the scourge that sought to intrude inside their bubble of protection.

Despite that, many rammed into the shield, displacing earth at a sickening pace. He didn't have much time.

Lark met his gaze, her hands still in motion, flinging dirt all around. "Good luck."

Conall nodded and knelt beside Shadow, wrapping an arm around his back. *"You ready for this, brother?"* he asked as he tugged the waterskin from his belt.

"Always, little brother."

Conall dumped the water into his palm and closed his eyes. Then he did something he'd only done once before. He called on all the elements in sync.

Warring sensations buffeted him. A cold chill crept up his spine. The air around him moistened and crackled with static. The ground below trembled and rattled his teeth.

The book told the story of a young mage who could transport below the earth. Her earth talent was so strong she could pass through layers of rock and dirt into the tunnels deep down below.

But the story had been a cautionary tale. The mage only managed the feat a handful of times before disappearing. A few days later, her waterlogged corpse was discovered floating in a deep well.

Would he be able to do what that mage had failed to accomplish? It was time to find out.

Conall clutched Shadow tightly. His eyes shot open. He met Ereni's blue stare one last time before the ground below opened up and the earth swallowed them.

Chapter 29

Kayda gulped. The ground opened up like an angry mouth, splitting apart beneath Conall and Shadow and sucking them down. An instant later it snapped back, reforming in their wake and leaving only a mound of loose soil as evidence of their disappearance.

It all happened so fast, if she'd blinked, she'd have surely missed it.

Please let them be all right.

Kayda shook off the thought and focused on the battle. She had to trust Conall to take care of his part of the plan on his own.

Lark's earthen shield was close to crumbling. Once it fell, there would be nothing holding back the vicious beasts. They'd been the first to reach this far inland, but while they'd been shielded, many warriors and mages had caught up. The scourge flowed around them all in a massive wave of fur and destruction.

Kayda gritted her teeth and called on her talent. The chill spread through her veins, cooling her even as flames licked her skin. When the shield fell, she was ready.

Fire flew furiously. She would make them pay for what they'd done.

Destroying her country. Sacking her city. Killing her king.

In the back of her mind, she knew if what Conall saw proved true, they were not the true villain. But it didn't stop her from unleashing her fury upon the beasts. It was as if every shred of rage she'd shoved down burst loose and flowed through her hands.

Kayda smiled, reveling in the destruction. Burnt hair and flesh stung her nostrils and the coppery tang of blood flooded the air as she watched the sea of beady eyes turn into a molten river of ash and flame.

The warriors from the boats spread around her. To her left, a small group of Sul fought in a ring, pole knives flashing furiously. Two archers remained protected in the center, shooting arrows above the warrior's shoulders wherever the scourge sought to pounce on the fighters unawares.

To her right, Clan Chief Aundrea and his son bowled through the crowd. Taul's axe and Aundrea's great two-handed sword hammered into the mass and sprayed blood in all directions, carving through the mound of beasts like they were shoveling snow.

Beside her, Lark and Ereni fought. Blasts of air and earth pummeled the scourge, unleashing death on all sides. Together, they pushed forward, gaining ground slowly until they mounted a small hill.

At this slight elevation, Kayda gasped and spun in a slow circle. The devastation spread out on all sides. From within the crowd, it was easy to lose track of just how many beasts swarmed the land. They carpeted the earth, so much that it was hard to glimpse any dirt beneath all the fur and teeth. It was truly mind-boggling.

Yet, still more came. They spilled out of tiny holes, popping up and jumping upon unsuspecting warriors. Even more poured out of a few larger holes, set within small hills like the one she stood on.

"Hey," Kayda yelled to Lark, sending a blast of fire ahead. "Can you block a few of those?"

Lark glanced at one of the hillside holes just as her falcon swooped down and snatched a scourge out of the air mid-leap. The crack of its neck snapping echoed in Kayda's ears.

Lark grinned. "Yeah, good plan."

Kayda led the way down the far side of the hill they'd mounted. Sure enough, there was a hole just like others she'd seen, cut into the very bottom of the mound. It was small enough a human would need to crouch down and shimmy through, but big enough to let a half dozen scourge out at a time.

"Go for it," Ereni shouted to Lark as she thumped to the ground beside her, hurling a blast of air that sent dozens of scourge scrambling backward. "We'll cover you."

Lark knelt down, filling her hands with charred soil. A heartbeat later, the thrumming in the ground intensified so much Kayda's feet buzzed in her boots. Then the mouth of the hole collapsed, crushing dozens of *ichneumons* and sealing the hole.

Kayda whooped. "That ought to slow them down."

With the multitude of tiny holes in the ground, caving in the large holes wouldn't stop the scourge completely, but maybe if they filled enough of them, it would turn the tide. It might give the fighters a chance to cull the massive herd while Conall sought the Unseen.

"C'mon," Kayda yelled, "Over here." She blasted fire in a wide arc, heading for the closest hillside.

They burst through the scourge, felling them mercilessly. Twice more, they stopped and collapsed a hole, each time heading further inland until they were so far from the main mass of fighters the sound of battle faded from an overwhelming din to a mere clatter in the distance.

The third hole they approached was set in a hillside much larger than the rest. The entrance rested on the hill's far side, and when they thumped down to the ground before it, the hill blocked their view of the ocean and most of the fighting.

It sent a shiver up Kayda's spine the moment she set her gaze inside the yawning hole. This one was large enough she would only need to duck her head to enter, instead of crawl.

A massive crowd of scourge lay in wait at the tunnel mouth. Unlike the rest, these weren't racing away, heading for them or to the larger battle beyond. These sat still, teeth bared, almost as if they'd been stationed there, guarding something within.

The eerie feeling that had first struck her only intensified as she set fire to the beasts and they squealed where they stood, unmoving even as they roasted to death.

Lark sank her hands into the earth, and the ground rumbled in response. But though the earth shook harder than ever, and flecks of dirt flew, joining the ever-increasing misting of white flurries, the hole refused to collapse.

Lark frowned, staring into the dark cave mouth. "I don't know why it's not working."

Kayda whipped around, pausing the fire flowing from her hands long enough to quirk a brow at the tunnel entrance, still standing stubbornly. "Try ag—"

"Funny finding you here, sister," called a voice from within.

Kayda gasped, her hand flying to her chest. It couldn't be. Surely not.

She shook her head, squinting into the dark. That voice. She would know it anywhere. Her heart skipped a beat.

"Tarquin?"

No, he was dead. She'd watched him die months ago, in the first battle here in the Abandoned Lands. He and his entire contingent of guards had been overwhelmed, swarmed by hundreds of the scourge. Eaten alive.

But even as she convinced herself otherwise, he strode out of the cave mouth, ducking his head until he halted before her and straightened to his full height.

Kayda's jaw dropped.

"No." She shook her head again, flicking it so strongly her braids whipped against her cheek.

How was this possible? She'd watched him die.

One of his blond brows arched, his voice dripping with malice. "Aren't you happy to see me, sister? Why am I not surprised?"

Beside her, Ereni stiffened at the sight of him. She turned from the crowd of scourge at their backs and blasted a wave of wind directly at him. The wind flew around him so strongly that just being in its periphery, Kayda nearly stumbled. But Tarquin only strolled on, his dark blond hair flickering, but his body unmoved.

Kayda's stomach plummeted.

Tarquin spared Ereni a glance and sneered. "Deal with them, will you?" He called back over his shoulder. "I've need of a private word with my little sister." His smile curved up as he lifted his hands.

Kayda caught a single glimpse of shadowy forms emerging behind him before the remaining scourge suddenly became unglued and burst into motion. They crowded around them and stacked atop each other, forming a wall of bodies much like the circular shield Lark had crafted out of earth.

Kayda stared, stunned.

Tarquin smirked.

"What? How?" Kayda backed up, coming close to ramming into the wall of scourge.

"What's the matter, Kayda? You look a little surprised."

That was an understatement if there ever was one. Kayda stared wide-eyed at the wall of scourge caging her. Her stomach churned uneasily. "Why are these vermin listening to you, Tarquin?"

From somewhere outside, male voices rang out, filled with violence, but their words slid through her ears, unheard. She could only stare at her half-brother. He looked exactly the same. Tall and strong. Still wearing that haughty smirk.

"I only took what I deserve."

"What you deserve?"

He sneered at her. "I will be the new king of these lands. Not just our country—all of them. A king for a new age."

"What are you talking about? The scourge will destroy us all." Despite herself, she couldn't stop a pleading tone from infecting her voice.

"Oh, but that is only the first step. After Father's had his fill, it will all be mine."

"Father is dead. And he never wanted—"

Tarquin's lips curled back. "Not that drunken fool. My true father."

Kayda gasped. No. Even Tarquin couldn't be that stupid. Could he?

"You allied yourself with the Unseen?" But even as the question spilled out of her lips, she knew it was true. That's why the scourge listened to him. And why he'd survived the attack that destroyed his men. "No." She shook her head vehemently. "How could you?"

Tarquin glared at her. "How could I? Easily." He stabbed a finger at his chest. "It should've been me. I should've been the special one. Not you. I was only righting a wrong."

Kayda drew back at the cruel glint in his eye. "But what the Unseen is doing is wrong. After he's finished, there'll be nothing left. You'll rule over a land of ghosts and bones. Can't you see that?"

Tarquin scoffed, waving a hand dismissively. "We're merely wiping the slate. Washing away the filth that inhabits this realm and starting anew. We're the cleansing fire that will render this world to ash and allow something stronger and better to rise from the ashes."

Kayda wobbled on her feet. "That's insane. All those people..."

Tarquin rolled his eyes. "There will be others. New rules. A society built in whatever way I see fit. No savages to the north and south to defy me. It will be a paradise."

How could he be so cruel? Willing to dispose of people like they were refuse tossed in a slop bucket.

Kayda planted her feet and squared her shoulders. "I won't let you."

Tarquin turned to stare at her full on, and he laughed. "You think you can stop me? Go ahead and try," he forced out between maddened chuckles.

Kayda raised her hand, her fingers twitching. "Please, Tarquin. I don't want to kill you. It's not too late to put an end to this. You can join us and defeat the Unseen."

He stopped laughing. "No." He stared pointedly at her hand.

Kayda gulped. Tarquin had seen her blast fire from her hands before. He knew what she could do.

"Go ahead, sister. Destroy me like you've always wanted to." He took a step closer. "Or are you too stupid and weak? I'll never stop. And do you know why? Because I don't want to live in a world where fate would choose an ugly, conniving little bitch like yo—"

Fire flew from her hands, cutting off his cruel words. Tarquin's clothes caught first, and his golden hair. Then his skin sizzled.

Kayda gagged but kept the flames flowing until he fell to a knee in front of her, his entire face blackened, and his clothing reduced to crumbling ash.

Then she backed away, a hand at her mouth, struggling not to vomit.

She expected him to fall fully after that. To slump face-first in the dirt and remain unmoving. But after only an instant, he started pushing up off the ground.

Kayda gasped again, her gaze glued to him as he rose. The damage her fire wrought stood out starkly. His flesh was black and red, covered in massive blisters.

But right before her eyes, Tarquin's skin began to heal itself. The blisters faded and disappeared. The redness receded, his skin returning to a pale, creamy white. His hair grew back, covering his head so quickly it was hard to remember it had just been burned to a crisp a moment ago.

When he rose to his full height and brushed the blackened remains of his charred clothing off his body, he was almost good as new, only a few tiny red marks and blisters remaining.

Tarquin strode to the piled scourge, seemingly unconcerned with his nakedness even though his breath clouded in the cold air and snowflakes landed on his shoulders. He grabbed one of the beasts by the throat and strangled it. The scourge made no move to defend itself, just whimpered pitifully until Tarquin snapped its neck.

Kayda's eyes bulged as the last of the redness and blisters faded away on Tarquin's skin.

"Blazes," she said. "What have you become?"

Chapter 30

Conall fought not to panic as darkness closed around him. The lamp dangling from his chest ensured it wasn't as complete as it could be. Even still, it was hard to remain calm as the earth dragged him down.

"Are you all right?" he asked Shadow, the comforting feel of his fur clutched tightly under his arm.

"Yes, I'm fine, little brother."

Conall sighed. That was good. Besides being uncertain this would even work, he'd also been unsure whether he could bring anyone with him. He'd convinced the others to stay above ground, but Shadow had insisted on coming. With the earth surrounding him like a grave, he was grateful for his bondmate's insistence.

They sank slowly through the earth. Conall's heart thrummed faster than a scared hare in flight. He'd expected to flash under, transported from one spot to the other in an eye blink like he'd done in the strange waking dream he'd experienced while the Palisade fell. But this was a whole different story. He fought through the descent, pushing aside the earth below while keeping a much smaller version of the shield Lark had constructed above intact around him and Shadow. It was slow going and exhausting, but it was working.

Long moments passed with nothing happening except for that slow sink. The air in their little shielded bubble grew stale, the same way it had when he'd been trapped below the snow with Quent. Conall forced himself to remain calm, praying they'd find a tunnel or cave, something to refresh their air supply before they passed out.

The surrounding ground, which had started out almost as chilled as the winter air on the surface, slowly warmed. He remembered the dream. The heat that had seeped off that red-lit tunnel where he'd first spoken to the Unseen. They must be getting closer.

Shadow stiffened at the same moment Conall gasped. The slow but steady movement changed to a sudden plummet and a shocking splash. Water flooded up from below, soaking the bottom of their shield of dirt and seeping into Conall's trousers.

"Don't worry, brother." Conall took a deep breath and pulled gratefully at the fresh air, ensuring their protective sphere didn't become waterlogged. But as the water trickled out to rejoin whatever underwater stream or lake it came from, Conall spotted a new problem. They'd stopped sinking. The ball of dirt and air was floating.

He banished a small section of dirt above his head and peered out, pulling at the fire in the lamp and sending four fireballs flying out the hole and across the ceiling. His eyes widened. It was definitely a lake. A huge one from the looks of it. He spun sideways and spotted water stretched out in every direction. The cave's roof hovered over his head, just out of reach, making it even harder to make out how big the chamber was or where it ended.

Shadow peered over his shoulder. *"What now?"*

Conall gulped. *"I'm not sure. Give me a moment to think."*

He wasn't having much trouble keeping them afloat. Granted, it required constant concentration and a steady stream of magic, but he could see them floating long enough to reach shore. The question was, how long would it take? How much energy would he be forced to spend in the process? How many people would be killed by the scourge while he and Shadow sailed?

Would it even be enough? He closed his eyes, concentrating on that vile wrongness. The further down they traveled, the feeling had steadily increased, but still couldn't match level he remembered from his dream. His instincts howled, demanding he listen.

The second option, then.

"We're going down."

Shadow cocked his head. *"Is that wise? What will we do for air? Ereni—"*

"I know. Let's just hope it's not deep." Conall petted him reassuringly.

Shadow nodded. *"I trust you."*

Conall took another deep breath, gripping Shadow even tighter. Then he banished the earth surrounding them, and let the water take them.

He kept a bubble of air locked around their heads, lifting the lamp close to his face. Wouldn't do to lose the light now that they sank into the black water below. Conall shivered as the water soaked his clothing. But though their legs and torsos quickly submerged, the bubble of air kept them close to the surface.

Conall kicked his legs. All the hope he'd held that the water would be shallow evaporated as his toes met no resistance. There was no way to tell how deep this water went. But that changed nothing. They had to keep going.

Using his talent, he forced the water to part below them, letting them sink further even with the air bubble around their heads seeking to buoy them. But as they dropped away from the surface—away from the air—a wave of exhaustion slammed into him.

Somehow he'd been able to maintain the bubble of air with the dirt wrapped around them, but underwater, it was a different story. The bubble slowly shrank with each breath they drew, forcing him to summon more out of thin air—or more like thin water. The exhaustion quickly compounded, making him dizzy.

How much longer until he passed out, and they drowned? Or how much of his life would this cost him? Ereni had lost months when she'd summoned a handful of bubbles to save herself and Lark. If this water was much deeper, he might start losing years.

Before the thought could make his stomach plummet as surely as he and Shadow sank through the water, Conall's feet touched bottom. He immediately pulled at the dirt and formed a shield, sinking back down into the earth. Slowly he forced the water out, watching in the lamplight as it trickled into the dirt and rock. The bubble of air stabilized, and the worst of his exhaustion lifted.

"Do I look older, brother?" Conall's voice wobbled in his mind and his shoulders stiffened as Shadow's golden eyes shifted across his face.

"No, you look the same."

Conall relaxed slightly, some of the tension lifting. *"Good, I'm glad that water wasn't deep—"*

His thought ended in a gasp as their shield of earth plummeted again. This time, the bottom wasn't met with a wet splash, but with a jarring thud. The earthen shield absorbed the worst of the blow, but Conall's legs still smarted from the collision.

He banished a section of the shield, lifting the lamp. They were in a tunnel. One with a red glow seeping through the air, along with a moist heat.

"I think we're here." Conall let the shield fall completely and stood on wobbly legs. The ceiling was too low for him to rise to his full height, but at least there was air and no water. He tugged his soaked clothes and set the lamp down so he could quickly shuck off his boots and spill out the water filling them.

Shadow shook out his fur, then shifted to stare down the long tube of dirt where the red light emanated. *"You sure this is it?"*

Conall shoved his feet back into his wet boots as that slithering wrongness crept across his skin, stronger than ever. *"Yeah, I'm sure. Let's kill this bastard."*

He took a step toward the light.

Chapter 31

Lark's stomach dropped as a wall of scourge formed around Kayda, blocking her and the smirking blond man from view. She and Ereni fought on, desperately flinging magic at an unending stream of vicious beasts throwing themselves at them from all sides.

Was that really the prince—back from the dead?

Whatever the answer, it didn't matter. She couldn't just let the bastard cut Kayda off from the rest of the battle. He could be doing anything to her in there.

She pulled at the earth, readying an enormous blast that would hopefully destroy the wall of vermin shielding the pair.

"Lark, look out!" Muse chirped, full of alarm.

The same instant, a deep voice spilled out into the night, and a bevy of shadowed forms appeared in the cave mouth, slinking out behind the wall of scourge. "Lady Death, we meet again."

A man with scarred arms was the first to emerge, an evil sneer twisting his lips. At least a dozen men joined him, all faces she recognized. The same men that stared at her with overt lust while she'd been trapped in that prison cell were here to greet her, clutching weapons in their fists, their faces full of amusement and rage.

Lark's stomach dropped. Blazes. She blasted the earth meant for the scourge in his direction. The man ducked, his reflexes somehow lightning fast, and the dirt pounded into the cave wall behind him.

"Bet you're wondering how we got here. Bet you thought we'd die in the bog or be eaten alive by the scourge."

Lark scrambled for a reply, tongue-tied in her shock, even as her hands went right back to moving, flinging a dart at a beast that leaped for her chest. He was right. She'd been sure she'd never see those men again.

"No one cares, Reg," Ereni shouted. She jumped up beside Lark while hurling a blast of air toward the men and a second behind her at the scourge. "Lay down your weapons or prepare to die."

The man's brows shot up as Ereni named him. "You witches are full of surprises, aren't you?" But he shook off his surprise and strode forward, a lecherous glint in his eyes as he scanned them. They both wore close-fitted cloaks and trousers, much more suited for battle than the normal skirts and dresses Lark was used to, but Reg's gaze lit on their simple attire like a starving man at a feast.

Lark spared a glance behind him and spotted a similar hunger on all the men's faces. It made her stomach knot like crazy, especially since none of them had moved to fight them. At least not yet.

A second man spoke up. "Bet if we drag them inside, we can have a little fun before the rest of the fighting reaches us."

"Not going to slit our throats?" Ereni shot back.

Lark's stomach dropped. Why was she goading them? Not that she could blame her. The thought of being dragged back into the caves with those men was worse than death.

Reg stilled in his tracks, staring at Ereni strangely. "She's right. These witches need to die." He growled, raising his spear and stabbing right for Ereni's chest.

Ereni dodged, blasting a wall of air at Reg and sending him sprawling backward on his ass.

But though Reg fell, a trio jumped at her next. Ereni spun sideways, barely staying out of reach of their blades and staves before pushing them back with another blast of air.

Lark's heart hammered as she fought by her side, sending darts of dirt in every direction. Muse swooped down and snatched a scourge who came close to landing on her back in the chaos. She snapped its neck.

Lark's breath came hard and fast. It was too much. The three of them against more than a dozen armed men and hundreds of ravenous beasts. They wouldn't be able to hold them off forever. But if they could just hold out until the rest of the fighting reached them, then maybe it would be enough.

She'd left her friends with explicit instructions to remain in the back of the lines. She'd even made Tiora and Dausius promise to stay close to Mika. Mika, Vespen, and a handful of other healers volunteered to care for the many injuries their force would be sure to receive. Lark knew Aren and the twins could handle themselves in a fight, but Ti and

Daus—not so much. She'd pleaded with them all to stay back. To stay safe. She hoped they'd listened.

But her friends weren't the only ones out there. The Doln warriors and Sul had been close on their tails not long ago. If she and Ereni could hold out a little longer, maybe they would catch up, and they might actually have a chance.

Even as hope spooled around her heart, she tripped, slamming hard to the rocky ground. A snarl filled her ears, and she jerked her wide-eyed gaze sideways, spotting a black and silver flash speeding straight for her throat.

The beast was impaled before it could reach her, the blade of a stave catching it in the ribs. A squeal of pain replaced the snarl an instant before the blade twisted viciously and retracted, flicking a cascade of hot blood across her face.

Lark turned, meeting the cruel stare of the prisoner who'd just saved her. But it was clear he hadn't done it for her benefit when he flipped his weapon around, aiming the blunt end for her forehead.

She could see it in his eyes. He would knock her unconscious and drag her off into the cave. Into the dark.

Lark dug her fingers into the rocky soil beneath her. The man drew his arms back, readying to thump the stave into her skull. Then a golden flash of feathers and fury shot into his face, wicked talons carving up his skin and tearing at his eyes.

The man shrieked, blood pouring down his neck. He dropped his stave and screamed, his hands flying toward his face, desperate to knock Muse loose.

Lark scrambled to her feet while they grappled. *"I'm up, fly,"* she screamed in her mind.

Muse unlatched her claws from the man's face, but not before he shot out his fist and slammed her into the cave wall.

"Muse, no!" Lark barreled between them and flung dirt at the man's bleeding face, using her talent to make sure it caught him in the eyes. He staggered back, scrubbing his face and yowling.

But one man down didn't mean she was safe. A pair of muscled brutes jumped up to take his place, one with a cudgel and the other a short sword. Lark dodged a blow from the sword but was too slow to avoid the cudgel. It slammed into her stomach in an explosion of pain, forcing the air from her lungs.

"I'm up." Muse screeched as she lifted off the ground. She flew right for the man holding the cudgel, momentarily blinding him and giving Lark the chance to catch her breath and scurry backward.

The sword came flying at her face again, but she speared a dart of dirt into the man's stomach before his swing landed, making his aim go wild. She sprinted away from the pair, scattering dirt behind her in a cloud, praying it would blind the men so she could regroup.

She almost ran into Ereni, who held a man immobile with her air talent, her fist outstretched. She calmly walked to his side and slashed his throat with her hunting knife. Blood spattered the ground and spurted into the air. Then Ereni dropped her fist and let the man's dead weight crumple to the ground.

Blazes, she was fierce. Lark made a mental note never to get on her bad side.

"C'mon." Ereni mounted the hillside, flinging a blast of air ahead of her. "Climb to the high ground."

Though Lark sent a wary glance back at the cave mouth—back to Kayda—still hidden behind the shield of scourge, she followed. Soon they made it to the top of the small hill, and Lark gasped as she caught a glimpse of the larger battle beyond their small clash.

Though the rest of their forces had only scourge to contend with, they weren't faring any better. If anything, they were worse. Blood soaked the ground, and far too many bodies lay in a tangle of limbs on the battlefield. Many more than their few healers could save.

The number of scourge had not lessened in the slightest, even after they'd plugged the few cave entrances. They swarmed across the land, overwhelming the tiny pockets of fighters with their immense numbers.

As she watched, a circle of Sul warriors fell, and the scourge piled on them so quickly they were lost to her view in the blink of an eye.

Lark's stomach churned as she swiveled around, forcing her gaze away from the melee behind them. From the cave mouth, a blast of fire roared, the heat so strong, a warm gust of air blew across Lark's face.

But then a handful of men emerged, scrubbing dirt from their faces and mounting the hillside.

The same villain who'd tried to slam her head with a stave clambered up the hillside. Lark locked stares with him, and her jaw dropped. His face, which just moments ago had been torn to shreds from Muse's talons, appeared to have partially healed already.

That shouldn't be possible. Did the men have a healer of their own?

The man sent her an evil grin, then stomped viciously on a scourge, grinding his boot into its back. The instant the vermin's squeals died, the rest of the gouges on the prisoner's face disappeared.

Lark bit back a gasp. What the blazes?

Ereni blew the men backward, and the air crackled from the force of her talent. But her brow was wet and her breathing erratic. Lark's own body slumped with exhaustion, her sore stomach heaving as she sent a hail of dirt pummeling into the scourge that sprang up at them.

How long could they last out here? How could they hope to defeat these men who had some mysterious way of healing themselves? She had no idea, but she wasn't about to stop trying.

Conall. Brother, you need to hurry.

Chapter 32

Kayda stared bewildered at Tarquin's healing body. How was it possible? She'd never seen anything like it.

Tarquin flicked a hand at the scourge, a sly smirk on his lips. The beasts moved in unison, the circle around them morphing into a wide wall that blocked the cave mouth.

Kayda gaped, watching them reform without him even speaking a word. How did he get them to listen? Did his pact with the Unseen grant him the power to control the beasts, too? It was all so strange. She was trapped, cut off from the battle, stuck with her brother, who'd become indestructible somehow.

Tarquin strolled over to a fallen man whose throat had been slit. Blood pooled around his neck and chest, soaking his dirty tunic.

"What's happening, Tarquin? I don't understand."

He knelt beside the man and tugged off his boots and his trousers, then quickly dressed in the fallen man's clothes, covering his nakedness. "Well, sister, I know you've always had a sick little thing for me, but I'd rather not fight like this."

Kayda shot him a disgusted look. "Don't even... That's revolting and not at all what I mean. How are you still standing?"

"That's all you have to say after trying to scorch me to death?" He straightened, adopting a mocking tone. "How are you still standing?" He bent at the waist and picked up the fallen man's discarded weapon—a short sword. "Isn't it obvious? I beat you at your own game. I was cheated out of the magic I deserved, so I found my own. And now, I'm going to enjoy watching you die."

Kayda backed away warily, forming a fireball on her outstretched hand. "Stay back, or I'll—"

"You'll what? Burn my clothes off again? Haven't you seen the futility in that? You spent your whole life with your nose in those books, yet you're still dumb as a rock."

Kayda trembled. He was right. He should be dead now, burnt to a crisp like anyone else would be after being struck by so much fire. But he wasn't.

How could she hope to defeat him when he would just heal himself?

Tarquin advanced, an evil grin on his face. He lifted the sword over his shoulder, pacing slowly toward her.

"Kayda, I'm almost there. Hold on."

Kayda stifled a gasp as Dru's voice reverberated in her mind. Yes! Dru would help her out of this mess.

"I'm stuck behind a wall of scourge in a cave mouth. Hurry."

She dodged a swing from Tarquin's sword, ducking under the blow and scurrying to the opposite cave wall.

"Where? I don't see you?" Dru replied.

Kayda blasted the fire on her hands at the wall of scourge. *"Look for the flames."*

Tarquin dove for her again. Kayda cut off the stream of fire and leaped away, but not before the blade caught the string holding the oil lamp around her neck. The lamp shattered on the floor. The oil ignited so quickly she barely jumped away before the flames engulfed her trousers.

Blazes. She didn't have much time before her source disappeared. She blasted another wave of flames at the scourge blocking the cave entrance. The reek of charred hair and flesh wafted through the air. Though many of them died, the beasts remained stacked, only squealing as the flames roasted them.

Tarquin didn't give her long to focus. He charged at her, his blade swinging straight at her neck.

Kayda dodged again, blasting a fireball at his face.

Tarquin grimaced as it connected, but paid his burning flesh no mind. Kayda's jaw dropped as his skin immediately began reforming before her eyes.

Then he flicked his hand, and the scourge shuffled around them, encircling them in a tight ring.

Kayda gulped. There was barely any room to dodge now.

Tarquin sneered down at her, his blackened, blistered skin already partially healed. He snatched another scourge off the pile and snapped its neck casually. Then he stomped out the flames lingering on the cave floor.

"Goodbye, Kayda." He lifted his blade, the metal glinting dangerously.

Fire blasted from the sky. A black shadow hovered just beyond the scourge. Druturion!

Kayda called forth her talent again, using Dru's flames as her source. Her blood ignited with liquid ice, chilling her body even as flames surrounded her. The scourge burst into flame from Dru, but Kayda aimed all her fire at Tarquin. She screamed, pelting him so intensely he staggered backward and dropped his blade.

After a moment, she relented and shoved her way through the scourges' burned carcasses, leaving her brother in a heap of ash and bloody blisters.

"Dru, you're back." She raced forward as he landed, a huge smile on her face, and clutched his neck.

"I am. Quick, hop on. We've got more vermin to kill."

Kayda vaulted atop his back. *"I hate to break it to you, but he's not dead, Dru."*

Even as the words filled her mind, Tarquin staggered to his feet behind them. The scourge he'd used as his puppets lay in waste, but somehow, he was healing himself yet again.

"Is that your brother? I thought he died months ago."

"Me, too. He's made some vile pact with the Unseen. No matter what I do, he won't die."

"We'll see about that."

Dru whipped around to face him and spewed fire in a molten stream. Tarquin dropped to his knees, his skin peeling and bubbling from the heat.

Kayda watched his smoldering body until more scourge diverted her attention, leaping at them from the outside of the cave. She blasted them back, but more kept coming, attracted to Dru like insects to a flame.

"C'mon, Dru. We have to fly. There's too many."

Dru cut off the stream of flame and burst into the sky. They left Tarquin in a pile of blackened flesh. But Kayda didn't hold out much hope that would be the end of it.

Dru flew low to the ground, and Kayda concentrated on destroying the scourge. Now that she was free from the cave, she could see the battle was not going as well as she'd hoped. Thousands of scourge swarmed up from the ground, and the fighters and mages struggled against the massive numbers.

Kayda's heart lifted as she spotted a white dragon barreling toward the coast. *"Bela's back."*

Belstasia dove, shooting blasts of ice at the scourge attacking the fighters near the coast. Their forces cheered, and it seemed like everyone fought with renewed strength. Surely now, with two dragons on their side, the tide would turn. Maybe they could actually win this fight.

Atop the hill, she spotted Lark and Ereni fighting back-to-back, sending wave upon wave of dirt and wind at armed men and countless scourge.

"Let's help those women on the hill."

Dru banked toward them, opening his mouth and spilling fire down at the ground. Kayda threw out her hand, adding her flames. Soon, they rendered the scourge to ash and set the men on fire.

Lark and Ereni whooped with delight. But Kayda gulped as one man brushed the flames off his body and rose off the ground. Then another.

"They're getting up, too?" Dru circled back, sending more flames at the men.

Blazes. Those men were just like Tarquin—somehow able to heal from her magic. How would they ever defeat them?

A thought struck her, and her stomach fluttered. *"Wait, there was a corpse on the ground in the cave that had his throat slit... If a mortal wound to the neck worked, then maybe one to the heart or brain would as well."* Kayda scanned the ground, spotting a few more corpses nearby that weren't moving. It must be true. They just needed to kill them quickly and get up close. *"Drop me back on the ground. You scorch the bastards from above, and I'll stab them."*

"All right. I'll stay close so you can use my flames as your source."

Dru dropped her next to one of the corpses, and Kayda snatched his discarded stave off the ground. She headed straight for the closest man as he skewered a scourge on the end of his blade, and the burnt skin on his face and arms healed.

He faced her with a smirk, but Dru wiped it off his lips the next instant, catching him in a blast of flame. Kayda strode up to the man as he dropped to the ground and shoved the stave into his heart.

She tugged the stave free and held her breath, half-expecting the man to climb back to his feet. But he stayed down. *"It works."* Kayda grinned. *"C'mon. Let's kill them all."*

Chapter 33

Crouching, Conall shuffled further down the narrow tunnel.

"How much farther, do you think?" Shadow's fur bristled. *"That awful feeling keeps getting worse. I'm not sure if I can bear it much longer."*

Conall shuddered. *"I don't know. I can feel it, too, but I still can't hear him."* That repulsive, crawling itch had returned with a vengeance.

"I wonder why the Unseen's only spoken to you, little brother? Even when it infected your mind at the fire moat, I still could not hear it, though our thoughts are connected."

Conall shook his head, ducking beneath a dripping stalactite. *"I don't know. But maybe we can use that to our advantage. If he can't sense you the way he can me, maybe he'll assume I've come alone if we don't speak."*

"Good plan, little brother. We must think of a signal. When you give it, I will stay silent."

Conall pondered that for a moment and settled for a double tap on his thigh. *"How's that?"*

Shadow inclined his head. *"I will watch for that movement."*

Conall sent him a half smile and crept forward. The eerie red glow increased with every step, as did the heat. Sweat slid down his back beneath his tunic, and his trousers stuck to his skin, the humidity making them slow to dry even with the heat baking him. He'd long ago shucked off his sodden cloak after stuffing all his supplies in his belt pouches.

In a few spots, holes in the walls and floor revealed a molten river of glowing, bubbling lava somewhere below.

Conall's eyes widened as he skirted the edge of a wide hole. The heat rose, crackling against his cheeks. *"Careful."*

Shadow sidestepped the hole deftly, though his tail hung low between his legs.

The tunnel ahead split, and Conall's stomach roiled as he stopped before the fork.

"Which way?" Shadow tilted his head, his golden eyes flicking between the two tunnels, each practically identical.

Conall rubbed his chin, then shifted his touch to his aching neck and shoulders. He couldn't just stand here forever, crouched and indecisive. But the wrong choice would cost them time and energy. Force them to backtrack and possibly lead to hundreds more killed on the surface.

Then the distant snarl of the scourge echoed down one of the paths, and he shuffled toward it. *"Keep a wary eye out, brother. Sounds like we're heading for a fight."*

He hoped he'd chosen right, and the presence of the scourge meant their leader was nearby, but only time would tell.

He pulled at the flame in the lamp dangling against his neck and readied a fireball as the beast's skittering claws and screeching grew louder. The chill of fire magic spread through his veins, and he shivered, though he welcomed the icy bite if only for a brief reprieve from the stifling heat all around.

He didn't have long to revel in the sensation. They rounded a bend and entered a wide, rocky chamber. But though the ceiling here was finally tall enough for him to straighten to his full height, there was a big problem.

Dozens of scourge blocked the path. Conall sent out wave after wave of flame. The answering shrieks of the vermin rent the air.

A few dodged the flames, leaping sideways and bouncing across the walls. A pair came at him, snarling, hate spewing from their beady black eyes. He gasped, certain they would leap for his neck and tear him to shreds before he could react, but both of the beasts ignored him and leaped straight for Shadow behind him.

Blazes. That was worse than if they'd come for him. Conall roared, turning from the huge crowd of scourge he'd already scorched.

Shadow caught the first beast mid leap, snapping its neck with his powerful jaws. But the second beast landed atop his back, and its claws sank deep into his hide, drawing blood.

Conall blasted fire balls at two more who leaped for his bondmate. His brow raised as they both ignored him once again, even though he was closer than Shadow.

Why were they not attacking him? It made no sense.

He shoved the thought aside and swung back to Shadow, where he grappled with the last scourge. The vile beast's jaw clamped down between Shadow's shoulder blades, holding tight even while he bucked and rolled, attempting to dislodge the beast.

"Stay still, brother," Conall shouted in his mind.

Shadow complied instantly, and Conall dumped a handful of water from his waterskin into his palm. Then he sent a globe of water to Shadow's back, fully submerging the scourge.

As the water surrounded the creature, it finally opened its wicked jaws and unlatched from Shadow's back. As soon as his bondmate ducked away, Conall sent the water and the scourge sailing into a hole.

The beast descended into the heated glow, the water sizzling as it evaporated.

Conall sucked in a deep breath and took a step toward Shadow. *"Are you all right, bro—"*

Conall staggered. His foot slipped in a puddle of blood, and he fell, smacking hard into the rocky cave floor. Pain, sudden and sharp, exploded behind his eyes, and the world twirled. Blearily, he lifted a hand to the back of his head and warm wetness coated his fingers.

Blazes. *This can't be good.*

Darkness reigned.

Chapter 34

The spearhead shoved into the charred man's chest. Kayda grunted as she twisted, then pulled out the spear with a wet *thunk*. She raced up the hillside to Lark and Ereni's side.

"Magic alone doesn't work," she yelled, slamming a scourge out of her path, which Druturion kindly roasted from his spot in the sky. "They need a mortal wound."

Lark's eyes widened, and Ereni nodded. Behind them, Kayda spotted more of their fighters closing in on their position. Belstasia's bolts of ice were turning the tide. But it wasn't time to celebrate. Not even close.

"Sister," a voice bellowed below. "Where are you?"

Even dragon fire had not been enough to kill him. A jolt of panic lanced her chest until she remembered the spear in her hands. It was time to end this.

Kayda spared a glance for Ereni and Lark. Lark sent darts of dirt shooting into a crowd of scourge. Four fell with spikes sticking out of their necks and chests. Even more flew off course, only to jolt back up to their feet and leap toward the pair again.

Ereni let one man get uncomfortably close. He raised a cudgel over his head, a menacing cry tearing out of his throat. Before he connected, Ereni's hand shot out. She held him immobile with what looked like nothing, but Kayda suspected from the crackle of static on her skin, it was a cage of air. Then Ereni strolled up to his side, lifted a blade off her waist, and stabbed the side of his neck. Blood gushed out, spurting like a red geyser.

"Sister!" Tarquin shouted again.

Well, it appeared that Lark and Ereni had things handled here. Especially now that several of their fighters closed in on the hillside. She smiled, spotting Jayan hovering close to a white-haired woman spewing out flames—Izora.

Kayda raced down the hillside, heading for the cave mouth. *"C'mon, Dru."*

Druturion followed, spreading flame around her path in all directions to keep the scourge at bay. Kayda lifted her hand, banishing the burning grass before her to clear a path through the fire. Her boots kicked up ash, and specks floated to her face, joining the cold snowflakes stinging her cheeks.

The snow fell in earnest, sizzling as it struck the fire and sticking to the grass everywhere else. The scourge's pelts were dusted with white, but the weather didn't slow their ferocity in the least.

Soon, their forces would begin to struggle, if they weren't already. The snow made everything slicker, and poor footing during battle could easily become a death sentence. The Sul, in particular, had never battled in these conditions. Kayda's heart ached, picturing Jayan and Lazar—all the sandborn who'd answered her call. Had she led them to their ends?

Tarquin's still healing face appeared before her, and she forced her worries aside. She could protect the Sul after she put her brother down—for good this time.

Tarquin smirked at her, then opened his mouth.

"Now, Dru."

The awful words he'd no doubt been about to spew were swallowed by a scream of pain. Fire cascaded around Tarquin once again. He shielded his face with his arms, and the skin peeled back, giving Kayda a glimpse of the bloody bone beneath.

Kayda marched up to him as Dru cut off the river of flame. She gritted her teeth and thrust the spear into his chest. She waited for the wave of remorse to wash over her, but nothing came. Even as she pulled the spear free, and his charred body crumbled to the ground.

Tarquin was no more. He'd never talk down to her again. Never plot against her and their kingdom. It was over.

Dru stiffened above her. The flames he'd been spraying at the scourge disappeared, and he roared as if in great pain.

"What's wrong?"

"Kayda. It's the Unseen. I feel him trying to take over." He shook his head and groaned.

"Fight it, Dru. You're stronger than he is. I believe in you."

The great black dragon wobbled in the sky. For a moment, she was certain he would come crashing to the ground, crushing her beneath him. But he suddenly stabilized, hovering easily once more.

"He's gone. I don't know how he reached me after our wish." He pivoted, sending another blast of fire into the scourge surrounding them.

Kayda pulled at the flame in his chest and added her own fire to the fray. *"Your wish?"*

"Yes, we—"

His explanation was cut off by manic screaming echoing across the snowy plain. Kayda raced sideways, rounding the hillside.

The sight that met her sent a chill down her spine. Belstasia had turned on them. Instead of blasting ice into the scourge, she sent great blasts of ice spiraling into the fighters on the beach. People fled in every direction, jumping aside and screaming.

"Bela!" Dru bellowed.

"Go," Kayda insisted. *"Stop her, Dru."*

Druturion took off like a shot across the sky. Kayda whirled around, her gaze on the scourge surrounding her. She couldn't afford to watch them grapple, not while she was surrounded by a sea of beasts.

She grimaced, realizing she'd just sent her source away. Kayda ripped the pile of handkerchiefs out of her tunic. She didn't need them to shield her breast from the lamp's heat any longer, but they could still come in handy.

She skewered them atop the spear and quickly shoved it inside a flame that'd already begun to sputter out on the ground. Luckily, the fire caught. It wouldn't burn for long, but maybe it would buy her enough time to reach Izora so she could share her source.

Kayda strode away from the hill and stopped as a strangled murmur reached her ears.

"Sister, don't leave. This isn't over."

Horror struck her, and she spun around. Behind her, a great clash exploded, no doubt from the dragons fighting, but she didn't turn to look. Her attention was entirely wrapped up in the nightmare before her.

Tarquin rose off the ground, the huge gaping hole in his chest where her spear had skewered his heart slowly closing. His skin reformed, his eyes burning with hatred and his smirk as haughty as ever.

"Did you think that little trick would work on me? Me!" He scoffed, staggering closer. "You can't defeat me. Not now. Not ever. As long as there is a single bone left in my body, I'll return to plague you." His smirk grew larger. "Not that you'll be around much longer to bother."

"What are you?" Kayda's brows sank, her jaw dropping with revulsion and disgust. "Why won't you die?"

She lifted her hand and sent more flames at him. But even as he writhed beneath the onslaught, his skin reformed. He flicked his wrist, and a line of scourge appeared in front of him, stretching out at his feet on cue so he could stomp on one with every lumbering step he took.

And like a curse from above, the snow shifted to sleet and fell in a great sheet upon them. Within a few instants, the fire atop Kayda's spear snuffed out, leaving her with nothing to draw from.

She cut off her stream of fire, shuddering as Tarquin stalked closer until he stopped directly in front of her. He smacked the spear from her shaking fingers. His hand shot out and seized her neck.

Kayda tore at his wrist, desperately seeking to dislodge his crushing grip. She couldn't breathe. The edges of her sight darkened. This was it. She was about to die.

Jayan leaped at Tarquin with his pole knife raised. He stabbed Tarquin's back. Blood spattered Kayda's face as the tip of the blade poked out from the spot in his chest that'd just healed.

Tarquin tossed her to the ground and rounded on Jayan with malice in his eyes. His hand shot out, and with a single strike to the chest, he blasted the huge, muscled Sul aside like he was a doll made of paper. Jayan slammed into the ground and rolled, landing on the hill's far side.

When he didn't jump back up, Kayda screamed, her throat hoarse and painful. She rolled up to her knees, ready to race toward him, but Tarquin snatched her hair, gripping a handful of her braids with an evil smile. "Get back here, you bitch."

Kayda grimaced, still on her knees, as her head snapped backward in his grasp.

Then a fireball slammed into his face.

Tarquin roared and shoved her to the ground. Kayda's head bounced on the hard dirt, her head swimming as Izora burst into view. She sent wave after wave of fire at Tarquin, her face filled with grim determination.

Tarquin, his skin sizzling, knelt down and lifted something off the ground. Her discarded spear.

Kayda fought to push through the pain. To rise and fight. But before she could recover enough to do more than lift up on her elbows, Tarquin sent the spear flying through Izora's chest.

"No!" Kayda screamed, watching with dawning horror as her grandmother tilted forward, falling upon the spear and driving it further within her chest. The fire on Izora's hands died, and her eyelids fluttered shut as blood poured out her open mouth.

Tears spilled down Kayda's cheeks. She reached out, wanting to run to Izora. To hold her in her arms and clutch her tight one last time.

But Tarquin had other plans. He grabbed her outstretched hand and slammed her to the ground again. His strength, even while his skin still smoldered from Izora's flames, was inhuman. He flung her to the ground like she was a bug he intended to stomp on.

Then he rounded on her as her head swam with dizziness and pain, the icy sleet smattering her face and mixing with the hot tears running down her cheeks.

Tarquin crouched by her side and stared down into her eyes. "I told you we would wipe the slate. I am the destroyer of worlds—the cleansing fire. I've become so much more than you could ever be, even with your little flames and your dragon. I am a god!"

How had it come to this? Tarquin had spent his whole life cutting her down with sly remarks and constant casual cruelty. Always acting like he was better than her. Like she was nothing. She could handle it when it was only directed at her. But this—he'd taken it to a whole new level of insanity.

Kayda stared up at her half-brother's crazed face. He truly meant it. There was no question he believed he'd become a god. He would destroy this world without a second thought, just like he had Izora.

Kayda's gaze flicked to the side. Izora lay next to her, the spear deep within her chest and the end of it caught on the ground, leaving her top half dangling in the air as her body slowly slid down the wood. The oil lamp on her chest swung in the wind, still burning brightly.

Tarquin's voice boomed again. "Any last words, sister?"

Kayda met his gaze. She stared back at the man who would happily hold a flame to the world and watch it burn. She couldn't let him get away with it. She wouldn't.

"You're wrong about one thing."

"What's that?" A sly smile crossed his lips as his fingers closed around her neck.

"You're *not* the fire. I am."

Kayda pulled at the flame in the lamp and sent it at him. Then she dug deep down inside. She grasped the pain welling within her for Izora and Jayan and let it flow through her, and the flame burned brighter and hotter than ever before. Just like back at the guard tower, it spilled out of her in a bright blast.

Tarquin staggered back, his eyes widening with horror before they popped and sizzled within his skull.

Kayda shook her head. It still wasn't enough. He'd said as long as he had a bone left, he would return. She had to make the flame burn long and hot enough that there would be nothing but ash.

Her talent screamed through her veins. She shivered uncontrollably; the icy sensation so strong her skin froze like she'd been dunked in the Northern Depths.

The flesh bubbled on Tarquin's skin, but he was still moving. Still trying to reach for her, to choke the life from her.

She wouldn't allow it.

Kayda flicked a glance at the coast where Dru and Bela hovered, battling each other with bolts of fire and ice. Her bondmate's words returned to her, replaying in her mind. "Even if I'm not with you, I'm there. Call on my strength." He'd never told her in so many words, but in that moment she instinctively knew. This was the boon dragons brought to humans they bonded. This power she had access to, the power to decimate her enemies, it came from Druturion.

She dug deep down and pulled at her talent with everything she had. A scream spilled out of her lips as the fire brightened, burning white hot. It seared her, bursting out from deep within her soul, drawing strength not just from her, but from her bond as well.

Tarquin's jaw opened on a silent scream even as his body burst into pieces, disintegrating.

That was the last thing Kayda saw before something within her exploded, and she crumpled to the icy ground.

Chapter 35

Conall's eyes flicked open. He rubbed a hand over his face, blinking repeatedly. "Not this again."

Conall floated on an undulating metallic sea. How had he returned here? This was supposed to be destroyed...

Whatever the answer, at least he knew what to do. He sighed, scanning the surface for a floating figure. There.

He jumped and landed next to a sleeping woman. One he recognized instantly.

"Delyth." He shook her shoulder gently. "Wake up."

Her eyelids fluttered open, and steely blue eyes speared him. "Conall?" Her head swung around, making her gray braid bob across the shoulder of her white mage robes. "Where are we?"

Conall stifled a groan. If she didn't even know that, then what were the chances she'd have any other answers?

"The Palisade. This was exactly how it looked when we brought it down."

Delyth's mouth opened on a silent oh.

"I have no idea how I ended up back here, though," Conall continued. "Or how you're here with me. Last I checked, I was searching for the Unseen, and you were—"

A thought struck him, and the word caught in his throat. Delyth was dead. Did that mean... Was he dead, too?

Would he ever see his friends again? Had he survived a magical trip through the earth, only to have a blow to the head end him?

"I'm dead, aren't I?" Delyth's voice was surprisingly steady for someone grappling with such news.

"I'm afraid so."

She gasped and splayed a wrinkled hand across her chest.

"I'm sorry, Delyth. I wish I could've saved you, but we were stuck on that barren island and—"

The look of surprise on Delyth's face vanished, and she waved a hand. "No, not that." She stared off into the distance, rubbing her temple and muttering under her breath so quietly Conall had to strain to hear her words. "That damn feather. I thought it was a dud. But it worked." A smile slowly spread across her face, the expression so reminiscent of her daughter it made his heart ache.

Conall leaned in, a single brow raising. "What feather?"

Delyth's gaze met his. "Hm?" Her smile fell. "Tell me, what's happened since I died? Quickly now."

Conall frowned, but then he filled her in on the events of the last few weeks. She listened quietly, and the urgency in her expression had him rushing through the tale, leaving out the finer details.

"And then I struck my head and passed out. I guess now that I'm here with you, it means I was the one who was destined to fall." Conall shuddered, picturing poor Shadow slumped distraught beside his cold body. Hopefully, the others would find him when they descended to finish what he'd started—defeating the Unseen.

Delyth squeezed his forearm. "Dear boy, you're not dead."

He met her gaze. "I'm not?"

"No. I've been given this one last chance to guide you. It was my greatest wish."

Conall's brow pinched. "I don't understand..."

"It's all right. You don't have to. Just know this; the Unseen, he will offer you things—wonderful, amazing things. But you must be strong and resist. He must be destroyed."

Conall drew back, trying not to let the offense bubbling within him color his tone. "I would never accept anything from him."

"That's easy to say now, but when he tries to hand you all your wildest dreams on a platter, you might think otherwise."

No. She was wrong. He'd never align himself with that sickening presence, no matter what he offered.

"Please, Conall. Listen. You have to know. The Unseen wants you and you alone. It has to be you who defeats him."

"Me?" His eyes widened. "Why does he want me?"

Delyth opened her mouth, but before she could speak, her body was rocked with a violent convulsion. Conall's heart sped up as he gripped her shoulders, trying to still her quaking.

Finally, her body quieted. She lifted her face to stare at him, and Conall swallowed a gasp.

She was changed. Aged just like the poor souls who'd held tight to the Palisade beside him so long ago. Her hair fell out in clumps atop her shoulders, and her face was so heavily lined and gaunt she looked only moments from death.

She cleared her throat and leaned closer, the voice escaping barely a whisper. "Some lines, once crossed, can never be redrawn. Don't—"

Her words were cut off by another round of convulsions. "Delyth." He clutched her tightly, until a tremor of his own ripped across his spine.

Blazes, that hurt. His arms detached from Delyth and wrapped around his middle instinctively. He clamped his eyes shut, praying for it to stop.

Please, make it stop.

The pain faded as suddenly as it had started, replaced with a new, strange sensation. A wet rasp grazing the back of his head.

Conall groaned. His eyes jolted open, and his hand rose to prod the sore, wet spot on his skull. He whipped his hand away when it encountered something rough and wet against his scalp.

"Little brother, you're awake."

"Shadow, were you just licking me?" he asked, incredulous, turning to stare at his bondmate's yellow eyes.

Shadow's tail flicked happily. *"I see you still have much to learn. It is helpful to lick a wound. The bleeding stopped, thanks to my help."*

"Thanks, I guess." He scanned Shadow, paying special attention to his back where the scourge bit him. *"What about you? Are you all right?"*

"Yes, it was just a scratch. I'm not bleeding anymore."

Conall sat up, staring into the cave's red-lit recesses as Delyth's words reverberated in his mind. *"I just had the strangest dream,"* he said, though a part of him was certain it had been no normal dream. He gasped, remembering the convulsions. *"Do I look different, brother?"*

Shadow tilted his head. *"No, a little banged up and wet, but the same as always. Why do you ask?"*

"It's a long story." He sighed, wobbling to his feet. *"I'll tell you once we get out here. C'mon. We've wasted enough time as is."*

They hiked deeper into the cave, stomping through the burned scourge's ashes. At the back wall of the large chamber, another tunnel stood. Conall ducked down, forced to crouch once again in the narrow dirt tube.

They walked long enough that his back and shoulders ached, but finally, they approached the entrance to another large chamber. This one was almost blindingly bright red, and so hot the sweat that had only trickled down his skin so far poured in rivulets.

He had a sudden urge to drain his waterskin, but his hand stilled before he removed it from his waist. He might need water magic more than he needed a drink. Best to conserve his source.

They crept inside the chamber. Here the roof rose again, allowing him to straighten, but the relief he felt was short lived. He fought down the urge to gasp aloud.

The chamber was enormous. Far larger than the last, perhaps as big as Flamesmoat, or at the very least, as big as all of Southmoat with some of Northmoat thrown in for good measure.

Bubbling pools of molten rock dotted the landscape, surrounded by great swaths of humongous circular rocks. And in the center, one rock stood out, larger than all the rest, made of a shining metallic substance that was unlike anything he'd ever seen.

"Ah, you've finally come. Just like I knew you would."

Conall flinched, and he tapped his leg twice, flicking a glance at Shadow. Shadow inclined his head in response, then tilted his jaw toward the center rock. Conall nodded, setting off on a straight course toward it.

No doubt Shadow could feel it as well. That revolting feeling emanated from that shimmering boulder. That was where he needed to go. He was certain of it.

Shadow darted sideways, leaping behind one of the huge round rocks. Conall's heart thudded harder being separated from his bondmate, but it was a wise plan. Maybe if they were lucky, they could catch the Unseen unawares.

Time to be the distraction. *"Yes, I've come. But not to join you, like you claim. I've come to destroy you."*

Laughter reverberated in his mind. That same sickening chortle he remembered so clearly. *"Why would you want to do that?"*

"Why shouldn't I?" Conall edged forward, only turning when he needed to dodge one of the huge boulders. *"You've set the scourge loose to destroy my home. You want everyone to die."*

"Not everyone. Some—yes. But they are nothing in the grand scheme. A trifling price to pay to get what I need."

"That's sick." He scanned all around, searching for signs of anyone in the vast chamber. So far, nothing. The place was quiet as a tomb, except for the bubbling lava. *"I'm here to make sure you don't succeed."*

"Even if what I need is you?"

Conall paused, fighting to tamp down his revulsion. Delyth was right, yet again. *"Why? Why me?"*

"I've waited eons for one such as you. Can't you see? Together, we will be unstoppable."

"I'll never join you." He took another step forward, craning his neck for any sign of movement. Where was he?

"Don't be so quick to refuse. Not after everything I've given you. It can all be taken away just as easily."

"You haven't given me anything."

The Unseen chortled again, and his laughter set Conall's nerves on edge.

"Where do you think you humans got that magic you waste, building walls that should've never existed?"

Conall's stomach dropped. *"That's not true."*

"Oh, but you don't believe that, do you? I told you I was the giver of gifts. The taker of lost dreams. The evidence is right there before your eyes, if you'd only look closer."

Conall's step slowed. He swiveled his head, scanning the chamber. What did he mean? His knees wobbled, and he rested a hand on the huge rock beside him. He only shifted a portion of his weight before his hand smashed through the side of the rock, shattering the fragile surface that wasn't solid at all. His eyes widened so much his vision blurred.

They weren't rocks. They were eggs.

Conall gazed inside the massive cracked egg. He spotted a body, at least as big as he was, but far different. The beast was winged and had a skinny tail wrapped around its shrunken, stunted form.

Suddenly, Delyth's cryptic last words began to make sense.

"What did you do to them?" But even as the question left his mind, something inside him revolted. He remembered the words in that ancient book. *"Dragons used to be the only ones who summoned elemental magic..."*

"Vile, disgusting creatures. I only spread the gifts they'd been so greedily hoarding."

Conall's stomach roiled, and his mouth watered so badly he almost heaved. The Unseen had killed all these young dragons, only to somehow siphon their elemental magic to mankind. How? Why? His head spun as he tried to get a handle on this insanity.

"All those years I spent searching for the perfect vessel. Someone worthy of all of my gifts. Finally, you've come to me."

Conall reared back, a hand splaying on his chest. *"Me?"*

"Of course. You can summon all elements. You have the gift of bonding. I knew if I spread enough magic through the humans, one such as yourself would arise. Join me and take what you deserve."

A vessel... What did that mean? It wasn't making any sense.

"Show yourself. Talk to me in the flesh," he cried out in his mind.

The Unseen scoffed. *"Not until we come to an arrangement."*

The coward. The Unseen wouldn't show himself until he agreed to his disgusting scheme.

Conall could play that game. But he couldn't sound too eager, not after he waltzed in threatening to kill him. The Unseen would never fall for it. Delyth said he'd make promises. Maybe he could pretend to be swayed by them.

"Why should I? I already have all the magic I need. You've admitted it yourself."

"Haven't you ever wanted more? Oh, the things I could give you."

"I'm listening." Conall left the egg behind and strolled toward the large rock in the room's center.

"How about your youth? Wouldn't you like the years back those witches stole from you?"

He was playing dirty. All those years he wasted tearing down the Palisade—he thought they were lost to him forever. *"You can do that?"*

"Mm-hm. Better than that—by my side, you will live forever."

Conall swallowed a gasp. Surely not. No one had that kind of power. *"That's not possible."*

"Don't you know how long-lived dragons were? I didn't just take their magic. It's all right here, waiting for me to gift it. How about your family and friends, hm? Wouldn't you like to give them the gift of perfect health and long life? I can arrange it."

"Y-you can?"

"Yes. All that and more." The Unseen's voice was a gentle purr, coiling around his spine, full of forbidden promises.

Even though it was impossible, he allowed himself to picture it for a fleeting moment. Lark. Ereni, and Violet. Shadow. All of them, living with him forever. They could travel the world, rebuild the farm. Anything they wanted for all of time—together.

He shook off the thought. No. He wouldn't allow himself to be swayed. Not truly. But for the Unseen's behalf, he had to act like he was considering it. In another life, he might've even wanted to take him up on his offer. It was certainly tempting.

"And what do I have to do for this gift?"

"You must swear to be my holy vessel. I cannot venture above without one. But together, we will rule the world. I've waited so long to find one worthy of my greatness. Out of billions of humans, it is you I've chosen. You should be honored."

"I-I need to think..." He let his voice trail off as if he were actually considering it.

"Don't wait too long. Even now, the last of the dragons battle above. After I turn them to our side, the silly war the humans have waged will be lost. I would hate to see your loved ones fall while you are considering my generous offer."

He was turning the dragons against them? Could he do that? But really, it wasn't too much of a stretch to imagine after everything else he'd claimed.

Conall rolled his shoulders back and strode forward confidently. *"All right, I've decided. I want to save them. Give me the gifts you've promised."*

"So, you swear it then? I have to hear it."

"Yes, I swear."

"Come to me."

Conall's feet dragged him forward as if they had a mind of their own, leading him straight to the metallic boulder in the chamber's center. He halted before it and stared up at the craggy surface as a hole opened in the rock's top.

Out of the hole, a creature slid, eerily reminiscent of a snake. It slithered across the jagged rock, its sinuous body a black so dark it seemed to suck all the light in the room toward it. It slinked closer, leaving a trail of gray sludge everywhere it touched.

His feet locked on the ground, Conall attempted to raise his arm. His stomach hurtled into his throat as his limbs refused to budge.

The creature slid closer, and the waves of revulsion emanating from it made him certain this strange beast was indeed the Unseen.

"Open your mouth," a gleeful voice commanded in his mind.

And though he wanted to do nothing less in his entire life, Conall's jaw dropped on cue. His heart hammered, his eyes bulging. Why couldn't he move? Was this disgusting thing controlling him already?

The vow—he'd made an awful mistake. He should've never let those words leave his lips.

The disgusting creature snuck closer, weaving across the rock's surface and dropping to the ground. Then it coiled up, no doubt preparing to leap atop his legs and slink all the way up to his mouth until it worked its way down his throat.

Conall gagged at the thought, but his traitorous body still refused to move. This was it. He was about to die.

A blur of gray fur leaped into sight, snatching the Unseen out of the air just as it jumped for him. Shadow bit down with a wet crunch and shook, only to toss the beast aside an instant later, yelping and rubbing his jaw with his paws.

But thankfully, Shadow's actions unlocked his frozen limbs. Conall jolted forward and raced to his side. *"Brother, are you all right?"*

"Yes. That thing's blood burns. But I'm fine." Shadow shook his head and coughed. *"Find him. Finish this, little brother."*

Conall nodded and rose. He scanned the ground, searching. There. He followed that nasty trail of sludge and found the Unseen cowering on the ground behind one of the petrified dragon eggs. Trying to find safety among the creatures he'd betrayed and slaughtered.

"Wait. It's not too late." The Unseen's voice had lost its cruel edge; it warbled, pained and full of panic. *"If you destroy me, all that I've given will die with me. Would you curse the world to live without elemental magic? Will you give up eternal life? The safety of your family?"*

Conall stopped before him and called forth his talent, using the flame dangling around his neck as his source. A cold chill seeped across his skin, but the sensation was barely discernible with the disgusting filth roiling around him being in the Unseen's presence.

As a fireball coalesced on his hand, he took another look at all the boulders surrounding him. There were so many. Hundreds.

"You really thought we'd do anything to keep your gifts, didn't you? But some lines should never be crossed. We don't want anything you've stolen. Here—have it back."

Conall sent the fireball at the Unseen and smiled as he watched him burn.

Ice cooled Conall's veins as the Unseen writhed beneath the flames. He wriggled and squirmed, letting out an unearthly screech as his oily black scales shriveled and cooked. The smell was horrendous, worse than garbage set out to rot in the summer sun. But Conall bore it silently, holding his breath through the worst of it. Once the Unseen stopped moving, Conall stuttered out a breath and killed the flames.

"Shadow." He raced back to his bondmate's side, sensing his discomfort through their bond even before he spotted him trotting toward him. Shadow met him halfway, pausing every few paces to rub his paws against his mouth. *"Here. Let me help you."* Conall grabbed the waterskin off his belt and poured the liquid in Shadows mouth, washing off the last of the foul black blood.

"Thank you, little brother. I think I'll be tasting that for days."

"I hope not." Conall peered inside Shadow's mouth as the water spilled out. *"Your tongue looks a bit swollen, but I think you'll live."*

"Conall!"

Shadow's warning was the only thing that saved him.

The Unseen, charred and still smoking from the scorching, leaped at Conall's chest.

Quicker than ever before, Conall called forth his talent. The very air sizzled, bursting with so much current every hair on Shadows body fluffed up instantly. Conall slapped the Unseen with a wave of air, knocking him off course.

The vile serpent shrieked, coiling back to strike. *"This isn't over. It will never be over!"* he hissed.

But Conall saw his chance. He didn't even bother to respond. He just sent another blast of air at him, knocking him back.

The Unseen's ruined skin sheared off in layers as he clung to the dirt, refusing to give up. *"You might kill me, but you won't win."* More of that black ooze poured out, hitting the ground and sizzling. The smell was so wretched Conall nearly backed away. *"You've already lost."*

"No. You have." With those words, Conall dug down deep. He pictured the faces of everyone he loved in his mind's eye. A rumble reverberated up his spine as he dug his fingers into the cool soil in his pocket and used it to loosen the earth beneath the Unseen. Then he sent a final blast of air at the villain, gritting his teeth and screaming.

The Unseen tumbled up, dislodging from the dirt and whipping into a hole soaked in red. An inhuman screech cut through the air, before choking off into a pained gurgle.

Conall crept closer to the hole's edge and stared down at the boiling molten rock.

"You did it, little brother. Nothing could survive that. Not even him."

Conall smiled weakly at Shadows assurance and decided to trust the evidence in front of his own eyes, no matter how much that vile creature insisted this wasn't the end.

He was wrong.

The Unseen was dead.

"Let's get out of here." Conall turned his back on the hole and walked away.

Chapter 36

Hundreds of voices screamed out in terror. Lark spun slowly, her eyes widening with horror as she spotted the cause. The white dragon, the one Kayda called Belstasia, sent great bolts of ice into the crowd.

But she wasn't attacking the scourge any longer. She was targeting the people crowded around the beach.

"My friends." Lark turned back to Ereni, who fought by her side atop the little hill. Together, they'd put down—for good this time—about a dozen prisoners. There were only two left she could see still fighting their way toward them.

"Go," Ereni shouted over the melee, her voice barely loud enough to be heard over the pained screams from the shore. "I've got this."

A spike of indecision warred within her. It was her fault these men were here. If she'd never freed them, they'd have died when Flamesmoat fell.

Then another bolt of ice pounded into the beach, spraying great gouts of sand into the air. The faces of her friends rose in her mind. She wanted them safe, but trouble had found them anyway.

"Muse, back to the beach. We need to help the others."

A blur of gold and brown darted through the sky above her. *"On it."*

Lark ran. She hustled through the crowd of scourge, felling beasts in every direction with blasts of earth.

Why had she insisted they stay so far away? She should've kept them with her, where she could protect them. Now they were being pummeled with ice and there was nothing she could do.

She pushed her legs like she'd never pushed them before. Snow and dirt kicked up in her wake, but she only ran faster. The snow battered her face and slicked the ground, but somehow, she kept her balance, even when countless warriors slipped and slid.

"She's heading for Aren," Muse cried.

Lark gulped, flicking her gaze to the sky as Muse flew directly toward the white dragon. Fear clawed up her spine. Muse would get herself killed, tangling with that huge beast.

"What are you—are you mad?" her own voice warbled in her mind, full of panic.

"Just a distraction. Hurry."

Even though she was already running faster than she'd ever run, Lark forced herself to race faster. The fighter's features blurred as she passed them. The muscles in her legs burned like she'd been doused in lava, but still she pushed. At this speed, she didn't trust herself not to hit the wrong target while she weaved between the fighters and scourge. She summoned the shape of a dart and clutched it tight in her fist, the vibration thrumming through her blood a welcome sensation as she barreled forward.

Finally, she glimpsed Aren's blond head peeking out from behind an overturned canoe, bow drawn, sending arrow after arrow into the scourge's ranks. His eyes widened as he spotted her racing toward him.

Belstasia was right behind him now, hovering in the sky, mouth open to spew more ice at the beach. A few of the fighters panicked, running and screaming, heedless of the scourge in their haste to escape the fearsome dragon. Aren stayed calm, using his bow to pick off beasts that leaped for the escaping fighters.

Muse darted in front of Belstasia, clawing and pecking at her eyes. But the dragon only shook her off, sending Muse flying aside and screeching in anger.

Lark's heart stalled as Bela opened her wicked jaw and a bolt of ice coalesced. She aimed down at the beach below. Right where Aren stood.

No!

With a final burst of speed, Lark jumped, simultaneously spinning the dart in her fist into a dirt shield. She landed in the sand next to Aren just as the ice slammed down, hammering the shield and shattering into thousands of tiny shards that pummeled into the sand harmlessly.

The blow made her shield collapse. Tiny flecks of dirt rained down on them as Aren turned to face her. "Lark, you're—"

His gaze flicked to the sky, and he stopped speaking just as a second dragon, this one black as night, slammed into the white dragon above them.

"Muse, are you—"

"I'm fine. Run before those beasts hit you."

She saw the sense in her bondmate's warning as the dragons started battling each other, throwing blasts of ice and fire. Most of the magic landed on its target, but whenever the dragons dodged, the ice and fire blasted to the ground instead, hitting whoever happened to be below, scourge and human alike.

Lark grabbed Aren's elbow, towing him aside. "The others, where are they?" She threw up a shield as they shuffled down the beach, away from the behemoth's battle.

Great sheets of sleet fell, sneaking between cracks in her dirt shield. Lark's teeth chattered as her sweat-soaked skin cooled beneath her cloak.

Aren frowned at the sound, wrapping his arm around her shoulder and shifting slightly, aiming for a circle of overturned boats further up the beach. "I left them here, helping Mika."

Lark breathed out a sigh as she spotted the circle of canoes, a dirt shield covering the top in a wide dome. Suddenly, a light flared further inland, white hot and blindingly bright. So bright, she was forced to shield her eyes and turn her head aside as she staggered across the sand.

"What's that?" Aren asked, squinting beside her.

"I don't know."

"Muse, can you see that from above?"

"Too bright. I can't focus on it." Her voice turned grave. *"But it's back where we just were."*

"Kayda." The word came out as a strangled whisper.

Aren's brow wrinkled. "What is it?"

The light cut off, and the black dragon roared so loud she thought her eardrums might burst.

Oh no. Kayda. What happened?

"I have to go back," Lark said.

They'd just arrived at the circle of canoes. She peeked over, spotting Dausius and Tiora, safe beneath the shield of swirling sand and dirt. Mika crouched over a man sprawled out on the ground, and the old, white-robed mage Kayda had brought back from Northmoat, Vespen, stretched out his hands, his face the picture of deep concentration.

Mazen and Meital were nowhere to be seen, and Lark's heart sped up for an instant until she forced it to slow. With their knife skills, she could count on them to take care of themselves.

Dausius spotted them approaching and dropped the bandages in his hand to sprint over. "Make a hole," he yelled over his shoulder.

Aren met her gaze and nodded as Vespen obliged, banishing a small section of the swirling dirt in front of them. "Be safe," he yelled, and then he released her shoulder and ducked beneath Vespen's shield.

Lark ran again, heading back to the hill where she'd left Kayda and Ereni. The sleet pelted her, raining down on her shoulders and face like tiny arrows. Her cloak was soaked, but she ignored the shivers and rushed toward Kayda, her stomach clenching.

As she approached, she spotted a brown ponytail bobbing, and a small smile tugged at her cheeks. Ereni was surrounded by a group of Sul and a handful of Doln warriors now, the front lines having managed to push through to their position.

Behind her, a great crashing *boom* rocked the earth. Lark halted as the ground shook beneath her, nearly throwing her to the ground. She swiveled backward, her eyes bulging.

Belstasia had fallen. She sprawled on the beach, laid out on her back. Dru hovered above her, watching as every scourge battling nearby stopped what they were doing and made a beeline for the fallen dragon.

Bela opened her jaw and aimed up at Dru. But before she could let loose, a scourge jumped atop her and dove straight down into her gaping maw. Two more leaped in right after, before she could snap her mouth closed.

Lark's jaw dropped. But she couldn't just stand there and stare. She whipped around and jerked back into motion as another one of those deafening bellows tore out of Druturion's throat.

Lark slowed down as she reached Ereni's side. She'd stationed herself above a crumpled man on the hillside.

She swallowed a gasp when she recognized him. Jayan, the captain. Was he...?

"He's still alive. Can you heal him? I'll cover you both," Ereni shouted.

Lark knelt at his side and reached into her pack. There was no time to examine him thoroughly, but if the huge lump on his forehead was any indication, he had a head wound, at the very least.

She slicked a handful of her mother's ointment—the one with countless ingredients—over his forehead. Then she wished. The tremor pulsed through her and shot into Jayan's skull. An instant later, he gasped and jolted up, his gaze jerking wildly while he sucked in huge gulps of air.

"You're going to be all right," Lark said.

He pointed, one long finger shooting toward the cave entrance as he struggled to his feet. "Kayda," he croaked.

Lark straightened and raced ahead of him, quickly overtaking Jayan's staggering steps. When she circled the hillside, her heart dropped.

Izora and Kayda were both down. The old nurse's blood spilled down her lips and onto her chest, a spear skewed through her heart, the only thing holding her up off the ground.

Bile rose in Lark's throat. The mage was clearly dead, so she sidestepped around her and raced to Kayda's side.

Kayda sprawled in a heap on the dirt, her head pressed into the snow, hiding half of her face. Lark's stomach roiled as she dropped to her knees beside her.

She reached out a trembling hand and shook her shoulder. Nothing. She slid her hand over her neck. No pulse. She slipped her hand in front of her nose and mouth, praying for a miracle.

She dug in her pack, slapping a handful of cream on Kayda's cold, lifeless cheek. She wished and wished—harder than she'd ever wished in her entire life for her sister to rise and live again. The magic pooled through her, rattling the earth beneath them both as it slammed into Kayda.

Still nothing.

A hand landed on her shoulder. She lifted her swollen eyes to meet Ereni's, steely blue and full of remorse.

"You can't heal the dead, Lark. I'm sorry."

Jayan screamed behind them, falling to his knees.

Grief tore at her heart, threatening to overwhelm Lark. But she couldn't give in. Not while they still fought.

Even though it killed her to leave Kayda behind, she rose to her feet and scanned the battle. The front lines had fought ahead of their position, affording them a bit of protection. But still the scourge came, an endless wave of gnashing teeth and razor-sharp claws.

Lark rolled her shoulders back, readying to run again so she could take out her righteous anger at her sister's demise on the enemy.

But then another crash shook the earth just beside her. Druturion landed next to Kayda and let out an anguished roar as he stared down at her lifeless body.

Suddenly, he clawed at his chest, his talons tearing at the scales on his front. Blood spattered the ground.

What was he doing?

Something golden flashed, fluttering to the ground among all the blood. Then Dru spread his wings and hunkered down, covering Kayda protectively beneath his outspread wings.

"Lark, the scourge, look!" Muse's voice rang out in her mind, full of—delight?

She swung around and gasped, her hands covering her wide-open mouth.

Everywhere she looked, the beasts fell, writhing and squirming on the ground. All around, fighters paused, catching their breath and staring, dumbfounded, at their enemies as they fought a losing battle with an unseen foe.

The Unseen.

Lark laughed. "He did it! Conall did it. He killed the Unseen." It was the only explanation that made sense.

Her laughter spilled out, boisterous and more than a touch manic, as she watched the vile creatures' shudder and eventually go still.

It was over. Blazes, it was over. They'd won.

But then her gaze swung back to Jayan, and her laughter died, choked off in a throat gone dry.

They may have won, but countless lives had been lost. Kayda and Izora were far from the only ones. Bodies littered the ground, and blood splattered everywhere, painting the snowy landscape a lurid red. What a steep price to pay.

Lark shivered, the sleet raining down on her like frozen knives.

A petite mage approached their group, and she shuddered, too, then she reverently tugged the lit oil lamp off Izora's chest and wrapped it around her own.

"Here." She lifted a hand, and the cold momentarily worsened before a blast of fire appeared on the ground before them, and the flame's warmth washed over them.

Ereni gasped. "Karina, stop. Stop. Now!"

The mage lifted a brow, but obeyed, cutting off the stream of fire. "I know it won't last long in this weather, but we can't all freeze."

Ereni scrubbed her face, blinking repeatedly. "No, that's not it. Your glow. While you summoned, you lost your blue glow. It's half-faded away already." She spun her head around and shouted across the battlefield. "No one summon! Something's wrong."

Just then, the ground rumbled off to the right. The dirt opened up in a small circle, and out of it, something rose.

"Conall!" Lark raced forward, arriving at her brother's side just as he and his wolf emerged from the ground. It reformed beneath him, the dirt covered by a thick layer of lush grass. She thudded into his chest before he could stand from his cross-legged position and caught him in a tight embrace. His arms wrapped around her instantly as he squeezed her back tightly.

Ereni arrived a moment later, her eyes wide. "Your glow. It's so red. It's barely purple anymore."

Conall cleared his throat. "When I defeated the Unseen, we lost our elemental magic with him. It was never ours to begin with. He stole it from the dragons and gave it to us as some twisted gift."

Gasps spilled out from the crowd gathered around them. Voices echoed, everyone no doubt relaying Conall's words far and wide.

Ereni glanced around at all the mages, and then down at her own hands. "That must mean after we use what magic we have left, it's gone for good."

Lark released Conall and rocked back on her heels. All that work she'd put in to become a healer was about to vanish. But what was the alternative? Letting the Unseen live and wreak havoc just to be a mage? With *stolen* magic, no less? The choice was obvious—Conall had made the right call.

Ereni helped Conall up to his feet and hugged him tightly. Then she drew back and nodded. "All right, everyone, save your talent. We'll use it to link to the healers and save all the injured we can."

The mages scrambled, preparing to follow orders.

But something about the words felt wrong. They twisted in Lark's gut as she stared at the fresh green grass she knelt on. She glanced up as a tinkling noise whispered on the breeze and caught a glimpse of Dausius approaching, his lanky arms swinging and a wide smile stretching his face. The rest of her friends followed in his wake, all of them covered in blood and mud and soaked from the sleet, but each of them wearing matching grins. All of them, still standing strong—together.

"Wait," Lark shouted. "Don't use your talent. I need it. We all have to link."

Ereni turned to her, brow raising. "What?"

Lark bounced to her feet, pointing at the patch of grass that was already quickly being covered by the icy sleet. "We need to save Dracwood. Heal it. Trust me."

Ereni glanced over at Conall. He met her eyes and nodded.

"Change of plans, all mages, come together and link with Lark," Ereni bellowed.

As the mages surrounded her, everyone linking hands, putting their trust in her, a rush of elation spread through her. This was right. Something deep down in her soul demanded it.

Conall had defeated the Unseen. Kayda destroyed the Unseen's greatest champion before succumbing to the prophecy and falling. This—this was her purpose here.

She met Dausius' gaze across the crowd as his tale from so long ago rang in her ears. They'd been stuck on a boat in the bog, watching the town of Bogsmouth burn after the scourge first ascended from the earth to plague their land. He'd told them all the tale of his lost love and her prophetic vision on her deathbed about the songbird who he was destined to save. She'd said—*together* they would save the world.

Conall and Ereni both grabbed one of her shoulders, completing the linked chain of mages. Lark sank her fingers into the earth, and she wished. She wished for the world to be as it was, before all this death and destruction. For all the charred earth and ash to disappear and green grass and trees to return to their rightful place.

Warmth flooded her and colliding sensations surrounded her. Tingles, chills, moisture and tremors, like nothing she'd ever felt, struck her body and sank into the ground. Power—blissful, healing power—drained from all the mages and spread through her hands and shot down into the ground like a shockwave.

Then it was over.

Lark rose from her spot on the icy ground, frowning.

Ereni's jaw dropped as she stared at the crowd of mages. "So much blue, gone," she whispered in a choked voice, tucking her head into Conall's shoulder.

Lark's heart thudded madly as she looked around. She despaired. Nothing had changed. The landscape appeared just as barren and destroyed as it had before they'd sunk the last of their magic into it.

"Lark, you won't believe this!" Muse called out, just as the ground rumbled beneath their feet.

Something shot out from the tiny finger holes she'd left in the small patch of grass. Jaw dropping, Lark backed away just as a massive willow tree burst free from the ground. She slipped in her haste and landed on her backside on the hard ground, her head craning up to stare at the gorgeous green tree in front of her.

Movement and gasps demanded her attention beside her. All around, wounded men and women staggered to their feet, shaking out limbs that had just been broken and staring down at wounds that had miraculously closed. She splayed a hand on her stomach, surprised to discover the dull ache from the cudgel blow had completely vanished.

Lark beamed, warm tears spilling into her eyes. *"What is it?"*

"That tree isn't the only one that just rose from the ground. The forest—Dracwood is regrowing. You did it!"

Lark stumbled up to her feet and raced across the field toward the ridge that hid the rest of Dracwood from the Abandoned Lands. After a long trek through the sleet, she finally mounted the hillside, and a huge smile broke out on her face.

All the trees the mages had been forced to burn to slow the scourges' advance stood once again. Dracwood was back. They'd healed it.

Chapter 37

Blackness surrounded her, and warmth pooled deep in her belly, buzzing through her veins. She could sense she was not alone. A familiar presence called to her, silently demanding her attention.

"Dru? Are you here? Where am I?"

"Kayda? Oh, it worked. I'm so glad it worked." His voice was strained, a quiet murmur in her mind, but nonetheless, her bondmate's words washed over her, calming the panic that fought to overwhelm her in the dark.

She rolled over, the pleasant warmth slowly receding as if it had seeped away into the cold hard ground beneath her. *"Why is it so dark?"*

"You are sheltered beneath my wing. I'm sorry. I'm afraid I don't have the strength to lift it presently."

Kayda lifted a hand and sighed as the leathery texture of Druturion's wing met her fingers. Following the curve of his wing, she scooched across the ground and laid a hand on a smooth scale on his side, then curled up beside him.

"I can't remember... Where are we now?" She leaned against his hide, taking comfort in his presence as something outside shocked her memory.

Excited chatter and whoops of delight echoed around her. She stiffened. That's right! They were in the Abandoned Lands fighting the Unseen. But why was it cheers she heard and not screams of pain and snarls?

"The battle. Do you remember now? We've won," Dru said.

Joy blossomed at his words, but then she quirked a brow, rubbing her aching skull. *"We have? I don't recall the end for some reason…"*

"That's because you were dead."

"I was—"

Dru convulsed beside her, his big body shuddering so forcefully he rocked the ground beneath her.

"Dru! What's wrong? Please, tell me how to help," she cried out beside him.

After a long moment, his body stilled. His voice returned to her mind, quieter than before. *"Nothing can help me now, I'm afraid. But it's all right. You're safe."*

"I'm safe? What about you?" Kayda's chest tightened, and she rubbed her hands across Dru's flank, desperate to soothe him.

"I've lived a long life, Kayda. So long, you can't even imagine. There's not much time. Please, you must listen."

Kayda nodded, then realizing he likely couldn't see her in the dark, she spoke, *"Yes, I'm listening."*

"Know that I don't have any regrets. But the magic I used to save you—it requires sacrifice."

What magic was he talking about? She knew of no magic that could heal the dead. Her throat constricted, and she clutched it as she asked, *"What sacrifice? Did you forfeit your life to save mine?"*

"No. My death was already sealed the moment the Unseen fell. The scourge, Bela, everyone who still shared a bond with the Unseen in some way, was destined to fall when he did. I will too—very soon."

"No. Dru. I can't lose you."

"You must go on, Kayda. You must live without me, as you did before we met."

"But you'll still be with me, won't you? That's how bonding magic works. The voices of your dead bondmate's live on, if only within your own mind. We'll be together always."

Dru shuddered again, and Kayda tensed. But this time, the convulsions only lasted an instant before he shook them off. *"No, Kayda. Not this time. The sacrifice demanded it. When I die, I'll be gone for good."*

She splayed a hand on her throbbing chest, her mind reeling. Ever since she'd learned about the strange quirks of bonding magic, she'd been afraid. She was terrified that the madness that infected her grandfather would one day be passed on to her. But now that Dru was dying, and leaving her for good, it didn't seem fair.

"It's all right, Kayda. I'm ready to rest. It's been so long. So, so long." Druturion sighed, his chest sinking and rising as the deep breath whooshed out of his body. *"I have one favor to ask, my friend. A final wish, if you will."*

"Anything."

Another convulsion rocked through him. This one went on for so long Kayda bit back a scream, certain he was about to die before revealing his last request. But then his shaking ended, and Dru sucked in a wobbly breath.

"I—need you—to—find them." His voice quieted even more, every word forced and clipped.

"Find who?"

"Our—eggs."

Eggs? Kayda gulped. He couldn't mean... Did he have young out in the world somewhere?

A flash of their conversation while she'd been imprisoned in Joria replayed in her memory. *You've given us a chance at a future.* Did that mean... had he and Bela procreated while they were in hiding from the Unseen?

"Where are they, Dru? I'll find them. I promise. I'll find your eggs."

Druturion didn't answer.

"Dru?"

When only silence greeted her, she knew he would never answer her again. He was gone.

Kayda sat in stunned silence, her heart shattering and stabbing outward, agony piercing through her core and deep down into her soul. Druturion—she would never speak to him again. It hurt. Blazes, it hurt far more than she could bear.

Eventually, the darkness beneath Dru's wing wore on her. The weight of it settled on her shoulders, stifling and ominous.

She had to get out. She had to escape.

Kayda crawled on the cold hard ground, her fingers reaching, scrambling for purchase. She couldn't breathe. She had to get out. Had to—

The leathery tip of Dru's wing slid over her scalp, and she pushed forward into the freezing air outside. Sleet rained down on her face and hands, but Kayda's panic only grew.

The darkness had not receded. Her eyes. Why couldn't she see?

Chapter 38

Conall stared out the porthole at the black night. The sea swelled, waves crashing against the hull in the storm's aftermath.

It had taken long hours to ferry everyone back to the ships. Even now, a few straggling canoes dotted the ocean with the last of the fighters on board.

He turned back to survey the room, and a wave of gratitude washed over him so strongly he almost collapsed from the force of it. All the people he loved most were still alive, crowded around him. Ereni sat in the single chair, cradling their sleeping daughter in her arms. Lark perched beside Kayda on the worn desk, holding her hand and humming softly.

When Kayda crawled out from beneath Druturion's wing, that had been the ultimate shock. But as soon as he saw her crouched there, her eyes wide open and changed from their familiar brown to an unfocused, startling crimson, the Unseen's word struck him anew. "Only two will *see* the next day." Kayda certainly wasn't seeing anything now, but at least she lived.

What he still didn't understand was *how*. Lark swore up and down that Kayda had been dead when she checked on her. That though she tried to heal her, her magic had no effect. The last of the elemental magic they'd sunk into the earth somehow miraculously healed all of their injured fighters, but Kayda was the only one who rose from the dead.

They'd tried asking her, but so far, Kayda had not said a word. Losing her bondmate and her grandmother had surely taken its toll. Not to mention everyone she'd lost already. Had she been struck not just blind but mute as well? Or was she in shock over the battle's end?

None of them knew for sure, so they'd decided to simply stay with her, patiently awaiting her words. Whether they came today, tomorrow, or never again, they would wait with her. They were family now. Not just by blood but forged in action. No matter what happened next, they would stick together. Conall was determined to keep both his sisters safe from now on.

"You still haven't told us about the Unseen. What was it like down there?" Ereni asked.

Conall shuddered. "It was awful. Just being near him—" He shuddered again. "He wanted to use me. Called me the perfect vessel. If Shadow hadn't stopped it, he would've slid down my throat and wedged himself inside me and used me like some kind of twisted marionette to take over the world."

"I'm glad that didn't happen," Ereni said. "I've never read about any creatures with that kind of power before. What was he, I wonder? Where did he come from?"

Conall shrugged. "I don't know. I don't know if we'll ever know, now that he's gone."

Ereni pursed her lips, letting the matter drop.

Maybe he should've grilled the Unseen for more answers. At the time, he'd only been worried about defeating him, but in hindsight, he couldn't help worrying that decision would come back to haunt him. Especially when he recalled the end of the cryptic message the Unseen had delivered to him. *Three will come, but only two will see the next day. Even then, it won't be enough...* The Unseen had been right about the first part of his message. The evidence was plain to see whenever he stared into Kayda's blind eyes. Would the second part of his message prove true as well?

"I wish I could heal you, sister," Lark said.

Conall shook his head gently. A mage who'd spilled into the bay had tried healing Kayda when they made it back on board. But even with the last of her magic, she'd not been able to return Kayda's eyesight.

Ereni tilted her head. "We'll figure something out."

Conall stole another glance out the window. "Maybe we should let her rest. It's getting late."

Lark patted Kayda's hand gently and peered at her closely. "What do you think, Kayda? I bet some rest would do you good. I can stay with you tonight, if that's all right with you?"

Kayda just stared blankly, her startling red eyes looking so strange.

Lark rose from the desk and tugged Kayda's hand. "C'mon, sister. I'll help you climb into the hammock. There's enough room for us both."

Ereni yawned, rising from the chair with Violet cradled in her arms. "I'm wiped, too. I might sleep all night and half the day as well."

Conall rubbed the small of his back, following Ereni to the door as Kayda took careful, mincing steps across the room at Lark's instruction. "That sounds like a plan. And then a huge meal when we wake. I wonder if the chef has any eggs?"

Kayda stilled. "Wait," she croaked.

Conall turned from the door, meeting Lark's gaze as a bright smile lit her face. "Kayda." She clutched her chest and let out a deep breath. "It's so good to hear your voice."

"Eggs. I need to find them."

Conall quirked a brow. "Do you want me to see if the chef is awake?"

Kayda shook her head vehemently. "No. No, not those kinds of eggs. Dragon eggs."

Ereni stepped away from the door. "Maybe we should sit back down."

They all filed back to their spots, Lark guiding Kayda as she spoke, "Druturion told me when he saved me I had to find them. Bela must've laid a clutch in the weeks we were separated."

Conall perched on the windowsill, the chilled glass pressed against his back, echoing the chill spreading through his veins at Kayda's news. "There are more dragons out there, somewhere? Did he tell you where to look?"

Kayda shook her head again. "I'm afraid not."

Ereni sank down into the wooden chair. "There was a book in the library at Mage Keep about dragons. If I'm remembering correctly, then we have time. Dragon eggs need many years to mature before hatching and a great deal of heat as well. I believe the book said the average was twenty."

"Well, that explains why the egg remnants I found with the Unseen were in a chamber surrounded with lava." Conall rubbed his chin. "We'll have to search for somewhere else like that. Maybe they buried them out in the Suland Waste?"

"Or maybe they're somewhere else entirely," Lark said.

"I think you're right," Kayda agreed. "The rumors of a land somewhere beyond the Orddon Ocean are true. Druturion confirmed as much to me. We'll need to scour the seas for his lost eggs." She sighed. "But at least now we know we have time. With all the chaos the battle created, we'll have a host of problems to deal with at home. Most of the crops we've stored will have undoubtedly been destroyed. So many people have been displaced from their homes. Not to mention the minor revolution in Joria we had a hand in starting will need to be dealt with in order to reestablish trade routes."

"We'll all help, of course," Conall insisted.

"You can count on us, Kayda," Lark agreed, squeezing her hand.

Kayda closed her eyes and rubbed her fingers across her eyelids.

"Are you all right?" Lark asked.

After a long moment of silence, Kayda nodded, a tentative smile spreading across her face. "Yes. I'm not giving up. Even if I never get my vision back, I won't stop until I find Dru's eggs. I owe him that much after he saved me."

"How did he save you?" Ereni asked. "I didn't think it was possible to heal the dead."

"I'm not sure. Whatever magic he used, he told me it required sacrifice. He's gone for good now, even from my thoughts."

Lark leaned closer, rubbing a hand gently across Kayda's back. "I'm so sorry."

Conall's brow scrunched, and he shot a glance at Ereni. She wore a pensive stare, her nose wrinkled, and her lower lip caught between her teeth. It seemed even with all the books on magic she once had access to in Mage Keep's library, she was just as stumped as the rest of them when it came to this new magic.

There was so much to do. Dragon eggs to save. A new portion of the world to explore. Political unrest to squash and scores of towns and homes to rebuild.

He wasn't sure how they would accomplish all of it, but he was sure of one thing—they could handle it. Together, they'd just defeated an evil force set on destroying the world.

The Unseen was wrong. He'd told Conall if they'd joined together, the two of them would be unstoppable. But Conall already had people in his life who could help him tackle anything. As long as his sisters stood by his side, nothing was impossible.

He glanced at all the strong, incredible women he was lucky enough to call his family and smiled. "So, what's first?"

Epilogue

Lark curled back the curtain on the carriage and peered through the glass. Sunshine filtered in between the new green buds bursting from the trees. Excitement welled in her belly. They were almost there.

She turned back to the interior of the carriage and smiled. "Are you excited to be going home?"

Conall spun toward her, peeling his gaze from the opposite window where Shadow and Sunny happily trotted beside the slow-moving carriage. "Yeah. I can't believe it's been so long since we left."

Kayda frowned from her spot beside Lark on the plush cushions. "I'm sorry for that. I should've arranged this trip sooner." Kayda's red eyes stared unseeing across the cabin, her head no doubt aimed at the sound of Conall's voice, but her gaze landing slightly askew.

"You don't need to apologize," Conall said. "It's just an empty plot of land. I've been happy to stay and help get everything sorted in Flamesmoat."

"We both have," Lark agreed, squeezing her sister's hand.

It had been a long, cold winter. Even with the land magically restored, there'd been so much to do. And without magic to rely on, everything had to be rebuilt the old-fashioned way. But now, spring was here and the hard work of the last few months was finally slowing into something approaching normal.

Her friends in the Wandering Bards were long gone. They'd agreed to be part of the peace forces Kayda sent to Joria to help set things right in the bustling port city, given the absence of the exploitive trade families who'd been ousted.

Well, most of them had. Lark's cheeks warmed. Aren stayed behind, determined to fulfill his promise to take her on a trip to Doln. They were planning to leave on the morrow, in fact, then they would travel to Joria to meet up with the rest of the Wandering Bards after.

But Lark had insisted on making this trip first. It wasn't so long ago that she'd left her home behind, determined to never step foot on the land again. Funny how that worked out in the end. She was on her way back, only to leave again.

Lark snuck another glance at her brother's face as he returned to staring out the window. A tingle of anticipation slid up her spine, and she had to tamp down the smile that fought to spread. She couldn't wait to see his face when they emerged from the woods.

"I see it. You weren't kidding," Muse chirped.

Lark's gaze shot out the window, but she couldn't spot Muse flying overhead with all the tree cover. *"How's it look?"*

"Just like you described it. He's gonna love it."

Lark couldn't still the grin then.

Conall didn't miss it. "What's got you so chipper?"

"Nothing. Just excited about my trip tomorrow," she lied.

"Hm." Conall cocked a brow. "You sure you want to travel all the way up north? It just started getting warm here."

"She'll have Aren with her to keep her warm," Kayda teased.

Conall shot Kayda a glare, not that she noticed. She probably wouldn't let his sour look bother her even if she could see it. Lark only giggled, squeezing Kayda's hand again. "You're right. I'm quite looking forward to that."

A gruff noise across the cabin made Lark's eyes widen. "Did you just growl at me, brother?" She chuckled. "I think you've been spending too much time with your hounds."

Conall rolled his eyes then met her gaze. His expression turned serious. "I want you to be happy, Lark. But you're still my baby sister."

Lark leaned over and patted his knee. "Hey, we just defeated an army of scourge. I can handle a trip with Aren to meet his family." She smiled warmly. "You don't have to worry about me. I am happy."

Conall grinned back. "Good."

The carriage jolted to a stop. Conall peered out the window. "Why are we stopping here?"

Lark reached for the door. "I asked the driver to stop just before we exited the woods. Let's walk the rest of the way." She opened the door and slid out before he could question her further.

Conall hopped out next, then lent a hand to Kayda. They hiked the final distance through the trees, and Lark's smile spread even wider at her brother's gasp.

"The house." He spun to face her, his eyes glossy and his mouth hanging wide open. "What? How?"

Lark giggled, staring behind her brother at the brand-new farmhouse perched in place of the burned-out shell she'd left behind last summer. Muse was right—it looked exactly the way she'd described it, an almost perfect replica of the home she'd destroyed. "We called in a few favors. Do you like it?"

"Do I like it? I love it." The longer he stared, the more his smile spread, until it practically burst across his cheeks. He squeezed Kayda's hand. "You had a hand in this, too?"

Kayda nodded, her own grin just as luminous. "It's the least I could do after—everything. I would give you more, but I had a feeling this was all you'd accept."

"You're right. It's everything I want and more." He breathed out a deep sigh, and his expression turned contented. "It's practically perfect."

Shadow and Sunny loped ahead as they started across the grazing field, barking and chasing each other merrily. Then the kitchen door popped open, and Ereni emerged, beaming, little Violet wrapped in her arms.

Conall stilled, his eyes gleaming. "I take it back. It *is* perfect." He smiled at Lark and squeezed Kayda's hand. "Thank you, both."

Conall rushed ahead, leaving Lark to follow more slowly, holding Kayda's arm. "He's so happy. And the house looks amazing. I wish you could see it."

Kayda sighed. "Me, too."

Lark's stomach clenched. "Kayda, are you sure you're all right with both of us leaving? I can always postpone..."

Kayda shook her head. "No. I want you to go. I appreciate everything you've both done for me these past months, but if I want to be taken seriously as queen, I have to learn to stand on my own." She tilted her head and aimed a grin at her. "I need this, too. I need to prove to myself that this"—she waved a hand in front of her red eyes—"won't hold me back."

"It won't," Lark said fiercely, squeezing her hand. "You were made for this, Kayda. My sister, the queen. Never forget, your family is so proud of you."

Kayda teared up, and she clutched Lark's arm, then pulled her into a hug. "Thank you, sister. I'm so glad I found you."

"Me, too," Lark said, squeezing her back just as tightly. "Now, how about we go see what our big brother thinks of his new house?"

Kayda pulled back and rubbed her cheeks with her sleeve. "After you."

Lark grabbed her sister's hand, took a step forward, and smiled.

The End

Also By

The Palisade Trilogy
Shadows That Bind Us — Palisade Trilogy 1
Muses That Align Us — Palisade Trilogy 2
Lines That Drew Us — Palisade Trilogy 3

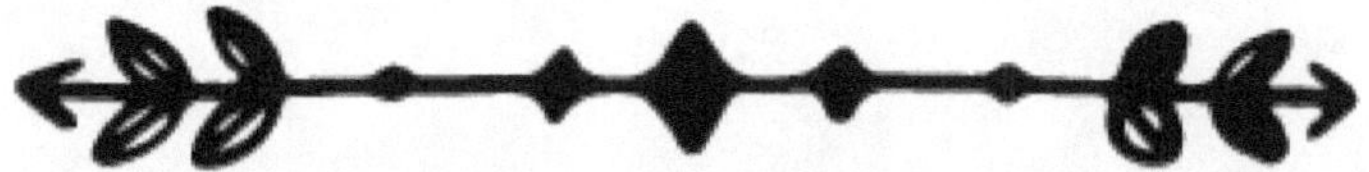

Sign up for my newsletter for a free standalone prequel novella that tells the story of how the Palisade was built centuries ago.
You'll find the link on my website amberlwerner.com

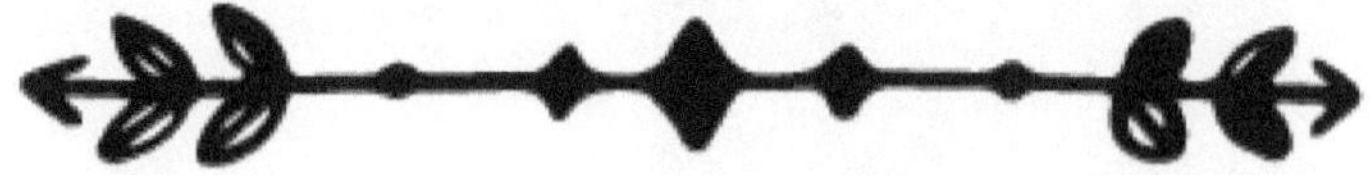

Standalone Short Story
Somewhere In Between

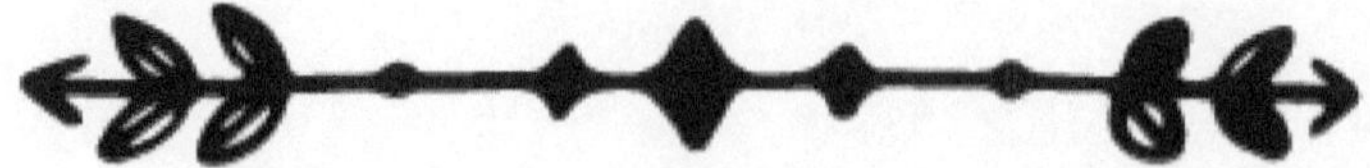

Want more in the world of Dracwood? Read The Blood Song Trilogy and discover what happens twenty years later.
The Odyssey Ring – A Blood Song Trilogy Prequel
Bloodfeather Lullaby — Blood Song Trilogy 1
Bloodfeather Heartsong — Blood Song Trilogy 2
Bloodfeather Symphony — Blood Song Trilogy 3

About Author

Amber L. Werner loves to write about magic, monsters and mythical creatures. She lives in Norristown, PA with her husband and two children. The Palisade Trilogy is her debut series.

Follow her Facebook page Amber L. Werner
Or Instagram amberlwerner

Sign up for her newsletter and receive a free novella.
Find it here amberlwerner.com